P9-ELR-058

ONLY YESTERDAY

S. Y. AGNON

Translated from

the Hebrew by

Barbara Harshav

Princeton University Press

Princeton and Oxford

nly Yesterday

Copyright © 2000 by Schocken Publishing House Ltd.,
Tel-Aviv, Israel

Introduction and Glossary by Benjamin Harshav, translator's note by Barbara
Harshav, Copyright © 2000 by Princeton University Press
Published by Princeton University Press, 41 William Street,
Princeton, New Jersey 08540
In the United Kingdom: Princeton University Press,
3 Market Place, Woodstock, Oxfordshire OX20 1SY

All rights reserved

Fourth printing, and first paperback printing, 2002
Paperback ISBN 0-691-09544-2

The cloth edition of this book has been cataloged as follows
Library of Congress Control Number 00021147
ISBN 0-691-00972-4

British Library Cataloging-in-Publication Data is available

This book has been composed in Electra

Printed on acid-free paper. ∞

www.pup.princeton.edu

Printed in the United States of America

10 9 8 7 6 5 4

CONTENTS

INTRODUCTION
The Only Yesterday of Only Yesterday | *vii*
BENJAMIN HARSHAV

Translator's Note | *xxxi*

ONLY YESTERDAY

Prologue | 3

BOOK ONE
A Delightsome Land | 37

BOOK TWO
Jerusalem | 193

BOOK THREE
From One Issue to Another | 371

BOOK FOUR
Epilogue | 482

Glossary | 643

The Only Yesterday of *Only Yesterday*

BENJAMIN HARSHAV

As Agnon felt that this strangely intensive bygone world happened "only yesterday," but was timelessly valid, so his own fictional world was alive, pervading all of modern Hebrew culture "only yesterday," and can — and should — stand beyond its ostensibly parochial landscape as one of the great literary myths of the twentieth century.

Shmuel-Yosef Agnon's Hebrew novel *Only Yesterday* (*Tmol Shilshom*) was written in Palestine under British Mandatory rule in the late 1930s, finished in 1943 during World War II, and published after the war in 1945. The prominent Israeli literary critic Barukh Kurzweil, a German Ph.D. in literature and a leading authority on his fellow Austro-Hungarian novelist, pronounced: "The place of *Only Yesterday* is among the greatest works of world literature." Those were not parochial sentiments of a "minor literature"; similar opinions were voiced by Leah Goldberg, Hebrew poetess and polyglot, translator of Petrarch and Tolstoy into Hebrew, and first professor of comparative literature at the Hebrew University in Jerusalem; and by Robert B. Alter, Professor of Hebrew and comparative literature at the University of California at Berkeley, a discerning critic and scholar of the European novel.

On the face of it, it is a simple story about a simple man, Isaac Kumer, who immigrated from Austrian Galicia to that cultural backwater, the southern Syrian province under Ottoman rule (the historical Palestine). He arrived with the Second *Aliya* — a few hundred secular idealists, mostly Socialist Zionists from Russia, who came to the Land of Israel between 1904 and 1914 to till the soil, revive "Hebrew labor" and the Hebrew language, and became the founding generation of Israeli society. Isaac, however, who believed in their ideals, drifted back to the fold of Orthodox Jewry, the Guardians of the Walls in Jerusalem.

Yet in this most unbelievable margin of all margins, the great themes of twentieth century literature reverberated. Among the main concerns of the book are "the death of God," the impossibility of living without Him and the impossibility of return to Him, the reversibility of the Siamese twins Homeland and Exile, the weight of the traditional Library and the hollow sound of inherited discourse, the power of suppressed eroticism, and the ambivalent and drifting individual consciousness in an age of ideology. The book was written after Schopenhauer and Freud, after Spengler and Lenin — and grounded in the most austere, minimal society, in an impoverished fossil of an ancient myth.

Summarizing the book would be a futile exercise since its strength lies not in events but rather in hesitations about events. The historical context is as follows: in the sixteenth through eighteenth centuries, when Jews were barred from most West European countries, the great majority of world Jewry was concentrated in the largest European state, the united Kingdom of Poland-Lithuania, which included what is today most of Poland, Lithuania, Belarus, and Ukraine. Between 1772 and 1794 Poland was dismantled by its neighbors, Russia, Austria, and Prussia (which later became Germany). The majority of Jews found themselves in a huge geographical ghetto, the Jewish Pale of Settlement in the Russian Empire, and a large community lived in Galicia, the southern part of former Poland, now incorporated into the Austro-Hungarian Empire. There was an enormous explosion of the Jewish population in the nineteenth century: from 2.2 million worldwide in 1800 to 7.5 million in 1880 and 16 million before World War II. The authentic Jewish territory in Eastern Europe was a network of small towns, where they constituted between one-half and two-thirds of the population. What united them was not an administrative hierarchy, but a dense cultural network, a religion with a Library of texts, a network of social and cultural institutions: separate Jewish schools, cemeteries, philanthropic organizations, hospitals and hospices, publishing houses, books and newspapers, a literature in several languages, as well as modern political parties and social organizations. All this was conducted in three private languages: Yiddish (for daily communication, education, politics, and modern life), Hebrew (of the Bible), and Aramaic (of the Talmud), as well as the languages of state and culture.

Agnon continues to call his homeland "Poland," though under Austrian rule its culture was increasingly Germanized; whereas the Jews in Russia rapidly accepted Russian culture and ideologies and were considered "Russian Jews." The revolutionary fermentation among Russian intellectuals, on the one hand, and the inferior status of Russian Jewry (deprived of the right of citizenship and disrupted by waves of pogroms), on the other, gave rise to a self-conscious literature and a whole gamut of political solutions and parties among the Jews of Eastern Europe, as well as the immigration of millions to the West and the US. This fermentation brought about a total transformation of the Jews, their languages, professions, education, their very place in general culture, geography and history, which we may call the Modern Jewish Revolution.[1] The Zionist immigration to Eretz-Israel was a mere trickle in a great stream — though its eventual results changed the nature of Jewish culture and identity as we had known it for two thousand years.

In the 1880s, a movement of Lovers of Zion (*Hovevey Tsion*) emerged in Russia, centered in Odessa, propagating the revival of the historical Land of Israel. In 1881, a small group of young intellectuals, who called themselves BILU (an acronym for "House of Jacob, come ye and let us go," Isaiah 2:5), immigrated to Palestine and thus started the First *Aliya*, the First Immigration (1882–1904). This was the first wave of Zionist settlers in Palestine, the so-called New Yishuv (the "new settlement" or "new population"). They built Jewish settlements (or "colonies"), supported by Rothschild and ICA (the Jewish Colonization Association), and became farmers on the land. Only in 1897 did Theodor Herzl proclaim the World Zionist Organization in Basel with the goal of establishing a Jewish State in Palestine by political means. Herzl's ideal swept the imagination of Jews

---

[1] See my book, Benjamin Harshav, *Language in Time of Revolution* (Stanford, CA: Stanford University Press, 1999).

everywhere, especially among the millions in Eastern Europe, but most Zionists paid the membership Shekel and stayed where they were. The real implementation of Herzl's dream came through the subsequent waves of immigrants, especially from Eastern Europe.

There was also an Old Yishuv of a few thousand Orthodox, mostly old Jews, who came "to die in the Holy Land," yet raised families and maintained a Jewish presence, mainly in Jerusalem and Safed. Many of them lived on the minimal "Distribution" (*Haluka*) given them by "Societies" (*Kolel*), according to their cities of origin, where the financial support came from. Traditional learning and reading religious books was a major preoccupation of the men.

The new Zionist immigrants regarded this subsistence off the Distribution, poor as it was, as the most abject, parasitic aspect of Jewish Diaspora life. Yet, as Agnon tries to show, winds of change penetrated these walls too: Some created neighborhoods outside the Old City walls — a symbolic as well as practical move — and established the first agricultural colony in Petach Tikvah ("The Opening of Hope"), some were artisans and supported their families with productive labor.

After the first wave of settlers ebbed, the Second *Aliya* arrived (1904–1914). Their ideological fervor was carried by young Socialist Zionists, mostly from Russia (fiercely debating between Marxist and anti-Marxist positions on Zionism). The immediate impulse was the pogrom in Kishinev in 1903, and the self-defense against the pogrom in Homel the same year (at the age of fifteen, young Rosa Cohen, mother of Itzhak Rabin, was one of the fighters and immigrants). The new pioneers intended to work the land, but work was scarce or nonexistent and the landlords of the First *Aliya* preferred cheap Arabic labor to the inexperienced Socialist bachelors. Collectives of Hebrew laborers emerged, reviving the Hebrew language in public communication and, after World War I, erecting the first kibbutzim. All in all, there may have been three thousand pioneers, most of whom abandoned the Land after a year or two; according to Agnon, only two hundred workers remained. (In 1908 there were sixty members of the Marxist party *Poaley Tsion* and ninety of the anti-Marxist Socialists, *Ha-Po'el Ha-Tsa'ir*). Their slogan was: "Hebrew land, Hebrew labor, Hebrew language." And though Hebrew sentences were spoken throughout the ages, between 1906 and 1913 the Second *Aliya* created the first Hebrew-speaking society, a Hebrew city, and Hebrew schools.

At the same time, however, there was an influx of secular Zionist immigrants to Jaffa and Jerusalem, and trade flourished. In 1909 Neve Tsedek, a Jewish neighborhood north of Jaffa emerged, which later turned out to be the beginning of the first Jewish city Tel Aviv; the first Hebrew high school, Gymnasia Herzliya in Tel Aviv, and the Bezalel School of Art and Design in Jerusalem were the pride of the New Yishuv. During World War I, Jews were persecuted by the Turkish authorities, some were conscripted into the Turkish army (fighting with Germany against the Allies), and some were expelled from Palestine. But after the war, when Palestine became a British Mandate territory where a "Jewish Home" was to be established, and a new wave, the Third *Aliya*, came from the Russian Revolution, the pioneers of the Second *Aliya* (Berl Katznelson, David Ben-Gurion, Meir Dizengoff) became the leaders of the Hebrew Yishuv.

This is the context Isaac Kumer enters. The rough outline of his story is as follows: Isaac Kumer was born to a poor family in a Jewish town in eastern Galicia. Losing his mother at an early age, he turned his father's little store into a Zionist club and brought it to bankruptcy. A naïve bachelor, unlike most of his career-oriented generation, he consumed the Zionist phraseology lock, stock, and barrel, adapted it to his religious discourse, and actually went to realize the Zionist slogans. He went to the Land of Israel to plow its soil and revive it as in biblical times. But agricultural work was not to be found, since the earlier immigrants of the First *Aliya*, landowning farmers in new Jewish settlements, preferred cheap Arab labor to the rabble-rousing young socialists. Labor Zionism, too, turned out to be a pipe dream. Almost starving, Isaac found work by chance as a house painter in Jaffa and then in Jerusalem, and instead of tilling the soil or building the country, he painted over old houses.

In Jaffa, he neglected the religious commandments and drifted into secular behavior, common among his generation. He became intimate with Sonya, the daughter of a well-to-do family in Diaspora and a Gymnasium student. Like most members of the Second *Aliya*, Sonya was Russian, and for some reason she flirted with this Galician simpleton and later rejected him capriciously. But when he ascended to Jerusalem, he wound up back in the Orthodox and anti-Zionist religious world of the Old Yishuv. Inexplicably, he fell under its spell and eventually married Shifra, the daughter of an extreme Orthodox fanatic, who was paralyzed and could not object to the match.

One critic called the book "the Epic of a period," and another described it as "the most weighty and important attempt in our literature to depict the life of the Second *Aliya* in the Land of Israel." Indeed, one construct that Agnon offers the reader is a faithful and meticulous historical reconstruction, including descriptions of buildings and neighborhoods in Jerusalem and mundane, humanizing anecdotes about legendary historical figures. Yet the documentary gesture resides only on the surface; behind its facade, enfolded in the novel's allusive and elusive, ironic and shrewd style, is a complex field of multidirectional and ambiguous meanings, raising a tangle of constructs, to be made by the reader and contradicted again, questioning all major aspects of the human condition.

The text is built on a series of ambivalences: Exile as a homeland versus the national Homeland as an exile; Jaffa versus Jerusalem; the liberated Sonya versus the Orthodox Shifra; subconscious drifting versus the dominant ideology of the collective Will, and so on. Actions and events "happen" to him, though usually he intended the opposite; and the motivations for those actions are always overdetermined, leaving the reader puzzled about which system of values is decisive.

But after several clues, planted yet unnoticed by the reader, there comes the powerful twist and the novel soars to Surrealist-Kafkaesque dimensions. Isaac playfully drips paint on a stray dog, writing "Crazy Dog" on his back in Hebrew. The dog Balak takes over the story: wherever he appears, he wreaks havoc, creates panic, and gets pelted with stones. Shifra's father is terrified into a stroke, and Balak has to flee into exile, to non-Jewish neighborhoods, where the Hebrew inscription on his back is illegible, and thus the dog becomes the embodiment of Exile. On the other hand, running around the city, he serves as the reader's guide to the precise geography and history of the neighborhoods and housings of Jews from various countries in early twentieth-century Jerusalem. The exuberant descriptions of Balak's predicament are among the most powerful chapters in the novel; the dog has been interpreted as an allegory of Jewish Exile, as Isaac's erotic projection, as the embodiment of the irrational, demonic force that subverts all Enlightenment rationality, as a guide to Jerusalem, and as a satire of its outlandish Orthodox society, as a Kafkaesque parable and a Surrealist vision; and he is probably all of those combined. Persecuted without understanding why, Balak really does go mad, and eventually bites his patron Isaac, who dies of the venom.

It was impossible for Isaac to stay in the fossilized religious world of Eastern Europe, which had come to a dead end and was abandoned by his peers; but, filled to the brim with a universe of codified discourse, it became impossible for him to live a normal, secular life. In the end, the improbable and irrational return to the outer reaches of Orthodox society was an anti-utopian move, a dead end, destined to fail, too.

In his tongue-in-cheek, "naïve" voice, Agnon takes on the great themes of Modernity in European literature from the most marginal margin possible. The Jews seemed absurd and alien in Christian Europe; they were further marginalized when they procreated and multiplied, according to the biblical commandment, and filled up hundreds of small towns that had been passed over by modern capitalism. The Zionists who called for an exit from Exile were actually marginal in Jewish society; and the "realizing" Zionist, who in fact carries out their ideals, was a mock-hero even in their own eyes. From the petit-bourgeois decency of Austro-Hungary, which had granted the Jews equal rights, and their beloved Kaiser Franz-Josef, Isaac went to that backward country, the decadent, despotic, and corrupt Ottoman Empire, and to its most marginal province, Palestine, where the Jews were doubly marginalized: by the Turkish governors and by the Arab majority.

The pioneers of the Second Aliya landed in this situation, with their Socialist and Tolstoyan ideals of settling the land. They were marginal to the religious Jewish society in Eastern Europe, which they fled, and were ostracized or feared by both the Orthodox Old Yishuv in Jerusalem and by the first wave of settlers in Palestine, the farmers of the First *Aliya*. Furthermore, the Second *Aliya* itself consisted of a few hundred Socialist-Zionist ideologically motivated bachelors, coming from the revolutionary ferment and anti-Semitic pogroms in Russia; while Isaac was a fuzzy-minded general Zionist, a Galician Jew, alien to their ideological fervor and erotic liberties. He drifted to the Orthodox society in Jerusalem, a "medieval" fossil, stuck away in a backward province of a decaying empire, a society with little productive labor (the ideal of his youth), living in poverty on the alms of the Distribution (given by the "societies" of their hometowns), and guarding the graves of ancient Jewish glory and the texts attached to those bare stones. The Old Yishuv was excluded from the new revival of the Land of Israel and excluded itself from the spoken Hebrew language and modern Hebrew literature. And Isaac was an alien intruder among them, too. It is hard to imagine a more exclusionary exile from all exiles.

Yet in all this historical specificity, some of the major themes of the twentieth century reverberate throughout the novel. They are not formulated in any ideological or philosophical manner, but are constantly evoked by this "naïve" witness and textual juggler. In a century that celebrated the Will and the will to power (Herzl's resounding slogan: "If you will it, it is no dream"), Isaac is constantly led astray by encounters and circumstances, always turning up in the opposite place from where he set out to be, and it is impossible to ascertain whether it is predestination, God's hand in the world, or blind and accidental fate that conducts this absurd existence. As Professor Boaz Arpali of TelAviv University put it, "The truths suppressed by the hero, the decisions he flees, the internal forces he shuns, knowingly or unknowingly or refusing to know, gather momentum in his soul throughout his life, and break out in the end, destroying both his soul and his life."[2]

---

[2] Boaz Arpaly, *Masternovel: Five Essays on* Temol Shilshom *by S. Y. Agnon* [in Hebrew], Literature, Meaning, Culture 23 (Tel Aviv: The Porter Institute for Poetics and Semiotics, Tel Aviv University, Hakibbutz Hameuchad Publishers, 1998).

The first sentence of the novel begins in the name of a collective "us," quoting the official Zionist line as an accepted fact, namely, that it was the fellows of the Second *Aliya* who brought our Salvation, our redemption from Exile. Indeed, in Hebrew, *Geula*, Salvation, is the opposite of *Gola*, Exile, locked in an interdependent binary opposition. It is the basic religious terminology, describing the timeless Jewish condition as Exile from their Homeland, to be redeemed when Messiah comes; yet here the language was secularized and transferred to the historical and political views of Zionism, which believed it could be a human task, performed in our generation: "Like all our brethren of the Second *Aliya*, the bearers of our Salvation, Isaac Kumer left his country and his homeland and his town and ascended to the Land of Israel to build it from its destruction and to be rebuilt by it." Etymologically, the word "homeland" (*moledet*) means "the land of your birth" and is used in Modern Hebrew literature as "fatherland" in the European sense. Thus, Tshernikhovsky's famous poem *"HaAdam eyno ela,"* which takes part in a dialogue between the national Homeland and every Hebrew writer's private homeland, like Tshernikhovsky's own very concrete birthplace in the southern Ukraine, begins: "A man is no more than a little plot of land / A man is no more than a pattern of the landscape of his homeland." And that is the homeland Isaac Kumer abandoned for the sake of the abstract "Homeland" of the Jewish nation. He did it, as the popular song of the pioneers proclaimed: *Anu banu artsa livnot ulhibanot ba* — "Us,[3] we came to the Land to build it and to be rebuilt by it." The notion was that, as the Land was neglected and desolate, so were the Jews in Exile; the pioneers going to the Land to work its soil would rebuild their own "Diaspora mentality" by rebuilding the land; they would create a New Man and a New Jew, not hovering in the air and living on air, as modern Jewish literature described him, but physically productive, with a straight back and mind, with roots in the soil.

---

[3] In Hebrew, *banu* ("we came") includes the past as well as the first-person plural; hence *anu* ("we" or "us") is redundant and betrays the Russian or Yiddish thinking of its authors.

The centerpiece of this sentence is a verbatim quotation from God's commandment to Abram (before he became Yahve's Abraham), sending him out to the Promised Land. This is how Isaac, the naïve and wholesome Zionist, understood the biblical phrase: as an injunction to go to the Land on God's mission. Yet what a terrible price to pay! As the King James Bible translated it: "Get thee out of thy country, and from thy kindred, and from thy father's house, unto a land that I will shew thee" (Genesis 12:1). The double root *Lekh-lekho* ("Get going! Get out of here!"), with its drastic, harsh ring in the East European context, sounded as an expulsion, and in Jewish Diaspora semiotics (as opposed to religious dogma), the Torah portion, "Lekh-lekho," became a synonym for expulsion. The last chapter of Sholem Aleichem's *Tevye the Milkman* is called *Lekh-Lekho* ("Get Thee Out") and describes the expulsion of the Jews from all Russian villages, even though they were born there. Quoting literally from the Bible and providing his own contemporary translation, as was the customary way of teaching Torah, Tevye tells Sholem Aleichem (in the original, the words in boldface are in Hebrew, their translations are in Yiddish): "What weekly portion are you reading now? Leviticus? With us, it is a different chapter: the chapter of *Lekh-lekho*." **Get thee out** — they told me — you must get out of here, Tevye, **from thy country** — from your own land, **and from your homeland** — from your village, where you were born and lived all the years of your life, **unto a land that I will shew thee** — wherever your eyes may carry you! . . ."

Agnon's contemporary Marc Chagall used the same biblical text in his painting, "The Red Jew" (1915). One scholar in Jerusalem used the Zionist intepretation and read it as Chagall's autobiographical message: Chagall returned from Paris to his homeland Russia in 1914. But Chagall read the Bible through Sholem Aleichem and Yiddish folk semiotics, where "The chapter of *lekh-lekho*" means simply expulsion from your home. Indeed, in 1915, hundreds of thousands of Jews were expelled "within 24 hours" from their hometowns and many thousands came to Chagall's Vitebsk. There is no trace of Russian Zionism or Chagall's homecoming here: an Eternal Jew, his face as white as death, is about to get up and leave his town behind.

This was the duality of interpretation faced by Agnon: the overtly Zionist and optimistic ideology was subverted by a Diaspora reading. And interestingly enough, Agnon changed only one item: instead of "get thee out . . . from thy father's home" (a sense of guilt that haunts him throughout the book), he says: "from his town," the decaying town that was Agnon's emblematic representative of Exile. As the language of the Bible betrays, Abraham was expelled to the Promised Land, and in many ways, so was Isaac Kumer.

And here is a link to the hero's name. Agnon's admired poet Bialik began his poem on the Kishinev pogrom of 1903 with: *kum lekh-lekho el ir ha-hareygo*, which in Hebrew means: "get up go thee to the city of slaughter." Why get up? And why is a conjunction missing between the two verbs (I Chronicles 22:16 says: "arise therefore, **and** be doing")? As the Hebrew critic Dov Sadan argued, *kum* here is in Yiddish (Bialik's daily language): "come, let us go," using the same biblical phrase, *lekh-lekho*, but this time he is told to come and see the city of slaughter. Agnon's protagonist is called Kumer, the one who came — to fulfill the commandment *lekh-lekho*, go thee to the Promised Land. Instead of Bialik's *kum lekh-lekho*, he heard *Kumer lekh-lekho*. But where did he go — to the Promised Land or to Bialik's devastation? In an important respect, the book is a sacrifice of Isaac, performed by himself.

When the book was published in 1945, before the establishment of the State of Israel, in a patriotic Zionist atmosphere, the opening sentence would have been taken seriously, at face value. It requires a long journey through the novel to discover that the opposite is true. The heroes of the collective myth, the laborers of the Second *Aliya*, are exposed as disillusioned and embittered remnants of an ideal, though Agnon does pay them reverent lip service. On the contrary, Agnon shows wherever he can that the Orthodox Old Yishuv also expanded beyond the physical and symbolic walls of the Old City. He set out to write the great epic of the Second *Aliya*, but wrote a novel about the escape from it. As Dostoevsky intended to write in *The Brothers Karamazov* "The Life of a Great Sinner," but didn't get to it and wrote a long antinovel that is a mere preamble to what should (and probably couldn't) have been written, so Agnon ended his book with a formulaic closure:

Completed are the deeds of Isaac
The deeds of our other comrades,
the men and the women,
Will come in the book, *A Parcel of Land.*

Which, of course, he never wrote.

Amos Oz, in his rich and sensitive writer's book about an admired writer,[4] makes it clear that Agnon's mode lies in overdetermination: every move, activity, or event is explained by so many motivations that none makes sense. He uncovers the ironies and contradictory subtexts behind the ostensibly naïve façade of Agnon's style and argument. And he correctly places it all in the perspective of Agnon's Exile/Fatherland dilemma. Thus, the introductory essay begins with a quotation from Agnon about himself, and Oz's striking interpretation:

> *Because of that historical catastrophe when Titus the*
> *Roman Emperor destroyed Jerusalem and Israel was exiled*
> *from its land, I was born in one of the cities of Exile. But all*
> *the time I imagined myself as having been born in*
> *Jerusalem.*[5]

> Those words, as all readers of Agnon know, are true. But,
> strangely enough, their opposite is also true. Had Agnon
> chosen to say: "Because of that historical catastrophe when
> East European Jewry fell apart, I became a Hebrew writer
> in Jerusalem. But I always saw myself as one who was born
> in one of the cities of Galicia and destined to be a rabbi
> there" — those words would also be true and right on
> target.

The tragedy of Agnon's vision lies in his perspicacity: long before the Holocaust, he saw the degeneration, ruin, and end of Jewish Eastern Europe; for him, there was no way back to the Diaspora. Yet, the

---

[4] Amos Oz, *The Silence of Heaven: Agnon's Fear of God,* translated by Barbara Harshav (Princeton: Princeton University Press, 2000).

[5] S. Y. Agnon, *From Me to Me* [in Hebrew] (Tel Aviv: Schocken Publishers, 1976), p. 85.

Zionist vision he embraced was far from a secure conquest, and its champions were far from idealists. Agnon's satirical view of the Makhersons and Makherovitches was relentless. There was no utopia in Agnon. But precisely for that anti-utopia in a utopian society, he could put the future in brackets and explore all problems of modernity in the fictional worlds of the past.

The quotations in the opening of the novel — from the Bible and from a pioneer song — are culled from Isaac's consciousness. The narrator presents him and his mind in the third person, thus either being faithful to Kumer's perceptions or creating an ironic distance, or both. Thus the narration is conducted on two levels in a Combined Discourse of the narrator and the hero's focus. The narrator leads the text and the hero is the observer. The narrator appears with his Royal We, sometimes representing the Second *Aliya* or the Zionist revival and collective ideology, sometimes representing Isaac's conscious or subconscious sensibilities, sometimes left alone with Isaac or serving as his voice, and always hovering just above him, yet shifting from reproducing his internal monologues to taking a distance and mocking him. Indeed, there is no specific person behind the "We," but an empty slot of a grammatical first person plural, to be filled in as variously as the text allows. And the same "We" takes over the dog Balak's consciousness in the second part of the book, interprets his innermost thoughts and observes him from the outside as well. There is no omniscient narrator here, for at every junction, the omniscience is suspended for the sake of a very focused point of observation: Isaac's, above Isaac, or the dog Balak's.

The fictional world of the novel is presented with very little concrete and descriptive material, but is rather reflected through Isaac's responses to it. A constant stream of consciousness drifts through his mind, yet it is not consciousness that we are offered directly, but strings of quotations and formulaic, pious discourse. If ever there was a text so pervasively using what M. Bakhtin called "alien discourse" (what has later been renamed "intertextuality"), it is surely Agnon's. Isaac has ready-made phrases, stories, anecdotes, and formulae for whatever his eyes encounter. And those are excerpted not just from the Bible and prayerbook, but from the immense Hebrew library. But there is no distinction between religious and other sources: he uses the phrases and images of the most popular Zionist ideology (the image of the man with his plowshare) as well as official Austrian propaganda, stories of the marvels of Vienna as well as the exploits of the early pioneers in Palestine. It is not a stream of consciousness here, but a *stream of textuality*: consciousness takes a back seat to the mosaic of textual excerpts and patterns.

As witness to an apocalyptic event in Jewish history, Isaac Kumer is similar to the narrator in Kafka's "Great Wall of China." Kafka's narrator is paradoxically both a simple laborer, ordered to do monotonous physical work on a national project, and a scholar of Chinese history, both within the process and above it in time. Isaac is both a simple house painter, even a simpleton who believes and understands anybody and everybody, and as learned a reader of the Hebrew library as Agnon himself. Yet all the use of traditional turns of phrases are not meant as specific allusions to specific texts, but rather serve as a stylistic layer which represents a textual culture, where the texts are preserved but their interpretations are shaken. Agnon's Israeli reader, who does not know that library, certainly perceives it so. Moreover, many Hebrew phrases and words that look like quotations actually have a subtext from Agnon's (and his character's) first language, Yiddish. Thus, in Israeli Hebrew, *bitahon* means "security," while in Yiddish it means quite the opposite: "you must have *bitokhn*" (the Yiddish pronunciation) means "to hope for the best" in a situation that is rationally hopeless, because the term derives from the phrase *betakh beHashem* — "trust in God" (rather than man).

In many ways, *Only Yesterday* is an abstract modern novel. From the beginning, reality is often not presented in individual situations and encounters, but in plural and in long catalogues. For it is not the external fact that constitutes the fictional world, but the summary of such facts in Isaac's mind, filled with categories and catalogues. When he leaves home, we are told: "Isaac parted from his father and his brothers and his sisters and all his other relatives and set out on the road." But for all his guilt feelings, we are not told here the names of his brothers and sisters nor how many of them there were. Traveling on a train is most convenient for that purpose:

The train rolled on between villages and hamlets, cities
and towns. Some were known for their great rabbis and
others were known for their famous cemeteries. Some
earned a name with the produce of their fields and the
fruit of their trees, the fish in their rivers and the minerals
in their mountains; and others earned fame with their
poultry and livestock and other things in heaven and on
earth. And yet other places have neither learning nor earning, but do have a Quarrel. Some sanctify the Name of the
Holy-One-Blessed-Be-He with the Kedushah, *We shall
sanctify You*, and others sanctify Him with *We shall bless
You*, and they wrestle with each other and create a Quarrel.
And another Quarrel, between Assimilationists and Zionists. The former want to be like all the other nations, and
the latter want to be Jews, so they wrestle with each other
and create a Quarrel. And yet another Quarrel, between
those who want Salvation by miracle and those who want
a natural Salvation, so they wrestle with each other and
create a Quarrel.

A neutral classifier summarizes his observations, takes no stand on
the available options, and empties them of any concrete content. Yet
between the lines, we learn about the futility of the Jewish Quarrels
that devour Diaspora society and willy-nilly are introduced to the
major theological issue of the book and of modern Jewish history: Is
Salvation to be brought by a miracle or in the normal course of nature — all this in passing on a train through named or nameless towns
and cities.

He arrives in the legendary capital of his Empire, Vienna,
and has several hours of free time on his hands. But first he delivers
a catalogue of all the remarkable places in the capital:

Isaac was all on his own and considered where he would
go. Would he go to Leopoldstadt with its splendid synagogues whose beauty is unsurpassed throughout the world,
or to the Prater, the joy of the whole city, or to the big
house called Bunch of Grapes, or to their church that has

a clock where every single one of its numbers is more than two feet high, or to the library where the Book of Psalms is written in gold letters on red parchment, or to the Emperor's palace, or to the Museum. Many were the things here that we heard about and now we can see them. And now we stand at the entrance of Vienna and we don't know where we shall go or where we shall turn. Isaac stood a while, his mind flitting from place to place but his feet aren't moving, for with so many things, his head is heavy and his feet are heavier than his head.

Even more remarkable is his hymn to the greatness of the Austrian Empire:

The train wound its way up, and wound its way down. High mountains flew by and snow lay on them, and even though Passover was already past, the snow didn't budge. And so, Isaac sits and rides through the realm of Austria, that same Austria that rules over eighteen states, and twelve nations are subject to it. One and the same law for the Jews and for the people of the land, their well-being is our well-being, for the Emperor is a Gracious King, he protects all who take shelter with him, Jew and non-Jew alike. Her earth is lush and fertile and the produce of her land is greater than the need of her inhabitants. She is blessed with everything and knows no shortage. One land makes wheat and barley and rye and beans and lentils and oats and corn; and another land makes potatoes and fruit of the orchard. One land makes plums for confiture and Slivovitz, and another land makes hops for beer. One land makes wine and another land makes tobacco and flax, and all lands are full of livestock, animals, and birds. Some give milk and butter and cheese, and some give meat and wool and skins and feathers. One land produces horses, and another land chickens and ducks and swans, doves, and pheasants, and bees make honey and wax, and her lakes and rivers are filled with fish and her mountains with silver and copper and tin and iron and lead for paint and salt mines, and coal and oil. And her forests make wood, and there are high mountains there, covered with eternal snow.

"Her forests make wood, and there are high mountains there, covered with eternal snow." There are no specific names for trees, no specific places in the mountains. He does not use the realistic technique of describing one of those provinces or talking to one person who may have boarded the train. We don't even know which province produces what product. And more important, Isaac does not confront this paean with his Zionist ideology; if this Empire is so rich and Jews have equal rights in it, why is he going to that desolate Palestine?

The paucity of realistic details reflects both the relatively undifferentiated world of lower class folklore and the Jewish Diaspora imagination, living in a fictional world of books, in a timeless Holy Land or Babylon, and not distinguishing between one tree and another or one mental situation and another. Nineteenth-century Hebrew dictionaries translated the names of specific birds or trees as "a kind of bird" or "a kind of tree." The great European fiction with its immense wealth of differentiated descriptive details of the physical world, nature, and civilization, as well as of states of mind, did not reach traditional Jewish society in Eastern Europe. The ways of resolving this situation (aside from writing a derivative European novel) were ways of abstraction and textuality.

The great Jewish writers of the twentieth century responded to this period of transition from a medieval, traditional society, religious in its framework and codified in its forms of behavior — to the world of modern, secular Europe, with its individualism, centrality of consciousness, and historicity. It was not a move exclusive to Jewish society, but here it was telescoped into a very short period of one or two generations, and dramatized by both the internal textual tradition of this people and the external pulls to their emancipation. Agnon, Sholem Aleichem, or Kafka evoked that fault line and gave it mythological forms. Sholem Aleichem knew he was not Tolstoy, that he could not describe aristocratic drawing rooms in exquisite detail because the authentic Jewish world was the world of the small town, the so-called *shtetl*, poor in physical objects, whose inhabitants lived in an imaginary universe, a mishmash of folklore and snippets of learning. He diverted the level of concreteness from actual events and their historical causes to the stream of speech of his garrulous protagonists. Even when a wave of pogroms washes over Russia, Tevye the Milkman says, "when they began talking about pogroms." Thus Sholem Aleichem erected a fictional world in Yiddish, using the most authentic material of the Yiddish language: its associative, rambling talk, filled with proverbs, idioms, stories, and asides, and studded with shards of distorted quotations from the Hebrew Library. Writing in Hebrew, Agnon mined the historical layers of the written Hebrew language and created an illusion of textuality, using both phrases and anecdotes from the Library as well as syntactical patterns that imitated the traditional books. Kafka, on the other hand, lost both the talkative Yiddish and the Library of texts. In his fictional work, Kafka moved out of the Jewish domain, yet his *realia* was just as poor in concrete details. He too resorted to abstraction, used catalogues of items in plural and presented the significant discussions of the "system" (in *The Trial*) in abstract, ideological terms.

In all of them, the front narrative was trivial; the real, profound issues were presented not in telling examples, but in the deep background, in ideological discourse. What remains concrete on front stage is *diverted concreteness*. Tevye talks, K. moves from one corrupt abode to another, Isaac changes places and jobs, but such concrete situations serve merely as occasions for verbal speculations and evocations, raising the great questions of human existence, the "rules of the game" in God's world, and the hierarchy of values or loss of them.

Thus, writing in Hebrew was not just a linguistic matter, but a resort to the totality of ways of seeing the world through the mountain of traces from a Borges-type of Library. That Hebrew Library entailed a panhistorical and transgeographical view of Jewish existence: it does not much matter where or when the characters were, the essential conception of the Homeland-Exile dichotomy remained eternal, until Salvation comes. There is very little here about any problems of the Ottoman administration or the Arab majority in Palestine, the Russian revolutions or technological advances, the building of Tel Aviv or the revival of Hebrew as a spoken language. Poverty in the most marginal marginality of Jerusalem under Ottoman rule also means exclusion from the technological age. Isaac's escape from the workers of the Second *Aliya* also means escape from the age of ideology. Yet the traditional religious view did not allow for Salvation by human hands, for the Zionists' "pushing the end" — thus, the impasse is given, no matter what end it may take.

Furthermore, at first reading, the novel sounds like a naïve and meandering story about a naïve and drifting house painter, until it explodes with the Mad Dog (the French translation is even titled, *The Dog Balak*). From here on (at least), all rationality is thrown to the dogs. But we must leave this part to the reader.

The discussion of the specific Hebrew substance of the novel, its ascetic minimalism, focusing on a nonintellectual, non-ideological antihero, must not obstruct our view of its deep European roots. Agnon was the last Mohican of Diaspora Hebrew literature, still able to invoke and visualize the religious world of the simple folk in East European Jewry, looking back from the territorial context of the Zionist revival in Palestine. Furthermore, Agnon did it while having read a library of European novels, though masking his modern concerns in the naïve language of the traditional Library and its "naïve" readers.

Boaz Arpali, who analyzed the genres intersecting in Agnon's novel, called it a "Master-Novel" or "Super-Novel," written by a "Super-Master": "*Only Yesterday* is a Super-Novel, for it includes several models and central aspects of the European novel since its inception. It is a conglomerate in which those models and aspects obtain new meanings and functions both in themselves and one vis-à-vis the other, thus creating new and exciting relations among them." The plot of the novel, too, is at least a double plot: "On the one hand, from its very inception, it is mainly a picaresque, panoramic, episodic and comical plot with a strong social orientation. On the other hand, it is a plot of character and destiny (or, perhaps preferably: character that is destiny), a dramatic-tragical plot, whose links derive from one another in a tight causal chain with a psychological-existential orientation. The first story emerges in a consecutive reading from the beginning onward, while the shock brings us to the second story, in a retrospective reading from the end to the beginning."

| *The Life of S. Y. Agnon*

Agnon was born as Shmuel-Yoysef Tshatshkes in the town of Butshatsh in eastern Galicia, formerly a part of the great Kingdom of Poland, and between 1772 and 1918 incorporated in the Austro-Hungarian Empire (today in the Ukraine). The Polish spelling of his and his town's name — Czaczkes of Buczacz — sounds almost grotesque, and his flight from the name was a symptom of his flight from the shtetl world.[6] In local parlance, the Jewish name of the town was Bitshu'tsh, and Agnon imitated the name in his fictional Shibush, a decaying, valueless, dying world, as portrayed in his novel *A Guest for the Night*. Hebrew critics made a great deal of this symbolic name, for its dictionary meaning is: breakdown, disruption, blunder — and this sounded like a death sentence on the Jewish Diaspora. Furthermore: breakdown is a cognate of Tomas Mann's *Budenbrooks*, representing the breakdown of the bourgeois world. Yet in the living language — the Hebrew incorporated in Yiddish — Shi'bush (pronounced: Shibesh) means: a worthless thing, a negligible value; if something costs a shibush, it practically costs nothing (derived from a worn-out penny, the smallest coin with the Emperor's face rubbed-of). And this perception evokes Y.L. Peretz's Yiddish romantic poem "Monish": "In kinigraykh Poyln / Nit vayt fun der grenets / ligt zikh a shtetele / groys vi a genets" ("In the Kingdom of Poland / Close to the border / Lies a tiny town / As big as a yawn.").

---

[6] The facts on Agnon's life are based primarily on Dan Laor's *S. Y. Agnon: A Biography* [in Hebrew] (Tel Aviv: Schocken Publishers, 1998); and on the still-classic biography of Agnon by Arnold Band, *Nostalgia and Nightmare* (Berkeley and Los Angeles: University of California Press, 1968).

In fact, considering the demographic structure of that time, Butshatsh was not a small shtetl but quite a large town, a center of a whole district, well connected to a network of similar towns around Galicia. It sent a delegate to the Galician Sejm and later to the Parliament in Vienna, as well as a delegate to the first Zionist Congress in Basel in 1897. In 1890, when Agnon was three years old, the town counted 6,730 Jews, about 70 percent of the total population, as was typical for towns in Eastern Europe. Since 1874, the town had an elected City Council (12 Jews, 9 Ukrainians, 9 Poles) and between 1879 and 1921 Berish Stern, the son of the head of the Jewish Kehilah, was mayor of Butshatsh — not quite a Jewish exile. The Jews engaged in trade (indeed they conducted the trade of agricultural products for the whole region) and in crafts: they were the tailors, furriers, carpenters of the area. There was also a vigorous political and cultural life: Hasidim, Misnagdim and enlightened, semi-secular, and worldly Maskilim, a Socialist party and a Socialist-Zionist party, and so on. Keep in mind that the language of the Austrian state, army, bureaucracy, and university was German (which was relatively easy for Yiddish-speaking Jews to acquire, especially when they had ties to German market cities, such as Leipzig), while Polish had an autonomous status in Galicia and many Jews studied in Polish Gymnasia. On the other hand, the Jews spoke Yiddish and had close relations to their brethren on the Russian side of the nearby border, and infused it with the two languages of study, biblical Hebrew and talmudic Aramaic (both together were called "The Holy Tongue"). Thus, the minimal education of boys was in five languages (girls often studied French, too).

Agnon was born on 8/8/1887, yet he claimed he was born on the 8/8/1888 (lucky number) which fell on Tish'a Be-Av, the ninth of Av in the year 5,648 since the creation according to the Hebrew calendar (which is simply wrong, because that date fell on August 17, 1888). The ninth of Av is a most significant date: it is a day of fasting to commemorate two events of apocalyptic proportions in Jewish history, the Destruction of the First Temple and the Destruction of the Second Temple. It is also, according to one tradition, the day the Messiah will be born. Agnon lived in a mythological universe, in the ahistorical world perception of Talmudic Judaism, where dates were less important as points in a chronological narrative but rather as significant moments in a universe of meaning.

In a similar way, Marc Chagall, who was born a few weeks before Agnon on the other side of the Russian border, claimed he was born on 7.7.87 (the actual date was June 24 1887, according to the old Russian calendar, which is equivalent to July 6 in the new calendar). But for Chagall, the magical number seven was an omen of his chosen destiny as an irrationally creative artist (see his "Self-Portrait with Seven Fingers"), while Agnon's fictional birthday was linked to the two great Destructions of the Jewish nation in the land of Israel (and perhaps, to the nation's Salvation, as mentioned in the first sentence of this novel). Did Agnon see himself in his innermost soul as the Messiah, the visionary prophet who would find the lost key of Jewish destiny or perhaps as the witness to two final destructions (as represented in his two great novels)?

Agnon received a traditional Hebrew education from the age of three until the age of ten, then was guided by several private teachers and embarked on an intensive course of study and reading. His father was a furrier, steeped in traditional Jewish learning, and praying in the prayer house of the Tshortkov Hasidic sect, whereas his maternal grandfather was a Misnaged (opposed to Hasidism). His mother was an avid reader of German literature, and at an early age, along with extensive readings in the traditional Jewish Library, Agnon learned Polish and German, read modern Hebrew secular literature as well as European fiction, as mediated through Yiddish and Hebrew translations, and read German literature as well as the fashionable Scandinavian novelists Ibsen, Biörensen and Hamsun in German translations.

He began publishing in Yiddish in 1903 and published stories and poems in Yiddish and Hebrew. When he reached the age of twenty-one, rather than being drafted to the army, Agnon left Butshatsh. After visiting Lvov, Cracow, and Vienna, in June 1908 he immigrated to Palestine, settled in Jaffa, in the new Jewish neighborhood of Neve-Tsedek, and worked as an assistant editor of a literary journal. Here, his first story, "Agunot" ("Abandoned Women") was published, signed: Sh-Y Agnon ("the teller of 'Agunot'"). In 1912, he lived for several months in Jerusalem, where Yosef-Hayim Brenner, the highest literary and moral authority among the Labor-Zionist settlers, published at his own expanse Agnon's most important early novella, *And the Crooked Shall Be Straight*.

In October 1912, like most members of the Second *Aliya*, Agnon left Palestine and returned to the Diaspora. He settled in Berlin, where he met Sh.Z. Schocken, a well-known German businessman, Zionist, and publisher, who became his lifelong patron. In 1918 *Und das Krume wird Gerade* was published in German. In 1920, Agnon married Esther Marks from Koenigsberg, with whom he had a daughter and a son. In 1921 they settled in Bad Homburg, but in June 1924 the house burned down, along with Agnon's library and manuscripts. In October 1924, Agnon returned to Palestine and settled with his family in Jerusalem. During the Arabic pogroms against Jews in 1929, Agnon was moved to the center of Jerusalem and his house in Talpiot was badly damaged. In 1930 he traveled to Leipzig, where his collected writings were being edited in Hebrew (published by Schocken in four volumes in 1932). In the summer of 1930 he also visited Poland and his hometown Buczacz, which served as the basis for his novel *A Guest for the Night* (published in 1939). In 1945, the novel *Only Yesterday*, written during the war, appeared in Hebrew. He was twice awarded the prestigious Bialik Prize for literature and twice (in 1954 and 1958) the highest Israeli award, the Israel Prize. In 1966, Agnon was awarded the Nobel Prize for literature, together with the Jewish-German poetess Nelly Sachs. Agnon died on February 17, 1970 and was buried on Mount of Olives in a State funeral.

This translation has enjoyed the generous support and assistance of many friends. I had the good fortune to work with the intelligent and supportive Dr. Brigitta van Rheinberg of Princeton University Press. Once again, James Ponet, "the Hillel rabbi" at Yale, was an eager participant in my search for sources. Parts of the manuscript were read by Robert Alter, Carol Cosman, and Michal Govrin; Esther Fuchs carefully read the entire book. All of them contributed helpful suggestions and comments. And, as always, Benjamin Harshav makes it all possible.

I attempted to discover allusions in the text to sources in the "Jewish library," and to track down their accepted English translations. In only one instance did I deliberately deviate from the original: in Book Four, Chapter One, the author presents an elaborate wordplay using biblical and talmudic passages to interpret the dream of a Hasid. Agnon used Deuteronomy 32:42 and Shabbat 12, while I used Exodus 6:1 and Miqvaot 5:5 to achieve the same effect. If there is some other world, where translators can discuss "deviations" with authors, I hope Agnon will understand.

Barbara Harshav

SEPTEMBER 1999

ONLY YESTERDAY

1 |

Like all our brethren of the Second Aliya, the bearers of our Salvation, Isaac Kumer left his country and his homeland and his city and ascended to the Land of Israel to build it from its destruction and to be rebuilt by it. From the day our comrade Isaac knew his mind, not a day went by that he didn't think about it. A blessed dwelling place was his image of the whole Land of Israel and its inhabitants blessed by God. Its villages hidden in the shade of vineyards and olive groves, the fields enveloped in grains and the orchard trees crowned with fruit, the valleys yielding flowers and the forest trees swaying; the whole firmament is sky blue and all the houses are filled with rejoicing. By day they plow and sow and plant and reap and gather and pick, threshing wheat and pressing wine, and at eventide they sit every man under his vine and under his fig tree, his wife and his sons and daughters sitting with him, happy at their work and rejoicing in their sitting, and they reminisce about the days of yore Outside the Land, like people who in happy times recall days of woe, and enjoy the good twice over. A man of imagination was Isaac, what his heart desired, his imagination would conjure up for him.

The days of his youth departed in his yearning for the Land of Israel. Some of Isaac's friends had already taken wives and opened shops for themselves, and they're distinguished in the eyes of folks and are invited to all public events. When they enter the bank, the clerk sits them down on a chair; when they come to a government office, the dignitaries return their greetings. And others of Isaac's friends are at the university studying all manner of wisdom that sustains those who possess it and magnifies their honor. While Isaac shortens his life and spends his days and his years selling *Shekels* to vote for the Zionist organization and selling stamps of the Jewish National Fund. His father wished to extricate him from his folly and set him up in a shop so he would be occupied in trade and become a man, but as soon as he entered the shop, the whole shop turned into a branch of Zionism. Anyone who didn't know what to do with himself went there. There were those who came to talk and those who came to listen, and those who just came and stood leaning on their walking stick and chomping on their beard, and the customers were dwindling and dropping away to other shops.

Even though there is a Society of Zion in the city, the talkers were fond of that store, because at the Society, you have to pay monthly dues, while here you entered and didn't pay. At the Society, everyone who comes in is dubbed a Zionist, and not everybody wants to be known as a Zionist, while here you were entitled to split hairs about Zionism to your heart's content and nobody called you a Zionist. And why are they afraid to be counted among the Zionists? Because the Sages of the Generation did not yet grant their seal of approval to Zionism and were hostile to the Zionists who make Societies for the Land of Israel thus annulling the Salvation that has to come by a miracle. All those who fear their words or are in awe of them are afraid to be called Zionists, but obstreperous individuals permit themselves to split hairs about it. They gather in Simon Kumer's store and find people like themselves and fire each other up with words that are food for the soul.

Thus passed the days of Isaac's youth, days that should form the foundation of a man's future. He didn't notice that he was spending them idly, or he did notice and wasn't worried, because his dwelling Outside the Land wasn't worth anything in his eyes, for all of Isaac's desire was to be in the Land of Israel. He remained alone in the shop, sitting and counting the Zionist Shekels he sold and making calculations, such as, if every single Jew gives a penny every day to the Jewish National Fund, how many acres can you buy with that small change and how many families could be settled on them. If a customer comes in to ask for some merchandise, Isaac glances at him like someone who is sitting on a treasure trove and people come and bother him.

2 |

When Simon, Isaac's father, saw Isaac's activities, he was bitter and depressed and worried. He would stand in the door of his shop and wring his hands in grief, or would sit on the chair and lean his head back and blow out his lungs inside him. If you haven't seen Simon Kumer, the father of Isaac Kumer, sitting in front of his son you never saw a father's grief. Before his son Isaac was grown up, his wife was his helpmate, and when she passed away leaving behind her a house full of orphans, Simon expected his son would help him. And what does the son do? Is it not bad enough that he doesn't help him, but he also drives the customers away to other shops? Simon neither quarrels with his son nor consoles him, for he has learned that neither quarreling nor conciliatory words will do any good. A curse has descended on the world, sons do not heed their fathers and fathers do not rule their sons. And Simon has despaired of getting any joy and satisfaction from his son and has started worrying lest his other sons learn from Isaac's deeds. He pondered the matter and agreed to send Isaac where he wanted to go. True, there is no prospect for the Land of Israel, but at any rate there may be some profit in that, for when he sees there is really nothing there, he'll come back to his hometown and settle down like everybody else, and the other sons will be saved and won't get dragged into this nonsense.

Simon didn't spare his son's dignity and would joke, For what reason do I agree to his journey? So he'll see with his own eyes that the whole business of the Land of Israel is a fiction the Zionists made up, and he'll remove it from his heart. Isaac heard and wasn't vexed. For the sons of Israel, if they aren't the sons of rich men or geniuses, grow up meekly, hear their disgrace and keep silent. And Isaac said to himself, Let Father say what he wants, in the end he will see that my way is the right one. Thus Isaac received his father's consent to the journey. From the day he was born not a thing had been done to his desire until that thing came and was done to his desire.

3 |

So great was the power of Isaac's trust in the Lord that even the town wags who make a joke of everything didn't laugh at him. His father began to think that perhaps God sent him to be a sustenance and a refuge for us. When Simon considered the journey, he started worrying and groaning and sighing, May I drop dead if I know where I'm going to get the money for the trip. Even if I sell all my wares it won't be enough. And even if it is enough, nobody comes in to buy, for Isaac has already made the customers forget the way to my shop. And even if my customers do come back they don't pay cash. All Simon Kumer's days were worries about money. Three generations had drawn their livelihood from the treasures their ancestor Reb Yudel Hasid had discovered, and the fourth generation finished off that wealth and didn't leave Simon Kumer, father of Isaac, son of the son of the daughter of Reb Yudel's daughter, even the remnants of remnants of those treasures. And now that he is pressed for money, no miracle occurred to him, and he didn't find a treasure as his ancestor did. Reb Yudel who had perfect trust in God was paid by the Holy-One-Blessed-Be-He to match his trust, while Simon his descendant placed his trust in trade, and trade sometimes brings honors to those who practice it and sometimes brings horrors on those who practice it.

Now a new worry was added to his worries, finding money for the journey. In those days there was some idle money among the well-to-do men of the city, for the royal authority had issued a decree against pawning, and they were afraid to lend to a Gentile who might report it to the government, yet they did take the liberty of lending to Jews at a fixed rate of interest. But where will a poor Jew get money to pay? And there's another problem here too, for Isaac won't find any work in the Land of Israel, and by the time his departure is paid for, he'll need to borrow to pay for his return.

Meanwhile, the time came for Isaac to be drafted into the army, and there was not a chance that he would be excused, for he was a healthy fellow and without the wherewithal to bribe the army commanders, and serving in the army meant profaning the Sabbath and eating forbidden foods. In spite of himself, Simon went back to pondering the journey.

Thus he went to the pawn shop and borrowed money for travel expenses and for clothes and footwear, for Isaac's clothing had laid him bare and his footwear wore him down because it was patched. He bought him clothes and ordered him shoes and a hat. Clothes of wool, shoes of sturdy leather, a hat of black felt, for they weren't yet experts on the climate of the Land of Israel and didn't know what clothes that Land demanded. True, they heard that the Land of Israel was a *hot land,* but they thought hot means beautiful, an in the poem of our bard, *the marvels of a land where spring blooms eternal.* For he is going to a place where they didn't know him and his clothes will show that he is from a fine home. Then Simon has six shirts sewn for him and ironed meticulously, because the ones he had showed more rips than patches, for ever since the day his mother died, no hand had mended them. If Simon had been blessed with wealth, he would have provided wedding garments for his son, but now he wasn't blessed, he provided him with supplies for the road. And he took a pillow and a featherbed from his wife's bed and gave them to Isaac. Then he took a valise and a sack, a valise to put the clothes and shirts in, and a sack to put the pillow and featherbed in.

4 |

Isaac parted from his father and his brothers and his sisters and all his other relatives and set out on the road. To the disgrace of his hometown, we must say that he parted from it without pain. A city that didn't send a Delegate to the Zionist Congress and was not inscribed in the Golden Book of the Jewish National Fund is a city you leave without pain.

Isaac came to the railroad station and bought himself a ticket, and boarded the train. He squeezed his sack under the bench and the valise he held in his hand and sat down wherever he sat down, his heart beating like those wheels beating their rhythm beneath his feet, and like those wheels, when they beat they travel on, so did Isaac's heart travel on. Yesterday he had worried lest there be some obstacle and he wouldn't go. And lo and behold, there was no obstacle and he is traveling. He had already left the borders of his hometown and was entering the limits of another city, and from that city on to another city. And if no mishap befell him on the way, in two days he would reach Trieste and sail on the sea to the Land of Israel. In his ruminations on the Land of Israel, he cleared his mind of every other matter, and even the Land of Israel itself seemed to grow more and more vague, for the pounding of his heart blurred his thoughts and the pictures of his imagination slipped away. Only in the moorings of his soul did Isaac see that he was transported from simple concrete things to a pleasant state of being.

The car was full of people from his hometown and people from other towns. Some were traveling for their own trade, and others were traveling for other kinds of business, and on their journey they started getting close to one another, as human beings would who chance to be in the same place and see one another as partners, if not in reality, then in conversation. Some talked about matters of trade and others talked about matters of state, some told news from their hometown and some skipped from one issue to another, like travelers who get excited about everything but don't linger long over anything. Unlike all of those, others sat in silence, because of the bad deals that got them in trouble. Some time ago the whole world rejoiced before them and now the whole world was sad. Maybe they will be exempt from a harsh judgment—from a light one they will certainly not be exempt. By the time you've got those deals in your hands, you're already in their hands. Isaac neither rejoiced with the rejoicers nor grieved with the grievers. Those businesses brought about by Exile were not worth either rejoicing or grieving about. Isaac had already shaken them off his hands and he would soon shake off the dust of Exile, like a man shaking something repulsive off his feet.

The train rolled on between villages and hamlets, cities and towns. Some were known for their great rabbis and others were known for their famous cemeteries. Some earned a name with the produce of their fields and the fruit of their trees, the fish in their rivers and the minerals in their mountains; and others earned fame with their poultry and livestock and other things in heaven and on earth. And yet other places have neither learning nor earning, but do have a Quarrel. Some sanctify the Name of the Holy-One-Blessed-Be-He with the Kedushah, *We shall sanctify You,* and others sanctify

Him with *We shall bless You,* and they wrestle with each other and create a Quarrel. And another Quarrel, between Assimilationists and Zionists. The former want to be like all the other nations, and the latter want to be Jews, so they wrestle with each other and create a Quarrel. And yet another Quarrel, between those who want Salvation by miracle and those who want a natural Salvation, so they wrestle with each other and create a Quarrel.

From time to time, the train stopped. Some got off and some got on. Some of them glanced at Isaac, for he had a pin stuck in his tie with the name of Zion engraved on it. Isaac didn't notice them, and if they said anything to him — he was silent. Isaac had removed himself from all arguments, and his heart was not moved by talk. Only yesterday, he was willing to argue about every Zionist issue, but today, since he is going to fulfill his words in deeds, all words are superfluous and supercilious.

Night began departing and the buds of morning started to appear. The train was approaching Lemberg, the capital of Galicia, home of most of the great Zionists of the Empire. Isaac broke up his trip and made a stop in Lemberg, to appear before our leaders and get their blessing before his ascent to the Land of Israel.

5 |

So Isaac picked up his valise and his sack and entrusted them to the guards. He smoothed the wrinkles in his clothes and entered the city. From students in his hometown, Isaac had heard of the coffeehouse where our leaders hold their meetings. A big city is not like a small town. In a small town, a person goes out of his house and immediately finds his friend; in a big city days and weeks and months may go by until they see one another, and so they set a special place in the coffeehouse where they drop in at appointed times. Isaac had pictured that coffeehouse, where the great Zionists gather to discuss the needs of the nation, as the most exquisite place, and he envied those students who could go there any time, any hour. Now that he had arrived in Lemberg, he himself went to see them.

And so Isaac came to Lemberg, capital of Galicia. Tall buildings rise high and higher and carriages move without horses, and bronze horses stand erect with bronze dignitaries astride them. And there are gardens planted in the city and stone figures spraying water from their mouth, and big synagogues built on stone pillars, and an old Jewish cemetery full of saintly and righteous ancestors protects the city. This city is a paragon of beauty, the joy of the whole land. Here sat the masters of the Torah, the interpreters of the sea of the Talmud and the interpreters of the *Shulhan Arukh*, and from here went forth most of the first Maskilim who wanted to rejuvenate our spirit, and here sat the Shepherds of Israel, the Champions of the Holy who could stop evil decrees, and like them were their righteous wives who, with their righteousness and their grace, overcame the persecution. If our misfortune is as wide as the sea and our troubles as multiple as the sand, there are pearls in the sea and jewels in the sand, the former are the Chiefs of Israel the Leaders of the Generation, and the latter are their proper wives who were given them by God for grace and mercy even in the land of our foes. Two cities there are in Galicia whose fame goes far and wide, Brod and Lemberg. The glory of Brod, her glory in the days of Reb Yudel Hasid, Isaac's ancestor, is departed now, but Lemberg still stands in her splendor. From the day the Jews came to Lemberg six hundred years ago until now, her light has not grown dim. Wherever you turn, in whatever corner you look, you find her greatness.

So Isaac walked along the streets of Lemberg. Before him and behind him, men and women are wearing expensive clothes like guests at a wedding, and heavy carriages run hither and yon, and people who look like Bishops walk around like ordinary human beings, and if not for the schoolgirls pointing at them you wouldn't have known that they are famous theater actors. And shops filled with all the best are wide open, and clerks in uniforms come and go. And a lot of other things can be seen in the streets of Lemberg and every single thing is a wonder unto itself. Isaac looked neither here nor there. Like that Hasid, his ancestor Reb Yudel, who blindfolded himself with a handkerchief a few years before his ascent to the Land of Israel because he didn't want to please his eyes with the beauty of Outside the Land, so did Isaac walk around with eyes shut tight. Before long he found himself standing in front of a splendid palace with several thick glass doors, running one behind another and turning nonstop, and a boy stands between the doors, dressed in blue and gold, and dignitaries and gentlemen come in and go out with thick cigars in their mouths. So Isaac stood still and didn't budge, transfixed by a spell. Who knows how long he would have stood like that if a man hadn't come along, spotted him as a provincial who wanted to come in, and brought him in.

Suddenly Isaac found himself standing in a splendid temple with gilded chandeliers suspended from the ceiling and lamps shining from every single wall and electric lights turned on in the daytime and marble tables gleaming, and people of stately mien wearing distinguished clothes sitting on plush chairs, reading big newspapers. And above them, waiters dressed like dignitaries and like lords on the king's birthday, holding silver pitchers and porcelain cups that smelled of coffee and all kinds of pastry. Everything Isaac had pictured in his imagination was nothing at all compared to what his eyes saw, and everything he saw with his eyes was nothing compared to the terror he felt at that moment. He began shriveling and shrinking until nothing was left of him but his hands, and he didn't know what to do with them. One of those dignitaries waiting on the guests came up and bowed to him. Then a miracle happened to Isaac and he started talking.

6 |

The waiter took him to a room with billiard tables where fat, stocky people in shirtsleeves were standing and holding colorful poles in their hands, and they were knocking the balls with the poles. The waiter said to one of them, This gentleman is asking for you. The Doctor put down his pole and came and stood before Isaac. And Isaac looked at him and was stunned. Could this be that shining icon gleaming on the walls of his house among the other pictures of the heads of the Zionists. When he realized that there was no mistake, he began to venerate him as he venerated his icon, and told him all his business.

The Doctor took him and introduced him to his companions, as if to say, If you're members of the group, share its vexations with me. And Isaac repeated to them, From the day I knew my mind, I gave my heart and soul to Zionism. I did not dread the scoffers and I suppressed my pity for my father and occupied myself with the needs of the Land of Israel. I sold Zionist Shekels and stamps of the Jewish National Fund, and I placed collection bowls on Yom Kippur eve in a few synagogues in the city. Oftentimes I was humiliated, but I paid no heed to it, but piled one deed on top of another, and now I am ascending to the Land of Israel to work her soil. And even though every day I spend Outside the Land of Israel is not reckoned in the number of days for me, I have broken up my trip and come to Lemberg to see our teachers and to receive their blessing before my ascent.

Neither his clothes nor his shoes nor his movements were cut to the style of those who sit in coffeehouses, they could even be called ridiculous; yet all his listeners were drawn to his words. Even though they were used to small-town people pestering them with their stories, they found in that lad what they didn't find in most of the youths. But they were amazed that he was going to Palestine. Anyone who is a Zionist and has the wherewithal goes to Conferences; if he's got a lot, he travels to the Congresses, for at that time they weren't accustomed yet to ascending to the Land of Israel, but every Zionist sits in his hometown and wins souls for Zionism. And if need be, they travel to Conferences and to Forums to deliver speeches. Some of them forsook their world for Zionism and were willing to give up their soul for it, but for the means they forgot the end, and strayed off into thinking that the end of Zionism is assemblies, and the end of assemblies is speeches, and the end of speeches is propaganda, and the end of propaganda is — propaganda. At first, the Land of Israel was the end of all ends for them, yet when they saw that the end was distant and hard and the means were close by and easy, they traded the distant and hard for the close by and easy.

So Isaac sat before our heads and leaders and feasted his eyes on them. And they looked favorably on him, too. This provincial who had been a nuisance to them at first was beginning to stir their heart. So they stood up and put on their coats and went with him to drink a cup of coffee. They treated him to coffee with cream that cost fourteen Kreutzers, and cake that also cost fourteen Kreutzers, which is twenty-eight Kreutzers, which is one thirteenth of the price of planting an olive tree in the Herzl Forest. And it was good that they invited him to eat and drink, because he had been so eager to see them that he had forgotten to eat and he was hungry. Yet our comrade Isaac didn't disgrace us, and didn't drink more than one glass, and didn't eat more than one piece of pastry, even though he was hungry and had never seen such fine pastry as that in his life.

So Isaac sat there before our heads and our leaders who were stirred by him. And since the hearts of our chiefs and our leaders were stirred by our comrade Isaac, they told him that even they might ascend to see what was going on there in Palestine. In those days, the Zionists used to call the Land of Israel Palestine. And when they got to Palestine, they would come visit him and would have their picture taken with him as he walked behind the plow. How happy Isaac was when he imagined himself standing among our leaders and our chiefs and the photographer is taking a picture of them together. Even the most humble of the humble doesn't run away from such an honor. Finally, they wrote letters of introduction for him to their colleagues in Palestine. And whereas he was the first one journeying to the Land of Israel and the first to ask for a recommendation, they lavished praise on him, and asked their comrades in the Land of Israel to support him and aid him and include him in their circle.

7 |

Isaac took the letters of recommendation and went to the railroad station. He collected his valise and his sack from the depot and boarded the train. The train was full of Jews and Christians, Jews who look like Christians and Christians who look like Jews. Isaac sat down and didn't raise his eyes to anyone, like a man who chanced upon great men and wouldn't dare lift his head. But when he heard their talk, his awe of them departed and he saw himself more distinguished than they, for they were traveling for their imaginary existence and he was traveling to the Land of Israel. He felt the letters and was glad as if he held a banknote hidden in his hand.

The train went on, sometimes fast and sometimes slow, swallowing between its wheels places whose names he had never even

heard of. How many cities there are in the world. There must be a
need for them. But Isaac has no need for them. If he hadn't stopped
in Lemberg, he would already have been approaching his destina-
tion. At any rate, he has no regrets, for during his visit to Lemberg,
he had greeted our leaders and had received letters of introduction
to their comrades in the Land of Israel. By now Isaac had stopped
reading the names of the cities. Other cities and other places
held sway over Isaac's heart, the cities and villages of the Land of Israel. But even in Galicia there are cities steeped in fond affection,
like Przemysl, because the prayerbook you prayed from in your
childhood was printed in the Holy City of Przemysl, and because
Przemysl is a Citadel, a fortress for the whole state. Like everybody
else in Galicia, Isaac thought that in the whole world there was no
Citadel stronger than the one in Przemysl, and now that the train was
arriving in Przemysl, he pressed to the window to see the Citadel,
and was stunned to find that you don't see towers or turrets or can-
nons or any of those things he had heard about. But he did see army
commanders, generals of legions of several nations with different col-
lars and colors, for every single legion has its own color. Officers of
the armies of the Emperor were strolling about the yard of the railroad station. Some with red and green and gray epaulets and some
had their beards and their mustaches shaved like priests. These were
the troops of General Windischgrätz, like those we saw in our hometown when they came there for war exercises. And there were also
cavalry and infantry, artillery and sappers, and officers of other troops
that you don't know what they're used for. Isaac's eyes were drawn to
see but his heart shriveled and told him, Don't stand at the window
and don't show yourself to them, for the sight of your face can bring
trouble down on you, for you have reached the age of military service and you are shirking and going to another land.

So Isaac went back and sat down in his seat and shrank up
so they wouldn't notice him, for you never know if, among the passengers, there are those who would denounce you, who would turn
you over to the authorities and you would not reach the Land of Israel. But blessed be all the passengers, all were proper Jews and none
of them turned him in or denounced him. And even though all of

them love the Emperor and wish him well and want his armies to be strong, they don't think of turning a Jewish boy over to the army.

After the train moved, Isaac raised his eyes. He saw before him dignified people, their beards black and shapely, their hats big and wide, and their shoes polished and shining. They sit comfortably and take cakes and brandy out of their bags and drink a toast and converse pleasantly with one another like well-mannered people. The train makes another stop, and broad-shouldered men with thick side-locks and wide belts come in. No sooner did they put their belongings down than they started reciting the prayer: *It is You, HASHEM, our God before whom our forefathers burned the incense-spices in the time when the Holy Temple stood as You commanded them through Moses Your prophet, as is written in the Torah*. All the passengers joined them and stood up for the afternoon prayers.

The train moves on and on and Reuben doesn't go where Simon goes and Simon doesn't go where Levi goes, but this one goes to this place and that one to that place. But at that hour, all their faces are turned to Jerusalem and their hearts are turned to their Father in Heaven, and all of them stand in awe and submission and great devotion and recite the afternoon prayers. Then the conductor came in and saw Jews standing at their prayers, so he withdrew and went to check the tickets of others who weren't praying.

8 |

The train moves on and on, and as it moves it embraces stations and villages, towns and cities. And at every station, the conductor announces the name of the town, and signs hang in the railroad stations, and wherever the train arrives, the name of that city shines on the sign. Cities whose names you never even heard roll by. And all of a sudden, your heart is shaken because the train has reached Tarnow, that same Tarnow that added a village in the Land of Israel. That village, Mahanayim, has already fallen to rack and ruin and its despondent inhabitants have left there. But your affectionate glance rests on every Jew who gets on the train from this city, for that person may have lent a hand to the Land of Israel or he may have been in the Land of Israel and returned here because he didn't succeed there.

A few years before, the newspapers announced that the farmers of Mahanayim were in trouble and distress and Isaac collected ten Crowns for them. Ten Crowns isn't enough to satisfy a host of hungry people, but it can show them that even in a wretched town like Isaac's, there is a person who pays heed to his brothers who work the soil of the Land of Israel.

The train moves on its way, disgorging passengers and absorbing passengers. People come with open hearts and strange pronunciations. Some look with angry eyes at Isaac because he is sitting in his seat while they are wandering from place to place, and some look with angry eyes because their heart is pressed and making a living is hard. Isaac ponders, those people are Hasidim of that Rebbe who didn't miss a time or place to revile and vilify the Zionists. Last year, Between the Straits, between the seventeenth day of Tamuz when the walls of Jerusalem were breached and the ninth day of Av when the Temple was destroyed, on the Sabbath when we bless the consoling month of Av, he sat amid his Hasids before the prayer and maligned the Zionists as was his wont. And when he passed before the Ark with the blessings for the new month and for *impending salvation,* he added a curse to the blessing and shouted at the top of his voice, But not through the wicked heretics in our time. And because he feared lest the Holy-One-Blessed-Be-He didn't know the Holy tongue, he translated his words into Yiddish, *Di epikorsim vus zaanen in inzere tsaatn.*

The train reached Cracow, a metropolis with everything in it. Here is an observatory where you see the stars of the sky in their orbits, and here is the grave of the RaMA, Rabbi Moses Isserlish of blessed memory along with the graves of other great Jews. Here the *Magid* came out and here the *Mitspe* is published. And at the gates of the city two enormous bones of a horrific beast stand erect, and the author of *The Paths of the World* wrote of them that no eye ever saw their like in all the lands of the globe. Jews wearing Shtraymls board the train, and their faces are like the faces of drawings engraved on the covers of old books. The train stayed for some time and started on its way again. And on its way, it made a stop here and it made a stop there. People get off and people get on. The Hasids keep decreasing and people whose business is greater than their Hasidism fill the train.

From the depths of the earth, from twisting tunnels, a mighty voice emerges. Such a tumult you never heard even in Lemberg or Cracow, for this place, Oderberg, is a railroad junction, and from here the tracks split and the trains spread out and go to many places. Since the train tends to stay here a long time, some of the passengers get out of the car and go to the railroad station. Isaac, who was scared to leave his seat lest he not find his car afterward, stood up and looked outside. He saw things that were simply amazing, like a kiosk full of newspapers. Or a man buying himself a newspaper, looking at it for a little while, and throwing it away. Newspapers did come to our hometown, too, but every newspaper counted a Minyan or two of subscribers, and after a year they bound it into a book, while here each man buys a newspaper all for himself, looks at it a bit, and throws it away.

9 |

Now the train left Galicia and entered the land of Silesia and the land of Moravia. Villages with thatch-roofed houses disappeared, and villages with tile roofs that turn black go on and on, and all the villages here are prettier than our cities in Galicia. And the villagers who board the car are dressed in city clothes. Their shirt doesn't come down over their pants, and the shoes on their feet are made of leather and not of straw. But the villagers themselves behave like villagers, they spit coarsely, and when they belch they don't cover their mouth, and their tongue is neither Polish nor Ukrainian, but a little like the former and a little like the latter, and it seems to have a singsong intonation. And at the side of the train they herd big horses and fat cows. And factories come after factories, and flatcars are coupled to the train full of chopped beets that look like sausages, and they make sugar from them, for there are a lot of sugar factories in this state, along with all the other factories and workshops. And they put out big chimneys as high as the sky with smoke rising above them. And at night flames burst from the iron pits and the crucibles.

And now we're approaching Vienna. The whole earth is engraved with tracks, and countless cars are flying in every direction.

You think you've come to Vienna itself, but you haven't even reached the outskirts of its outskirts.

And when the train pulled into the railroad station, the station looked like a bustling metropolis, and not a small one either, but a big one. And a jubilation erupted and rose and dignitaries and officers and gentlemen and ladies were pouring in, and in front of them and in back of them were porters loaded with bags and trunks and valises and suitcases and all kinds of fine vessels, as if they were transporting gifts to a king. Some hurry and run and some stroll and lounge. Isaac sometimes hurries and sometimes strolls, and doesn't know whether to stand still or to walk on, whether he is jostled or whether he is moved about in the throng. But he does know that he has to go to another train that is going to Trieste. Yet the masses of people blocked his way, and it seemed he would never get out of here. And even though he had about twelve hours until his journey, he began to fear he was late, and if he wasn't late yet, he surely would be late. He drew in his limbs and hunched up his shoulders and stooped over and threaded his way through the crowd with his belongings until he emerged into the open. He came upon a clock and saw that he still had the same twelve hours until his trip, and he pondered, If that is the case, I shall go and see the city. He deposited his belongings in the checkroom and was all on his own.

Isaac was all on his own and considered where he would go. Would he go to Leopoldstadt with its splendid synagogues whose beauty is unsurpassed throughout the world, or to the Prater, the joy of the whole city, or to the big house called Bunch of Grapes, or to their church that has a clock where every single one of its numbers is more than two feet high, or to the library where the Book of Psalms is written in gold letters on red parchment, or to the Emperor's palace, or to the Museum. Many were the things here that we heard about and now we can see them. And now we stand at the entrance of Vienna and we don't know where we shall go or where we shall turn. Isaac stood a while, his mind flitting from place to place but his feet aren't moving, for with so many things, his head is heavy and his feet are heavier than his head. So he waved his hand in resignation, and entertained the idea that a person who is going to the Land of Israel can forgo the whole world. Yet Vienna is Vienna and can't be dismissed with a wave of the hand. His feet moved by themselves, and he was dragged along with his feet. But there are so many things and you don't know what to look at first, either at her towers or parks, or at her statues or at the abundance of Gentiles. There are so many things here, and since there are so many, he sees and doesn't see. And a vague thought comes to him, Maybe here in this place where I'm standing now Herzl stood. And Isaac recalled something that not everybody remembers, that if it hadn't been for Herzl, we would have lived out our days in Exile and would not have ascended to the Land of Israel. Suddenly a voice that sounded like chanting pierced the air, and at the peaks of the towers, clocks began drowning each other out with their sounds. And hour after hour comes rolling in, and you listen, and how do you know whether it's for good or for bad. And the sounds rolled down from the peaks of the towers, and the expanses of the world tremble at their sound, and passersby stand still and set their watches, some with satisfaction and some with dejection. And Isaac prayed for himself, May the hours pass quickly and may I get to my place. But since the hours went on slowly, he had time. So he opened his mouth and asked where the Emperor's palace was. They told him the way. He came to the Emperor's palace and saw the tall gendarmes guarding the palace, and he saw the gatekeepers garbed in red and wreathed in loops and stripes, with many buttons sparkling on their clothes. And Fortune smiled on Isaac and he saw the Emperor's band playing the anthem. And if he had stayed there longer, he might have seen the Emperor himself, for sometimes the Emperor gets up off his throne and goes to the window for a little while. But we didn't wait, for we were in a hurry to travel.

After departing the Emperor's palace, he went to the Prater, the joy of the whole city. We don't know if he went there on purpose or not. According to the natural order of time, nighttime had arrived. But this night is not a night. Countless street lamps turn night into day. And water fountains entwined with all kinds of fire make all kinds of shapes of water. And a kind of melody is played, as if the trees in the parks were singing and playing. And the folks are also playing and singing. Even if you had a thousand eyes you still couldn't see it all. But at every single thing he saw, his pleasure was not complete, like a person who goes astray and is derailed, and cannot get to the place he longs for. And when he realized that, he rushed back to pick up his belongings and betake himself to the Southern Railroad Station, where you leave for Trieste. And before he went, he bought himself roasted potatoes and roasted chestnuts from vendors in the market, for all day he had had nothing to eat, for his food was packed up in his valise, and his valise was stored in the checkroom.

10 |

The train wound its way up, and wound its way down. High mountains flew by and snow lay on them, and even though Passover was already past, the snow didn't budge. And so, Isaac sits and rides through the realm of Austria, that same Austria that rules over eighteen states, and twelve nations are subject to it. One and the same law for the Jews and for the people of the land, their well-being is our well-being, for the Emperor is a Gracious King, he protects all who take shelter with him, Jew and non-Jew alike. Her earth is lush and fertile and the produce of her land is greater than the need of her inhabitants. She is blessed with everything and knows no shortage. One land makes wheat and barley and rye and beans and lentils and oats and corn; and another land makes potatoes and fruit of the orchard. One land makes plums for confiture and Slivovitz, and another land makes hops for beer. One land makes wine and another land makes tobacco and flax, and all lands are full of livestock, animals, and birds. Some give milk and butter and cheese, and some give meat and wool and skins and feathers. One land produces horses, and another land chickens and ducks and swans, doves, and pheasants, and bees make honey and wax, and her lakes and rivers are filled with fish and her mountains with silver and copper and tin and iron and lead for paint and salt mines, and coal and oil. And her forests make wood, and there are high mountains there, covered with eternal snow.

The train skittered between cities and villages, snaked its way between mountains and valleys, lakes, and streams. Then it threaded itself into a long cavity, crept on its bowels and crawled along slowly.

Darkness grows thick and black smoke rises. The red lanterns lighted in the car are wrapped in heavy mist. The wheels wrestle on the dark tracks, and it seems as if it's not the wheels that are turning but the tracks are moving beneath them, and along with them, the walls of the tunnel are running behind the train, reluctant to part from it. But the train prevailed. No sooner did it get rid of the walls than the tunnel grabbed it once again. The train roared a dreadful roar that rattled the walls of the tunnel and finally it shook off the tunnel and emerged, and a great light suddenly shone and greeted the passengers. And once again, forests are waving their trees and streams are peeping from the valleys and dales. By day the sun illuminates them and at night the moon smiles with light, sweet to the eye and pleasing to the heart. And from the high mountains comes a wind like a wind rising from the snow.

Passengers come and passengers go and officials change places with other officials. Some passengers are tall and dignified, wearing green coats and black leather pants and a green hat with a feather, and other passengers wear pink coats and speak a coarse German tongue that grates on the ear. And they too disappear and others come, speaking in a singsong. The night has passed now and in the train window a blue strip suddenly appears, stretches and widens with no limit and no end. People who were in the train with Isaac stood up and called out happily, That's the sea. That's our sea. Isaac stood up and looked at the sea. That is the sea which is a branch of the sea of the Land of Israel.

11 |

Dawn broke and the train approached Trieste. All the cars in the train were filled with valiant women, fat and stout, with suntanned faces, loaded with heavy baskets full of chickens and eggs, fruit and vegetables. Most of the passengers jumped up from their seats and helped the women arrange their baskets, looking pleased and smug at the produce of their land, like sons returning home and seeing it filled with all the best. Some asked how their sisters were, and others asked how the fruits of their gardens were; some asked what this one was doing and what that one was doing, and others joked with the women, and the women joked with them, until the train entered the station and all the passengers jumped up and got off. When Isaac had entered his car, he saw only those who were in the car; now that he got out, his eyes were confused by that population. And Isaac picked up his belongings and went down to the city. This was the city that was the end of all his journeys on land and the beginning of his journey by sea.

The city is big and noisy and large palaces loom up. All kinds of wares whose like Isaac had never seen before in his life he saw now in Trieste. And everything here is unusual and unfamiliar. Instead of horses — donkeys. Even the fish in the market are strange, even the fruit and vegetables. And a kind of warm bluishness permeates the space of the city and a smell of soaked grass wafts there. Carriages run and their noise is swallowed up in their rubber wheels. But a great turmoil rises from the city. A lot of people are here, and among all those many people, not a single one pays heed to Isaac.

Isaac walks around in the markets of Trieste, in one hand his sack and in the other hand his valise. The sweet sun he left three days ago in his hometown had grown old before its time. Spring it was when Isaac left his hometown and here it is summer. Endless sweat drips from his forehead and all his limbs are weary. Where will he go and where will he turn and where will he buy a ticket here for a trip to the Land of Israel? And Isaac put down his bundles and asked passersby, and they replied in a tongue that was incomprehensible to him. More than from their words, he learned from their gestures. Isaac set off for the sea. Innumerable ships are standing in the harbor of Trieste. Some came from distant lands and others are leaving for distant lands. Among all those ships stands Isaac's ship. The next day it sets off, and whoever buys himself a ticket buys himself a place on the ship, and is entitled to board it at once. Isaac bought himself a ticket and bought himself food. He ate a little and he drank a lot and he got onto the ship.

12 |

Isaac boarded the ship and found his place. He untied his sack and opened his valise and changed some of his clothes, for he took pity on his good clothes not to rumple them during the voyage so that he would enter the Land of Israel with them ironed. And after he found a place for his belongings he went to tour the ship. Aside from the crew, there wasn't anyone there.

The day began to turn dark and small lanterns illuminated the ship. The crew went to eat their supper and as they dined they sang in German and in Italian, hymns to the sea and other songs. The waters of the sea turned dark and stars flickered in the firmament, and the moon rose from the dark water and the black waves swayed silently. Little by little the sailors' singing stopped and silence spread over the sea. All that was heard was the sound of the waves lapping the boards of the ship. Isaac took out bread and sardines and sat down and ate supper and looked at everything around him, until his limbs started to grow slack and his eyes began to close. He stood up and packed the leftovers of his dinner and made himself a place to sleep. It didn't take long before he was lying down.

Isaac lay down alone on the big ship by the light of the stars in the firmament and the voice of the waves in the sea. Never in his life did Isaac lie down alone and never in his life had he slept outside. Never in his life did Isaac lie down alone because in his father's house there were only four beds. In one bed Father slept with little Vove, the son of his old age, and in another bed Isaac slept with his brother Yudel; and in the other two beds his sisters slept. And never in his life had Isaac slept outside, unlike rich boys who are used to outings and sometimes happen to sleep outside.

So Isaac lay and looked at the firmament. And since the stars that illuminate the sea are the same stars that illuminate the land, he looked at them and thought of his hometown, for it is the way of the stars to lead the thoughts of a person as they are wont. Isaac wondered and pondered, Now that I'm lying here, my brother Yudel is alone in Mother's bed, for ever since Mother passed away, he and his brother had slept together in her bed. (And before Mother passed away, every night a place would be made for them, a kind of bed made of boards placed on chairs, two on each side.) Or maybe Yudel was joined by Vove, our little brother, so Father would have more room. What does Yudel put under his head, now that Father gave me the pillow that was on the bed? Yet we shall leave Yudel and Vove and think about other things. Now that I'm here, the people of my hometown wonder why they don't see me, and maybe they ask about me and are amazed when they hear that I have gone to the Land of Israel. Some envy me and others are sorry I went, for as long as I was in the city I was busy selling Zionist Shekels and stamps of the Jewish National Fund, and now they've got to take care of selling them. I do hope the revenue won't decline.

And Isaac thought a great many other thoughts, and all his thoughts were about his hometown. The streetlamps have been lit by now and the city elders are sitting down to get a breath of fresh air, and girls are strolling between the marketplace and the post office, and students are escorting them, and maybe the girls are thinking about Isaac, because he went to the Land of Israel. Never in his life had Isaac paid any heed to girls. If his passion struck him, his heart carried him to the fields and vineyards of the Land of Israel. As he came to the Land of Israel, he saw a well in a field with flocks lying nearby, and a big stone lies on the mouth of the well, and it takes the strength of more than one or two men to roll it off. The village girls came there to water their flocks. And Isaac rolled the stone off the mouth of the well. They watered their flocks and returned to the village. The whole village was amazed, How did they manage to get back so fast today. And the girls said, We chanced upon a young man from Poland who rolled the stone off the mouth of the well, just as you pull a cork off the mouth of a flagon. And they said to the girls, Where is he, why did you leave him there? Call him and he shall dine with us. And they went out to call him and bring him with great honor, and a few days later he married one of them. Or perhaps this was how it was: Arabs were there and didn't let the girls draw water from the well. Isaac chanced by there and drove out the Arabs, and the girls filled their ewers and told their fathers, A fellow from Poland saved us from the Arabs. And they said to the girls, Where is he , etc.

But as he lay down alone on the big ship and the offspring of the sky looked graciously upon him and the waves of the sea rocked him, his heart swelled and he thought thoughts he wasn't accustomed to. At last, he cleared away all those thoughts and started thinking about himself, how he had given his soul to Zionism and how people used to make fun of him, and now that he was ascending to the Land of Israel, it was he who was making fun of them, for what importance do they and their words have if they don't lead them to action, and what was the difference between them and all the other denizens of the city, the former live out their days in Exile and the latter live out their days in Exile, neither of them want to move until the Messiah comes.

After he thought about their deeds in general, he began detailing the deeds of every single one of them one by one. Here's Reuben Leyb Weissbier, who is the first at every party and reads all newspapers before everybody else, and when Isaac came to ask him for the farmers of Mahanayim, he didn't give him a cent. You'd think maybe he can't give, but when it comes to giving money, that's where his Zionism ends. The same with Hirsh Wolf Atamanut, and the same with most of the Zionists in town. They'll give you prooftexts from the Talmud that the air of the Land of Israel is healing, but when they travel for their health, they go to Karlsbad and other places Outside the Land of Israel. And as for the young Zionist students we hoped would bring a new spirit of life to Zionism, they're willing to put off every Zionist meeting to go walking with a girl. Many more things Isaac pondered about the people of his own circle in his hometown. Some of them caught the trivial and turned it into the essential, and some heaped trivial on top of trivial and came up with trivial images.

And then again Isaac began musing on girls, and not because he was fond of them, but because of his sisters, who see their girlfriends strolling in a city street while they themselves don't show their faces outside because they don't have summer hats. How little Pesyele rejoiced when she put on her brother Isaac's new hat, danced around and said, Look, I've got a hat too, I've got a hat too. Finally, he dismissed all his thoughts and started thinking of sleep that would certainly not come, since he was lying in a new place and was lying outside, while he was accustomed to sleeping in a room with all the windows closed, and he might catch a chill and would probably get sick. And there was no Jew here to take care of him. Isaac was not a melancholy type who sees every illness as the beginning of death, but neither was he one of the optimists who don't stir their heart off their worries. All his thoughts came to an end only when weariness took hold of him and he fell asleep, for in three days on the train he hadn't slept but just leaned his head on the wall and dozed off for a while.

Who knows how long he would have slept if not for a flood of water that reached the place where he was lying. For day had dawned and the sailors were washing the deck and the water hit his bedclothes. He shook himself and jumped up from where he was lying. He scurried to fold up all his bedclothes and put them in his sack and put the sack wherever he put it. He washed his face and hands and put on his Tefillin and recited the morning prayer and drew out the prayers, since all the days on the train, he hadn't put on Tefillin except for the first day on the way to Lemberg, when they formed a Minyan on the train. After he fulfilled his obligation to God, he took out bread and sardines and sat down to eat.

13 |

By the time he sat down and ate, all the serenity of the ship had ceased. The crew were running in haste and in panic. Some were tugging heavy chains and others were hoisting big cargoes. Some were tying up all kinds of objects and others were bringing coal. The ship was in an uproar all around. And in the uproar and the confusion, men and women were boarding, dressed like lords and ladies, and in front of them and in back of them were porters loaded with trunks and packages. Soon the ship's siren was heard. The ship jolted out of its moorings and began moving. And now she left the waters of the harbor for the mighty waters of the sea. The lords and ladies disappeared and the commotion that had been there ceased. Every single one of the crew stood at his post to do his job, the work of the ship.

Isaac was left alone on the ship. The lords and ladies went in to dine and the crew were at work among the big boilers and the other covered places. Isaac looked at his belongings and saw that they were in their place, and he went on a tour of the ship. He strolled up and down and checked the thickness of the boards of the ship and everything his eye fell on, as he pondered to himself, It wasn't on a big, handsome ship like this that my ancestor Reb Yudel traveled, for in the days of Reb Yudel Hasid, there were not yet any steamships, but only sailboats that cruised the sea at the whim of the wind. Many troubles befell Reb Yudel at sea. Your common sense cannot grasp how he could endure them. But he did endure them all and accepted them lovingly, as if the Holy-One-Blessed-Be-He had been merciful to him by sending him torments at sea, so that he would enter the Land of Israel cleansed. Once a big tempest came at sea and the waves were about to swallow the ship, even though they knew the Hasid was going by the will of the Blessed-One. But that Hasid stood up and was not afraid, for he said, Whatever the Holy-One-Blessed-Be-He does, for good He does it, and if this be the will of the Blessed-One, it must be good. And with this knowledge, he grew greatly excited and became all joy. And the waves saw his pleasure and were ashamed and went away. As they went away, the ship was standing in the middle of the sea and there was a danger that it would get stuck there and would not move. All the passengers on the ship were terrified and scared that pirates would come and take them into slavery or that they would die of hunger and thirst, and would become food for the fish of the sea. They howled and lamented and wept, Is it not bad enough that they wouldn't get to the Land of Israel, but they wouldn't even get to a Jewish grave. And there was great weeping on the sea, as if they had already fallen into the sea and all the creatures of the sea were coming to eat their flesh. And that Hasid was joyful, for all the acts of the Holy-One-Blessed-Be-He were equal in his mind, and hence it didn't matter whether they moved or didn't move. He stood and chanted a wonderful melody, *To the Lord for all His deeds*. And the winds heard and came to appease him. They bore the ship, as porters bear burdens on their shoulders, until they brought it to the Land of Israel. And all the feats of Reb Yudel Hasid in the Land of Israel are told and retold in the courts of the Rebbes at the Melaveh Malkah Meal, the farewell to the Sabbath Queen on long winter days, and sometimes they get up from the meal and still haven't finished telling the events that happened to Reb Yudel Hasid.

Isaac strolled about, up and down, and looked hither and yon. A high sky stretched above his head and a great sea opened beneath his feet, and between sky and sea travels this ship we're sailing to the Land of Israel. And like that firmament above, the sea below is all a mighty blue, that keeps breaking open at the bottom of the ship and raises white waves, and the white waves curl up, turn dark, and sink. Sometimes a white bird descends from the sky and hovers over the ship, then rises back to the firmament and disappears in the blue mist, and sometimes a sailor passes by Isaac and blurts out a strange word. Once or twice one of the lords of the first class emerged, came and stood with his lady next to Isaac and said something to him. When they saw that his conversation wasn't likely to shorten their voyage, they left him and went on their way. Once again he was alone between sea and sky. And he didn't know that on that same ship were other Jews who were also going to the Land of Israel.

As he stood there, two people, an old man and an old woman, appeared. Isaac looked at them and was amazed, for he had thought there were no other Jews here but him. And they too were amazed, for they had thought there were no other Jews here but them.

The old man took his pipe out of his mouth and greeted Isaac, while the old woman nodded fondly at him. The old man asked Isaac, What are you doing here? Said Isaac, I'm going to the Land of Israel. The old man was amazed, Was it usual for a young man to go to the Land of Israel? Said Isaac, I am going there to work its soil. The old man began to be even more amazed. Wasn't the Land of Israel all made of synagogues and prayer houses? Wasn't the Land of Israel designated for prayer, and what did working the earth have to do with the needs of heaven? He concluded that that fellow belonged to the cult of Zionists who want to strip the Land of its holiness and make it like all other lands. He began fulminating at Isaac, like old Jews of that generation, who looked at us as if we came, God forbid, to turn the world into heathenism. He began arguing with Isaac. Isaac wanted to answer him as he had been taught. But he changed his mind, Why should I argue with an old man who is going to add another grave in the Land of Israel? When the old man started scolding him, Isaac countered his argument with prooftexts from the Torah, quotations he had found in Zionist pamphlets. The old man grew angry and said, You are twisting the Torah. By the time they parted from one another, they had become enemies.

People traveling together on a ship, even if they have something against one another, since the Lord-Who-Is-In-Every-Place has brought them together in the same place, they overlook their principles and treat each other amicably. And so it was that when that old man saw Isaac again, he removed the wrath from his heart. And to keep from falling into a quarrel, he let go of everything controversial and talked with him as a person talking with his friend.

The old man asked Isaac, Do you have any relatives in the Land of Israel? Said Isaac, What do I need relatives for, all the Children of Israel are comrades, especially in the Land of Israel. And the old man smiled and said, In the Sabbath blessing, say that and we shall answer Amen, but on all other days it's hard to make it without a relative, especially in a new place you don't know. Isaac asked the old man, And you, who do you have in the Land of Israel? The old woman answered, We've got a daughter in Jerusalem, married to one of the prominent men of Jerusalem, and, Thank God, they also have a daughter. And as the old woman mentioned her relatives, she started singing their praises.

Isaac looked at her dismissively, These people the old woman was praising, who are they? They too came only to add dust to the dust of the Land of Israel. Isaac is an expert in the deeds of those who eat the bread of the Distribution, who come from all lands to Jerusalem and study Torah in idleness and run from grave to grave, until they flicker out and die and add graves upon graves. And between one thing and another they create quarrels and stir strife and put Jerusalem into shame and disgrace. And surely that Reb Fayesh, the old couple's son-in-law, is one of those. As for Isaac, all the people of the New Yishuv are related to him, if not by blood, then by heart. Is there anything that brings hearts together like a mutual idea? And aren't all of Isaac's thoughts like their thoughts, to work the Land and to restore it from its destruction? Look at Isaac, his hands are delicate as a maiden's, but they are eager to do any work. And when the ship reaches Jaffa, he'll go to a village and pick up a hoe and work. Too bad his ship doesn't hurry as fast as his heart.

The old woman asked Isaac, How come we don't see here on the sea the big crocodiles that run after every ship to swallow it along with its passengers, and therefore sharp knives are attached to the ship to cut up the crocodiles so they won't swallow the ship, and here there are no knives and no crocodiles? A lot of questions that woman has, as is usual with those who travel the roads and sail the seas, who see new things they have never seen before in their lives, or who don't find on their way all they have heard about, and they are puzzled and ask questions. But our comrade Isaac took his mind off the sea, as if he were already in the Land of Israel and already seeing himself hobnobbing with the notables of the New Yishuv, whose pictures embellished the walls of his house. Today their memory is lost and their names are forgotten. But in those days, when we ascended to the Land of Israel, all mouths talked of them and all newspapers were full of them. Today those newspapers themselves are forgotten. But blessèd are the chroniclers who grant them two or three lines in their books.

Meanwhile, the old people had arranged for their journey and rented themselves a private cabin from the sailors and ate and drank and slept and enjoyed the journey, unlike our comrade Isaac who, in his excitement about the Land of Israel, didn't arrange for his journey and didn't prepare enough food and didn't rent himself a bed and wallowed on the deck and all the people of the ship leaped over him if they had to and if they didn't have to.

15 |

The food Isaac bought for the trip turned bad, and when he got up on the third day, he found his bread moldy and his fruit rotten and the rest of his food was not fit to eat. So Isaac went without food until his knees buckled with hunger, and he was ashamed to ask the old man, for Isaac was the son of fine citizens who would rather die of hunger than ask for charity, and here the sea air stirred his appetite more than on all the days when he was on land. He hoped for a miracle that would restore his food. But the food thwarted his hope and wasn't restored, on the contrary, it grew even more rotten. And when he tasted it again, he was about to vomit up his mother's milk. He was assailed by such despair that he feared the hunger would drive him out of his mind, since the sea air and the smell of cooking from the kitchen piled appetite on top of his appetite, and along with the yearning for food he was assailed by thirst. Then he cast out his shame and went to the old man. Isaac said to himself, I won't ask myself, but if he gives — so much the better. He found him reciting the blessing after food and "the slice of bread for the poor" was set before him. Isaac saw the slice of bread and began devising stratagems to get it into his hand so the old man wouldn't notice anything. Indeed, he could have taken the bread and the old man wouldn't have seen, for the old man was sitting with his eyes shut, as pious Jews do when they devote their heart to their Father in Heaven, and he surely wasn't thinking about his bread, but Isaac's hands went slack and he couldn't stretch them out. And he returned from the old man with his soul much hungrier. So he dropped his body in the aft part of the ship and pondered the slice of bread that could save him from hunger. He decided to go to the chef or to the waiter, maybe they would sell him something to eat. He took his teapot and came and stood in the doorway, as if he were requesting hot water for tea. The assistant cook saw him and filled his teapot, for the cooks are accustomed to ship's passengers coming and asking for hot water and giving them a tip for their trouble. In those days, there weren't many passengers on the ship and the cook didn't have anything to do, and was glad to chat with a person. He recognized that Isaac was hungry, brought him bread and cheese, and from then on the cook gave him food and drink all the days of his journey. And Isaac was not ungrateful to his benefactor and gave him a gift of a vest of hides that you wear in winter over a shirt and under a coat. It was the garment Father had given him before he set out on his journey. And the assistant cook wasn't ungrateful and protected him from the crew who treated him with contempt. And Isaac wasn't ungrateful and returned his favor, and when the assistant chef was about to paint the kitchen furniture, Isaac helped him. And that was good for Isaac, because the long journey on the sea bored him, and all the pamphlets and journals he had taken with him became alien to him, and the books he could have borrowed from the old man were far from his soul, for what were an old man's books, the Law of Israel and the Mishnah, and The Way of the Righteous, and The Hebrew Heart, pious books that a fellow like Isaac wouldn't look at.

And so Isaac spent his time with the chef and the chef was good to him. But as he was good for his body, he was bad for his soul, for when he heard that Isaac was going to Palestine, he started speaking evil of its Arab inhabitants. Isaac pleaded their cause, that they were sons of our uncle Ishmael, and Ishmael is the son of Abraham and the brother of Isaac. And the more the other man slandered them, the more he praised them. And the more he praised them, the more the other man slandered them. And from his slander of the Arabs, he came to slander the Jews, for it is known that the uncircumcised hate the circumcised. Sometimes they hate the Ishmaelites, and sometimes they hate the Israelites, and sometimes they hate both of them. But he did treat Isaac well in all matters of the body, for the Gentiles still treated the individual Israelite well, even if they hated the Israelites in general.

16 |

For ten days, Isaac shook on the waves of the sea. It was springtime, comfortable days for those who travel the roads and sail the seas. Every day the sun shone and every night the moon gleamed. Sometimes the sound of a bird was heard soaring in the air and sometimes another ship was seen, for more than one ship was traveling on the sea. Some were going to the Land of Israel and some were returning from the Land of Israel, and some were going to other places. Sometimes a silhouette of a human settlement was seen in the distance and sometimes other things appeared. For even though the sea is only water, it is not empty of other things. Every day Isaac would talk with the old man and the old woman, and every day he would get his food from the kitchen. Four times the ship made a stop, unloaded and loaded, let people off and took people on. People whose like Isaac had never seen came on board, some came from Bosnia and some came from other countries. Some were going to Alexandria in

Egypt and some were going to the Land of Israel. Some on their own business and some to serve God. Isaac didn't understand their language and they didn't understand his language, for they were Sephardim and spoke Spanish and he was an Ashkenazi and spoke Yiddish. And when he started speaking with them in the Holy Tongue, and they replied in the Holy Tongue, they didn't understand what he said and he didn't understand what they said, for he spoke the Ashkenazi dialect and they with a Sephardi accent. But when their heart was full, they would point to the East and say, The Land of Israel, and kiss their fingertips.

Between one thing and another, the ship got to Alexandria in Egypt. And when we got to Alexandria the whole ship filled with men, women, and children. Some had lots of clothes and some had lots of belongings, some had been wandering far and wide and some were returning to the Land of Israel. Some were happy and some were sad. Some were happy that they were returning to the Land of Israel and some were sad that they were leaving all the good things Outside the Land. Out of love for the Land of Israel, Isaac ran about and served them, tied and untied their packages and brought them hot water and played with the babies, gave his finger to a crying baby to suck and helped the mothers of the babies to dress them and put on their shoes. Meanwhile, they took his place and didn't even leave him room to rest his bones, or needless to say, his belongings. He had put down his sack and his valise in one place and found them someplace else. He thought they were in the first place and found others in their place. He went to look for his belongings and found them scattered about. And his mind too was scattered and his spirit was broken. His soul was weary and he wanted nothing but rest. Rest we didn't find, but only weariness. And if not for the weariness, our heart would have become empty. At the end of ten days, the ship reached Jaffa.

17　|

Our ship reached Jaffa, the gateway to the Land of Israel. A Jew arrives in the Land of Israel, leaps off the ship and kisses her soil, in the joy of weeping and weeping for joy. Isaac showed neither joy nor weeping, but spread his lips in a grin, and didn't jump out of the ship, for until a doctor came to examine the passengers of the ship, no one was allowed to leave.

The crew tied ladders to the ship. Strange people climbed up on board. Some pushed on top of others and some in front of others. Some were half naked and their faces were dreadful and their loud voices went from one end of the ship to the other. Even in a dream they would have terrified us. The ship's crew stood and looked at them, some laughing and some contemptuous. Men and women and their belongings were snatched up and disappeared in little boats standing near the ship. Isaac stood still in this turmoil. His lips parted, but his grin had been removed. Wherever he turned there was noise and crush. He wiped the sweat off his face incessantly, and when he wiped his face he seemed to be wiping away his sweat with a hotter sweat. The ship's crew pushed and were pushed. They blurted out curses and ran. Their faces turned dark from the soot of the smoke and the coal dust. When will the noise stop and when will we get out of here? A thousand times he is pushed from place to place, and he no longer feels his feet. It seems he has recoiled and is crawling on his belly. The doctor came and examined the papers of the ship's passengers. And some new people dashed around, searching among the ship's passengers and looking here and there. Suddenly they fell upon the immigrants, some weeping for joy and some in the joy of weeping.

Isaac forgot why he was standing here and what was in store for him. Next to him stands that old woman who traveled with him on the ship, hugging another woman in her arms, and weeping over one another. And when that other woman stopped weeping on her mother's neck, she grabbed the old man's hands and wept over them, as he stroked her and said, There there, hush. Isaac assumed that this was the daughter the old people had talked about on the ship and he envied them, for as soon as they entered the Land, they had a loved one. If he hadn't been ashamed, he would have approached her and wouldn't have been so orphaned. He began imagining that the old people were telling him, Come with us, and that woman was letting him stay in her house, and he found rest from his wanderings on sea and on land, for he had been on the sea ten days and three days he had traveled on land. But events are one thing and imagination is another. By the time the imagination spun its imaginings, the people he was with descended with that woman into a small boat and Isaac remained orphaned many times over.

Then two or three people came, one snatched his sack and one took his valise and another one pulled him. Isaac assumed that they had been sent for him to ease his entrance into the Land of Israel, and he said to himself in rhetorical figures, Our Mother Zion sent her sons to greet their brother who has returned to her. He wanted to show them the letters the dignitaries of Galicia had written about him so they would know that they weren't mistaken about him. But before he could take them out, he found himself sitting in a small boat rocking between cliffs and rocks.

The boat rocks down and up between the terrifying waves, and foam, turgid white and green-and-white, rises upon them, and salty water strikes his face and his hands and stings his eyes. The sailors lead the boat by its nose, and curses and cries rise from boat to boat. The sailors strike their oars and conquer the hard water, as they curse and shout back and forth to one another. Mighty rocks rise erect from the sea to butt the open boat and she dodges them and they get angry and roar, go down to the sea and lie in wait for the boat, and go back up and spray their foam on the boat and its passengers. But the boat keeps on rowing, and before Isaac knew if he would get out of it alive, a sailor grabbed him and hoisted him up onto dry land.

BOOK NE *A Delightsome Land*

On the Soil of the Land of Israel

1 |

Isaac stood there on the soil of the Land of Israel he had yearned to see all the days of his life. Beneath his feet are the rocks of the Land of Israel and above his head blazes the sun of the Land of Israel and the houses of Jaffa rise up from the sea like regiments of wind, like clouds of splendor, and the sea recoils and comes back to the city, and does not swallow the city nor does the city drink up the sea. An hour or two ago, Isaac had been on the sea and now he is on dry land. An hour or two ago, he was drinking the air of other lands, and now he is drinking the air of the Land of Israel. No sooner had he collected his thoughts than the porters were standing around him and demanding money from him. He took out his purse and gave them. They demanded more. He gave them. They demanded more. Finally, they wanted *baksheesh*.

When he got rid of the Arabs, a Jew came and took Isaac's belongings. He led him through markets and passages, alleys and yards. Trees with abundant branches rose up, and strange cattle were chewing their cud. And people wrapped in turbans mock in their own tongues. The sun is blazing above and the sand is burning below. Isaac's flesh is an enveloping flame and his sinews an ardent fire. His throat is hoarse and his tongue is like parched soil, and his lips are dry and his whole body is a jug of sweat. Suddenly a light breeze blew bringing life in its wake. But as suddenly as it came, so it disappeared. And once again he seems to be inside a case of fire and a pool of boiling water. He looked in front of him and was stunned. His escort had brought him to a yard and taken him into a dark house full of sacks and bundles and belongings and packages and baskets and crates and boxes, and told him they were setting the table and would soon call him to dinner. Isaac rummaged around for those letters our leaders in Lemberg had written for him to show the landlord that he wasn't mistaken about him.

The landlord wasn't mistaken about Isaac, but Isaac was mistaken about the landlord. This house was an inn and the landlord was an innkeeper and all his efforts with Isaac were simply to be paid for room and board. If Isaac had gone with others who had attached themselves to him on the boat, he wouldn't have had to wind up in this hostel where the food was thin and the bedbugs were fat, the bugs sucked his blood by night as their owner sucked his blood by day. Or maybe those who attached themselves to him first were also innkeepers whose affection was all for the sake of money. Isaac justified the judgment meted out to him and accepted everything lovingly. Isaac said, Tomorrow I'll go out to the field and I won't need this fortune I brought from Exile, and it didn't matter if they took a lot from him or a little.

Isaac spent that day and all that night in the hostel. He drank a lot and slept a little and waited for dawn to go to a village. When day broke and he wanted to go, the landlord said to him, Eat first and then go. When he had eaten and got up to go, he said to him, Where are you going? He told him, To Petakh Tikva, the Opening of Our Hope. The landlord said, The wagon's already gone. He wanted to go to Rishon Le-Tsion, the First of Zion, and he told him, Today the car doesn't go there. He wanted to go to some other place, and he told him, Arabs attacked that place and destroyed it. And so with every place Isaac wanted to go to, the owner of the hostel found something to delay him. At that time, the hostel was empty, had no guests, and when a guest wound up in the hostel, the innkeeper held on to him until his money ran out. Isaac fathomed the innkeeper's mind, and he got up and went to find himself a cart.

2 |

Isaac went out to look for a cart. As soon as he took one step, both his feet sank in the sand. This is the sand of Jaffa that digs underneath you to swallow you up. As soon as you stand on it, it runs out and turns into holes on top of holes.

The sun was strong in its dominion and beat down on Isaac's head. His eyes were filled with salt water and the fire lapped it and boiled it. His clothes are heavy and his shoes are blazing like coals. The ironed shirt he donned in honor of the Land sits on his heart like a soaked Matzo, and the hat rains salty dews down on his face.

Shapeless houses are strewn over the sand, which rises above their thresholds and rubs into the walls. The windows are closed and the shutters gleam in the sun. No sign of life is evident in those houses, but puddles of slops standing full and smelling foul indicate that human beings dwell there.

Isaac walks around in the wasteland of Jaffa. No man on earth, no bird in the sky. Only the sun stands between sky and earth like a dreadful being that won't bear any other being in its presence. If he isn't burned in fire, he will dissolve in sweat. Isaac no longer feels his clothes and shoes, for he and they have become one single mass. In the end, even the sense of himself was stripped from him, as if he were removed from himself.

God took pity on him and he didn't lose his head. Isaac knew the road he came from and knew that he could go back to the hostel. He made his heart obstinate and didn't return. He said to himself, Today I'll get to the settlement and I'll go into the forest and dwell in the shade of a tree and no sun in the world will overcome me. An imaginative man was Isaac and he imagined that the people of the settlements had planted forests to dwell in their shade.

Soon after, Isaac left the desert of sand and reached a dwelling place. Camels and donkeys and mules loaded with wares were standing around as if they bore no burden. Nearby sat a few Arabs with long, multicolored tubes in their mouths, and their eyes were raised to the sky. Nearby stood a few Jews and debated with the Arabs.

Isaac encountered one fellow. He said to him, "Pray, my lord, where might I find here a vehicle going to one of the settlements of the Jews?" The fellow held out his hand and greeted him. He welcomed him, saying, A new man, a new man. Isaac nodded in reply and said, I arrived yesterday, and now I want to go to Petakh Tikva or Rishon Le-Tsion. Does my lord know where I might find a vehicle?

The fellow replied, "Does my loydship see dose green trees standin in a line? If it may please my loydship, he'll toyn toyd dose green trees; and dere my loydship would please to find de carriages my loydship is seekin, both dose dat journey to Peysakh Tikvoy and dose dat journey to Rehoyvis and to Rishoyn-le-Tsioyn, and dose dat journey to de udder dwellins of our brudders, children of Isroyel, who dwell on de holy soil in de Holy Land." All that to make fun of him for talking in his Ashkenazi Hebrew of the Exile. Isaac got into conversation with him, and in the end they went into a coffeehouse to drink lemonade.

When they entered they found a group of young men, sitting both silent and slovenly. They raised their weary eyes to Isaac and looked at him. One of the group stretched out his hand and greeted him and said, A new man comes, hissing as if he were hushing his thoughts and calling Hush hush. Isaac returned his greeting and said, Yesterday I was fortunate enough to ascend to the Land of Israel. And as he spoke, he waved his hat like a fan and blew a breeze on his face, he wiped his sweat and said, It's hot here, hot here. Someone exclaimed in amazement, The springtime isn't over yet and he's already hot. And another one looked at Isaac's clothes and said, The sun gets hot from patriots like you.

Isaac ordered lemonade for himself and his companion and the companions of his companion. He drank and didn't quench his thirst, and drank again and didn't quench his thirst. As soon as the beverage entered his body it came out on his face. He held his glass and wiped his sweat, wiped his sweat and drank some more. At first that drink is sour and sweet and finally it scratches your guts and leaves an insipid taste in your mouth. His companions ordered black coffee to get rid of the taste.

One of them asked Isaac, What's new in the world? Isaac, who thought there was no world except for the Land of Israel, replied, I'm a new man in the Land and haven't yet heard anything. On the contrary, perhaps I shall hear from you what's new in the Land. One of them answered, News you want to hear. Well then, hear. This place what is it, a coffeehouse, right. And this man talking to you what is he, a laborer in the Land, right. And this day what is it, a day like any other day, right. If so what is the laborer doing in the coffeehouse on a weekday? Except that he pursued all the Effendis in the settlements of the Land of Israel and didn't find any work. And why didn't he find any work, because their work is done by Arabs. And why doesn't he turn to construction work? After all a Hebrew school is being built here in Jaffa with money from a Jewish donor supported by the committee of the Lovers of Zion in Odessa, and they surely need workers. But the building supervisors turn us down and say that they have already given the construction work to contractors, and the contractors turn us down, because it's easier for them to work with foreign laborers, since the foreigners cost them less. And since they won't say that they're turning us down because, by their accounting, we cost them more than what they need to make a profit, they slander us, saying that we don't know the work. It's not enough that they take away our livelihood, but they also dishonor our name. Why are you looking at me? Don't you understand a human language?

Isaac understood yet didn't understand. He understood that they were building a Hebrew school, and didn't understand the actions of the contractors. He understood that that man walked through all the settlements, but didn't understand that he couldn't find anything. And why didn't Isaac understand, after all he did know Hebrew, but that man spoke with a Sephardi accent, and mingled Russian and Arabic curses with words that had been invented in the Land. How much Isaac loved the conversation of that man, held in Hebrew and in the Land of Israel.

Another man added, The officials of our national institutions, some of them get the salary of a governor, and complain about us laborers that we want a salary of two or three Bishliks a day. And they, who are no wiser than we are, think they have some superior wisdom and they made themselves patrons of the Yishuv, and they placed themselves in offices and write memoranda, while we pull the skin off our bones and take a leading part in all troubles.

Someone pointed at Isaac and said, Why are you scaring him? Said the one who spoke first, Shall I compose an idyll of the Land of Israel for him? And the other one said, That I leave to the poets and the tourists, and I ask you all, are you the only ones suffering? Aren't there people here who came before us, and if we tell all the troubles that befell them, time would run out. They came to a wilderness, a place of harsh malaria, and gangs of highwaymen, and harsh laws and evil governors. If they built themselves houses, the king's officials came and destroyed them. If they sowed, their neighbors came and threw their beasts on the grain. If they drove them out, they went to cry to the government that the Jews attacked them. And if some of the harvest remained, they didn't know if they should sow it next year or use it to bribe the clerks not to twist their laws against them. And what they rescued from humans was taken from them by Heaven. But they didn't despair and they endured all the troubles and they maintained the Yishuv through their suffering and turned the deserts of the Land of Israel into homes and vineyards and fields. And as he mentioned their suffering, he told of their heroism, and as he told, his companions told more and even more. Thus they sat and told tales about afflictions and tales about heroism, about those in the plain and about those in the mountains, about those in the sands and about those in the swamp. About those who eat the harvest of their fields and about those who are eaten by the Land. It is small, our Land, and how great are its troubles. And since they were telling about the settlements, they told about their founders. And as they were telling, they were amazed at themselves that they hadn't noticed the heroism of those founders before now.

How Isaac loved that hour when he sat in the Land of Israel in the presence of laborers of the Land of Israel who were telling of the building of the Land of Israel. The Land of Israel was acquired with suffering, and he who loves the Land of Israel and lovingly accepts her suffering, is privileged to see her being built.

As they sit, hunger begins to oppress them. One of the group stood up and said, It's lunchtime. Anyone who had a Bishlik or half a Bishlik began pondering whether to eat at noon or in the evening, and anyone who didn't have a cent in his hand was exempt from superfluous contemplations. It was hard for Isaac to leave the group so he invited them all to dine with him. He really did want to go to the settlement, but it was worth it for him to while away a day with them.

They sat and ate together. They ate to satisfy their hunger, and he who wasn't used to the food of the Land of Israel ate little, and even that did not accord with his habits. After they ate and drank, he paid their expenses. How heavy is the currency of the Land of Israel and how many kinds there are there, Francs and Megiddos and Bishliks and Matliks. If all the coins were put in one side of the scales and all the food in the other side, the coins would tip the scales.

CHAPTER TWO

Tells a Little and Slurs Over a Lot

1 |

At last, Isaac reached the settlement. Who can describe Isaac's joy when he saw the houses of the Jews in their settlement crowned with fields and vineyards and olive trees and citrus groves. These are the fields and vineyards and olive trees and citrus groves he saw in a dream and now he sees them awake. At that hour, Isaac was like a bridegroom about to enter the marriage canopy and lacks only a best man.

Isaac entered the home of a farmer to hire himself out as a worker. He found him sitting on a glassed-in verandah, drinking tea. The sun settled on the glass and the trees in the garden waved their shadows like a fan and a serene calm was spread over the farmer and his table. The farmer sliced himself a piece of sugar and sucked and drank, and looked with favor on Isaac. Isaac greeted the landlord and the landlord returned his greeting and said calmly, A new man, a new man, like a landlord who gets satisfaction and joy from a guest.

Isaac replied humbly, It has been two days since I was privileged to ascend to the Land of Israel to work its soil. Perhaps there is work for me here in the field or the vineyard or the citrus grove. The landlord sucked the sugar in his mouth and took a sip from his glass and replied calmly, Others have been here before you. Isaac envied the others who had been here before him at work, and was sorry for himself that he had tarried so long because of the hotel owner. At last he put off his sorrow and his envy. Thought Isaac, If I didn't find work with this one, I'll find it with somebody else. And as others have been fortunate, so shall I. He bade farewell to the landlord and went on his way.

When he went, he began to worry that he hadn't behaved decently to the landlord, for it was right to stay a bit and show him affection for receiving him kindly and being willing to take him on as a worker if others hadn't been there before him. He relied on the heart of the farmer not to be vexed with him, for he was in a hurry to find work.

Isaac went to his neighbor. He did not look favorably upon Isaac nor did he look upon him pleasantly. It is a sin to tell that he didn't even return his greeting. Isaac gave him the benefit of the doubt, perhaps sorrow had befallen him and his heart wasn't open. He began seeking words to console him. The farmer looked at him angrily and said something in Russian, which Isaac didn't know. The farmer's wife came and told him he should take himself to our neighbor, and she pointed him to the left. Isaac apologized to her for bothering her and her husband. She shook her head in sorrow for the Jewish fellows who trudge needlessly from place to place asking for work. Isaac took his leave from her and went to her other neighbor.

Isaac straightened his tie and fanned his face with his hat and knocked at the door. No answer. He knocked again, and no answer. He went around the house and found another door. He knocked, and no one opened. He hung onto the window ledge and looked inside the house. He saw that the room was empty. He went and hung on another window. He heard a kind of throbbing, and saw mice scampering in the house. Amazing. An empty house and the neighbors don't know.

He turned away and went to another house nestling among trees and flowers and surrounded by an iron fence, trimmed with copper flowers and a bell hanging at its entrance. Isaac found the gate open and didn't have to ring the bell to announce his coming. He wiped his shoes and straightened his tie, ascended stone stairs and entered a handsome vestibule full of handsome furnishings, such handsome furnishings and such a house Isaac had not seen in his hometown. He was proud of his Jewish brother and his spirit was humbled, as are small people who come upon a big house.

Isaac found a fellow standing in the vestibule like a pauper at a gate. His clothes and sandals indicated that he was a laborer, but it was hard to imagine that any laborers in the Land of Israel wore such paltry clothes as these. Meanwhile, Isaac took his hat off his head and held it in his hand, the way that fellow was holding his hat.

Words came from the room inside in a language Isaac didn't know, but he did know that it was French. The door opened and a lady came out, made-up and perfumed, and well-dressed. She closed the door behind her and said something in a language Isaac didn't know, but he did know that it was Russian. And she turned around at once and closed the door behind her. The fellow said to Isaac, You don't have to wait, because in her answer to me you find an answer to your question. Isaac grasped his meaning and knew there was nothing for him here.

The fellow took off his sandals, picked them up, and left. Isaac trudged after him and went with him. They went down the stone steps and closed the gate behind them. The bell sounded. Isaac looked upon the ground and saw that his companion was barefoot. His feet shriveled up in his shoes, as if they were pricked by thorns. The fellow spat and said, Had any tea? Isaac looked at him and was stunned. What did tea have to do with this? But since he was tired, he trudged behind his comrade, who walked along silently, his sandals in his hand.

2 |

The sun set and adorned the village with the gold of its fire. The streets began filling up with old men and young men, women and maidens. Old men went to pray, and young men came out to greet the coach returning from the city, and women came to greet their husbands returning in the coach. And others came for no good reason. Some spoke in the manner of the village and some measured their shadow.

Tranquility prevailed over the whole village and a kind of mellow warmth bubbled out of the ground. The trees gave a fragrance above and the bushes gave a fragrance below and the setting sun adorned folks' faces and made them affable. Suddenly the earth opened up and a plethora of Arabs covered the village. Gangs of three, one plodding along behind the other. Soon the whole village was filled with Arabs and soon the Jews were dissolved, turned into an insignificant minority. Isaac got scared, as if he had come upon a Gentile market fair. His comrade put a hand on his shoulder and said, Look at those people, they're laborers who work for our brothers the farmers. How much dust they raise. Come my friend, let's pour a cup of tea down our throat.

They got up and walked until they came to the edge of the village, to one of the ruins remaining there as an example of the first houses. Isaac's comrade walked around the ruin and went with him into a room whose walls were broke open and whose ceiling was ramshackle and whose floor was part dirt and part stones, and two holes peeping from the door let in the light. The host put his hand on the guest's shoulder and said, My house is your house. He sat Isaac down on a bed and told him, Soon we'll drink tea.

He went out and brought water from the cistern, put on a kettle and a kerosene lamp. He put on the kettle and lit the wick. The wick caught fire and illuminated the room. The host spread a sheet of *The Young Laborer* on an upright box, as if he were spreading a cloth on his table, and looked upon Isaac amiably. He took out bread and olives and tomatoes, and said, Take and eat.

Never in his life did Isaac feed at someone else's table and never in his life had he tasted olives and tomatoes. For he did not yet know that tomatoes are fit for human consumption, for in his hometown, they call tomatoes fools' apples, and clever people won't put a finger on them. Suddenly, Isaac finds himself sitting at someone else's table and tomatoes are placed in front of him. Hunger came and told him to eat. He took a slice of bread and two or three olives for which the Land of Israel was famous and wouldn't put a finger on the tomatoes. When he tasted the olives he twisted his mouth. The host smiled and said, Just as you twisted your mouth from them today, so you will be happy with them tomorrow, have a tomato. Isaac took a piece of tomato, ate a little of it, and put it down, like a person who says no to your sweet and no to your sour. His companion looked at him and said, If you want to be one of the Land of Israel, eat what you find. Give me your glass and I'll pour you some tea. Isaac gave him his glass and the host poured him tea, which he liked better than all other drinks. In fact, Isaac wasn't used to many drinks, but of all the drinks he had drunk, he didn't enjoy any of them as much he enjoyed that drink at that time.

After he drank his fill, he looked at the host and pondered, I gave a proper rejoinder to that old man on the ship who asked me if I had relatives in the Land of Israel and I told him that all the Children of Israel are comrades, especially in the Land of Israel. Better a close friend than a distant relative, for among all his relatives he didn't find one who loved him even halfway, because they disagreed with him for being enrapt in Zionism, and differences of opinion led to differences of heart. Among Isaac's relatives there are Hasids, and among Isaac's relatives there are Maskilim. The Hasids among them see him as a kind of heretic, the Maskilim among them see him as an errant Hasid. The former keep him at a distance because of his apostasy and the latter keep their distance from him because of his excessive Judaism. And still others of Isaacs relatives see him as an idler who doesn't lift a finger to make money. His schoolmates from the Heder and the prayerhouse weren't close to him either. Rich ones because he was poor, and poor ones couldn't stand him because he was arrogant about his Zionism. To make a long story short, until he ascended to the Land of Israel, he hadn't found himself a comrade. When he did ascend to the Land of Israel, he found himself a comrade.

This comrade was named Rabinovitch. If you saw ten Russian Jews, know that nine of them are called Rabinovitch. In Isaac's hometown, there was no one named Rabinovitch. From books and newspapers, Isaac knew that name, for it is the name of several famous writers and Zionists. Isaac was fond of Rabinovitch for himself and he was fond of him for his name.

Rabinovitch asked Isaac, Would you like some more to drink? No. Well then, we'll put out the machine and light the lamp. When he lit the lamp, mosquitoes and other wingèd insects found their way there, leaping from here to there and from there to here, from the face of the host to the face of the guest, and from the face of the guest to the face of the host. If Isaac twitched his shoulder, Rabinovitch jumped up and killed a scorpion on the wall with his sandal. He threw it away and said, They're frequent guests in my house. Why are you trembling like this? Now let's talk about your affairs a little. So, you came from Galicia? Tell me, why are the people of your country so remiss about ascending to the Land of Israel? Perhaps they're waiting for Emperor Franz Josef to lead them here in golden cars. It seems to me that, aside from Rabbi Benjamin and Doctor Thon, I haven't seen anyone from Galicia. Are they from your hometown? No? But you do know Rabbi Benjamin's essays?

3 |

A voice was heard at the door and a fellow came in. He greeted the host and looked at the guest in amazement. Rabinovitch said, I am honored to introduce you to our new guest, oh dear, I forgot to ask his name, so let's call him brother in sorrow. The fellow held out his hand to Isaac, greeted him, and said, And I'm a comrade in calamity. And so he wouldn't think he was hiding his name from him, he said, That really is my name, Comrade in Calamity.

Comrade in Calamity Gorishkin is his name, for Gore means Calamity in Russian. And why is he called that? Because wherever his comrades came to look for work and didn't find any, they did find Gorishkin. There's no work at all in the field or the vineyard or the citrus grove that he didn't try, and there's no work that he wasn't pushed out of by the Arabs. Only one place was left him by the Arabs — in the wine-press, and so he is about to go to Rishon Le-Zion or to Zikhron Ya'akov, perhaps he'll find work to do there.

Rabinovitch examined the kettle and saw that it was hot. He took a glass and poured him some tea and said, You surely haven't eaten dinner. Take and eat. Gorishkin said, Let me think first, when did I dine. Rabinovitch said to him, Eat first and then we'll deal with the chronicles of hunger. Here's bread and here are olives and here are tomatoes. Put sugar in the glass and sweeten your life.

Gorishkin sliced himself a big slice and ate heartily, and sweetened his meal with sweet tea, and looked at the tomatoes like a hungry man who sees a tasty dish. Rabinovitch said to him, Take a tomato and add spice to your bread. Gorishkin said, Where did you get this nice fruit? Rabinovitch smiled and said, From the place where all the tomatoes come, from the gardens of the Arabs. Gorishkin picked up a tomato, caressed it with his eyes, and said, A delight to behold, a delight to behold. He sank his teeth in it and licked its juice from his mustache.

Rabinovitch said to him, And you still complain about our farmers? Gorishkin looked at him in amazement. Rabinovitch added, Let's be grateful to the farmers who don't give us work, for because of that even you and I enjoy a fresh tomato. Gorishkin said, If there's no work, where does the money come from, and if there's no money, where does the tomato come from? If I do get work, I don't have time to look for tomatoes. For our farmers in Judea don't grow vegetables and they wait for the vegetables the Arabs bring them, just as they bring them chickens and eggs. And when do they bring? When the laborers are at work and can't go out to the Arabs to get tomatoes from them, and I add spice to my bread with old herring that dries up my guts, because I can't go into a hostel and buy me something hot to eat because the owners of the hostels demand that I pay the money I owe them.

Rabinovitch twirled the ends of his mustache and started humming a song to the melody of *Du schönes Mädchen:* Oh what a fool you are, how and why. If the farmers give me work I've got no time to buy tomatoes, now that I'm idle, I've got time to buy tomatoes.

When he had eaten and drunk, Gorishkin went back to talking about the Land and the work and the farmers and the laborerers, until he came to that story that some farmers were about to invite laborers from Egypt. It's not bad enough that they flooded the village with Arab laborers, but now they wanted to add Egyptians to boot and endanger the Yishuv with foreigners from outside.

Rabinovitch knew that Gorishkin knew that the farmers had already changed their mind, but to let him get rid of his anger, he didn't stop him. Gorishkin sensed that. He changed his tone of voice and said, But, to the credit of *The Young Laborer*, it did warn of the danger. And even though Gorishkin is a member of *Poalei Tsion* and doesn't approve of *The Young Laborer*, because it is too spiritual, that didn't prevent him from praising it for standing in the breach, and the village committee had already issued a circular letter denying the matter, and even though everybody knows the truth, there's some benefit in that denial, so everyone will see that the world hasn't gone to the dogs.

Rabinovitch sat and smiled. He seemed to be smiling at his comrade who thought the village committee was scared of a newspaper article and the farmers were scared of a circular letter. But in truth, he was smiling at himself and at his comrades, who hadn't yet shed their naiveté. Gorishkin said to him, Why are you laughing? Rabinovitch said, If I had money for the trip, I would go up to Jerusalem and put my hoe in the Bezalel Museum. And once again he smiled. But the sadness in his face betrayed that he wasn't joking.

4 |

The first watch of the night burned down and Isaac's eyes closed. The host saw that he wanted to sleep, consulted with Gorishkin about where to lodge the guest, for Rabinovitch's bed was too narrow for two. And even if he makes a bed for himself on the floor and gives the bed to the guest, he probably wouldn't find rest in it, for it is wont to fall apart and drop whoever is lodged in it. They went over the names of several of their comrades, the teacher whose home was open to guests and the laborers who were taken to the hospital in Jaffa and their beds spend the night without their lodgers and are ready to receive guests. Rabinovitch tapped his forehead and said, Didn't Yarkoni leave at dawn to go Outside the Land and they haven't yet rented his room, let's take our guest there and he'll sleep on a respectable bed in a fine room, for Yarkoni is from a rich family and his flat is the finest one of all our comrades.

The host extinguished the fire and took Isaac. The three comrades left and entered the village. The houses were concealed among the barren trees and the fruit trees, and between the trees water pipes sprouted and watered the orchards. The summer harvest gave off an aroma and the smell of scorched brambles mingled with the fragrance of roasted manure bubbling up from the Arab villages surrounding the Jewish village. Sometimes you could hear the sound of jackals' howling and sometimes the sound of a cow from the barn. Sometimes the sound of a wild animal dominated and sometimes the sound of the cattle of the human settlement, and between those sounds, the sound of water in the pipes was heard irrigating the earth and making the trees grow.

The whole village slumbered, some on down and some on straw, some slept the sleep of repose and some slept the sleep of toil. The villagers weren't concerned with politics or other unsettled issues that don't concern the settlement, but everyone minded his own business and slept when it was time to sleep and woke up when it was time to work. There were no quarrels there, aside from the small squabbles found wherever there are human beings. Sometimes the zealots in Jerusalem wanted to spread their influence over the village and there were mischief-makers who were drawn to them. But every squabble stopped as soon as it started, for the earth doesn't allow its workers to get involved in nonsense. About two thousand Jews dwelled there at that time. Owners of fields and vineyards made a living from their grapes and the produce of their fields, and owners of citrus groves made a living from their citrus groves. And anyone who left his fields uncultivated hired himself or his livestock to others, and anyone who had money in hand made a living from the money in his hand, and artisans made a living from their trade. And they also stood on the ground, some worked their land by themselves and some used others. Aside from them, there were about thirty or forty shops in the village, which made a living according to the place and the time.

The comrades soon came to Yarkoni's room. Yarkoni's room was bigger than Rabinovitch's room and pictures from French journals hung on the walls, and nevertheless it didn't deserve all that praise. His comrades stayed with Isaac to get him accustomed to his place. They looked at the pictures and talked again about all the things we used to talk about. That night Isaac learned what he hadn't learned all the years, for all the years he had seen the new Land of Israel as one body, and that night he learned that it too was split into many sections.

Isaac lay down on the bed of laborers and covered himself with the blanket of laborers. The bed was made of many boxes beside boxes, the kind they bring tins of kerosene in, and on it was a layer of straw and stubble. Isaac was tired from the wanderings of the day, and when he lay down he dozed off. When he dozed off, he was shaken, sometimes by the buzzing mosquitoes who caroused on his face and sometimes by the loathsome crunching of the mice promenading back and forth. He hit his face and beat all around with his shoe until his hands grew slack and he fell asleep. Meanwhile came the Lord of Dreams and scared him with his dreams.

Isaac was waiting for light. As day began to dawn, sleep descended on him and he dozed off. As he dozed off, all the donkeys that came with the Arab men began braying and the chickens the Arab women brought to market began clucking. Isaac covered his face up over his ears. If the blanket hadn't been full of holes, he might have been saved from the noises, but since it was full of holes, the noises permeated and punched holes in his ears. All of a sudden, the whole room was filled with sun and speckled on his eyes. He tossed and turned in his bed until Rabinovitch came and said, Let's get up and go, maybe we'll find some work.

CHAPTER THREE

In the Labor Marketplace

1 |

Our two comrades, Isaac Kumer and Yedidya Rabinovitch, set off to hire themselves out as laborers. The air was pure and the earth was neither hard nor raked, and the trees were shining with the morning dew, and a good smell stretched from one end of the village to the other. The firmament had been white and was starting to turn blue and warm up, and birds and butterflies were flying in the heights and singing. Isaac forgot all his torments, and expectation and hope rejoiced his heart.

Isaac and his comrade came to the marketplace where farmers come to hire laborers. Masses of Arabs came shouting and shrieking, like enemies who come to lay siege to a city. But the tools on their shoulders indicated that they came not for war but for work. Shriveled in their torn clothing stood a few of our comrades, each of them holding a small basket, with half a loaf of bread and two or three cucumbers. Some of them stood with eyes completely indifferent to everything. While the sad eyes of others bubbled with hope and fear. Hope of finding a daily livelihood and fear that the Arabs might get there before them.

The firmament turned blue and the sun grew warm. The birds were still heard, but their voice was weary and wearisome, and flies and mosquitoes and gnats were humming and fluttering on the green pus in the eyes of the Arabs and on the baskets of food in the hands of the fellows. Finally they traded places. Those who had surrounded the bleary eyes came and surrounded the food and those that had surrounded the food came and stood on the bleary eyes.

Fat Victor came, his heart as thick as his flesh, riding on neighing Fatma, a fine and graceful mare, the finest and smartest mare in the village, and a tropical hat sat on Victor's head shading his fat eyes and leaving just a crack of laughter, and he's wearing cloth garments and holding a leather whip. The whip rises on its own and its shadow runs to and fro, the air recoils and flees for its life, uttering a kind of moan, like a person flogged and moaning. The fine and smart Fatma stands still and doesn't budge, for Fatma knows her owner's soul that he doesn't mean her but those human creatures who forgot today what happened yesterday, and she savors a bit of that joy when her master tells those ragamuffins, Don't you see that I don't need you, and they stand ashamed and embarrassed, as they stood yesterday and the day before yesterday.

Nahum Teplitzki comes up, a short man with his shoulders hunched and his greenish eyes dripping because he can't stand the light, he shuts an eye and opens an eye and clasps the shanks of his donkey, and bites his thin lips out of envy and hatred. Hatred for the ragamuffins who see themselves as the élite of the nation, and envy for that fat guy who knows how to deal with them. Once upon a time Nahum too was one of the ragamuffins and went out to the market like one of us to hire himself out as a laborer. All of a sudden, his mother's brother Spokoyny acquired an estate and made him the steward. Nahum Teplitzki rides on his donkey and whip in hand, shouts Yallah, Get a move on, and many of our comrades are terrified of his voice.

Behind him came two others, riding on mules with patched whips in their hands. Not because they are old are they patched, but because they use them a lot to break them in. The four employers stand, one of them is the representative of a veteran Zionist in Jerusalem, and three come on their own behalf, and opposite them stand our comrades their eyes beckoning to them to hire them as laborers and they will make a daily living.

The fine Fatma stands and ponders. Do those beasts who came with their owners know what is going on here? But, even though the mules were endowed with too much sense of hearing, they stood still as if they didn't hear. And the donkey too, with his long ears, as if those ears were created in vain. But in truth nothing escaped them. And the donkey stood and pondered, It would serve that bastard riding on me right if I threw him off, but if I throw him off here the ground is loose, and it's not worth all the blows he'd give me afterward, but I arm myself with patience, and when we get to a rocky place, I'll throw him down, yet I fear he will never get his punishment, for when we get to a rocky place, he gets down and goes on foot. The donkey began braying in despair and breaking wind. The mules smiled and dropped their dung.

Victor looked here and there, and in their imagination it seemed he cast a favorable eye on our comrades to hire them as laborers. But imagination is like a passing shadow that has no reality at all, and like flying dust, you can't sow on it or bring forth bread from it. While their imagination entertained them, Victor lashed the whip in his hand until the air was divided into several airs. He turned to the Arabs and hired some of them. And among those that Victor left, Nahum hired; and among those that Nahum left, his two comrades hired.

Embarrassed and ashamed, we stood on this earth we had come to work and preserve, and if yesterday and the day before yesterday we didn't find any work to do, we still hoped to sustain our hungry soul with work we will get today, whether a little or a lot. And once again *we were slung out as out of the middle of a sling* because of the great evil and disgrace, our strength left us and we didn't open our mouth.

But our comrades, who at first didn't seem to care about anything, suddenly were shaken and a fire was kindled in their eyes, until we were shocked and retreated. They cast their baskets to the ground and returned to the earth its petty produce and began rebuking the employers. In their rage, their words got confused and it was impossible to understand a word. Their hands grew slack and they said, Wretches. Not about themselves, but about those who were given the Land and kept us away from it. Victor looked at them and his fat, yellow eyes danced in their sockets like eggs in a skillet. He wanted to answer our comrades with the same kind of confused and stammered words they threw at him, but his laziness weakened his heavy tongue. He raised his whip languidly and said, Don't you see, I've already got all the laborers I need. And his three comrades used the same words as Victor. And in fact they did have all the laborers they needed, since of all the Arabs that were there, not one remained. How the fine Fatma rejoiced when she saw Isaac's face. And if not for her excessive pride, she would have shared her joy with the other animals. Fatma looked with one eye, peeping and examining whether those bearers of humans sensed what had transpired here. Soon, the whole marketplace emptied out and only our comrades were left, covered with the dust of the Arabs' feet.

The sun began to blaze in the firmament and heat up the earth. The trees grew warm with that warmth that weakens the heart and relaxes all the limbs. The grass of the field began to shrivel and the flowers in the gardens lowered their heads. The dry nettles burst and emitted a sound of desolation. For a while, our comrades stood and looked at the earth that absorbed the footsteps of their rivals for work. At last they shaded their eyes from the flaming sun, and at last this one returned to his house and that one to his bed. Rabinovitch put his hand on Isaac's shoulder and said, Come, let's drink some tea.

2 |

Our two comrades, Isaac Kumer and Yedidya Rabinovitch, went off to drink tea. And a few of our comrades joined them and went with them, for every single one of them lacked something to make tea, either a wick for the kerosene stove or a piece of sugar for the tea or tea for the sugar, while Rabinovitch is a host who's got all those things and his hand is spread out to slice a piece of bread for those who don't have any, just as their hand would be spread out to slice the bread if they had had any.

Rabinovitch put on the kettle and spread a sheet of *The Young Laborer* on his upright box, like a person spreading a cloth on his table. He took out bread and olives and tomatoes, and anyone who had a piece of bread in his basket or cucumbers took them out and put them down. Our comrades sat themselves down on the host's bed and on the floor of the house and ate and drank. When they had eaten their fill and quenched their thirst, they began discussing that issue they found it hard to resolve all those days, how to make the farmers realize how much evil they were causing themselves and all of the Children of Israel when they reject the Hebrew laborers and nod their head at the Arabs and shake their head at the Jews.

While we're on the subject of the farmers' deeds, we should assume that the laborers spoke angrily. After all, we came to build the Land and in the end they won't let us stand our ground because of an imaginary profit, for the employers mistakenly think that the Hebrew laborer is expensive and the Arab laborer is cheap. And they don't see that everything a Hebrew laborer earns returns to them. He rents himself a room in the village and buys his groceries in their shops, while Mahmoud and Ahmed take their wages from the village and spend it in the Arab cities and not a penny that goes out from Jewish hands returns to them. According to the farmers' deeds, the laborers should have spoken angrily. But in fact, they spoke as a lover who appeals to his friend's integrity. And this is what sustained them, shifting their eyes from themselves to the good of the community. Moreover, they called on their brothers in Exile to ascend and come to work the Land with them. And their words were not in vain. There were those who heard the call and came. And if some of them went back, some did settle in the Land. And if the times betrayed them, they did not betray the Land. They added villages and settlements and strengthened the workers, and provided the lips for Hebrew speech, and restored a bit of our honor that had been exiled. Because of them, the first immigrants began to raise their head, and because of them, all who came after them could stand tall.

3 |

What happened to our comrades today happened to them tomorrow. Wherever they went to seek work they didn't find it. Some rejected them out of pity and some rejected them because of something else. Out of pity, for, they said, how will a Jew exploit his brother Jew. Because of something else, since it was still the widespread opinion that a Jewish laborer is expensive and doesn't accept authority. But both the former and the latter said, Most of the young laborers had kicked over the traces of Torah and the pious deeds of the religion, and it is a good deed to keep them away, so that our sons won't learn from their actions. If a farmer gave work to a Jewish laborer they saw him as a strange man. If a Jewish laborer worked for a Jew they saw him as privileged.

Isaac walked about in the Land of Israel, among the fields and vineyards of the Children of Israel. The fields make wheat and the vineyards make grapes. Both field and vineyard are full of Arabs, and the owner of the field or of the vineyard or his steward moves among them riding on his animal. He scolds them and jokes with them, and they accept his scolding with love and laugh with him at his jokes, and take a break to pray and to eat, and extend the eating and extend the praying. The Arabs know that the land won't run away from under their feet. Unlike them, Isaac walks about like an idle person and doesn't eat and doesn't rejoice, for the money in his pocket has run out and he doesn't have any work. Things were good for Isaac as long as he was in his hometown. Fields and vineyards he didn't have there, but he wasn't hungry. And if Exile is a disgrace there, he found some solace in loathing Exile and in anticipation of the Land. And when the people of his hometown made fun of him, they weren't making fun out of hatred. And when they said to him, If you're wasting your time, where will your food come from, he would answer, There in the Holy Land, there in the villages of our brothers, I will take up the plow and I shall know no care. Now that he lives in the Land of Israel and walks about in the village, no one says to him, Come to my vineyard, hoe my citrus grove, work with me in my field. Back in the hotel in Jaffa in his first days, Isaac sensed that everything wasn't going well, but he made a distinction between city dwellers and village dwellers. Now he is forced to see that there is no difference between them, except that the former like to bring a person close for their benefit and the latter like to keep him at a distance for their benefit. Out of idleness and out of grief and out of lack of food, Isaac's strength wore out and he got sick. One day, he was in bed with fever and one day he would look for work and not find it. At first, his pockets were full of Francs and Magidis and Bishliks; now he doesn't even have a Matlik to buy quinine. Before he goes to borrow a penny, they come to borrow from him.

As he walked about in the village, Isaac saw those inhabitants who had come to the Land emptyhanded and now own fields and vineyards and houses full of good things, not by virtue of observing the Torah and pious deeds, for the *Biluim* were free thinkers and their feet too are on the ground, but because they're Russians and I'm from Galicia, and even the one small village the Galicians put up fell to rack and ruin. And there are people here who came from Russia and are also shriveling with hunger and idleness, but since he was concerned with his own sorrow, he didn't pay heed to theirs. And as Isaac walked about in the village and saw fields of thorns, his heart screamed, What difference would it make to their owners to call on me to destroy the thorns. But no one called on Isaac to destroy his thorns. Isaac was dwelling with Rabinovitch and Rabinovitch's comrades and ate what they ate and went hungry as they went hungry and dreamed with them of going up to the Galilee, for the people of the Galilee are not like the people of Judea. The people of Judea prefer the Arab laborer to the Hebrew laborer, even for tasks the Hebrew laborer does well, because his master can't treat him as a slave. While the people of the Galilee accept Hebrew laborers and treat them like brothers. At first, the people of Judea did accept Hebrew laborers, especially since pruning and grafting demand talent and knowhow. When the Arabs learned those skills, they fired the Hebrew laborers and hired themselves Arabs, who subjugate their minds to the minds of their masters. And so our comrades dreamed of ascending to the Galilee, but since they didn't have money for the trip, they stayed where they were and demeaned themselves at the farmers' doors. At last, Isaac loaded his belongings on his shoulders and went to Jaffa.

4 |

Isaac returned to Jaffa and went looking in all kinds of offices and departments and institutions, and found there a host of suffering and depressed and weary people standing and shivering with malaria, and an ink-stained secretary humming words to them that were hard to understand. And why didn't Isaac go to the leaders of the Yishuv, after all the dignitaries of Galicia had given him letters of recommendations to their comrades in the Land of Israel, but he knew by now that they weren't worth the damage to his shoes. And in fact, once he did go to one of them, a Mr. Makherovitch, whose speeches made the whole Land of Israel quake. He found him standing before a map of the Land of Israel with a delegate of an association of Zionists in Exile, showing him on the map some lands to buy and what can be done with them. Isaac was ashamed to disturb with his trivial business a man who was occupied with the most sublime matter. He stood and looked and was amazed and stunned. That wasn't an illustrated postcard of a colony, but a map of the whole Land of Israel, and the one standing before the map acted as if the whole Land was at his disposal and he could distribute it as he liked to whomever he wanted. Mr. Makherovitch glanced over and saw Isaac. Isaac took out his letters and offered them to him. Makherovitch looked at them and said, Well, hmmm . . . , like a person who says, You're impressed with them, believe me, there's no point being impressed. And he didn't ask Isaac anything and didn't tell Isaac anything. From now on, Isaac wouldn't go to any activist. Maybe some of them would give him good advice, but as he was seared by this one, he was wary of the embers of others.

Since he was unemployed and didn't have anything to do, he went to the port. Ships are going and ships are coming. Porters and stevedores load and unload all kinds of wares whose like we have never seen. The whole port is humming. Merchants and agents, clerks and customs brokers are moving and shaking, and beverage sellers laden with jugs and cups tinkle their instruments and the smell of coffee bubbles up into Isaac's guts. The Lord of Imagination takes hold of him and paints all kinds of imaginings before him. Isaac lifted his eyes and saw himself as if he had come here on business. By what right did he come here on business? Because a merchant who travels the seas hired him. They were traveling the seven seas to distant islands. A big storm came on the sea and capsized their ship. Isaac leaped into the sea and took his boss with him, and carried him on his back until they reached land. And his master took him home and told him, You saved me from death and I'll save you from hunger. He immediately ordered his clerks to make a just account of all his property that he had left and divided it equally with him. And that property that fell to Isaac's lot was many times greater than the share of all the activists of the Yishuv put together.

Isaac walks about and the Lord of Imagination walks about with him. But miracles don't happen to every person, especially not to a fellow like Isaac, who isn't worth it to the Lord to do him a miracle even in a natural way. So Isaac returned from the port much more tired and exhausted than he had been before. He dragged his feet along the paving stones, crooked and broken as they were, and in the endless blazing sand, where your feet are roasted like meat on coals.

The Lord of Imagination left him because he failed to wear himself out with him in difficult places. Isaac saw before him a cave, one of those caves the first immigrants used to sleep in, for Jaffa was a ruin for many years and a person couldn't find an apartment in Jaffa, and all those who ascended to Jerusalem to carve themselves a grave there would sleep in niches and caves, until they found a camel to ride up to the Holy City. Isaac betook himself to the cave to cool his weary soul from the heat and to sleep off the hunger a bit. But the hunger didn't let him shut his eyes. So he lay there with his eyes wide open and said, How much can a person's troubles darken his mind, until he fools himself and sees the imaginings of imagination. And since he wasn't important to himself at that time, he dismissed his thoughts of himself. And since he dismissed himself from his mind, his heart became the home of thoughts for honest and naive people, like Reb Yudel Hasid his ancestor and his three virgin daughters, who, when they were over their heads in troubles, the Lord summoned up for them a cave and they found a treasure. Isaac raised his head slightly and peeped into the cave and said, But here there is no treasure. And he laughed at himself for expecing to find a purse of coins here or two or three pennies to buy him some bread. Needless to say that he didn't find anything, but we do need to say that he was sad because he didn't find anything, for he had no hope or expectation of finding a penny in a natural way to buy him something to save his soul from hunger.

CHAPTER FOUR

Work

1 |

May you never know such things, good friends. Isaac would have despaired if the Lord had not taken pity on him and brought relief to
him from somewhere else. Once upon a time, he wandered around
the city. He came to the German colony and went into the Baron's
garden to relax and he fell asleep. When he awoke, he saw an old
man standing over him holding a green pot with a paintbrush in it.
The old man told him, Take the tools and finish your work. The old
man apparently hired laborers and mistook Isaac for one of them, or
perhaps he saw that he had fallen asleep because of hunger. He took
pity on him and gave him work so that he would be paid and buy his
bread and not starve to death.

Isaac took the tools and followed the old man. He showed
him a fence to paint. Thus Isaac started working by chance. That
work was easy and didn't require any previous training. All he had to
do was dip the brush in the paint and pass it over the fence pickets.
In the evening, his employer paid him his fee of two Bishliks, and
told him, When I see that you're not a slacker, I'll give you more.

Who can describe Isaac's joy? How many days and how
many weeks had he vacillated about earning something for bread and
tea, and suddenly two whole Bishliks fell into his hand all at once as
wages for work, and on top of that, he was promised more tomorrow.

Isaac bought himself bread and milk. He dipped his bread in
the milk and ate, something he hadn't done for days on end, when
all he had to eat and drink was dry bread and water, and didn't have
an extra penny to buy tea. When he had eaten his fill, he stretched
out on his bed to prepare for the morrow.

The Lord of Thoughts came to him and said, May you not come in vain tomorrow, when your employer finds out that you're not a painter and fires you. And may this meal of yours not be the last of all your meals. Nevertheless, Isaac didn't despair. Isaac said to himself, He who made me a miracle today and dropped two Bishliks in my hands all at once will make me a miracle tomorrow and I won't starve to death. He raised the blanket and covered himself up to his neck. He shut his eyes and fell asleep.

Pleasant was his sleep. From the day he had entered the Land, he hadn't enjoyed sleep as much as that night. His bed absorbed him and was good to him. Even his regular enemies, the flies and mosquitoes, made peace with him and let him sleep.

Isaac lay there until dawn. When it grew light, he began to fear that he would be late and his work would be given to someone else. He looked at the window and saw that the day was still at its start, and he knew he wouldn't be late. He began to fear that his employer was one of the missionaries who are good to Jews to trap their soul. And he did right to fear, for it did happen to him in the neighborhood of the Germans, where there are several converts. For exiles from Russia once ascended to the Land of Israel and didn't find anything to eat and were shriveling with hunger. The missionaries latched onto them to cure the sick and feed the hungry, and when they treated them to food and drink and medicine, they would also give them an ounce of their faith. Within a month or two they changed their religion and left the fold of Israel, for that is the art of the missionaries who cure the body and collect the soul. When Isaac pondered it, he stood up and put on his Tefillin and prayed with great devotion, and strengthened his belief in the God of Israel that He would not abandon him and not cast him away and would make his way straight before him and prepare him a livelihood in ways that are legitimate and not forbidden. After he finished his prayers, he recited the Thirteen Principles and the Chapter of Reverence for God. Then he dipped his hands and ate what was left over from the night before and went to the German neighborhood. And the old man welcomed him warmly and gave him work. And in the evening, he paid him three Bishliks and told him to come the next day. Isaac grasped his

money like an amulet. Never in his life had money been so important to Isaac as those Bishliks he earned in the Land of Israel.

2 |

Even though Isaac hadn't learned any skill, he was expert at many
jobs, like most sons of the poor who fix and paint their furnishings by
themselves, and thus teach themselves how to do any work. Especially Isaac, who was the oldest of his brothers and made them toys,
like *dreidls* for Hanuka and rattles for Purim and bows for Lag
B'Omer, and a Sukkah for the holiday of Sukkoth, and whatever had
to be done, he did. Even the days when he helped the assistant cook
on the ship stood him in good stead, for he learned from him how to
hold a brush. Now that he had chanced upon the work of painting,
he took care to do it well. The old man saw it and became fond of
him. And when he finished his work, he took him to his neighbor,
and when he finished his work there, he took him to another neighbor. If he didn't find work today, he found work tomorrow. From now
on, he was rid of the dread of hunger.

Many stories were told about that old man. Some are legend
and some are truth. And even the truth is like legend. They said about
that old man that his father was a teacher of children in some city in
Poland. And he too studied Torah but when his soul was not sated
with the bread of Torah he went to seek some secular bread. He left
his city for another city and that other city for another city, and wandered around from place to place until he came to the cities of Germany. He came to Germany and didn't find anything to keep him
alive. He was found by an old man from his hometown who had been
stranded there in his youth while seeking his fortune. The old man
pitied him and hired him to watch over the dead until they were laid
to rest, and also to study a chapter of Mishna for the ascent of their
soul. On top of that, he hired himself out to fast on public fast days
for those who bought themselves out of the obligation. On top of that,
he shoveled snow and swept the streets. And still he wasn't rescued
from hunger. He wandered around until he wound up in London,
and expected the Jewish leaders to come to his aid. But before he got
to the Jewish leaders, he fell into the hands of a vile lord of poverty

who took him to the missionaries. They gave him bread to eat and clothes to wear. And his body became heavy and his soul light. And his body became dearer to him than his soul. He exchanged the light for the heavy and the pleasant for the unpleasant. The missionaries found him an easy job with some general. Later, the general was appointed minister of war in some state in Africa. He took his servant with him and made him his adjutant. Eventually the general died and the king appointed him minister of war in his place. All his life, that convert expected to return to the God of Israel, but one day he was busy with the war against the king's enemies, and the next day he was busy marrying off his daughters, until he was busy and sunk in his error. Such is the skill of the Evil Instinct, when a man gets himself into a bad deal, he won't let go of it until it ruins him. Later, he got sick and went to Europe to consult the physicians. The physicians told him, Don't go back to Africa where it is hard to live, and don't return to Europe where the chill is harmful, but ascend to the Land of Israel, where the climate is moderate. He came to Jaffa and built himself a big house and planted himself a fine citrus grove and expected to return to the God of Israel, but because of his daughters, whom he had married off to dignitaries of other nations, he delayed returning and didn't return. If the faith hadn't grown weak in that generation, he would have returned immediately and sanctified the Name of Heaven, but the Jews he chanced to meet were slack in performing pious deeds, and he was light about it. He thought to himself, Since I don't go to church and I don't kneel to the Cross, I'm like a Jew. He behaved like a Gentile and saw himself as a Jew. But there was one good thing about him, that he strengthened the Jews and let them earn their living. On that day he saw Isaac's trouble. He took him and stood him on his feet.

3 |

Isaac paid his debts and became his own master, bought his groceries in the shop where he wanted, and ate where he wanted. And needless to say, he rented himself a room, for since the day he returned to Jaffa he had slept in the vestibule of a doctor who went abroad to be cured and left a guard to guard the house, and the guard let him sleep with him. Meanwhile the doctor died and they sold his belongings and rented the house and got rid of the guard and took away Isaac's place. Isaac moved from comrade to comrade and from room to room. Until the day he rented himself his own room. He also bought light clothing and a light hat and light shoes that walk on the sand and don't sink in it. No longer is he bothered by the sun in his heavy clothes and doesn't add to her warmth. The Land of Israel gives a new soul to the nation, but every single person has to tailor his clothing according to his own body. Because of his new clothes, his nickname, The New Man, was forgotten, a name they had stuck on him the day he entered the Land, and is synonomous with Nincompoop. The Land, too, expanded for him, since when he was ashamed to meet his creditors, he had detoured around their shops. Now that he doesn't owe anyone a penny, the whole Land is open before him, wherever he wants to go he goes.

Another thing Isaac did. He bought himself a spirit stove and a teapot and cups and pitchers and bowls and spoons and bread and tea and olives. He makes his own dinner and doesn't waste his time in restaurants, whose pleasure is small and whose cost is great. He spends his day with others and at night he returns to his room and lights the lamp and draws water from the cistern and puts on a teapot and drinks tea and eats whatever his heart desires, bread and tomatoes and olives. Isaac has now learned to appreciate olives, which satisfy the heart and guard against malaria. If a guest comes to him from the city or the villages, they eat together and drink tea and rejoice with a glass of wine. You think the blessing of wine was created only for the rich! A glass of wine also kisses the mouth of a simple laborer. After they eat and drink, Isaac makes up a bed for his comrade. The Land of Israel is mild for her inhabitants and they don't need luxuries. All a person needs is a roof over his head and a stone floor beneath him, and if he puts his clothes under his head and covers himself with his blanket, he gets his sleep.

CHAPTER FIVE

Isaac at His Work

1 |

Isaac is still a novice at work, for his brush leads him and he doesn't lead his brush. He dips a brush in a pail and puts the paints on the objects without thinking before he acts. He lays it on thick where he should be sparing, is sparing where he should lay it on thick, and if something perfect comes out of his hand, it's only by chance. We shall not offend Isaac's honor if we count him among the painters who are called smearers, who stretch out their hands with paint and rely on the brush to do what it does, just so they get paid. After a few days, he learned a bit from experience. But every rose has a thorn, for the routine of work made a habit of the same mistakes he kept making. And even if he recognized that he was doing wrong, he didn't know how to correct it, because he hadn't learned this craft and wasn't experienced in it.

To learn the craft properly, he should have gone to an artisan, and served as his apprentice for a year or two. After he became expert enough, he would work for him as a laborer for a salary of two Bishliks a day. But two Bishliks a day aren't enough to support him, let alone during those two years when he doesn't get any salary. And furthermore, there wasn't anyone to teach him. The ten painters who lived in Jaffa weren't accustomed to using assistants, not because they are destined to become their competitors, but because they have no need for them. There are painters in Jaffa who don't have work in the city and go seeking work in the villages, and there are those who take any job that comes their way. When people move, they work as plasterers and whitewashers, and in the winter, they make crates for oranges for export, for painting jobs aren't found in every season and the work doesn't support those who do it. Isaac, who was a bachelor, supported himself with it, those with a lot of children couldn't support themselves with their craft.

Isaac worked at his craft and supported himself, sometimes less and sometimes more. In the end, he found his craft tedious, for if you're not expert at a craft, it grows tedious. All that time, Isaac didn't have a moment of satisfaction. By day he was depressed as he worked and at night he saw the other painters shrug their shoulders at him and say, You're a painter? You're not a painter, you're a smearer. And if he dozed off, in his sleep he peeped out of a box or a cabinet to see how the artisan does it. What the artisan does is to fill his brush with paint and throw it in his eyes and blind him. If he climbed up to the top of the roof to look from there, the artisan pulls the ladder down from under him and he falls into a can of paints. Thus Isaac despaired of improving, and pulled his yoke with an anguished heart, like those who learned their craft in a casual way and work like a donkey in a mill, turning the millwheel with blinkered eyes until he wears out his soul and dies.

2 |

One day Isaac went to the inauguration of the synagogue of the Artisans' Center in Jaffa. When he arrived there, most of the people were already drunk. Sheinkin, who had already concluded his speech, sat at the head and sang a tune without words, and the heads of the synagogue bim-bammed after him, bim bim bam, nodding their heads and snapping their fingers. And the rest of the people, every one with a glass in hand, this one drinking and that one pouring into his comrade's mouth and another one dancing in front of a barrel of wine that was bottom up. Isaac wasn't a member of the Center, but when it comes to drinking on a joyous occasion, they don't distinguish between members and nonmembers. They brought him a glass. He saw one man lying in a puddle of wine and folks were teasing him. Isaac asked what that was. They grinned and said, *Let the young men now arise and play before us*, he's as drunk as Lot. He felt sorry for him. He put down the glass and went to him. He stood him on his feet and propped him up and took him to his room and lay him on his bed and took care of him until he recovered from the wine.

That man, Yohanan Lightfoot by name, was a jack-of-all-trades. And even though we don't approve of a man who is a jack-of-all-trades, we think differently about that artisan, whose Creator blessed him with blessed hands, and everything he did he did well, either in iron or wood or stone. He was tall and slim and his face was creased. And when he spoke, all his lines laughed, and his small eyes sprayed sparks of laughter and derision. They called him Sweet Foot. Why? Because once he slept in a vineyard in Sarona and a snake came and bit him on the foot. He went to a doctor. The doctor told him, The only thing we can do for you is take off your foot, otherwise the venom will spread throughout your body and you'll die. He went to the synagogue to pray for himself. On his return, he fell down with arms and legs outspread and wept loudly. An old Arab passed by and asked him why he was crying so hard. He told him. The Arab examined his foot and told him, Wait until I come back. He went and brought a donkey loaded with halvah. He wrapped the swollen foot in halvah. The halvah sucked out the venom and he recovered. They started calling him Sweet Foot until his name stuck.

He lived in the sands near the sea, far from folks, in a hut he had made for himself, and he brought good soil and planted himself a few vegetables and a few flowers, and went to work only when he ran out of food. And whatever work he did, either for himself or for others, he did for his own enjoyment. And sometimes he left his work before he finished and all the coaxing of his employer couldn't help at all. And even though all Jaffa knew his ways, they showed up at his door and sought him out, for he was an expert artisan and everything that came from his hand was perfect and handsome. He lived without a woman, and sometimes a woman came to his house and sat with him until he said to her, Thus far, my sister, from now on this man wants to scratch his foot. One of those who used to come to his house was a rich woman, the widow of an American rabbi, who married Sweet Foot, and after the feast of the wedding week, they got divorced. Sometimes she came to his house to discuss matchmaking and to see if he was alive, because he didn't eat like other people, but made do with raw vegetables from his garden or dipped his bread in the juice of figs he had cooked for several days. And when she came she brought two baskets with her, one of food and one of drink, and she sat with him until he told her, Thus far, my sister, from now on this man wants to scratch his foot. And he withdraws and sits in front of his hut and strums an instrument or teaches his dog clever tricks.

3 |

It was not long before Isaac went by Sweet Foot's place. Sweet Foot saw him and called to him. As they sit, he tells him some of his adventures. His father, a native of Kishinev, was a painter of icons. He left his city and his icons and went to Odessa to paint there in the theaters. Later he returned to Kishinev and opened a workshop for icons, and fifty laborers worked in his shop. His father had a friend who had ascended to Jerusalem after the pogrom in Kishinev. He wrote to Father, Come to Jerusalem and I promise you an abundant livelihood. Father, who was religious and didn't drink a drop of water without blessing it before and after, when he heard that you could live in Jerusalem the Holy City, he took his wife and sons and ascended. He found a good living in Jerusalem, the Russians bought all the icons he made and paid him nicely, and all the other Christians, guardians of the churches in Jerusalem, would quarrel over him, this one said, Fix my icon, and that one said, Fix my icon. And an Armenian mediated between them, since Father didn't know all the languages in Jerusalem. There is no church in Jerusalem that Father didn't work in, and everybody was satisfied with him because of his skill and because of his integrity. The young Greeks saw it and envied him. They came to him to study, and thought that when they learned the craft, the world would no longer need the Jew. And Father, who was a good man, consented to teach them. And he wasn't afraid they would compete with him; on the contrary, he laughed at the competitors, who often did him a favor, for they would come ask him to fix what they had broken, as in the Christian church on the Via Dolorosa and in their churches in Bethlehem and Hekeldama, where they needed Father to fix what was damaged. Now Father doesn't do anything, but sits and recites Psalms. But before he left his craft, he painted the Hurbah of Rabbi Yehuda the Hasid, the ruined synagogue in the Old City of Jerusalem, and did it very very well, as he didn't do for any Gentile. And he didn't take money, for everything he did he did for the sake of Heaven. At first, Father hoped his son would be a painter too, but the son didn't want to, for, ever since he was a child, he was excited by real crafts, and even before he was four years old, when he heard the sound of a hammer, he would put down his food and run to the smithy, and Father swore to expel the smithy from the street. Now Sweet Foot turned his attention to Primus stoves, whose sound no one could resist, since wood and coal had become expensive and everybody started using Primus stoves. And so he invented a vessel like a wreath to put around the top of a Primus that insulates and decreases the noise. Similarly, he is busy making a kind of crown for a candle since, on summer nights, the windows are open and sometimes a wind comes and puts out the candle, and if it's the Sabbath, it's a double grief. And so he is making a kind of crown to put around the candle to stop the wind. He had started making a lot of other things, but he doesn't know which to do first, for as soon as he turns to one thing, the other things come immediately and tickle his fingers and want him to tend to them.

Isaac sat at the feet of Sweet Foot and engraved every word on his heart, fearing he would stop talking. Sweet Foot didn't stop, but on the contrary, went on talking, for it had been a few days since anyone had happened by him, aside from his ex-wife, who pestered him with her matchmaking, and when he got rid of her and a person came by to talk with him, his mouth opened like a gushing spring. And there was something special in his conversation, for Isaac learned things from it that he had wondered about, and he was also instructed about matters that hadn't occurred to him. And when he bid farewell to him, he said to him, When you come by this way, drop in on me.

4 |

Two days later, Isaac came by that way. At this time, Sweet Foot was busy feeding his dog and didn't look at the guest. Isaac saw that he was in the way and turned to leave. Said Sweet Foot to him, Tomorrow I'll be working at such-and-such a place. If you want, come and work with me, but I don't guarantee that you'll find me. And as he talked, he picked up the dog and lifted him to his face. He looked into his eyes and asked, Had enough? Then he turned his face to Isaac and said, If you find me, you find me, and if you don't find me, you don't find me.

The next day, Isaac came and found him busy at work. He squinted his small eyes and laughed. He put down his brush and said, I knew you'd come, and you came. And you even brought the tools of your trade with you. Brave man. I see that you have understood the nature of human beings, that if they put doubt into your heart you know there's no room for doubt. Now take your brush and dip it and we'll learn from one another what to do and what not to do. In truth, I like to do what others don't do and I don't do what others do do. But I advise you to do as every artisan does.

Isaac picked up his brush and worked with him. Sometimes he would take his brush out of his hand and correct the spot and sometimes he would laugh and say, You seem to have learned from all the painters in the world. I am sure you will become a smearer like them. In the evening, he took him to his hut and shared his food with him, as they sat in the light of a concave lamp without glass, for glass is wont to break, and he gave up on it before it broke. And as they sat together, he told him about all kinds of work and about all kinds of human beings, and about the kinds of women who think a man can't get along without them. Indeed a man should stay away from them. And if he doesn't stay away from them, it's a sign that he's like them. And if he's like them, he's certainly superfluous. One female sex is enough for the world.

The second watch of the night had passed and Sweet Foot was still sitting and talking. The sound of the sea grew louder and its waves crashed noisily as if they were knocking on doors that didn't open, and a damp, chilly wind began to blow. A bluish light mixed with sulfur glittered, and sea and land seemed to jolt. The dog barked in his sleep, he scratched his skin and pulled in his scared bones. And once again a terrifying light flashed from one end of the sky to the other and the sea roared a mighty roar. Isaac felt his bones dozing off, but his heart was awake. The lamp suddenly went out and Sweet Foot broke off and said, Tomorrow we shall not go to work. He stood up and offered him his bed. Isaac went home. Sweet Foot called after him, But tomorrow after tomorrow we will work.

Two days later, Isaac got up early in the morning and went to him. He found him standing and warming up some drink made of fruit juice. Sweet Foot saw Isaac and said to him, Since you've come, sit down, and since you're sitting, drink. Isaac reminded him of what he had said the day before yesterday. Sweet Foot began laughing and said, You've got a memory, just like a calendar. And as he spoke, he pulled the dog's ear and asked him, What do you think, Sweetiepie, about that gentleman? Then he picked up some junk, and about every single piece of junk he told a few tales. Just as Isaac resigned himself to the fact that the day would be wasted, Sweet Foot took him and said, Let's go.

He locked the door and put the key in front of the dog and said, Run. Put it away. The dog took the key in his teeth and ran wherever he ran, and came back and rubbed his head on Sweet Foot's shoes. Sweet Foot patted his head and scratched his neck and lifted him up to his face, opened his mouth and looked at his teeth, put him back down on the ground, and said, Now run and don't be too wild. He tapped him on the back affectionately, and said to Isaac, Let's go.

They walked until they came to a big house, a kind of mansion. The owner stood on the doorsill of the house and it seemed that he was about to take out all his wrath on that artisan who was late in coming. Sweet Foot rubbed his nose like a man who came to survey his property and found a man there he didn't need. The owner lowered his shoulders and began flattering the artisan. Sweet Foot paid no heed to him and said to Isaac, If you want to start, let's start.

They worked there two days, at last Sweet Foot got fed up with working. He dropped it and said to Isaac, You work and I'll come and fill in after you. When he came back Isaac asked him, Have I done well? Sweet Foot looked at him and said, A man should know that by himself. He saw that he was sorry. He picked up the brush and passed it back and forth until he had smeared over everything

Isaac had done, and he stayed there until midnight painting the whole thing over. When he summoned him the next day, Isaac asked him in a whisper, What can a person do to satisfy you. Sweet Foot laughed affectionately and said, What do you care? No matter what, I won't be satisfied with your work.

5 |

Isaac saw that he was still far from perfection. Nevertheless, his soul was relieved and his hand grew light. And that skill that had been closed to him started revealing things to him which even Sweet Foot didn't reveal to him. And he stopped asking if he had done well, and even Sweet Foot didn't say anything to him. Either he despaired of him or he regarded him as an artisan like all other artisans in Jaffa. One way or another, Isaac's soul was relieved and his hand was light, like an artisan who is expert and trained in his craft.

No longer did he see himself in his dreams climbing to the tops of the roofs to watch how the artisans work. Nor did the artisans any longer throw paint in his eyes to blind him. And even Sweet Foot who mocked him during the day and would call his brush burst, looked graciously on him in his dreams. And when Isaac lay supine on his bed after his daily toil, he dozed off and slept and drew strength and life.

In those days, Isaac rejoiced at every new day and every new job. And not only because he got paid, but also because he was fond of his craft, for he could do in reality what he had pictured to himself in imagination. His limbs were at ease and the order of his days was fixed. If he had work to do, he worked, if he didn't have work to do, he sat in his room and read a book, or he wrote letters to his father and his brothers and sisters, and at night he would stroll on the seashore and in the other places and go visit Sweet Foot or somebody else. And when Isaac would dress in his fine clothes, he looked like all the sons of good families who left their father's house and wound up here in the Land of Israel.

Days of Grace

1 |

His days passed smoothly. His livelihood was at hand and there was no need to worry about tomorrow. And now he was used to the climate of Jaffa. The sun didn't crush his brain by day and the damp of night didn't weary his bones. He feared neither the winds nor the heat wave. And when people grumbled about the *Hamsins* that sucked their marrow and dried their skin, he would say, On the contrary, I like the *Hamsins*, for I bathe in them as in a pool of sun. Whether he exaggerated a lot or whether he exaggerated a little, this was a display of goodwill and affection for the Land.

A special affection did he feel for the sea. At first he was terrified to approach it lest it rise up and wash him away; now he goes into it and isn't scared. And on summer days, when he leaves his work, and needless to say on Friday evenings, he bathes in the sea. But some of the excitement he felt when the sea appeared to him for the first time on the way to Trieste still stirred his heart. And just as he is amazed at the sea, so he is amazed at himself when he bathes in it and at the children who play in it. That water that can cover the land, schoolchildren play in it and aren't afraid. And that is nothing compared with the Gynmasium students who make human pyramids in the sea, and when the pyramid is very very high, they all jump off into the water at the same time. And one of them makes himself into a boat and his friends sail on him. And sometimes someone disappears from the group and reappears in a boat standing in the sea far away from the land.

On days when the sea rages and you don't bathe in it, Isaac walks on the beach. Terrifying waves rise from the sea and strike one

another, and rise up to the land and pluck up the sand, and the sand
is undermined, and the storm roils the depths, and the sounds of
mighty waters rise from the bottom of the sea, and the whole world
trembles and quakes, and you stroll along and aren't afraid. Behold,
there's a small river in our city which is a drop compared with the sea
and not a year goes by when it doesn't sweep away cattle and vessels
and even houses, but this sea doesn't go over its bounds which the
Holy-One-Blessed-Be-He delineated when He created the sea. And
on the morrow a person goes out and sees that the sea has made peace
with itself and its waves are smiling at one another with greenish eyes
and bluish eyes, and the sand is gleaming before them like a fop's illuminated mirror.

Now we shall turn to things that are essential to human life
and shall talk a bit about the foods that are special to the Land of Israel. Even the foods that were alien to Isaac at first became tasty to
him. Eggplant fried in oil and tomato sauce, and the other dishes
they eat in the Land are his daily food, not to mention olives and
tomatoes.

Isaac took thorough pleasure in apricots. We didn't learn
about them in the Torah, and we didn't hear about them until we
came to the Land of Israel, and suddenly they appear to us, and behold they're good and exquisite. The Holy-One-Blessed-Be-He loves
the Land of Israel and gives more than He promises. He promised us
a land with wheat and barley, etc., and He also provides other good
and fine fruits. And when does He provide? Between Passover and
Sukkoth, when the oranges were gone from the market. With one
hand He takes, and with one hand He gives.

Before you've had your fill of them, the whole market is rejoicing at grapes. Grapes like those you never ate in your hometown.
On the second night of Rosh HaShana, Father used to buy a bunch
of grapes to make the blessing "that we have lived to see this time,"
and if he didn't bless with grapes — currants are even better, for Father is a poor man and buys second-rate goods. And here, for a penny
you buy an ounce or two of sweet, good grapes. And how many kinds
there are here, and the taste of one isn't like the taste of another. Like
all our comrades who come from northern lands, Isaac knew that

there were white and black grapes, but what he didn't know is that both of them are divided into many kinds, and every kind has its own name. And now that he does know, he selects from the good kind and skips over the mediocre kinds. However, we must say that even the mediocre ones merit a blessing.

While the grapes still fill the market, another fruit is already peeping at you. The Sabra, that prickly pear they use to build garden hedges and when a person steps on it with his shoes it pricks his sole, is also a fruit worthy of a blessing and sweet to the heart. The eyes of the Lord wander throughout the Land, and when He wants to, He bestows a good taste even to the thorns of the hedge. Arabs sit at the slopes of every street and for a penny they peel you enough prickly pears to fill your belly. And while you're preoccupied with the prickly pear, another Arab passes by with a basket of Damascene strawberries on his head.

Between one thing and another, the market fills up with heaps and heaps of big watermelons, bigger than a man's head. Their rinds are green and white flecks sparkle on the rind, and their inside is red and rejoicing, and black seeds look out from them, and you eat the core and spit out the seeds, and throw away the rind. You recall autumn nights in your hometown when you saw the market vendors sitting in the light of small lanterns with watermelon halves in front of them, and your mouth yearned to savor that sweet fruit, but your pocket was empty, and you couldn't buy yourself even a small piece of watermelon. And here, you buy a whole watermelon and eat it for a day or two.

Even before the watermelons are gone, the whole market is filled with figs. The fig is a fruit with no rind outside and no pit inside, and is eaten as it is, it enters your mouth unmediated, as an object that is purified of all junk, and remains all good. Even before the figs are gone, the whole market is filled with dates sweet as honey. These fruits that we ate in the Diaspora once a year on the fifteenth day of the month of Shvat, the New Year of the Trees, one fig and one date, to bless with them, to rouse with our blessings the force of the supreme values to bestow the holy profusion unto the fruits of the Land of Israel, here you buy an ounce or two of them for a penny.

Even in the Diaspora, figs and dates are the sweetest fruits in the world, but in the Land of Israel, they are many times sweeter, for not like the taste of fruit in Exile is the taste of fruit where it dwells. And between the figs and the dates come the pomegranates. Before we came to the Land of Israel, the pomegranate served us as a parable, for instance, he ate its core and threw away its rind. When we came to the Land of Israel, that parable became reality. From the fruits the Land of Israel is famed for, we turn to the other fruits the Land grows for her inhabitants.

Big, good oranges fill the Land, and their fragrance is like the fragrance of a world that is all good, and a kind of light envelops them, like the light that comes from gold, and their good taste stays in the mouth. All the time you were outside the Land, you may never have got yourself a whole orange, and if you did buy one — you certainly didn't buy two; and here they give you three or four for a Mat-lik. The surplus of Jaffa, which is blessed with good fruit, treats you generously and gives abundantly.

Next to the orange comes the mandarin, the baby of the tree of the Land of Israel, and the little sister of the orange, which captivates you with the warmth of her beauty and her fragrance and her taste, and wraps herself in a light wrap, and if you desire her she is unpeeled easily.

And now, our brothers weary in the *Hamsins* and the sun and all other things which sap a man's strength in the Land of Israel, didn't you know that in the season of the oranges, the sun weakens, and a pleasant chill spreads and flutters, and sweet clouds are suspended in the firmament, and the sun peeps from them with sad affection, and it seems to us that we really are in a Delightsome Land, especially here in Jaffa where there is no snow and no cold, but there are good winds and a sweet sun. Here a man doesn't have to fear that his blood will congeal from the chill and a man doesn't have to fear the cold, and even when it is cold, the sun rises in the firmament and warms us pleasantly. The Holy One Blessed Be He knows that we are poor and can't make ourselves warm clothes or heat our oven, so God provided a comfortable climate we can endure. And when Isaac recalled his father's house in the winter, when the ground beneath the bed sprouted ice and frost and everybody was sick from the chill, he didn't know whether to sigh for them or to rejoice for himself.

2 |

Little by little, Isaac uprooted his mind from his hometown and was getting used to the conditions of the Land. The cherries and the currents and the Canaanite strawberry and all the fruits, big and small, which he was used to in his city, were departing his memory. He also turned his mind away from the other food and beverages he was used to in his hometown. And just as he had grown accustomed to the climate of the Land, so he also grew accustomed to her language, and mingled Arabic and Russian words in his speech, whether he spoke Yiddish or whether he spoke Hebrew, like all our comrades in the Land.

In other things too, he behaved like most of our comrades. He didn't go to synagogue and he didn't lay Tefillin and he didn't keep the Sabbath and he didn't honor the religious festivals. At first, he made a distinction between the Commandments of commission and the Commandments of omission; but in the end, he didn't distinguish between commission and omission. And if he chanced to violate one of the Commandments of Thou Shalt Not, he didn't worry.

He didn't do that because he thought a lot about faith and religion, but because he dwelled among people who came to the conscious conclusion that religion and such things weren't important, and since they didn't see a need for religion, they didn't see a need for its Commandments. On the contrary, as people who cherished truth, they would regard themselves as hypocrites if they observed Jewish law when their heart was far from it. Nevertheless, a trace of an idea prevailed in Isaac unwittingly, a vague idea that didn't become clear, but it guided his acts. For the Land of Israel was divided into the Old Yishuv and the New Yishuv, the former behave this way and the latter behave that way. And since he belonged to the New Yishuv, why should he behave like the people of the Old Yishuv. And even though some of his ideas changed, as far as that was concerned, they didn't change. And even though they didn't change in this matter, he did long for the days of yore, for his father's house, for the Sabbath and the festivals, yet he didn't go into a synagogue but sat silent or hummed an exalted tune, until he forgot the gloomy reality with all its distress. In this, Isaac was not alone. In those days, Jaffa was full of young fellows who had studied Talmud and had practiced exegesis, and when they gathered together, and their hearts would assail them, they would sweeten their sitting with Hasidic stories and Hasidic tunes or with homilies. The generation before them sang songs of Zion, for this generation those songs became trite, and when the yearning soul yearned it went back to seek what was lost. Anyone who could sing sang tunes he had brought with him from his hometown, and anyone who could tell tales sat and told tales, and the Lithuanians who don't know the Hasids pretend to be preachers and expound homilies. And here a thing happened that did not happen to their fathers, the sons of Misnagdim found delight in Hasidic tales and the sons of the Hasids found delight in the words of homilies, and they didn't distinguish between the imitation and the original, because of the desire to exalt the soul. Out of their affection for those things whose tang is mostly in Yiddish, they sometimes gave up Hebrew, on condition that the things were not said in public; in a small party of friends, they weren't sticklers about their language. Isaac was different from most of our comrades in two things, he didn't belong to any political party and he didn't court girls. He didn't join a political party because he was wholeheartedly with Zionism as a whole, and he didn't court girls because he didn't. If he had sought them, he would have found. In these two things, Isaac was different from the rest of our comrades, and maybe in one more thing he was different from them, that sometimes a thought of repentance stirred in his heart, but since he had gotten used to not observing the Commandments, he appeased his good instinct with an easy Commandment that wasn't exacting, like reciting the Shema at bedtime. And that he did not so much as a Commandment as a remedy for sleep.

Isaac had no better days than those. His bread he found, not in abundance, but not with grief either. And he lived in a room of his own, not like most of our comrades who lived three or four in one room. This is hardly comprehensible. A poor boy, the son of poor people, who slept with his brother in one bed in a crowded house, wasted six and a half Francs on a room of his own. But Isaac followed the ways of his forefathers, for the way of poor people who come from well-bred families is to cover up their poverty and keep the eyes of people away from what happens inside their homes, so that they won't be seen in their poverty. Hence, he rented a room for himself and spent what he spent, just so they wouldn't see him in his poverty.

But a room of your own has something good about it, for when a person is free from his work, he can sit and read books. And we must say that Isaac did not deprive himself of what was good for him and read a lot. He expanded the scope of his knowledge and learned things he hadn't known before. Aside from the books he read in his room, he also read in the Sha'arei Zion Library. And Alexander Ziskind Rabinovitch was good to him and didn't keep any book from him, except for books in which he found heretical matters, since he thought that most of the troubles that befall Jewish boys come from the harmful opinions they learn from heretical books, and so he hid from them every book that might damage them. He also read newspapers and journals in Hebrew and Yiddish. Some he read for pleasure and some he read to acquire knowledge. There were things he understood and things he didn't understand because he lacked the basics of knowledge. But even in those he didn't understand, his reading wasn't in vain, for when he heard his comrades talking about them, he didn't stand there like a dummy.

There's another advantage to a room of your own, that it's conducive to dreaming. And even Isaac, who hadn't wandered away in dreams ever since the day he had ascended to the Land of Israel, would sit within the walls of his room and see a good dream, for instance, that his brother Yudel came to him, and he brought him to his room. *Thou who art majestic on high, Who abidest in might*, Isaac who didn't even get a bed in Father's house, lived in a room like a bourgeois. And, good comrades, isn't this in itself worth the rent of a whole room. And, God willing, if two or three extra Francs drop into his hands, he'll buy himself a chair. For the time being, he's got only the chair he's sitting on, but he was already considering buying himself another chair. In truth, our comrade Isaac really isn't looking for much, yet a man should complete his set of furniture and add a chair. For anyone who's got a room, his comrades come to him, and it's befitting for him to have a chair ready to seat a guest.

As we said, our comrade Isaac wasn't looking for much. With the money he earned, he satisfied his needs. Isaac wasn't used to delicacies, and wasn't eager for special treats, but every day he did buy himself an ounce of milk and sometimes even an egg, and of course bread and fruit and vegetables, and sometimes he would go in an eatery and eat a hot soup with a small piece of meat, for you had to heed what folks feared, that if a person doesn't eat meat, his bones get soft.

And this too Isaac did. He bought himself cloth and had six new shirts made, for the ones he had brought from his father's house were torn, not because they weren't strong, but because he wore them to work. And for the shirts he bought he had to thank the convert to Judaism who did his laundry and hinted to him that it was time to make himself new ones and he obeyed her, even though in another matter he didn't obey her, when she told him to let her launder the garment with ritual fringes too, for in her innocence, that convert never imagined that there are Jews who do not fulfill the Commandment of ritual fringes.

3 |

Isaac was perfect both inside and out. What does a Jew need — bread to eat and a garment to wear and a home to live in. And he had all three. And now he was adding one penny to another to buy himself winter clothing. And he amused himself by saying, After I buy myself some winter clothing, I'll add one penny to another until they make up ten or twenty Francs and I'll send Father some payment on the debt Father borrowed to pay for my trip. If Isaac hadn't given that cook the leather vest, he wouldn't have needed another garment for winter and would have put that money aside for Father. But what was done was done, and he had to do it, for the cook supported him on the sea. In any case, he didn't stop thinking about that vest, which was Father's main protection against the cold. And Father didn't think about himself and gave it to hm. Now that the days of winter came there and a fierce cold prevailed there, what would Father do without that vest?

At that time, Isaac thought a lot about his father. Now that he was far from his town and his home and all his quarrels with Father had ceased, Isaac saw his father's deeds, how great was his compassion for his sons and daughters, and how much he toiled for them. Things he had at first taken for granted now assumed greater importance in his eyes. In truth, Isaac's father was no different from all the simple people, but even a simple Jew, when you look at him up close, you see that he is exquisite and distinguished.

To make a long story short, Isaac's days are serene. And nothing changes the order of his life. A new chair he didn't yet buy himself, nor did he buy himself winter clothing, but he did buy himself new friends and didn't abandon the old ones for them.

4 |

Our comrade Rabinovitch also settled in Jaffa. There was a clothing store in Jaffa and its owners were old and it was hard for them to tend to customers. Once one of our comrades had to leave the Land and Rabinovitch went with him to buy himself some clothes, for our comrade Rabinovitch is an expert in clothing since, for many years before he ascended, he worked in his father's clothing store. The owners of the store sensed that that ragamuffin was an expert, and began chatting with him until they asked him if he wanted to work in the store with them, and he accepted.

Two years Rabinovitch had spent in the Land. There wasn't a village he hadn't been in. If he found work one day, that day he ate. If he didn't find work, he went hungry. He got fed up with the vicissitudes of the times and went to work in that shop. Two years Rabinovitch had spent in the Land, and some think he was even in the Galilee. But the Land did not think well of him and was cruel. His hoe grew rusty and his teeth grew blunt with hunger. When he had a chance to make a living from something else, he turned over his tools to somebody else and settled down in the city. When our comrade Rabinovitch left his father's store, he didn't imagine that he would return to trade, since his mind was all on the village, in the end he left the village and went to the city.

Rabinovitch works in the store and earns more than he spends. And he eats and drinks like a human being and lives like a human being and wears nice clothes and patent leather shoes. Isaac used to say to Rabinovitch about that, You love yourself in those patent leather shoes, and I love you because I remember your crooked sandals. In truth, Isaac was fond of Rabinovitch all the time, but he liked to remind him of the day they met when he saw him walking around in his crooked sandals.

Even though Rabinovitch had abandoned his hoe, he hadn't abandoned the idea of the conquest of work. He was a member of Ha-Po'el Ha-Tsa'ir and a subscriber to the journal *The Young Laborer*, and was more punctual about paying than in the days when he was a laborer, and he takes special care to preserve the newspaper. When he was a laborer, he used the newspaper *The Young Laborer* as a tablecloth for his bread and olives, and now he puts the issues down and there are no grease spots on them, but in the past, there wasn't any article he didn't read and now he tosses it aside and doesn't give it a glance until the landlady or one of her daughters comes and puts it in the closet.

Rabinovitch's landlady straightens up the room and fixes his meals and makes his bed and mends his linens and darns his socks and cherishes him like a member of the family, even though he's a Jew and she's a Christian. And the same is true of her daughters, who are very fond of the tenant, who gave them back their tongue. Before Rabinovitch came to live with them, they were about to forget a human language, for the Christians regard them as Jews and the converts pretend not to know them so that the Gentiles won't say that birds of a feather flock together. Their forefathers who were Jews would have adorned them with gold coins, but the girls themselves who were born Christian, no one pays attention to them or seeks their company. The early days when their forefathers would serve their prayer house were gone. They had been cantors and sextons and priests, and even rose to be bishops, and lords and ladies, and consuls and the wives of consuls would come to hear their homilies. And now the girls stand in the prayer house squeezed, pressed into a corner and everybody gives them a wide berth. And as the Christians treat them, so do the Jews. But the Christians stay away from them because their ancestors were Jews, and the Jews keep their distance from them because their ancestors converted to Christianity. At first the new Christians got along all by themselves, for every year there were more new Christians. But when the Zionists came, the Jews stopped changing their religion, and thus they expire among themselves.

And why did their ancestors decide to change their religion? When they ran away from their home because of the persecutions and ascended to the Land of Israel, they found the Land ruined and desolate and didn't find anything to live on, so they wallowed in the trash without food and no housing, until they got sick from hunger and suffering. The missionaries got hold of them and cured their diseases and quelled their hunger, and as soon as they recuperated, they were baptized into Christianity. They said, What do we care if they sprinkle a little water over us? But the water sprinkled on the body reached the soul. They made a bald spot in Israel and left the community. And so did others. And then destruction seemed to come upon the foes of the Jews. Something suddenly happened and changed the face of the Land. From Russia and Romania and other countries, Jewish youths ascended, and not like their fathers, to hew themselves graves in the Land, but to plow and to rake its soil. Some were amazed at them and said, The Land doesn't have the power to feed a human being and the Jew doesn't have the power to work its soil. *For they have sown the wind, and they shall reap the whirlwind.* Until everyone grew discouraged, they went and bought themselves land and made themselves settlements. They plowed their soil, sowed fields, planted vineyards, dug wells, and built themselves houses. The Land produced a harvest and the vineyards ripened their bunches of grapes. They relished the great peace and brought bread out of the earth. And those who left the community of Israel were cursed and perished. And those who remained were rotting among themselves.

That woman and her daughters walk around in the wooden house they inherited from their ancestors in the German Colony.

Sometimes they wonder at that Jewish tenant who behaves as if the whole Land were his, and they give praise and thanks to God for sending them a man who resurrected them to themselves. Sometimes one of the daughters raises her eyes to Rabinovitch and takes them back, for Rabinovitch is taken by another, by Sonya Zweiering. Sometimes one of the daughters raises her eyes to Isaac and takes them back, for Isaac is modest and doesn't raise his eyes to a woman.

CHAPTER SEVEN

Isaac Parts from His Friend and Finds Himself a Girlfriend

1 |

Like most of the fellows of Galicia in that generation, Isaac was excellent and modest. Men friends had Isaac, but no girlfriends. The
whole time Isaac lived in his hometown, he hadn't talked with a
woman, aside from his mother and his sisters, like the sons of good
families who don't know women before they are betrothed, aside
from Gymnasium students and university students who broke out of
the fold and court girls, and there are girls who respond to them and
stroll with them in public. And as Isaac behaved in his hometown,
so he behaved in the Land of Israel, he paid no attention to women
and didn't seek their intimacy. And perhaps it didn't occur to him
that a fellow like him could get close to a girl, even though he saw
that some of his comrades did. The habit Isaac had adopted in his
youth stood him in good stead in his manhood. And as he got used
to it, that was it. The merit of his mother also stood him in good stead,
so that he wouldn't behave frivolously in matters where others behave frivolously. And when his mother appeared to him, she didn't
appear withered, as she was just before her death, but as she was in
his childhood, when it seemed to him there was no mother more
beautiful in all the world. Sometimes she appeared to him as on Yom
Kippur, wearing white garments, her voice full of compassion; and
sometimes she appeared to him as in the early days when she still
wore a bluish chapeau Father had brought her from the fair. Sometimes part of her appeared, like a white hand stretched out to him, as
when they sent him to congratulate her when his sister was born. And
sometimes all those forms came together into one whole form, and
it was clear to him that there was no woman in the world like his

mother. And since his mother died, another woman who would come take her place would be modest and pious as his mother. Ugly sufferings did not afflict him, the frailties of human beings didn't hurt him, by virtue of his mother who was perfect in her qualities. And even when his faith slackened, his modesty did not.

2 |

And so it happened that Rabinovitch left the Land. When he went to work in the shop, he went only to get away from the disgrace of hunger, but eventually he forgot the original reason and once again became a merchant as he had been in his hometown, but all his years he lived in his hometown he made the shop secondary and the Land of Israel the essential; when he went to work in a shop in the Land of Israel, once again he made the shop the essential. And the expertise he brought from his father's house and the dread of hunger hanging over him stood him in good stead to make his name and he was fortunate that everyone was satisfied with him. The customers, because he gave them what they wanted; and the shopowners, because he could win the hearts of the customers. The activist and the merchant, the shopkeeper and the clerk buy there regularly; for from the day Rabinovitch started working in the shop, they have found clothes that fit them. And even someone with a crooked back or a bulging pot belly finds a solution from an iron hoop that tightens his coat collar and adapts the coat to his body. And after the customer pays, Rabinovitch spreads out the garment and smooths it and stands him in front of the mirror and shows him the fine merchandise he has bought. A person who buys merchandise from a shopkeeper in the Land of Israel isn't used to lavish service, especially after he has paid, for most of the shopkeepers in the Land of Israel regard customers as if they were created only for their profit, and when a customer sees Rabinovitch's affection, he is drawn to his shop.

Rabinovitch saw that there were finicky people in the Land of Israel who like their clothes to be à la mode, and when they travel outside the Land, they have their clothes made there, for the clothing dealers in the Land of Israel bring their merchandise from Vienna after it has gone out of style there and is sold cheap, and it isn't cut to anybody's size. He started coaxing his bosses to import good merchandise and hire expert tailors to supply the needs of people with good taste, but his bosses didn't listen to him and didn't want to change their habit, for they had gotten used to spending a little and taking in a lot. To make a long story short, they didn't want to change their habit and he didn't want to change his mind. He started looking for another shop, and found a fine shop whose owners employ permanent tailors, who sew clothes for rich Christians and for generals of the Turkish army; but this shopkeeper hired his salesmen from his family, and since Rabinovitch wasn't a relative he didn't hire him. Rabinovitch began considering Beirut and Egypt. But as he considered leaving the Land, he said, I better go to Europe where I'll learn something I won't learn in the lands of the Levant. And as for the conquest of work, this profession also needs conquering. Even though it was already in the hands of the Jews, not all Jews, especially those who are finicky about their clothing, have their clothes made in the Land of Israel because they don't find the clothes they need. Yarkoni, the son of rich people, whose father sends him money, went to study agriculture, and I who don't have a rich father and don't have money, I'll go study the ways of commerce, and from agriculture and commerce the Land will benefit. And so our comrade Rabinovitch left the Land of Israel, as others had done before him and as others do after him, coming as dreamers and leaving as doers.

3 |

Rabinovitch boarded the ship with all the others who were leaving the Land of Israel because the Land didn't absorb them, so they leave the Land and return Outside the Land. Some are glad to get away from the suffering of the Land and some are sad for they don't know what they will do Outside the Land. When they ascended to the Land, they knew why they ascended, when they descend and go outside the Land, they don't know why they are descending. Different, perhaps is our comrade Rabinovitch who knows why he is leaving, he is leaving to return and establish a clothing shop here, so everyone will find clothes that fit him. Three years Rabinovitch wasted in the Land of Israel, now at last he knew his calling. And since he knew his calling, he took action and withdrew from the Land of Israel for the sake of the Land of Israel, for he trusted in the future when all those who reproach him will say on the day he returns, You did well to leave, because it was for the good of the Land that you left. Just as the Land needs people to work the soil, so it also needs expert merchants.

That day was the Sabbath, a day when all the Children of Israel, even a person who doesn't keep the Sabbath, rest from their work, and so, many people accompanied their comrades who were departing. Some weep for their comrades who are leaving the Land of Israel, and some envy them for going to Europe, just as their comrades wept for them and envied them when they left their hometown for the Land of Israel.

Isaac also accompanied his comrade who was about to sail off on the sea. From the day Isaac ascended to the Land of Israel until now, he hadn't been on a ship, and now that his comrade is leaving the Land, Isaac boards the ship to be with him until his departure.

The big ship stands in the sea of Jaffa, the same sea we've already forgotten, the sea we sailed on to the Land of Israel and we didn't imagine that someday it would take us Outside the Land. A smell of coal and of sea blended together. Sometimes the smell of coal takes the upper hand and sometimes the smell of sea. And another smell, a good smell of food and baked goods, comes from the ship, the smell of a world where folks sit comfortably eating and drinking and are well dressed, like those lords and ladies who stand on the deck and look at the sea.

Rabinovitch is busy with his valises and all the other matters of travelers before departure, and Isaac stands a bit apart from him so as not to disturb him if he can't help him, for Rabinovitch is a nimble man and likes to do things by himself. Isaac stands there and looks at his comrade tying and untying and untying and tying, and thinks to himself that his comrade has already gone off. And he pities him for having to wander off to faraway places, and at the same time that he pities him, he also envies him, for those faraway places have become close to his heart. Isaac remembers all the cities and villages and mountains and rivers he passed on his trip to the Land of Israel, and all the mountains and rivers and cities and villages he saw on his trip and didn't pay attention to because his eyes and his heart were in the Land of Israel, now they all come and stand before him in his mind's eye, and every place is more beautiful than the last. Tall buildings rise and pleasant parks are spread out and delightful statues spray water and well-dressed people sit in the café and a smell of thick cigars wafts up with the smell of cakes and coffee. Mountains and hills emerge, and a smell like the smell of snow sprouts up from the mountains, and primeval forests wave their trees, and rivers caper between valleys, and jolly palaces hum, and pleasure carriages run, and lords and ladies sit together on red cushions of velvet and silk. And suddenly all the fine places disappeared, and once again Isaac saw himself in the place where he is standing, in this city of Jaffa that his comrade was leaving. He and his comrade are still standing on the ship, but soon one will sail out of the Land and the other will go back to Jaffa. And once again days will come with no change, no transformation. Day follows day and week follows week, and once a week or once every two weeks comes a letter from Father, and once a week or once every two weeks he writes to Father. The letters Father writes to him and the letters he writes to Father all seem to be made from the same model, and they don't add anything except sighs. Isaac looked around and saw people about to set sail. And Isaac began thinking, I won't move from the ship until it reaches Europe and I get to those places where people live in peace and enjoy the world. And as for traveling expenses, I'll hire myself out to the sailors, like some of our comrades who left without a penny and worked off their passage as members of the crew. Shall I miss my furniture, shall I miss my tools? At that moment, it was easy for Isaac to leave the Land of Israel, just as, years before, it was hard for him to get to the Land of Israel. And he didn't ask what he would do in Europe and how he would support himself there, for he had nothing but a simple craft and he wasn't an expert in that. As he stands on the ship, he sees himself in Europe, getting rich, dropping in on his hometown and settling his father's debt, and giving him something to live on and a dowry for his sisters and pulling his brothers with him and making them rich. How much the people of his hometown envy him, some envy him because he was in the Land of Israel, and some envy him because he dwells in big cities. And both the former and the latter envy him because he is rich.

As he sees a dream of Europe, the ship's horn signals that it is about to sail. Rabinovitch grabbed Isaac and gave him a farewell kiss. When Isaac parted from his father and his brothers and sisters, they kissed him and wept on his neck, but the kiss of a comrade he had not tasted until that moment. He looked at his comrade's patent leather shoes, which were shinier today than on any other day, and he turned his head away to suppress his tears. A sweet blue dallied in the sky and a deep blue fluttered up from the sea, and the world was white and fresh like that almond tree in bloom, and something throbs in the air like something a man's soul yearns for.

As Isaac stands there, he sees Sonya Zweiering, Rabinovitch's girlfriend, embraced in Rabinovitch's arms and both her arms caress his neck and her hat slips down over her ear. Her face is sickly and pale. At that moment, Sonya looks like a sick lad.

The ship's horn sounds once again. The sailors run urgently and hastily. Some are preparing the ship for the journey and others are urging the visitors to get off the ship. Sonya drew herself up and stood on Rabinovitch's shoes and gave him one last kiss. Rabinovitch turned to Isaac and said goodbye. He took a handkerchief out of his pocket and wiped his shoes. Sonya and Isaac went down the ladder of the big ship into a small open boat. The big ship moved at the top of its voice and sailed off onto the open sea, and the little boat wagged in the water of the port.

4 |

The two of them sat in silence. The sailors slapped their oars and guided the boat between waves and rocks. Jets of salt water sprayed high. The water is chilly and the chill is briny. Sonya looked back. The big ship is moving away and Jaffa looms ever closer. No pleasant surprise is in store for her there. Sonya thought about the three or four fellows she had come across in the Land, and also about one Russian journalist, a friend of her father who taught her Hebrew, who would take his rings off his fingers when he was about to embrace her. Between them came Grisha, whose rage cannot be endured.

Even when he embraced her, he glared at her with nasty eyes. If not for Rabinovitch, she would still be in his hands. As she pondered, the boat reached the port.

Sonya jumped out and climbed up onto dry land as quick and vigorous as a lad. The sailors saw her and smiled with good will and affection. Behind her Isaac got out with the help of two sailors. Sonya shook her dress and smoothed its wrinkles. Men and women appeared, they had also gone to bid farewell to their comrades who were leaving the Land and they too are returning to the city. Sonya stood still and said, Those are going and others aren't coming, and the Land is growing empty.

The square of the port is abuzz with stevedores and sailors scurrying around. Stevedores to their own houses and sailors to houses of pleasure. Customs officials leave the customs house, and warehouse clerks go out to welcome them. Mailmen of the six postal services in the Land scurry around, tossing letters and newspapers in one direction and newspapers and letters in another, mail the ships had brought from Outside the Land. Five or six Jews in Sabbath clothes gaze at the full bags of the mailmen and request and implore, Is there something for me, is there something for me? If the mail-carrier is in a good mood, he gives them. If not, he replies, A good Sabbath, and turns away from them. And they retreat, looking around to see if anybody noticed them. Sonya raised her eyes and said to Isaac, Next Saturday we'll get a letter from Rabinovitch.

An autumn silence enfolded the square and the silence was wrapped in a chill. The world shrank and there was a smell of sea water mixed with a smell of rotten oranges. Isaac and Sonya fell silent until they left the sand of the port and entered the street of the city. Sonya stood still and picked a bunch of jasmine, smelled it, and tossed some behind her, and said, I'll polish my shoes. She put one foot on the box of a shoeshine man and raised the hem of her dress. The shoeshine man straightened her foot and stroked her shoe. He picked up his brush, spat into it, dipped it in polish and started rubbing until the shoe gleamed like a mirror. Isaac remembered the moment when Sonya had stood on Rabinovitch's shoes and kissed his forehead. And Isaac passed his hand over his forehead and peeped into his hand. And Sonya put the other foot in front of the shoeshine man and urged him to make it very very nice, as if this foot was the main one. Afterward, what happened, Isaac asked himself and answered himself, Afterward Rabinovitch took out a fine silk handkerchief and shook the dust off his shoes with it. Finished, Sonya called out, paid the Arab his fee and walked off, and Isaac walked with her, sometimes close to her and sometimes a bit distant from her.

In silence, they reached the main street, with its big shops and consulates and offices, and the shop where Rabinovitch had worked. Since it was the Sabbath, the shop was closed and didn't notice that Rabinovitch had left it and descended Outside the Land. And above the shop is a balcony and on it is a white sign with blue letters of the information office. Many times Isaac had stood in that office with comrades as dejected and dog-tired as he. A mute sadness circled his lips.

Sonya looked at the sign of the closed shop and said, Rabinovitch left and won't come back so fast. Like Yarkoni, like Rabinovitch. They come in shouting at the top of their voices and go out stealthily. Now Gorishkin considers himself unique in the world. Do you know Yael Hayyot? Gorishkin is courting her friend Pnina. If you don't know her, you haven't missed anything. Did you see Gorishkin's mustache, like two bananas hanging vertically on his face? Sonya brought the bunch of flowers to her nose and smelled them.

Isaac shrank before Sonya. All his answers were simply yes or no. If a bon mot had fallen into his mouth he would have said it. Even though she isn't important to him, she is important because she is his friend's girlfriend.

In silence he walked beside Sonya. Since he wasn't used to women, he walked carefully, as if she was the daughter of lords and dukes. This behavior amused Sonya and annoyed her, annoyed her and amused her. She looked him over and asked, Is this how you act with a woman back in Galicia? Isaac lowered his eyes as he blushed, and said, Never in my life did I talk to a woman, aside from my mother and my sisters.

Many times had Sonya met that Galician and had wondered what Rabinovitch saw in him that he was so close to him. She looked at him and closed her eyes. She straightened the two points of her collar and passed her hand over her heart.

When they reached Neve Shalom, with the flowers in her left hand, Sonya pointed to one alley and said, Here's where I live. She seemed to want to tell him something, but thought better of it, gave him her hand and said goodbye. Sonya entered the alley and Isaac went home.

CHAPTER EIGHT

Sonya

1 |

Jaffa, belle of the seas, ancient city. Japheth, son of Noah, built it and gave her his name. But of all the Greek beauty of Japheth, all that remains is what human beings can't remove from her, and their city changes with the nature of her inhabitants. Her white houses gleam in the hills of sand, and her green citrus groves crown her with fruit trees, and the luster of her sun hovers over her, and the sea breeze blows among her dark cypresses, and the blue of the sea plays with her sands, and a good smell wafts from her vineyards and from all the other desired trees that desired to settle in Jaffa.

Like all big cities built in ancient times, Jaffa has seen mutations and permutations. Many peoples have warred at her gates, some demolished her foundations, and others built her up on her own heap. Egypt governed her first, then came Assyria and Babylon. The Philistines settled in her, and other nations nested in her walls, until the Holy-One-Blessed-Be-He took her out of their hands and gave her to us, the Sons of Abraham His beloved, seed of Isaac His only son, the community of Jacob His firstborn son. To the shore of Jaffa the city of Tyre brought cedars to build the Temple of our God in Jerusalem, and from Lebanon to the sea of Jaffa cedars were brought to build the Second Temple. The Hasmonean kings made war there, and the ships of the heroes of Israel sailed in her sea to plunder and loot the spoils of war, when the wicked Roman Empire ruled over them. And for our many sins, Jaffa slipped out of our hands and the Romans and Byzantines destroyed her. After them came the Arabs and after them the Franks, after them Egypt and after them the Turks. And even though it was under the yoke of foreigners, we found there a bit of refuge in the shadow of Ishmael. And even if Jaffa is not sanctified with the sanctity of the Land of Israel, it has become the gate to the Holy Land, for all those who ascend to Jerusalem the Holy City ascend first to Jaffa. And at the end of days, all the silver and gold and precious stones and gems lost by all the ships in the open sea, the open sea will vomit them up to Jaffa for the righteous at the end of days. For many generations Jaffa was not inhabited by the Children of Israel because of the ban of the ancients not to settle there permanently so as to increase the settlement of Jerusalem, and because of the dread of the Knights of Malta who invaded the cities of the shore. When the ban was lifted and the strength of the Knights of Malta dwindled, Jaffa was once again a city in the Land of Israel.

In those days when we lived in Jaffa, Jaffa grew to be a big and bustling city. Ships came from far away and brought their wares, and Jaffa sent its produce to distant lands. Tourists who came to travel through the Land didn't pass over Jaffa, and from the settlements of Judea, men came to Jaffa every day on business and women came to buy supplies. Neve Tsedek and Neve Shalom were already standing. And before them, the Templars built their houses. About forty thousand people inhabited Jaffa, maybe more, including perhaps five thousand Children of Israel, Ashkenazim, Maghrebians, Sephardim, and Yemenites. Some lived in the sands in Neve Tsedek and Neve Shalom, on the seashore and in the Agami quarter, and among the citrus groves on the way to Sarona. From Neve Tsedek to the port is a half-hour walk, and from the port to the end of Agami is a half-hour walk, and you still haven't circled all of Jaffa. There are places in Jaffa that seem to you like the end of the city and are only its center, for big citrus groves go on there, and after the citrus groves, houses emerge, and after the houses, again citrus groves and houses. Here a house is hidden in the shadow of a citrus grove, and here a house is peeping out of the citrus grove, and sometimes there's nothing there but a stand of fig trees or a group of vines or pomegranates. And the settlement of the city hasn't yet ended, for overnight a new house pops up. There are places in Jaffa where you don't find a friend or acquaintance, and when you return to your own neighborhood you find them all, for they all live in three or four neighborhoods close to your neighborhood. And if you don't find all of them — some of them you surely find, those you have removed from your mind and those you think about. And sometimes you come across a person you had removed from your mind, but he may well raise a lot of thought in the future.

2 |

Let us return to Isaac. Eight or nine days hadn't passed before Isaac happened to meet Sonya. Great was Sonya's joy when she found Isaac, for a letter had come from Rabinovitch with regards for Mr. Kumer. Amazing that, all the days the letter was wandering on the road, they hadn't come across each other, and when it came they did come across each other. In fact, it isn't really a letter, but just a picture postcard, but it is a sign that he is thinking about us.

Sonya held out the card and read it to Isaac. Finally she gave him the card and said, Please read. Indeed, he doesn't have to read it to her, for she has already read it, but if he wants to read it to her he may read it. There isn't much trouble here, for all that the writing on the card takes only three lines, and one line doesn't concern her, but only Mr. Kumer. So, said Sonya, he wrote this card in Alexandria, and Mittelman he doesn't mention. Don't you know Mittelman? We have a friend named Mittelman. Haven't you heard about him?

Sonya looked down at Isaac's shoes, and said, You haven't heard of Mittelman, who owns the shoe factory? For three years, Mittelman lived with us in the Land, in the end he got up and left. When he left he had enough money to travel only as far as Alexandria, but not to Russia. And with the money his mother sent him for the trip he bought himself nice clothes and good shoes and a new hat, so he wouldn't put the Land of Israel to shame, and he trusted that the sailors would let him work for his passage on the ship. When he told the ship's crew, they went and informed the shipping clerks that there was a Jew here who wanted to cheat them out of his fare. And the shipping clerks were anti-Semites, and members of the Black Hundreds. When the ship docked in Alexandria in Egypt, they put him off with a reprimand and hurled his belongings after him, and the

Jews accompanying him didn't recognize that he needed help, because he was dressed like a rich man. So Mittelman stood on the shore of Alexandria with no money and no friend. He recalled that there was a branch of Carmel Wine there and somebody from the Land of Israel was its leader. He went there and didn't find him. He wandered here and there and looked hither and yon, until he started worrying about his feet because of the walking and about his eyes because of the looking. He saw a shoe store, stood still and peeped in the window to collect his thoughts. The owner of the store came out and saw a well-dressed man wearing new shoes, standing and looking at his wares. He thought he was a professional man, brought him into the store and showed him some of his wares. Mittelman's head didn't follow the shopowner's shoes, so he started showing him more, and ordered coffee for him. Then his tongue loosened up and he started talking. He talked about this, that, and the other. About the manufacture of shoes in general and about the manufacture of shoes in the Land of Israel and in Syria. About the decline of craftsmen in Germany, where factories are driving them out of business and leave them with nothing but patching up shoes, but that is not the case in the Near East, where industrialization doesn't yet exist, but there is room for capitalists to hire laborers and make whatever shoes are needed locally. And here Mittelman began lecturing on Jewish sandals and on Greek sandals, and what kinds of shoes are popular among the inhabitants of the Land, and what kinds of leathers are found in the Land, and what kinds are imported from Outside the Land, what shoes are good for the cities of the shore whose soil is sandy and what shoes are good for the mountains and the rocky ground. And as he talked, he mentioned customs duties and rates of exchange, and such things. Mittelman is no charlatan and doesn't intend to lead folks astray with his words, but since our Yishuv is new and there isn't anything here, people talk a lot about everything the Land needs, and everybody regards himself as an expert. And maybe Mittelman chanced to hear something about the profession or come across an article and read it, for since there are too few books and too much time, a person reads whatever comes to hand. Moreover, Mittelman was a moderate man and his speech was mild. He didn't budge from there until the store owner invited him to lunch. He did-n't budge from there until he told him, Come work with me. And he agreed to work with him. And he knew no more about shoes than any other two-legged creature, but in a short time he learned all he needed to know. Mittelman is a diligent and clever man, and if a per-son had work here in the Land, he wouldn't have to go Outside the Land. To make a long story short, before long he married the store owner's sister and became a partner in his business. And now he owns three stores in Alexandria, and his hand extends over the whole land of Egypt. That's it, my friend, the intelligent ones leave and the weak-lings stay. What will happen to the Land, this is a question that has no answer. And here we are at the Laborers' Club. If you like, we'll go in. Nowhere in Jaffa can an intelligent person find tea and a news-paper on a winter night except in the Laborers' Club. The newspa-pers I don't care about, but a cup of tea I am willing to drink.

3 |

Sonya doesn't read newspapers. By the time the newspapers reach the Land, they have grown old and their words are history. And she doesn't like history, but she does like the Scriptures. And for that she has to thank Doctor Schimmelmann, who lectures to a group of young women on the Prophets. Before Dr. Schimmelmann came, she didn't realize that there was anything interesting in the Scriptures, but first we have to correct its text. You learn that the Prophets weren't idlers, but were people like you and me, who lived the life of their time and suffered the pain of their generation. If you like, they were the journalists and orators of their period. With Dr. Schimmel-mann's emendations, there are prophecies that read like modern ar-ticles. The same is true of the narrative part of the Holy Scriptures. If you like, they're oral feuilletons, for we can't say that there were newspapers in their day. And even satire you find in the Bible. Open the Book of Jonah and you've got a biting satire on a nationalist prophet who withheld his own prophecy and didn't want to proph-esy to the Gentiles.

From Dr. Schimmelmann, Sonya's conversation came round to the other great men of the Yishuv, to Makherovitch who doesn't let a day go by without giving a speech, and Professor Schatz who created the Bezalel Art School. The Professor was now making tablets of olive wood that say: Jew what did you do today for your Nation and your Land?, so that a person should hang a tablet in his house and see and remember and do. From Schatz's feats, Sonya's words came round to two big assemblies that were in Jaffa, one concerning the agricultural laborers whose housing shortage in the settlements keeps them from putting down stakes there, and another assembly about establishing an organization of half a million people to present a petition to ICA to urge them to do real work in the Land of Israel. From those assemblies, Sonya got to the workers, who are called workers only because of their yearning. For nobody gives them work. From the workers, Sonya got to the activists of the Yishuv, who regard the Hebrew worker as if he were undermining their deeds and scaring the capitalists off of settling in the Land. From the activists of the Yishuv, Sonya got to the farmers of the settlements, who ask what we need Jewish workers for, since we've got Arab workers. From the builders of the Yishuv, Sonya got to Zionism, whose activities were carried out mostly by young men and women. Isaac drank in her words, words like Sonya's a person doesn't say unless he has thought about them a lot. And someone who can think like that is endowed with great wisdom.

Isaac doesn't belong to any sect and doesn't join any collective. He hasn't become a member of either *Ha-Po'el Ha-Tsa'ir* or *Po'alei Tsion*. And even though there isn't a person in the Land who isn't a member of a party, Isaac didn't join any party. It's enough for Isaac that he's a Zionist. And that he is a Zionist is really shown in fact, for he did ascend to the Land of Israel. As the son of poor, wretched, and ineffectual parents, Isaac grew up in a world where all people are conditioned and stand from their birth in the place where their fortune put them, higher ones on top and lower ones on the bottom. If success favors a person, he rises. The more he's favored, the more he rises. And the idea that people can change the laws of nature and human beings can improve themselves if they have the will was not only inconceivable to him, he even poked fun at it. Back then in his hometown he made fun of the socialists who wanted to change the order of the world, which never changes. And if he dismissed the socialists with mockery, he complained and grumbled about the Labor Zionists because they mix Zionism together with socialism. And when they made a chapter of the Labor Zionists in his home-town and came to Isaac, he told them, How can you mix two things that don't go together, and are often opposed to one another, for then you're getting yourself into something and its opposite. And in fact, Isaac's propecy did come true, for when they heard that Davis Trietsch was coming to town and the Zionists wanted to make a party in his honor, the Labor Zionists didn't know what to do, whether to honor him, but he did own a factory for wooden goods in Jaffa and the workers there were on strike, or whether to demonstrate against him, but he was a famous Zionist. Just as Outside the Land Isaac maintained his Zionism as it was originally given, without any addi-tional opinions that aren't essential to it, so he maintained it in the Land of Israel, too. And he wondered at our comrades, for after all they ascended to the Land to rebuild it and in the end out of irrele-vant ideals, they make war on the farmers, which sometimes leads to strikes and inhibits the work of the Land. Isaac recognized the strug-gle of the Enlightenment, and needless to say, our war against the as-similationists, but how can Zionists who come there to work the Land make sects on top of sects that crush the Land into sections. And since he wasn't a member of any sect and didn't go to assemblies, he didn't know much about the issues of the Land, and if an issue of the magazine *The Young Laborer* fell into his hand, he read the poems and stories and critical articles, but not the news articles. Now that he heard Sonya talking, even things everybody had already hashed over were like a new teaching to him. Moreover, it's nicer to hear things from a living person, from a young woman, than to hear them from irascible speakers or to read them in a squashed paper groped by many hands.

From the founders of Zionism, Sonya got to ordinary human beings, the ones you don't know why they came and what brought them here. They heard a rumor and they came. Blame the Zionist preachers who go around the cities of Exile and stir up the rich to buy themselves property in the Land of Israel. The rich aren't stirred, but the poor are roused, the ones who don't have a livelihood there, and think that if they come to the Land, every single one will immediately be offered a colony. Colonies aren't offered them and not everybody can work, and even those who are willing to work don't find work, and they go to the dogs.

And Sonya went back to talking about the distinguished men of the Yishuv and about our national institutions. No doubt they're bona fide Zionists, but their acts are far from Zionism. And, Sonya expatiated and said, Have you ever considered that most of our activists, are followers of Ahad Ha-Am? That's no accident, but there's an ideology here that comes essentially from fear. Those good people, who are afraid of any real action, for them it's convenient to dream of a Spiritual Center, that the whole Land will be filled with schools and small children will be knowledgeable about Judaism and so forth. But we need work, life, a nation working its own soil that brings bread out of the Land.

From the national institutions, Sonya got to the officials of the institutions and to Orgelbrand who had rented Rabinovitch's room. And as she mentioned Rabinovitch, she started talking about him. A marvelous quality, Rabinovitch has, that he accepts every single thing as inevitable, but he doesn't bow to it, and is ready at any time to break out of its domination. People like Rabinovitch aren't revolutionaries or innovators, but under certain conditions they become partners in building a society.

Sonya didn't conclude all her praise of Rabinovitch. For, aside from that virtue she found in him, he's got a good quality that outweighs all other qualities, that is love of his fellow man. And here Isaac began telling some things Sonya knew and some she didn't know. Now Rabinovitch lives in Berlin or Vienna, and he has probably already found what he was looking for. A person like Rabinovitch never gets lost. If you saw Rabinovitch looking for work from the farmers and saw him afterward measuring a garment for a Kaymakam you know that any place is his place. In a year or two Rabinovitch will return to the Land of Israel and return to his work. Said Sonya, In a year or two, he'll return with his boss's daughter, whom he got from her father along with a dowry.

That was a bad joke. A person like Rabinovitch is as true as gold and doesn't betray for a dowry. And maybe it was Sonya who made Rabinovitch leave the Land so he could get rich and come back and take her and give her a life of pleasure and honor. This idea that his friend had left the Land of Israel because of Sonya elevated her in his eyes, even though he wasn't happy with her words.

Sonya sensed that Isaac was seared by her words. She placed both her hands on his as a gesture of reconciliation. Isaac blushed and dropped his eyes, as if, in the touch of Sonya's hands, there was some affront to Rabinovitch's honor. She glanced at him and was puzzled.

CHAPTER NINE

In the Workers' Club

1 |

A meager light illuminated the two rooms of the club. The tables and chairs and other furnishings weren't the kind of accoutrements that expand the mind. Some were bought from those who descended Outside the Land and some came from volunteers, and sometimes a person comes to the club and sits on a chair he loathed in his own house and here he was glad to sit on it, for the other chairs were even worse.

That night was an ordinary night. There were no conferences or assemblies. Our comrades sat there, some were drinking tea, some were reading newspapers, some were talking with one another. Some weren't reading or drinking or talking, but were sitting by themselves and thinking. They were thinking about this, that, and the other. About yesterday that had passed and about tomorrow that was to come. Many are the days here, and every day is as turgid as sooty glass that muddies the lamplight. Was the woman at the buffet so busy she didn't have time to clean the lamp, or because she doesn't have anything to do, she doesn't do what she has to do.

At the end of the table sat Gorishkin, reading a book. Gorishkin sat and didn't think, neither trivial things nor sublime things, but just sat and read. Gorishkin isn't one of those who think a man dredges everything up out of himself, but he knows that anyone who wants to be a writer has to read a lot and study a lot and expand the scope of his knowledge. Gorishkin has already left behind all his own thoughts and wants only to be the writer of the Land of Israel. A new life is taking shape in the Land and it needs its writer. He hasn't yet started writing because he doesn't have a corner of his own, for he lives in a room with three or four of his comrades, and the room is about the size of an egg and the table is about the size of an olive. And there's no space there to spread out paper. And mainly, because he hasn't yet made up his mind whether to write things as they are, that is, to copy from reality, or to make his books novels. On the one hand, his heart inclines to things as they are, for there is no truth like the truth of actions, and on the other hand, novels are likely to appeal to the heart and lead to action. For the time being, he reads every book that comes to hand, for, aside from expanding a man's mind, books, to quote Bialik, are like dung to a field for a person with talent, and to quote Simkha Ben-Tsion, like dew to the flowers.

Our comrade Gorishkin is sitting and reading a new book, for the librarian took pity on him and lent it to him before he had read it himself. His head is sunk in the book and the branches of his mustache run from line to line, like pointers for children, and he doesn't see Sonya or Isaac. Isaac, who hadn't seen him since the day he met him at Rabinovitch's, wanted to go ask him how he was, but it wasn't proper to leave Sonya. And Sonya doesn't notice anything, for it doesn't occur to her that someone would want to leave her for someone like Gorishkin.

Next to our comrade Gorishkin sat a fellow over a cup of tea. He sipped it slowly because his money was limited and he had to make do with one cup as if it were two. For a long time he had been idle until he was exhausted with idleness and hunger, and finally found work to do, and when he began working, he got sick. He girded his loins and paid no heed to his illness, for if they knew he was sick, they would fire him immediately. Sometimes he got the upper hand and sometimes his illness did. Suddenly he found himself in the hospital. He spent two months there and came out. Was the doctor mistaken when he told him he was healthy. If the doctor was mistaken, he isn't mistaken. His bones are soft and all his limbs are scattered abroad and dispersed. He picked up his cup and drank drop by drop, like a man who uses glue to glue one thing to another. He sat before his cup and pondered, So I got sick again and since they put me out of the hospital, they won't take me back. So what shall I do? To go back to work, I can't, since I'm sick, and to sit idle I can't, because I have to eat. So what will become of me? If there's no food, there's no strength, and if there's no strength, there's no food. Your prophesy has come true, Father, when you saw me preparing for a craft and said, I see, my son, that you've got two right hands, and you will wind up an artisan, not a merchant and not a rich man, may you not have to starve. Your prophesy has come true, Father, your blessing hasn't. He turns here and there. Here they're quibbling about current events and there they're discussing literature. Here and there, no one has an extra penny to lend him in his hour of need.

2 |

Not all faces are alike. While that fellow sits in his grief, Puah Hofenstein sits happy for she has received good tidings that her brother had managed to escape from Siberia and is on his way to the Land of Israel. And Madame Hofenstein's joy is shared by Ossip the anarchist, her brother's comrade. Ossip sits nearby with his thick stick, the stick we joked about, saying that it gets thicker as its owner grows more shriveled from day to day. Ossip doesn't show his joy, but only mutters, Hmm, hmm. But his stick tells us he's happy, for if not, the stick in his hand wouldn't be dancing.

Ossip is shriveling more and more and it's no wonder. For Ossip left a vast land and came to this little Land, which is as impenetrable as a rock. The Arabs speak a language you don't know. And the Jews are divided into several tribes and several languages, and every tribe is a nation unto itself and a language unto itself. Sephardim and Ashkenazim and Yemenites and Mughrabians, etc. Reluctantly you have to give up on all those whose language you don't know. All you've got left are the Ashkenazim. If you count all of them, there are no more of them in the Land than in a middle-sized city in Russia. And they're divided, too. The members of the Old Yishuv settled in the Land mainly to be buried in its soil, and the members of the New Yishuv are either Effendis with wealth or destitute ragamuffins. Anyone with a grain of sense sees that the ragamuffins should regard the Effendis as enemies, yet in the end, they cooperate with them to increase their wealth, and they don't let you open your mouth to argue with them, because you can't speak the

Holy Tongue. Another trouble here is that you haven't got a liveli-hood. But thanks to Puah Hofenstein who shared her meals with him he was saved from starvation, because of the fraternal bond between him and her brother. And even though food and drink are better than starvation and thirst, his pleasure wasn't perfect, for as long as you sit before her, you see yourself sinking into the abyss of the indulgent bourgeois life you escaped from.

There were others in the club too. Like Princess Mira Ramishvili Lordswill and Masha Yasinovski Lordswill, the ex-wives of Vittorio Lordswill, the wonderful musician, famous all over the world. Those women had opened a millinery salon. Princess Mira Ramishvili Lordswill and Masha Yasinovski Lordswill don't usually come to the Laborer's Club, so why did they come? Because once Tsina Dizengoff came to have a hat made for the winter season and told them that she saw in the newspaper the name of Prince Ramishvili, and Prince Ramishvili had been Mira's husband before she met Lordswill. So she and her friend Masha came to see what the newspapers write about the Prince. Across from them sat Sasha Tugendherz, who had gotten a good job in the Russian consulate. And Sasha hadn't yet argued anything before the consul.

Our comrade Joseph Aronovitch was also here. He was still dressed like all our comrades in the settlements, with threadbare gar-ments on his body and oversized sandals on his feet and a torn straw hat on his head, even though summer was already over and the rains would soon come. And in his hand, he wasn't holding a leather bag, as editors do, but his pockets served as the editorial briefcase for *The Young Laborer*.

Silman saw him and told him he was preparing an issue for Purim. Aronovitch looked at him out of the corner of his eyes and smiled at him. Suddenly the mockery was gone from his eyes and the lines of his forehead filled with great sadness. And Aronovitch told Silman, You want to publish a Purim paper, to rouse laughter and mockery with the jokes you make up. But if you heed my advice, you'll take from what is happening in the Land, things as they are, without embellishing anything, and I guarantee you that you'll make them laugh more than all the humorists in the world, even though woe is us from that laughter. Aronovitch immediately reminded him of actions that had been done and actions that were about to be done, and every action was more ridiculous than the last. And more ridiculous than the actions were their actors, who boast as if the whole Yishuv depends on them. And even if every day were Purim and every day you publish a comic newspaper, you still wouldn't be able to tell everything. And maybe a Purim paper shouldn't take from reality, for things we see as painfully ridiculous, and that every sensible person weeps over them, are used as material for propaganda in the Diaspora. Silman looked at Aronovitch, whose face was full of grief and began laughing, for laughter is nicer than grief. Aronovitch looked at him and was amazed, for those actions should make you weep and not laugh.

And there were also others in the club. Printing press workers and building workers, workers who have no specific skill, and workers who were out of work and looking for work, and workers who left their work because of illness and became secretaries, this one in the SHILOH Company, whose initials stand for Sail Home Israel to the Land of Hope, and that one in *Akhuzat Bayit*, the committee preparing to build a new neighborhood in Jaffa. The whole club consisted of two rooms, one room for eating and drinking and another room for reading, but no one is strict about reading in the place for reading and eating and drinking in the place for eating and drinking, but this one eats and reads and that one reads and drinks. This one comes in and that one goes out. This one is a member of *Ha-Po'el Ha-Tsa'ir* and that one is a member of *Po'aley Tsion*. The Purim event is already forgotten, when our comrades got into a fight and the fight spilled out to the street, and the Kaymakam of Jaffa got permission from the Russian Consul and sent Arab Ottoman police to make order and thirteen Jews were wounded.

Falk Spaltleder entered and ordered two portions of hamburger and a loaf of bread. And even though he was hungry as a dog, Tsippa Shoshi, the girl at the buffet, didn't pay attention to him because at that moment she was busy with Tshernipolski, who had been measuring several countries with his feet. People are wont to stroll in the Land, from Jaffa to Kfar Saba and from Kfar Saba to Hadera and from Hadera to Zikhron Ya'akov and back. And if they're a bit more adventuresome, they go up to the Galilee and to Metullah. While our comrade Tshernipolski swallowed up the entire Land, its length and breadth, with the soles of his feet, all the way to Mount Hermon, and didn't miss a single village. In one place he stayed overnight and in another place he drank pomegranate juice with snow, and in one village he saw a wedding celebration and in one village he saw something, but he won't tell. A person has to conceal his feelings, for by concealing them in his heart they bear fruit. And once upon a time he sat on the crest of a rock at sunrise to eat his bread and garlic. And he felt in himself a kind of stirring that not everyone feels. If he wanted, he would have written a great poem with a few hundred stanzas about that. A poem like that, Tsippa Shoshi my dear, such a poem that Tshernipolski would write is worth all the poems of Pizmoni.

Gorishkin put down his book and sat and pondered, That tale I read here also happened to me, if not really the same, then something similar, but it didn't occur to me to write, and that writer came along and wrote and made a book, and I sat and read his book, and tomorrow others will come along, and the day after tomorrow others, until there won't be a person left in the Land who hasn't read it. And when I come along and publish my book, they'll say, We've already read all that. It seems to me that the essence of a writer is his speed. If he's fast and writes, he wins, and if not, others come along and take what's his. The time has come for me to rent a room of my own with a table. I don't ask for a desk with a green cloth, like those teachers in Jaffa who all make themselves a desk and put a basket full of torn paper in front of it so people will regard them as writers. All I need is an upturned barrel, just so I can spread a piece of paper on it.

3 |

Gorishkin raised his eyes and saw Sonya. He thrust his book in his pocket and went up to her. He saw Isaac and asked how he was. Said Sonya, And about Rabinovitch you don't ask? Said Gorishkin, Why do I have to ask, if you had something to tell me about him, wouldn't you have told? Said Sonya, In fact, I don't have anything to tell about him because he doesn't write to me. Said Gorishkin, If he had something to write, he would write.

Said Sonya, You returned to Jaffa. What are you doing here? Said Gorishkin, I'm doing what I haven't done for days and years. I'm working, I'm working, Sonya. Where? she asked. And Gorishkin took the two ends of his mustache in his fingertips and said triumphantly and proudly, I'm working at the building of the girls' school, with clay and stones. Said Sonya, Good for you that you found work. Said Gorishkin, It found me. At long last they've got to hire Jewish workers. And we're flaying the skin off our bones just so they won't find empty excuses to reject us. So what does Rabinovitch write? Sonya laughed and said, Didn't you just say if he had something to write he would write. Said Gorishkin, Which means that he doesn't have anything to write. Said Sonya, That's not so, you must say he's got lots of things to write and so he doesn't write at all. Let's go, said Sonya to Isaac. You're going? asked Gorishkin. Sonya turned her head back and said, Say hello to Pnina. Here she comes.

Pnina said to Gorishkin, I didn't know you were here. Said Gorishkin, If you had known, you wouldn't have come? Said Pnina, That's not what I said. Said he, But in your heart, that's what you thought. Said she, Does a person know what's in his comrade's heart, aside from writers? Said Gorishkin, Believe me, Pnina, they don't know anything either, but when you read their words it seems to you that they do know. Said Pnina, What's that in your pocket, a new book? Said Gorishkin, The book is a new book, the content is old content. If you like, the same thing happened to you and to me. The very same thing? she asked. And if there are some changes, that doesn't change a thing. Let's go, said Sonya.

Sonya doesn't look down on Pnina or Gorishkin. Pnina is a much more honest and pleasant girl than Yael Hayyot, whom Hemdat is wooing. And if she bores you — it's her naïveté that's boring. And Gorishkin is also an honest man. Before she met Rabinovitch, she used to go out with Gorishkin, and she is grateful to him for not wooing her too much. In fact, no man woos a woman unless she is willing. However, she remembers Gorishkin kindly for not making her do that, so that she could look Rabinovitch in the eye even when

Gorishkin was with them. Now Rabinovitch has gone and includes her in his letters to Isaac Kumer. That Galician, it seems his heart is blank. Has he really not spoken with a girl in his life, or is he just saying that to make himself interesting?

When they emerged from the dark lane of the club and came to the crossroads, Sonya took her leave of Isaac, even though she hadn't yet come to her house. For no reason, as we people of the Land of Israel say, she took her leave of him. As she took her leave of him and went off, twice she told him goodbye: Shalom, shalom.

CHAPTER TEN

At Sonya's Place

1 |

A few days after that night, Isaac saw Sonya walking in the street. He waved his hat and went toward her. In fact, Isaac should already have tried to see her because he got a letter from Rabinovitch, and in that letter, Rabinovitch asked how Sonya was. What does our friend Rabinovitch write? Our friend Rabinovitch writes almost nothing. If Madam wants to read it—please. Sonya took the letter and read, Ohhh, said Sonya, a person goes to Europe and finds nothing there but bad wine in Brindisi and sailors who beat each other up over a prostitute. At any rate, our Rabinovitch isn't willing to fight over a girl. Rabinovitch was deserving of Sonya's praise, for he didn't fail to write them. Yet in the end, she chides and mocks him. Isaac bowed his head in embarrassment, so as not to look at her while she is mocking, but her face didn't turn away from him. This was not the face he had seen on the ship when Sonya stood on Rabinovitch's shoes with her face glued to his. Isaac glanced at her from the side and once again was embarrassed. But his embarrassment was divided, half of it tremulous and half of it rejoicing. Said Sonya, Look, you say of Rabinovitch that every place is his place. There's a bit of truth in that, but I say not every place a person acquires is flattering for him. Are you in a hurry, Kumer? No, then let's stroll a little.

So Isaac walks with Sonya. Sometimes next to her and sometimes behind her, as she tries to match her steps to his steps. Passersby ask how she is. Some of them are teachers, some of them are writers, some of them are clerks. And though they are noted people whose name you find in the newspapers, she replies to their greetings rather casually. So they went through a few streets and a few alleys until they came to her house. Sonya stood still and said, Here's where I live. Are you busy? No. Then come in.

2 |

Never in his life had Isaac seen a girl's room, and suddenly he finds himself sitting in Sonya's room. The room is neither small nor big, but is medium size, and it has two windows, one window looks onto the street and has a curtain hanging on it, and one window opens onto a narrow alley where not everyone can pass. In the room is a bed and a sofa and a small table and a closet. The bed is covered by a colorful blanket embroidered with a yellow dog carrying a stick in his mouth. And under the sofa is a yellow box full of glasses and bowls and plates and spoons and knives and forks, all of Sonya's crockery. And in the closet her dresses are hanging. And on top of the closet is a round hat-box. The room also has a lamp and a washbasin and a pitcher and two glasses, and a picture of Berele, our comrade who was killed by Arabs. Sonya didn't know Berele, but because she had taken care of his be-reaved mother who came to prostrate herself on his grave, the woman gave her his picture. And because all our comrades were fond of him, it seemed to Sonya that she knew him better than anybody and was more fond of him than anybody. And sometimes she chides Berele's girlfriends who consider themselves closer to him than she is. Isaac didn't raise his eyes from the table, and whatever he saw in the room, he saw only by short glances, split into several details.

Her dress is handsome and light, wraps her body and taps on her limbs. Most of the girls wear such a dress, but not every girl brings her dress to life like Sonya, for the dress gambols on her, as if it too were alive. And another secret Sonya has, her shoes, which were made for her by the cobbler from Homel, that most women don't know. Their shoes are made by Greek cobblers, and those women don't know that there's a poor Jewish cobbler here, and the shoes he makes give you an upright body and a fine posture. That cobbler de-serves gratitude, but Sonya keeps her secret and doesn't reveal it to her girlfriends.

Sonya is not exceptionally beautiful. Rachel Heilperin is bet-ter looking, Leah Luria is better looking, Asnat Magergut and Yael

Hayyot are better looking. Even other girls who aren't famous beauties may be better looking than Sonya. As for her face, it's freckled. And her eyes are neither black nor blue. And as for her hair, it's bobbed and of indefinite shade. But all the defects gathered together in Sonya endow her with charm. Not for nothing did that Russian journalist, the friend of Sonya's father, who taught Sonya Hebrew, say, There's nobody like you, Sonya. That sinner already considered himself old, but when he met Sonya, his heart became young. As Sonya attracts the hearts of old men, so she attracts the hearts of young men. Grisha was attracted to her, Yarkoni was attracted to her, Gorishkin was attracted to her, not to mention Rabinovitch. Now Isaac sits before Sonya, because he is the friend of Rabinovitch who is Sonya's friend. Isaac isn't shrewd like all our other comrades. But there is something about him that attracts the heart. Sonya doesn't know what it is. We who do know what it is will explain. There is in our comrade Isaac what there is in most young sons of Israel who have not yet tasted sin either in deed or in thought, and that is what endowed him with charm. Sonya passed her right hand over her head and smoothed her hair. Her hairdo is masculine, although she is not. When Isaac saw Sonya on the sea, she looked like a lad, now he sees her as a maiden, whom our comrade Rabinovitch liked better than all our women comrades in Jaffa. Maybe Isaac was sitting and maybe not. Even though he isn't experienced with women, Isaac does know that as long as the hostess is standing, it's not fitting for a guest to sit. And if he does sit, he sits tentatively.

Sonya bent over to the sofa, and from the box underneath it, she took out a small wicker basket and two flat plates and knives and paper napkins to wipe their hands. She stood up on tiptoe and brought down some oranges from the top of the closet. And then she put the oranges in the basket and set it on the table. She sat down, picked up a knife and peeled, and placed before Isaac a peeled orange sliced into sections. Isaac took a section and ate, while Sonya peeled a second and a third. Eat, Mr. Kumer, eat, said Sonya softly; there's a lot here. Isaac took another section and told Sonya of the first time he had eaten an orange. Once upon a time, Mother, may-she-rest-in-peace, was sick and Father got her an orange. Mother di-

vided the orange and gave some to every single child. At last nothing
was left for her. Sonya said, Yes, yes, Outside the Land, oranges are
expensive, while in the Land of Israel they are literally rolling in the
street. Once the priest's wife from her hometown ascended to the
Land of Israel and came to see Sonya. Sonya put a heap of oranges
before her. Said the priest's wife, Sonichka, you treat that expensive
fruit the way we treat potatoes. Said Sonya, And where you are, you
treat potatoes the way we treat oranges here. Yes, yes, said the priest's
wife, a person doesn't appreciate what he's got, but likes and appre-
ciates what he hasn't got. Yes, yes, Sonya repeated the words of the
priest's wife, a person doesn't appreciate what he's got. Sometimes
you find perfect wisdom in simple speech. Isaac wiped his hands and
picked up a Bible from the table. He looked at it and saw a line erased
here and a verse written there. Said Sonya, That belongs to my girlfriend, who corrected it according to the emendations of Doctor
Schimmelman. You know Doctor Schimmelmann, don't you? He
speaks like a prophet and researches like a professor.

 As Isaac was about to leave, Sonya said, Now that you've
been in my house, I hope you'll come back. Isaac answered, Sure,
sure. Isaac knew that his sure's were dubious. But in his heart he
thought, If we meet again and she tells me to come in, I won't refuse.
On my own I won't come. As soon as he had left he wanted to return.

3 |

The moon stood in the sky and the citrus groves were fragrant and
the sea uttered its voice, not the voice of mighty waters, but the voice
of a quiet humming. Even if you hadn't been sitting with a girl like
Sonya, you saw that this night was not like all other nights. The moon
plays with the world and the universe is happy, and the fragrance of
oranges wafts from every citrus grove and every tree, that's the fragrance of oranges close to you and if you stretch out your hands to a
tree and pluck off a fruit, the owner of the citrus grove won't scold
you, for oranges roll around here like potatoes Outside the Land
The distress of hunger and the disgrace of wandering from farmer to
farmer and from office to office, and all the other things Isaac had
experienced — were nothing now but a memory. Our comrade Ra-

binovitch was foolish to leave. At that moment, Isaac didn't long for Rabinovitch, Isaac did long for something but he didn't know what. The moon played by itself. It hid between the clouds and shone through them.

As he walked, Isaac came to the German Colony. The Negro guard saw him and recognized him because he had painted the homes of the residents of the Colony and frequented the home of Bra-bra-no-rish, the man of many clothes. The guard opened the little gate for him and let him in. He went in and started strolling around.

Mr. Orgelbrand came out, as he was wont to do every night before going to sleep, for every sleep that is not preceded by a stroll is heavy. There are people who stroll around for no good reason, but not Orgelbrand, for all his times are calculated, and he allocated this short time for a stroll. In the past, Orgelbrand lived on the sands at the sea and the sea roiled his sleep. When Rabinovitch left the Land, he came and rented his room. And now he's happy about the change. No longer does he have to weary his legs in the sands, but walks on solid ground. And when he comes back from work, he sits down at the window like a person sitting in his garden, looking at the trees and bushes and flowers standing peacefully and not lacking anything. And he doesn't lack anything either. He gets his pay every month and eats his fill and dresses well and is respected by folks, but it is that peace that made him start feeling the lack of something and if you lack that something, you lack everything.

Jonathan Orgelbrand is one of the clerks of the Anglo-Palestine Company, and a distant relative of Sonya's, and is ten years older than Sonya, maybe more. At first, he expected Sonya to see his nature and overlook his years, then Rabinovitch came and destroyed his hope. When Rabinovitch left the Land, his hope for Sonya returned, since anyone who leaves the Land of Israel doesn't come back so fast. And if he does come back, he doesn't come back to old things. Hence the contact between Sonya and Rabinovitch was broken, even though it ostensibly still exists, and Sonya is unattached and it is no crime if you think about her. Suddenly he found her walking with Isaac Kumer. He really doesn't have anything against

Mr. Kumer. He's a worker like all other workers in the Land, at any rate, if Sonya hadn't been walking with him, he wouldn't have noticed him.

Orgelbrand hung his stick on his arm and pulled his cap down on his forehead, the black cap he wears at night in front of his house. His good, languid eyes expanded because the cap shrank his forehead and because he saw Mr. Kumer. Since the night is fine and the moon is shining and he found a person to talk with, he started talking. First about the moon, which is twice as big here as Outside the Land, and then about other things that are different in the Land of Israel from all other lands, and about the people of the Land of Israel who are different from other people, and then about the ways of commerce, and from the ways or commerce, he got to the Ango-Palestine Company.

Isaac Kumer stands there, a little painter from a little town in Galicia, before Mr. Jonathan Orgelbrand, a certain clerk of the Ango-Palestine Company, and hears things about an issue that had excited him in his childhood, when two doctors from Lemberg came down to his hometown and delivered lectures about the Settlement Fund and about shares that give the Children of Israel possession of the Land of Israel, and would give their owners great profits. Like most matters that start with a bang and are forgotten, so Isaac had forgotten that matter too, until he came to Jaffa and saw a big building with a sign on it, and a lot of people roaring and pouring there, this is our bank, which the Zionists Outside the Land are proud of and say, May we live to be attendants in it. Many times, Isaac had chanced to see the director of the Anglo-Palestine Company riding in a carriage from his house to the bank and from the bank to his house, with a liveried attendant sitting in front, and everyone who sees him bows down to him, and Arabs call him Father of Money. Some merchants complain about the director that he doesn't lend them money in time of need, and some activists grumble that if he's offered land to buy he doesn't buy. Maybe he's right, for he knows the Land and knows what should be done and what shouldn't be done, and maybe the merchants and activists are right, for the Anglo-Palestine Company wasn't created only to make money, but to support the Land and its inhabitants. Whether it's one or the other, it's great to hear from a certain clerk of the Ango-Palestine Company certain things about the Anglo-Palestine Company that the whole Yishuv can be proud of.

Orgelbrand dropped the subject and asked Isaac, What does our comrade Mr. Rabinovitch write? Isaac answered, What does our comrade Rabinovitch write, trivial things he writes. Orgelbrand dropped his eyes as if he were ashamed of his question and said, To you he doesn't write, to Madame Zweiering he writes. Isaac answered, To her too he writes almost nothing. Said Orgelbrand, How can it be that he writes almost nothing to her? As he spoke, he became alarmed at his own words. Mr. Orgelbrand didn't intend to stick his nose so far into other people's business.

4 |

Jonathan Orgelbrand makes a good salary and is respected by folks. There are merchants who cast their eye on him for their daughters, and there are daughters who cast their eye on him for themselves. And still he wasn't yet married, even though he was already past his prime, and of all the money he earns he doesn't have enough left to build himself a house, for he spends most of his money on various relatives who are no longer related to him. From the first day of his life, Jonathan Orgelbrand has borne the yoke. First with his father, who ruled him ruthlessly because he wanted to teach him the trade of hatmaking while he wanted to study office work, to be a clerk, because the clerk sits in a warm building on a swivel chair, and everybody tips his hat to honor the clerk, not like that hatmaker who makes hats for everybody and nobody tips his hat to him. As long as his mother was alive, he suffered his father's rule. When she died and his father married another woman who brought him three daughters from her first husband, Jonathan ran away to the city of Baruch Zweiering (Sonya Zweiering's father), a distant relative on his mother's side. Mr. Zweiering gave him room and board and found him comrades from good families to teach him language and literature, for in those days folks were good to one another and helped one another. Orgelbrand was a diligent student and didn't waste a minute, like a person who yearns to reach a certain status in society and knows the value of time. And what status did he want to reach, the status of a clerk. And not because the clerk sits in a warm building in a swivel chair, but because he was inclined to that, for he had already become a man and turned his mind to his future.

Before long he went to work in a bank. First as a lowly secretary, and then as an assistant clerk, and then as a full clerk. He heard that they were about to establish a bank in Jaffa and needed expert clerks. He, who was drawn to Zionism and saw himself as an expert, took a pouch full of letters of recommendation with him and ascended to the Land of Israel.

He came to the director of the Anglo-Palestine Company. The director looked at his letters and said, Let's see if you're as good as they are. He examined him and found that they had written scarcely half the truth about him. So he gave him a position and raised his wages several times. When Orgelbrand ran away from his father he had nothing but the clothes on his back and a new hat he had taken unbeknownst to his father, and was supported by others, and now he has three suits and supports others with his money, for when he started getting paid, he started helping his father with money, first occasionally, and then on a regular basis. Then the father died and his widow married somebody else because people said that man could support her. But he couldn't support her, for he was a sick man who needed to be supported. She wrote anguished letters to her stepson. He took pity on that wretched woman and started sending her money, as he had sent his father — at first to support the family, then additional money as a dowry for her oldest daughter, then for the second one, then for the third one, and aside from that, he sent money for the husband's medical treatment. Things had reached such a pass that he spent half his salary on his father's widow. And by now he was used to that, as something natural.

One day, he encountered Sonya Zweiering. He recalled all the favors of her father who had brought him into his home and fed him and gave him whatever he needed and hired teachers for him until he reached wherever he reached, and now his daughter lives here among strangers and needs to be taken care of like all the other girls. And out of his pity and his affection, he started thinking, If I were married, I would bring her into my home and repay her for all the benefits her father granted me. But what should he do, since he is a bachelor and has no home, and all the nice things he should do, he can't do. It occurred to him that maybe God willing, she would take a shine to him. He still wasn't clear about what he wanted. When it did become clear to him, he got scared of the boldness of the idea, even though he didn't stop thinking, Perhaps and maybe.

As he wavered between the various possibilities, he found Sonya going out with Rabinovitch. He curbed his feelings and tried to take his mind off her. But he invited her and Rabinovitch to his home, and offered them fruit and sweets, and accustomed himself to seeing them as a couple. And he was already considering what gift he would give them for their wedding. Then Rabinovitch left the Land. Orgelbrand understood that the package had come undone, that if they had been a couple, he wouldn't have gone, or she would have gone with him. He began turning his mind to her again. Suddenly he found her walking with Isaac Kumer. Once again he wanted to take his thoughts off her, and didn't succeed, but on the contrary, would ponder and say, And if Rabinovitch the merchant isn't a match for her, even less so is this Kumer, this laborer. And if you say, Isn't she going out with him, it's the way of the world that lively girls go out with fellows until they find their mate and wash their hands of the others, and we cannot change that custom.

CHAPTER ELEVEN

Mutations and Permutations

1 |

Let's go back to the main issue. One day Isaac came home from work. He put on his best clothes and went out for a stroll. What made Isaac put on his good clothes on a weekday and go out early? If you had asked him, he couldn't have answered. Not every day are a man's actions in his own hands.

As he walks, Sonya comes toward him. Her light shirt flutters over her heart and a new hat is on her head, a girl's hat that gives her face the bloom of a handsome girl. She too went out early, just like Isaac. Even though she didn't have anything to do outside, she was happy she went out, for the day was declining and the time had come to get a breath of fresh air.

Sonya is happy and joyful and the freckles on her face scattered like golden lentils. Her eyes smile at Isaac and on her lips is an accommodating smile that is neither stunned nor amazed to find Isaac.

Isaac asked Sonya, What did Rabinovitch write? Sonya replied, That's just what I wanted to ask you, did he write to you? I haven't gotten a single word from him. Rabinovitch had planned to do great things Outside the Land, and hadn't done any of them. He is ashamed to write the truth, and he doesn't want to lie, so he keeps silent.

Since they came upon one another, they joined one another and went for a stroll. And not just at that time, but whenever they met, they would stroll together.

2 |

At first their conversation was about their comrade Rabinovitch. Isaac told how he met Rabinovitch, and how Rabinovitch treated him with love and affection. And Sonya told how she met him, and when she knew him it seemed to her that she had known him forever. That is hard to put into words, because there's a contradiction here, for if you hadn't seen him before, how does it seem to you that you know him? Maybe because of an imaginary reminiscence that unwittingly brings hearts close together.

Isaac Kumer and Sonya Zweiering walk together because he is Rabinovitch's friend and she is Rabinovitch's girlfriend. And even though Rabinovitch isn't with them, his image goes before them. Sonya, who is an expert in human beings and likes to paint their portraits in words, talks about Rabinovitch until it seems to you that he is standing before your eyes.

Isaac was fond of those hours when he strolled with Sonya and chatted about Rabinovitch. If Rabinovitch isn't here, his mate is. And here Isaac had to admit that he had no cause to complain about his friend for courting Sonya, for aside from the fact that she is a handsome girl, her mind is astounding. Whether she is talking about Rabinovitch or whether she is talking about other people. There are things Isaac feels and can't explain, and Sonya comes and gives them a Hebrew or a foreign name and everything is nice and clear, for Sonya attended a general school and acquired general knowledge, something he doesn't have, because all the learning he received in Heder and the study house allowed him to read a Hebrew newspaper and a Hebrew book about Judaism and Zionism and Zionism and Judaism. And one more thing. Sonya is the daughter of educated people, a girl from a big city, while he is the son of a poor shopkeeper, a boy from a small town where there is nothing except trying to make a living and gossip and slander.

With time, they talked less about their friend Rabinovitch. Sometimes they started with him and then sailed off to another subject. And if they came back to talk about him, they themselves felt that there was nothing new to add to the matter of Rabinovitch, and all they had to say they had already said. Nevertheless, they did mention him. Sonya would say, Too bad for Rabinovitch, while we're strolling here and the stars are taking shape in the firmament and the waves of the sea are skipping on the sand like a cluster of lovers assembling for a meeting of love, he's probably sitting in coffee houses and irritating his eyes with his cigarette smoke. And Isaac adds, Just as we think of him, so he thinks of us. Isaac brought up the subject of Rabinovitch a lot, but as he spoke he saw that his words had lost their warmth and he was talking only to fulfill an obligation.

With time, they stopped mentioning him. And since they didn't mention him, they mentioned their own affairs. They talked about this, that, and the other. Sonya told Isaac about her father and her mother, about her boyfriends and her girlfriends, about everything a girl of a good family tells and isn't ashamed of. And by now Isaac was an expert in Sonya's affairs, as if he had known her since childhood, and he was grateful to her for considering him worthy to tell him things that were important to him, both in their own right and because of Sonya. And he also told her about his father and his mother, and about his brothers and his sisters. And to make those things sound proper, he changed them to make them seem more worthy. Perhaps Sonya doubted his words or perhaps she believed the things he added to the truth.

Isaac wasn't forgetful, and needless to say he wasn't a liar; but he had heard things from his comrades about the status of their father's house and those things amazed him at first, now they rose up in his mind's eye when he spoke with Sonya, and he used them to embellish his father's house for her. If Isaac had told things as they were, he wouldn't have lost face in Sonya's eyes, for Sonya was a girl from Russia and read Russian stories that make troubles endearing and make the poor precious. But Isaac was a Galician fellow from a poor family who were ashamed of their poverty, and if his imagination hadn't helped him out, he would have been ashamed to tell Sonya.

And since they grew accustomed to one another, they also talked about current events, for even if those don't capture the heart as in bygone days, a person should know them. And in that Sonya shone, for she was an expert in what was done and what should be done and isn't done. And she casually mentions an article by somebody or other about settlements and says that the writer wasn't precise. Sonya, who heard a lot and read books, can make her way among ideas, unlike Isaac who, even if he looks at articles about the settlements, doesn't understand the meaning of the words, not to mention foreign words, for he lacked the basics of an education. Isaac may know who Warburg is or Franz Oppenheimer, but Sonya is an expert in their plans. A lot Sonya heard in meetings and a lot she got from her friends, some of them leaders of parties, others writers of articles.

3 |

Isaac should have been happy that a handsome, educated girl treated him as her friend, something he had never achieved before in his life. For until he ascended to the Land, he hadn't talked with a girl, except for his sisters, and even in the Land, he hadn't had a chance to talk with a girl. We already said that Isaac did have men friends but he didn't have women friends. But precisely where he should have been happy he was sad, for his heart rebuked him, saying, She belongs to your comrade. Says Isaac, But what am I doing? I'm just talking to her. And his heart replies, You're stealing her heart away from him. And Isaac is stunned, What is this stealing the heart? Because I'm talking with Sonya am I stealing her heart away from Rabinovitch? And his heart replies, You better stay away from her before you get too close. Isaac ponders and says, Maybe I should stay away from Sonya, but not all at once.

Habit becomes nature. When they met, she held out a hand to stroll with him. At first, they strolled among folks and then they turned to side paths, then they went off to the Baron's garden, the garden that became a salvation for Isaac, where the old Baron found him and helped him earn his bread. Once the Baron found him as he was strolling with Sonya. He was friendly to him, picked a flower and gave it to Sonya. And it wasn't only the Baron who was friendly to him because of Sonya, but many people are friendly to him because of Sonya, for a lot of fellows are courting her and she neglects them all and is occupied only with him. So he should be happy. But the open wish is undermined by the hidden cause.

4 |

Once, a week went by and he didn't see Sonya. Isaac decided, I'll go to her house. Before he could go, she came to his house. That hour was strange. It was night and the lamp was lit over the table, and on the table was a book. A little while earlier Isaac was reading a story of fiction or nonfiction. The door was perhaps open and perhaps not. Once or twice Isaac looked at the door. Suddenly, Sonya is standing in the room. And all that is nothing compared to Sonya.

Sonya was strange at that hour. Her mouth was somewhat open and her tongue was between her lips as if she were licking them. She opened a book and put it down. She picked up a dish in one place and put it in another place. Isaac spoke and wasn't answered. He was silent and she didn't notice. He stood up and sat her down on his chair, and since he didn't have another chair, he sat on the bed. It would have been proper if he had sat on the chair and she on the bed, for the chair wasn't safe and those who weren't used to it found it hard to sit on it. But Isaac wasn't used to guests like Sonya and didn't know what he should do. And since it is more comfortable to lie down than to sit with no support, he stretched out on the bed.

As he lay he peeped up at Sonya. And she looked at him. She looked at him and shifted her eyes away from him, shifted her eyes away from him and looked at him. His face blushed and his eyes grew dim and his heart began to pound. He held out his hand to Sonya, like someone who doesn't know what to do, or perhaps he intended to beckon to Sonya to sit down next to him on his bed, for sitting on the chair certainly wasn't comfortable. She came and sat down next to him. A sweet warmth bubbled up, a kind of experience he had never known. And Sonya was still silent. And he was silent too. It occurred to him that it wasn't proper to be silent. He said to her, I haven't seen you in a few days. Said she, You haven't seen me. Said he, I haven't seen you. Why? Said she, Even now I'm amazed at myself that I came here. Said he, Why are you amazed? Said she, I really didn't mean to come to your place. Said he, How did that occur to you all of a sudden? Said she, Is there any sense to these rendezvous? Isaac took her hands in his, as if he were afraid he would lose her.

Her hands inflamed his hands and his heart. Her head sank slightly on his shoulder. He sat up straight and stroked her head and pressed it to his heart like an amulet. At last she lifted her head and he kissed it. This was the kiss that had been preserved in his mouth ever since the hour his mother died. And Sonya kissed Isaac too. But this kiss was not a virgin kiss.

After midnight, Isaac walked Sonya home. The sky was deep and blue and many stars were set in it and the ground was soft as a carpet. That is the sandy ground of Jaffa, by day it digs underneath you and by night it appears like fine silk. The sea is fragrant and its waves rock pleasantly. At some distance from the shore a ship is floating. We don't know who is there on that ship. At any rate, Sonya's friend isn't there. He is thousands of miles away from the Land of Israel, wandering from place to place and not finding a place for himself.

Let's go back to Isaac. In the afternoon, Sonya found Isaac in the street. Isaac dropped his head and wanted to turn into a side street. Isaac was ashamed of two disgraceful acts at that hour, one, that he had disgraced Sonya and two, that he had disgraced their friend. Isaac's face blushed and his eyes grew dim. Sonya smiled at him and took his hand affectionately and asked, Why don't we see you? And Isaac asked himself, What does that mean, they don't see me, it hasn't even been a day since she was at my house. By the time he pondered her words, a billow of warmth came and flooded his heart as when she laid her head on his heart.

CHAPTER TWELVE

Isaac and Sonya

1 |

From now on, Isaac changed his ways. He began to be fussy about his clothes and shaved his beard twice a week, once on Friday evening like everybody else and once in the middle of the week. If he has work he comes home after work and washes his face and hands with soap and puts on clean clothes, and eats something, and runs to Sonya's place. If he doesn't have work, he reads a book and sleeps a lot and swims in the sea and straightens his room and tends to his things and prepares for Sonya, who comes in the evening. And when she does come she stands on tiptoe and leans her head back, her hat drops off, and she stretches out on the bed and shuts her eyes. At that moment, the white buttons sparkle on her blouse and the freckles on her face turn dark. And he comes and sits next to her and counts the buttons on her blouse, and says, One and one more, up to eight. If he counted nicely, she says, You counted nicely, and she rewards him for his trouble. If he made a mistake in his counting, she caresses him and says, Didn't you ever study arithmetic? And since arithmetic cannot be learned casually, they leave off their arithmetic and sit like that, until she slips out of his arms and says, Light the lamp. He stops and lights the lamp and spreads a tablecloth and brings bowls and spoons and forks and knives and they eat together everything he has prepared beforehand. Sonya looks and laughs at him for acting like a housewife, not like those who eat out of the paper they bring the food home in from the store. And since she laughed at him she appeases him, and doesn't appease him like those girls who kiss until they're a nuisance, but places her mouth on his mouth and the hair on her upper lip, which is usually not seen, caresses you until you're

| 131

about to die. When they had eaten and drunk, they go out for a stroll. And on their way, they rest on the seashore or on the hill of sand called the Hill of Love, or they go into Café Hermon and eat ice cream.

2

Café Hermon stands at the edge of Neve Shalom, near Bustrus Street. You enter a hall where, during the day, in the doorway, a pitch-black man sits bent over a green lattice table with large and small bills and coins, like those moneychangers who sit in the doorways of houses in the street and count coins. Since we haven't got two pennies to rub together, we'll leave him and dwell on the café, where at night the café owner stands, his face red as a honeycake and his beard flaming like a pomegranate bud, and his multicolored eyes staring at everyone who goes out or comes in or looks at the flies eager to enter that candy box. Those who are thirsty or hungry and don't have time come in and eat and drink standing up. If they do have time, they come into the yard where the ground is covered with seashells. And little wicker tables and chairs painted green stand among the palm trees that are lit by lanterns, except on moonlit nights when their light isn't needed.

This café isn't like Arab cafés with their narghilas and gramophones and parrots; nor is it like the café in Lemberg with silver dishes and china dishes and waiters dressed like lords serving the guests. Here, you find a higher virtue, for wherever you turn you see writers and teachers and clerks and activists. Some of them cool themselves with a cold drink and some of them warm themselves with a hot drink and when they drink something hot a kerchief is wound around their neck to absorb the sweat. Some of them talk about Mendele, whose old age did not disgrace his youth, and about Bialik, who suppresses his poetry and doesn't publish any poem. Next to them sit the other distinguished people of the Yishuv. Some praise the Odessa Committee and some slander the German Zionists who took over the Jewish National Fund and regard the Land of Israel as a stepdaughter of Zionism. Some discuss the domain of Rothschild, the Famous Donor, and some discuss the quarrels of Petach Tikva and the squabbles of

Be'er Tuvia. Some mention *The Young Laborer,* which attacked Dizengoff and the Anglo-Palestine Company in one issue, and some mention Rabbi Benjamin, who even writes about current events as if he's writing poetry. Next to them sit the other people. Some of them play chess and some watch their moves. Some of them face the chessboard and some turn their back on the pieces. Over them stand the kibitzers, who know how to advise them where it is advisable to move and where it isn't. Far away from those, near the wall of the café, stand men in shirtsleeves and collarless, and play ping-pong, and a little boy runs and picks up the balls that roll here and there. And sounds rise from the seashells on the floor, as if the animals inside them are shrieking under your feet. And nevertheless, the whole yard is tranquil as if all the tranquillity of the world had gathered here.

Isaac, who comes from a small town where there are no cafés and people don't sit in groups and don't know what ice cream is, is amazed to find himself suddenly sitting among famous people all Zionists talk about. Sometimes Isaac asks himself, Can it be that these people sipping lemonade are the ones you read about in the newspapers? If only the Zionists of his hometown could see him in such honor! In truth, the Zionists of his hometown had declined in his eyes, but even so, they should see who he was sitting with. Isaac was especially amazed at Sonya, who converses with those famous people, and even with the writers, as if they were her friends. Before Isaac ascended to the Land, he had made do with pictures of the writers, and today he sees a living writer. There sits our warm-hearted story writer Simha Ben Zion beaming. At that time, folks were still fond of the words of writers and their faces were illuminated by the light of their affection. There sits Simha Ben Zion wearing brown cloth clothes shiny as modest silk, and like that silk, his brown eyes are shining, and a poetic cravate is knotted at his collar, and his whole being is like a handsome column of poetry, and everything that comes out of his mouth is the verse of a poem. We are familiar with the stories of Simha Ben Zion. Now he sits face to face with us, and some of his words even reach our ears.

Dizengoff comes in wearing a light white jacket buttoned up to his neck, and on his head is a hard black hat, neither concave nor square, and under his arm is a loaf of bread. That day Antabbi was dining at his table and some guests came to honor him and didn't leave a crumb of bread, and the Yemenite housekeeper comes at seven o'clock, and he is accustomed to getting up at six, and sometimes he is attacked by hunger at four or five, and goes out to get some bread, so he'll have some ready, and on the way, he comes into the café.

Dizengoff sits down on a willow chair and his body fills the seat. He put his hat on the table and the bread on the chair in front of him, and rubbed his hands together as if preparing for some hard work. He looked with his gray eyes at the café owner, who brought him ice cream, and waved his hand over the little bowl as if he were shaking off a fly and said, What's that in front of a man? Just look at it and it's gone. So the café owner ran and brought him another portion. Before he could bring it, his assistant has already anticipated him, for he knows that that gentleman isn't satisfied with a little bit. Dizengoff thrust the spoon into this bowl and into that bowl and looked around to see which of his personal friends was here.

In fact, all the persons of Jaffa are his personal friends. And if there is a person here who is irritated with him, he is silly. And as for that article, "Jupiter Is Raging," that *The Young Laborer* published against him, he has already given them a devastating reply in Ben-Yehuda's *Ha-Tsvi*, and Mordechai Ben Hillel Ha-Cohen has also answered them as they deserved. The main thing is that we must do, do and do, until there is no time for intrigues. And isn't he the first of the doers, even for the laborers and the improvement of their conditions? Yet they took the wrong path. And so he wrote explicitly, You're making war on the whole Yishuv, the Old and the New, as if you were the only ones who remained after the Flood, and aside from you no one else is pained by the rupture in the nation and by the crisis of the Yishuv. You've set yourself the goal of the conquest of work, but that goal is beyond your reach, and the war itself became your goal, for you carried on a war front and back. A justified war and a sweeping war, a war for the sake of war, and the whole Land is full of the trumpets of war and victory. But woe unto such a victory. For if in fact all the settlements and all the national institutions are so rotten that they are all opposed to Jewish work — if so, who are you toiling for? Why do you deceive yourselves, and don't you know, if today everyone in Petach Tikva embraced *Ha-Po'el Ha-Tsa'ir* and demanded of you, Give us Hebrew laborers instead of Arab laborers, would you be able to supply them all the wagon drivers and orange pickers and guards they need? The work of the Yishuv demands back-breaking toil, and we aren't used to such work. We need simple laborers, yet the immigration gives us make-believe laborers with big demands who can't adjust to the life of a laborer. His steely eyes are veiled like a general commanding his troops and finding them weak. He wants to scold them but takes his eyes off them so they won't see that he is filled with pity for them.

As he senses his own valor and the weakness of others, his heart whispers to him, All your deeds are nothing but failure. A lot of things he tried to do and succeeded in nothing. Was all my energy and my strength created in vain? What does *The Young Laborer* say, That gentleman knows that the *Ha-Po'el Ha-Tsa'ir* organization is working, while those gentlemen, that is I and my comrades, are yawning, they, that is, I and all the other excellent people of the Yishuv, see *Ha-Po'el Ha-Tsa'ir* as a rising force, and they're scared that, God Forbid, their communal activity won't show. Were they joking, those innocent fellows, don't they themselves say there's enough work for honest people who really want to work and not to fight, and if such activists arrive, they will certainly find work both outside *Ha-Po'el Ha-Tsa'ir* and along with *Ha-Po'el Ha-Tsa'ir*.

Dizengoff isn't vexed about being insulted. But he is sorry that those young people who are plotting war against him stay away from him. In his hometown, all the young people used to come to him, and here in the Land of Israel, a mountain has risen up between them and him. There are fellows here that his wife Tsina should meet, and they seem to keep pleasure away from his house. His house is full of teachers and writers and clerks and activists, but no young man shows himself in his house.

As he ponders, he saw Simha Ben Zion. Dizengoff says to Simha Ben Zion, You're here? And they come and sit together. And you don't know if Dizengoff came to Simha Ben Zion or if Simha

Ben Zion came to Dizengoff, and they indulge in a discussion, and everyone pulls up their chairs and sits down to listen. Some esteem Dizengoff and some are fond of Simha Ben Zion, and when they come together, the light of one illuminates the other, and everyone basks in their light.

3 |

Never did Isaac have better days than those. Isaac is involved in the Land like all our other comrades who know that they have no other place in the world and are absorbed into the Land for good or for bad. Little by little, Isaac started forgetting his hometown and his father's house. The cramped apartment where one of two dark rooms serves as a kitchen was exchanged in his imagination for the houses of the dignitaries of Jaffa who have spacious yards inside and balconies outside. Here there are no damp walls of a dark kitchen, where his big sister Frumtshe stands in front of her empty pots and their little brother Vove holds onto the hem of her threadbare dress and cries, I'm hungry, I'm hungry. His sisters gather round his voice and poke fun and say, Come on, come on, everybody who wants news, you'll hear something new that you've never heard before. There's a hungry person among us. Vove stretches out on the floor, lies prostrate, and bleats because everybody is making fun of him. Father comes from the shop and hears all that wailing. He puts his hand in his pocket in case there's a coin there to buy his son a bagel, and he doesn't find any. Father turns his face to his daughters and asks, What do you want from the child? They reply, We don't want anything, but Vove wants to eat. Father scolds them angrily and says, You're turning my house into a theater. I don't want a theater. And they scatter, one here and one there, and he goes and wets his fingers on the window and recites the evening prayer, and goes to bed without supper just as he had gotten up early in the morning without breakfast, and he groans in his sleep pursued in his dream as he is when awake by usurers and creditors.

And when the truth shifted from its place, delusions and imaginings came to Isaac. Father is portrayed in his mind's eye as a person who resides in a spacious dwelling and respectable guests come to

him, including Gymnasium pupils and university students. They sit
and drink tea and discuss world events. And as they sit, they glance at
the daughters of the house. This one glances at this girl and that one
glances at that girl. Father smiles and says to himself, My daughters
are destined for people greater than you. And all his sisters go out in
handsome clothes with handsome hats on their head, hats like the
ones Princess Mira Ramishvili makes. And when they go for a stroll,
they turn neither this way nor that way, like well-bred girls who know
their distinguished pedigree, just as he had portrayed them to Sonya.

But the power of imagination slackened and his sisters went
back to being as they were, with their threadbare dresses and their
down-at-the-heel shoes, and muddy strings hang from their ears instead of earrings. Isaac was furious at them, Why are they like that
and not the way he wants to see them? As soon as he swallows his
anger, the postman throws him a letter from Father. Isaac reads tearfully and every letter of the alphabet stands out like a painful thorn.
Isaac wipes his tears and says, Oh my God, what does Father want to
tell me, didn't I know that things were bad with him? Isaac picks up
the note again and sees disjointed letters there, where Blomtshe
Leah, his little sister, wrote a greeting to her dear brother. Isaac tries
to read, but the letters don't combine into words, because she didn't
learn to write, because she doesn't have shoes and can't go to school.
Isaac says to himself, If God helps me and an extra penny falls into
my hand, I'll send it to Father to buy her shoes. The Blessed Lord
who is better than His creatures did put an extra penny into Isaac's
hand. But Isaac didn't send it to Blomtshe Leah to buy shoes, but
bought jam to sweeten his meals with Sonya. His heart rebuked him.
And he replied, It's enough for Father that I don't ask him for money,
like some of my comrades who bother their fathers to send them some.

Enough for a father that his son doesn't ask him for money,
but supports himself and buys his own clothes and shoes and lives in
his own room all by himself. Of all the craftsmen in Jaffa, nobody is
dressed like Isaac. Not to mention his dwelling. Some of our comrades live two, three, and four in one room. But Isaac lives all alone
in his own room all by himself and can entertain Sonya anytime at
all. And blessed be Sonya, who doesn't keep away and comes to Isaac.

Just as he is satisfied with his actions, so he is satisfied with his craft. In truth, he ascended to the Land of Israel only to work its soil, but since the Land didn't want that, he took hold of this craft of painting. And we must admit that he did well, for it does give him a livelihood, and he doesn't depend on anybody in the world. He's the boss and he's the laborer and he's the one who gives himself his work. If we look at it, his lot is better than most of the people of Jaffa, for most of them depend on others. A clerk on his supervisor, a teacher on his principal, and the principal himself depends on the Odessa Committee. Not to mention the laborers. If they are agricultural workers, they depend on the farmers; and if they are factory workers, they depend on the factory owner; and the factory owner and the farmers depend on the moneylenders. While Isaac Kumer is his own master. He picks up his brush and his paintcan and works, a day or two here, and a day or two there, he takes his pay and he goes on his way. And something else too. Most craftsmen are stuck in one place, the tailor at his needle, the cobbler at his last, the carpenter at his wood; while Isaac wanders from place to place, among many people, and many come to look at what he's doing. When a house is re-painted, all the neighbors come to see it. Two things attract a person's heart, a new house and a house that was painted. A house, because it separates him from the world; and paint, because it's a higher model of the colors of the firmament, which appeal to the human soul.

Isaac stands at his work. A pot of paint in front of him and a paintbrush in his hand. He dips his brush and moves it back and forth and knows from the beginning what the end will be. Isaac learned a lot from Sweet Foot, and what he learned he learned well. We shall not offend the honor of craftsmen if we count Isaac among them. His hand is as light as his soul and his soul is as light as his hand. From the lightness of his soul, he jests and draws funny pictures, sometimes to astonish people and sometimes to please the children and some-times for himself and his own enjoyment. If you met Isaac in the be-ginning, you'd be amazed that this fellow with nine measures of grief poured over his face could do such a childish thing. But don't be amazed, for human beings are wont to change, like those walls he is painting. And that's a mistake most of the world makes, when they see a sad person when he's happy, they say maybe he's not himself. And in truth there are many qualities in a person from the beginning of his creation, and everything happens for many reasons. Yesterday he was heavy as lead and now he's light as a bird. And in Isaac, what is the reason? If you like, it is the proficiency he has acquired in his work. If you like, it is Sonya. If you like, it is both. In the past, he saw his work as secondary to his livelihood, now he sees it as the main thing. No longer does he have to go beg for work from the farmers or the clerks of the institutions. And in the evening, when he comes home from work, he changes his clothes and goes to Sonya or Sonya comes to him. Blessed is he who has someone close who brings him close to himself.

4 |

By now, Isaac has forgotten the purpose of his ascent to the Land of Israel. In every single thing, a Jew carries out his mission, and there's no difference if he plows and sows or mixes paints. Some of our comrades ascended to work the earth and are idle, while Isaac is a craftsman. Some of Isaac's comrades envy Isaac. Some ascended before he did and still don't have any work to do. And by now they have stopped praising work as a repair of the soul and the resurrection of the nation, but want to work as salvation from hunger, for hunger screams from their belly and salvation tarries.

He comes across veteran laborers whom he saw at first as aristocrats because they had come to the Land a year or two before he did, now there's no difference between him and them, except that most of them are idle and he's working. And because they are idle, they don't earn anything, and because they don't earn anything they lack bread and they borrow a Bishlik or half a Bishlik from him. And if they don't pay him back, he doesn't put a lien on their property. All Children of Israel are comrades, especially in the Land of Israel, Isaac told that old man from Hungary he met on the ship to the Land of Israel, and Isaac doesn't belie his words. No longer do they belit tle Isaac for being from Galicia, even though his accent declares his origin. Nor is he impressed by the accent of his comrades, which, just between us, is nothing to be impressed by, for you can see the influence of the Russian accent in it. Our comrade Isaac isn't an Austrian patriot, and doesn't distinguish between one Jew and another, yet he does have a bit of pride that he was born in the shadow of the kingdom of grace, where everyone is equal before the Emperor, Jews as well as non-Jews, not like those Russians who are persecuted in their own land.

Those were good days for Isaac. He makes a living and is satisfied with his work. Some work he does for Jews and some for Gentiles, some for Ashkenazim and some for Sephardim. Sometimes he paints the inside of a house and sometimes the outside, for most of the houses of Jaffa are built of stones drawn from the sea which aren't polished properly and are then whitewashed and plastered and painted to enhance its charm for folks. In the past, they built with big, distinguished stones from the remnants of palaces left over from ancient times, now that they build with porous stones, they paint them red. To make a long story short, every day he has work, for every day new houses pop up from the sand. A person rises early in the morning and sees an empty lot, comes back at night and doesn't recognize it, for they have brought beams and stones there and have started building a house. Four generations ago, this Jaffa didn't have a Minyan, and now it is being built. And even the painters we considered superfluous don't go looking for work in the settlements anymore, and don't take scraping work, but are busy with their craft and support their family. New immigrants come, and owners of lots put up houses for them. Isaac earns more than at any other time. He goes to work in the morning and comes home in the evening, and prepares himself for Sonya, for in the evening she went. And after they dine together they go out walking, sometimes to the Baron's garden and sometimes to the seashore or on the hill of sand called the Hill of Love. Young men and women sit there in couples and sing "Take me in under your wing," and other languid songs, and a wind blows among the sands bringing good smells from the vineyards and from the desert where the big city of Tel Aviv was later built, and the firmament spreads out its black blue and stars twinkle above and smile to the Land below, in appeasement and yearning, and the waters of the sea lie in their lair, sometimes going on silently and sometimes flooding furiously, but not flowing over their boundary. Happy is he who sits in the shadow of a beloved soul and is not solitary and forlorn as a desert.

5 |

How good were those days, and better were the nights. Isaac does his work and sees a reward in his toil. By now Isaac has forgotten the days when he went hungry, and has taken his mind off everything that muddies the spirit. When a letter comes from his home he reads it and tosses it aside to reread it, but he doesn't, for he is busy with his craft. And when he comes home from work in the evening, he has to prepare for Sonya. And when he comes home from Sonya and goes to bed, he is immediately overcome by sleep and doesn't feel the night departing. Days and nights that were long are now so short you wonder at how and when they passed.

Isaac comes back from Sonya's, happy and goodhearted, and since he is happy — he is happy with everyone. There's a night guard near Isaac's house, a poor and wretched Arab who has nothing but his dog. Isaac comes and chats with him. He pulls the dog's ears and praises him to his face. Said the guard, What do you say my brother, this dog is handsome. A dog that was stolen from me was handsome. His skin was as brown as the eyes of a doe. Said Isaac, Brown skin you want? Tomorrow, you'll have a brown dog. Said the guard, You've got one like that? Said Isaac, You want a red one, tomorrow you'll find a reddish one. Said the guard, A kennel of dogs you have, my brother? Said Isaac, Not even the tail of a dog do I have. Said the guard, You conjure them up by magic? Said Isaac, Various colors do I have, and if you want, I'll paint your dog brown or red or yellow or green. Said the guard, Never have I seen a green dog. Said Isaac, Yet I can make you a green dog. The guard laughed and they laughed together.

Said Isaac, I saw a dog that held a stick in its mouth and didn't let go of it for a moment. Said the guard, Was it made of sugar? Said Isaac, No, of silk. Said the guard, Such a dog doesn't bite and such a stick doesn't beat. Said Isaac, Who knows? The guard rolled back his lips and laughed. Said Isaac, Don't you believe it? Said the guard, I would take the stick out of the dog's teeth and hit the dog with it. Said Isaac, Who is like unto you? You even hit your own women. Said the guard, He who is worthy of the stick gets beaten. Isaac laughed and the guard laughed.

Good were those days and good were the nights, and good was Sonya to Isaac. And even though she is an educated girl from a well-to-do family in a big city, and he is a simple fellow from a poor family in a small town, they are seen as bride and groom. In truth those words, bride and groom, are not customary here. But Isaac who thinks the way our forefathers thought, savors many flavors in those words. And sometimes he imagines writing to his father and announcing the whole thing to him, and Father and his brothers and sisters would all be joyous and happy. And his brother Yudele would send him a poem in honor of the event, for Yudele is a poet and writes poems. And people would come and congratulate Father and would be stunned and amazed. This Isaac who doesn't know any living language won in the Land of Israel an educated bride who studied in a Gymnasium. And the fact that his fiancée studied in a Gymnasium was likely to make an impression in a town where there wasn't even a Gymnasium for boys. And so the envious won't say she has some defect, Isaac intended to ask Sonya for a picture to send to Father so folks would see. And even though the image of Sonya doesn't show the whole nature of Sonya, it can still indicate that she is handsome. And when Isaac reviews Sonya's nature in his mind, he loves her twice as much. And if their comrade Rabinovitch pushes himself between them, Isaac shifts his eyes away from him as if he isn't there. If Rabinovitch persists and doesn't budge, Isaac hides his head in Sonya's lap.

CHAPTER THIRTEEN

Between Sonya and Isaac

1 |

Good were those days. But the days that came after were not good. Blessed is he who had his first kiss with a maiden whom others had not yet kissed, and woe to him who kissed a maiden whom others had already kissed before him. For no special reason, Sonya changed her ways with Isaac.

Isaac came home from work as he did every day. He brought up water from the well and washed his face and hands, put on clean clothes and prepared for Sonya. He waited but she didn't come. And as is the wont of a man waiting for a maid and she tarries and doesn't come, it seemed to him that never in his life had he needed her as at that moment. Time slows down and doesn't budge. God forbid, maybe something happened to her? Seven times a minute, Isaac got up to go to her and seven times a minute he jumped up to see if she was coming. When his patience ran out, he went to her house.

Sonya lived in a small alley that has no name. You can't consider it in Neve Shalom, for a desert of sand separates them. And you can't see it in Neve Tsedek, for a group of houses separates them. Those are the houses of the Odessa engineer who ascends to Jaffa every autumn and builds himself a house to live in and when he returns to Odessa at the beginning of summer, he sells the house.

Isaac went to Sonya's house. His knees trembled with fear, perhaps she is sick, for if she was healthy, wouldn't she have come? Sonya is sick, Sonya is sick, Sonya is sick, Isaac said, like someone muttering incantations over an illness, and maybe they've already taken her to the hospital. And all the while he's trudging here, he should be running to the hospital. He raised his eyes and saw that he was standing at her room and that there was light in the room. Isaac understood that everything he had imagined was truth, Sonya is lying sick and the doctor is standing over her, taking her pulse and writing her a prescription. I shall hurry, said Isaac, as long as the pharmacy is open, and bring her the medicine.

In the end, all his worries about Sonya evaporated. Sonya isn't sick, Sonya isn't sick, Sonya isn't sick, he repeated three times, against those three times he had said before. On the contrary, Sonya is healthy, Sonya is healthy. And she is sitting and waiting for me. There is a spirit in man. Sometimes a person changes his habit to add spice to his actions. Every day Sonya has been coming to me and today she wants me to come to her. I was a fool not to think of that. A new joy enveloped his heart and he forgot all his grief, and already saw himself opening the door and Sonya coming and jumping to meet him, stretching out her warm hands and caressing his head. He shut his eyes and held his breath, and inhaled a hint of those things he saw in his imagination.

2 |

Sonya didn't jump up to meet Isaac and didn't stretch out her arms to hug him, as she did when he was mistaken in his calculations. Sonya sat silent on an easy chair she had bought that day from Princess Mira, and a lamp was lit in front of her, and heaps of stockings were laid on her lap. Since the day Isaac first met Sonya, he hadn't seen her mending a stocking, now all her stockings came together and asked her to mend them. Sonya went on with her work, as if she didn't see Isaac.

His knees were about to give way, but his anger seemed to hold them up. With an effort he said, You didn't come to me. Sonya replied, It seems I didn't come to you. Why? he asked. Sonya answered, If I didn't come to you, you came to me. Said Isaac, But this welcome you give me is a bit strange. Said Sonya, If you had sent me a telegram that you were coming, I would have ordered all the women dancers of Damascus in your honor. Isaac asked with affected docility, May I sit down? Said Sonya, If you want to, sit. He took a chair and sat. Said Sonya, Not that chair, there are threads on it.

Isaac stood in the room he knew by heart, ever since that night he came here for the first time, when they strolled together and talked about Rabinovitch and Sonya said, Look, you say that anyplace Rabinovitch is is his place, but not every place a person achieves is flattering for him. The room is neither small nor big and it has two windows, one window looks onto the street and one window overlooks the narrow alley where no one passes. And in the room is a bed and a sofa and a table and a closet. And the bed is covered with a colorful blanket, embroidered with a yellow dog carrying a stick in his mouth. And over the bed hangs a picture of the murdered Berele. And even though the whole world meant nothing to Isaac compared to his grief, he turned his attention to that blanket whose edge was tattered and he was indignant with Sonya; before she tended to her stockings, which was not at all appropriate when he came to visit her, she had better take care of the blanket so it won't get even more tattered.

3 |

Said Sonya, Didn't you want to sit down? Isaac replied, I see that you're in a bad mood. Is there a reason for that? Said Sonya, Anyone who knows the first thing about logic knows that there is nothing without a reason. Said he, Well then, what is this reason? I'm busy, said she. Said Isaac, Apparently I distract you from your work. Do you want me to go? Said Sonya, Excuse me for not seeing you out. You see that I've got a lot of work. What do you think of this chair I bought today? Said Isaac, It should be repainted. Said Sonya, No need. I'll put a cushion on it and cover its flaws. Said Isaac, If there's no need, there's no need.

Mme. Puah Hofenstein entered. Good evening, Mme. Zweiering, said Mme. Hofenstein and adjusted her eyeglasses; good evening, Mr. Kumer, I almost didn't see you. I see that I'm disturbing. Said Sonya, On the contrary, I'm glad you came. Said Mme. Hofenstein, You're busy, Mme. Zweiering? Said Sonya, When a person sits idle and hasn't anything to do, he checks the holes and cracks and takes things out of them that he wanted to destroy, and takes care of them, just to keep himself busy. Said Mme. Hofenstein, Tolstoy already said that ever since the sin of the First Adam, a man can't sit idle. And so you're mending your stockings. A nice thing to do. Stockings are something you can't do without. I came to Mme. Zweiering to ask if you can come to the kindergarten tomorrow, I want to take a day off.

Said Sonya, Are you going to greet your brother at the port? Mme. Hofenstein blushed and stammered, My brother isn't coming yet, and who knows if he will come, I might go on an outing tomorrow. With Ossip, Sonya thought to herself, as if it were a simple matter for Puah Hofenstein, principal of a kindergarten, to leave the children because she desired to go on an outing with Ossip.

Puah Hofenstein loves children and her whole life depends on the little ones in the kindergarten. And even if they gave her the whole world, she wouldn't leave her young chicks. But something extraordinary happened. Ossip is about to return to Russia. Why? Because he escaped from serving in the army and his father has to pay a fine. And he's a poor man and doesn't have the money to pay. So Ossip is returning to Russia to serve in the army and release his father from the payment. And Puah Hofenstein wants to spend one day with him before he goes.

Never had it occurred to Puah Hofenstein that her heart could accept a person like Ossip, for nothing binds him to the Land, neither working the Land nor the Hebrew language. And even she, that is, Puah, doesn't bind him at all. And she doesn't know that it is she who made Ossip leave the Land, for ever since she pulled him closer to her, he saw himself falling into a deep pit of petite bourgeoisie. Things had reached such a pass that once he had even shined his shoes in her honor. But he took vengeance on her, and as he left her house, he rubbed one foot on top of the other and soiled them.

Never had Sonya seen Puah Hofenstein as a woman, or Ossip as a man. To her, the two of them were like an idea. Now that they are going on an outing, they were exalted in her eyes, and she said to her gently, Mme. Hofenstein can rely on me, I shall do my best to take your place. Although I doubt that there's anyone here who is worthy to take your place. Isaac took his leave as Mme. Hofenstein was wiping her eyeglasses and watching him with dim eyes.

4 |

After he had taken a few steps, he suddenly stood still, like a man who has lost something and needs to look for it. He squinted his eyes and scrunched up his nose. And when he scrunched up his nose, his heart also scrunched up. The sky was full of little stars, but the night was dark, and in the darkness, Sonya's lamp shone. Well, said Isaac to himself, well, I came to her, I came to her, because she didn't come to me, she didn't come to me, and she sat there, she sat there, with stockings on her lap, on her lap, because stockings are wont to be torn, and when they're torn, they have to be mended, mended. At any rate, what is amazing is that just when I came to her, just at that time, she was mending her stockings. And that Hofenstein woman suddenly fell into the house as I was sitting with Sonya and she was telling things about the sin of the First Adam. And once again he saw Sonya's stockings lying in her lap, and all the anger in his heart was uprooted from his heart and a new affection caressed his heart.

Why am I holding the handkerchief in my hand? Did I want to wipe my tears? I wasn't crying was I? But it seemed to me that I wanted to sneeze. It seemed to me, but I didn't sneeze. Achoo. When it seemed to me I was going to sneeze, I didn't sneeze, and now when it doesn't seem to me that I was going to sneeze, I did sneeze. Now let's go. Let's go, since there's no point standing still. Indeed, I'm not standing still, since I'm walking. And I'm walking because I'm not standing still. This is clear to everyone, even to someone who didn't learn the first thing about logic. Sonya is an educated girl, and as for me, if I hadn't met Sonya, I also would have increased my knowledge, since before I met her I used to sit at home and read books. On the other hand, there's no denying that I did acquire some knowledge from her, but knowledge a person acquires from fleeting conversations is not like information a person acquires from an assiduous reading of books. So, because of the sin of the First Adam. Didn't his sin come from Eve, so why do they hang the sin on Adam?

5 |

Isaac arrived at his house and went into his room, and came to his bed, hesitating whether to take off his clothes. She is sleeping, Isaac whispered, and even if she isn't sleeping it's impossible to go back to her at this hour. Now I have nothing to do but get into my bed. Whether I shall sleep — is doubtful.

He took off his clothes and shoes, shook the sand out of them and lingered over every single piece of clothing. Finally, he got into bed and wrapped himself in his sheet, shut his eyes, and recited the She'ma at bedtime. He drew out its words and repeated every single word, like a person returning in the dark of night to a dark house and examining all his keys to find which one of them will open the lock. Finally he opened his eyes wide like a child waiting for his mother to come tell him good night. Finally his eyes closed by themselves and he fell asleep.

When he woke up in the morning, he was puzzled. Where did that sleep come from? I didn't expect it and it came. And I didn't even dream any dreams, not bad dreams that come to scare you, and not good ones that end in disappointment. Or maybe I did dream and I forgot. How many stockings did Sonya have, twenty, thirty, when she mends them all, she'll come to me.

He got out of bed and made himself breakfast. The milkman came and brought him milk. And even though he still had all the milk left from yesterday, he took his daily share and ate what he had made yesterday for his supper with Sonya, amazed that he was eating heartily, and pondered, Sonya is still sleeping, sleeping. Or maybe she's already out of bed, for she promised Hofenstein to take her place. And when he said Hofenstein, he felt a kind of small revenge at her that he didn't attach Mme. to her name, as people dubbed her. After he cleared the dishes off his table, he examined his socks which needed mending, and left for work.

At noon, he left his work and went to shave his beard. Afterward, he went to the inn and ate lunch. Afterward, he returned to his room and prepared himself for Sonya, a tune stuck in his head, How many stockings are there, twenty, thirty, when she mends them all she'll come to me. He was certain she would come, and he kept checking his room and fixing something, until the day passed and he began to fear she would come before he finished his work. The day passed and Sonya didn't come.

6 |

Sonya didn't come. And since he thought that she was ashamed of behaving unruly with him, he felt pity for her and wanted to overlook the rules with her. He went to her to hold out his hand to her in peace. And he pitied himself too, for his solitude.

Puah and Ossip returned from the outing. She was tired but happy. Ossip walked ahead of her, holding his stick, as if that was all he had left from the whole outing. Mme. Hofenstein saw Isaac and said, her voice half shrieking, half childish, The outing we made today I shall never forget. We were in Kfar Saba and we got as far as Antipatros. We live in our own Land and we don't know it. And the Arabs are the complete gentlemen. One Effendi invited us to his house and was very hospitable to us. What shall I tell you, Mr. Kumer. The salad he fed us was the equal of all the delicacies in the world. And a samovar he's got, a real samovar, a Russian samovar. It was Mr. Eisenberg of Rehovoth who gave him that samovar. Too bad we can't speak Arabic. But we understood one another. Didn't we, Ossip? How did he tell you, *Khorosho*, just like a born Russian. How healthy are his wives' teeth! I don't believe that legend that there are rich Arab women who pull out a healthy tooth and make themselves a gold tooth because they envy us European women. I would give all my silver and gold just to have healthy teeth like theirs. By the way, Mr. Kumer, just between us, I don't have even an iota of gold, aside from a gold Napoleon I'm keeping for the rent. A Spanish proverb says, More beautiful is the tooth that's healthy than any jewel of the wealthy. I see that you are in a hurry and I don't want to delay you. Just tell Mme. Zweiering hello for me, and please thank her for being so kind as to take my place in the kindergarten. I don't know what came over me to leave the marvelous children and go on an outing. But that outing was worth it. Wasn't it, Ossip?

Ossip nodded and said, Hmmm. And with that Hmmm, he raised his eyes and looked angrily at Isaac. It seemed to him that that little Palestinian was judging him. Where are you going, Ossip? asked Mme. Hofenstein in a panic, as Ossip set out to go. Hmmm, answered Ossip, I've got to buy something for supper. What do you mean, exclaimed Mme. Hofenstein, didn't we agree to eat at my house? Well, Mr. Kumer, what did I tell you? What? asked Isaac in confusion. Mme. Hofenstein smiled and said, You've already forgotten what I told you. Didn't I tell you to say hello. . . . Yes, yes, said Isaac and went on his way.

7 |

The lamp that lighted his way to her room last night also lighted his way this night. But this night, his steps were shorter. If he hurried and took a long step, he lingered after it for a long while.

Sonya sat like yesterday in the chair she had bought from Princess Mira and a small cushion hung on the top of the chair and covered the places where the paint had flaked. As he entered, her face grew long and her lips formed a bow, and a kind of double chin embellished her chin and lent her a measure of femininity. Her double chin gathered into her neck and her chin rose toward Isaac and her lips opened a bit. She looked at him without amazement. Even though she wasn't waiting for him, she understood that he would come, and since she understood that he would come, she wasn't amazed.

At that time, she wasn't busy with her stockings. But she was busy with that blanket, the one Isaac had thought needed mending yesterday. Sonya held out her fingertips with the needle between them to Isaac, and went back to her work.

Isaac stands in front of Sonya and doesn't dare look into her face. Because of that, he looks at the blanket on her lap, and from the blanket the dog scowls at him, like the furious Grisha we all hate. Isaac turns his head back to the other side, but the blanket recoils on Sonya's lap and the stick sways in the dog's mouth. Isaac's shoulders recoil and he brings his face back to Sonya and the dog once again looks at him with furious eyes. The image of Grisha comes and stands before him and Isaac's heart is filled with wrath and envy.

Why am I thinking about him, and since I am thinking about him, Sonya is also liable to think about him out of telepathy. Suddenly he was terrified for maybe he thought of Grisha because Sonya thought of him. And once again, his heart was filled with envy, although he knew that even if Sonya thought about Grisha, her thoughts wouldn't be in Grisha's favor.

Gradually, his envy dissipated. And since envy dissipated, his anger returned to burn in his heart. And as is the wont of soft men who know very well that their wrath is not effective, he swallowed his anger. And as is the wont of human beings like Isaac who don't know that their qualities aren't constant and nevertheless put everything on their ability and their will, he was satisfied with himself that he had succeeded in restraining his anger. And since he swallowed his anger, he began talking gently. Sonya scowled at him. Isaac was amazed. After all that, she's still angry? Soon she'll recognize her fault and will appease me. But I won't be appeased toward her.

Sonya didn't try to appease Isaac. On the contrary, her face grew more and more hostile. He began to fear that she might say harsh words to him. He anticipated that and started saying affectionate words. Sonya looked at him and her heart was filled with wrath for that solemnity in his words.

And here we must admit that there is a bit of truth in it. Isaac spoke in a tone, like a petit bourgeois on a holiday. And that solemnity drove her out of her mind and made her angry. And since in anger she didn't find Hebrew words, she began speaking to him in Russian. And he didn't know Russian. Sonya sensed that and said, I forgot that you're a Galician, and she spoke Yiddish to him, the way you talk with simple people who don't use the language of educated people. Sonya, who wasn't used to Yiddish, spoke half Yiddish and half Russian; and he, who didn't know Russian, didn't understand most of what she said. Thus, the wall between them rose higher until he saw himself distanced from her. When Isaac began to feel Sonya's remoteness, she was already cutting her mind off from him. Sonya said to herself, For two or three kisses do I owe him anything? And does this fellow think that a girl's kiss enslaves her completely? At any rate, I'm not enslaved to him. The time has come for him to get it out of his heart. Where would I be if every single fellow I've kissed saw himself like this Galician?

Isaac didn't know what was in Sonya's heart. And the more she pushed him away, the more he tried to come close. And whatever he used to get close, she rejected him with the same thing. He began saying words she had been fond of and he didn't know she was fond of the words not for themselves but because she was fond of the one who said them, and when the cause ceased, the fondness stopped. She scolded him, Do me a favor, don't bore me. Isaac was amazed and astonished, for everything he did he did because he knew she was attracted to it, and in the end, she scolded him.

CHAPTER FOURTEEN

Brief Commentary on the Preceding Chapter

1 |

This change, when did it begin? Perhaps the prologue was like this. One day she found him wearing new clothes. She glanced at him and she seemed to be looking at him affectionately, suddenly she said, There was a Hebrew teacher in our city, round as a herring barrel, who wore blue socks like the ones you're wearing. Isaac didn't understand that she intended to make fun of him, for what was there to make fun of blue socks, especially since in the Land of Israel, where people aren't fussy about the way they dress, especially with socks that are covered by trousers. When he sensed her mockery, he was offended by her words. And when she saw that he was offended, she didn't leave a stone unturned and there was nothing she didn't tease him about.

And still Sonya would come to him. Until that day when he waited for her and she didn't come. So he got up went to her. But she put on an amazed expression. And he went off and was insulted.

Isaac thought that Sonya would come and appease him, for she must have sensed that she hadn't behaved decently. He sat with a furious expression to teach her good manners. What did she do? She didn't come at all and didn't give him a chance to teach her good manners. He began to give in to her just so she would come. What did she do? She didn't come, and didn't give him a chance to show her he had given in. His face became pallid and he sat and waited for her. Now his anger was calmed and an affection he had never known throbbed in his heart, the affection that starts with yearnings and ends with madness. He sat all by himself and enumerated for himself some of her movements which, when she used to come to him would make him happy, and now that she doesn't come, he's despondent. How lovely was Sonya when she would enter his house, threw her head back and her hat dropped off, and she stood before him full of affection. If he hadn't seen it, he wouldn't have imagined that her presence alone was rejoicing. And since he recalled those times when she stood before him, he recalled how she stretched out on his bed and he sat with her and put a finger in her hair, took a comb from here and thrust it in there, his fingers quivering and just the memory of that quiver took his breath away with its sweetness.

What can we tell and what can we say? Isaac sat and waited for Sonya and she didn't come, not when the sun went down and not when the stars came out, not yesterday and not today. He has already straightened up his room and lit the lamp, he spread a cloth and set the table. Everything was ready for the meal, all that was lacking was Sonya to come for supper. There stands the new jar of jam Isaac bought to sweeten Sonya's supper, and the virgin in the picture on the jar bares her teeth and smiles at him. Can it be that Sonya isn't coming today either? Sonya doesn't come, not today and not the day after today and they won't sup together and they won't stroll together, not in the Baron's garden and not on the seashore, and not on the hill of sand that lovers call the Hill of Love. Wherever you turn there you find couples. But Isaac and Sonya you don't find together. To jog his memory, Isaac goes back over all those places where he used to stroll with Sonya, even though he knows that all his walking is in vain. Ah, Isaac, our comrade, pursues Sonya and doesn't find Sonya.

2 |

Why did Sonya change her way with Isaac? We can't say that her heart was throbbing for Rabinovitch, and we can't say that she was attracted to somebody else. True, that moneychanger who sits in the door of Café Hermon sent a matchmaker to her. And as for Mr. Orgelbrand, Mr. Orgelbrand keeps silent, even though he knows that she isn't intended for Mr. Kumer. Did she turn her attention to Gorishkin who swallows books like quinine and blurts out the stories of his memories or the memories in the form of stories? As far as we know Sonya, she isn't paying any mind to him. There are others who ask for her hand, and she doesn't heed them. Sonya knows that in the Land of Israel, there are more men than women, and if she stretched out a finger, seven bachelors would come. In the past, when she went out with Rabinovitch, maybe if he had said, Marry me, she might not have said no; when he left the Land, he ceased to exist for her.

On the other hand, Isaac's mind did return to Rabinovitch. There wasn't an hour that he didn't think about him and there wasn't a day when he didn't feel pangs of conscience. Even though Rabinovitch's affairs with Sonya had ended, Isaac doesn't see himself as innocent, for if he hadn't clung to Sonya, Rabinovitch wouldn't have gone away from her, for ever since the day that Isaac came close to Sonya, Rabinovitch stopped writing to them. When torments come to a person, he starts rummaging around in his deeds and believing in Divine Guidance, whose eyes wander all over the earth. If so, he had to stay away from Sonya, but he said you don't mend betrayal with betrayal, I shall take her for a wife, maybe I'll atone for that sin. If he had observed sufficiently, he would have left Sonya and gone on his way. Such matters happen every day, and a person doesn't see it as his obligation, especially since Sonya doesn't ask anything from him.

3 |

Sonya doesn't ask anything from him because it isn't respectable for a girl to ask, especially a proud girl like Sonya who receives many requests for her hand in marriage and rejects them — so Isaac thought. And because of that, he felt he should open up to her and make it easier for her. That decision brought something good, for he took his mind off Sonya's deeds, and set his mind to doing what he had to do, and between one thing and another, he again pictured to himself what he had pictured in his imagination before the quarrel, that is, that he writes to his father, I am betrothed to a maiden, her name is thus-and-so, and these are her virtues, Father reads the letter and is amazed, and so is the whole town, that a girl from a big city who stud ied in a Gymnasium would give her hand to Isaac. What do the envious say — this is the power of the land of Israel. But they admit that Isaac achieved what they didn't. That's how Isaac pictured to himself things that were determined in his heart before the quarrel, but he lacked that joy that made him happy at first when he wanted to inform his father. Instead, the imaginary picture was much stronger than at first.

Isaac decided to talk with her about the main purpose, and in his naïveté, he thought he would make her happy. In those days, when Isaac decided to tell her to enter the bond of marriage, he didn't find Sonya. And if he did find her, he didn't find an opening to talk to her, either her face was sealed or her lips were clenched, and a face like that and lips like those block the tongue and suppress speech, especially in a matter that needs an open face and smiling lips. Nevertheless, Isaac was sure that someday things would change for the better. With his common sense, he didn't grasp that his affairs with Sonya were finished. His trust in the future was the trust of logic, for since everyone saw them as a couple, how is it possible that they would go their separate ways as if there was nothing between them?

Attempts

1 |

Isaac began neglecting his work. And when he started neglecting he
went on neglecting. Yesterday he found his brushes frayed and today
he forgot where he was wanted. If he bought a new brush and recalled where he was wanted, he postponed his work for other reasons.
All the time that Sonya came to him, he worked; when she stopped
coming, he stopped working. One day he bought himself some new
clothes and went to Sonya's. Sonya wasn't impressed with his clothes,
for Sonya's views changed and even if he was wearing blue socks, she
didn't care.

Sonya's views changed. And if there were fellows who didn't
take their mind off her, Sonya took her mind off them. Just because
she wears a woman's dress, isn't she better than some of her male
comrades? And because sometimes nature overcame her and she was
drawn to somebody, was she condemned never to get rid of him?
Sonya had already managed to uproot a lot of things from her heart,
and if she recalled them they didn't rouse her very much. She even
went to the barber and cut her hair. How amazed the barber was at
her when she stood on her long upright legs like a lad and ran her
hand over her head. And we were also amazed at her for she started
treating herself like those women with bobbed hair whose feminine
grace was removed by their Creator.

2 |

A few years Sonya had lived in the Land. A thousand things Sonya
had tried to do and hadn't succeeded in anything. Before she came
to the Land of Israel, like some of her classmates at the Gymnasium,

she had been caught up in ideas that were anathema to the monarchy. Once, the secret police found forbidden writings at the home of one of her friends, among them a letter Sonya wrote containing harsh things about the government. Her father was scared and sent her to the Land of Israel to keep her out of prison.

Sonya ascended to the Land of Israel, and her father, Mr. Barukh Zweiering, a veteran Zionist, expected that, since she was in Jaffa, she would enter the Hebrew Gymnasium in Jaffa and finish school in a Hebrew atmosphere, the wish and desire of a Hebrew Zionist. She came to Jaffa and didn't enter the Gymnasium. We thought that all the teachers would be vying for her, since she came from a Russian Gymnasium, which was better than that Hebrew Gymnasium in Jaffa, whose founders had never seen a Gymnasium in their life. When she took an exam, it turned out that she didn't know Hebrew. For the next year, she acquired some Hebrew and took the exam. It turned out that she had forgotten most of her learning. They wanted to put her in a low grade, but that was beneath Sonya's dignity. She gave up the Gymnasium and turned her mind to nursing. Mr. Orgelbrand intervened with the treasurer of the hospital, Mr. Simon Rokeah, and with Dr. Pikhin the physician, and they accepted her. In those days, girls weren't yet serving the patients, except for Mrs. Tempelman, the head nurse, who was sent to us from Hamburg. Mrs. Tempelman trained her and devoted a lot of attention to her, for as Mrs. Templemen said, sick people need consoling hands, and there are no consoling hands like the hands of a woman, who from the beginning of her creation was made for those who need help. Sonya would walk among the beds wrapped in white clothes with a white cap on her head and a thermometer in her hand, with her eyes on the patients, and it was as if the Creator had created her for the sake of those garments. And we also imagined that a nurse had sprung up among our women friends. Everyone was pleased with Sonya. Especially Dr. Pikhin, who always regretted everyone who was idle, and expected her girlfriends to follow her example. Within seven or eight days, she began to slack off in her work. She said, A hospital was created only to make sick people healthy and healthy people sick. She left the hospital and went to Rehovoth to work in

the vineyards. There she did as much as she did and didn't do anything, and except for a song written about her by the poet Pizmoni,
she didn't achieve anything. So she ascended to Jerusalem to enter
the art school, Bezalel. All the young artists were happy she came.
Some wanted to paint her as Ruth, others wanted to paint her as
Helen. And she could surely serve as a model for both of them. Even
though she looked more like a Northern type. But on the other hand,
it can be assumed that Ruth the Moabite also had something northern in her, for the redhaired David came from her, and the anti-
Semite Chamberlain wrote that King David was an Aryan type.
Sonya strolled with the young artists on the walls of Jerusalem at
night, as the students of the Teachers' College gazed at her with love
and longing, for in their lives they never had the good fortune to stroll
with a girl at night. Sonya spent a month and two months in
Jerusalem and came back to Jaffa. She said the nights were beautiful
in Jerusalem, but the days were tedious. The sun burns like fire and
the dung smells and the city is drenched with sadness and the sticks
in the road trip your feet, and you jump over the hills and leap over
the rocks like those goats that smell, and the water is rationed, and
whatever corner you turn it's either garbage and dirt or a beard and
sidelocks. And when you turn to one of them, he flees from a woman
as from a demon. And everyplace in Jerusalem is called Moshe, either Ohel Moshe or Zikhron Moshe or Yemin Moshe or Mizkeret
Moshe. If you want to get to one of those places, you forget which
word is attached to Moshe, and you go from Moshe to Moshe and
don't get to the Moshe you wanted. While Jaffa is full of gardens and
vineyards and citrus groves, and there's the sea and cafés, and young
people, and every day new faces, some who come on ships from Outside the Land and some who come from the settlements, some you
want to see and some who want to see you, some you chance to meet
at assemblies and some you stroll with on the beach and on the Hill
of Love with and they don't talk about Apollo and Venus and Beatrice and other creatures who have been dead for thousands of years,
but talk about living people, whether you love them or hate them,
they're close to you in time and place. Even Doctor Schimmelman
in his lectures on the Holy Scriptures adapts his words to the time

and place. And when the people of Jerusalem talk to you, they don't call you by your name and don't address you directly in the second person, but say She, Madame, Lady, Her Honor. And when you call a man by his name and address him in the second person, he turns scared eyes on you as if you had violated good manners. So Sonya came back to Jaffa. One day she had to get her teeth fixed. When she was at the dentist, she decided to study for that profession. When she saw how hard it was, she changed her mind.

Sonya lived in Jaffa like the other girls from good families who got a monthly allowance from their father. She attended assemblies and heard speeches, listened to the lectures of Doctor Schimmelman and engaged in public works, and when the print-shop workers in Jerusalem went on strike, she went with our comrades to collect money for the strikers' fund and she did her mission well, for even bourgeois people who complained about the strikers gave generously. Some gave anonymously and some gave because Sonya persuaded them. To make a long story short, Sonya lived in Jaffa and ate from what her father sent her.

But her father's business was destroyed and his livelihood suffered. He sent her money every month and attached letters of grief to it. Mr. Barukh Zweiering, father of Sonya Zweiering, wrote, My dear daughter, I sent you your share of money this month too, but God knows if I shall send you anything next month, for time treats me rudely and the ways of trade are desolate, and big merchants, dignitaries, whose sun of success had shone upon them, had gone down nine degrees backward, let alone me, a poor man, who brings my bread with my very soul, for I am only a middleman, and my advantage is that I stand between the big merchants and the small shopkeepers who bring their merchandise through me, and when the oaks fall, all the trees of the forest shake. Won't your fine talents stand you in good stead to find some job, big or small, to provide you with a sufficient livelihood? For all those who come to us from Palestine to win souls for Zionism, they all testify that the sun of success shines in the Land and the whole Land is flourishing, and those who won't hide their hands in their pockets will find a hundredfold return in their work. And you, my dear daughter, hasn't God graced you with a good mind, and if you work, you'll succeed, for the God of Zion will be with you and will help you find the life of your soul as is the wish of your father who does not know what tomorrow will bring.

Harder than the letters of her father were the letters of her mother. Sonya's mother didn't praise her or mention her sublime talents, but complained about her and about her brothers and sisters. Oh God, has such a thing ever been heard that grown children make an old and infirm father support them and don't lift a finger to ease his load? For if your father falls under his burden, you will all fall with him. And you, Sonya, are adding distress to our distress, for whenever the time comes to send you your share of money, I see your father's face fill with sorrow and suffering, for he doesn't have any ready cash. And the money he sent you today he took from the IOUs entrusted to him. God willing, he will succeed in repaying them before they hold him and choke him, saying Pay Up. And Sonya, you sit in the chosen Land like the birds of the field who don't toil and don't know want. But what will you do when the hail comes down, and strikes the bird until it has no strength to fly?

Sonya took these things to heart and was sad. In a month or two, she might not have a penny and might not be able to pay her rent and buy food, not to mention to make a dress or shoes for herself. There was nothing left but to throw herself on the sea. Yet she loved life, and life demands money, and there is no money because her father can't send her any, and she's not used to earning her keep. Sonya had a friend who was a kindergarten teacher who worked in Madame Hofenstein's kindergarten. Once that kindergarten teacher got sick. Sonya went to the kindergarten and told the principal that her assistant couldn't come. Madame. Hofenstein clasped her hands and shrieked, What shall I do with all the children, I've only got two eyes. Can one pair of eyes watch over three dozen snotnoses? Sonya saw her grief and took pity on her. She told her she'd help her a little. And she immediately started taking care of the children. She endeared herself to them and they didn't let go of her until she promised them to come always. The principal saw it and said to her, Miss Zweltering, a great task and a holy task and a sublime task is entrusted to you. I'm amazed that you haven't yet realized your task. Perhaps the lady would like to work with me, if not for my sake, then for the darling, dear tots. Sonya listened and accepted. And even after her friend recovered, Sonya came to the kindergarten every day. She divided her day, half to the children and half to studies, to learn German to go to Berlin and study that profession. And since she was busy all day, her heart wasn't free for love affairs.

Sonya immersed herself in studies that didn't stick in her head. The years she had spent in idleness made her hands too proud to hold a textbook. But Sonya is resolute and when the book falls from her hand she picks it up even seven times, even ten times. Too bad that Sonya doesn't see a blessing in her study. Harder than that is the German language. Good God, to chatter a little Hebrew with a Jewish tot in the Land of Israel, does a kindergarten teacher need to go from the Land of Israel to Berlin to study German? But in everything else, Sonya is a great success. Everyone who sees Sonya playing with the tots says, Blessed are the tots in the care of that kindergarten teacher, especially when they see the toys she makes for them. Not in vain did Sonya want to enter Bezalel. Sonya has hands that every kindergarten teacher can envy. The kindergarten teachers envied Sonya and intrigued against her, and if she hadn't been clever, she couldn't have foiled them. Sonya is a clever girl and knows the time for everything, knows how to bring somebody close and how to keep them far away, and whatever she does she does with common sense and taste, so that everyone who is hurt by her places the blame on himself and scrutinizes his own deeds, and wants to get close to her again, and the more he wants to get close to her, the farther away she keeps him even though she doesn't mean him any harm.

3 |

The rainy days passed and the heatwave strikes. The sun stands in the firmament and roasts itself in its fire, and the earth is yellow and hot, and between heaven and earth lies a yellow air like a polished copper mirror heated in an oven, and a voice seems to whisper in the space of the world, lulling a person's bones. The city is tired and the sea lies like a corpse. Anyone who can sits in his house, drinks something hot and something cold, and wipes his sweat. But Isaac goes his way between the kindergarten and Sonya's house, in case he might find Sonya on the road.

The roads are full of piles on piles of dry sand and a yellow sun dwells on them. A glazier walks and calls out, Glazier Glazier, and tablets of light come from the glass in his arm and walk with him, and Yemenite kiddies run after those shining tablets to grab them. Loaded camels lying on the ground raise their necks and stand erect on their long legs. Arabs come, some with fruit and some with vegetables, and shout at the top of their lungs. And women come out of their houses to buy fruit and vegetables. The donkeys bray at them and a stray dog barks. Across from them stands a child blowing up a glove he found, slapping his jaws with it and laughing.

Isaac walks around and makes guesses about Sonya. Sometimes they're in his favor and sometimes not. Isaac grumbles, Who cares whether I find her? And he looks to see if she's coming. Suddenly, the shriek of the train sounds. Isaac shakes himself and thinks, The train from Jerusalem is coming already. And he's amazed at himself that he recalled Jerusalem, and is amazed at himself that all the years that he has been in the Land of Israel, he hasn't ascended to Jerusalem even once. And once again he makes guesses about Sonya. Sometimes things look good for him and sometimes not. Said Isaac, Won't I see her now either? He gazed and saw Doctor Pikhin. His little pipe is in his mouth and his doctor's bag is in his hand. Isaac is ashamed of himself for being idle. He turns and goes off. And as he walked, he came to Bostros Street. He walked the whole street to the clothing store where Rabinovitch worked before he left the Land. Isaac glanced into the store and entered.

The two storeowners were going over their ledgers. The younger one raised his eyes and greeted Isaac. But from the greeting it was as obvious as if he hinted to him, Even though I know you're a friend of Rabinovitch, you don't have the right to come here for no good reason. Isaac held his hand out toward a pile of clothes and said, I want a suit. And he repeated, I want a suit, to show him that he had come to buy some clothes. The younger one took a suit out of a heap of clothes and said, Try it on. When he wanted to put the pants on, the older one said, No need. They're certainly not short. And if they're long, you can fold the hems, and when they tear, you can make yourself patches from the leftovers. After he bought the suit, it turned out that it wasn't ugly. He went and bought himself an ironed shirt like the one he had worn the day he entered the Land. The shirt made him sweat and he had to change it, which is the way of superfluous things, it's not enough that they're superfluous, but they entail other superfluous things. Isaac's other clothes aren't comfortable either. The new ones haven't got used to him, but are likely to make an impression. And for that reason, he doesn't take them off. And as he walks, he goes into Sonya's house and doesn't find her. Since he doesn't find Sonya at home, he goes to the kindergarten. The kindergarten teacher sees him and nods to him, and a child calls him Uncle. Isaac doesn't notice them because his heart is busy with Sonya.

Even at night, Sonya doesn't come to Isaac, for in those days Sonya was accepted into the dramatic guild and is preparing for her role in "The Weavers" by Hauptmann, and has no time for idle matters. But Isaac in his fine clothes isn't working at all, for you don't work in fine clothes. And he doesn't come to the Laborers' Club, for if he went in there in his new clothes, he would be astonishing, and he doesn't sit with Sweet Foot, whose hut is full of junk and old tools. But since he is a political person by nature and can't exist without company, he began to visit Mr. Orgelbrand.

4 |

Mr. Orgelbrand leaves his work an hour or two before dark, goes home, and eats. Clerks are not wont to work too much, especially bank clerks, especially in the Land of Israel, where all their work is done in six or seven hours, and even those hours don't bruise their fingers too much. Between one hour and the next, they bring them a cup of coffee, and between one coffee and the next, lemonade. And so Mr. Orgelbrand leaves his work an hour or two before dark, goes home, and eats, and sits in the window and looks at the trees in the garden and smokes a little pipe. For when Mr. Orgelbrand went to Doctor Pikhin to consult him about his nerves, Pikhin told him,

Medicines you want, I won't write you a prescription for medicines, just buy yourself a little pipe, and when you sit alone in your room, fill the pipe with tobacco and smoke. And if today you don't find any sense in smoking, tomorrow you will.

When Isaac comes, Orgelbrand takes his pipe out of his mouth and says, Isn't that amazing! My father didn't smoke and I sit and smoke. And why do I smoke, because Doctor Pikhin ordered me. You know Pikhin? He's a clever and gracious man. A member of Bilu. Someday there will be a generation who will look at us as we look at the members of Bilu. How old are you, Mr. Kumer, twenty-four? I thought you were young. Anyway, you'll live to see them point at you and say, that old man is one of the last old-timers of the Land of Israel. And everybody will look at you like a miracle, because everyone who has money to travel returns out of the Land. We should call it our ascendance there. If we leave the Land, our name will stand after us.

Isaac sits facing Mr. Orgelbrand, and even though Mr. Orgelbrand is a clerk, he behaves like a brother to our comrade and offers him figs and dates that come from outside the Land. Mr. Orgelbrand isn't attracted to sweets, but he does like to have sweets in his house, so that if a guest comes, he has something to offer him; in the past when Rabinovitch and Sonya would come to his house, he would sweeten their stay with fruits like those.

The landlady and her daughters are happy about Mr. Kumer, even though they don't talk with him very much because he isn't used to politeness, and yet they like to see him in their house. And when he comes, they say to one another, Come and see, Mr. Kumer is from Austria and Mr. Orgelbrand is from Russia, and yet they're comrades, just as Mr. Kumer was a comrade of Mr. Rabinovitch, who was also Russian. Is there a nicer nation than that, who treat each other as brothers and friends? While we Christian daughters of Christians dwell among Christians and no Christian pays any heed to us. Gone are the early days when our forefathers were cantors and preachers in the church, and consuls and barons would come to hear. Once a party of bishops came from Scotland and when they heard our grandfather go to the Ark, they said, close to us, that with such a melody the Lord our Savior would pray to his Master.

Orgelbrand hears their talk and gazes in the air with shining eyes. He too longs for his Creator, and sometimes his soul is weak to pour itself out to God. Last year at Rosh Hashanah, Orgelbrand did something and went to pray with the teachers and activists in a congregation they made for themselves in the auditorium of the Sha'arei Tsion School. One teacher went to the Ark and one teacher read the Torah and one activist blew the ram's horn, and Mordechai Ben Hillel preached before the blowing of the ram's horn. You can't say the prayer wasn't proper, and you can't say there wasn't a hint of an idea in the sermon, but the heart wasn't refreshed. At a time when human beings believe and a man can't imagine that he can get along without prayer—prayer is prayer. Now that belief suffers and a man knows he can get along without prayer, even when he does pray—his prayer isn't prayer. I fear, Mr. Kumer, that you haven't completely understood me, so I shall explain further, everything a man does and knows that he doesn't have to do doesn't help him these days. I don't ask you to pray all day long, but if you need prayer, do your praying regularly and don't do your praying haphazardly, for everything that doesn't have a fixed time is put off for anything that comes along, and if so, it is put off and put off. If you admit that you owe money to the bank and sometimes you pay and sometimes you don't pay, you're not reliable to me. Excuse me, Mr. Kumer, for making a parable about you, I really should have made it about me and all our comrades, clerks and managers, teachers and writers, merchants and activists.

Even though Isaac didn't ascend to the Land of Israel for Torah and prayer, like that old man he met on the ship and like all the other old people, he was sorry that faith had slackened. If his faith hadn't slackened, he wouldn't have done what he did. And since he recalled what he did, he recalled Sonya. In fact, he hadn't taken his mind off Sonya for even one hour, but he was wrong to think that all his thoughts about her were only because he wanted to repair his acts with her. If we observe the matter, we shall find that Orgelbrand's attraction to Sonya was worthier than Isaac's, for Isaac is attracted to

Sonya as if to repair the sin he had committed, while Orgelbrand is attracted to her for herself, because he loves her. And so the two of them sit together, Isaac Kumer and Jonathan Orgelbrand, and don't mention Sonya, but each of them is thinking of her, one out of hope deferred and the other out of heartache.

5 |

When the room becomes small for them, they go for a stroll in the Baron's garden. And when Orgelbrand is in a generous mood, he invites Isaac to Laurenz's café, for Orgelbrand doesn't go into Café Hermon, where all the groups talk about the director, but goes to Laurenz, where most of the customers are Germans and have no business with AFEK, and even the Jews who come there want a rest from business. Orgelbrand treats his guest to a glass of beer or a cup of punch and orders a cup of tea for himself, drinks two or three drops and puts it down, for those Germans who are experts in everything don't know how to make tea. And on the Sabbath, when the air is pleasant and the road is comfortable for pedestrians, they go out to Sharona and drink warm milk fresh from the cow. Orgelbrand is respected by the people of Sharona, and sometimes a farmer comes out to meet him and sits with him in front of his house and tells about the first settlers, why they left Germany and came here, and why their sons left their father's deeds and behave like all the rest of the nations. The Jews say as the Christians behave so the Jews behave, and we say as the Jews behave so the Christians behave. Both Jews and Christians have deserted God and God has deserted them, and the noose is hung on the neck of the Jews, for all good things are promised the Jews if they keep the Torah, and it's not enough that they don't keep the Torah, but they also take paths that are no good and take their lives from this world and from the world-to-come. Once they found an old farmer from Haifa who had served Baron Rothschild as a carter, when the Baron came to see Zikhron Ya'akov. The Baron asked him, What do you say about my deeds in the Holy Land? He said to him, The Baron shouldn't scatter his millions for nothing. It's not money that makes a settlement, but love of the land and love of work, and those Jews don't know what is land or what is work. But the Jewish Baron is stubborn and doesn't listen to what others say, he scattered many millions and didn't succeed much.

Once or twice, Orgelbrand walked with Isaac to Petach Tikva, and they visited several landlords, and in every single house, they were greeted with tea and marmalade. There are houses where Isaac had been soon after he ascended. The landlords don't remember Isaac, for he was only one of many who asked them for work, and who can remember them, but Isaac remembers them, this one sitting on the porch and drinking tea and reading *HaShiloah* and sucking sugar and getting rid of him just like that, and this one's wife telling him maybe he should apply to our neighbor, and when he came to the neighbor's house he found it locked. Now they set the table for him. And after the meal the daughters play melodies of Bach and Beethoven and Mozart and Rubenstein. Many times Isaac heard about them and didn't know what they were like, suddenly he finds himself sitting at a full table and well-dressed girls are sitting and playing their melodies. And if the girls are pleasant to Orgelbrand, Isaac doesn't envy him, for all of Isaac's thoughts are only on Sonya. After an hour or two, they parted and went to the hotel, where at night the stagecoach left. The hotel owner was one of the first farmers and his house was open to guests. When they ate, everybody would come and he had nothing left except his house, so he allowed himself to accept payment.

The guests sit among the tall cypresses in the garden that shade them with a sweet gloom. And with them sit some of the local people, the young educated fellows who own fields and vineyards, who haven't yet given up their early ideals they brought with them from outside the Land, and even things that ostensibly made them forget the loss of money, like giving work to Jewish laborers, and in their naïveté they say, After all, aside from coming to build ourselves we also came to build our Land, and the Land is nothing if there aren't laborers. Accountants laugh at them and show them with clear evidence that they will lose their money and their property will decline at last. And some of the accountants complain about them that they should be sued, and tell them why don't you use Jewish laborers, for your work is done by Jews and your property is crumbling.

And sometimes they too feel remorse, for perhaps the accountants are right. For the time being they live on the money they have and several Jews live with them and they treat their laborers as comrades. They sit down among the cypresses in the garden and talk about current events and about issues of the settlement, about the Baron and about PIKA, about the truths of Ahad Ha-Am and about the beginning of Petach Tikva, about the first ones who have gone to their rest and about others who have gone wherever it is they have gone. Only the cypresses planted by the owner of the garden grow and don't move from their place.

And so Isaac sits in the village hotel where he had gone with Rabinovitch soon after he ascended. If only they could stand on the ground. But since they couldn't, one is wandering around outside the Land and the other is like a guest for the night. For the tree of the field is man's life, says the Torah. If he is worthy, he is like a tree whose roots are deep, if he is not worthy, he is blown like a leaf.

Isaac took his mind off those days when he went around here in this settlement from one farmer to another asking for work. Now he sits like a guest who has bought his place with his own money. And like a guest whose money buys him his place, he doesn't worry about bed or board. Once a farmer came from Mayan Ha-Ganim to take dung, and when he saw people sitting and talking, he came and sat among them and told that, before the Sabbath, he had been in Jaffa and there he heard that Brenner was about to come to the Land of Israel. Brenner wrote that, since a Jew has no other place in the world I shall go and try, perhaps there is a place for a person in the Land of Israel. How happy we were at that news, for of all the great writers there was no one here in the Land except for Sh. Ben Zion, and if one or two came to see the Land, they'd spend three months here more or less, and return outside the Land. Like our leaders and chiefs who said that Diaspora needs us. Diaspora didn't need them. And if it did need them, it needed them to set an example, that you can be a Zionist and live outside the Land. And so we were glad about the rumor that Brenner would come to dwell among us. But not all who hear were glad, for this writer isn't wont to cover up all that his eyes see.

The cypresses are enveloped in shadows and people are sitting and talking about days gone by and days to come. No one knows if the days to come will be better than the days gone by, at any rate this hour which is not past and not future is beautiful. Isaac's heart was sweetened and he thought, Too bad I didn't bring Sonya with me. And that fool doesn't feel that even if he had pleaded with her, she wouldn't have come. Weren't his affairs with Sonya finished by now? Whether they were or not, his grief certainly wasn't finished.

CHAPTER SIXTEEN

Pioneers

1 |

Isaac and Orgelbrand got up in the morning to return to Jaffa and found the stagecoach filled to bursting. Because of the honor due to Mr. Orgelbrand, that many people need his services, the passengers agreed to huddle together and made room for him among them. Orgelbrand returned to Jaffa and Isaac had to wait until the next day, for in those days, the stagecoach went from Petach Tikva to Jaffa only once a day. Isaac could have gone back to Jaffa on foot, for from Petach Tikva to Jaffa a normal man can walk in three hours, and what is a walk of three hours to a fellow like Isaac, and he wasn't even afraid of Arabs, for the Arabs had learned by now that not every Jew is born to die. But Isaac decided to wait until the next day and to see Eyn Ganim in the meantime. That settlement of workers, founded in the bad days, at a time when many people were forced to leave the Land because they didn't find any work to do, is precious to us as a living and faithful testimony that our existence in the Land is possible.

Isaac picked himself up and left the boundaries of Petach Tikva and walked to Eyn Ganim. The red and black soil that used to produce thorns and briars, lizards and scorpions, now grows trees and vegetables, chickens and cattle, houses and sheds, men, women, and children. During the day the men work in Petach Tikva, some are hired by the month and some by the day, but at night they come back from their work and work hard for their own village.

How is it that a place that was desolate of any settler becomes a settled village? Yet in those days when it seemed to us that we had nothing to do in the Land, a small group of comrades who were devoted to the Land said, We shall not move from here. They gathered together and made themselves an association to make a settled village, that is to buy themselves so many dunams of land and work their soil. On a day when they found work with others, they would do their own work after they were done; and on a day they didn't find work, they would work all day long for themselves. They had no money to support themselves, and of course none to buy a strip of land, for they were dayworkers, and not every day is there work, but their determination and their will strengthened their force and overcame all obstacles. And this is not the place to list all the details, which are known.

So they bought themselves a plot of land, and every day after they returned in the evening from their work in Petach Tikva, they went out with their wives and children and weeded the thorns and turned over the dust and molded bricks. And water they didn't have, for the well was far away from their settlement, through sand and thorns and briar, and they walked barefoot, for they were sparing their shoes. But they didn't spare themeselves and brought water from far away to mold bricks and they built little houses for themselves. And near those houses you find good land that rewards those who work it. They plowed and sowed and planted. And water they didn't have, for the well was far away from their dwelling place. But they didn't spare their efforts and brought their water from far away to water their gardens. The gardens grew and flourished and made fine shoots, whose praise was on every tongue, and many people came to buy them. And they didn't sell the shoots, but grew them into good trees. Toiling men, who suffered hunger and disease, who should have bought a little quinine with their wages to relieve their malaria, but they reined in their wishes for the sake of their hope. And the women too. Even the most tender and delicate of them would take from her own mouth and feed her babies. And daughter like mother, son like father. That's Eyn Ganim, the first settlement of Hebrew workers in the Land of Israel, who earned their place with their work.

2 |

Let's go back to Isaac. Isaac walks around among the small houses and the young shoots wearing Sabbath clothes like a tourist, and wherever he turns a young shoot, a chick, or the window of a house peeps at him, and between house and field a red kerchief flashes on the head of a woman who rules over house and field. You have surely heard of the first people of Petach Tikva and about the first people of Rishon Le-Tsion and about the Bilu people and about all our other brothers, the settlers in Judea and the Galilee, in the Sharon and the Shomron, in the plain and in the mountain, with what suffering they took possession of their place, but the toil of the first pioneers seems like an ancient legend to us, their heroism makes the suffering forgotten. While here, where the suffering of the toilers is still new, no matter how much you are amazed at their heroism, you can't ignore the grief of their toil. Nevertheless, Isaac considered himself deprived. Why? Because he wasn't blessed like the people of Eyn Ganim. But now he didn't ascribe the failure to others who rejected him from work on the land, but he ascribed the failure to himself for not enduring the ordeals and for fleeing to the city. Unlike our comrades in Eyn Ganim who stuck with the soil until they got to whatever they got to.

Isaac looked in front of him, but his eyes were behind him. He thought about himself and about those who were uprooted from the Land, and were wandering around all over the world. Even Rabinovitch is wandering around Outside the Land, and even though he left to return, it's doubtful he will return. And when he remembered Rabinovitch, he remembered Sonya. And when he remembered Sonya, his heart grew sad. He went back to thinking about himself and about those who left and about what that German farmer told him, It's not money that makes a settlement, but love of the land and love of the soil, and the Jews don't know what is land or what is work.

3 |

Suddenly there was a peep from one of the chicks poking around in the dung, and it was answered by another chick from a woman's apron. Isaac lifted his eyes and saw a woman whom he had met in the barn of Petach Tikva soon after he ascended, when he and Rabinovitch were looking for work, for in those days, there weren't any cafés in the settlements, and anyone who wanted to lift his spirit would go to the barn. Young and handsome was that woman when we first saw her, and now she looked like an old woman. Like most of our sisters who work in the house and the field, lines and wrinkles furrowed and incised her face, bestowing splendor like drops of grandeur. Isaac knew her by sight, but not up close, for until he met Sonya, he hadn't talked to a woman. The woman looked and saw Isaac. She said to him, Don't you want to see my farm? Isaac bowed his head and muttered something, like someone who admits his guilt. And what guilt is it, it is the guilt of all of us who came to work the land and didn't work it.

That woman smiled at him and took him and showed him a group of chicks her hen hatched, and showed him orange saplings and lemon saplings her husband had planted. And finally she showed him two children any mother would have been proud of. And after she showed him all the great things and wonders not every woman can boast of, she brought him tomato juice and looked favorably with beautiful eyes on every gulp he gulped. After he drank, he held the cup because its base had fallen off and it couldn't stand. She took it out of his hand and said, You think I made that juice for pleasure and indulgence, but when the Land gave us fine, first-rate tomatoes, my husband said, We won't eat the tomatoes, but I'll take them to the market, and he thought about what he'd do with the money he'd get for them, like that peasant woman in the folk parable who found an egg and delighted in imagining the good things the egg would give her and as she did, the egg fell out of her hand and broke. And so my husband took his tomatoes to Petach Tikva and didn't find a person to buy them because the Arab tomatoes are cheaper than our tomatoes. Ashamed, he came back with the tomatoes and swore to bury them in the ground. So I quickly made juice from them.

While they were talking, Pnina came. She saw Isaac and said, Here something was done, not like in our Jaffa. And Pnina's words had a triumphant tone for everything that was done in Eyn Ganim, and on the other hand, a sorrowful tone for herself and for Jaffa. To work the soil Pnina ascended to the Land of Israel, and in the end she is wallowing in the city, like Yael Hayyot and Sonya Zweiering, but they are city girls and she isn't, she's a village girl and deserves to settle on the soil. Gorishkin was partly to blame, for whenever she wanted to uproot herself from the city, he found things to keep her. So it was when our comrades went up to the Kinneret she wanted to go along with them, and the same when she wanted to go to Ben Shemen. It's not good for a girl to rely on men, for most of them want their own good. Pnina looked at Isaac and asked herself, That fellow who isn't flooded with theories, why does he live in the city? That must be Sonya's fault. For if not for her city notions, Isaac would have done by now what the Land needs. It's not good for a man to run after girls, who are all egotists.

Two members of Eyn Ganim came; they weren't working that day because they had to go to Jaffa to apply for a loan to buy a cow. They saw Isaac and looked at him the way you look at a tourist, even though they knew he was an artisan, but someone who works in the city isn't like someone who works in the field. And even though there is also conquest of work in the city, there isn't conquest of the soil in it. And without soil, we are bereft of a foundation, eternal nomads.

Little by little, our comrades' hearts changed in Isaac's favor. This one drew him to survey his property with him and that one showed him something you don't see everywhere. And what did he show him? A pit he dug in his yard. Why? To collect manure, to improve his land with it. The pit is still empty, since he doesn't have a horse or a cow to make manure. But he had already prepared a receptacle for manure in case he succeeds in buying a cow.

Isaac stood among our pioneer comrades and was happy about this one's farm and that one's pit, for in those days we were generous about our comrades and rejoiced at their joy as if it were our own joy.

CHAPTER SEVENTEEN

A Light Conversation

1 |

After Isaac parted from the people of Eyn Ganim, he strolled at the edge of the settlement, thinking about everything he had seen and heard. And it seemed to him that he had already seen and heard such things. Where had he seen and where had he heard? For, from the day they had laid the cornerstone of that workers' settlement until now, he hadn't been there. He recalled one of those stories they tell about his ancestor Reb Yudel Hasid, who, once in his wanderings to collect money for dowries, wandered into a village and spent a Sabbath with one of the Thirty-Six Just Men, on whom the world stands. And Isaac started thinking about the things they tell about that hidden saint. That hidden saint dug mud for the daughters of Israel to plaster the ground of their houses in honor of the Sabbath, and on the Sabbath he would speak nothing but the Holy Tongue, and would not call his residence a home, for the residence of a man in the false world is not a home. And when Isaac contemplated those things, he smiled and said, And I, Isaac, descendant of Rabbi Yudel Hasid, spent a weekday not with a hidden saint, but with a host of hidden saints on whom the world stands, and even on weekdays they speak the Holy Tongue, and they dig pits for manure to improve the earth of the Land of Israel. And as for their homes, homes built by the hands of their residents certainly deserve to be called homes.

And thus Isaac thought and walked until he came to the barn. That was the barn where we would sit into the night. Isaac was in good spirits, like a man strolling for his own pleasure. He began singing one of those songs they used to sing in the barn at night.

In Petach Tikva
Oyfn shayer
vu a glet iz volvl
un a kush nisht tayer

In Petach Tikva in the barn,
As everyone can see,
Kisses aren't expensive,
Caresses are for free.

After Isaac walked around the barn, he went into the Laborers' House and looked at the announcements and the newspapers. And since the air was fine and a good smell rose from the citrus groves and the jasmine bushes, he left the Laborers' House and went out for a stroll. He came to one of the ruins of Petach Tikva, where he had eaten his first meal on the first night he came to look for work. Great was Isaac's hope that day when he came to Petach Tikva the first time and great was his pain on the day he left Petach Tikva. Later that pain departed from him and other pain came. Isaac looked at that ruin where he stayed with Rabinovitch. Those days weren't good, but his heart was pure of all blemish.

A man glanced at him and said, Aren't you that Galician I saw at Yedidya Rabinovitch's? You haven't gone back Outside the Land? Isaac replied, I am that Galician, and it looks like I haven't gone back Outside the Land. So he greeted him and invited him to his room. As they entered, the bell from the citrus groves was heard. Said the host to the guest, It's time for lunch. Sit down and we shall eat. He took out three or four oranges and half a loaf of bread and they ate and drank tea from a burnished brass samovar.

That man was called by two names, one name was Menahemke the Rabbi and the other name was Menahem Who Stands. Menahem Who Stands, because he did everything standing up. And Menahem the Rabbi, because when his father the rabbi died and left a house full of orphans and the community had no money to support the orphans and to pay the wages of the rabbi, they sat Menahem in the rabbi's chair until they found his older sister a bridegroom who was fit to serve as a rabbi and Menahem left his place and ascended to the Land of Israel. He came to the Land of Israel and went to Petach Tikva and looked for work with the farmers like all our other comrades. When he found work, he just plain took it, and when he didn't find work he didn't complain. He would say, Just as I am entitled to ask for work, so the employer is entitled to tell me, I don't have any for you. Any work that came his way was proper in his eyes even if it gave a lot of trouble and a little pay. He used to say, I don't refuse any work, and even if they appointed me Hakham Bashi of all Turkey, I would take it. In fact, he hated the rabbis, and hated anything that had even a grain of dust of the rabbis on it. Once upon a time, two disputants wanted to make him a judge, and he didn't want to, even though he was hard up for money at that time. And since he knew there was no work at all times, he saved on his needs. He became so stingy that once he moved from one apartment to another and took the straw of his bed with him, even though it was crushed with age. But he was meticulous about wearing clean clothes and washed his laundry every Friday night, and if he found a rip he would mend it himself. He also insisted on choice tea, and he had a burnished brass samovar which he took with him from his father's house as his inheritance. Just as he was fussy about clean clothes, so he was also fussy about his apartment. He had no books except for a volume of Talmud he studied. And when he studied, he studied standing up at a reading stand he had made for himself. If his legs became numb from standing, he took off his shoes, put down a bottle and stood on it.

2 |

Isaac told Menahem some of the things that had happened to him in the Land of Israel. Menahem stood on his feet as was his wont, blowing on his cup and listening. When Isaac finished the story of his adventures, he smiled and said, You see, Rabbi Menahem, I ascended to the Land of Israel to work it and preserve it, and in the end, what am I, a painter, a smearer. Menahem blew on his cup and was silent. Isaac closed his eyes and began talking about the Land and about work. In the end, he grew excited and talked about the Religion of Work.

Menahem looked at him with hard eyes, nodded his head, and said, Religion of Work, Religion of Work. People who dismiss the essentials of religion took on that pleasant notion, like those modern poets who mention God's name in their poems, even though they and the readers of their poems don't know the Lord and don't want to know the Lord. You want to hear my opinion, then listen. A person has to work, for if he doesn't work, what will he eat? I myself have no need for ideas, not about the Land and not about work. It's enough for a man that he was blessed to dwell in the Land of Israel. And may we not have to be ashamed of the Land.

Menahem lowered his eyes and added, In general, a person has to behave a little modestly toward the Land of Israel. And a person shouldn't see himself as if he were doing a favor to the Land. I haven't yet seen all the greatness that the thinkers of thoughts have done here. And if a little something was done, it was done against their will. A Land, as it is written the eyes of the Lord thy God are always on it, such a Land shouldn't be as they want, for the eye of Divine Providence, as it were, is different from the eyes of planners and advisors, whether they are old or whether they are young and the youngest of the young, whether they write "Truth from the Land of Israel" or whether they lie for the sake of the Land of Israel. But the main trouble is not in ideas, but in the caviling those ideas involve. A greater trouble than that is the trouble of men of action who want to turn idle words into action. Needless to say, our salvation won't be as they imagine, but when we achieve complete salvation, they will be the first to be fed up with it. I've already talked a lot, but this I will tell you, every Jew must try with all his might to dwell in the Land of Israel, for the origin of the nation of Israel is in the Land of Israel. And since the Land is destroyed and desolate and it is hard to dwell in a place of destruction, we must repair the place and make it a place of settlement. If so, if the main thing is to restore it from its destruction, then what does it matter if our work is done by foreigners, as the foolish farmers say. That has an inherent answer, for from the day the Gentiles came to our estate, the Land has not been built, but on the contrary, all the nations, one after another, destroyed it more and more. The hand of Providence was here, for the Land is waiting for

us, the sons of the Land, to rebuild it. Straight words, proved by reality. Once again I talked a lot. If you want to prove the futility of idle
words, you have to prove it against your will with words. I see that you
won't return to Jaffa today, and you need a place to spend the night,
so stay with me. I won't make a bed for you, but I will make you a
place on the ground. Hospitable people offer their bed to the guest
and they sleep on the ground, but not me, so that I don't give myself
an excuse to say that I am fastidious and need a bed, and so I found
myself stopped from doing something that every person should do.
So sleep here, and if you need to go about your business, come back
here for supper, for I eat my main meal at night, and there's clean
bread and olives and halvah in my house, not to mention tea from
the samovar.

3 |

Isaac didn't return to Menahem because he went to the Laborers'
House to hear the lecture of Falk Shpaltleder on Peretz's stories. And
by the time the lecture was over and the discussion ended, it was midnight. A barrelmaker gave Isaac his place on a pile of barley in the
cellar of a farmer in Petach Tikva, and he himself went somewhere
else, for the place was too small for the two of them to sleep.

And before the barrelmaker took him to his room, they went
to the laborers' hostel to drink a cup of tea. A few of our comrades
sat and ate and drank and argued about Shpaltleder's lecture and
about Peretz himself. From here, they came to the issue of languages
in the Land. But some of our comrades didn't take part in that debate, for they had already made a rule that in the Land of Israel, a
person must speak Hebrew, and they were strict about their language, not to utter one word that wasn't Hebrew. Most especially
Herzl Spivak, that is Naftali Zamir, who later drowned in the Lake
of Kinneret when he saw an Arab drowning and jumped in to save
him. Naftali Zamir was adept in the treasures of the Hebrew language and made light songs from them and composed tunes for
them. And when he was in jolly spirits, he would speak in rhymes.
He didn't attend Shpaltleder's lecture, for he hated him with utter
hatred, because he sees our devotion to the Land as something

whose time has passed. Why? Because in most enlightened countries, most of the peasant sons leave their soil and go to the city. Neither did he like our devotion to Hebrew. Shpaltleder said, At a time when great newspapers are coming out in Yiddish, and great literature is created in that tongue, and writers and journalists live on it , you want to exchange it for a dead language. But we honored Shpaltleder, for we are generous and more generous to our opponents than we are to those who love us.

Shpaltleder entered with a loud noise, tossed his hat on the table, rumpled his flourishing pompadour, and said, Fellows, I'm as hungry as a dog. Is there something to eat here? He saw that everyone was debating and no one hurried to bring him something to eat. He said to them, Why such words, such vain patois? Said Naftali, Bring him meat to eat, tender or raw. Said Shpaltleder, And will you bring me with it something other? Said Naftali, A kid cooked in the milk of its mother. Said Shpaltleder, But such abomination the Torah forbade. Said Naftali, A man of your stature should be afraid? Said Shpaltleder, Your rhymes drop down like cattle dung. Said Naftali, Open your mouth and I'll fill up your tongue. Said one of the group, Who knows a word without a rhyme? Said Naftali, He who doesn't will have a hard time. Said someone else, I know a word. Said Naftali, I hope it's one we've not yet heard. Said the man, Like Falk Shpaltleder. Said Naftali, He has plunged down and touched the nadir. He responded, Your rhyme doesn't rhyme, Naftali, you fail. Said Naftali, If you speak truth, all my toil's to no avail. He said to him, Because "leder" is spelled with "e," and "nadir" with "i." Said Naftali, If I spell it with an "i," has it gone awry? He said to him, But the rhyme doesn't follow the rules of the game. Said Naftali, Well, nadir and Shpaltleder now sound the same. Said Shpaltleder, You couldn't find a nicer rhyme for my name? Said Naftali, Any rhyme I'd find would fill me with shame. Said Shpaltleder, And you, what's your name, Mr. So-and-so? Said Naftali, Oh, dear, I forgot it, how I don't know. Said another, And if the Angel of Death asks you the same. Said Naftali, I'll answer the dead don't know their own name. Said Shpaltleder, Give me something and I'll eat. Said Naftali, Something not a kosher treat. Said Shpaltleder, Shut your mouth, young man, don't say another word. Said Naftali, Not for me, but for you no praise has been heard. Said Shpaltfeder, You saw that he has no merits. Said Naftali, I'm treating you just as you treated Peretz.

Between this and that, they brought Shpaltleder some meat and wine to try, he devoured everything in the wink of an eye, and ordered them to bring him more because he was hungrier than before, for ever since he had entered the ring, he hadn't bothered to eat a thing, had just sweated like a bear that is dumb, and his guts were rumbling like a drum.

He tapped the bowl with his fork to hasten the waitress and said, Because the Jews got used to waiting for the coming of the Messiah, they got used to waiting for every single thing. But I want to see my food immediately. As his comrades were enjoying his wisdom, he saw Naftali. He said to him, Now I'm ready to have fun with your rhymes. Naftali restrained his anger and began rhyming against Shpaltleder.

> Renew my joy, Oh Lord of hosts,
> And fill my throat with tender roasts.
> Give me food for my salvation,
> Send reward for all my merits,
> And overlook my peculation,
> And what I said of Y. L. Peretz.
> And if you find my words are foul
> And in your eyes they are a crime,
> Recall my hungry guts do growl,
> And call for sustenance all the time.
> If you won't hear the words I scream,
> I'll talk of Mendele Mokher Sfarim,
> Like moths I'll hurl my words to crash
> On Sholem Aleichem and Scholem Asch.

Menahem waited for his guest. The samovar stood and hummed and he stood and studied until daybreak. And at daybreak, he didn't lie down to sleep, for never in his life had he put his head on a pillow during the day. And since he didn't have any work outside, he studied all day and completed his tractate of Talmud. And since he didn't have any other tractate, he went back to the beginning, saying, Their words are intended for a person's every season and every moment, and sometimes you catch on the hundred and first time what you didn't grasp the hundredth time. And he pitied the folk in the fields who don't know how good is the Talmud for those who study it.

Back in Jaffa

1 |

The next morning, Isaac got up early and returned to Jaffa. It turned out that Pnina sat in the same carriage as he. Their eyes met and she didn't seem to look favorably on him. In truth, Pnina felt nothing in her heart against him or against anybody else in the world, but the grief peeping out of her eyes made them hard. For she went to Eyn Ganim because she wanted to tear herself away from the noise of Jaffa and smell the smell of earth and see her good girlfriend. She tore herself away from Jaffa and smelled the smell of the earth and saw her friend, and finally she is returning to Jaffa and her friend is about to go back Outside the Land. What did her friend tell her? Every person is commanded to come to the Land of Israel, but even God didn't order them to waste all their years here. Pnina thought to herself, Now that my friend is about to go back Outside the Land, I should multiply my strength, but what am I and what is my strength, even if I multiply it a hundredfold. Just because I picked geraniums or oranges, am I entitled to see myself as if I had done something? And once again, her grief flickered in her dark handsome eyes, as a daughter of Israel who wants to do only good, but isn't offered an opportunity. Isaac felt her eyes turning favorable and started talking with her. He talked about this, that, and the other. About Eyn Ganim and its inhabitants, about Petach Tikva and the laborers' house there, and about some of our comrades who are avoiding it, forbidden to enjoy any benefit from it, because it was built with the money of the Zionist Agency, and they see every institution of laborers that the laborers don't build by themselves as if it has a grain of charity on it, and a genuine laborer has to stay away from it. And after Isaac told

Pnina everything he had seen and heard from the time he left Jaffa, he wanted to tell her some of Menahem's words. But as soon as he started talking, his tongue grew mute and he fell silent. And when he fell silent, he started looking at things until he reached Jaffa.

2 |

Isaac returned to his regular deeds, or we had better tell the truth, it wasn't to deeds that he returned, but to a life of idleness. But before he went to Petach Tikva, Sonya was the cause of that idleness, and after he came back from Petach Tikva, other causes came. Or we better tell the truth, he himself was the cause. No matter what it was, Isaac recognized that it wasn't good for him here and he should go somewhere else.

In those days, Isaac heard about a shoemaker in Jaffa who left his trade and his wife and his little children and ascended to Jerusalem and settled in the prayer house of the Braslav Hasids. A simple shoemaker sewing shoes did something because his soul longed to repair himself. Isaac wouldn't do that, but he did know that a change of place would change his luck for the better. There are people who, wherever they are, live their lives as they want to. Isaac wasn't one of them. Isaac didn't have a weak temperament. For you see, when others satisfied their Zionism by saying words or collecting Shekels, you find him ascending to the Land of Israel. And that is not an easy matter. And if he had found work in the field or the vineyard, he would have settled on the soil, and we would sing "The Song of the Earth." But in spite of himself and not for his own good, Isaac became what he became, that is, seeking work with his brush and his bucket, and we tag along behind him. For the time being, Isaac dwells in Jaffa and every day he expects some change. Either for good or for better, we won't abandon him in the middle of the road.

Here we have to tell a few things about Sonya. Sonya spends her days in the kindergarten and her nights in the drama society. And just as she succeeds in one place, so she succeeds in the other. And there are already a few lovers of the Hebrew theater who prophesy that Sonya will be a great actress. A great actress she didn't become.

At any rate, Gorishkin wrote in his notebook what they said about her. Gorishkin doesn't omit a thing from his notebook. For the time being, those things have no importance, but someday his words will be seen as the cornerstone of the history of the Land of Israel. And since Sonya is busy she doesn't pay any heed to Isaac. And since she doesn't pay any heed to Isaac, Isaac doesn't know what to do and what not to do.

CHAPTER NINETEEN

Isaac Parts from Sonya and Ascends to Jerusalem

1 |

Many times, Isaac wanted to ascend to Jerusalem, but didn't. All the while he was idle, he didn't have money for the trip. When he began working and earning, he was afraid to leave his work lest it be given to others. Meanwhile, he met Sonya. When he met Sonya, he forbade himself to leave her and go to another place. When she began to stay away from him, he once again considered ascending to Jerusalem.

Once he found Sonya and accompanied her home. On the way, the conversation turned to Jerusalem. Said Isaac, I haven't been there yet. Said Sonya, Anyone who has a drop of blood in him and not colored water goes and sees. And said Sonya, There isn't a place in Jerusalem that I didn't visit. All the things I saw! The art school Bezalel and Professor Schatz, Ben-Yehuda's study and the desk where he wrote his great dictionary when he was in prison. And said Sonya, All the days I spent in Jerusalem, I never once tasted sleep. By day I went to see the antiquities and at night I strolled on the Old City walls with the Bezalel students and we danced in the light of the moon.

A pale flush suddenly covered her face, as on that night when Isaac first kissed her. Isaac saw it, and his heart trembled in him like the gold down that trembled on her lip. He stretched out his hand and stroked her head. She bowed her head and said, Let's go. When they came to her house, she held out her hand and told him goodbye. Before he could tell her goodbye, she disappeared.

In those days, his heart was divided. He wanted to ascend to Jerusalem and he wanted to stay in Jaffa. Meanwhile, he neglected his work and strolled around a lot. Once Sonya found him in the street and was amazed that he was idle. He told her, I am ascending to Jerusalem and I have neglected my work. Sonya nodded at him and said, At last, as a person loathes his friend who pestered him too much and tells him, At last you recognized that you should leave, and she didn't ask when he'd come back, but she did ask when he'd go. Said Isaac, I am going to Jerusalem to look for work. Said Sonya, You will surely come to say goodbye to me. And she held her hand out to him and left.

2 |

Isaac sent his belongings to the railroad station and went to Sonya's to bid her farewell. You're going? said Sonya. I'm going, said Isaac. Well then, said Sonya, I won't keep you. She sensed that her words weren't fitting, changed her tone, and said, When does the train leave? Isaac whispered, In an hour. Sonya said, I'll put on another dress and accompany you to the railroad station. She put on her best clothes and went with him.

On the way, she repeated her question, When does your train leave for Jerusalem? Isaac stammered, In an hour it leaves from here. Well then, said Sonya, why are we hurrying? Let's go into the café and say goodbye over some ice cream. You agree? He nodded. Sonya pretended she didn't see and said, Why are you silent, say yes. Fine, said Isaac, let's go into the café.

They went into the café and ordered ice cream. By the time they tasted it, it had melted. When Sonya pushed her bowl away, she looked at Isaac and passed all her acquaintances before her mind's eye. Sometimes they were this way and sometimes they were that way, and Isaac always levelled with her and never sinned against her. She took his hand and asked his forgiveness. She considered and said, After this melted ice cream, we should drink coffee, strong and bitter coffee. You want to? Isaac replied, Yes, I do. Said Sonya, Your voice is weak, as if you lost your strength of will. I wonder if you have even a hint of will. In all your life, Isaac, you never asked me for anything. Isaac woke up and said, In all my life I never asked you for anything because it seemed to me that I don't lack anything with you.

Sonya raised her eyes and gazed at him, and he looked at her too. From the day he had met her, she hadn't been as beautiful as she was at that moment. He took her hand and asked her, Sonya, will you write to me? Said Sonya, I'll write to you, I'll write to you. Isaac closed his eyes. Sonya gazed at him and asked him, Why did you close your eyes, Isaac? He whispered, I am reading your letters. Said Sonya, With your eyes closed you read. He opened his eyes and said, In all my life I've never seen a letter from a girl. Said Sonya, In all your life you've never seen a letter from a girl? He closed his eyes again. Said Sonya, Letters that weren't written you read. Isaac shook his head and a halo beamed over his closed eyes.

The café owner brought two cups of coffee. Sonya laughed and said, I wanted to drink a strong and sharp beverage with you, and he brought us coffee with milk. If you want to taste real coffee, go to the Arabs, as Rabinovitch and I used to do. You're sad again? You want to leave me a slice of sadness before your trip. When does your train leave? Said Isaac, It's already time to get up. Well, said Sonya, get up and let's go, but with head held high and body erect. Yes, yes, said Isaac, with head held high and body erect. Said Sonya, You're repeating my words. Yes, yes, said Isaac. Sonya laughed and said, Stop your yesyessing and give me your hand. She took his hand and lifted him out of his chair. She quickly paid their check. She took a chocolate bar and went into the German bakeshop, took some baked goods and gave them to Isaac for the road. She linked her arm in his and went with him. He shortened his steps to lengthen the way. But the way was short. In only a little while, they came to the railroad station.

The train was delayed. Everyone who came and was afraid he was too late started grumbling about the Turks who don't know their schedules, they write on the board that at such and such hours the train arrives in Jaffa, and in the end it doesn't arrive. Isaac didn't complain or grumble. On the contrary, it's nice that the train is late, may it not come at all. He started imagining that he returned with Sonya to the city and rented himself a room in the German colony like Rabinovitch's room, and there. . . Isaac hadn't finished all his thoughts when the rumble of the train was heard rattling in. Isaac boarded the train and pushed into a car as Sonya waved her hand-kerchief at him and called out goodbye goodbye goodbye.

3 |

The train jolted and moved. Those who had taken a seat sat as if they were afraid the seat would be taken out from under them. Those who didn't find a seat wandered around with expressions of rage and expressions of pleading. When all the passengers found themselves a seat and arranged their belongings, they started introducing one another and started talking, about Hakham Bashi, about whom a quarrel was still going on, and about the other kinds of quarrels that were increasing. Finally, they dropped general issues and talked about their own issues, finally they talked about the committee of all communities and the Distribution of charity, which involves both matters of the community and matters of the individual.

Isaac sat in a seat somewhere. Sometimes it seemed to him that he was still walking next to Sonya and sometimes it seemed to him that he was wandering and didn't know why he was wandering or why he was going. He raised his head and looked around. All the people were strangers to him, and even he was like a stranger to himself. He recalled the day when he accompanied his friend Rabinovitch and compared Rabinovitch's leaving with his own. How did it happen, Yedidya Rabinovitch traveled Outside the Land and he accompanied him and found Sonya. As he was comparing and thinking, he took out the chocolate Sonya had given him and broke off a piece. He saw a child looking at him and gave him the piece. The child's father jumped up, snatched it out of the child's hand, threw it out the window, and scolded the child's mother, shouting, Cow, where are your eyes, don't you see what he's giving the child? Isaac's neighbors sensed the insult and wanted to get him away from that foolish Hasid who didn't know that Chikilld is kosher. As they talked, Isaac asked them about lodgings. They began discussing which lodging is good, Tallisman's or Rabinovitch's. And if it's Rabinovitch's, is it Rabinovitch from Warsaw or Rabinovitch from Grodno? And since they mentioned the two Rabinovitches, they started talking about them, that if one of them moves, his competitor immediately rents himself a house across the way for his own hotel.

And when they mentioned the hotel, they mentioned the early days when there wasn't a hotel in all Jerusalem. Some mentioned it as a defect, some mentioned it in praise, for since Jews were fond of the commandment to offer hospitality, it didn't occur to a Jew to make a living out of it, but anyone who saw a guest, rich or poor, would bring him into his home and feed him and serve him beverages and offer him a bed and take care of him, for free, better than all hotel owners take care of their guests, for even a wink of their eye is for money.

Why did they mention Rabinovitch here, Isaac asked himself. And if chocolate is kosher, why did that Hasid throw it away? They're advising me to stay at Rabinovitch's, and so I'll stay at Rabinovitch's. Isaac raised his eyes to ask which Rabinovitch they advised him to go to. A man noticed him and gestured to him, as he would gesture to his comrade to listen to what people are saying.

The passengers sat and recalled the early days and all the good qualities the Children of Israel could boast of. On the train there was a scholar, one of the great scholars of Jerusalem. He said to his comrades, I hear that you're talking about hotels. Well, then, I shall tell you what happened to me on that subject. Once I went to collect money for the Etz Hayim Yeshiva fund and came to Rishon Le-Tsion. My comrade, Rabbi Hayim Dov, found me and said to me, What are you doing here? I told him. And you, what are you doing here? He told me, I was appointed ritual slaughterer here. I asked him, How is your livelihood? He told me, Thank God, I get a little livelihood from my craft, and what it doesn't give me is given by another livelihood. What? He said to me, I opened a kind of guest hostel they call a hotel, and I ask you to stay with me. You know that my house, Bless God, is absolutely strictly kosher. He immediately picked up my belongings and brought me to his house and set before me a table filled with all kinds of delicacies and offered me a clean bed and took such good care of me. Three days later when it came time to go, I wanted to pay him. He smiled at me and said, What's that, am I a hotelkeeper to take money? I knew you needed lodgings and so I gave you lodgings.

Isaac sat and rubbed the little finger of his left hand with the index finger of his right hand. Well, thought Isaac to himself, well, I'm going to Jerusalem. At any rate, I have to admit that Sonya treated me nicely, and even gave me food for the trip. But if she hadn't given me chocolate, I wouldn't have been shamed. And so in an hour I'll come to Jerusalem because I am riding on a train to Jerusalem, and that's something I know even though I never studied logic.

The train jerked slowly as it was wont to do. It made a short stop here and a short stop there until at sundown it arrived in Jerusalem. Everyone took his belongings and leaped over his companion and didn't see him. Isaac remained alone in the railroad station and didn't know where to go, like most people who come to a new place. A carter came and took his belongings. Isaac trudged along behind him and got into the cart.

BOOK TW *Jerusalem*

CHAPTER ONE

Outskirts of the City

1 |

The cart is traveling between cliffs and rocks, hills and peaks. Some wear faces of wrath, some of menace, and all of them erupt like little volcanoes rolling down onto the crushed earth at their feet, and the crushed earth writhes like a snake twining around the cart and twisting its chains around it. Before the earth can swallow it up, the horses are pulling the cart out and the earth is dropping off in chunks and clods, limb after limb.

The carter looked back. He saw a group of people walking up the hills, groaning from the hardships of the road. He slowed his horses, held up a few fingers, and said, For so many pennies I'll take you to the city. But those misers were more fond of money than of their bodies, they passed up the ride and chose to go by foot. The carter growled at himself for wanting to help those ingrates who, for three or four cents fare, would linger on the road and would miss the evening prayers. He waved his whip and cracked it in the air. The horses picked up their feet and raised dust until they were covered with it and so was everyone walking on two legs with his belongings in his hands. The cart went on again, ascended mountains, descended to valleys.

A wind came and started blowing. It shook the dust and flapped at the rocks. The air began to change, and a still small voice was heard like the voice of wailing in the mountains. Suddenly a sad stillness enveloped Isaac's heart, as if they came to bring him tidings and he didn't know if those tidings were for good or for bad. And because the measure of goodness is greater than the measure of calamity, he looked forward to the good; and because his heart was slack, he feared that it wasn't good. The carter turned the horses and led them gently, and he whispered a melody of prayer.

Isaac looked before him and his heart began pounding, as a man's heart pounds when he approaches the place of his desire. And because he was somewhat consoled by the voice of the old man sitting and singing melodies of prayer, he removed the gloom from his heart. Before him, the wall of Jerusalem suddenly appeared, woven into a red fire, plaited with gold, surrounded by gray clouds blended with blue clouds, which incise and engrave it with shapes of spun gold, choice silver, burnished brass, and purple tin. Isaac rose up and wanted to say something. But his tongue was hushed in his mouth as in a mute song. He sat down as if carried away by a sitting dance.

The carter asked Isaac, Where do you want me to take you? Isaac pointed toward the wall of Jerusalem. Said the carter, The Old City you want? Isaac shook himself and said, Take me to Rabinovitch's inn. Said the carter, You point to the wall but you want to go outside the wall. Which Rabinovitch do you want? The one from Grodno or the one from Warsaw? Said Isaac, Which one do you advise me to go to? Said the carter, If it's my advice you're asking, don't go to either one of them, but go to Shoel Hershel Tefillinski. Said Isaac, Well, then, take me to Tefillinski. Said the carter, You changed your mind, young man? Didn't you first want me to take you to Rabinovitch? Which Rabinovitch do you want? Said Isaac, I forgot which one they told me. Take me to Tefillinski.

2 |

Tefillinski's hotel stands on a steep hill, half of it is hewn in the rock and half seems steeped in a dungheap. You ascend to the rock side on crooked steps and come to a hall three times longer than it is wide and that has rooms on both sides, like the houses of rich Arabs who marry many wives and make a section for every wife. How many years and how many cycles and how many jubilees has this place stood within the desert of Jerusalem entangled with the fearsome rocks and stumbling blocks and hurdles, and putting forth thorns and briars, and no one paid any heed to it. When the Jews started building themselves houses, the Arab who owned those grounds went and built himself a house in the middle of his field and lived joyfully with his wives and concubines. Until the envoys of the Angel of Death came, who grow entwined in every person against his own good, especially in old men in the hour of their enjoyment. And when he saw that there was no wisdom nor understanding nor counsel against the Angel of Death, he took his wives and his concubines and returned to the home of his forefathers inside the walls of the Old City, to give back his soul in the place where he had received it. When he was dead, his sons came and rented the house to Jews and Shoel Hirshl Tefillinski came and rented it and made it an inn.

Shoel Hirshl is an innkeeper who knows how to treat guests, for he was trained from birth for this metier. In Heder, and afterward in Yeshiva, when tourists came to see the institutions of learning, and the students pretended they didn't see them and swayed over their books so the tourists would see that they were diligently studying Torah, he clung to the guests and told them things they liked to hear. He did the same at the Western Wall and every place tourists come. When he grew up and got married, he put the dowry in Yeshiva bonds. But a curse befell the bonds and he was left without a cent. He accepted God's judgment and didn't quarrel with the treasurers of the Yeshiva, but on the contrary he defended them, and silenced his comrades who were in the same predicament, saying it was out of love of Torah that the treasurers did what they did, that they wanted to increase the money of the Yeshiva students so they would study Torah in wealth. And if they erred and lost all the money, it was proper to grieve for them and not to cause them grief. Later on, he went to the treasurers of the Yeshiva to consult with them about an inn he wanted to establish. They encouraged him and gave him an apartment of a Society. He expanded the place but the place wasn't enough for him. Then he went and rented that Arab's house and made himself a big inn.

Shoel Hirshl walks around among his rooms with a smooth charm on his lips, not a charm to deceive folks, but one that comes from a happy mind and generous eyes. He tries to help every single guest, both for his good and his pleasure, either with a sharp rumor or with a wise saying from the Torah. He shares a hot drink with this one and a cold drink with that one, with this one a drop of brandy, with that one a pipe, and he behaves like one of the guests, whether he likes them or not, just so they like him. And his wife helps him in her own way. She stands in the kitchen between four kerosene Primus stoves and does the cooking. And a little orphan girl helps her, brings up water from the cistern and coal from the cellar, peels vegetables and plucks chickens, washes the floor and lights the stove with the big kettle for the tea drinkers, and does all the other things that have to be done in an inn, for her forefathers, who came to settle in the lands of the living, died before their time and left her in the hotel and didn't leave her anything but the mercy of Heaven. Shoel Hirshl added his mercy to the mercy of the Holy-One-Blessed-Be-He and gave her lodging in his house until Heaven would have mercy on her and she wouldn't need the mercy of folks, whose mercy is greater for themselves than for their fellow men. And since she is small and can't do everything an inn needs, Shoel Hirshl brought Manoah Shtapaneshti, who shortened his name and calls himself Noah, to help her a little in the inn.

Noah, that is Manoah, was born in a ship on the way to the Land of Israel, when his father and mother ascended with some Romanian refugees who had bought themselves a field in the Land of Israel, where Zikhron Ya'akov was later built. While they were still on the ship on the high seas, it was decreed that Romanian exiles were not allowed to set foot in the Land. They wandered around the sea for a month, two months, three months. Whenever they came ashore, they were returned to the ship, and when they returned to the ship, they were returned to shore. They wandered from one port to another and were not allowed to land. At last, with bribes and pleas and interventions and supplications and temptations, they were allowed to enter the Land. They ascended to their soil, an earth filled with boulders and rocks and cliffs with no paths and no roads, far away from any settlement. They were robbed by robbers and slandered by slanderers and everything they had left was taken and they were left with nothing but the bones in their skin. They sat among the mountains with no food and no livelihood. Things reached such a pass that on the eve of Shavuoth, the holiday of the giving of the

Torah, they were forced to pawn a Torah scroll. And if not for Lord Oliphant who lived in Haifa in those days and rushed to their aid, they would have been wiped out of the world by hunger and the diseases of starvation. Rothschild heard of it and sent Elijah Sheid to them. Sheid built them several small houses, made some plans, and went on his way. At that time, the chairman of the committee in whose name the property had been bought met his death. So Turkey descended on their property, since he died without heirs, and according to Turkish law, the property of anyone who dies without heirs falls to the government. Finally, with bribes and pleas and interventions and supplications and temptations, the government gave up the inheritance and their property remained in the hands of its owners. In those days, Rothschild made a tour of the Land and came to pay them a visit. He saw that the place was beautiful and he was taken with it. And he named it after his father Jacob, Zikhron Ya'akov, and built spacious stone houses and drew water through pipes to every house and planted vineyards and fruit trees of all kinds and carved out a winepress for them and made roads and streets and hung lanterns in them, and appointed a Rabbi and a ritual slaughterer and a Cantor and a chorus of singers and a doctor and a pharmacist and a medic and a hospital and a pharmacy and a school and a warehouse for merchandise. And so the fearsome rocks turned into a settled city that looked like one of the handsome cities of Europe. Anyone who was blessed to endure the bad years was blessed with the good years. The fathers of Manoah weren't blessed and died in the bad years.

Manoah was left an orphan, lost both his father and his mother. He wallowed on the dungheaps of Zikhron Ya'akov like all other abandoned youngsters, street-sweepings, suffering from hunger. Serving the muledrivers and carters and tending the horses and donkeys, for a wage of leftover food and wornout shoes and torn trousers. Reb Haim Dov took pity on him and brought him to Jerusalem to the Diskin Orphanage. There he spent as much time as he did and didn't see a sign of blessing. There was a Baghdadi woman serving at the Grodno Rabinovitch's inn, who had been slandered that she had curried favor with a Samaritan in order to marry him. Her whole family joined against her and married her off to Manoah.

They made him a garment and bought him a tarboosh and Manoah became his wife's helper in the inn where she worked. That woman was not content with her husband, for she was mighty and irascible, and he was skin and bones, modest and miserable. She grieved and vexed him and sometimes raised her hand to strike him. Manoah, who was accustomed to suffering, neither protested nor complained. Thus a year went by and the world thought the match had succeeded. But that woman didn't think so. She went to a fortune teller who cast her lot and it turned out that she was to ride on a sea camel and her husband was to eat thorns. And it seems that the fortune teller hit on the truth. For within a month she sailed in a ship to Beirut, and the Arabs call a ship a sea camel, and Manoah ate thorns, for before she ran away and left him without a divorce, his wife borrowed money from the innkeeper and Manoah had to work off his wife's debt. Shoel Hirshl heard about it and made a deal with Manoah's boss, the Grodno Rabinovitch, and he took Manoah and brought him to his place. And he shortened his name, for it was enough for that skinny Manoah to be called Noah.

Noah wore a squashed tarboosh and tattered clothes hung on his body and he dragged his feet in patched shoes and every three or four days he added a patch to them. From the prayer at dawn to the Shema at bedtime, he ran errands for Shoel Hirshl and errands for the guests, and did all the jobs nobody else could do. And sometimes he linked the Shema at bedtime to the prayer at dawn, for he didn't have enough time to sleep. Because of that his mind is confused and he says things a sensible person doesn't say. Says Noah to Shoel Hirshl, I'm worried about you, Reb Shoel Hirshl, I'm worried about you. Says Shoel Hirshl, Fool, what are you worried about me? Says Noah to Shoel Hirshl, I'm worried that you'll go to hell. Says Shoel Hirshl, Why? Says Noah, Because there is no mercy in your heart for me and you work me harshly, and up above there in Heaven they see, they see everything you do to me, and they've got a Jewish heart and they're full of mercy for a man from Israel. Shoel Hirshl replies, Go to your work and don't be a fool. Says Noah, I'm going to my work, I'm going to my work, if I don't work, you'll throw me out into the street. But I have to tell you, Reb Shoel Hirshl, I'm afraid for you, I'm afraid for you. Says Shoel Hirshl, You already told me. Says Noah, And what results? Eh? Shoel Hirshl replies, What results is that you are a fool. Said Noah, A fool I am, a fool I am, at any rate, a Jew should have a little mercy in his heart for a fellow Jew. Shoel Hirshl laughs and says, It's forbidden to have mercy for a fool. Says Noah, I know that Reb Shoel Hirshl is a learned man, but there in Heaven there are greater learned men than him, and maybe they don't teach that. Says Shoel Hirshl, What don't they teach? Says Noah, That it's forbidden to have mercy on a fellow Jew. Says Shoel Hirshl, If they had mercy on the children of Israel, they wouldn't have imposed a fool like you on me. Go to your work, Noah. Noah returned to his work, pondering to himself, How many years are a man's life, seventy years. And a weakling like me certainly won't live long, and is not required to live long, and when I die those in Heaven will have mercy on me. In this world they say it's forbidden to have mercy on a fool, and in the next world they say, on the contrary, it's a Commandment to have mercy, and they have mercy on me.

3 |

When Isaac entered the hotel, the hotel owner came and wished him good day and spoke with him as if he had known him from the day he was born. He asked him all kinds of things, sometimes in a respectful tone and sometimes in a contemptuous tone, depending on what Shoel Hirshl's heart required at that time and depending on the look on Isaac's face. And meanwhile, he studied him to figure out what kind of a person he was, for when fellows like him ascend to Jerusalem, they usually stay with their comrades. And if they don't have comrades, they go to the Turkish bathhouse and spend all night there, and the next day they go and rent themselves half a room or a third of a room. Isaac, who didn't have a comrade in Jerusalem and didn't know about that custom of the seminarians and the Bezalel students, needed an inn, and since the carter brought him to Tefillinski, he came to Tefillinski.

After Isaac took his bags to his room, he ordered dinner. They brought him a thin slice of bread and eggs cooked in sesame oil. He wanted to change that taste with the pastry that Sonya had given him for the road. He remembered all that had happened on the train with the chocolate, and he left the pastry and didn't eat it. He ordered a cup of tea. He drank and enjoyed it. And in truth, the hot drinks in Jerusalem are finer than all the hot drinks in the world for they are made with rainwater and there is nothing finer for tea than rainwater.

When he had eaten and drunk, he went into his room and got into his bed. Satisfaction he did not find from his bed. Either because of himself or because of his roommates. And he began thinking about what was in store for him in Jerusalem. And because he was in low spirits, melancholy images rose in his mind. He turned over and started thinking of everything that had happened to him with Sonya. Then his thoughts began speaking aloud. And his roommates thought he wasn't in his right mind. Isaac surely was in his right mind, but the earlier troubles that had oppressed him struggled to come out, to make room for the later troubles.

CHAPTER TWO

An Apartment in Jerusalem

1 |

After he ate breakfast, he wrote in his notebook a few places they had told him at the inn, and he went out to find himself an apartment. He went to several neighborhoods and asked in several houses if there was a room to rent. Some were nice to him, but the room was not nice; or the room was nice to him but the landlord was not nice; or they didn't know what he was talking about, for there are landlords who dwell in their homes and don't know that there are homeless people with nowhere to live. So he wandered from place to place and from courtyard to courtyard until he had gone through most of the day and hadn't found himself a room. He was about to return to his inn, for by now he was weary of running around and his mind was confused from the many rooms he had seen and the many people, and he resolved to seek tomorrow what he hadn't found today. On the way he came upon the Russian Compound. He saw that the place was spacious and handsome, and peace and quiet dwell there and its walls separate it from the noise of the city and a good wind blows there, so his soul was refreshed and he sat down to rest.

Old people of the generation, who are fond of every stone and every corner of Jerusalem, tell that a son of Israel was about to buy that place, but couldn't come to an agreement with the owner of the field about the width of the road. The buyer claimed that there had to be six cubits so that two camels loaded with sacks coming toward one another could pass; and the seller said that all he needed was the width of one loaded camel, which was three cubits. Neither of them yielded and the lot and three lots adjoining it were sold to the Russians. And the hearts of all the other Children of Israel in that generation were opressed within the Old City walls, in the alleys of the Arabs, without sunshine or a green garden. And they ruined their eyes without light and grieved their soul without air to breathe, and they are reconciled to their suffering and console themselves with the end of days, for in the future the Land of Israel will return to the Children of Israel, and every Israelite will sit in his house, built and perfected like a palace fit for a king. And if a son of Israel had a little money he rented himself a house from a Gentile and bought himself the right of possession. How? He would go to the sages of the city and they would give him a document of possession for the house and the courtyard. In his courtyard, he rents out a corner of an apartment here and a corner of a room there, and takes rent at the standard rate in Jerusalem. And anyone who would come to expropriate his right of possession will be persecuted, for the rate for apartments has already gone up because the Gentiles desired to devour Israel voraciously, and there are not many houses in the city, and those with the right of possession see themselves as landlords by virtue of the agreement they made with the sages and the city elders of Jerusalem, with the power vested in them by the lords and deputies, the officials of Istanbul.

2 |

And what did the Gentiles do? They bought houses and courtyards and lands and built houses and gave every single person of their Society, rich or poor, an apartment for free, except for the houses they built for pilgrims, which stand empty all year long. And they go on and buy more lands in the city and outside the city. Once the Armenian church wanted to buy lands and didn't have any money. They got a loan of forty thousand gold Lira from the government treasury. When the time came to pay, the Armenian bishop went to Istanbul and reached an agreement with the authorities that they would collect from every male one penny a year more on his taxes. Within three or four years, they had paid off the debt. The Armenians bought the southwestern part of the Old City, along with fields and villages outside the city, and from the money of the apartments and stores that they rent to the Children of Israel, they bought more land and built houses and stores. And the Greeks bought the north-western part, along with fields and villages outside the city, and from the money of the apartments and stores that they rented to those who are not members of their Society, they bought more land and built more houses and stores until they surrounded all Jerusalem. And the Russians bought that lot and built their church and houses for their priests and their monks and their pilgrims who come every year from Russia to kiss the dust of the tomb of their Messiah.

And the Children of Israel were still dwelling between the tight walls and were pressed in small courtyards they rented from the Arabs, and every single courtyard was filled up with several stories, and every single story was filled up with many apartments, and not every house has windows, but some houses get their light through a little opening in the ceiling and some houses get their light through a hole in the wall above the lintel or through an opening to the air of the courtyard where there is a cistern and where the women do their laundry, and below in the lower courtyard are outhouses that are cleaned only once every few years. And a house could still be bought for a sack of rice, but in all those times only a rare person bought a house for himself. And when new immigrants came they didn't find a place to lay their head and slept in the street until they found shelter in an Arab house that was still being built. Jerusalem began to contemplate a solution. Then the Lord planted in their heart the idea of going outside the Old City walls, to buy land and build houses. And it was a hard thing for the officers of the Societies to invest money in trees and stones, when they had to support the poor and the destitute. And anyone who didn't worry about the poor worried about himself, for all the roads outside the Old City walls were dangerous, for there was no settlement there aside from the Russian Compound, and when the gates of the Old City were locked at night, everyone outside the wall was unprotected. Those who were more fond of their body than of building Jerusalem remained where they were; those who were more fond of building Jerusalem than of their body went outside the walls and bought themselves land and built themselves seven houses, a house for each person, and they called their settlement Nahalat Shiv'ah, the Estate of the Seven, because there were seven of them. Those were the first seven houses outside the walls, except for the houses of Judah Tura and the houses of Moses Montefiore, which had been built about ten years earlier.

Those seven houses were neither elegant nor splendid, but they did have one advantage, that they expanded the border of Jerusalem and strengthened the Jewish settlement, for the people of Jerusalem weren't accustomed to leave the gate of the Old City and go outside, except during the week of Passover, when they circle the walls of the Old City. When Nahalat Shiv'ah was built, they began going out even on other days to ask how their brothers of Nahalat Shiv'ah were faring. And on the first day of the month when women don't do any work, they go out in groups wearing their Sabbath clothes. And their relatives and relatives of their relatives accompany them: they go out Jaffa Gate and pass by the Arab café, go up mountains and come down into valleys until they come to Nahalat Shiv'ah. And as they walk, they are stunned and amazed that even in the destruction, the air of Jerusalem revives the soul. One person says to his companion, If I could, I would have built me a house here. And his companion replies, Let us ask mercy that we live to see the day. Within seven or eight years they built Meah Shearim, bought a plot of land, and built a hundred houses for a hundred members. Others learned from them and did the same, and others followed their lead. Before long, Jerusalem was crowned with new Jewish houses.

3 |

Jerusalem sits there like an eagle bearing its young on its wings. There are separate neighborhoods for Ashkenazim and separate neighborhoods for Sephardim, and there are some where Ashkenazim and Sephardim dwell together. There are some whose residents are Yemenites or Georgians or Mughrabites or Persians, and there are some where several commuities dwell together. There are some which have unfortunately gone out of the hands of the Jews, and there are some whose name is forgotten because they were so small. And you don't have one single neighborhood that doesn't have a synagogue, and there are some that put up several synagogues and study houses and religious schools and Yeshivas and everything a son of Israel needs for his body and his soul. When Jerusalem expanded, the importance of the right of possession disappeared and all the money invested in it went for nought. But the houses that were built still exist and they too are expanding, some add a room and some build an attic, some add two rooms and some add two stories, and no longer does a man say, The place is too strait for me to stay in Jerusalem.

Let's go back to Isaac. As he sat, his weariness left. He walked down to Nahalat Shiv'ah. He saw a big house, taller than all the other houses. He said to himself, This house is full of apartments, maybe there's a room here for me. I'll go and ask. He went in and found a vacant room. So he stayed there and paid his rent.

Isaac Buys Himself a Bed

1 |

That house where Isaac found himself an apartment was called the house of the convert, after the owner who changed his religion. That convert had a lot of houses, and this was one of them. Every single house he had inherited from his English wife, who immigrated with her daughter from London to dwell in Jerusalem in the city of their Messiah. He was a tall and corpulent man and was something of a writer. Even though he claimed that he himself believed in poly- theism, he didn't believe that there was even one person in Israel who would believe that. And if a Jew came to him to convert, he would ask him why he wanted to change his religion. If the Jew told him he was poor and had no means of support, he would give him money and add travel expenses for him to go to London and con- vert again and get double the money. But if the Jew told him that he wanted to change his religion out of conviction, he gave him a good scolding and told him to get out and tell it to the Gentiles, I don't believe you. That's what he used to tell us to endear himself to us, and he told the Gentiles something else to endear himself to them. Since he had despaired of finding favor in the eyes of God, he wanted to find favor in the eyes of man. But anyone from whom the Omnipotent does not take pleasure, people do not take pleasure. The Children of Israel because he denied his people and his God, and the Christians because they didn't believe in his loyalty. Since pious people refrain from dwelling in the house of a convert, he had to rent apartments cheaply and could not insist that his tenants pay him a year's rent when they moved in, as was the custom in Jerusalem.

The whole house is settled and inhabited. Below are shops and warehouses and cellars, and above them are apartments opening onto the courtyard, with metal balconies surrounding them in the shape of a closed square. Families and single men and women lived there. Some of them are professionals and some of them have no particular craft, but are willing to do anything. Some of them are artists and writers and some of them are close to art and literature. And among them live hatmakers and seamstresses whose hands work and whose hearts turn to that je-ne-sais-quoi. Isaac got a room in the apartment of a teacher who lived with his wife and sons and daughters, as well as his wife's sister's daughter, but we're not concerned with her because he guards her and keeps everyone away from her but himself. And Isaac's room has its own private entrance. A private entrance has advantages and disadvantages. It's an advantage that the tenant isn't dependent on the opinions of others, he comes in when he comes in and goes out when he goes out, and doesn't have anything to do with his neighbors. It's a disadvantage that, since he doesn't have anything to do with his neighbors, he grows lonely, especially if he's not an artist or a writer. Isaac was a simple housepainter and the neighbors showed no inclination to get to know him, especially since he was a Galician and they were Russians. And he wasn't eager to get close to them either. That room, like all rented rooms in Jerusalem, was empty, there was nothing in it but four walls, a ceiling, a floor, a door, and a window. Since Isaac hadn't brought anything with him from Jaffa except for his bedclothes and his small utensils, he had to buy himself a bed, the first necessity of a room. And so he went to the city to buy himself a bed.

The day burned like an oven and the sun inflamed the whole world and the whole world was yellow and dry like the air that stands still between heaven and earth, and like the dust that sticks to a person's body and covers his eyes and fills his ears so much that he doesn't see and doesn't hear anything but a kind of mute humming that parches the soul and drowns him in boredom. With every single step, his strength wanes and his bones dry out and his tongue is dry as dust. Only his feet still trudge on. And so he trudged along behind his feet, until they brought him to Meah Shearim.

2 |

As a city within a city, Meah Shearim dwells within Jerusalem. It has no palaces or castles, no gardens or citrus groves, and none of the other things that expand the mind. But, let it be remembered to Meah Shearim's favor that if not for Meah Shearim, we would be pressed and oppressed between the Old City walls and wouldn't find a house to live in for ourselves and our children. When Jerusalem saw that the Israelites were coming from all lands and that the Ishmaelites were raising rents from year to year, a hundred distinguished citizens of Jerusalem got together and made an organization to build themselves houses outside the walls. They bought a big, broad valley of thirty thousand cubits, and dug cisterns and built themselves houses, and erected synagogues and study houses, Heders and Yeshivas, a bathhouse and shops, everything a Jew needs for his body and his soul. In the beginning they wanted to sow wheat and plant citrons for an Esrog there so a person could harvest wheat from his own field for Matzo and take his own Esrog, but the holiness of Jerusalem is too holy and you don't plant gardens and citrus groves in it, and you don't sow or plant because of the stench, for sowed land is loaded with dung, and dung stinks. So they changed their mind and didn't sow and didn't plant.

Forlorn and solitary stood Meah Shearim at first within the desert of Jerusalem. Between Jaffa Gate and Meah Shearim, there wasn't a single house, except for the seven houses in Nahalat Shiv'ah and the houses in the Russian Compound. Ten houses were built there in Meah Shearim at first, a room and a corridor for every family. And every night a candle was lit in every house for fear of robbers and thieves, and one of the men of the house gets up every night and studies Torah, for Torah defends and saves. It wasn't many years before the rest of the members came and built themselves houses. Meah Shearim filled up. And the area around it was also built, and the neighborhood seemed to be swallowed up within Jerusalem, but it stood by itself and didn't blend with the city's neighborhoods. And it still stands as a city within a city.

A yellow sadness settled over the neighborhood that day, and even the sound of the Torah, which hums every day, was weak and weary that day. And no wind blew in the narrow streets, the width of one loaded camel, and every house huddled against its neighbor, for when they built Meah Shearim, they didn't know what measure to allocate to the streets, they remembered the Mishnah Baba Qamma, A camel which was carrying flax and passed by in the public way, and they went and hired a camel and loaded it with flax and measured how much room it took. And the houses they built row upon row, each house attached to the next, to gain two half walls, on the right and on the left. And anyone who was enriched by the Omnipotent added an attic years later, or a balcony for the holiday of Sukkoth.

3 |

Isaac entered the gate across from Nathan's Houses. Iron pylons were fixed in the gate to prevent carts from coming in and enclosed the yard in a kind of cage. Two rows of shops are set there within the wall, one row across from the other, and the shopkeepers sit there in front of their shutters, some sit with legs folded beneath them as the Sephardim sit, some sit bent over like the Ashkenazim. And in front of every shop, below on the ground, in the shade of the shutter, sits a lame man or a blind man, an invalid with missing limbs or a man covered with sores, and in front of him sits a Charity box, and flies and mosquitoes dance between their eyes and the sun fries their wounds and makes the Charity box glow. Isaac, who hadn't seen a pauper stretch out his hand all the days he was in Jaffa, looked upon them in amazement. When he realized what they wanted, he quickly gave this one a penny and that one a penny, until he gave something to all of them.

Isaac drags his feet between the houses and the shops. The shops are wide open and the eyes of the shopkeepers are closed shut as if they want a bit of sleep. If not for the flies and mosquitoes, they would have laid their heads on their hands and dozed off. Across from the houses and shops old women peddlers sit in front of their delapidated shutters and their drooping lips move as if they are praying or chewing. As Isaac walks, he comes upon a dog. The dog looked at the human creature who had bumped into him and who didn't kick him, and Isaac looked at the dog he came upon and who didn't bark at him. After a while, Isaac soon came to a shop of old furniture and stood still.

The shopkeeper glanced at him and asked him something. Isaac was silent and didn't reply. Said the shopkeeper, I thought you were a Sephardi and I addressed you in the Spanish tongue. You want to buy something? He immediately offered him various wares, a samovar for tea and a narghila for smoking and Bukharan garments and a music box and a wedding ring. When he heard that he wanted a bed, he jumped up and said, An iron bed I bought today from a German teacher, a Gentile, and here it is right in front of you. The shopkeeper started praising the bed for its springs and for its mattress and for the gilded knob at the head shaped like a bird. And that bird, my friend, has the advantage that you don't need to feed it. When the shopkeeper saw that he still hesitated, he told him, I'll tell you something that will go to your heart. You see that bed, no matter how much you rummage around in it you won't find a bedbug in it, because it belonged to a Gentile, and the heathens are meticulous about cleanliness, as it says in the Talmud.

Isaac asked the shopkeeper, How much are you selling it for? The shopkeeper wanted to tell him, but he decided not to rush and started praising the bed and praising the Germans, for whatever comes from their hands is made well, unlike our brothers the Children of Israel, quite to the contrary, for if they make a piece of furniture — tomorrow you can throw it in the garbage, because every day we are waiting for the coming of the Messiah so why should we worry about tomorrow. But just as the products of the Germans are strong, so they themselves are firm and impudent. If you heard, my friend, how much that German asked for that bed, you'd have spat in his face. But I'm not asking you for even half. After all, you're a Jew, even though your sidelocks are cut and your beard is shaved, probably with some salve, for as the Talmud says, a man will not abandon what is permitted and do what is forbidden. I say in truth, a beard is fitting for a son of Israel and even, quite the contrary, for a Gentile. With my own eyes, I saw an image of the King of Prussia, may I live to see the King Messiah, and his beard is full. So, my friend, how much will you give me for that bed? Pay two Bishliks and it's yours. If you don't pay two, pay a Bishlik and a half. If not a Bishlik and a half—one Bishlik. Or to be reasonable in every regard, half a Bishlik. By your life, I'm ashamed of your words. You look like a modern person and you haggle like a charity case. Isaac understood his words and added more money. He called a porter to take his bed. The porter untied his ropes, loaded the bed on his shoulders, and tied it. And even though he had been fasting for two days, yesterday a voluntary fast and today a fast on account of a bad dream, nevertheless he walked quickly and not carelessly, for by now his external limbs were accustomed not to be dependent on the internal organs, for the ones inside were created for eating and drinking, while the ones outside were created for work and carrying. And furthermore, he was glad, for that night, he had been shown a bed in a dream and he had worried lest the time had come for him to die, and now that he had chanced upon this bed, he interpreted his dream favorably, for this was the bed Heaven meant. He walked behind Isaac until they came to his room and they put up the bed between the door and the window. Isaac paid him his fee and stretched out on his bed.

4 |

The silence of a heat wave lay upon the house and the courtyard. The warehouses and the shops, the merchandise and its owners were dozing as they do on the day of a heat wave. Isaac felt good that he had rented himself a room of his own without roommates and had bought himself a big bed. He was so tired that he went without eating, even though he hadn't eaten since morning and was hungry. It wasn't long before he jumped out of bed as if he were stung by a scorpion. A scorpion hadn't stung him, as we learn in the Talmud, a snake and a scorpion never bit anybody in Jerusalem, but a host of bedbugs came out of the walls of the house to greet their brothers in the bed, and on their way, they came upon Isaac. Even before that and during that came mosquitoes and little flies, the kind that were called little flies before the war, and after the war people started calling them sand flies. As he was busy with them, he heard the sound of a mouse. The cakes Sonya had given Isaac called forth a mouse.

In the meantime, the courtyard woke up, as courtyards do in Jerusalem on hot days when they wake up in the evening. Isaac lit a candle and examined his bed. While the candle was in his hand, a mosquito stung him. He threw the candle down and licked his hand. A mosquito came and stung his face. And between this and that, the sand flies stung him. He went back to his bed, fortified a place for himself, and fought his foes. But they were many and he was one. He clasped his hands and curled up to reduce their domain.

In the meantime, the neighbors finished eating their dinner, and from every apartment and every room they came out to their balconies for a breath of wind and told one another about the heat wave and the dust, until the first watch of the night ended. Two or three times, Isaac jumped out of his bed and went out to the balcony and stood there, for he hadn't yet bought himself a chair. Finally his legs collapsed and he returned to his bed, sleep fell upon him and he dozed off.

5 |

As he lay sleeping, a north wind blew and brought a good change to the air. And when he woke up, a clear and fine day was sparkling. The air was steeped with a fragrant moisture, and a wind wafted in the air like the smell of dew on flowers in the morning. Isaac forgot everything that had been done to him yesterday. It is a good quality they have in the Land of Israel that a good day makes you forget a bad day. Since he had gone to sleep without eating, he got up hungry. He stretched his bones and jumped out of bed, washed his face and hands and got dressed, and went down to the street to buy himself some food. The shops were already open and the day's work had begun with happy faces and grumpy faces, depending on a person's lot and the desire of his Creator. As he wanted to enter a shop, he saw a group of Georgians selling biscuits and cakes and wafers. As soon as he wanted to go to them, he saw a cook shop and went in.

Half of that cook shop is above ground and half is sunk in the ground, and a chimney rises above the door and smoke climbs from the chimney. You bend and go down and stand in the room whose length is equal to its width and its height is as tall as an aver-

age man. People sit there drinking tea and eating wafers. And anyone who has an extra penny orders himself a cup of cocoa or an egg
or a piece of herring or a vegetable meal, all depending on his pocket
and his belly.

Isaac ordered himself a cup of tea and two twin cakes, that
have more puff than dough and more absence than presence. Since
he ate and wasn't full, he ordered those things that fill a person's grat-
ification, bread and eggs and cucumbers and sundry things. When
he ate his fill, his mouth became light and he started talking with his
neighbors. Since they were people of Jerusalem, and on that day the
air of Jerusalem was fine, Isaac began with respect for the city and
praise of its air, which refreshes the soul and strengthens the body,
not like Jaffa that makes you sweat a lot and melts the bones in your
body. And since the people of Jerusalem are amiable and hospitable
people and their interlocutor was from Jaffa, they agreed with him a
bit and differed with him a bit, and even when they differed with him,
they deferred to his city. They said, Even though a person should
hear praise of his city, especially praise of Jerusalem, which is a Commandment, you can't dismiss Jaffa, for the sea is there and a person
washes off his sweat, not like Jerusalem where you drink cistern
water. And there are drought years when the cistern doesn't fill up
with water and you need to buy it from the water carriers and from
the water hoarders who make themseles a lot of cisterns and raise the
price of water according to how thirsty a person is, and sometimes a
poor man doesn't have a drop of water to wet his mouth. And sometimes the whole city is in that trouble, rich as well as poor, for there
are years when the skies are shut and the cisterns are emptied. And
once upon a time, no rain fell that year and on the night of the Seder,
they had to wash their hands in wine, and a miracle happened and
that night so much rain fell that some houses melted. One story led
to another and another story led to another, and everyone told something he had seen with his own eyes or heard from his father who
heard it from the elders of Jerusalem, and his comrade testified that
he had heard the very same thing.

Who knows how long Isaac would have sat there, except that
at that moment a tall, thin fellow came in, his head was leaning on

one shoulder and a small cap was on his head and an artist's palette was hanging on his arm and a sheet of a picture was in his hand. The smell of paint spread and Isaac remembered his craft. He went and sat down across from him and said, I see that you deal with paints, perhaps you know some of my fellow artisans, the housepainters in Jerusalem. The artist leaned his head from this side to the other and looked at him with one eye, like a person who looks at something that isn't worth wasting two eyes on, and said, I don't paint with paints, I draw with the Holy Spirit. And he ordered the owner to bring him two cups of tea, one for breakfast and one to pay the body that had stood with him on the Old City wall to draw a picture that our forefathers never pictured. Isaac bowed his head and left in shame.

What that painter didn't do, another painter did, for at that time Jerusalem was full of painters, who came from many places to study the art of painting with Professor Boris Schatz in Jerusalem, and as is the way of human beings, some are friendly to folks and others are not. The one Isaac first came upon was not friendly to folks, the one he found afterward was friendly to folks and Isaac was helped by him as we shall soon see.

CHAPTER FOUR

The Man We Alluded to at the End of the Previous Chapter

1 |

Near Isaac's apartment stands a group of houses. People who were content with little built themselves those houses, people who were content with even less came to dwell in their cellars. When Isaac left the restaurant, he saw the sign of Samson Bloykof the painter, whose name he had heard and whose pictures he had seen in several Hebrew and foreign almanacs, and his frames are found in the home of every Hebrew teacher in Jaffa and Jerusalem. Those frames are of olive wood in the shape of a Magen David inlaid with seashells, but the teachers of Jaffa who have a literary bent put the pictures of our writers and poets in them, the greatest one in the middle and his satellites around him, including pictures of themselves, for there isn't one single teacher in Jaffa who doesn't see himself as a writer, unlike the teachers of Jerusalem who see themselves as sages and who put pictures of our great sages including pictures of themselves in those frames. Bloykof was Isaac's fellow countryman, and now that he found himself standing before his house, he took heart and went inside.

Samson Bloykof was about thirty years old, suffered from a weak heart and weak lungs, and knew that his death was near, and so he worked diligently to accomplish in his life what he wouldn't accomplish after his death, for when a person is dead, he can't paint, and furthermore, at the moment when he is passing to the nether world, all his images return and pass before his eyes and are thousands and thousands of times sweeter and finer. And he wants to stretch out his hands and paint. And his hands reply, We are already delivered to the earth, for dust we are. And he wants to cry but the tears don't come, for his eyes are closed with shards. Bloykof, who knows all that and isn't a fool like the foolish artists, wants to work as long as he can, and wants to return to the world a little bit of what the world has given him, and if not really a little bit, then a little bit of a little bit. He no longer paints the pictures that made him popular in his generation, and he doesn't make frames for pictures, but paints what Heaven shows him. And even though he knows himself that he is the slightest of the slight and keeps neither Torah nor Commandments, he knows that Heaven is gracious to him and gives him strength to see and to paint, and the Omnipotent Creator of the World must have a special intention for future generations to know the splendor of Jerusalem, even in her destruction. And they will know that there was one Samson Bloykof who looked favorably upon her.

His round face is wreathed with a yellowish beard and his blue eyes smile from their sockets a smile that comes from satisfaction and a good heart. And Samson Bloykof really does have satisfaction and pleasure, for every single hour things that rejoice his heart appear before him. There are things he saw eye to eye and didn't pay heed to them, and now they come and stand before his mind's eye, and he sees that they are more beautiful than they were, and he knows how to draw them. Carpets of flowers that cover the valleys and hills in the month of Nissan, bluish mountain slopes in the east, a solitary plant in a field, a small reed burgeoning out of a rock, an old woman crying at the Western Wall, a porter lying in the shadow of a wall and sleeping the sleep of toilers, and a little bird dwelling in the beard of an old man sitting at the cistern in his courtyard and dozing off over his book — all those rise up in his mind's eye, and as they rise up before him, so they rise up on the canvas with exquisite colors he extracts from his tube of paint. Years ago, Bloykof ascended to Jerusalem with the first Bezalel students, he painted paintings and made frames for pictures which made him famous in the Land. Finally he made his own artists' house. And so that he wouldn't have to paint pictures for money, he made signs for shopkeepers. But there is no great demand for shop signs, and his income is few and far between, so he paints out of hunger and out of extreme yearnings. Sometimes hunger gets the upper hand and sometimes yearnings get the upper hand. But since an artist cannot conquer hunger, but he can conquer his yearnings, he removes his eyes from hunger and paints paintings. If his heart afflicts him because of his illness, he silences it and tells it, Are you better than the lungs? And if his lungs afflict him, he silences them and tells them, Are you better than the heart? And he goes back to his craft and does his work. And if hunger attacks him, he strikes his stomach and says, Are you more distinguished than I am? Even if I die of hunger, I don't say a word.

2 |

When Isaac knocked on the door, Bloykof flinched and shook, and he cursed and insulted him in his heart as we tend to do with anyone who comes to divert us from our work. But his anger quickly turned to pity and he greeted him nicely because man is created in the image of God, and because Bloykof was a good and hospitable man. When Isaac told him what country he came from, Bloykof welcomed him and clasped his hands very affectionately and didn't let go of them, as if they rolled up all Galicia and gave it to him, for Bloykof was inordinately fond of his homeland, and everyone who came from Galicia was like a greeting card sent from there.

All the time Bloykof had lived in Galicia, he was not attracted to its inhabitants; when he left there, he began to love them. And there were several reasons for that. And the entirety of all the reasons is that he sees himself in Jerusalem, among the Russians, as a herring in a cage, for those Russians, even though their heart is open and their hand is generous and their mind is determined and most are brave and responsible, they lack something we people of Galicia are given in abundance. And since Isaac Kumer is a son of Galicia, Bloykof was extremely happy to see him, and didn't budge from his affection until he sat him down in front of him and showed him some of his paintings. And that's not something Bloykof does with everyone, for not everyone is worthy of the artist's cares. Finally, he revealed some of his intentions to him and explained some of his paintings to him. Indeed, not every fine painting needs interpretation, but since most people see and don't know what they're seeing, the artist has to guide their heart. On the face of it, it's enough for the artist that he paints, and sometimes even if he doesn't know what he is painting, at any rate, he knows more than his interpreters, not to mention those who claim to be patrons of the arts. As he talked, he showed him a bunch of pictures that could be mistakenly attributed to him, but they were just the creations of various people who had nothing of their own, but who looked at his pictures and imitated their model. You wouldn't think that would preoccupy him, for everything that is not real doesn't catch the truth, and all that is real has its own truth and doesn't need to borrow from others, hence every imitation is essentially flawed, and there's no point bothering with what is flawed, but the critics attacked us, mentioning the names of the forgers along with his name. And if you say that among the things the imitators imitate, there are things that look like what I drew myself, I tell you that they don't look like mine, and if they do look like mine, what need is there for them, since mine already exist, and they can't deny that mine exist, for if mine didn't exist, how would they imitate them?

Samson Bloykof and Isaac Kumer sat down. Bloykof talks and Isaac listens. And Isaac doesn't understand everything Bloykof says, but every single thing that comes out of Bloykof's mouth caresses his heart and makes him forget his troubles a bit, and it seems to him that all his life he yearned for nothing but this hour, and it seems to Bloykof that everything he says was kept in his heart for this man. And isn't it a little puzzling, for Kumer is a simple housepainter and has nothing to do with art, but Bloykof is confident that if he talks with him, he is surely worth it. And so he goes on talking.

And so they sat, one talking and one listening, and they didn't hear the door open. And when the door opened, Mrs. Tosya Bloykof, Samson's wife, entered with two baskets in her hands, one with fruit and vegetables and one with other food. Samson jumped up to greet her and called out, Tosya, and drawled out the name Tosya as if she was suddenly revealed to him. He looked at her for a while with a bit of affection and a bit of criticism, the way he looked at his wife after she had been gone from him for some time. But he immediately shifted his critical eye away from her and looked at her with complete affection and tremendous love as he had done from the time he had first seen her. As he looked at her he turned his gaze to Isaac, and didn't rest there, but turned his face back to his wife and said, A guest has come to us. You may think just an ordinary guest, Tosya, so I tell you he's from our homeland, a son of Galicia. You may think just an ordinary son of Galicia, but I tell you that he understands art. You think he told me so, but no he didn't, but with the insight of an artist I recognized that he understands. Put down the baskets, Tosya, and say hello to our guest and be nice to him, for I tell you that he deserves a nice welcome. Just as he praised the guest to his wife, so he praised his wife to the guest, that if not for her, he would already be lying in the cemetery on the Mount of Olives. Not because she takes care of him, but because it's worth living when a man's got a wife like that with him. As she put down the baskets, Samson grabbed her two hands and embraced them and kissed them. Mrs. Bloykof looked at the guest with an embarrassed smile, and scolded her husband for not letting her say hello to their guest, and apologized to the guest for appearing before him in a housedress, for she hadn't yet had time to change her clothes because she had to hurry to the market before the hands of all the women in Jerusalem had groped the vegetables. And as she spoke she went and brought Isaac a cup of cocoa. Isaac, who had had breakfast and had eaten more than his fill, thanked the hostess for her kindness and said that he had just eaten and drunk and was still sated. Samson jumped up and said, Don't say I'm full, for I don't believe you, for never have I seen a full man in Jerusalem. Drink, my dear, drink, boy, the advantage of cocoa is that it's drink and food at the same time, it quenches your thirst and satisfies your hunger. In truth I say, of all the beverages in the world, I love brandy, but it doesn't love me because the doctors denounced me, and when I take a drop in my mouth, it vomits itself up with what remains of my lungs.

Mrs. Bloykof went to the corner where the kitchen was, for the whole apartment was one room with two beds, and the cradle of their only daughter who died two years before, and a long table where the painter painted his paintings, and other things a man and woman need. She came back and begged the guest to swear he wouldn't go until he had had lunch with them. She enumerated all the dishes she had made for that lunch, and looked at him fondly, as did the daughters of Israel of that generation who valued guests. Isaac felt her eyes and his heart felt good, but since he was full and since he wasn't used to sitting at the table of a man and wife, he was a bit embarrassed and apologized to her that he couldn't eat with them, since he had to go look for work. Said Bloykof, If it's because of work, you don't have to hurry, for there's nothing going on. First eat and then we'll go over the names of the painters in Jerusalem, maybe one of them will hire you, and may you make a little bit of a living. Oh, a living, a living, whoever invented you doesn't love folks, and whoever keeps you away from folks surely doesn't love folks. I often wanted to find a trick to get around making a living, but I'm busy with more important things than making a living and don't have time to get involved with tricks. And maybe it's good that my time isn't free for that, for if I found it, who would enjoy it? Of course, the scoundrels who use the power of others to imitate them. Thus not only art would be forged, but everything would be false. And what face, my dear boy, would our world have.

3 |

So Isaac remained at Bloykof's house until after lunch. In honor of the guest, the host left his work and talked with him about everything an artist is wont to tell and praised Isaac for leaving Jaffa and coming to dwell in Jerusalem, for you don't have a single hour in Jerusalem that doesn't have something of eternal life. But not every person attains it, for Jerusalem is revealed only to those who love her. Come, Isaac, and let us embrace one another that we have been blessed to dwell in Jerusalem. At first, when I compared Jerusalem to other cities, I found a great many disadvantages in it, at last my eyes were opened and I saw her. I saw her, my brother, I saw her. What can I tell you, my friend, can language tell even the slightest bit? Pray for me, my brother, for the Lord to give me life, and I will show you with the brush in my hand what my eyes see and my heart feels. I don't know if I believe in God, but I do know that He trusts me and He revealed to my eyes to see what not every eye sees. If I was allowed to paint, I would have painted thus. Who's here? Mrs. Bloykof again.

What did you want to say, Mrs. Bloykof? No, my dear, I don't want anything except rest, but rest I don't find, that woman is wont to disturb me. Sixty times a minute she comes and says, Shimsi, my sun, perhaps you want bird's milk, Shimsi, my sun, perhaps sky blue I shall spread beneath you. And perhaps she does it out of love, no she doesn't, she's afraid she'll be widowed and will have to wear black, and black doesn't become her. And here Samson grabbed his wife and kissed her mouth, and immediately wiped off her mouth because he suffered from all kinds of contagious diseases, and it would be too bad if she got sick, for she is a Galician, and the people of Galicia are good people, but there's a difference between eastern Galicia and western Galicia, for the people of the west are like Poles, and Poles are like Russians. And we know well what the Russians are. And here Bloykof laid his hand on Isaac's shoulder, closed his eyes, and said, I see that I am destined to die among the Russians, and I hired one of our own people from my hometown to say Kaddish after my death and study a chapter of Mishnah.

And said Bloykof, As you know me, I won't set foot in the holy places. I leave that to those who run from one holy place to another holy place. It's enough for me to be in Jerusalem. But there is one place in Jerusalem that I visit once a year on Shavuoth, and that's the tomb of King David, because King David is dearer to me than all the Jews in the world. A mighty king who was preoccupied all his life with wars with Goliath the Philistine and all the other wicked men, and even the Jews, on the contrary, certainly pestered him a lot, and nevertheless he took time to play on the harp and to make songs for all the miserable and depressed — how can I not love that king? And so, every year on Shavuoth, in the morning, I go to his tomb. And when I go to David, I don't eat anything, not even a drop of cocoa, so that I won't feel superior to the poor and the destitute who stand and recite the Tikkun all night. And I wear my handsome shirt woven with red stripes that I wore on my wedding day, and my best clothes, as befits a man who is going to a king. Last year on Shavuoth, I went as usual to the Old City. And that day there was a heat wave, as usual here in Jerusalem, for every Shavuoth such a great heat wave comes over the city that you think you've been thrown into a fiery furnace.

But I don't deign to notice the heat wave or anything about it, and I walk on and meditate on the King of Israel, how he took his harp and played it, and as I walk, the sound of those sweet melodies he made into psalms sweetens my way. And even though I don't know any melody by heart, I do know that if I open my mouth and sing, all those melodies will come out by themselves and join together into one song. But I'm a polite man and I don't open my mouth. And that melody keeps playing all by itself until I want to cry from its sweetness. My head suddenly started spinning and my legs collapsed. You think it was because of the heat wave or because I hadn't eaten breakfast, and so I tell you, no, but because of that sweetness. And now I no longer feel my legs or my head, but I am fluttering in space like a string that broke away from the harp and flutters in the air. A man over sixty years old came to me, with a full beard and long sidelocks, and took me and brought me to the alley of the Karlin study house and sat me down on a stone and brought out a cup of brandy and put it to my mouth, and sliced me a piece of sweet cake. After I came to, I was amazed, a Hasid with a full beard and long sidelocks, how does he take care of a clean-shaven man in a short coat? I'm not wont to hide my thoughts and I said to him, If you had known that I was a sinner you certainly wouldn't have given me your brandy and cake. He smiled at me and said, Why are you proud of your transgressions, you haven't got any strength in you to sin, after all, you don't even have the strength to drink that little cup of brandy. I took a liking to that Hasid and asked him, What city are you from? He told me the name of his city and it turned out that we're from the same city. When I heard that, I didn't let go of him until he told me where he lived and everything about him. A few days later, I scraped together all the money I had in my house and went to him, and found him sitting over a book, and his house was like the houses of all the poor and destitute in Jerusalem. I said to him, I came on business. He put his handkerchief on his book and said to me, From the day I was worthy to dwell in Jerusalem I have left all my business and I deal only in Torah and prayer. I told him, That's the business I've come on. I give you five Bishliks and I'm willing to add more, up to eighteen Bishliks, if you promise me that you will say Kaddish after my death. I immediately put before him all the money I had, those five Bishliks. He lifted his hands to me joyously, and said, Blessed is he who bestows good things upon the guilty. The money I shall take, for I need it, but to say Kaddish after your death I cannot agree, for if I die before you what shall I reply to the Divine Court, that I took money improperly, but I have an old father, and the wife of the Rabbi of Shutz, may she rest in peace, promised him that he would live a hundred and twenty-seven years, and she was a great saint and showed great wonders, for she had the rod of Rabbi Meirle of Premishlan. And you, as one can see from your face, are no more than thirty, and even if God gives you seventy years, my father will still be alive seven years after you, for he's now close to eighty. Let's go to him, he's a merciful man, and he'll agree to your wish. We went to him and I placed my request before him. He accepted the responsibility. And he even added a promise on his own to study a chapter of Mishnah for the exaltation of my soul.

Mrs. Bloykof wiped the tears that were rolling on her young and handsome face. And even Isaac's eyes were excited and shed a tear. Samson straightened up to his full height, smiled and said, I was poking fun at you, I don't want to die, great work is waiting to be done by my hand and I promise you that I won't leave the world until . . . Even before he finished his words, he started wheezing. His neck turned red and his veins were stretched and his face turned blue like a spleen and his fingers turned pale, as if the blood abandoned them. He swayed back and forth and shouted, S'blood, that wheezing doesn't let a person talk with his friends. Why are you croaking at me, did I do anything to you? He looked at Isaac and said, What do you say to that, they shout and bleat like a beheaded heifer. Mrs. Bloykof quickly wiped the phlegm off his mouth. Samson gently caressed her hands and said, So where were we?

CHAPTER FIVE

Before the Painters of Jerusalem

1 |

Within four or five days Isaac became an affiliate of the painters of
Jerusalem. The wages his boss paid him were meager, nevertheless
he consented, for others wouldn't agree to give him even that paltry
wage. Isaac went to work as a daily laborer, from sunrise to sunset.
From Jaffa, Isaac had brought fine colors he had bought from a shopkeeper from Odessa, and the painters of Jerusalem called them the
colors of the Viennese, after Isaac, since Isaac is from Galicia and
Galicia is located in the states of His Majesty the Kaiser and the capital city of His Majesty the Kaiser is Vienna, the city of Kaiser Franz
Joseph, who spread his grace over most of the Ashkenazi residents of
the Land of Israel and took them under his wing to defend them
against the wrath of the oppressors.

Isaac was affable to his companions and his companions
were affable to him, as craftsmen in Jerusalem tend to be affable to
everyone. For their spirit is low and their mind is humble, for they
are lowly and humble in the eyes of the officers who give them Charity according to the number of souls in their family, and don't add to
their allowance any special money that comes from time to time, as
they do for the Torah scholars and other privileged people. But Isaac
was from Outside the Land and most of the Jerusalemites see everyone from Europe as if the keys of wisdom had been turned over to
him and they consult him on all difficult matters. Isaac didn't put on
airs with them, but on the contrary, humbled himself and replied,
You surely wanted to do thus and so, and what you wanted was right.
If they told him, That didn't occur to us, he replied, You clowns, you
want to test me. And they are astonished and don't know what to be

amazed at first, either the naïveté of an Austrian or the humility of Isaac. It wasn't long before Isaac won the hearts of his companions and they gave him a good name, as a person who knows how to use his colors, which is not true of every painter. We don't know if Isaac was more adept in his craft than all the other painters in Jerusalem or if his companions thought he knew more than they did. Either way, both those factors were of great benefit to Isaac. Things reached such a pass that once, the Russian Consul needed a painter and Mr. Solomiak brought him our comrade Isaac, for Russia will do nothing in the Land of Israel without first consulting with Mr. Solomiak, and when Mr. Solomiak heard the praise of Isaac Kumer, he brought him to the Consul. And what happened to Isaac with the Russian Consul happened to him with the Austrian Consul and the German Consul, for in the Land of Israel, when the Consuls see what their colleagues are doing they hasten to do the same, for they get nervous about their honor and are quick to show Jerusalem their power. And what happened to Isaac with those, happened to him with the French Consul, and he praised Isaac to Antebi. And when Antebi heard Isaac's praise explicitly from the French Consul, he tied the cravat in his collar. And when he went to welcome the Pasha, Antebi told him, Here, I'm sending you one of the artists of our school to repair what time has damaged in the parlor of His Supreme Highness. And who did he send him? He sent him our comrade Isaac Kumer. And our comrade Isaac wiped every winespot off the walls of the Pasha's parlor which he and his colleagues had spilled in their drunkenness on the days of Ramadan, and he painted the walls to the Pasha's pleasure. And the Pasha was grateful to him. And when they needed to repair their temple on the Temple Mount and wanted to bring painters from Egypt, the Pasha said, Here, I'll send you a Jewish fellow. Next to him, all the Egyptian craftsmen are like a mosquito in front of a camel, and he sent them our comrade Isaac. And Isaac may have been the only one to enter the Holy of Holies and to practice his craft in the place of our Temple which all the other craftsmen of Jerusalem are afraid to enter for we are defiled by corpses and do not have the ashes of the heifer. Too bad our comrade Isaac isn't much of a a storyteller and can't tell what his eyes saw there. Isaac didn't make much money, for anyone whose hands are clean, who doesn't cheat and isn't mean, who does his best and doesn't rest, will never see his labors blessed. But Isaac's needs were few and his food was cheap and his rent was low and he could support himself and even have new clothing made. And Isaac did need new clothing, for the clothes he brought with him from Jaffa were light and the climate of Jerusalem is hard, and anyone who doesn't know that is liable to come to misfortune.

Not every day does Isaac work for lords and consuls, pashas and mosques. Isaac's main work is with landlords, ours and theirs. Some have warm hearts and good taste and are glad to embellish their houses with handsome colors. And some are stingy and miserly and grumble and are angry that they have to invest their silver and gold in paint. And as for wages, some are generous with words and crown you with gold for your fine work, and when the time comes to pay up, they deduct a Bishlik here and a Matlik there. And some are difficult people who are envious of others' good, and the laborer has to take great pains to get a penny out of them. At first, Isaac hired himself out to others. Then he started working sometimes alone and sometimes with others. At that time, he was working with an old man and a boy from a family of painters in Jerusalem. The old man's son, the boy's father, left for America to try his fortune. But they found a filament in one of his eyes and didn't let him in. So he went somewhere else and didn't come back. The old man took the grandson to teach him the work. The old man's strength was gone and the grandson hadn't reached half his strength. They work humbly and don't raise their eyes above their hands.

2 |

Our comrade Isaac doesn't raise his eyes above his hands either, and does his work in total silence. What is there to say? If we take everything into account, we'll find that silence is better even than those things we must say. How much trouble and suffering would we have spared ourselves if we weren't enthralled by language. If not for the excess of words Isaac said to Sonya, he wouldn't have confused his heart and wouldn't have sinned and betrayed his colleague. What did

Isaac have left of all his conversations with Sonya? She's in Jaffa and he's in Jerusalem, and between Jerusalem and Jaffa rise high mountains. Once Isaac came upon a prayer house and there was a preacher there, Reb Grunam May-Salvation-Arise, who preached to the congregation, castigating the sinners whose instinct tempts them to commit sins, and when their instinct sees that they are drawn to sin, it raises the price of the sins to them, to wear them down, and at last it draws the sin to one place and the sinners to another place, until their eyes bulge and they don't enjoy anything. Like those who tease dogs, show a dog a chunk of meat and when the dog jumps up to catch it, they remove the meat from him, until he finally goes mad with desire.

Isaac mixes his colors and passes his brush over the window shutter. Before it became a shutter, it was a tree growing among the trees of the forest and the Holy-One-Blessed-Be-He blew wind over it and brought rain down on it and made dew flourish on it and birds nested in it and chirped and sang there. Then came woodchoppers and chopped down the tree. The birds dropped off and fled. And all the cares of the Holy-One-Blessed-Be-He seemed to be in vain. Then the wood was taken from place to place, on rivers and seas and over land until it came here. A carpenter saw it and bought it. He planed it and polished it and made it into boards. He joined the boards together until it became a shutter. The shutter was set in a wall to keep off rain and wind and sun and birds. Now Isaac stands at the shutter and passes his brush over it and spreads paint on it, just as Isaac's companions are doing with the other windows. Isaac picks up his eyes and glances outside. Mountains and hills, steep and rising, and deep valleys descend, and silence settles there, and another silence comes and swallows the first silence, and cliffs and rocks rise up and grasses sprout in the cracks, like the blisters of a rash, and a sort of gray blue purple light shines on the blisters, which aren't really blisters but grass. And the light capers among the rocks and all the rocks sway like a flock. And a sound emerges from them like a shepherd's pipe. When Isaac was a child, he learned that Joseph the saint was a shepherd and Our Teacher Moses was a shepherd and King David was a shepherd. Now he stands in the place where the shepherds of Israel stood and lambs and goats graze and an Arab shepherd shepherds them. Isaac's heart is stirred and he begins to sing Hemdat's songs. How many days, how many years had gone by since the day Isaac first read that song, how many sorrows had Isaac gone through, but whenever he brings the song to his lips, his heart pounds like the first time, like a man who is tempted in his trouble to joy and rejoicing. Isaac's two companions heard it, raised their heads amazed and astonished, for never in their life had they heard a man singing as he worked.

The boy asked Isaac, Are you a cantor's assistant? Said he, Why? Said the boy, Because I heard you singing. Said he, I was singing for no reason. Said the boy, Are you a Zionist? Said he, Why? Said the boy, I heard that the Zionists are always singing "Our hope is not yet lost." Said Isaac, What else did you hear about the Zionists, pal? Said the boy, I heard that they want to hasten redemption through all kinds of sins. Said Isaac, Why through sins? Said the boy, The Messiah, Son of David, comes only in a generation which is all innocent or all guilty, and since it is easier to sin than to keep the Commandments, so they sin.

Isaac heard and didn't reply. Gone were the days when he was eager to win souls for Zionism. It's enough for him that they're not eager to influence him. Nevertheless, he is still influenced. For better or for worse, who are we to know? Externally, he already looks a little like the people of Jerusalem, and maybe internally too. And when his fellow painters stop working to recite the afternoon prayer, he also stops working and prays. And if they eat a small snack together the size of an olive, he joins in the blessing. If not for Bloykof the painter, Isaac would become a complete Jerusalemite. Milk and honey Isaac did not find in Jerusalem, but he did attain a state of equanimity.

CHAPTER SIX

Private Thoughts

1 |

Isaac didn't make much of an impression on folks. There are a lot of fellows like Isaac and you don't pay any heed to them; Isaac excels neither in looks nor in conversation. If you chanced to talk with him, you wouldn't be eager to talk with him again. And if you meet him in the market, sometimes you don't recognize him. Unless you're fond of Isaac, a fellow like him doesn't exist for you. He is average height and his face is broad on top and narrow on the bottom. His eyes are calm and do not sparkle. His walk is heavy like a craftsman whose pace is weighed down by his tools. On weekdays he wears white pants and a short coat of green satin with black stripes, and under the coat is a brown shirt, and a tattered hat sits on his head, and all those garments are speckled with paint. His shoes are flat and his fingernails shine in his black fingers and his hair burgeons on the back of his neck. And when he puts on his Sabbath clothes he looks like a young man from Meah Shearim who fancied himself a Maskil. There are seamstresses and milliners who have complaints about him. Such a fellow shouldn't push himself into that house whose tenants are all teachers and writers and artists and activists.

Those milliners and seamstresses who crush their bodies to make a living didn't show favor to that painter. Other fellows won their hearts, fellows whose deeds are like those in novels. Some of them were already exiled to Siberia and some of them had part in the assassination of a Russian General Governor, some took part in the self-defense organization against pogroms, and some organized strikes. Now they dwell here in the Land of Israel like sheep hidden by the shepherd from the wolf. Some day they would emerge from the pen and tear the wolf and the shepherd to pieces.

Since there are neither factories nor rioters in Jerusalem at the moment, there is nothing to do here. So they sit here and split hairs about the affairs of the world and give lectures and deliver speeches, and in the evening they come to the seamstresses and the milliners, drink tea and eat sweets, borrow a Bishlik from this one and a Bishlik from that one. And the milliners and the seamstresses enjoy and are happy to give a hand to people with a sign of heroism marked on their forehead by fate. Even though those women need those pennies themselves to buy bread and milk, for Jerusalem is a city where you don't earn money every day, and that work in a narrow room with stuffy air and without healthy food saps a person's strength, and even though the days last longer here than anywhere else, nevertheless a person ages faster here than anywhere else. No longer does the mirror smile at their approach, no longer does it show a girl's face with round red cheeks, but shows a countenance as furious as those rocks of Jerusalem that look at you with rage. What was left for them in Jerusalem that they wanted to live there? If not for the People's Center and two or three people who usually visit them in the evening — all their lives would be a gloomy experience. In their youth, in their father's house, every one of them was a substantial being, every ball added luster to her shine and desirable fellows sent her love letters, and here when many of those girls are gathered in one place, each one is more wasted than the next, and all of them are wasted and wasting away. And the days go on, and every day is long. It seems as if it will never end, and it does flow to an end, and so do weeks and months and years, spinning their web on you like that spider who spins a net at the mouth of the cave and no one comes to rip the web.

2 |

Isaac didn't notice his female neighbors or their ways. No image of their activities took shape in Isaac's heart. From the day he had ascended to Jerusalem, he had lowered his eyes into himself and fenced himself off from all sides. After a day's toil, he returns to his room, drops his tools, and lies down on his bed, like a porter unloading his burden and putting it down, or like a burden the porter unloaded. After a while, he gets out of bed, washes his face and hands, and waits until they dry in the air, so as to use fewer towels that need laundering, and the water here is sold in small measures. If he had strength, he made tea or cocoa and two or three eggs. If he didn't have strength, he took a slice of bread with a tomato or olives and ate and drank cold tea left in the pot since breakfast. After he ate and drank, he picked up a book. If he had strength he sat and read. If he didn't have strength, he dozed off over his book, sometimes with a bad conscience that he wasn't doing anything for his soul, and sometimes with pleasure, like toiling people who enjoy the little bit of sleep like a windfall that comes inadvertently. A hard war between body and soul. One wants rest and the other wants knowledge. As the world goes, the strong defeats the weak, while for Isaac Kumer, the weak defeats the strong, that is the afflicted body defeats the educated soul. He recalled Sonya and thought about her, not with great affection did he think about her. The suffering she caused him reduced the affection of her memory. At any rate, a bit of consolation he found in the suffering, that perhaps it would wipe away that sin.

But he didn't linger much either on Sonya or on Rabinovitch. Father's letters took him out of a domain that wasn't his into a domain that was. And thus he sat with his head in his hands and his eyes open and observant. And when he observed, his father's house appeared in his mind's eye enhanced with more desolation, the kind of sadness and desolation that is in his heart. It was night now and they hadn't yet lit the lamp there because they were saving kerosene. Yudele returned from evening prayers and takes Vove and sits him on his knees and rehearses words and their meaning with him, for Vove is already old enough to go to school, but doesn't go to Heder, because Father doesn't have money to pay tuition. So Vove sits on Yudele's knees and repeats everything he learned. Vove chirps, *Av* is father, *le'troakh* is bother, *keder* is Tartar, *kadosh* is martyr. *Le'lekhet* is to go, *sheleg* is the snow, *betsek* you can think is dough. At the same time, his sisters stand at the window and watch the passersby because they don't have hats and can't appear outside. What's in store for Frumtshe and Pesseyle and Zisa and Blumtshe Leah and Sarah Itil?

Maybe a widower or a divorcee with a house full of children will come along and marry one of them to cook his food and mend his shirts and raise his sons. In the end, they won't even have that pleasure of standing at the window in the evening. While he follows his heart's desire and runs after the shadow of Sonya and closes his eyes to their suffering. In fact, when he was going to Jerusalem, Sonya treated him pleasantly, but what was all that maiden's pleasantness compared to his sisters' grief, and what was all the pleasantness of a brief moment compared to all those days when she offended him. Before he left she promised to write to him. Let's see if she keeps her promise.

It was not for our good that we went back to Sonya, but we won't linger on her because of Father's image that appeared to us. Father returned from the store and sits and counts his money to see if there is enough to pay a week's interest. If we hadn't gone to the Land of Israel, Father wouldn't have had to borrow and the interest wouldn't be devouring him. And perhaps he would have laid by a little dowry for Frumtshe. How old is Frumtshe? At any rate, she had already come of age. Does the daughter of poor people have a hope of finding a bridegroom when fellows are eager for a dowry? Here in the Land of Israel she might have found a mate, for fellows in the Land of Israel don't run after money, but just as they don't run after money, so they don't run to get married. They can't even support themselves, so how will they support a wife and children? Because they have a hard time making a living, some of them leave the Land. If Rabinovitch hadn't left the Land, he would have married Sonya. Now that he didn't marry Sonya, he would have done well to marry Frumtshe. And even if she isn't what he used to tell Sonya about her — her real virtues are even finer than the ones he made up for her.

Av is father, *le'troakh* is bother, *rakevet* is train, *tal v'meter* means dew and rain. Dew we praise in the summer, and rain — in the winter, for the Land of Israel needs dew in the summer and in the winter rain, for all the requests we pray for we pray for the Land of Israel. What is the Land of Israel? The Land of Israel is the name of a place where our brother Itzikl lives. What does Itzikl do in the Land of Israel? Itzikl sits under his vine and under his fig tree and eats carobs. And when do we eat carobs? I don't know. On the fifteenth day of the month of Shvat we eat carobs. No no no. What do you mean, no no no? No no no. I didn't get anything on that fifteenth day this year. You didn't get anything, but you should know that on that day everyone eats figs and dates and raisins and carobs and other good fruits that are the boast of the Land of Israel. And why doesn't Itsik send us his fruit? Isaac sent, but the Kedar came and snatched them away. What does Kedar mean in Hebrew? Are you stubborn, Vove? If you are, I won't teach you, and when Isaac comes and talks in the Holy Tongue, you'll stand like a dummy and won't know what he's saying. Tell me, Vovele, is that nice? Vove slips off Yudel's knees and started crying. And even Yudele started crying, longing for the Land of Israel.

Sara Itil says to herself, We have to eat supper. Pesseyle nods at her and says, Yes Yes, we have to eat supper. Bluma-Leah asks, What will we eat today? Zisa answers, Meat and fish we will eat, and she laughs as she speaks. But since it's not nice to make fun of the hungry, she turns back to her big sister and asks, Isn't anything left from dinner? Her sister answers, The dinner we ate today was from the leftovers of yesterday. And she presses her face to the window so they won't see her tears, even though they can't see her, since they haven't yet lit the lamp. For it's a sin to waste the two or three drops of kerosene left over from the other day, because Father doesn't have money to buy kerosene because he has to pay interest on the money he borrowed for our trip to the Land of Israel. How old is Sweet Foot? Isaac asked himself. At any rate, he's at least ten years older than Frumtshe, but he's taller than most of the fellows. And if his face is withered, his eyes are young, and when he looks at a person not every person can resist those eyes. How many inventions has he invented, how much they could improve the life of folks, but he jumps from one thing to another and doesn't have time to finish. If Frumtshe were here, she would take care of him.

All the sons of Israel are comrades, especially in the Land of Israel. For a long time, Isaac had suppressed in his heart the answer he gave that old man on the ship, now both of them live in Jerusalem and they might run into one another, but if so, what do we gain?

Their ways are so different from one another. How good Isaac felt when he traveled by ship to the Land of Israel. How many hopes had Isaac hoped. Now all his hopes have gone. The money Father borrowed for his trip he didn't return, and if a miracle doesn't happen, the creditors will descend on Father's house and take the pillow from under his head. That tale of Reb Yudel Hasid and his three sons who came upon a treasure, was that really true? But surely it was Reb Yudel Nathanson, who was very rich, who gave a dowry to Pesseyle, the daughter of Reb Yudel Hasid, and people who are fond of miracles made up the story about the treasure. Whether it's this way or that way, we don't gain anything, for benefactors like Reb Yudel Nathanson aren't around these days, and those who trust in God like Reb Yudel Hasid certainly aren't around. So, what difference is it to us if we conjure up a miracle that happened to Reb Yudel and he came upon a treasure or if he came upon a rich man who gave him a dowry for his daughter? If we look at the events of the world we see that it's easier for the earth to open up its treasures than for a rich man to open his hand to a pauper. In fact, our generation doesn't lack rich benefactors either, but all their righteousness doesn't stand the pauper on his feet, but makes it easier for him to exist in his poverty. Let us leave off musing and return to the world of action. Isaac does his work, sometimes alone and sometimes with others, sometimes for dignitaries and consuls and sometimes for simple landlords. Honey and milk Isaac didn't find in his toil, it was enough for Isaac that he attained a state of equanimity.

A State of Equanimity

1 |

The state of equanimity spread its state over him. Everything that came upon him he accepted magnanimously, he didn't grumble and didn't complain. He had gotten used to the caprices of the sun and the whims of the winds. The dry heat waves that lap the marrow of a man's bones, the dust that shrivels the skin, the yellow light that sears the eyes and the air that infuses boredom, and all the changes in the climate didn't drive him out of his state. If he found work, he worked, if he didn't find work, he wasn't depressed. On days when he was idle, he went to the library and read a book, and in the evening he went to the People's Center to read newspapers. And if there was a speaker or a lecturer there, he sat and listened, and didn't get up from his seat until all the discussions were over, whether they were a repetition of things that had already been said two or three times over, or the opposite. And even if he returned home half dead, he returned to the People's Center the next day for the same things.

In the People's Center, Isaac met all kinds of people, including a few of the fellows from Jerusalem, who came there secretly, keeping it from their fathers, for anyone who went to the People's Center they regarded as a heathen and a heretic. With their heavy clothing and black felt hats and their very motion, which looked as if they had to account for every single movement before they made it, and especially with their thirsty eyes, they stood out from all the other visitors to the People's Center. That thirst in their eyes was partly a thirst for the real purpose the world was created for, for what makes the world worth living in, and partly a thirst for a bit of freedom in life. They don't yet have any image of that real purpose and they don't yet know what freedom might be, but they hope that here, in this place, among modern people, they will find what their soul longs for. Whenever those fellows saw the people of the People's Center, they were puzzled about them. On the face of it, they looked like everybody else and were even inferior to most of the people they knew, but since one mustn't say so, they humbled themselves and said, Of course our imagination is low and we aren't capable of seeing the brightness in them, and they lived in wait for the day when they would be worthy of having it revealed to them.

As long as they were young, they studied in the Tree of Life Yeshiva. When they grew up, they held out their hand to the tree of knowledge. They left the tree of life and started seeking a path in life, not with Torah studies and Charity, for their eyes were already opened and they saw how much harm comes to those who study Torah and accept Charity. There were four comrades. One wanted to study a trade that supported those who practiced it, and one was eager to buy himself a piece of ground and bring bread out of the earth like those exceptional individuals of Jerusalem in an earlier generation who founded Petah Tikvah, and one wanted to study medicine, and one hadn't yet decided what he would do.

A man does not do everything he wants to do, especially in Jerusalem, which is not blessed with handiwork. Each one held onto what he found, just not to go back to the Yeshiva. The one who wanted to learn a trade went to work in a shop, and the one who wanted to bring bread out of the earth became a clerk in a charitable institution, and the one who wanted to be a doctor became a proofreader at a printing press and copies manuscripts for the sages Outside the Land, and the one who hasn't yet decided what he would do sits and studies languages. Six working days, they are busy at their trade. Comes the Sabbath, comes rest. When rest comes, the soul desires its pleasures. And what pleasures the soul desires are pleasures the body enjoys too. They gather together and go outside the city and stroll around, for outside the city, among the high mountains in the invigorating air, a person's mind expands, especially in Jerusalem, where every four cubits grants a person knowledge and wisdom. And Isaac accompanies them. And even though they are learned in the

Torah and their fathers are dignitaries of Jerusalem, they don't put on airs with Isaac. On the contrary, they embrace him because of his craft. If they did not attain a trade, they are fond of those who do practice a trade. As young people who filled their bellies with the new books, they despised Charity, even though their fathers lived on it. And they enjoyed it too, for you don't have one single livelihood in Jerusalem that doesn't have a little bit of Charity in it.

You don't have one single livelihood in Jerusalem that doesn't have a little bit of Charity in it, and you don't have a person in Jerusalem who doesn't talk about Charity. If he gets it, he complains and grumbles that they give him neither enough to die nor enough to live. And anyone who doesn't need Charity slanders both those who get it and those who give it. But you must know that if not for Charity, may the enemies of the Jews starve to death like the Jewish people, for there is neither trade nor industry in Jerusalem, so where would they make a living? And as for the officers, who presumably hold onto most of the money in their own hands, we have never seen them riding in carriages in parks and citrus groves during their lives, and at their death, they don't leave any fortune and wealth. The elders of Jerusalem still remember Reb Yoshi Rivlin. Twenty-five years he was a writer and a supervisor of Charity, by day he would wear himself out with the poor and at night he would wear himself out over his learning, and never in his life did he see any good and he bent his shoulder as if to bear troubles and suffering with a good heart and a modest mien, and all the money that came to Jerusalem was distributed by him, and he didn't eat meat or drink wine even on the Sabbath and holidays, but made do with black bread and black coffee. And when he passed away, he didn't leave his widow and orphans food for even one meal, but he did leave behind him eleven neighborhoods that he added to Jerusalem.

2 |

Like all the other members of the Second Aliya, Isaac found Jerusalem already crowned with a few neighborhoods, and he regarded its suburbs and hub as one city. And he didn't know that at first all Jerusalem dwelt inside the Old City walls, and all those places that are bustling today with so many people were a wasteland, and when the gates of the Old City were locked from sunset until dawn, anyone who remained outside the walls was in danger of being robbed. When Isaac accompanied his Jerusalem comrades, he heard from them how those neighborhoods were built and when they were built, at a time when the Land was full of violence. And about who built them, people of Jerusalem who lived on Charity who dwelt among a riffraff of bribe-taking, bloodthirsty foes. And those Jerusalemites didn't spare themselves or their families for the settlement of Jerusalem. We who are close to them in time see their faults and not their virtues. But if they hadn't expanded the border of Israel, Jerusalem would have been shrunk between the Old City walls and all those places would be desolate.

By now Isaac had forgotten some of his first opinions, but his opinion about Charity he didn't forget. When he walked in the neighborhoods and saw their houses, he was amazed, for people we heard were idlers and obscurantists and remote from any settled life were the ones who expanded Jerusalem and prepared a place for future generations.

Isaac also learned that a young man can revere God even if his forefathers weren't Hasids. Isaac was from Galicia, from a small town, which was divided between Hasids and Mitnagdim. All sons of Hasids were educated in Heders and study houses, and all sons of those who were not Hasids went to schools and universities. The former were raised to follow the Torah and the Commandments and the latter became free from performing the Commandments. But sons of Mitnagdim who followed the Torah and the Commandments Isaac hadn't seen until he met his Jerusalem comrades. And to what degree were they Mitnagdim! Once the subject of Hasids and freethinkers came up, and one of them said, The head of our Yeshiva said that there is hope that a licentious student will repent, but a student who becomes a Hasid won't ever repent.

3 |

On weekdays, every one of them is busy at his work, and on the Sabbath they rest from work, gather together and go out to stroll in the city and the surrounding area. Isaac accompanied them. Sometimes they walked around the Old City walls and its seven gates, and sometimes they left from Damascus Gate and went to the Cave of Zedekiah, where King Zedekiah fled from the Chaldeans, and the cave goes underground all the way to Jericho. And opposite the Cave of Zedekiah you see the yard of the dungeon where the Prophet Jeremiah was imprisoned and the cistern where Jeremiah was thrown and the rock Jeremiah sat on and lamented the Destruction. From there they went to the Gate of Flowers, where Nebuchadnezzar, King of Babylon, camped when he came to destroy Jerusalem, and where the wicked Titus conquered Jerusalem. From the Gate of Flowers, they went to the Gate of Tribes, where the tribes came up to Jerusalem. From there they went to Lions Gate where four lions are carved. For once the Ishmaelite King dreamed that if the walls of Jerusalem were not built, lions would tear him to pieces, so he built the wall and ordered them to carve in it the lions he had seen in the dream. From Lions Gate they went along the eastern wall and came to the Gate of Mercy. That was the gate where Ezekiel prophesied *This gate shall be shut, it shall not be opened, and no man shall enter in by it; because the Lord the God of Israel, hath entered in by it.* And it is still shut, for the Ishmaelites shut it because they fear that Israel's prayer will triumph there and the Messiah will come. From there they went down to Yad Avshalom and came to Gihon, where Solomon was anointed King of Israel, and there is the ritual bath of Rabbi Ishmael the High Priest. And its waters can cure all kinds of diseases, but are not good for drinking, for from the day Israel was exiled, the waters lost their taste. From Gihon they went down to Shiloah, whose waters pour forth four times a day, and those places are adorned with green gardens whose blooming never stops all the days of the year, for they are watered by the waters of Shiloah, and there were the gardens mentioned by Nehemiah in his book. And from there they went to Eyn Rogel and sometimes went to visit Arzef.

Arzef was a native of Jerusalem, and like most natives of Jerusalem, he studied in The Tree of Life Yeshiva, and many of the dignitaries and rabbis of Jerusalem were his comrades. And there are those who think he knew Talmud better than some of them. What made Arzef choose that strange craft of stuffing the skins of animals and birds and insects and reptiles no one knew. Arzef lives alone like the First Adam in the Garden of Eden, with no wife and no sons and no cares and no troubles, among all kinds of livestock and animals and birds and insects and reptiles and snakes and scorpions. He dwells with them in peace, and even when he takes their soul, they don't demand his blood in exchange, since they enter the great museums of Europe because of him, and professors and scholars flock to his door and give him honorary degrees and money. Arzef doesn't run after money and doesn't brag about the honorary degrees. Let those who get all their honor from others brag about them. It's enough for Arzef to look at his handiwork and know that never in his life has he ruined any creature in the world, on the contrary, he gave a name and remainder to some birds of the Land of Israel who were said to have vanished from the earth. Some of Arzef's comrades had made wealth and honor for themselves. Their wealth and honor are as important to Arzef as empty casuistry. Some of Arzef's comrades practice numerology for the names of the wealthy of Israel. Their numerology is as important to Arzef as the research of most of the sages of Jerusalem. What is important to Arzef? Important to Arzef are the livestock and animals and birds and insects and reptiles mentioned in the writings of the Holy One and in the two Talmuds, that dwell in the Land of Israel. Arzef hunts them and throws away their flesh and fills their skin so they will be preserved. All that Arzef does on the six days of work, and on the Sabbath he rests like everybody else, spreads a mat in front of his house, lies and reads Yosiphon and the Fables of Foxes. Yosiphon because there are tales of human creatures there, and the Fables of Foxes because there are tales of livestock, animals, and birds there.

Arzef doesn't like guests because they pester him with their questions. But if guests come to him, he doesn't reject them, but tells them not to touch any stuffed animal, for the stuffed animals are irascible. If the visitors listen to him, it's fine; if they don't, Arzef roars like a beast or a bird of prey. And even if they know it's Arzef's voice, they get scared and run away.

Isaac's comrades were experts in the merits of Jerusalem and could tell about the city and its chronicles, its builders and its destroyers. And sometimes they cited a biblical verse about an event. Whenever Isaac heard he was amazed. Isaac knew, of course, that we had seers and prophets, but he didn't know that their words still lived and existed, and most of their words or some of them relate to issues we see here in Jerusalem. In his Heder, Isaac had learned a little Scripture and in the study house where he prayed in his youth, there were some torn books of Holy Writ he had never looked at. For he was used to the light books a person reads to keep boredom at bay or to acquire information. All of a sudden Isaac stands in Jerusalem at the place where Isaiah and Jeremiah and the other Prophets stood, and their words are still ringing among the stones of the place.

Isaac's comrades walk with Isaac and tell about Jerusalem of the past and about Jerusalem of our own day. Some of the stories seem to us like stories of legend yet in fact they are events that happened, for Jerusalem is experienced in miracles, for the eyes of God roam in this city, and He doesn't remove His vigilance from her even in her destruction. And some of the stories aren't stories, but since they were told about Jerusalem, the human heart is drawn to listen.

From praise of Jerusalem, they come to praise of their forefathers, the men of Jerusalem. Some of these stories seem legendary to us, but in truth they were events that actually happened, for their forefathers were great men and great events happened to them. Isaac hears and is also stirred to tell about the feats of Reb Yudel Hasid, his ancestor, whom the Lord raised from the dust, but when he came to tell he couldn't connect one thing to another. In his childhood, when his grandmother was still alive and told the wonders the Lord did for His pious follower Reb Yudel Hasid and his three modest daughters, Isaac didn't have the intelligence to understand. In his youth, when his aunts would tell the tale of Reb Yudel their grandfather, Isaac was eagerly pursuing other stories which were wont to mock the Saints and the Hasids. Now when he longed to tell, he didn't know how to begin because he wasn't expert in the chain of events. Isaac was like his father who, if you asked him to tell even one thing that happened to his ancestor, he groans and says, What do I know, one thing I do know, in the past it was good and now it's no good. Someday, the deeds of that Hasid will be forgotten, as if they had never existed. And there are already progeny of that Hasid who forget the whole tale and say that the poets of Brod made up those things to amuse themselves. But it is Yudele's merit that he began setting the tale of his ancestor to rhymes, for Yudele is a poet and can make rhymes like the poets do.

Isaac walks around Jerusalem and his spirit is roaming somewhere else. There too it is the Sabbath, and there too it is summer, but the times are different, that is we're not twenty-five years old anymore but are seven or eight. And Isaac's grandmother has already finished the weekly Torah portion in *Tsena Ve-Rena*, the women's Yiddish Bible, and comes and sits down outside on the stone bench in front of the house. Her hands are laid on her knees and a kind of sweet sorrow spreads over her wrinkled face. A few of the neighbor women gather together and come and sit with her and she tells them in the same sweet, sad voice the wonders of the Lord that He did for His pious follower Reb Yudel Hasid. Sometimes the women groan and sometimes they raise their voice in joy. But she doesn't change her voice. A few years have gone by now. The old woman has already departed this world, and of all the women who listened to her stories not many are left. But that tune still plays, and from it Yudele makes the tale of Reb Yudel.

Isaac lifts his eyes as if he is seeking his brother and he sees his comrades. He surveys them all and thinks to himself, This one is worthy of this sister and that one is worthy of that sister. And right away he remembers that they dwell Outside the Land and knows that this one will never meet up with this sister, and that one will never meet up with that sister. Those who descend to America bring their brothers and sisters to them after a year or two; but as for those who ascend to the Land of Israel, it's enough for them if they themselves don't return outside the Land. The money Father borrowed for Isaac he hasn't yet returned, and how can he hope to bring his sisters up to Israel?

4 |

At that time, Isaac moved out of the convert's house. Ever since the day he had come to live in the convert's house, he had not been happy with his room. In summer because of the heat and in winter because of the cold, by day because of the dark and by night because of the mice. One day, it turned out that one of his neighbors brought his mother from Russia and she couldn't live with her daughter-in-law. Isaac agreed to leave her his room and he rented himself a room in Zikhron Moshe.

That neighborhood was built a year before we ascended to the Land of Israel, and is better than the other neighborhoods, for it was made according to a fixed plan and the laws of health. Every house stands by itself, and a street goes down the middle, and trees are planted on the sides of the street, which will provide shade on sunny days and branches for Sukkoth. And even though a wise doctor warned not to plant trees, for trees need water and water brings mosquitoes and mosquitoes bring malaria, nevertheless they planted trees, and they stint their own mouths and water them, and a woman measures her little children on them. Just as the neighborhood is exquisite, so are its residents. They are pleasant to God and pleasant to men, and don't persecute one another because of their opinions. Some of them are merchants and shopkeepers and some are teachers and writers. Some of them write for the newspapers and some are secretaries in Charity institutions. And because their houses are bigger then their incomes, they rent out a room or two. Students of the teachers' college live there, modest young fellows seeking knowledge and speaking Hebrew, humble and docile people. Once it happened that they didn't come to the seminary and the teachers imagined that the students were on strike, and when they went to look for them, they found them sick in bed, for the bad food and the foreign studies sapped their strength and made them ill.

Isaac became friendly with four of them from Galicia, who had sneaked out of their father's house, with a Tefillin bag in their hands and a little food in their clothes and a good hope for the future. Unlike Isaac, they didn't ascend to plow and sow, but to study Torah and wisdom on the Holy Soil in the Holy City on pure Holiness in the Holy Tongue. And they maintain the Torah out of poverty and accept suffering gladly and don't rebel, but on the contrary, sing songs of Zion and its hope, and stir longing for the Land in the heart of their comrades in Galicia. And even though they are scholars and seminary students and Isaac is only a laborer, they are friendly to him and affable with him. And when they heard that he has a girlfriend in Jaffa, they saw her in their dreams ascending to Jerusalem and coming to Isaac and they would get to meet her, for when they were awake, they didn't meet a girl up close. One of the group set his longings in rhymes and published them in *The Young Laborer* or maybe somewhere else. Their dream didn't come true. Sonya didn't ascend to Jerusalem and didn't come to Isaac. But she did keep her promise to write him letters.

5 |

Sonya kept her promise. Once a week she wrote to Isaac. Her letters are better than Isaac's and longer than Isaac's, and another advantage of her letters is that there is nothing superfluous in them, whether she writes about herself or whether she writes about others, and even things that have nothing to do with Isaac take on importance and charm for him. Sometimes Sonya amuses herself and attaches to her letters matchmaking notes from some shopkeeper who owns a big store in Jaffa or some farmer who owns fields and vineyards, who want to marry her even with no dowry. Foolish lads, you think Sonya will take on the yoke of marriage. Those matchmaking notes Sonya sends to Isaac for sheer amusement do some good, for from them you learned that everyone sees Sonya as being unattached, and Isaac doesn't have to see her as if she still belonged to Rabinovitch, and his guilt is purely gratuitous.

The day a letter comes from Sonya is a happy day for Isaac, like one of the early days when Sonya was close to him, but in the early days his heart struck him and now he is calm, and if his spirit rouses him, he binds it up in words and writes to her. And even though our comrade Isaac isn't used to writing, he occasionally finds a pretty word in his quill, and when he puts it on paper it soothes his soul and calms his body. If Isaac recalls all those good hours he saw with Sonya and longs and yearns and wants to see her, he evokes in contrast all the bad hours he saw with her of late, and finally he returns to a state of equanimity, as if there is no difference if Sonya is here or if Sonya is not here.

In time, the letters decreased. He wrote her at length and she answered him briefly. He wrote her briefly and she didn't answer him at all. He wrote her, Why don't you write so often? She answered him, What shall I write you? Nothing's new and all that's old grows older.

He also began to write less. He wants to write a lot and he writes a little. He wants to write a little and doesn't write anything. Sometimes he composes a long letter in his heart, and when he sits down to write, he sees that it's not worth writing; week in and week out go by and he doesn't write her and she doesn't write him. Even though the two of them are doing the same thing, that is, not writing, he complains about her because she stopped first and because it's easy for her to write, go to the post office, take paper and ink and write on the spur of the moment without any toil or exhaustion; while it's not like that for him, who needs peace of mind and calm of soul. When a few weeks passed without a letter from her, he recalled those notes she attached to her letters and wondered if she was betrothed or had set her sights on someone else, not exactly for marriage, but for no good reason. That girl had a strange power, she did whatever her heart desired and her heart didn't admonish her for her acts. Isaac knew he should be jealous but he wasn't. Didn't he care about anything? Does a man see his fiancée given to someone else and remain silent? A person can accept suffering and even rejoice in it, to regain his balance, but to see his fiancée given to someone else and to be silent, not every man can bear that.

Once one of his acquaintances came up from Jaffa to Jerusalem and brought regards from Sonya. Isaac didn't ask him if she told him to ask how he was or whether the man did it on his own. And when he parted from the man, he didn't send regards to her. Had Isaac let him open his mouth, the man would have told him things he longed to know. But Isaac didn't let him open his mouth and he didn't open it himself. After he parted from him, Isaac sat and grumbled, Somebody who doesn't have anything to do with Sonya sits in Sonya's city, and I sit here far away from her. He realized that he should go down to Jaffa. And since it wasn't clear to him what he wanted there, his soul vexed him, as a man's soul is vexed whenever his thoughts aren't clear. After a few days, his thoughts began to fall into place, and every single thought received a shape and speech, but they were divided. One said Go to Jaffa and loosen your bonds, and another one said, No, on the contrary, tighten and strengthen them. And one mocked and said, Before the sand disappears from Jaffa, jump down there and fill your hand with sand and weave yourself a rope and tie your Sonya with it so she'll be attached to you forever. When Isaac imagined going down to Jaffa and standing before Sonya, his heart wasn't arrogant, but he saw himself as someone who forces himself to do what he cannot do. Isaac sensed dimly that all his power was nothing but the power of the love of others for him, and when that love was lacking, any little thing could intimidate him. Therefore, he was afraid to appear before Sonya and left the matter hanging in the air.

CHAPTER EIGHT

The Curtain the Artist Pulled

1 |

The state of equanimity transformed Isaac's face. Never in his life had his heart been haughty or his eyes arrogant, and when he reached that state, he hung his upper lashes on his lower lashes, like a person whose educated soul has completed its activities and his whole body took on meekness, which was manifest in his walk and his speech and his voice. Once Bloykof looked at him, and said, What is it, Kumer, you've abandoned your world. Another time Bloykof looked at him and said, There's a special quality you've got and I don't know what it is. Too bad you weren't born an artist. Because a person doesn't become an artist unless he is born an artist, but he can learn an art that is an art, so he started teaching him sign-painting. Isaac found sufficient reason not to go to Sonya in Jaffa, and he found a new craft to occupy him.

The very first day Isaac came to Bloykof's house, Bloykof treated him like a brother. Now that he became his pupil, his brotherly feeling was doubled. Isaac savored the taste of friendship as in the days when he was with Rabinovitch. Isaac didn't compare Bloykof to Rabinovitch or Rabinovitch to Bloykof, for even when Rabinovitch didn't have work, he was a practical man, while Bloykof floats in the upper worlds even when he is busy with practical things. But they do have one quality in common, a self-effacing love of friends and affection for comrades.

Bloykof was an experienced teacher and knew how to make his pupils love their trade. When he sat with Isaac to teach him, he told him, Here's a sheet and here are paints. Ostensibly, they have nothing in common, but you want to mate them. So, try to make the mating succeed, so that everyone who sees them will say, Those paints were created only for the canvas and the canvas was created only for the paints, and needless to say, the letters and the images have to be exquisite, for if not they'll haunt your dreams. How much I regret those frames I made and most of the paintings I painted. I was foolish and I thought everything preceded from ideas and I didn't know that the main thing about painting is painting. A person who scatters his fingernail clippings everywhere has to return after his death and collect them. And what's true of the fingernails is so much truer of a person's handiwork, which is the essence of his existence in the world. How much grief and suffering are in store for that man when he'll have to go into the houses of those who bought his pictures and see their faces in the frames he made. That kind of reincarnation I don't wish even on my enemies. And you must know, Kumer, that I hate my enemies. There may be good people who love even their enemies and forgive them, I'm not a good man and I'm not likely to forgive. The quantity of love is limited and I keep it for those I love. Pick up your brush and don't spare your efforts, for you are not the main thing, but what you do, and what you do isn't the main thing, but the act itself. And don't say, Is it worth it for me to put all my strength into that shopkeeper's sign. His merchandise will rot, but the sign you make must be beautiful.

2 |

At that time, Bloykof's strength was sapped. He didn't yet know that his death was at hand. Because he was accustomed to thinking about death, his heart became inured to death. If his brush fell out of his hand because of weakness, he would stretch out on his bed and close his eyes and paint in his mind all that he would do if he were healthy. Since the paintings of the soul are many and there was not much time, he would overcome his weakness and go back to his work.

His wife saw and brought him novels and read to him to keep him in bed. He wasn't happy with the novels because he couldn't bear tales of people and their exploits, and because they separated him from his visions, and he would get rid of the novels and jump out of bed and go back to his work. Once she came on a book about livestock, animals, and birds. She lay him down against his will and read to him. He lay with his eyes closed and listened and yelled, Oh, I see, Oh, I see. When Tosya grew weary from reading, he wanted to hear some more. That went on for a day, two days, three days. And she's got a house to run and all the housework is on her, to sweep the room and shop at the market and cook the food and run to the pharmacy to buy medicine for her husband. And on top of all those troubles is the trouble of guests, you have to feed them and make them a cup of cocoa, the cocoa that serves as both food and drink at the same time, for Bloykof's income isn't big enough to give a guest food separately and drink separately. And as for Bloykof, when he was interested in one thing, he was wont to shift his eyes from everything else. He lay on his bed with his eyes shut and she read to him, and he stopped her from going to the market or the shop, and when it came time for dinner, they didn't have anything to eat. Isaac noticed that and started bringing all kinds of food and fooled them about his shopping. Tosya was amazed that he paid less than she did, and she let him buy all the food for the house. If she came across an extra penny, she paid his expenses, if she didn't, she asked him to wait until God brought her relief.

God didn't bring her relief, but on the contrary, He brought distress and bitterness. Isaac kept his eye on her, and not only did he take pains for her and bring food, but he also took pains to soothe and comfort her. There are those who bring flowers and those who bring trinkets, and you can get along without flowers and trinkets, but you can't get along without bread and food. Bloykof saw what Isaac did and was pleased with him, for he was behaving like an artist and didn't insist on those outpourings whose artistic form is dubious. Isaac would have done well if he had sent something to his father, who wore himself out to pay his creditors their interest. But Father's distress is far away and Bloykof's distress is close by. Moreover, if he sent something to his father, he would have to send ten or twenty francs all at once, while for Bloykof he pays it out in dribs and drabs and spends only Matliks and Bishliks.

By now, Bloykof has stopped teaching Isaac. But Isaac didn't stop coming. And when he came he didn't come empty-handed.

Tosya takes one of the oranges Isaac brought, peels it and gives it to her husband. Bloykof sucks it and says, What a delight, what a delight. At that time, Isaac's eyes wander off to another place and another time, a time when his mother lies sick and Father stands over her and asks, Do you want anything? Mother smiles with blue, dry lips and doesn't reply, for if she does want something, does he have anything to give? Isaac drops his eyes from Mother's smile and Father's grief. His sister Frumtshe comes and picks up the basket and goes to the market to buy something and returns from the market with nothing because she went without a cent. Their little brother Vove goes out to meet her and takes the empty basket from her hand and puts it on his head like a hat, and says, Come see my new hat. And he is amazed that his brothers and sisters don't laugh at how clever he is and don't tell him, Wear it in good health. At that time, Isaac sits at home or in the shop and counts the number of settlements we've got in the Land of Israel, and Father sits and counts all the excuses he's already given the landlord who is demanding the rent. Isaac sits and counts how many good things are in store for him in the Land of Israel, and Father sits and counts how much grief is on its way to him. He hasn't found any of those good things in the Land of Israel, and Father hasn't yet finished his counting of troubles. And both times, those in the past and those in the present, merge into one long trouble. Once Bloykof looked at him, and said, What is oppressing you so much? Said Tosya, We have to find him a nice girl. She invited for him one of those girls who came to her house. He didn't look at her and she didn't look at him. Obviously Isaac won't attract the heart of every girl.

3 |

Bloykof got rid of the books and sent his guests away, he pulled the curtain in the room and sat behind the curtain. From the day Bloykof knew his mind — his mind was given to two things which are one, life and death, but minor matters kept him from devoting his whole mind to that, and now that he tastes the taste of death every day and knows that the purpose of life is death, he dared to create images of life and death. He was aided by the stories his wife read him about livestock, animals, and birds, which he had already forgotten, but a kind of reflection of a reflection of them remained in his heart.

And so Bloykof sits inside the partition and before him is a canvas of four cubits and on it he paints a leopard and a snake winding around the leopard, choking it with its rings gleaming in an array of colors. From dawn to dusk, Bloykof plies his trade, he puts spots on the leopard and makes hatchmarks on the snake. The snake is life and the leopard is death. The leopard strikes the head of the snake to crush his brain, and the snake winds himself around the leopard and strangles him. And behold the miracle, ever since he has been occupied with the image of death, he inhales life, and it seems to him that he is getting better, and his wife coaxed him to come out for a stroll with her, like most of the intellectuals of the city who go for a stroll in the evening, like Mr. Ben-Yehuda who strolls every evening with Mrs. Hemda. And she didn't know that all his strength derived from his work and if he turned away from his work, his strength would turn away from him. She would invent things to make him stop working, so that he wouldn't get too worn out. That made him angry and he scolded her. She was alarmed and wept, for never in her life had she heard him scold her. When he went back to his work, she came and stood in front of him so he would appease her. If he understood her intention, he put down his brush and hugged her, but if he was too steeped in his work, he glared at her. She threw the curtain behind her and sat and wept. She sat behind the curtain on this side and wept and he stood behind the curtain on that side and groaned and coughed. When she heard him coughing and groaning, she came and threw herself on his neck and hugged him, as he divided his eyes between her and the picture he was painting.

CHAPTER NINE

Accounts

1 |

Isaac stayed away from the Bloykof house and didn't even come to bring products from the market. For, from the day the artist pulled the curtain, he regarded his guests as if they were conspiring against him to interrupt his work, until they finally stopped coming.

Once, on Friday afternoon, Isaac was coming home from work at the house of a Christian member of the sect of the Sabbath Keepers who had a bathhouse on Jaffa Road, and at noon on Friday the man locks the bathhouse and stops all work. Isaac was going to the barber to shave his beard, for he hadn't yet bought his own razor, something he did later on. That was the afternoon hour when the teachers are coming out of school and the clerks are coming out of the bank and going to shave their beards and cut their hair. He waited a long time and his turn didn't come, so he decided to give up the shave and spend the Sabbath at home reading a book, and for the walls of his house a person doesn't need to beautify himself. He picked up his tools and left. He walked along with a pot of colors hanging on his arm, and on his shoulder hung a small ladder, and he was looking ahead like an artisan who has finished his work and was about to take his rest and pleasure.

2 |

The city was still bustling as on all other days, but signs of preparation for the Sabbath were already obvious. The merchants and shopkeepers who aren't busy selling food lock their shops and their hearts are boasting that the Lord gave them a livelihood that doesn't make them wear themselves out until dark, and they can enter the Sabbath with tranquility, and as they lock their shops, they jingle their keys to let the neighbors know that the Sabbath is approaching. On the other hand, all the grocers run from box to box in their shops, from a measure of wet goods to a measure of dry goods. They measure oil by the *Issar* and weigh sugar, they pour kerosene and cut halvah, they tear up paper and make wrappers, they make bundles and take coins from anyone who pays, and they write in their notebook who didn't pay, they give change or ask for more, and they exchange thick candles for thin ones and thin candles for thick ones, whatever the customers want. Here a woman urges the shopkeeper to hurry up and there a shopkeeper urges a customer to buy something and go. Here a baby is crying whose bottle is broken, and there a pauper insinuates himself forward to ask for alms. Here a wine dealer measures wine for the Kiddush, and there a belligerent man yells that the candles they sold him last Friday didn't have a wick. And on the street between the shops a beadle from the court runs to paste up announcements and skips past the places where he should paste them to teach the onlookers not to run after him. As he runs and they run, they bump into schoolchildren going to put the Cholent in the public oven. The owner of the oven stands and yells. At some he yells for lingering, and at others he yells for hurrying, he yells at some whose bottles don't have proper corks and are likely to spill, and he yells at others whose bottles are too tightly corked as if they're afraid he'll drink from them. Between this and that, you hear the Bible read twice and its translation once, and a Bar Mitzvah boy reciting his Haftorah, and the smell of fish and the smell of other Sabbath dishes envelops you. Old men come out wearing Sabbath clothes, this one is going to his prayer house and that one to the Western Wall. This one has a kerchief wound around his neck against the chill, and that one has a kerchief wound around his neck in case the Sabbath boundary has been desecrated. The weekday sun has not yet set and the splendor of the Sabbath has not arrived, but everyone who is fond of the Sabbath leaves his work and hurries toward it an hour or two before time. As soon as the schoolchildren see the old people, they come and push their way among them, spilling shells out of their mouths and saying, Shabbas, Shabbas. Sabbath, Sabbath, whispers one old man in a sweet voice, as if he were given a taste of the World to Come. And he looks at the firmament to a Sabbath up above, and runs to the Western Wall to receive the Sabbath that is waiting for the sons of Israel who will be blessed with its blessings. As the Land prepares for the Sabbath, the face of the firmament changes and other faces are flickering above. It is not yet really the Sabbath, but a taste of the Sabbath is already gleaming.

3 |

Isaac strolls along leisurely, enjoying the view. For six days he worked from early morning to late at night, now, as he left his trade, he will return to his room and take off his dirty clothes and put on clean clothes, and won't move until after the Sabbath. Isaac dallies a bit here and a bit there and glances, and calculates how much he has earned and how much he has spent, and what things he will buy to celebrate the Sabbath. Even though our comrade Isaac isn't careful about keeping the Sabbath, he does tend to buy some special food for the Sabbath. When he added up his accounts, he found that he had five Bishliks left. A shame to touch them, for if he saved another five and another five and another five, he might succeed in putting together ten francs and sending them to Father. And that was about to happen, for he stayed away from Bloykof's house and didn't spend anything on him anymore. Isaac was happy at his sacrifice for Father and also that he hadn't shaved his beard, both because he saved the cost of shaving and because he would have to sit at home all day of the Sabbath and rest from his toil, for he can't appear in public when he's not tidy.

4 |

Isaac shifted the pot of paints from his right arm to his left and shifted the ladder from one shoulder to another, and pondered things that were close to his eyes and far from his heart, as well as things that were far from his eyes and close to his heart. He heard a voice shouting *Charity Will Save from Death* and he came upon a bier. Isaac didn't ask who died and didn't wait to hear. Jerusalem is a city where most of the inhabitants are old people who come from all places to die here, so what's remarkable about burying a dead man? A person who passes away to his reward is taken to the Mount of Olives and buried in a grave he bought while he was alive, and then the people return home peacefully. Many a time on rainy nights, Isaac came upon members of the Burial Society running to the Mount of Olives to bury a dead person, and many a time he saw them returning with their clothes streaming like springs, and they were shivering with chills and suffering from malaria. There are people who complain about the members of the Burial Society that they make a living from the dead. Even harsher are the words of Rabbi Obadia of Bartanura, the commentator of the Mishnah, about the Society leaders of his day who were careful not to lose even the least little thing of the dead person's property and legacy, and they libeled those who visited the sick, saying that they took money from their houses and put it in their own cotters. And woe to the man whom they set their eyes on. Therefore, many were afraid to visit the sick lest they be suspected. And the situation of the sick who have no acquaintances in the city was very bitter. And the Society leaders knew no mercy and did not deviate from their evil ways.

As Isaac recalled past generations, he recalled what the people of Jerusalem tell about their first forefathers, who had left houses full of delicacies for burial in the city of Our God. And as he recalled those old people, he recalled Reb Yudel his ancestor, that Hasid who lived a life of woe, and when fortune smiled on him and he became rich, he left his city and ascended to Jerusalem. And in those days his city was a big city, full of learning and wisdom, and folks honored him for his wealth and for his piety, and he could have lived out his days in wealth and honor. Yet he left his honor and ascended to Jerusalem. And who knows if a man is present at the hour when his soul departs, for Grandmother Frumit died before him. Isaac felt sorry for his ancestor. But in his somber mood, he found a little consolation, for if our grandfather is buried here, then we too are embedded in this soil, like those whose forefathers created the Yishuv. Isaac pondered, How come I didn't remember before now, and now that I have remembered, I should visit my ancestor's grave, even though it's hard to imagine that I'll find it, for it has been over eighty years since the day he passed away, and his grave has certainly sunk and its place is forgotten.

Isaac looked at the pallbearers who were hurrying to bring the dead man to his rest before the entrance of the Sabbath, and he looked at the funeral procession and didn't find anyone he knew there. And they didn't seem to know the dead man either, but they came upon a chance to fulfill the Commandment to accompany the dead and they accompanied him a few paces to perform the last honors.

He asked one of the pallbearers, Who's the dead man here? He replied, One of the freethinkers. Another one said, Free among the dead, says the Bible, and you shouldn't speak ill of the dead. Yet another person asked, Who is it who died? They answered him, A painter from Nahalat Shiv'ah. Someone else interrupted and said, Why not Professor Schatz? Another one said, Blessed be the True Judge, I saw that painter last Shavuoth at the tomb of King David. He hadn't yet filled the measure of his years and he has already passed away. Someone else answered, Is it only old people who are entitled to die? Sometimes even a young man finds himself dead.

Isaac understood what he understood, and was about to pass by the bier and return home and eat and drink and go to bed to rest and enjoy. He stood still and looked at the rickety poles tied with thick ropes, and on them lay Bloykof who died and a small group walked behind him. Some go and some come. Isaac picked up his feet and started running after the corpse along with all his tools. He could have put down his tools in any shop and accompanied the corpse to the cemetery, but at that hour his eyes and his heart were blocked by the death of his comrade. So he walked with the pallbearers, paint-stained, a pot of paint hanging on his arm and a ladder hanging on his shoulders, until they placed Samson Bloykof in the ground and poured dirt on him.

Samson Bloykof died at noon on Friday, and they hurried to bring him to the cemetery before the entrance of the Sabbath, and there wasn't time to announce his death to his comrades before he was buried.

5 |

At night, after dinner, a few artists and writers and teachers and activists went down to his widow to console her. Professor Schatz came, wrapped in a white Bedouin robe. And along with him came the director of the rug department of the Bezalel art school also wrapped like his teacher in a robe. And along with them, Kleinhof the writer who boasted that he was one of the first to write an article about Bloykof and made him famous in the world. Then came Gilboa the writer along with Mantelzak the painter who suppressed his usual behavior and didn't bear a grudge against Bloykof at that moment, even though Bloykof had called him a smearer. Then came Spokoyni, whose portrait Bloykof had painted. Now that Bloykof was dead, it occurred to Spokoyni that the journals would jump and publish some of his works and would certainly publish that picture which was praised as a success by all the experts. Spokoyni was satisfied and a little dissatisfied, satisfied that his name would be publicized in the world and dissatisfied lest, in the process, the widow would remember that he hadn't paid for the picture. Finally came our friend Eliezer Karstin the humble and modest painter who plied his trade in art and never sought greatness for himself. He wasn't one of Bloykof's coterie and wasn't fond of his paintings. But he showed up when he was in need and hid when the time came to pay up. Karstin mourned Samson Bloykof who died and was sorry for Tosya who was widowed, and sought how to grant help to the widow with some of his own bread without shaming her.

The widow Tosya lay ill and a woman who served as a nurse from time to time took care of her. Everyone who entered the house went to the widow and clasped her hand and said something, with a sheath of mourning on his face. Isaac came too. Since he had joined the funeral procession, he hadn't had time to change his clothes, and since he wanted to spend the Sabbath at home, he hadn't shaved his beard. Thus his simple countenance was evidently the countenance of a simple craftsman, and people were amazed at him pushing his way in among teachers and writers and painters and activists. One maiden, whom Mrs. Bloykof had once invited for him, glanced at him. She looked at him with smiling eyes and said, Did you ever think that Samson would leave us suddenly? Isaac looked at her in amazement. Even though he saw them bury Bloykof, his mind had not come to terms with the artist's death.

After a while, most of the consolers went, and only those who were close remained. One stretched his hand toward the wall and pointed to the new picture which wasn't finished and said, He certainly took pains for his widow. They began discussing the livelihood of the widow and where she would get her sustenance. One of the visitors withdrew from the group and his comrade and three or four others accompanied him. Soon the cellar emptied out and the only ones remaining were Isaac and that woman who was taking care of the widow. Mrs. Bloykof raised her eyes to him and said, Mr. Kumer, you're here. He nodded to her and began weeping. She sat up in bed and said, Do you think I'm responsible for his death? Isaac screamed, Who, you? Said she, I also tell myself that I'm not responsible for his death, but when I saw him wasting his strength, I asked him to relax a little. And he didn't listen to me, until his brush dropped out of his hand and he died. Please, Mr. Kumer, bring the picture close to me, the one standing on my table. No, leave it in its place. No, bring it close to me. And Mrs. Konstantinovski will be good enough to light the lamp for me. Isaac brought the picture close to her. Tosya looked and said, The paint hasn't yet dried and he's already lying dead. Tosya didn't weep or shed a tear. But her grief muddled her eyes. At last, she held out her hand to Isaac and said, When you have some free time from your work, come visit me. Goodbye. A good Sabbath to you, answered Isaac, tearfully. Mrs. Bloykof was jolted and said, Today is the Sabbath. And she began to weep loudly.

6 |

The Sabbath passed. For the pious, in Torah and prayer, eating and drinking and sleeping. And for the average person, in eating and drinking and sleeping. For Bloykof's widow, how did it pass? For Bloykof's widow, it passed in sorrow and mourning. And for Isaac too. A thousand times a day, Isaac said, Bloykof's dead. And as he said it, he repeated, Bloykof's not dead. But in his heart Isaac knew that if he went to Bloykof's house, he wouldn't find Bloykof. And when

Isaac felt that, he turned his head to the wall and wept. And so Isaac spent most of the day in his room. The bristles of his beard pricked his face like mosquitoes. And a mosquito seemed to be pricking his brain. And when the day began to decline and the walls of his room began to turn dark, he felt gloomy and couldn't bear his grief. He got up and went out. And when he went out into the street, it seemed to him that something wasn't right. In fact, there was no change outside, but there was a change in his heart and he imagined that he saw the world changed. When he saw that nothing had changed, he was amazed that everything was in its regular order without any change. And when he saw girls wearing Sabbath clothes strolling in the street as they did every Sabbath, he was again amazed. His heart told him, Why are you amazed at them, do they know what you've lost? And again he felt the loss he had lost. Isaac found a little consolation in those who recite Psalms and those who study Talmud, whose loud voice was heard from the synagogues and study houses. And he wanted to go into one prayer house, but he didn't because he wasn't used to prayer houses. He walked down Jaffa Road, and from there to Jaffa Gate and from there inside the Old City wall and from there to the Western Wall.

A silence of holiness hung on the stones of the Western Wall. One Minyan was concluding the afternoon prayers and another Minyan was reciting the afternoon prayers. And among those standing was Eliezer Karstin wrapped in a black cloak. After they finished the prayers, Karstin leaned his head on the Western Wall and said Kaddish. There was one man there who enjoyed Karstin's alms and knew that that painter was the nephew of the Rebbe Reb Naftali Amsterdam, one of the great leaders of the Musar movement. He came to him and asked him if he had a Yortseit today since he was saying Kaddish. Karstin told him, I had a comrade and he died without sons. He asked him, What's his name? He told him. He said to him, Good things are brought about by good men. An old man in my neighborhood promised that painter to say Kaddish after his death. I'll go and tell him.

Once again, the friends of the deceased gathered to discuss the support of his widow. Since it's impossible to resolve the problem on the spur of the moment, they put the matter off to another time. Isaac couldn't make a decent decision either. At one moment, he wanted to advise her to open a restaurant and at the next he wanted to give her other advice, which he couldn't accept. Meanwhile, Isaac stood by her in her hour of need and was grateful to her that she didn't make things hard for him.

Once a shopkeeper came to the cellar to order a sign, and he didn't know that Bloykof was dead. At that moment, Isaac chanced to drop in. Said Isaac, I'll make the sign. He made the sign and gave his fee to Tosya. Said Tosya to Isaac, My husband Samson left paints and brushes and canvas. Take them and let's make a partnership and we'll divide the profit. Isaac agreed to the partnership, and thought to himself, Even if there's no livelihood here, there is enough to assist the widow honorably.

One day Isaac found a man in her home acting like the head of the house. Mrs. Bloykof sensed that they were wondering about each other. She told the guest who Mr. Kumer was and she told Mr. Kumer who the guest was, it was her brother-in-law, the husband of her deceased sister. The day her father got the news of Samson's death, her brother-in-law went to Trieste, where he went every year, for he was a merchant of southern fruits; and he left all his business and came.

Eight or nine days later, Mrs. Bloykof wrapped up Bloykof's paintings, put them in the cradle of the dead little girl, and gave them to whoever she gave them to. And that man left them wherever he left them until the moths attacked them. Tosya returned with her brother-in-law to her hometown, after she had suffered great hardships with Bloykof, and now that Bloykof was dead, her brother-in-law was willing to marry her. Artists grab the best women for wives. But the lives of artists are lives of grief and suffering and most of them starve to death in their youth, and so even an ordinary man can win a handsome and desirable woman like Tosya.

CHAPTER TEN

Orphanhood

1 |

After Bloykof died and his widow left the Land, Isaac was left without a friendly home. In truth, for a few weeks before Bloykof passed away, he hadn't gone to the artist's house, and when Bloykof died he withdrew into himself. In those days, Isaac hid from his comrades and sat by himself a lot, wondering at the world full of suffering followed by death. And in his thoughts, he enumerated all his comrades who had died. Once he went to his neighbors from his homeland, the seminary students. He came and found only two of his four comrades, for one of them was sick and was taken to the hospital and one got married and went to live in his father-in-law's house.

That woman was lame, and it was hard to find a match for her because of her defect. And that defect was the result of an act, for once, violating the prohibition of the holiday, she went to the grave of Simon the Saint and broke her leg and became crippled. Don't the graves of the Saints bring healing, and how did an accident happen on the grave of the Saint? But she went to show off her new dress, got her legs tangled in her dress and broke her leg. But the Saint had mercy on her and sent her a mate and blindfolded his eyes so he wouldn't look at her defect. And because he didn't look at the defect of a Jewish girl, he won a wife and support.

His two comrades laughed at that fool who was tempted by the bread of fools. But when they look at their own meager bread that they cut up into pieces as tiny as olives and are never sated by it, they justify what he did. Not every Amnon wins his Tamar, and not every Solomon finds a Shulamit. How much their hearts had hummed when they lived Outside the Land and read in the novel *The Love of*

Zion about the splendor of the excellent daughters of Zion. Now that they dwell in Jerusalem, they haven't yet seen that splendor. Perhaps the Sages were right when they interpreted the Song of Songs as a parable and an allegory.

Our two young comrades lie on their rickety benches with torn bedding beneath them, and books in their hands. A lot of things are written in books, but the main thing is missing from the book, how you sustain the body in hunger and thirst, in evil illnesses and the other ravages of time. If they had stayed Outside the Land, they would have been married off to women and dressed in good clothes and lived like human beings and eaten and drunk like human beings and been appointed to everything in the Society and would have supported Zionism, bought a Shekel and contributed money to the Jewish National Fund and subscribed to the Hebrew newspaper, and educated fellows would have flocked to their door and talked about Ahad Ha-Am and Mendele and Bialik and about the change of taste in literature and poetry. When their fathers were young, Y. L. Gordon was considered the leader of the Hebrew poets, and when the fathers of their fathers were young, Adam HaCohen was considered the leader of the Hebrew poets, and before Adam HaCohen, Naftali Hertz Vesseley was considered the leader of all the poets. Now, Vesseley is derided and no one remembers Adam, and they even scratched Gordon out of their heart, and every mouth bleats, No one dares disagree that there is no poet like Bialik. But times change, and from time to time, taste changes, and a new generation may arise that won't savor all the flavors we savor in Bialik. But why should we worry about tomorrow, we have enough to worry about today. If they withstand all the troubles and complete their studies and don't fail their examinations, they'll find a position in a school and will find their daily bread. But man doth not live by bread only. There are a great many other things a man's heart yearns for. Meanwhile, their time is running short. Even when there were four of them, it was hard for them to pay the rent. Now that there are two, it's that much harder.

Two or three times, Isaac went to visit his comrades. At last he stopped going to them. As long as Bloykof was alive, Isaac seemed to leave all his friends for Bloykof. Now that Bloykof was dead, he had lost the taste for friendship.

2 |

Isaac has been living in Jerusalem for almost a year. Breakfast and supper he ate in his room, and for lunch he made do with what he had taken to work in his basket. If he didn't have any work to do, and if he did have an extra coin, he put on his best clothes and went to the Georgian restaurant where most of the bachelor intelligentsia ate their meals. Since our comrade Isaac wasn't eager for luxuries, he gave up dessert and his meal suited his pocket. There were some diners who gave Isaac a friendly welcome and there were others who didn't, for Jerusalem is not like Jaffa. In Jaffa everyone sits together. In Jerusalem, craftsmen sit in one place and members of the intellectual professions sit somewhere else. Once Isaac heard that Lydia Rosenberg, the pampered secretary of the principal of the Hilfsverein Society School, complained that a housepainter was seated at her table. Isaac thought to himself, If Sonya was with me, they wouldn't look down on me.

All that time he lived in Jerusalem, he hadn't heard anything about Sonya, except once when he got regards from her. And it's not clear if she sent him regards or if the man who gave him her regards did it on his own. She even stopped writing letters to him. Sonya was preoccupied with other things. But Isaac thought about her again and ruminated about what he was going to write to her, but he hid the words in his heart before writing them. When he saw that he didn't get them down in writing, he sought to do orally what he didn't do in writing. And he began thinking about going down to Jaffa. What Isaac did with his letters you already know, so now I shall tell what he did with his trip. At night he would say, I have to go. Morning came and he didn't go. Isaac came out of his state of equanimity. And when he looked at himself he said, That's not how I pictured my world. But if that's my lot, so be it.

Isaac's world really wasn't so bad. He made a living, and if it wasn't prosperous, it was enough for his needs. And from the day Bloykof died, Isaac's yoke was lighter and he didn't have to skimp on his own bread for the sake of others. And from the day Mrs. Bloykof went Outside the Land, he didn't have to share with her what he earned making signs and dedication tablets. But it is not given to every man to be happy with what he's got, and he is sorry for what he hasn't got. Isaac began disparaging his brushes and paints, which he had to substitute for the spade and the plow, and he didn't remember that never had he held a plow or a spade. And since he examined that, he examined the origins of things and the sequence of their development, from the day he lured his father into giving him travel expenses to the Land of Israel, to the day he became close to Sonya and took her heart away from Rabinovitch, and finally she took her heart away from Isaac too. What did Isaac have left of all those things? He deceived his father and he deceived his friend and his friend's girlfriend. And what did he have left? Desolation and grief and remorse and shame, like the parable the preachers tell about the cunning of the Evil Instinct that tempts man and seems to show him all the delights of the world in his hand until he drags his feet behind him like a dog, and finally he kicks him as you kick a mad dog.

CHAPTER ELEVEN

Inside Jerusalem

1 |

A covenant is made with every city that stamps its seal on its inhabitants, especially the city of God, most exquisite of all cities, where the Shekhina never moves away from it. And even if the Shekhina is hidden and covered, there are times and seasons when even the most simple son of Israel who was blessed to dwell in Jerusalem will sense it, each to the degree of his sensibilities and to his merit and to the light of grace that illuminates his soul, and by virtue of the suffering he has suffered in the Land and that he accepted with love and did not complain.

All the time Isaac lived Outside the Land, he kept the Sabbath and laid Tefillin and prayed every day, as taught by the precept of men. When he ascended to the Land of Israel, he hung his Tefillin on a peg and lifted the other Commandments off his neck, he didn't keep the Sabbath and he didn't pray. When the fear of his father was lifted from him, the fear of his Father in Heaven was also lifted from him. Isaac was young, and hadn't pondered much and made no calculations with his Creator, like most of our comrades in those days. When he ascended to Jerusalem, he started changing. Sometimes on his own initiative and sometimes because of others, for instance when he worked with the Jerusalem painters and the time came for afternoon prayer and the painters stood up to pray, he also stopped work and prayed with them. And if he ate with them a piece of bread as tiny as an olive, he would join the prayer and say grace after his meal.

2 |

Isaac's fellow painters invited Isaac to all the celebrations in their homes. Those people, who flay their flesh to make a wretched living and all their days are grief and suffering, when they get a festive meal, they change and become happy. Twenty or thirty of them gather in a cramped apartment and spread a cloth, put out a bottle of red wine and a pitcher of brandy and some peanuts and sunflower seeds, and slices of honey cake from coarsely ground flour, and pieces of watermelon. And on winter days, they crown the table with oranges from Jaffa whose fruit is big, and from Jericho whose fruit is sweet. Everyone pours himself a little drink, and drinks a little and congratulates the host and all the guests, and slices himself a small slice of cake, and doesn't eat immediately, but puts it with his glass so the host will see that he is enjoying his feast. If he has a good voice, he sings a tune, and if he is a joyful fellow, he tells a joke that entertains everybody, and if he's a Talmud scholar he proffers a fine oral sermon or subtle reading on the weekly Torah portion or on a Bible verse, and concludes with some numerological acrobatics on the political events of the day.

From issues of Torah, they come to tell about Torah scholars, the first Rabbis of Jerusalem, who quashed persecutions with their prayers and removed evil decrees and brought down so much rain that the Gentiles were amazed and stunned, and bowed their heads to them. And it's no wonder, for everyone who sanctifies himself and is truly in awe of the Lord and all his actions are for His Name, Blessed-Be-He, the Almighty loves him and is happy to do his will, as we say in the Psalm of David, He will fulfill the desire of them that fear him. As was the case with our teacher Kalonymos the miracle worker, who sacrificed himself for the Sons of Israel so much that he violated the Sabbath and the punishment for that is being stoned to death, and so that Saint commanded that everyone who sees his grave shall throw stones at it, and you still see a heap of stones on his grave. And since so many years have passed, the stones should have risen as high as heaven, but they must come down from heaven and take those stones away, and they must have a reason for that which we can't grasp. From our first Rabbis, we come to the Rabbi who wrote *The Light of Light* and to the sages of God's House, to the supreme saints, the masters of mystical intentions, who are like the ministering angels. And there are those who tell about Jerusalem, that the Shekhina has never moved away from it and even the Gentile inhabitants of the Land don't reject it, even in its destruction, and it always rests on the Western Wall, which, even though it is desolate, in its holiness it stands, and all the deeds of the Gentiles and their abominations don't touch it. And some tell about the Western Wall that in the past they didn't come there with shoes on their feet, but took them off and left them at some distance from the place, not like today when people come in their shoes. Our forefathers who were closer to the Destruction follow the laws of the seven days of mourning, while we who are close to the Redemption follow the rules of an ancient mourning. And when they tell of the first generations, they tell of those awesome sights in the heavens that were seen in Jerusalem until the year 1840 and stirred every heart to repentance.

Most of all, they were fond of telling the feats of their forefathers, who wandered around on the roads for a year or two or three, until they came to Jerusalem. Some of them were rich Outside the Land and lived in fine, big houses, and they left all the luxuries Outside the Land and ascended and came to Jerusalem, and they made do with dry bread and lived on a dungheap that disgusted even the dogs, and they were as happy as if they lived in a royal palace, because they were dwelling in Jerusalem. And if they saw a fine house they wept and said Jerusalem, Jerusalem, how have you doffed the garb of your widowhood and donned fine clothes? And some of our forefathers were great rabbis, mighty in Torah, and when they came to Jerusalem, they didn't publicize themselves because they didn't want to enjoy the crown of the Torah in the place of the Torah's life and they sat in the marketplaces of the city as harness-makers and cobblers wrapped in Tefillin and making a living from crafts they had clandestinely learned Outside the Land for the sake of Jerusalem, and no one knew their greatness until someone from their city chanced to come here and knew them and the Rabbis of Jerusalem forced them to leave their work for the work of Heaven. And when they did leave their work, they didn't call a craftsman to their home, but did everything with their own hands because of the honor of the craft, and they decreed that their sons should practice a craft, for a craft sustains those who practice it. And since the weary hearts are stirred by the feats of their forefathers, holy men who serve the Lord, one of the group stands up and takes off his shoes and sits on the ground and recites Bible verses of trouble and mourning, like the essence of man is dust, and like For our soul is bowed down to the dust: our belly cleaveth unto the earth. While that one sits and weeps, someone else stands up and dances to God with a song of joy, For we are Your people and You are our God, and all the guests join in, some with singing and some with clapping, until the time for prayer comes and they stand up to pray and return to their homes.

3 |

Isaac was most excited on Sabbath eves, when the city stops its give and take and gleams with the light of the Sabbath. This is the light of the Sabbath whose splendor glows even in the rotten generations. The sun has not yet finished its course in the firmament, but beneath the heavens, on the earth below, a great change is already visible. The air is transformed and a kind of hidden joy rises. All the shops are locked and all weekday business comes to a halt. The streets of Jerusalem are emptied of carts and the Holy Earth dwells in silence. No wheel turns, no whip lashes. The expanses of the world are silent, and a holy calm is ignited by the silence of the city. At that hour, the old beadle goes out from the Great Synagogue of Rabban Yohanan ben Zakkai and calls out, The time for lighting candles has come! At that hour, someone jumps from the homeless shelters on Mount Zion and goes up to the top of the roof of a tall house and blows the ram's horn to warn the nation that the Sabbath is coming. Opposite him, one of the Sadigura Hasids jumps up to the top of the roof of the Great Synagogue, Tiferet Israel, with a brass trumpet two cubits long in his mouth, and blows. Immediately, they come out of the rest of the synagogues and climb up to their roofs and blow until their voice is heard outside the Old City walls. Yeshiva students dressed in Sabbath clothes come and climb up on the roofs of the tall houses in the new city and ring big bells in their hands to announce that the time has come to light candles. And in every house and every courtyard, people hurry to prepare themselves to honor the Sabbath. Some savor the Sabbath dishes, for those who savor the Sabbath gain eternal life. And some search through their clothing lest they have forgotten something that is forbidden to carry on the Sabbath, and others urge their little sons to arrange the prayer books for the Sabbath; some put oil in glass lamps and others pour some red wine into the oil to make it beautiful; some set the table and others don Sabbath clothes. Anger vanished from their faces and every speech is soft and good, and from every house and every courtyard shine many candles, and the whole city is like a palace adorned with candles and lights. Here a lamp is lit and there a lantern. Here a bowl of olive oil and there pure white candles. Here two candles for remember the Sabbath day and keep the Sabbath day, and two tablets of the Covenant, and there ten candles for the Ten Commandments. Here seven candles for the seven days, and there twelve candles for the twelve Tribes of Israel. Here as many candles as there are people in the house, and there candles without number. There are houses and courtyards where you don't see the light of a candle all the nights, and when the Sabbath comes, the whole house is lit up. There are women who used to drop a coin into the box of Rabbi Meir Ba'al Haness and say a special prayer every Sabbath eve before they lit the candles, and now they themselves are supported by that Charity, like people who deposited their money in a secure place and take it out in their hour of need. Now all of Jerusalem has ceased its work and from every house and every courtyard come old and young, dressed in Sabbath clothes, their faces glowing with the light of the Sabbath. People who aren't important in your eyes on weekdays are exalted at that hour. Gone are angry faces and every eye is shining. Some go to the synagogues and study houses and others go to the Western Wall. Some walk slowly and others hasten, as their multicolored robes in all handsome hues are dragged over the stones of Jerusalem and cloak the streets of Jerusalem in velvet and satin. At that hour, all kinds of handsome hues appear in the sky overhead, either because the Sabbath garb is reflected in it, or the Sabbath garb is handsome because the shine of the firmament is reflected in it when the Sabbath enters. Often, our comrade Isaac followed behind those going to pray until he came to the Western Wall and stood and read with them *Give thanks unto the Lord, for he is good: for his mercy endureth forever*, as if he too merited that mercy the Holy-One-Blessed-Be-He bestows on those who keep His commandments.

How beautiful is the entrance of the Sabbath at the Western Wall. The holy stones, whose holiness shines to us through the darkness of our exile, are even holier in the sanctity of the Sabbath, and the Children of Israel, who draw holiness from it, its remembrance and preservation, they will be redeemed. Isaac stands and prays, either by heart or from the prayer book. Sometimes his heart is drawn to the simple and charming melodies of the Mitnagdim and sometimes to the melodies of the Hasids, sometimes to the melodies of the Hasids who are excited at the awe in their heart, and sometimes to the melodies of the Hasids who are exalted by the flame of their prayer. And within every single melody, in Isaac's heart his own melody sings with a blend of the melody he got from his hometown. In his amazement Isaac removes all his sins from his heart and sees himself as a newborn babe with no sin, pure of all blemish as in those early days when he was a lad with the lads of his hometown — with an addition of holiness from the holiness of the Sabbath in Jerusalem. How beautiful is the light of mercy to the soul that yearns.

4 |

But that mercy is not forever, for the quality of mercy is revealed only at times, especially to a person who isn't worthy for the light of mercy to shine on him incessantly. Much as we try to justify Isaac, we must say that he was no better than all our other comrades. What can words add to it? We all want the good, but that good we want isn't the real good. This matter has to be explained and I shall try to explain it.

When we studied Torah in our youth, we knew that everything written in the Torah exists forever. And the only yearning of every single person of our nation was to carry out the Commandments and good deeds as told in the Torah. Later, other books fell into our hands and we found in them things we hadn't imagined. Doubt entered our heart. And when we entered the house of doubt, we began slacking off in the Commandments. And if we kept some of them, we kept them so as not to make our parents angry. When we ascended to the Land of Israel and became free of Father's yoke, we also removed the yoke of Torah. Some removed the yoke out of fondness for freedom, and some removed the yoke because they mistakenly thought that the Lord demands of us only a good heart and to do mercy. And here came some of the sages of the time and reinforced us in our errors with their articles and their research, who said that most of the Commandments are just products of Exile. Because when the first sages saw that we were exiled from our Land, they began to fear lest we disappear among the Gentiles. So they gave us a great number of Commandments to distinguish us from all the other nations, for as long as the Children of Israel lived on their own soil, what did the Prophet demand of them? A good heart and to do mercy. And the same for the future, when we return to our Land. Now that we are returning and the danger of mixing with the Gentiles is abolished, there is no more need for the positive Commandments, as they said in the Talmud, the Commandments will be abolished in the Hereafter. That or something close to it is the error of the sages of the time and we followed them. And we didn't notice that the early days have passed and the days of the Messiah haven't yet come, and the Exile is still going on and on.

Those ideas dominated Isaac's generation. And even though Isaac himself wasn't concerned with ideas, he put aside the Law and put off the yoke. Therefore, as soon as the light of divine mercy was revealed to him, it was extinguished. Like that lantern whose sides burst and the candlelight inside it cannot survive. Here is Isaac standing at the Western Wall and the divine light illuminates his heart, but when he returns to his home he returns to his own state. So very sadly Isaac sits there. No white cloth is spread on his table, and no Sabbath candle illuminates his house. No wine for the blessing and no plaited loaf of bread. A small lamp is lit as usual, but on all nights its light glows and on the Sabbath night its light is dim, for on the Sabbath night the eyes of the sons of Israel are bigger than on all other nights and need a double light. Isaac recalled Sabbath nights in his father's house. Father returns from the prayer house dressed in Sabbath clothes and thanks the Lord for all the mercies He has done unto him and will do unto him and unto all mankind and greets the Sabbath with awe and love and joy, even though he borrowed for his Sabbath because of his poverty. And when he recalled his father he recalled all his troubles at home and outside and his running from lender to lender, for Father has not yet settled his debt and pays interest on the interest. Even harsher than that is the issue of his brother who is eager to ascend to the Land of Israel to work the soil like Isaac. And even Father who consented to his oldest son's journey only to keep his brothers from being dragged after him, even he wants Isaac to help his brother ascend to the Holy Land to work its soil and be sated with its goodness, for all hopes have come to an end, and there is no end to the pressures of a livelihood. And what will Isaac do? The truth he is ashamed to write, and a lie he won't tell.

5 |

In the meantime, Isaac got used to Jerusalem and Jerusalem got used to him. And if the sun beats during the day, the chill of the Jerusalem nights is refreshing. How good is a wind! When it blows, folks' limbs become light and comfortable on them.

Isaac is settled in Jerusalem and knows the city and its neighborhoods. There is not one single neighborhood in Jerusalem where Isaac hasn't worked. Here he painted walls and there he painted doors, here he painted houses and there he made signs for shops as he had learned from Samson Bloykof. All work brings those who practice it among folks. The tailor with his clothing and the cobbler with his shoes and the barber with the hair on your head and all the other craftsmen, every single one according to his craft. But most of all is the painter whose craft brings him among a lot of people all at the same time, for when the walls of a house are being painted, the neighbors and the neighbors of the neighbors come to watch the painter at work. And so Isaac got acquainted with most of the communities, Ashkenazim and Sephardim, Babylonians and Aleppans, Mughrabites and Yemenites, Georgians and Bukharans and Persians, Hasidim and Mitnagdim, educated people and average people. Sometimes Isaac works for those who mourn Jerusalem and sometimes he works for those who are helping to destroy her. Sometimes he does his work alone and sometimes he hires a comrade to help him, or his comrades hire him to help them. For one reason or another, Isaac came upon that old painter he had worked with when he first ascended to Jerusalem. The old man had gotten much older and still practiced his craft, for his grandson followed his father's example and followed him to America to seek his fortune, but fortune can't be sought, and here are his mother and his brothers and his sisters and his wife and his son, and they don't have anything to eat, and they gaze at his hands. The people of Jerusalem are strange people. From everyplace, people ascend to Jerusalem and the people of Jerusalem leave Jerusalem. But the Holy-One-Blessed-Be-He punishes those who leave His city and doesn't give them rest in any other city, but while He punishes them He also punishes those who love her. For an old man like this one deserves to sit in the study house and study a chapter of Mishnah, while this old man has to weary himself twice over.

Let's come back to Isaac. Sometimes Isaac does his work alone and sometimes he does it in company. Sometimes he hires himself out to someone else and sometimes he hires himself a laborer. And sometimes that laborer was himself a craftsman and Isaac had worked for him. What goes around comes around. Yesterday a man is the boss of others and tomorrow a slave to his slaves. Sometimes Isaac worked in this neighborhood, and sometimes he worked in that neighborhood. To make a long story short, you don't have one single neighborhood of the neighborhoods of Jerusalem our comrade Isaac didn't frequent.

Two Friends Will Meet But Mountains Never

1 |

In those days, Isaac worked in the Hungarian houses in the western part of Jerusalem, near Meah Shearim and Beit Israel, where there are about fifteen big houses with three hundred apartments for the members of the Hungarian Society who live there three years for free, and sometimes more, according to the wish of the donor and the officials who run the Society. All the houses are alike, and each apartment has two rooms and a small corner where the women cook their dishes. And a big yard paved with stones goes between one row of houses and another, and there is the cistern. Just as the houses are all alike so are their tenants. All of them are dignified people who keep the Torah and the Commandments, who serve their Creator with a full belly. And they don't yield to anyone either in earthly matters or in heavenly matters, and they punish any person who is not like them, by persecution and contempt and ostracism and refusing Charity and expulsion.

    That day was hot. Isaac was working outside. The sun tossed sparks of fire and the cobblestones of the yard burned like fire. The air turned white like the ashes of a stove when a fire is lit in it, and the gutters and the eaves and the iron bolts of the cisterns and the iron at the stairs of the houses and the brackets and the balconies and everything that sees the sun was ablaze. A smell of cooking and baking and frying wafted from the houses, and the smell went from house to house and from yard to yard and wound up outside, as if everything that was cooked and baked and fried on an ordinary fire came to be cooked and baked and fried on a fire from above. And from the three Yeshivas, from the Yeshiva of Hatam Sofer and the

Yeshiva of the Katav Sofer and the Yeshiva of Beit Ha-Meir, rose a sound of Torah, worn out and sated, sated and worn out. In competition, a teacher's voice was heard reading to his little pupils.

The teacher stands before his pupils and reads, When Israel was a child, then I loved him, and called my son out of Egypt. That is, when the children of Israel were in Egypt they were like a child who has not tasted the taste of sin, therefore I loved him, as the Scripture says here, When Israel was a child, then I loved him, and it also says I loved you, But the Lord hath taken you, and brought you forth out of the iron furnace, even out of Egypt to follow me and I showed them miracles and wonders, I broke the sea before them and I brought manna down to them and gave them the Torah and many other good things I did to them, as we learned in the Humash. And now, children, listen to me, what does the Prophet then say, As they called them, so they went from them. As I called them and I brought them to the Delightsome Land, that in all other lands there is no better one, and I gave them good Prophets to teach them the good way, so they went and fled from them. They fled not to me, but they fled to idols and graven images. Where are you looking, wicked ones, may the Angel of Death snatch your eyes, ye wicked ones, I'm teaching them the word of the Living God and they turn to idols and graven images. Isaac felt that the schoolchildren were looking at him through the window. So he turned back to his work. He found his brushes dry and the water jar empty. What Isaac left the sun drank, and what the sun left Isaac drank, and there wasn't enough left in the jar to wet your lips. He picked up the jar and went into a house to ask for water. The lady of the house recognized him and said, Aren't you the one who traveled with us on the same ship?

Isaac looked at her and recognized her. He held out his hand to greet her. Yet the old woman hid both her hands behind her and called her husband and said, Moyshe Amram, Moyshe Amram, come and say hello to a guest. Moyshe Amram came out and looked at Isaac, then frowned, then took off his glasses, then looked at him again. Finally he asked, Who is this guest? Said the old woman, Don't you recognize him, and me, as soon as he came in, right away I recognized him. Said the old man, That means your eyes are better than mine, or let's say as they said, a woman recognizes guests better than the man. Wait a bit and don't tell me who he is. Isn't he. . . Before he could finish, the old woman interrupted him and asked, So, who is he? Said the old man, Isn't your name Jacob? He told him, Isaac's my name. Said the old man, Blessed Be He Who reminds what is forgotten. I remembered, I remembered. He greeted him and asked him, What brought you here? Said Isaac, I was at my work and I was thirsty and I came in to ask for water. Said the old woman, I'll pour you some right away, right away I'll pour you some. Said the old man, What's this, Disha, will he stand here and drink? Come Isaac, come into the parlor. The old man went in with Isaac and sat him down on a chair. The old woman brought him a pitcher of cold water. Isaac drank his fill. The old man asked him, How did you get here? Didn't you want to go to the settlements? All that time, the old woman stood and looked favorably on Isaac. Everyone who knows about Isaac will feel Isaac's joy. Ever since the day Samson Bloykof died, he hadn't been so happy with anyone.

Isaac sat with the old man, who asked him how he had fared. What did he do after he came off the ship in Jaffa, and where did he go first, and how did he become a painter, and hadn't he ascended to work the land? And he also asked him how many villages of the children of Israel there were in the Land of Israel, and how much a farmer earns from the produce of his fields. What do they sow and what do they plant? And how do they transfer their businesses to the Sabbath Goy, do they take him as a partner for one hundredth part, and so on and so forth. And he even told Isaac how he behaved Outside the Land, that he had never allowed himself to act with cunning, not in matters of the Sabbath and not in matters of Passover, when others behaved loosely. And Thank God, he didn't lose anything. On the contrary, by virtue of keeping the Torah Outside the Land, he was blessed to ascend to the Land of Israel. And may he succeed in upholding the Torah in Jerusalem as he had upheld it in his hometown. So they sat and talked for an hour and another hour. Before Isaac could answer one question, the old man had asked another question and for every single question he asked, he told many things. Like old people, everything reminds them of something else.

The old woman sat across from them and looked affectionately at Isaac and at her husband, whose soul was refreshed by the
guest. And when her husband fell silent for a while, she came and
reminded Isaac of their trip on the sea. How much had passed by
now, but she still imagines that she is rocking on the ship, and at night
when she can't sleep because of the heat and the mosquitoes, she lies
in her bed and raises in her mind's eye the open sea and the blue
water, how one wave butts the other and they finally make peace.
And she does that even now when the sun is burning and no wind
refreshes the person. *M'darf nit zindign*, a person must not sin, Isaac,
said the old woman and tapped her mouth, but sometimes it seems
to me that the trip to the Land of Israel was better than coming into
the Land of Israel, not to mention dwelling in the Land of Israel. A
person must not sin, but if only our settling in the Land of Israel were
like our journey to the Land of Israel. Let her talk, Isaac, said the old
man laughing, his mourning evident on his face. It's the way of
women to grumble and complain. There's nothing new under the
sun, Eve back in the Garden of Eden wasn't satisfied. But we must
learn from experience not to become like the First Adam who was
tempted by women and was punished. You married, Isaac? No? How
come? From what you say, you make a living, and even if a man
|doesn't make a living, God Forbid, he may not live without a
woman. The old man looked at Isaac with compassion and said to
him, May The Blessed Lord help you find a mate. Amen, answered
the old woman pleasantly, Amen, may it be His will.

Happy and goodhearted, Isaac left the old man's house. Two
mountains will never meet, but two humans will. Isaac never imagined such a fine reception. All the time they were Outside the Land,
they hadn't come together, in the Land of Israel, they did come together. All sons of Israel are comrades, especially in the Land of Israel. That old man asked a lot of questions. Things Isaac had never
thought about, but since the old man talked about them, he became
fond of them. *M'darf nit zindign*, Isaac; Isaac repeated the old
woman's words and laughed to himself, what were all those transgressions of that modest woman. A person must not sin. Suddenly his
sin came and stood before his eyes, and a great sadness embraced his

heart, and like Menashe-Haim in his day, he pondered to himself, How easy it was not to do that. But what was done can't be taken back. A man who committed an offense does not cleanse himself of it unless he repents. But here, what good does repentance do, for repentance itself comes as an offense, for if he married Sonya, what good would it do Rabinovitch? Master-of-the-Universe, what should I do and what must I not do?

2 |

A few days later, Isaac returned to the old man's house. But the second coming is not like the first coming. Not only did the old man not greet him with a smile, but he greeted him with rage. May that not befall you, good friends, Isaac thought Reb Moyshe Amram would be happy with him, but in the end he showed him an angry face. At first those old people pull you close together, and when you are close, they push you away.

When Isaac saw that he wasn't wanted, he stood up to go. The old man said to him, Are you in a hurry? Said Isaac, I'm not in a hurry. Said the old man, Then why are you wiggling around to leave? Said Isaac, I see that I'm superfluous here. Said the old man, Why do you see what is superfluous and you don't see what's missing? He pointed at his chin and told him, If you neglected your beard Outside the Land, in the Land of Israel, who forces you to do that? Isaac played the wise guy and inundated him with words from the Torah to placate the old man, he told him, I heard that growing a beard is one of the Commandments dependent on the Land. The old man jumped up as if he had been bitten by a snake. But he immediately sat back down, took Isaac's hand, and said to him, My friend, why are you telling me innovations? Isn't shaving the beard forbidden by the Torah? To smooth things between them, the old man placed his hand on Isaac's and said, Sit down and rest, sit. If you're not rushing to afternoon prayers, you don't have to run. The old man called into another room and said, Shifra, Shifra, bring some treats for my guest.

A beautiful and pious lass entered and brought water and jam. She poured water for Isaac in a clean glass and said, May the gentleman please savor it. The old man looked at her fondly and said to Isaac, My granddaughter, my daughter's daughter. Before Isaac could look at her, she had left. At that moment, Isaac's eyes grew dim and his heart began pounding. What was Isaac like at that hour? Like the First Adam when the Holy-One-Blessed-Be-He took one of his ribs and stood Eve before him. Isaac shifted his eyes from that lass since he regarded himself as Sonya's mate. But the eyes of his heart came and showed her to him. Isaac was sad. But a pinch of joy sweetened the sadness.

CHAPTER THIRTEEN

Memorial Stones

1 |

Isaac finished his work in the Hungarian neighborhood and everyone was satisfied with what he had done. Blessed hands has Isaac and
everything he does he does well. Too bad the artisan himself isn't as
handsome as his work. He wears a short jacket and has neither sidelocks nor beard. It's amazing that Reb Moyshe Amram, the father-in-
law of Reb Fayesh, is nice to him. But Reb Moyshe Amram is new in
the Land and in some things he behaves as he would Outside the
Land. It would be interesting to know what Reb Fayesh will say when
he sees that Polak frequenting his house.

Isaac finished his work in the Hungarian Houses and is already working in other places in the city. New houses are being built
and even the old ones want to be restored. This one because it was
time for it to be restored and that one because it saw its comrade
being restored and wanted to restore himself. Isaac sometimes works
in a new house and sometimes in an old house. He paints doors and
shutters, walls and ceilings, whatever the landlord wants and whatever the house needs.

2 |

Isaac has another trade, too, making signs and painting memorial
stones. From all over the globe and from distant islands, generous
philanthropists establish houses and courtyards, memorials to the holiness of the Lord and His Land, to His Torah and those who study
it, so that every person with love of Jerusalem in his heart and with
means erects a memorial to himself in Jerusalem, builds a house and
dedicates it, buys a courtyard and dedicates it. And when the Holy-

One-Blessed-Be-He remembers His children, He looks first at Jerusalem, sees those houses and courtyards the Children of Israel built in Jerusalem, nods His head affectionately, as it were, and says, This people have I formed for myself, etc., is there a nation in the world I exiled from its land and its eyes and its heart are still on it. And everyone who dedicates a house in Jerusalem puts up a memorial stone, to give him a good place and a name in its walls, and writes his name, and his extravagant generosity is an eternal memory unto the last generation. He who is righteous, his Charity stands and his name is forgotten. He who is not righteous, his name remains and his Charity is enjoyed by those who are unworthy. Our comrade Isaac, who made his name for his paints that can endure rain and wind and snow, was called on to paint in color the writing on the tablets. How long do his colors last? Once upon a time, Isaac wrote on the skin of a dog and the dog wandered around a few months, wallowed in all kinds of dung, and the writing wasn't wiped off. And what did he see fit to write on the skin of a dog? That will come in due time.

Where are those handsome tablets painted in handsome colors by Isaac's hands? Did they overpraise Isaac's colors? But before you ask about the tablets, ask about the houses. Some of them were destroyed and some of them passed into the hands of foreigners. And even some of the neighborhoods have gone out of our hands. How much money was sunk in those houses, how many souls sank in those neighborhoods. Now a Jew doesn't set foot there, neither benediction nor blessing is heard there. At any rate, the righteousness of the volunteers was not in vain, for when the Children of Israel lived in those houses, they begot sons and daughters who were to build Jerusalem finer and more beautiful than it was, and may they never be interrupted.

And so, aside from houses and furnishings, Isaac paints signs and tablets. You don't find one single neighborhood in Jerusalem where you don't see Isaac's colors. And even our brothers, the Sephardim, who are fussier about crafts than the Ashkenazim, admit that this Ashkenazi, this Isaac Kumer, is an outstanding craftsman, and when one of them wants to put up an eternal name for himself, he calls on Isaac to paint the tablet, and needless to say, so do our brothers, the Ashkenazim. To make a long story short, you don't have one single neighborhood of the neighborhoods of Jerusalem where you don't find the colors of our comrade Isaac. In Even Israel and Beit Israel and Knesset Israel and Mahane Israel and Mishkanot Israel and Ezrat Israel, and in Ohel Moshe and Zikhron Moshe and Mazkeret Moshe and Yamin Moshe and Sha'arei Moshe, in Beit David and Beit Joseph and Beit Jacob, in the Ornstein Houses and the Bukharan Houses and in the Horodna Houses and the Werner Houses and the Warsaw Houses and the housing of the Volyn Society and the housing of the ChaBaD Society and in the housing of the Byelorussian Society and in the houses of Mendel Rand and in the houses of Simon the Saint, and in the houses of Samuel Strauss, in the houses established by the officials and administrators of the Holland and Deutschland Society and in the houses of the Sephardi community and in the houses of the Mughrabite community, in the courtyard of the Ostreich Galicia Society near Meah Shearim and in the houses of the Ostreich Galicia Society in other places, in Mahane Yehuda and in Mazkeret Tsvi and in Mishkanot Sha'ananim, in Nahalat Yakov and Nahalat Tsvi and Nahalat Shiv'ah, in Sha'arei Hesed and Sha'arei Pina and Sha'arei Tsedek, on the gates of Torah houses and prayer houses and on the gates of hospitals and on the gates of ritual baths and in all other places.

CHAPTER FOURTEEN

Stray Dog

1 |

Once, Isaac was working in the neighborhood of Rehovoth, called the Bukharan quarter. A rich landlord of Bukhara ascended from his hometown to Jerusalem to pray to God in the holy places and to prostrate himself on the graves of the Patriarchs and Matriarchs beloved of God, cherished by the Almighty. When the time came for him to return to his place, he was brokenhearted to leave Jerusalem the Holy City, for all who leave seem to fall into Hell. But his business in his hometown was extensive and his wife and his sons and his daughters urged him to return. He said to himself, I just came here and I already have to leave. I'm like a bird flying off into the air, when he flies his shadow flies with him. He delayed his journey from ship to ship and lingered a little bit more and a little bit more, and at night sleep wouldn't come because of his grief at having to leave here. Heaven took pity on him and planted in his heart the idea of making himself a memorial to the Lord. And since the Holy-One-Blessed-Be-He loves the poor, he considered building a house for the poor. He built a stone house and put up a marble tablet in it, that the house was for the poor and must not be sold or redeemed until the coming of the Redeemer. And as Isaac Kumer became famous as an expert artisan and his colors are never wiped out, he commissioned him to paint the tablet with exquisite and handsome colors. And he didn't haggle with him, so he would do good work and not stint on the paint. Isaac took his brush and embellished the tablet with his colors. The name of the donor he painted in gold and the words of the ban in red and the poor in black, and each of the other words had its own color, until the tablet rejoiced in its hues.

Isaac looked and was glad, as an artisan who chances to work for a generous person and didn't have to cheat in his work. As he was about to wipe his brushes, he chanced on a stray dog, with short ears, a sharp nose, a stub of a tail, and hair that looked maybe white or maybe brown or maybe yellow, one of those dogs who roamed around in Jerusalem until the English entered the Land. Isaac picked up one of his brushes and didn't know if he wanted to threaten the dog with it or if he wanted to wipe it off on the dog's skin. The dog stuck out his tongue and gazed at him. You can't say he wanted to lick the brush, for paints are salty and a dog doesn't like salt, but he didn't want the owner of the brush to put his brush away with no result. Isaac's arm stretched out and his hand started trembling. He reached out his brush to the dog, and the dog reached himself out to Isaac. Isaac just stroked the dog's skin, like a clerk stroking the paper before writing. Once again he dipped his brush and leaned toward the dog and wrote a few letters on his back. We don't know if, from the start, he meant to write what he wrote, or if in the end it seemed to him that he wrote with malice aforethought. But why should we get into that doubt, we had better look at his acts. And so, by the time Isaac stood up, he had written in calligraphy on the dog the letters d-o-g. He patted his back and told him, From now on, folks won't mistake you, but will know that you're a dog. And you won't forget you're a dog either.

The dog liked his contact with a human creature who has a kind of dripping vessel when the sun is at its height, when the Land is scraped and the air is dry and there isn't a drop of moisture in Jerusalem. Therefore, it is no wonder that he didn't take off, but was still waiting for his moisture to drip on him. Isaac saw the dog standing and looking at him. He said to him, What else do you want? Isn't it enough for you, dog, that I wasted a whole brushful of paint on you? But the dog wagged his tail and barked entreatingly. Isaac smiled and said to him, Are you crazy? You want me to make spots on your skin, or do you want me to paint your name in gold? The dog lifted his wet nose and barked a weak, obsequious bark. Isaac's hand began to tingle, like an artist whose hand approaches his work. He rubbed it on his clothes to get rid of the tingling, but it kept on tingling. So he dipped the brush and stretched out his hand. The dog stretched himself toward him and looked at his brush as if with curiosity. In truth, there was no curiosity here, but there was a flirtation, he raised himself a bit and raised himself a bit again until between him and the brush there was just a margin of nothing. The brush started dripping. The brush didn't dry out until the words Crazy Dog were written on the dog's skin.

Isaac looked at the dog and was happy. When our Rabbis in the Land of Israel excommunicated a person they would tie notes to the tails of black dogs saying, So-and-So, son of So-and-So is excommunicated, and they would send the dogs throughout the city to warn the people to stay away from him. But never before had anyone written on the skin of a dog. But there is no new thing under the sun, everything man does and will do has already been done before him and before that. And Jerusalem still recalls that once they excommunicated a sage who wanted to correct the Yishuv against the will of the Keepers of the Walls, and they brought a pack of dogs and wrote on their skin, Heretic Banned and Excommunicated. Isaac looked here and there like an artist whose artistry has succeeded and looks to see if people have noticed it. That happened in the afternoon, when everyone is eating dinner, and there wasn't a person outside, for even those who don't have anything to eat sit in their room out of shame. Isaac was sorry people didn't see. But he consoled himself with the thought that they would see later on. He kicked the dog to make him wander around the city and advertise his deed. The dog opened his mouth wide and peered at him in amazement. He treated him with affection and in the end he kicks him. He lowered his eyes. That one's eyes smile and his feet are angry. Don't his feet know that he's just having fun? In the meantime, the dog's spirits drooped and the tip of his nose turned cold. He dropped his tail and stood with his tail drooping and his spirits low. By now, Isaac was no longer thinking about the dog and packed up his tools and meant to go to his boss and collect his pay. The dog jumped and started getting under his feet. If he turned this way the dog was walking behind him, if he turned that way the dog was plodding behind him, and between here and there he raised dust. Isaac scolded him angrily and chased him away. But the dog wound around Isaac's steps and raised his face toward his brush. He hit the paint bucket and almost turned it over. Isaac hit his leg and it bled. He barked a vague bark and then a whining bark, picked up his feet and started running.

2 |

He ran and didn't know where he was running. And wherever he ran he came on something that hurt him. Here he was pricked by a thorn and there he was hit by a bracket in front of a wall, here by a ram's horn and there by road markers. From the hair on his head to his toenails there wasn't a limb that wasn't hurt. He stood still and looked at those who wished him evil and was angry and bitter that he left the place where he was living and went to a place of calamity. He barked a bark of, Oh, woe, in me that human parable is fulfilled. The dog deserved the stick and got a beating. He looked at himself sternly and said, Why are you lying prostrate like a stinking carcass, pick up your feet and go. So he raised his tail and lifted his feet from the ground and started running nimbly and lightly, like dogs who run on their toes and not on the soles of their feet like men and bears, who roll the soles of their feet from the heel to the toes. And so he ran lightly and nimbly, until he came to his place in Meah Shearim.

And when the dog came to Meah Shearim and jumped to his hole and wanted to sit quietly and rest from his suffering, all of Meah Shearim was shocked, and all those who walk on two legs, men, women, and children, started running in panic. The dog thought they were running to hear a sermon from the preacher. And since everyone ran, the dog thought that Rabbi Grunam May-Salvation-Arise was preaching, for his sermons were all the rage in Jerusalem, for he knew what sins they committed and what they had to do to repent. And as the dog's mood was heavy at that moment and he didn't say, How goodly are the feet of the children of Israel when they ran to hear moral reprimands, but he twisted his tail and said, How blind are the eyes of the Children of Israel who see and don't know what they see. This screamer, even his knees don't move when he groans. Only human creatures can be led astray like that, for man looketh on the outward appearance. But he too, that is, the dog, began running, like dogs who, if they see human beings running, they immediately run after them. As soon as he ran he knew he was mistaken. There is no Reb Grunam here and no sermon, but there is something here that never had been before. He sniffed a little here and a little there and nothing came into his nose. He raised his voice and asked, Where are the feet going? And everyone who heard his voice and saw him and the writing on his back picked up his feet and fled, wailing, Crazy dog, crazy dog. When there are many voices screaming at once, they can't be heard, but a wail added to them is heard. That wail went from one end of Meah Shearim to the other, and the farther it went, the less it was understood. He decided to wait until folks calmed down and then he would ask once again. Meanwhile, he opened his mouth wide, up to his eyes, as if to make it a companion to his sight. But the shopkeepers began shooing him away with ounces of iron and liters of stones, so he inferred that the court had sent to examine the weights. He started shouting, Arf Arf, I can't swallow all the defective weights and conceal them from the eyes of those agents of the court. If the weights weighed as much as they should, they would have killed him, but the Holy-One-Blessed-Be-He had compassion on the dog and made them light. The dog shouted, Where is Heaven? Your sons have sinned and I am beaten. When he shouted, all the men, women, and children hid in their houses and locked their doors. Meah Shearim emptied and there wasn't a creature left outside, aside from that dog.

Hunger came and began oppressing him, for all that day he hadn't tasted a thing. For when he left his hole in the morning to hunt for his food a lot of things happened to him that made him forget eating. Now that he was idle, his guts rattled inside him and shouted Arf Arf Arf, carve us some food, Arf, Arf, something to eat. He tricked his guts and looked here and there, as if he didn't know who was shouting. He saw an open butchershop, its smell rose and its meat was left behind. And not only the butchershop, but all the shops in Meah Shearim were open. And all kinds of food was left behind. And if he wanted he could fill his belly and eat, and no one would stop him. But in amazement, he didn't touch the meat or anything else. And when his guts were amazed that he refrained from the meat, he was amazed at the crowd who were so agitated and so paralyzed. He peered in all four directions. The world was empty and emptied. Sometimes a human face peeped out of a window. When he looked at it, it immediately disappeared. Suddenly the sound of an instrument was heard, one of those instruments that sound on the hour. The dog pricked up both his ears to hear, for by nature he loved all kinds of sounds, and meanwhile he wanted to know what time it was. He started counting, one two three and stopped, for what do we gain if we know what time it is and we don't know who the lord of the hours is, a European or an Arab? He gazed at the sky and looked at the stars and the constellations arrayed in their order as on every night at the hour when the Children of Israel enter to recite the evening prayer, and here no one was going to pray, not to the synagogues and not to the study houses or the prayer rooms and not to the simple Minyans. His heart filled with pity for those souls wandering around in the world without Kaddish. How many legacies did they leave so they would be remembered with the recital of the Kaddish and a chapter of the Mishnah, and here no one opens his mouth to say a word of holiness. The dog raised his muzzle to the locked houses and to the closed shutters and started shouting. We mustn't attribute unusual thoughts to a dog, such as that he intended to rouse the dead to rise up out of their graves and come to argue with the living, but we can imagine that he wanted to rouse the living to be charitable toward the dead. When he saw that there was no response, he stopped. And even though he stopped, he didn't spare his voice and shouted again. When he saw that all his shouts were in vain, he wagged his tail in despair, stood up, and went on his way.

3 |

He followed his tail to the right and it led him to Sha'arei Pina. He sniffed a bit here and a bit there and jumped up to the Vittenberg Houses. He sniffed a bit here and a bit there and went around a few houses and a few courtyards and entered the Warsaw Houses. He sniffed a bit here and a bit there and went to the Ornstein Houses. He sniffed a bit here and a bit there and took himself off among the rocks next to the Bukharan Houses. At that time, young couples were sitting there, lads and lasses, as they are wont to sit there on summer nights, telling each other things that even the First Adam didn't say to Eve in the Garden of Eden. When the dog sniffed the smell of human beings, he jumped for joy and came and stood among them. And in his joy, he raised his voice until it was heard from rock to rock. Those who were lovely and pleasant heard, and their vow that even death wouldn't divide them was forgotten. A fellow's fingers twined in a girl's hand dropped away, and the fellow and the girl dropped away too and fled, for a rumor was already circulating that a mad dog was straying in the city. This one fled here and that one fled there and the rocks once again stood like rocks of the wilderness with no person and no love. And the dog too stood like a stone with no love and no person. But amazement spread over his face and a question twitched in his mouth and hung on his tongue, What is this, wherever human beings look at him, there is either stoning or fleeing. His solitude struck him and he was sad. He raised his nose and his ears. No sound of the steps of human beings was heard, and no smell of humans arose.

Suddenly he heard a sound. But that sound was nothing but the sound of his heart pounding. Weakness overcame him. That weakness became like a creature in its own right and the whole body was obliterated by it. Finally he felt every limb separately, as if this was the pain. And once again his guts went back to rattling and hunger returned to pester him. He left the rocks and returned to Meah Shearim.

All the houses in Meah Shearim were closed and not a person was outside. Yet all the shops were open and all kinds of food was left behind. He took whatever came to his mouth and ate his fill. And after he filled his belly with all kinds of food he went to his hole. He walked around it and walked around again and went in. Sleep descended on him and he dozed off.

4 |

Sleep at night is good, especially for one who is hounded by day. Especially when the pursuers are silent and don't interrupt your sleep. And a cool wind blows and weakens the stings of the fleas and mosquitoes. And so the dog lay in the dirt of his hole and felt in his flesh a bit of that sweet oozing when a sore heals, and you indulge in pleasure, as if someone is petting you fondly. And all the events that had happened to the dog when he was awake seemed like a dream to him now. He wagged his tail at intervals as he wags it in a dream and whined vague whines. But when the second watch of the night came, the time of shouting for dogs, and he wanted to stand up and shout, a heaviness came over his body and he couldn't stand up. But Meah Shearim rose and stoned him with its shadows, until he was all covered by shadows, and from the shadows leaped the skeleton of a wolf, who then turned himself into a jackal and a fox and a kind of dog unlike any dog in this world. The dog's hairs stood on end, even those hairs that were stippled by the painter with two words that mustn't be mentioned. The skeleton's bones began rattling and saying, Don't be scared, for we are your father and you are our son. May you not dream such bad dreams. Even the heathen, who worship the stars and the planets don't see their afterworld so harsh.

One dream came and another dream passed, and with them passed the night. The dog emerged from his hole, looking here and there. His soul was not happy and his spirit was not easy. He lowered his head toward his tail. His tail was still in its place, but something was slightly out of order. When he looked again, he saw heaps of meat and fish and fruit and vegetables and loaves of bread and cakes and cookies baked in oil and pretzels and challahs lying in the garbage. All kinds of food the shopkeepers threw away because of the danger that the mad dog had touched them during the night and deposited venom on them, when they had left their shops open and ran away. If the Holy-One-Blessed-Be-He hadn't left his food in his guts, he would have come back and eaten and no one would have prevented him. He strolled among the heaps like a smug merchant and didn't know what to do. He considered taking from everything here and bringing it to his hole and digging himself some other holes and hiding all that food, as the fruit vendors do. Before he could consider what to do, all Meah Shearim came out with wooden instruments and stone instruments and ceramic instruments and glass instruments, and with pots and pans, with jugs and jars, with tins of kerosene and stoves of earthenware, with broken lamp shafts, with glass beads and rings made like a pot below and like a lens above, and they started stoning him. And everyone who wasn't hoarse from yesterday shouted at the top of his lungs. The dog raised his voice and shouted Arf Arf, What is my sin and what is my crime, what do you want from me and what evil did I do you? And he shouted until they ran away and hid. Before the dog could take account of everything his eyes had seen and his ears had heard, a stone was thrown at him. Before he could observe where it came from, a second one and a third one hit him. He picked himself up with a wail and began running. Where did he run and where didn't he run. From Meah Shearim to Nathan's Houses, and from Nathan's Houses to the Hungarian Houses, and from the Hungarian Houses to the Srebenbirgen Houses, and from the Srebenbirgen Houses to Sha'ar Shekhem, and from Sha'ar Shekhem he returned to all the neighborhoods he was used to. And thus he ran from neighborhood to neighborhood and from dead end to dead end and from courtyard to courtyard until he came to the houses of the convert in Nahalat Shiv'ah. He made water and ran on. Since he was in several places and didn't find a place for himself, we imagine he went to Jaffa Gate and entered the Old City inside the Wall, but we don't know if he went in through the gate or through the breach cut by the government in honor of Kaiser Wilhelm, for when Kaiser Wilhelm ascended to Jerusalem, the government cut a breach in the wall of Jerusalem in his honor.

CHAPTER FIFTEEN

Changing Places

1 |

And so he went inside the Wall and stood between Jaffa Gate and the
Austrian Post Office. At that time, everyone was eager for letters coming from Outside the Land and didn't notice the dog. And he didn't
notice them either because he was eager to find his way. After he
looked this way and that way he took himself off to the upper market, and from there to the vegetable market in front of the street of
the Jews, where there was a cool wind, because it is roofed with
stones. How many things did he see, and what didn't he see! The
things that dog saw in passing writers of travel books never see. From
the vegetable market he went to the Aladdin market and from there
he sneaked into the serpentine street. And he passed through and
over obstacles and hurdles, and jumped and leaped through a multitude of paths, bent and blocked, curving and contorted, pocked and
putrid, perpendicular and precipitate. And he marched proudly
among garbage and manure, among houses of the Ishmaelites,
mournful and gloomy, like their owners who came from Morocco
the land of Mughreb, and in their lairs they lodged like animals in
ambush. He sniffed a bit here and a bit there, and went to the Hamidan Market and from Hamidan Market to the homeless shelters. And
when he came to the shelters, he wanted shelter for his bones, and
not only did he not find shelter, but whatever bones of his that had
emerged intact from Meah Shearim were about to be broken. For in
those days, the city was full of Heders and Yeshivas, that produced
mighty geniuses, who still live amongst us here to this day, and even
in their early childhood they could read and write. And when they
saw the dog and everything that was written on him, they surrounded

him with stones like a viper. And if he hadn't run away in time, who knows if he would have lived out the day.

And so he fled for his life and ran away and came to wherever it was he came and sat down wherever it was he sat down. And it looked as if he sat down among the Gentiles. It's not known where he sat down first, whether among the Greek Orthodox or the Greek Catholics, the Gregorian Armenians or the Catholic Armenians, the Syrians or the Marronites, the Copts or the Ethiopians. Among the Franciscans or in the other monasteries, the Presbyterians or the Lutherans. But it is known that he didn't leave a single place that he wasn't in, like those Jewish apostates who trudge along behind anyone who gives them more. The nations of the world who do not know the Holy Tongue were not scared by what was written on his skin and treated him as they treat dogs and he didn't want for anything with them.

And so he settled down among the Gentiles and ate and drank and played with his comrades. Sometimes he would bite them and sometimes they would bite him, sometimes playfully and sometimes for something else. Especially since in those days, the Syrian *Putirta* was revealed to them, which was like the challah of their feast days. But satisfaction he didn't find because of the confusion in his heart, for he was flabbergasted, could it be that the Children of Israel, merciful sons of merciful souls, suddenly became cruel, and Ishmael became merciful. So he would scrounge around in his mind, but the dog mind wasn't capable of grasping the truths of things.

Meanwhile, food he had in abundance. But his pleasure wasn't complete, for all those days his thought was bound to Meah Shearim and to Sha'arei Pina and the neighborhoods near them, like that tail that was bound to his behind. And so he kept on wondering, Could it be that the Children of Israel are cruel and the Ishmaelites are merciful, otherwise, how can you explain that incident, that the Jews throw you out and the Gentiles bring you in. In the end, he came to the conclusion that there must be some trace of a defect in him that made folks hate him, for he didn't yet ascribe the rupture to others, as do those human creatures who see themselves pure as angels and others they see as devils and demons. In truth, no creature is free of flaws, but the flaw in him is different from theirs. If so, why is it that the Children of Israel see his flaw and the Gentiles don't see his flaw? Or perhaps the flaw in him is a flaw in the eyes of the Children of Israel, but for the others it isn't a flaw.

2 |

That question pierced his brain and confused his mind and sapped his strength and didn't let him rest either by day or by night. And even though he sapped his strength with his thoughts, he didn't lie down on his belly and didn't wait for salvation to come by itself, but started chasing after remedies. Some remedies helped him for a little while and hurt him in the long run, and some helped him in one limb and damaged his other limbs, like remedies that cure one limb and endanger the entire body. He started getting angry at the remedies that cheated him and laughed at himself for believing in them. Meanwhile, his body grew rusty and he wanted to wash. But everyone who knows the problem of water in Jerusalem knows how exhausting it is to find a little bit of water for washing. In his mind's eye, he passed all the bathhouses in the Old City and outside it. The bathhouses of the Turks at Lions Gate and at the Western Wall and across from Hezekiah's Pool, and the bathhouses of the Jews in the synagogue of Nishi, facing the houses of the Karaites, who are called inverted Jews, and the bath of the Mughrabites which is always cool, and even finicky men who don't attend any bath all year come there on Yom Kippur eve, and the ChaBaD bath and the bath in the courtyard of the abandoned woman. From the bathhouses inside the Old City walls, his dog's mind came to those outside the wall, to the one on Jaffa Road of the sect of the Christian Sabbath Keepers, and — not to mention it in the same breath — to the Jewish bathhouses in every neighborhood. But in every bathhouse he found a flaw. In the baths of the Turks because of the jokers who are liable to pour a bucket of boiling water on him, and because of those seminarians who have no place to sleep and spend the whole night there, for if they saw him they would spread the word of his disgrace. In the courtyard of the abandoned woman, because everyone who bathes there emerges as dirty as a broom on Passover eve. And it's doubtful if the water there is water. And once upon a time, those who had to dip in water came in to dip and had to bring a knife to remove their crust. So, in every bathhouse he found a dull side. And as for those outside the Old City walls, sometimes a dispute erupts in one of them and those who get the upper hand lock the bathhouse and take the key away and your trouble is in vain. And the one belonging to the sect of the Sabbath Keepers? If we weren't afraid of far-fetched hypotheses, we would say that his spirit did not approve of its owners. And we won't be too far from the truth if we say that the dog said, Make up your minds, if you recognize the Sabbath, why do you neglect the rest of God's Commandments. And why didn't he think of the pool of Mamila? Because on all the days of sunshine it is a wasteland, and it differs from a valley of dung only by name. And Baedeker was wrong when he wrote that it is full of water, for he saw it in the rainy period, but in the rainy period most of the houses in Jerusalem are filled with water. To make a long story short, one day passed and another day came. His limbs grew rusty and his whole body stank. And even his hair got sick, aside from those two words the artisan had written on him, which stood firm and shining in their blaze of colors, for Isaac was a master painter and his colors don't get erased. Meanwhile, all kinds of rashes and fleas attached themselves to him and made themselves the owners of his head and his tail and on his whole body. Not to mention the lice. These modest creatures wherever they cast their eyes, there are rashes or boils, and even in sleep, he had no rest from them. The dog wagged his tail and shouted, in turn, sometimes in torment and sometimes because it seemed to him that he was told in a dream what to do. When he woke with a start he saw himself as that German that the German poet wrote a poem about, Here I stand, a miserable fool, and I am as wise as I was. And when at last he reached the conclusion that he had to take action, every bathhouse took on nine measures of humility, and said, I'm not worthy, I'm not worthy. But he sacrificed his honor. And which bathhouse did he decide to go to? The bathhouse of the Oren Stein Houses. We don't know why he chose a bathhouse in the new city, but we do know why he chose the one in the Oren Stein Houses, since every neighborhood has its own pack of dogs who don't let any outsider dog into their turf. But that isn't the case with the Oren Stein Houses, which stand between two neighborhoods, between Zikhron Moshe and the Warsaw Houses, and the dogs divided the neighborhoods between themselves, one pack took one neighborhood and the other pack took the other neighborhood, and they left the Oren Stein Houses to their own devices.

3 |

The dog lay on his guts to examine his steps, what road would he take. Finally he picked himself up and walked to wherever it was he walked. Meanwhile, the day grew dark and the Muezzin ascended to the top of the turret and called out whatever it was he called out. The Arabs heard and left their work and cleared out a pure place for themselves. They washed their hands and their feet and rinsed their mouth and dabbed water on their forehead and their hair and turned their face to the south. And they raised their hands and said whatever it was they said and picked themselves up and sat on their knees and straightened up and raised their hands. The sun declined and the stars began coming out and filled the sky, and every star gleamed like a raindrop. The dog looked at the sky and said, Sky sky, if only you were a river and the stars in you dripped water, this wretch wouldn't have to move his wornout bones around seeking water. After he looked at the sky, he brought his face back to the earth and found himself a niche to sleep in. He circled it a few times and checked to see if there wasn't a snake there and went in. Sleep descended on him and he dozed off. He was shown a big river with all kinds of water coming out of it. He folded his tongue into the shape of the palm of a hand. But when he was about to drink, the water took off and ran away. He spurred on his legs to rush and to scurry, Oh, you apostates, why won't you hurry! Don't you know, I am rushing, can't you see? Add your road to my road and your strength to mine, why will you whisper together against me. May your mouth be covered with dust for a spell, may your fathers' forefathers go straight to Hell. His legs flew out like an arrow from a bow, he ran in panic, like a deer and like a doe, like a bird who flees a net of cunning, he sped off, leaping, running. And so he ran at the speed of light, turning neither left nor right, didn't delay, he lowered his tongue like a jar to a trough, his lips were dry and his throat was rough, and the water makes a sound and there is no water to be found. It went away as it came up to the rim, and his legs collapsed and his eyes grew dim.

He fell down and closed his eyes. But he saw that the water was fruitful and multiplying and everything around him was filling up, and there was nothing between him and the water except two or three leaps. He gathered all his strength and went toward it. But his legs failed him and brought him down. His heart filled with wrath and he bit his legs and screamed at them to get up, or not even a piece thin as a cow pat would he leave of them. They were wounded and couldn't stand. He started jumping like a chicken and leaping like a frog and coiling like a snake and hurling himself like an arrow and tumbling down like the scapegoat. Suddenly he realized there was no water here, but only hallucinations, like the springs and streams that appear to travelers in the deserts. He threw himself on the ground and said, A fool it was who followed his eyes. Now even if they showed us four mouths of the rivers of the world we wouldn't budge. He examined his legs and licked their wounds and soothed them and promised them to bring them to a valley below Bezalel where healing grass grew. As he was tending to his legs, he was shown a brook full of water. He straightened his back and leaped into it. But that brook was a looking-glass, like the ones barbers hang in their shops. And when he leaped into it, he was hurt and wounded and his ribs were broken. In the morning, Balak wondered, What is that? All night long we lay still, and how did our bones get broken? He stretched his bones but they wouldn't stretch. He spread out his legs but they wouldn't spread out. Meanwhile, his eyes closed and he dozed off. He saw that he was running, as he had run all night long. But at night he ran for water and now he was running and didn't know why he was running. It seems that he saw a reflection of his dream, or a kind of secondary dream. He shook himself and barked, barked and shook himself. He hung out his tongue and looked around. Then he got up and went to the place where he had decided to go, that is to the Oren Stein Houses, where there is a bathhouse and there are no dogs. And he had the good luck that no Jew encountered him and they didn't see his writing. Then he came on a group of Hasids. And he had the good luck that they didn't notice him, for at that time they were coming from a blessed celebration and were too drunk and were busy finding a proper place for their feet, so they wouldn't slip and fall into the cisterns and ditches. Then he came upon an old man. And it was his good fortune that that old man was blind. Then he came upon a young fellow. And it was his good fortune that that fellow had trained his eyes not to look upon This World. Then he came upon a Jewish lady. And it was his good fortune that she couldn't read without vowel signs. When he saw that they didn't say anything to him, he imagined that his flaw was repaired and that he no longer had anything to fear. And he assumed a measure of arrogance, as if the whole world was reconciled with him.

4 |

The dog walks around with an idea to grapple, and pampers himself like a worm in an apple, and the thoughts of his heart cruise and soar, on the torments of the wicked and his own good score. He took a step and jumped up one more time, and uttered his parable in rhetoric and rhyme, Woe to you, damn bastards the fleas, you tortured my soul and don't give me peace, your mouth never shuts from morning to night, as if on coyotes you sharpened your bite, I'm telling you, your end, as the start of it all, your end will be bitter as wormwood and gall, in abysses of water will you sink and drown, like the soldiers of Pharaoh you will go down. And let us add woe to the crawling lice, who feed on my flesh like they're in paradise, sucking my blood my heart's travail, swear by my head and swear by my tail, that by the time the sun appears, you'll be gone from foot to ears. And you mosquitoes, angels of destruction, I shall sweep away your nasty destruction, and you will have no salvation, no relief, because you gave me so much grief, and on my blood that you have drunk, like the bird of the king, you've made yourselves a song to sing. And you, dunghill of vomit and feces and clay, you smeared on me plaster to lead me astray, here I stand on top of your height, and you won't know your place by this time tonight. Not in vain my words will go off to and fro, revenge for my woes I shall wreak on my foe. And thus in an ornate tongue did he speak, like poets who prattle optimistic chic, and he polished his body, may your honors excuse, and jumped down to the bathhouse without any ruse. Sweet is optimism, to your soul and blood, but in the end come bitterness, mire, and mud.

And when he smelled the water, he stretched his legs, barking with joy. His loins were suddenly filled with quaking and all his limbs with fear and shaking. False teeth and trusses and shoes, wet towels and things that men will use, whatever came to hand, whatever they found, they threw at him fast, in anger profound. Stockings and slippers that give you a wrench, for no one can ever endure their stench. The dog sees that his luck does not hold, for he is in danger wherever he looks, and he fled inadvertently, lo and behold, to a house full of books. And thus our schlemiel, in full compliance, entered the library, Treasure of Science.

And there sit wise sages, the finest minds of the ages, concocting word pictures, and correcting the Scriptures, quoting their quotes and writing their notes, their hands holding quills, books piled up in hills, with pamphlets so ample and notebooks to sample, they multiply and increase and grow without cease. A camel who bore them would fall down afraid if a complete total ass didn't come to his aid. And they copy and write avoiding imbroglios, from many old books and some ancient folios, and compose compositions one after another, for the sake of wisdom and the good of their brother. And as they sit, each in his seat, wisdom on his head and knowledge at his feet, a lowly creature did appear, the dog who had fled in panic and fear, their quill pens dropped out of their hands and they trembled, their breath fell off and they scrambled, and the books they were copying they didn't even mention, for to fleeing they turned their attention. And the dog fled too. And not because of a primeval ban on the library, but because he feared that the books would be his tomb. And as the dog ran away and fled, he came to the houses of the Ethiopians. He stood there, as if he were under a spell, for all his life he had seen their roofs as black, and today they were painted blue. At last, he moved his feet and turned to the crooked street and passed the house of Ben-Yehuda and the street of the consulates, and it looked as if he meant to go to the Russian Compound, and from there to the Old City, through the new gate, to Bab el Jedid. But his feet led him to Jaffa Road. And here they suddenly had a dispute, two feet wanted to go to Mahane Yehuda and one wanted to go to Sukkat Shalom and one didn't want to go either here or there, and every single foot teases its comrade and says, I'm acting on behalf of our master and am going on his mission. Meanwhile, they sit idle and don't do anything. A cart passed by and the carter saw the dog. He stretched out his whip and struck him. And if the horses hadn't suddenly run, he would have hit him again. The dog shook himself and shouted. His legs heard and became alarmed. They all jumped together and started running, until their strength ran out and they stood still at the school of Alliance Israel.

The dog looked at the doors of the school and saw two hands clasped in brotherhood and friendship. Envy entered him, and he envied the human creatures whose hands don't move from one another and he sighed for himself who was persecuted by them. That fool didn't know that as far as hatred and persecution are concerned, all are equal, men as well as dogs. As he sat at the gate of the school, he wagged his tail and said, Here they teach all kinds of wisdom, maybe they'll teach me why they hate me. His soul longed to know and his heart began yearning. But he was polite and didn't go in suddenly, but stretched out on the doorsill of the building and waited until the teachers came out, saying to himself, Slowly, slowly. And as he sat, his mind got into a whirl, and as his mind whirled he started thinking, Maybe the calamity came from that man with the wet instrument, for until the hand of that man touched me I wasn't hated and hounded. He recalled that day when he wandered into the neighborhood of the Bukharans and came across that wet instrument that dripped a cool moisture and he recalled that moment when the owner of the tool kicked him and all the troubles that had attached themselves to him ever since. He thrust his head toward his back, as he was accustomed to do because of the fleas. And he saw strange signs. It came to him that those signs were the handiwork of the owner of the instrument. And since his mind was calm he didn't shout and didn't throw a fit, but took heart and said, Everything is for the best. If I hadn't been thrown out of the bathhouse I would have

bathed by now and all those signs would have been wiped out, now
that they threw me out of the bathhouse and I didn't bathe, I may
find out the truth. At that moment, all his suffering was naught compared to the search for truth. And once again he turned his head back
to see what were those signs and what was that truth. But all his pains
were in vain because he couldn't read. He was amazed and stunned,
Everyone who sees me knows the truth about me, and I, who possess
the truth itself, I don't know what it is. He shouted loud and long, Arf
Arf Arf, this truth, what is it? And while he was barking he returned
his tongue to his mouth and scolded himself sternly, Fool, shut your
trap and don't scare folks. The teachers will come out soon and reveal the truth.

As soon as the bell rang, the principal came out. The dog
jumped at him and licked his stick and looked at that gentlemen with
pleading eyes. And even though that gentleman was perfumed with
various fragrances called eau de cologne, which a dog's spirit is not
comfortable with, the dog hid his nose from them and didn't notice
their smell, and he held himself out like an ignoramus who holds out
a letter to the expert to hear what is written there, and all the while
he whispers, Please sir, see what is written here. The principal saw
letters, took a pair of glasses and matched them up with his eyes, and
started reading, as was his wont from left to right. He connected the
letters and joined them: BLK, and read: Balak. He smiled and said,
The people of Jerusalem are experts in Humash and know that there
was a wicked man Balak and so they name their dogs after him. He
patted the dog's head and chirped at him, Balak. But from right to
left, the Hebrew letters read: KLB, dog. And the dog heard that he
called him Balak and was amazed, but not offended.

Well then, we can call him Balak, too. And what was his
name, perhaps he had a name and it sank and perhaps he didn't have
a name, as in some communities, where a man whose sons don't survive doesn't name his son in order to confound the Angel of Death,
so he won't know that there is a creature so-and-so. Balak wagged his
tail and said, That's it, exactly what I said, that grief came to me only
through others. Because some dolt wrote things on me, do I deserve
to be persecuted?

Truth has a covenant, that all who seek it seek the whole truth. Balak too. Since he paid heed to the truth he wasn't content with some of it and sought to know the whole truth. He stood before the legs of the principal and called out, Arf Arf Arf, give me the interpretation of things, give me the true truth. The janitor came out and saw the dog and what was written on his back. He picked up his feet and ran away. Said Balak, He knows the truth, he knows the truth, but what shall I do since he ran away with it. And Balak was still far from the truth, at any rate investigating the truth was a bit of consolation for his sorrow, as in the verse of the divine poet

> Blessed art thou, spirit of Inquiry, for you console me
> When billows of despair overcame my soul.

CHAPTER SIXTEEN

The Old and the Young

1 |

All the time Isaac was on the ship with the old man, they weren't close to one another because of their differences of opinion and their different concerns, for one ascended to build the Land and the other ascended to dig himself a grave. When they met years later in Jerusalem, the two of them were drawn to each other. Needless to say Isaac, for he was alone and forlorn and longed for the company of human beings, but so was the old man who sat inside his house among his close relations. If they had met right after they had ascended, they would have behaved as they behaved on the sea, but time, which makes close people distant, brings distant people close. With time, Isaac had changed some of his opinions, and so did Reb Moyshe Amram. Reb Moyshe Amram had thought the whole Land of Israel was made of synagogues and study houses and all its inhabitants were Godly scholars. In the end, most of those here are idle and quarrelsome, and they make of the Land a farce. And if there are people whose intentions are all for the sake of God, like his son-in-law Fayesh, not every good intention legitimates every act.

And another reason. All the time Reb Moyshe Amram lived outside the Land and stole an hour to study Torah, his Torah would revive him. When he was blessed to dwell in Jerusalem, and to sit all the days before the Book, the Torah lost its taste. He started paying heed to people's conversations. At first he was amazed at their talk, then they began shrinking in his eyes. And in the end he was disgusted with them. Needless to say, he disliked their bans and excommunications, but also the clandestine dealings of the Distribution, which is the main support of Jerusalem and the secrets of the

Societies and the administrators and the inspectors and the treasurers and the synagogue officers, the things all Jerusalem wrangles about, were too ugly for his attention. As active people who spent their whole life in the real world find no point in those empty issues the world's idlers toil over. But for the love of God and the awe of Jerusalem, he held his tongue. When he discovered Isaac, that fellow who earned his own livelihood with his own hands, his heart was drawn to him. And when a few days passed and he didn't come, Reb Moyshe Amram said to his wife, What is it, Disha, our fellow doesn't show up at our house. Said she, Too bad we didn't ask him to come. Said the two of them, We should have gotten close to him. Reb Moyshe Amram repeated, All the days he was on the ship with us, my mind wasn't comfortable with him, and now my heart is drawn to him. Said Disha, But I, the first time I set eyes on him, I saw he was a decent fellow. Said Reb Moyshe Amram, Your pity preceded your sense. Said Disha, Is it possible not to pity him, a fellow living in a strange land without any family. Said Reb Moyshe Amram, Shame on you, Disha, for calling the Land of Israel a strange land, but there is some truth in what you say. Here he has no rind and no kind. Harder than that, he lives without a wife. You remember, Disha, how he would brag and say all the children of Israel are comrades, especially in the Land of Israel. Where are his comrades? Once Isaac put off shaving his beard. He said to himself, That beard can show itself to that old man. He put on his Sabbath clothes and went to him.

2 |

Isaac knocked on the door and Shifra came out to him. Said Shifra, My grandfather is going to Meron for Lag b'Omer and he went to the city to repair his eyeglasses before the trip. And where is her grandmother? Said Shifra, She and Mother went with him. Isaac was disheartened and wanted to go back. Said Shifra, The gentleman is tired from the heat, may he come in and rest a bit. Said Isaac, Tired I am not, but I will come in and wait until he comes back and will tell him goodbye before his trip. Too bad, too bad he is going away. Many times I wanted to come see him, and I don't know why I didn't come, and now that I did come he's going away. Shifra offered him a chair and he sat down. As soon as he sat down she went out.

Isaac sat there in the house of Reb Fayesh, the father of Shifra and son-in-law of old Reb Moyshe Amram. Many times Isaac had heard of the Keepers of the Walls, members of the Hungarian Society whose sting is evil. And here he is sitting in the home of Reb Fayesh, the most zealous of the zealots. Said Isaac to himself, It's easier to get into the home of the zealots of Jerusalem than to get into the home of the farmers of the settlements.

Isaac looked around. It was a stone house and its windows were open to the fields and the valleys and the dales and the hills. The sun cooled itself outside and didn't pour out its wrath inside. The floor stones were washed with water and a refreshing moisture still rose from them. The walls were light blue and white and a round lamp hung down from the middle of the vaulted ceiling to the table, where a cloth was spread over half of it, as if for a meal. And in fact the table was set for a meal, for on weekdays, Reb Fayesh used to eat his meals alone, especially on those days when prayers of supplication are said. The rooms and the cloth and all the household objects were clean and neat, each one in its place.

Isaac began pondering and began comparing Shifra's house with Sonya's house. For on the last days before their estrangement, when she started working in the kindergarten, she didn't keep her room neat and her table wasn't set. When she invited Isaac to eat at her house, she didn't put the olives in a bowl or the cheese on a plate or the bread in a basket, but placed them in front of him on the bare table without a cloth, wrapped in paper, as she had brought them from the shopkeeper. And an annoying lamp with sooty glass was smoking. Once Isaac said something to her. Sonya laughed and said, Am I a German girl to be fussy about such things? Isaac's room isn't handsome either. If we want to make an analogy, we would compare it to a turgid space where windows were opened so people would see its desolation. And his furnishings—four or five kerosene cans pushed together serve as his bed (for the German's bed that Isaac bought in Meah Shearim was conquered by fleas. Nothing helped, neither Lysol nor carbolic acid nor the milk he used to block their nests, nor the paints he used to paint his bed, until he threw it out and made himself a bed of cans like most of our other comrades in the Land of Israel) and two more upright boxes served as a table and closet. But Isaac is a bachelor, and as long as a man is a bachelor. . . Who's coming? Shifra? And in fact, as he had guessed, so it was. Shifra came in and brought bread and salt and a knife, and Reb Fayesh came in behind her, with his hands washed. For it was Reb Fayesh's habit when he came in to eat to dip his hand outside and Shifra comes and brings him bread and salt and a knife and he sits down and eats. Reb Fayesh made a blessing on the bread and sliced it and sighed and ate, closing his eyes and directing the intention of a served table to rise and repair the sparks that fell into the sin of the First Adam and were swallowed in the heart of the dust. Isaac looked at him and saw that he was enraged, and didn't know that the thrust of the host's rage was the guest. The day Isaac came the second time, Reb Fayesh was already annoyed, and now that he came a third time he was enraged. Anyone who knows how fond the Children of Israel are of the Commandment of hospitality will be amazed at Reb Fayesh's rigor, but anyone who knows Reb Fayesh won't be amazed. Even if Isaac were an ordinary Polak, Reb Fayesh wouldn't be easy about him, but especially since Isaac wore short jackets and a free-thinker's hat on his head and didn't grow sidelocks and a beard. Even though a razor hadn't passed over it for a few days, you could see on his face that he was clean-shaven. Even those who are more moderate than Reb Fayesh aren't easy with fellows like Isaac, and especially Reb Fayesh, who regarded all those wearing short jackets as criminals.

Shifra came back in and brought her father a cooked meal and a spoon to eat it. For Reb Fayesh, anything that was not absolutely necessary was a luxury and a person who guards his soul will keep away from it; therefore Reb Fayesh gave orders in his house not to bring him any utensil unless he needed it, a knife for bread and a spoon for food. Reb Fayesh took a spoonful of soup and said something to Shifra. Since he spoke in the Hungarian tongue, and Isaac didn't know the Hungarian tongue, he didn't pay any heed to the words. If he had been in control of his eyes and they weren't gazing at Shifra's face, he would have recognized from the way the host twisted his lips that he meant him. Meanwhile, Isaac sat and pondered, If I were clever, I would have worn the long coat I brought from my hometown. It's hanging in my room on the peg and no one enjoys it except the spiders who spin their homes on it.

Meanwhile, Shifra left and Reb Fayesh finished his meal. He shook the crumbs out of his beard, put the knife away, and drummed his fingers on the table. Shifra came and brought him the fingerbowl and a towel. He dipped his hands and closed his eyes, and said, By the rivers of Babylon, in a sad, lamenting melody. Finally, he recited verses of thanks and blessed the food in a melody of supplication. After he recited the blessing, Shifra came and removed the cloth. Reb Fayesh said something to her. Isaac didn't know the Hungarian tongue, but he recognized that he wasn't wanted here. He stood up and left.

The sound of a dog shouting Arf Arf Arf was heard. The hair of Isaac's beard stood on end for he hadn't shaved in honor of Reb Moyshe Amram and was sorry that Shifra saw him in disarray. Arf, Arf, Arf, the dog shouted again. Isaac recalled the dog on whose skin he had written Crazy Dog. He turned his face to Reb Fayesh's house and said, Crazy Dog should have been written on you and your skin.

On the way, Isaac saw Reb Moyshe Amram walking with his wife. Isaac turned aside. Disha said to her husband, Look who's walking here. Reb Moyshe Amram took off the new glasses and called, Isaac, you're hiding from us. Said Isaac, I heard that you are about to go on a trip and I didn't want to delay you. Said Reb Moyshe Amram, You heard right, we're going to Meron. What did I want to tell you, many times I asked about you. I thought you were angry at me because of what I said to you. It's impossible to talk here with a person and not offend him. Outside the Land, every Jew is a Jew. And if he's strict about observing the Commandments, he's called a kosher Jew. And if he's very careful, he's called a Saint. But here the whole community are holy people, and because of too much holiness in them, each person sees his fellow man as if he doesn't fill his obligation, for holiness has no limit. How is your work? For thou shalt eat the labor of thine hands, says the Scripture, but plumb the depths of the Bible, Thy wife shall be as a fruitful vine. And you are still without a wife.

The Lord will send you your mate. And so we're leaving here. And I don't know if I'll see you again. As the proverb says, A mountain and a mountain will never meet, but a man and a man will, but my legs are like two mountains, and I too am like them. When I saw you on the ship, I didn't like you, and now that I do like you, I am leaving here. Where are you, Disha? Here? And I thought you had left me and went on your way. The new glasses don't want to get used to my eyes.

CHAPTER SEVENTEEN

Back to Balak

1 |

Balak found rest for his body, but consolation for his soul he didn't find. He was sorry about what had slipped away from under his feet and was not happy about what had come into his hands. The entire world was not worthwhile for him as was the place he was exiled from. Between one thing and another, he settled down among the nations and was melted among the Gentiles and defiled himself with the cooking of the heathens and his heart was numbed and he couldn't distinguish between Jewish holiday and Christian holiday. But a convert for spite he didn't become, and he would still wake up in the second watch of the night and shout properly, for in the second watch, dogs shout.

The evil men of Israel are like dogs. But the evil men of Israel sometimes repent and sometimes don't repent. And even those who do repent don't repent on their own, but repent because of the Shofar on the Day of Judgment, for when they hear the sound of the Shofar, they tremble in fear and dread, while Balak did repent on his own, and it was in the month of Tamuz when the Shofars are still sleeping that he decided to repent. He had enough of the goodness of the Gentiles and was fed up with them. That month when the Angels of Destruction direct the sun, and because of its heat, offenses increase and sparks of purity succumb to the evil spirits, that month whose sign is Cancer, which engenders hot and bad air and all those who are afflicted with cancer are never cured, but will die of it, that month of Tamuz didn't kill Balak's heart, but on the contrary, Balak donned so much strength in it that he flung insolent words to the heavenly Cancer. What did Balak say, Cancer, Cancer, Crab, you are full of legs and yet you recoil backwards, and I who have only four legs my whole desire is to go forward.

Balak was still lying on his belly and eating and drinking more than his fill. But he was willing to give it up and throw away all his pleasures. And when he looked at his belly bursting with too much food and pulling him down, he barked and said, My belly, my belly, you've got it good and I've got it bad. You fill yourself up while my mind flies away from me and becomes empty. His belly growls at him like an army drum, as if all the hosts of the Sultan came down on him in war. Balak pulls his tail between his legs and barks to himself and says, Wouldn't it be better if this belly that stuffs itself on the food of pagans would enjoy the food of the Jews.

From too much thinking, his soul grew weary and he dozed off. The Lord of Dreams came to him and showed him things in his dream that he had thought about when he was awake. And when he woke up from his sleep, he didn't know what was real here and what was a dream. And since he was tired from so much eating and drinking and so much sleep, his senses were lax about distinguishing things. To make a long story short, both awake and dreaming, and dreaming and awake, he saw himself coming and going in the houses of the children of Israel. Here he snatched a piece of Kugel and there they threw him a spoonful of Cholent. And they also tossed him unkosher slaughtered animals and unkosher food, for the Torah says, Ye shall cast it to the dogs, etc., for there weren't yet many sinners in Israel eating unkosher slaughtered animals and unkosher food, who steal from the dog and eat what is his.

Balak was especially fond of the chickens called Kapores, with which the children of Israel atone for their sins, and they throw their guts on the roofs or in the courtyard. But even on other days, Balak didn't lack anything. Sometimes he filled his belly with the dough they used as glue to paste up posters against the secular schools, and sometimes with the dough they used to paste up all other excoriations, for he pulled off the dough and ate it. Like those dogs mentioned by our Sages of Blessed Memory to illustrate the verse, Sin lieth at the door. There are dogs in Rome who can make a living cleverly. How? The dog goes and sits in front of the bakery and pretends to doze off so the baker won't be on guard against him, and so the baker dozes off for he trusts the dog, and the dog gets up and drops the bread on the ground, and by the time the baker gets up and picks up the loaves, the dog has already eaten and gone on his way.

But the Lord of Dreams who granted him good dreams at first turned away from him. When Balak entered the courtyard of Jews and stretched his mouth toward the guts of Kapores, a few strange four-legged birds came and snatched them away from him. He went to the posters and found them put up not with raw dough but with nails.

Balak didn't heed his bad dreams, and resolved to return to Meah Shearim. But like that animal of the sign of Tamuz with many legs who retreats its body backward, so did his legs retreat him backward and postponed his return.

2 |

The days of heat were at their height, Jerusalem was enveloped in hunger and thirst and dust and all kinds of diseases, God Forbid, malaria, dysentery, and influenza were going around the city and all kinds of flies and mosquitoes and fleas and gnats sport with the blood of the children of Israel. A person sits in his house like a corpse without a family and without a grave, a person goes out to get medicine at the pharmacy, and by the time he stands before the pharmacist, a dust storm comes and covers both of them. And they stand facing one another like a heap of dust. This is the dust of Jerusalem that doesn't cease throughout the days of heat.

There is no bad without good. This dust covered Balak's skin and concealed his writing so that he looked just like any other dog. Balak had no calmer days than those days when Jerusalem was enveloped in dust and the children of Israel were weary from heat and thirst. Balak didn't hate the children of Israel, but as he realized that when the children of Israel were depressed and despondent they were dangerous, he rejoiced at their calamities and said, Those calamities know who deserves them and they visit those folks in abundance. And when he came upon a single Jew, he would bark at him to scare him. Things had come to such a pass that once upon a time, there was a Jew from the Society of Libeshow, the most destitute of all societies, where a person's entire income was no more than twenty Rubles a year, with which he bought for himself and his household a piece of herring as big as an olive, and Balak encountered him and barked at him. The pauper was scared and threw the herring away. And even though Balak was naturally disgusted by herring, which was all the rage in Jerusalem, nevertheless he poked around in it and refused to eat it just to spite the Jew. Lo and behold, said Balak, all the time I didn't provoke the Jews, they irritated me, now that I provoke them, they are meek with me and don't tease me. Balak knows he's not acting nicely, but his evil instinct incites him to bark. What does the evil instinct tell him? They're ingrates, they kick the charitable and give Charity to those who do evil, show them your teeth and they'll respect you. Not like your father who said, Be nice to folks, and not like your teachers who said, When the dog is trying to please folks and doesn't bark what does a man say? I am the ruler over the animals, there's something in my eyes that shuts up a dog's mouth. And since he knows that there isn't anything in his eyes that gives him dominion over the dogs, he flatters them and gives them whatever they need. And not like your mother who said, Endear yourself to folks and you won't have to raise your voice in vain, but like Sammael who is called Dog and is in charge of Hell and shouts Arf Arf. Yet his heart shrieked at him, Will a mouth that ate their bread snap at the hand that feeds him?

3 |

But in those days when he resolved to return to Meah Shearim, he taught himself to subdue his mouth and not to snap if he didn't have to, but he just sat and considered what he would do and what he wouldn't do. And when at last he came to that conclusion that he had come to many times already, that he had to go to Meah Shearim, he started finishing up his affairs and leaving place after place he had inhabited. Within a few days he was ready to go.

He went out of Jaffa Gate to Jaffa Road. And why didn't he go through Nablus Gate, for that would have been shorter? But near

Nablus Gate are more than two hundred houses called the Houses of Nissim Bek. Georgians live there and Aleppans and Babylonians, and the Lord gave the Babylonians an angry heart and they can get angry at him and stop him, and the Aleppans who naturally go along with all folks will certainly join the Babylonians, not to mention the Georgians, who are ignorant of Torah and do what others do, because they think that's what's written in the books. Therefore, Balak chose to go through Jaffa Road, where there are banks and businesses, and human minds don't have time for things that have no cash profit.

And so he went to Jaffa Road and turned neither left nor right, not to the Pool of Mamila and not to other places, but went straight ahead until he came to the bathhouse of the sect of the Sabbath Keepers. And when he came to the bathhouse of the sect of the Sabbath Keepers, he didn't turn to Hotel Kamenetz to rummage in the garbage bins, nor did he turn aside to the Russian Compound to fool around with the monks, but went on the road that leads to Meah Shearim. He took one pace and went back two paces, he went back two paces and took half a pace, amazed that he was going and wasn't afraid. With so many thoughts, he grew weary and sat down to rest. He thought perhaps he should go back the way he came and go to Meah Shearim some other day. Balak, who wasn't one to dismiss his thoughts, immediately turned his head back. His tail came and went in front of him. Balak picked himself up and went behind his tail. His head came and returned behind him. The long and short of it is, all of Balak's reversals at that time happened all by themselves, as if his limbs ruled him and he didn't rule them. He looked at them harshly but didn't bark. His limbs sensed his anger and compromised with one another, and went back to walking until they reached Musrara, a place close to Meah Shearim. He saw a big house surrounded by an iron fence and stones and trees surrounding the house and leaning over to the public. And even though the dust covered them and their greenery couldn't be seen, his sense of smell recognized that they were trees. He said to himself, Until the day cools off, I shall sit in the shade of a tree and rest a bit and deliberate my course. He looked at his feet to see if they were willing to go with him. They obeyed him and went with him.

He went in among the trees and found himself a hidden place. He sat and looked out. He saw a few schoolgirls, some Ashkenazim, some Bukharans, some Georgians, some Aleppans, some Medeans, some Sephardim, some Persians, some Yemenites, and some from all the other ethnic communities in Jerusalem, and all of them wearing blue dresses and all of them grimacing their faces and twisting their mouths, and strange and various sounds were coming out of them. He recognized that they were speaking the tongues of a Gentile nation, but which nation he didn't recognize, even though he knew seventy tongues like most of the dogs of Jerusalem, for the tongue of that nation was not yet common in the Land, but since that was a school founded by our brothers the sons of Israel in England, he put two and two together and understood that the language was English. He smiled to himself between his teeth and spoke to himself, The daughters of Israel are intelligent, and just as their brothers learned the tongue of the Alliance Israélite and the tongue of the Gehilfsverein, so they will also learn that tongue. If Sholem Aleichem were here, he would make a fine story. He would take a girl from this school and marry her off to a boy from another school, he doesn't know her tongue and she doesn't know his tongue, they get fed up with their lives and go to the judge to get a divorce, but the judge, who doesn't know foreign languages, doesn't understand what they want and doesn't open a case. They return home without a divorce, adding insult to injury. The husband sees that languages were created only so that humans will not understand each other, and takes matters into his own hands. His hands carry out their missions and hit and beat and wound. And she is a pampered woman worn out by learning and she has no strength to hit. So what does she do? She takes one pot after another and throws it at her husband, until all the pots are thrown and broken. Since the pots are broken and there's nothing to cook in, the man has nothing at home. He goes down to Jaffa and sets sail for distant lands. The woman is left with no husband and no livelihood and she goes and hires herself out as a servant. The mistress of the house speaks Russian or Yiddish with her and she replies in English. The mistress of the house is angry that the servant dares to know a language the lady herself doesn't know, and the servant doesn't think much of her mistress because she doesn't know English. The mistress torments her so much that she runs away from her to another place, and from there to another place, and every place she goes they expel this woman because they don't understand her language. That miserable woman goes back home and sits forlorn and sad with no livelihood, with nothing.

CHAPTER EIGHTEEN

Encounter on the Road

1 |

Balak sat wherever it was he sat and laughed at the woes of the children of Israel. Meanwhile, the day began to grow dark. He recalled where he wanted to go and recalled all those calamities that came upon him from there. He thrust his feet into the ground and folded himself and lay back down and shrank up, and it looked as if he wouldn't budge from here. Suddenly, his ears pricked up and he started sniffing and spinning his tail like half of a wagon wheel and he stood up and went away. And where did he go? To a place we doubted he'd go. And since he knew that the place was a place of danger, why did he go there, for it is forbidden to get yourself into mortal danger, but just then, he saw Reb Grunam May-Salvation-Arise, and Reb Grunam's cloak was dragging below his feet. He stuck to him and hid in the hem of the cloak and went in with him, and folks didn't notice that a dog was walking with Reb Grunam.

And when Meah Shearim saw Reb Grunam, they began running toward him, for everyone is eager for words of ethics and they love chastisement. They showed him love and affection and asked him to preach. Reb Grunam shrugged, one eye turned down to hint to the Holy One how meek was that man, and one eye turned to see how many are those who wanted to hear him. At last, he raised both his eyes to heaven to tell the Holy One that we are far from boasting and preaching in public, but since a Commandment has come to us to be fulfilled, to bring human beings back to repentance of course it is desirable for the Almighty that we preach. He turned to the crowd and said, Bring me a bench out to the courtyard of the big synagogue. Perhaps I'll say a word or two.

All Meah Shearim gathered together and came to hear him, for Jerusalem wasn't yet filled with theaters and circuses and places of entertainment, and they yearned to hear preaching. They immediately brought a bench out to the courtyard. Reb Grunam mounted the bench and people held him up on all sides. Balak huddled in the hem of Reb Grunam's cloak and mounted with him. Reb Grunam wiped his nose with the hem of his cloak. And why with the hem of his cloak and not with his sleeve? Because with his sleeve he filters the water before drinking. He rubbed his eyes and glared straight ahead. They started predicting what the sermon would be and what he would preach. Paupers robbed and widows exploited and orphans enslaved and bad judges who become prominent and there isn't anyone to tell them what to do. Moreover, that year was a drought year and the reservoirs raise the cost of water, and a poor person can't afford water anymore. And needless to say, the activities of the Societies which aren't always legitimate, because they give more Distribution to anyone who has a lot, and to anyone who doesn't have anything, they don't give even the little bit he deserves. And there are a few more harsh issues here, and there is no one to stand in the breach. Even those who came intending originally to kill time, started looking with respect at Reb Grunam, who was about to denounce the flatterers who fill the city with enmity and hatred and envy and the evil eye and quarrels, and make Jerusalem a disgrace in the Diaspora.

Reb Grunam spread his legs and stood submissively, and moaned a few times, the moans preachers moan before a sermon, and shut his eyes so they wouldn't seek honor. And once again he spread his legs, for it seemed to him that something was pressing them. And if he hadn't spread his legs, Balak wouldn't have survived. And here we must praise Balak, who controlled himself and didn't eat Reb Grunam's shoes. Not because he was sated just then, and not because he feared that Reb Grunam would tie a ban on his tail, but because he was fond of sitting in the presence of Reb Grunam. But, from praise of Balak, we come of necessity to censure of Balak. Why did Balak like to wallow in the dust of Reb Grunam's feet? Because of the rebuke to the children of Israel, which he heard from the

mouth of Reb Grunam, for in those days Balak's heart was full of resentment against the children of Israel because of those calamities
they had caused him, and he found satisfaction in their humiliation.
Balak lay in the place where he lay and Reb Grunam stood in the
place where he stood. And Reb Grunam already threw out his first
identity and took on a second identity. His head, drooping like a vessel declared unfit whose owners threw it into the garbage, now stood
erect. And he too stood erect and started jumping up, jumping and
preaching.

2 |

God created one thing against another. On the one hand, He made
synagogues and study houses for the Torah and prayer, and on the
other hand, He made shops for merchandise. On the one hand, He
made preachers and castigators and sermonizers, and on the other
hand, merchants and shopkeepers. While Reb Grunam stands and
preaches, a shopkeeper stands in the door of his shop and sells pottery to an Arab. The Arab examines the pots to see if they're not
cracked, and Reb Grunam examines the deeds of the Jews. And the
voice of Reb Grunam and the sounds of the empty vessels blend together. Reb Grunam shouts, Who is making noise? And all the listeners shout, Close your shop. Said the shopkeeper, All day long I
haven't seen a penny and now that God brought me a customer, you
want to ruin my livelihood. A sturdy Mughrabi night guard, one of
those who are feared in Jerusalem, happened by. He grabbed the
shopkeeper and shook him this way and that and shouted at him, Jew,
close your shop. The shopkeeper pulled himself out of the
Mughrabi's hands and said to him, Where were you the day they
robbed my merchandise from the shop? When you want him he
doesn't come, and when you don't want him, he comes. Did you see
that one, the zeal of the Lord of Hosts hath eaten it up. Just as
Grunam is trying to make a living, so am I trying to make a living.
The guard took the shopkeeper and flung him around until he was
about to give up the ghost, and all the children of Israel were shouting at him, Shaygets, Shameless, Arrogant, We'll uproot you. When

the shopkeeper saw that trouble had overtaken him, he closed his shop and went off frustrated.

Reb Grunam's voice grew louder and both his eyes were filled with mucous, the mucous folks mistake for tears. All the women started weeping and making their husbands weep and all Meah Shearim was filled with weeping. Reb Grunam raised his voice and screamed, Woe unto us for the Day of Judgment, woe unto us for the Day of Rebuke. A man walks in the marketplace and he doesn't think he is a sinner, but I say that he is a sinner and a criminal. How? A cart stood harnessed to an ox and an ass, and that man took a pinch of snuff and sneezed and the animals were shocked and moved, and he has violated the prohibition Thou shalt not plow with an ox and an ass together. A man stands in the synagogue and prays in public and responds Amen, you would think that here in a holy place he is clean of all transgression, but I say to you that he is a sinner and a criminal, for who doesn't respond Amen with all his might.

Gentlemen, you all stand here today in our holy town of Meah Shearim, and here a man should be clean of all transgression. And what do we see, Gentlemen, there isn't one among you who isn't a sinner. Here's a man who sat all day fasting, wrapped in a Prayer Shawl and crowned with Tefillin and he completed one hundred blessings, not over coarse food, Heaven Forfend, for he fasted, and he lies down to sleep and recites the Shema and gets into his bed and shuts his eyes so as not to see evil and doesn't entertain any alien thought, Heaven Forfend. You say he is clean of all transgression. But I say to you, Gentlemen, woe unto him, that man who fasted all day and studied all day and didn't walk without Tefillin and prayed all day long and recited the Shema with devotion and did not engage in idle conversation and no profane word crossed his lips and no trace of an alien thought rose to his heart, nevertheless, this is a sinner. How? Gentlemen, here I am telling you, and why won't I tell you? Better you hear it from my mouth and not from the mouth of the Angels of Destruction, for if you hear it from the mouth of the Angels of Destruction, it's impossible to repent, but if you hear it from my mouth, you still have time to repent. For that man slept and the

Yarmulke fell off his head, it's not enough that he sins physically, that he violates the prohibition against baring your head, but he also makes his holy soul sin. How? For just then, his soul rose on high and wrote his deeds of that day. And there, they say to the soul, My daughter, have you written everything? Says she, I wrote everything. They say to her, And you didn't forget anything? And she replies, I didn't forget anything. They say to her, Perhaps you've made a mistake. And she swears she didn't make a mistake. Immediately all seven heavens are shocked at the false oath and fling her down and she returns to the body, and what does she see, woe to the eyes that see such a thing, she sees him lying with his head uncovered. Lest you say this matter is over and done, I say to you it is not, but that one sin produces another. The next day, he gets up early to go to the study house and says, *My God, the soul You placed within me is pure.* Gentlemen, it is not bad enough that he lies bareheaded and sins physically and makes his soul sin, but he gives false testimony about himself.

At that moment, the whole audience was shaken. If you turn this way, woe, if you turn that way, alas. If they sit in the study house, woe, if they get into their bed, alas. Reb Grunam knows they want to hear one word of consolation, but his heart is bitter as wormwood and he cannot bring any words out of his mouth except words bitter as wormwood.

During Reb Grunam's sermon, sleep descended upon Balak and he dozed off. He saw all kinds of dreams and became alarmed. He wagged his tail and barked in his sleep. His voice blended with the voice of Reb Grunam, but fortunately for him, Reb Grunam's voice was strong and they didn't hear the voice of the dog. After Reb Grunam concluded his sermon and they were about to recite the evening prayer, Balak woke with a start and sneaked out from between Reb Grunam's legs and pulled himself out of Meah Shearim, so as not to press his luck. And thus he walked until he came to the Hungarian Houses. We don't know what made him go here and not somewhere else. Anyway, he didn't lose anything. He came to the Hungarian Houses and found himself a corner to hide in. He sniffed a bit here and a bit there and circled his place a few times and checked to see if there weren't those harmful reptiles. He went in and curled up. Sleep came to him and he dozed off.

3 |

The moon disappeared in its clouds and light winds began blowing and swaying the olive trees and the dew descended upon them and their fragrance wafted. Balak stirred and peeped into the sweet darkness, and listened to the bells of the camels who come in caravans to bring us food and subsistence. The song of the bells and the nocturnal dews calmed Balak's spirit and took away the anger that permeated his body like venom. Balak looked at the body of the world and feasted his eyes on the nocturnal sights, and was glad that his Creator had given him the intelligence to sleep during the sermon and to be awake at night, when good dews descend and cool winds blow and a good smell comes from the trees, not that smell that human creatures perfume themselves with, but the good smell that the Holy-One-Blessed-Be-He perfumes His world with. And when Balak saw himself steeped in this tranquility, he was proud, as if he were the only one who could enjoy the goodness of creation. But he who is haughty is brought low in the end. An evil wind began rattling, saying, All that tranquility may be only fleeting, for no one saw you when you came in, but in the morning, when the Holy-One-Blessed-Be-He lights up His world and they see you, they'll come against you with sticks and stones, and may you not pay for your enjoyment with your body. He grew dejected, and his nose seemed to stop its moisture. He started lamenting his bad luck, and even when he was enjoying himself his enjoyment wasn't complete, because of his worry about tomorrow. He looked around to see if they weren't coming to pester him. He saw that the whole world was sleeping and there was no reason to be afraid. His spirits revived and he lifted his tail and wagged it to and fro, as if all his worries were fleas and mosquitoes. He lay down in his place and relied on the people of that neighborhood not to get up soon, for those Hungarians aren't like the other people of Jerusalem, for they had come to build their houses in a lush place, then livelihood is provided for them and their sleep is sweet.

And so Balak lay as if the whole night were his. He began shaking his voice in a song as if he were alone in the world and no creature heard him.

The Song of Balak

I look at the land
No candle will quake
With the stars of God Almighty
I stay awake

On the face of the earth
There isn't a sound
In the cleft of the rock
On the clods of the mound

And over my paths
No one will hobnob
And why, oh my soul,
In vain do you sob

The night is still deep
Far away is the dawn
Your eyelids are closed
And your eyes are shut down

All over the land
No one passing now
All flesh is silent
Bow wow wow

And thus Balak sang and didn't see that Reb Fayesh was here. And what brought Reb Fayesh out in the dead of night and darkness? Reb Fayesh went to hang up posters of excommunications, which he was afraid to hang up in daytime lest those who were excommunicated tear down the posters, and so he did his work at night, and by the time they woke up early in the morning, the whole city knew who was excommunicated and outlawed. Balak wasn't involved in politics and didn't stick his head into any quarrel. He didn't distinguish between one society and another or between one ethnic community and another. In this respect, Balak was truly unique in his time. Therefore, it is no wonder that he didn't pay heed to any of those excommunications, which were hung up every morning. And if he did pay heed to them, he did so for his enjoyment, for example, if he was hungry he pulled off the dough they use to paste the excommunications and ate it. And just as he didn't care to know what the documents were, so he didn't care to recognize who wrote them. When that man appeared to him, that is Reb Fayesh, the dog thought in his innocence that he was also enjoying that sweet darkness that enveloped all Jerusalem. Balak was filled with love and affection for that human creature who was awake like him, and all that was in Balak's heart at that moment rose up to his tongue. And when Reb Fayesh approached him, he gave him a welcoming bark to tell him, Even though I don't presume to be your equal, I'm informing you that I'm here too. Reb Fayesh was startled and his lantern slipped out of his hand and the candle went out and the pot fell and the dough spilled out of it and the excommunication posters were scattered and began flying away. And Reb Fayesh's soul also flew away. That Commandment began clinging to him and said to him, What's wrong with you, don't be afraid. And it tempted him until his soul returned. He started running and gathering up the posters. Those scraps of paper made their own inference. If Reb Fayesh, an emissary of the Commandment, is running, we who are the Commandment itself should run even faster. They immediately began rolling away and striking him in the face. And every single note cackles with those words Reb Fayesh wrote on it. In his innocence, Reb Fayesh thought that the forefathers of the excommunicated rose up from their graves and came to take vengeance on him, for the notes were white as shrouds of the dead. He screamed a great scream and ran. And the notes ran after him. Reb Fayesh came upon the dog and kicked him. The dog screamed and Reb Fayesh was startled and fell down. All you emissaries of the Commandments, may you not be startled as Reb Fayesh was startled. Balak saw the downfall of that man and was stunned, What is the matter! Just a little while ago, he was walking around on two legs and now he's down on four. I'll go and smell him, maybe the creature isn't a human, or maybe he needs help and I'll be kind to him. As he was smelling him, Reb Fayesh was jolted awake and fled for his life. Balak stood ashamed and embarrassed. All you who are kind, may you not have such shame.

4 |

The night was pleasant and a cool wind blew. That coolness strengthened Balak's bones and his spirit too. On most occasions, Balak liked the heat, but on those days of great heat, he was drawn to coolness. He consoled himself for his grief and said, What did that Jew do to me, because he ran away from me am I defective? As folks tell when they throw a dog into the river he comes out and shakes himself and goes back to being a dog as he was. And even though he mentioned the issue of water only as an example, his mouth filled with saliva, for all through those days most of his thoughts involved water, and when he said water, his mouth filled up immediately.

Never in his life had Balak seen seas or rivers or brooks or canals or ponds or springs. He had heard of them only by rumor. And like folks whose foolishness is greater than their wisdom and who haven't any idea of the ways of the world and think that everything they haven't seen with their own eyes is a fiction, so Balak thought the seas and the rivers and the brooks and the ponds and the springs were made-up fictions. And like those folks whose foolishness is greater than their wisdom, when they long for something, they immediately believe it, so Balak began believing in the reality of all the waters in the world, but he thought they were made by human hands. How? They dig a cistern like that ritual bath in the Rand Houses and in the Oren Stein Houses, and they put slivers of ice in it, like the ones the soda vendors bring from Jaffa and the sun shines on them and they melt and become rivers and brooks and seas. You drink from them, you quench your thirst, you bathe in them, you remove the weariness from your body.

By the time Balak rummaged around in his mind, the second watch of the night ended and the hour came when all heavenly creatures and all earthly creatures recite poetry. But where is the water that we say, *When he uttereth his voice there is a multitude of waters*? Where are the rivers of *let the floods clap their hands*? Where are the springs that will recite poetry? Jerusalem is wiped dry as a desert. If not for two or three Minyans of trees and stalks and desert plants, no poetry would be heard in Jerusalem. At that hour, the voice of the beadle was heard saying, At the light of thine arrows they went, and at the shining of thy glittering spear. Jerusalem shook itself out of its sleep and from every house and every hut and every shed and every courtyard all kinds of slops began to be poured into the street. Before Balak had time to quench his thirst, the sun shone and nothing was left of them but mounds of filth.

CHAPTER NINETEEN

Leaves the Dog and Concerns Only Reb Fayesh

1 |

More dead than alive, Reb Fayesh was brought home. His blood was chilled and his limbs were paralyzed. His tongue was stuck to his palate and his thoughts were scrambled. Out of an unclear consciousness, he pondered, Our Rabbis said that envoys of the Commandments come to no harm. So why was I harmed? Can we suspect the Lord of passing judgment without justice?

The Holy-One-Blessed-Be-He does not pass judgment without justice. Whatever He does, He does well in its time and its season, for He had warned the Children of Israel not to attack one another, but because of the voices of quarrel, His voice was not heard, the voice of the Almighty. Many of them were afflicted, in their fortune or their body, and they haven't yet learned the moral. For, they said, A habit that found favor in the eyes of our forefathers could it be unclean for us. And they didn't know that there are things that were beautiful in ancient times and ugly in modern times.

Reb Fayesh's thoughts gradually ceased. His limbs fell still and his thoughts left him. Sleep descended upon him and he dozed off. Torah and Commandments, good and evil deeds, Hell and Paradise, This World and the World-to-Come went off, and nothing was left but this body sunk in pillows and blankets and sweating. His lips rounded and were covered with saliva. At times they looked blue, at times purple. At first Rebecca diligently wiped them. When she saw that it was endless, her hands slackened and she left him alone. But Shifra didn't leave him alone. As a butterfly spreads her wings on a gray day and shakes them, thus Shifra hovered over him with a colorful rag in her hand and wiped his lips. If he stirred — he looked straight ahead, like someone glancing into the clouds, and went back to sleep.

Reb Fayesh's bed is surrounded by neighbors and the neighbors of neighbors, friends and half friends. Some nod their head in grief and others offer consolation and say the Lord will take pity. Both the former and the latter discuss that unknown illness and tell stories in praise of the sick man. Reb Fayesh wasn't aware of them or their words, or he was aware of them and didn't pay any mind to them.

Meanwhile they sent for the doctor. The doctor examined the sick man and prescribed some drugs for drinking and oil for lubrication. He took his fee and went on his way. And as he left, he said he'd come back, and if necessary, he would prescribe other drugs for him. Another doctor summoned after him did the same. Except that one was a German who spoke German and ordered them to get his drugs from the German pharmacist and the other was a Greek who ordered them to get his drugs from the Greek pharmacist. Neither of them did any good for the sick man, neither with their examinations nor with their medications. Gentiles who raise dogs in their own houses, how should it occur to them that the disease came from a dog. Reb Fayesh lies without a tongue and without speech and they don't know what happened to him. Too bad for Reb Fayesh. People like Reb Fayesh aren't born every day. Now that he is sleeping, we'll talk about him a bit and tell a bit of his story.

2 |

Reb Fayesh was born in a small community in the state of Slovakia to a pious father and mother who observed the Commandments. They rented fields and vineyards from the nobleman and brought forth bread from the earth with toil and tedium. Even in childhood, signs of purity were visible in him, for he didn't behave like those mischievous boys who turn their heart away from the Torah and run away from school to seek in the orchards and pick fruit, but he would hide at home and study Torah. Because of their poverty, his parents couldn't hire a teacher for him and they made do with any vagabonds seeking work in small villages, who showed him the shape of the letters and their combinations. When he could combine letters, he clung to the Yeshiva students who went around on the Sabbath eve for their food, and he would give them his own bread if they taught him a chapter of the Pentateuch. His father and mother saw that Fayesh's soul longed for Torah and deprived themselves for their son and didn't notice that their livelihood wasn't enough for them, and every Sabbath they invited a student to their house to teach their son. When Fayesh was about ten years old and studied Talmud on his own, they sent him to a Yeshiva. He acquired perfection in the ways of the Lord and didn't enjoy the pleasures of this world, not even those that are obligatory. Because he was born under the sign of Mars, his Rabbi advised him to study the laws of kosher slaughter. He carried out the imperative to love your craft and he hated the Rabbis and honed his butchers' knives. When he was still a fledgling, the people of a small town called on him affectionately to be their slaughterer. He responded to their call and became a slaughterer. And he too was affectionate to them. For in that community, the diseases of the time had spread, schools had been established to teach the children Christian languages and foreign wisdom, and Reb Fayesh stood in the breach to erect a fence, and rescued his community from total extinction. With the dowry he received from his father-in-law, Reb Moyshe Amram, he hired teachers to teach the children what a Jewish soul needs, and he himself supervised the teaching, and examined the students, and checked the teachers' interpretations, for in those days, in some places people popped up who looked pious and who inserted into their teaching foreign interpretations that were taught in modern schools which call themselves seminaries for Rabbis. Just he was involved in the needs of the children, so he was also involved in the needs of the grownups, things like ritual baths and Eruvs and burial practices. And just as he was involved in the needs of grownups and children, so he was also involved in the needs of the smallest children. He would cajole poor pregnant women and give them money for a Brit and would circumcise their sons. When the sons excelled, he saw them as a return on his money. If he found a trace of heresy in any one of them, he would tell him, Boy, push back the sidelock, for I want to smack your jaw.

3 |

Reb Fayesh could have enjoyed his life and filled his belly with meat, but he was fonder of a tiny bit of Wild Ox in the World-to-Come than of all the living animals and birds in This World, and was rigorous about disqualifying meat as unfit even in cases when most legal rabbinical opinions would have permitted it. The butchers started screaming that he declared their animals unfit just to upset them, and people from the community wrote letters of appeal to all the sages of the generation about butchers who don't believe their kosher slaughterer and claim he declares unfit and forbids meat and makes unkosher all that is kosher. The sages of the generation were divided. Some relied on Reb Fayesh who was known for his outstanding reverence for God and all his deeds were for the sake of Heaven, and they wrote to the people of the community to remove the enmity from their heart and obey him; while others wrote explicitly that he banned where there wasn't even a shadow of a doubt, and warned him not to deprive the people of his city of meat, and if not, the people of his city were authorized to remove him from his position as ritual slaughterer and to accept another ritual slaughterer. But Reb Fayesh behaved as usual, until the butchers threw him out of the slaughter house and brought in another ritual slaughterer. Reb Fayesh put up his knife and took up his pen, and started writing against the new ritual slaughterer whose ritual slaughter was impure, and he warned the people of his community to save their soul and not to defile themselves with broth of abominable things, for there is no transgression worse than eating forbidden foods that stupefy the Jewish heart. And for our many sins, many communities in the land got a bad name because of lax ritual slaughterers, and the people ate and stuffed themselves on unfit meats, and harmful ideas overcame them until they became licentious and were lost from the Community of Israel. Thus Reb Fayesh would warn the people of his city until the butchers began to fear his words and tried to appease him and bring him back to the slaughterhouse, but he wouldn't come back, for he had already taken a vow to ascend to the Land of Israel, for he hoped to build a new life in the Holy Land, for Outside the Land he did not have any sons. It wasn't long before he fulfilled his vow.

4 |

When he ascended to Jerusalem, they gave him an apartment in the Hungarian Houses and a Hungarian Distribution, which is better than most of the Societies, aside from the money his father-in-law gave him, and the money given him by the butchers who feared lest he would pray against them in the holy places. Reb Fayesh was released from care about this world and gave his whole mind to the World-to-Come. He began inquiring about the desires of heaven and seeking sins, in order to purify the antechamber before the great hall of the World-to-Come. Bans and excommunications that had already been forgotten, he restored to their former glory, and he even added on to them. He issued stern warnings against transgressions that people stomp underfoot, and he made a crown for his head of Commandments people neglected. Proclamations and announcements were published by him every Monday and Thursday, until the walls turned black with them. And if need be, he wrote new excommunications. And in that matter, Reb Fayesh was superior to all writers of excommunications, for most writers of excommunications in Jerusalem used high-flown rhetoric and a person can't grasp their meaning, while Reb Fayesh, who had never in his life looked at books of rhetoric, wrote in a language everyone could understand. Moreover, he wasn't afraid for himself, for there are those who are wary of ostracism and bans because sometimes the same measure of justice strikes the excommunicators themselves; and he wasn't afraid of any man, not even of a pious scholar. Reb Fayesh would say, If he is acquitted in the Court of Heaven, I shall go and stand at the entrance of Paradise and not let him enter. Until Reb Fayesh ascended to Jerusalem, he was concerned with Torah, when he ascended to Jerusalem, he was completely taken up with current needs. Reb Fayesh would say, When the Angel asks me, Did you set regular times for the study of the Torah, I will tell him, Sometimes abrogation of the Torah is what keeps it alive, and I trust that he will nod at me and tell me, Congratulations.

Some of Reb Fayesh's comrades are mentioned among the builders of the Yishuv, but Reb Fayesh isn't mentioned except for one regulation he issued that guards be placed at the entrances to synagogues on Simhat Torah to prevent women and men from mixing. In truth, there is no difference between Reb Fayesh and them, except that they issued a lot of sons who saw the generation change and all boast of building the Land, and they declared that their fathers were the real builders of the Yishuv; while Reb Fayesh had only one daughter and there was no one to declare anything about him.

5 |

It wasn't long before his name became known in the city, and on every single issue, the Rabbis asked Reb Fayesh's opinion. Envy entered the heart of his colleagues. They began worrying that power would pass into his hands. And even though both he and they had the same intention, to uproot heresy and to purify the antechamber, even so, his colleagues' minds weren't easy about him, for a man has a vested interest, especially about Commandments, for everyone wanted the Commandment to be done by him. Satan started dancing among them, for in that generation the freethinkers were not yet important, and Satan desired to dwell among the pious. A strong dispute erupted between Reb Fayesh and his colleagues. He bans and they allow, he excommunicates and they release. He pastes up excommunication posters and they tear them down, some openly and some secretly. But Reb Fayesh mocked their efforts. If he found his proclamations torn down, he wrote other proclamations harsher than the first, and hung them up at night when everyone was sleeping. That night, Balak found him and what happened happened.

When he got sick, his colleagues forgot what they had done to him, but were sorry for what the Holy-One-Blessed-Be-He had done to him. And they sighed about Reb Fayesh who ran like a deer to do the will of his Father in Heaven, and now he is laid in his bed like a dove struck by a vulture. That Reb Fayesh who was a vessel full of purity is lying like a broken clay pot. Reb Fayesh should have spent his days and years in enjoyment and in the end he is sick and oppressed with suffering. Not to denounce the severity of the judgment did they intend, but to break their own heart recalling that if the Holy-One-Blessed-Be-He doesn't favor even a great man like Reb

Fayesh, what can we infer about human beings who have not ac-
complished such good deeds as Reb Fayesh?

Reb Fayesh lies amid his pillows and blankets, and his loved
ones and friends surround his bed, all of them respectable people,
pious and perfect, men of renown and men of action, the first in all
practice of the Commandments. But Reb Fayesh doesn't notice
them and doesn't know where he is. Reb Fayesh squints his eyes and
makes an effort to remember where he is. A kind of mist rises, like
the mist that rises from the waters of a river close to the holiday of
Sukkot, and that mist enters his clothes and they are permeated and
a chill emanates from them and a cold sweat emanates from him. He
looked straight ahead and didn't see any river, but he knew that the
river was nearby, and there are the young boughs where they take
twigs for Hoshana Raba. Now he and his comrades are going to cut
boughs for themselves. And other lads who aren't from the village are
also coming to cut branches. And he urged his comrades to run so
the strange lads wouldn't get there first. That mist began to thicken
and started swallowing up his comrades until they were enveloped
in the mist and disappeared, and the only one left was him. And the
other lads who came from other places also disappeared. And they
didn't disappear within the mist, but ran away because of the village
dogs who chased them. He walked on alone and came to the young
branches. He plucked as many as he plucked and loaded them on
his shoulders. And he heard a pleasant voice coming from the
branches on his back. He began to fear that it was the voice of a panther, for everyone who hears that voice is tempted and follows him
until he comes to his hole and the panther sucks his blood. He was
scared and trembled and threw away his branches. The branches
began flagellating one another. He raised his voice and shouted for
help. Reb Fayesh's colleagues saw that he was moving his lips. They
bent their ears to hear. Reb Fayesh looked at them in fear and
shouted, Dogs. His words became confused and he fell silent.

Rebecca saw all that had happened to her husband. But her
heart couldn't accept that calamity. Is it possible that Fayesh, who
had never been sick in his life and had never been idle, could be
lying in bed and nothing happens? This body that was nimble to

carry out all Commandments and good deeds, how can it spend its days and nights with no Torah and no prayer? Great was Rebecca's grief for her husband, and greater than her grief was the amazement of her heart. This amazement sometimes made her forget the truth, and she would imagine that his illness would pass and Fayesh would be himself again, but they had to hasten his cure, and the doctors and nurses and medicines weren't doing that. She would come to his bed and examine every single one of his movements and wait to hear something from his mouth, for who could give advice better than Fayesh. And sometimes she would come to hear a word or a rebuke from him. But no word came from the mouth of Reb Fayesh and no rebuke was heard on his tongue, but his eyelashes were stuck like a man who fell asleep from a heart attack. She would consider and seek something to say, and would talk to him and say, Fayesh, have pity and compassion on your wife and tell her a word. Don't withhold your pity from me, if not for my sake, then for Shifra our daughter. Sometimes Reb Fayesh would look at her with eyes that stood like two clods of lead, but mostly he didn't notice her.

Rebecca didn't despair and when she left him and went away from him, she would come back to him immediately, lest he would consent to tell her something. Since Fayesh was silent, she would lift her eyes to heaven and say, Master of the Universe, how can you leave him lying there with no Torah and no Commandments? For You surely know that he walked before You with an innocent heart in private as in public. Please take pity on him, You don't have many like him in This World. When she saw that the Holy-One-Blessed-Be-He didn't respond to her prayer, she would go back to her husband and say, Fayesh, Fayesh, why are you silent? Why don't you pray with me? For the Holy-One-Blessed-Be-He yearns for the prayer of a Saint, and if you pray He will surely hear your prayer. And since she knew herself that she wasn't as important as her husband, she would take Shifra and lead her to the sick man and say as she wept, You pray for father. The two of them would stand and weep over the sick man and weep for one another.

CHAPTER TWENTY

Isaac Comes and Goes at Reb Fayesh's House

1 |

When Reb Fayesh got sick, the doors of his house were opened to Isaac. Reb Fayesh lies like a silent stone and has no control over his limbs, his hands and his tongue don't obey him, and the rest of his body also seems removed from the world. Only his eyes are still under his rule, but they were changed too, as if he had abandoned the world and withdrawn his attention from it.

Two or three times a week Isaac came to feed the sick man. Praise to the healthy man who tends the sick, especially a sick man no one tends. At first, the neighbors came in, after a few days their number decreased, and after a few more days no one came in. Some stopped coming because they were busy with community needs, and some refrained from coming because they didn't want to sit with women, and others didn't come because of both reasons together. And there was one more reason, they remembered what Reb Fayesh did·to them when he was healthy. God Forbid they should bear a grudge against him, but even Solomon said be not righteous over much. And his father-in-law and mother-in-law, where were they? In Safed. Reb Moyshe Amram saw that he couldn't live with his son-in-law, and if he lived in the same city as his son-in-law and didn't live with his son-in-law, folks would have said that they didn't get along. And when he ascended to Meron on Lag b'Omer, he saw Safed and found its setting beautiful, and he rented an apartment there. Rebecca wrote her father and mother and didn't get a reply. Either the letter remained in the post office in Jerusalem or their letter remained in Safed. For sending a letter through the Turkish post office is like throwing it into the Dead Sea.

Isaac supports the sick man, and sometimes brings food. He is used to such things from his experience with Bloykof. And when he brings he brings stealthily so Shifra won't notice, and he claims that it cost less than he really paid. Great are the compassionate who lie for the good of others and enjoy more than any liar enjoys from his lie for his own good. His pocket is small and his coins are few. He is only a laborer who works a lot and earns a little. But he shrinks his belly and expands his hand and does mercy to three souls.

The market is crowned with fruits and vegetables. Isaac selects the finest and doesn't haggle, for things bought generously are a double blessing. From the fruit market, Isaac goes to the egg and poultry market. Isaac is not an administrator or an inspector to buy a chicken, but he buys eggs. In that year when we ascended to the Land of Israel, eighteen eggs cost a Bishlik, and at the Kinneret, our comrades bought thirty for a Bishlik. When the railroad track began going out of the Land, they started exporting eggs to neighboring countries and their price rose a lot.

The shopkeeper sits in the doorway of his shop like a hen sitting on her eggs. He remembers days when he got up early and went out to where the roads meet to the village girls to buy chickens and eggs from them and went around all day long with his baskets. Now he sits in a shop like a merchant. Isaac puts his hand in his pocket and clinks his coins and says to the shopkeeper, How many for a Bishlik? The shopkeeper responds, Seven for a Bishlik. Says Isaac, Seven for a Bishlik, but nice ones I want. Says the shopkeeper, Nice ones I sell. From today? From today. Says Isaac, Then, choose for me, it's for a new mother. For Isaac is sly in purchasing and knows how to trap people with his words. So the shopkeeper won't say to himself, Can't this young fellow eat an old egg, Isaac tells him it's for a new mother so that he'll give him nice ones. The shopkeeper puts his hands in the box or the basket and takes an egg and examines it in the light and gives it to the customer, takes an egg and holds it up to the light and gives it to the customer. And Isaac takes his wares and brings them to Rebecca.

Rebecca asks, How much are these eggs? And she sighs because her hands are empty and she hasn't any money to pay, for they deduct from her Distribution the fee for the doctor and the medicine and other expenses that don't seem to do any good. Says Isaac to Rebecca, These eggs cost me nothing. How is that? I painted a chicken coop and they gave me eggs as my fee and I brought them to you, since I eat in a restaurant and I don't know what I'll do with them. From the beginning of the world until now, we have never heard of anyone painting a chicken coop. But Rebecca hears and believes. And as for the grapes he brought, that was from his friend from the Sharon Valley who came up to sell his fruit in Jerusalem and gave him a basket of grapes. Lest you think that Isaac ran out of lies, a few days later, he came back and brought eggs, for ever since he painted that chicken coop, the hens began laying more because its color is white and they think it's daytime. And when the egg sellers saw that, they hired him to paint their chicken coops and paid him with eggs, and they were going to give him some every week.

He who has an egg boils it and makes himself a meal. If he has grapes he adds grapes to it. The Holy-One-Blessed-Be-He feeds the world with His good things. Some take their sustenance from living things, some take their sustenance from things that grow in the ground, and some take their sustenance from both together. Until Reb Fayesh got sick, he supported his household with hens and fish, since Reb Fayesh got sick he supported it with similitude. But mercy of the Lord is from everlasting to everlasting, if the livelihood is deprived, He invents compensation for it and if you lose it here, it is raised somewhere else. Isaac doesn't weary of making up new things every day. If his pocket is small, his imagination is big. Every day he makes up something, just so Shifra and her mother won't lack food.

2 |

But the quality of grace isn't always rewarded. Evil neighbor women began looking at Isaac and slandering Shifra. And when he comes, Rebecca asks him if her neighbors noticed him. And when he sits down, her eyes and Shifra's eyes seem to ask him to get up and go on his way. Not as at first when they brought him a glass of cold water and jam. Jam imported from Outside the Land in colorful jars with a smiling virgin painted on them may be sweeter, but it doesn't have a real taste. For that jam isn't made of fruit grown by the sun that warms your limbs by day and the moon and stars that light you by night and poems and songs aren't sung as it is made. In vain do you spread your lips, naughty girl. Your smile doesn't please Isaac's heart. He likes Shifra's light smile better than the smiles of a thousand painted girls.

Shifra is a thin girl and you can circle her with the ring of a bolt. Her hair is the color of nuts and her lips aren't thin like her father's or full like her mother's. Her eyes are more closed than open, either because of fatigue or because of piety. Eyes like those are usually called dreamy eyes. And her mother calls them eyes of gold. And in truth, a golden thread did seem to stretch from them. And it is this thread that bound Isaac's soul to Shifra's soul.

3 |

At that time, the season of Muharram began, the season of moving, when people move out of one apartment and into another. Everyone who moves into a new apartment renews something in it and changes its color, for not all tastes are the same. Some like one color and some like another color, and some don't like this color or that color, but a blend of many colors. Some say tastes depend on the stars. A person born in the sign of Mars likes red, in the sign of Jupiter likes white, and some say it all depends on bile. Those with black bile are drawn to black, and those with green bile to green. And both admit that even bile is dependent on the stars, for bile is attuned to a person's sign. Others say, on the contrary, everything follows from the banners carried in the desert, that every single tribe had a flag and a color on every single flag, like the color of gems on Aaron's breastplate. And the heart of every single Jew is drawn to the color of his banner.

Isaac stands in a house and grinds colors and dissolves them in water and dips his brush and paints the walls and the ceiling. This grain which is nothing but dust can change the way things look. If you want, you draw angels and seraphim with it, if you want you draw Devils and Demons and Ghosts. And since those are days of work and not of idleness, Isaac shuts his heart and fills his hands. No longer will you see him playing with dogs and writing on their skin, now he's busy renovating houses for their inhabitants. Too bad for Isaac that, of all those houses, there isn't a house waiting for him in the evening after he finishes his work and wants to relax with folks. All the time he was busy he didn't notice that. When the moving season ended and Isaac's hands grew light, his soul grew heavy. And when he returned to his room, his heart was bored inside him. After a few days, he overcame his hesitations and went to Reb Fayesh's house.

And before he went to Reb Fayesh's house, he changed his clothes and washed his face and hands. Even a painter sometimes wants to see his hands clean and to see himself dressed in clean clothes. And since the day had already declined, he went to the market to buy himself food for supper. Isaac walks around in the market and considers what to buy. The coins in his pocket slip into his hand. Round are the coins and they roll from hand to hand. A little while before they were in Isaac's hands, a little while later they are in the shopkeeper's hands. What will Isaac do with all those things he bought, for there are more than a single man needs. On the other hand, there are people who need them and don't have them.

Rebecca opened the door to him and greeted him with tears. A letter came from her father and it didn't contain good news. He is also sick and needs pity, and when he gets out of bed, he will do as much as a weak man can do. He'll go to the graves of the Saints to pray for his son-in-law. And what he agreed to do his spouse has already done, but on her way back from the graves, she slipped and cracked her leg and now she is lying sick, and they can't return to Jerusalem. It was a miracle from heaven that they reached Safed safely, and you can't test God twice.

Isaac sits facing Rebecca and Shifra, and each of them is sad in his own way. Isaac is sad because of the two old people, and Rebecca is sad because of her father and mother and because of her husband, and Shifra is sad because of her father and mother and because of her grandfather and her grandmother, and because of herself. Before nightfall she went out to fetch water from the cistern, and she heard a neighbor woman saying to her friend, Did you see that girl who hung on his neck like the crucified hanging on a crossroads;

and the words clearly were said about her. Because Isaac comes to ask about her father, does that give the neighbor women the right to slander her.

Isaac asked Rebecca, How is Reb Fayesh? Rebecca pointed to his bed. Isaac looked and said, Nothing has changed. Rebecca answered, Nothing has changed, and she looked too. Reb Fayesh's face was shriveled and dark. His eyes, that used to pierce the face of anyone who saw them, were slack, and his drooping lips were moving, as if he wanted to say something but his tongue didn't obey him. When Isaac stood up to go, Rebecca remembered her neighbors and said, Are you going? And she lit the way for him, covering the lamp with her apron.

CHAPTER TWENTY-ONE

With His First Comrades

1 |

Tranquility settled on the city and its houses settled into tranquility. And the people inside the houses are a quiet nation, secure in its God. Every house shines and every window stretches out peace to you. And between the thorns of the towers, the moon shines. The local stones are reconciled with you and the trees in the field wave their leaves. And a very faint voice rises from the earth, and you follow the voice. And here comes a caravan of Ishmaelites with their camels bearing the goods of the Land of Israel. And you imagine you are walking with them until they return you to your father.

But there are nights when Isaac doesn't find peace, not at home and not outside. He goes into his house, and the walls of the house press him. He goes outside, and heaven and earth join together to grieve him. If the moon is shining, he sheds his heart inside him. If it isn't shining, the world is dark for him.

Like most single people, who have a hard time living alone, he goes to the People's Center. Even Adam, the First Man, who lounged in the Garden of Eden with ministering angels standing before him and roasting meat for him and filtering wine for him, the Holy-One-Blessed-Be-He said it is not good that the man should be alone, and that applies even more to someone who doesn't have ministering angels standing before him. Isaac goes to the People's Center to soothe his mind a bit in the company of human beings.

Some lavish heaps of praise on the People's Center, as a gathering place for the educated people of the city, seekers of knowledge, and supporters of the renaissance of Israel; and others are complaining and say, A People's Center should be it, and it isn't. The weekly

Young Laborer, which can't be dazzled, once published comments about the People's Center, and from the day those comments were published, nothing has changed, and when you come in here, it seems as if your eyes had come only to confirm those comments.

You enter a fenced courtyard which grows thorns and stones, and you come to a big hall, with two rooms on this side and two rooms on that side. In one room sits the librarian and lends books; and in another room sit all those who want to spend one of the spare hours the day is full of; and in another room, the heads of the committee gather to discuss the issues of the People's Center; and another room serves as a kind of cafeteria. And anyone who hasn't yet decided what room to enter strolls in the hall. On the other hand, in the courtyard, girls walk around, to and fro, arm in arm, and they chat. What do those girls chat about? They chat about the endless boredom and that there isn't a man here to stir their heart a bit. On the other hand, in the gatehouse sits a seminarian who sneaked in here clandestinely, and he shrinks himself up so they won't notice him, for if they do notice him, they will throw him out of the seminary with a reprimand, for the principal of the seminary ordered his students not to go to the People's Center, for all who come to the People's Center are heretics and apostates or revolutionaries. The student sits and shrinks himself up so they won't notice him. But his thoughts, which he can't control, are expanding. Many are the thoughts in a man's heart, and the essence of all his thoughts is about women and about love. When the Holy-One-Blessed-Be-He created a man He produced a woman from him. Since man transgressed, he has to pursue woman all by himself. That student sits there all by himself and whispers to himself Bialik's poem, Take me in, they say there is love in the world, what is love? And he wonders, Doesn't Bialik, that great poet, know what love is? An ordinary man, why does he need to know? The eyes and heart of that student are enveloped with tears, like those girls whose shadows are enveloped at evening. Says one girl to another, Come, let's go inside, they've already lit the lamp.

When the lamp is lit, they pick up a paper to read it, or they sit and talk with one another. Their talk doesn't refresh their soul, like a person who talks to himself in the mirror. If there is someone there who knows how to deliver a speech, they ask him to deliver a speech. If it seems worthwhile to deliver a speech, he gets up and delivers a speech; if not, he doesn't deliver a speech. Somebody comes along, climbs up on the stage and reads a story by Sholem Aleichem. People from Outside the Land sit and laugh, people of Jerusalem drop their heads onto their shoulders and doze off, until they are awakened by the sound of applause, and they also applaud so people won't say they don't understand literature, as they wonder what's so funny here and what's the reason for the applause.

But sometimes, a spirit of life enters the walls of the People's Center, as on nights when there's a party or a lecture, especially when the lecturer is from Jaffa. What's the difference between the sages of Jaffa and the sages of Jerusalem? In literary matters, the sages of Jaffa are stronger, for they know literature and are acquainted with literary figures. In science, the sages of Jerusalem are stronger, for they know German and draw their ideas from the source, not like the sages of Jaffa who learn from Russian books translated from the German, and no translator is an expert in the language he is translating from. But the sages of Jaffa have an extra advantage, they speak excitedly. Aside from science and literature, there are also lectures on current events. Those lectures on current events attract a big audience, for even in Jerusalem which is withdrawn from the world, people long to know what's happening in the world. On occasion, writers and scholars and activists from Outside the Land drop in. And once upon a time, a caravan of forty tourists who ascended to the Land and shook up the whole Land came to the People's Center and all of new Jerusalem gathered to honor them and carried them on their shoulders. Speakers delivered speeches while they were carried and when they were put down.

Sometimes ordinary guests drop in, from Jaffa and from the settlements, who come to Jerusalem for their business or for their health, and they come to the People's Center to welcome the educated people of the city, the best people of the New Yishuv. You can spot them by their light clothing and their suntanned faces and a few qualities unusual in Jerusalem. They sit, the people of Jerusalem, sons of the capital city, and are pleasant to their brothers, with magnanimity and largess, as distinguished citizens of Jerusalem who know themselves that they are above the whole world because they are blessed to dwell in Jerusalem, and they weave into their conversation words that were coined by the Language Committee, and they boast about the art school, Bezalel, which has all kinds of artistic activity, from the rug at your feet to the turban on your head, as well as household utensils and ritual articles, and they brag about their Library of the Treasures of Joseph, which is loyal to the Hebrew spirit and the ingathering of the exiles of our books, from the beginning of Jewish printing to our own day. And as they talk, they mention the sages of Jerusalem who will promote the wisdom of Jerusalem in the world, for you don't have one single sage in Jerusalem who hasn't written several books, some of them are still in manuscript and some of them are still in thought. And needless to say, a great writer will appear and write a novel about Jerusalem, a novel in two parts, one part about the divine Jerusalem and one part about the earthly Jerusalem. That part about the divine Jerusalem has to include all the yearnings and longings of the elders of the generation that sustained the Yishuv with their suffering. And that part about the earthly Jerusalem has to tell about the building of Jerusalem and her activists and builders.

Mr. Nehemiah Gedalia Posek, an old man of about fifty, with a jolly face and small eyes, one of the founders and supporters of the People's Center, is lavish in praise of old Jerusalem. And even though he belongs to the New Yishuv, he was involved with the Rabbis and the inspectors, and he is an expert in every single institution, for every single thing in Jerusalem, either of young people or of old people, is close to his heart.

Mr. Nehemiah Gedalia Posek sits wearing a black coat, which may be either the garb of the pious or the clothing of the educated, and on his head is a creased black felt hat he bought Outside the Land when he went to the Congress in Basel, and he looks very affectionately at the people listening to his words, and he praises the Rabbis of Jerusalem who can get along with every person, and they manage the city wisely, for you need great wisdom to manage the city that contains people from all over the Exile, and every single person is an Exile in and of himself. Just as the Rabbis know how to manage the city, so the inspectors and the officials know how to manage the Societies and the other charitable institutions, which are the main source of income of Jerusalem. During the time when the Temple existed, Jerusalem was supported by the Temple, now the city is supported by the coins of Charity, for Jerusalem is not like all other cities that have trade and industry, but Jerusalem has Torah and prayer. Mr. Posek adds, When such-and-such an institution was founded and when such-and-such a Yeshiva was founded, how much income and expenses they have, who are those at the head of the institutions and who are the heads of the Yeshivas, what did they do Outside the Land and when did they ascend to Jerusalem, and he advises everyone who comes to Jerusalem to visit the institutions of Charity and the institutions of the Torah. And don't be afraid of the zealots, but on the contrary, learn from them to be zealous as they are, for the essential thing is the lack of it, that zealotry has ceased in Israel and every person yields his opinions out of false tolerance.

2 |

Once Isaac came to the People's Center and found some of his first comrades with whom he had looked for work among the farmers and in the doorways of the offices. They thought Isaac had left the Land of Israel, and Isaac thought the same about them, and suddenly they find themselves together in Jerusalem. This soil they had wanted to work and preserve holds onto them and doesn't let them leave it.

Isaac sits with his first comrades and talks with them about the farmers of Petach Tikva and the vine growers of Rishon Le-Tsion, about Victor and about Teplitsky and about the tobacco they planted in Nes Tsiona, about the clerk in the information office in Jaffa and about all the other clerks and offices that have already passed and gone out of the world or which were about to be abolished, for everything that does not have the spirit of life doesn't live. And as they talked, they mentioned Rabinovitch and Sonya, the sea and Jaffa, its vineyards and palm trees. They talked about everything under the sun. Because of the length of their talk and for love of brevity, we shall omit their conversation. Isaac is fond of his comrades and invites them to drink a cup of tea, and makes them love the tea we drink in Jerusalem, for it is made of rainwater, and he orders them the fine cakes of the Georgian baker. They sit together and talk about Rabinovitch, whom they haven't heard anything from, and about the many Rabinovitches who followed his example and left the Land of Israel, and from one Rabinovitch to another Rabinovitch, they talk again about Sonya, who prepares herself every day for another profession.

So they sit, our comrades, and talk about themselves and about others, about the parched sun in Jerusalem and about the big sea in Jaffa, about the sweat and about the sand, about the Distribution and about work and about Judea and about the Galilee, about Jerusalem and about Jaffa.

That day, Isaac left his work and took a holiday to show his comrades Jerusalem. He showed them anything and everything. The shining lighthouse built especially to see the sun rise from its top and the houses and the courtyards that don't see the light of the sun. The Tiferet Israel Synagogue whose roof was built by the donation of the Austrian Emperor, and the four synagogues of the Sephardim and the cave where Elijah the Prophet was discovered. The Beth El Synagogue and the ruin of Rabbi Judah the Hasid. The Yeshivas and the Karaite Synagogue, and needless to say, the Western Wall, the remnant of our ancient splendor. And before Isaac led our comrades inside the Old City walls, they visited the streets of the Bukharans and the houses of the Yemenites, the Bezalel art school and Ben-Yehuda. Mrs. Hamda Ben-Yehuda treated them nicely and showed them the table she brought to Ben-Yehuda in prison, and she also showed them the big cabinet where the entire Hebrew language was gathered in, from, In the beginning God created, to the words she herself created. A lot of things there are in Jerusalem, the eye is not filled with seeing.

The two days Isaac spent with his comrades seemed to him like one long holiday. As he led his comrades through the streets of Jerusalem, Isaac felt how fine that city was. What is Jaffa, and even the sea of Jaffa. Jerusalem is unique, for all the space in the world, he wouldn't have changed his dwelling here for any other city. Suddenly, his heart clenched, like a person who has to go on an urgent journey. Why do I have to go, and where do I have to go, Isaac asked himself. And before he replied to his own questions, he knew he had to go down to Jaffa and see Sonya, for as long as he hadn't finished his business with her, he wasn't free. Why do I have to be free, Isaac asked himself. And before he replied to his question, he shifted his mind from the trip and started thinking about Shifra, as if he had already finished all his business with Sonya and was permitted to think about Shifra. And since he was permitted to think about Shifra, he thought about her, as if Sonya didn't exist. Since he recalled her, he said to himself, Tomorrow or the day after, I'll go to Jaffa and finish my business with her.

CHAPTER TWENTY-TWO

From Place to Place

1 |

As usual on most summer Sabbaths, Isaac kept to his room because of the dust and because the restaurants of Jerusalem are locked to customers. He ate what he ate and drank what he drank, things that bore a person's kidneys, stretched out on his bed and took himself off to another place. He began imagining the room where he was born and the room where his mother died and the room where he lived before he ascended to the Land. And for every single room, he recalled what happened there, until he came to think about the nature of time.

Time is divided into several times, past, present, and future. Past and future are two definite periods separated from time as one thing is separate from another, but the past has a beginning and an end, while the future has no end. He who is confident looks forward to what is to come, he who is not confident worries about his future. The optimist forgets the past, the pessimist doesn't forget the past. But the present, even though it is separate from time, is not really time, but is the median between past and future and supports and is supported by what was before it and what will be after it. Now I'll come back to my starting point, to my city and my place. What is my city doing at this moment? At this moment, my city is waking up from the Sabbath sleep and drinking something hot or something cold, tea or fruit juice, and eating cakes filled with fruit or with sweet cheese and raisins. After they have eaten and drunk, they put on Sabbath clothes and go in a group to the forest and sit in the shade of trees and fear neither the dust nor the sun. Afterward, they go back to their houses and from the cellar they bring up jars and pitchers of sour milk and sour cream, and they eat the Third Meal and drink cold sour milk before and after.

Isaac lies on his bed and in his heart he accompanies the people of his city. Flies and mosquitoes come. He shoos away the mosquitoes and the flies, and all kinds of thoughts come. Isaac ruminates about things he has already pondered and doesn't want to think about. And here, here in the Land of Israel, a person sees neither sour milk nor sour cream, neither butter nor cheese (for the children of Israel were not yet producing dairy products in the Land of Israel). Once, Isaac was in Rishon Le-Tsion. He caught cold and feared for his throat. He asked for a glass of warm milk. He saw the landlady giving the infant tea mixed with egg yolk instead of milk because there was no milk there. And the Arabs' butter is full of hair and filth, and their cheese is hard as a rock, and its smell — washed goat hide smells better. And even if they scald it with boiling water to get out the filth, its smell doesn't go away.

Isaac shuts his eyes but doesn't really shut them, like a person who shuts the window and leaves a little crack open, and once again he looks over his city and the forest of his city and the trees in the forest. Hordes of mosquitoes come and assault his eyes. When he shoos away the mosquitoes, hordes of thoughts come and with them Jaffa with Sonya. Says Isaac to himself, It looks like I've got to go down to Jaffa. That thought started rattling in him, and he knew there was no way of getting out of the trip, that he had to finish his business with Sonya, for as long as he didn't finish with her he seemed tied up. And when Isaac saw that there was no way of getting out of the trip, he put his head on the pillow and shut his eyes. But sleep didn't come. He put on his clothes and went out.

2 |

A white hot sun turns white over the city and inflames the dust. No bird chirps, no bird flies, all the streets are silent and mute, you don't even hear the hum of the telegraph poles. And packs of filthy dogs are lying prostrate, and flies and mosquitoes are dancing between their eyes. If Isaac veers toward the houses, bad smells come out of them, if he veers toward the street, carcasses of cats and mice stink.

He walks in the middle, and the sticks in the roads smite his feet. Isaac walks without knowing where he will go. So, he goes to the People's Center. In the People's Center they are busy arranging benches and tables, for on Saturday night, Falk Shpaltleder will lecture on Peretz's folk tales. And because the organizers don't need him, Isaac withdraws. He plods along to Jaffa Road. The shops are locked because of the Sabbath and the houses are closed because of the heat, and the whole street is like a wasteland with no inhabitants. He turned and went to Jaffa Gate. As he went so he came back. And as he came back, once again he didn't know where he wanted to go. In fact, Isaac did know where he wanted to go. But an iron wall stops him. It's strange, he's from Galicia and Shifra is from Hungary and the Lord summoned them to Jerusalem, and he can't get to her. Since the day he knew Reb Fayesh's house, Isaac hadn't seen as clearly as at that hour how far he was from there. And after all, sometimes Rebbeca was nice to him, but even when she was nice to him she was thinking, How many saintly men and women live in my neighborhood and the Holy-One-Blessed-Be-He didn't find anyone to be gracious to a sick man except Isaac. And Shifra, what does she think? Shifra's heart is blocked like a virgin and she doesn't think of Isaac. If her father told her, Go and marry him, she wouldn't have refused. Now that he is bereft of his words and doesn't say anything, who is she to think about Isaac.

In his mind's eye Isaac reviewed everything that happened to him. He wanted to ascend to the Land of Israel and he ascended. He thought he was alone and Sonya was given to him. And here he skipped over everything that happened to him until his mind came to Shifra. He thought and walked and as he walked he came to Meah Shearim.

3 |

Meah Shearim is vanquished by the sun and steam rises from every house and every courtyard, and in every room and on every bed a person is dozing. Balconies overhang the windows, and women's kerchiefs and men's cloaks are spread out on them because of the heat, and the sleepers of the Sabbath are resting from the annoying heat and from the Sabbath food. And the entire town seems to be sleeping the sleep of the Sabbath, and the Sabbath itself is also sleeping. And if not for the sound of the study houses twittering and reciting the Tractate Shabbat and the Tractate Aboth, you would think the Eternal Sabbath had arrived. Isaac enters a study house to hide from the sun. There he found Ephraim the plasterer sitting with a group of children and reciting Psalms with them.

Ephraim had no children, but he did have many troubles, and every single trouble that came to him, he shook his head and got rid of it. Every midnight he gets out of bed and walks around Meah Shearim and calls and wakes people to serve the Creator, and every day he does his work, and half of every cent he earns he gives to holy things. With that money he rented himself a prayer room and hired a preacher to study the portion of the week in public. And since a person has to do repair by himself, aside from the things he does with his money, on the Sabbath afternoon Ephraim gathers little boys from the street and recites Psalms with them. And since the little ones are little and don't know how sweet are the songs and paeans David King of Israel recited to the Holy-One-Blessed-Be-He, Ephraim attracts them with sweets, and after every book they finish he gives them candy.

Ephraim stands before the children and recites Psalms with them. He reads a verse and they read a verse. Ephraim reads, I was glad when they said unto me, Let us go into the house of the Lord. And they read, Our feet shall stand within thy gates, O Jerusalem. And he snatches the words and savors them in his mouth as if he suddenly felt that he too was worthy to stand in Jerusalem, and he repeats the verse a few times. Isaac looks at him and Ephraim notices him. He hunches his shoulders and looks at him affectionately, and repeats in a beautiful melody, Our feet shall stand within thy gates, O Jerusalem. Jerusalem is builded as a city that is compact together. Isaac felt that he was keeping the children from reciting Psalms, for they were looking at him and not looking at the book. He withdrew.

Isaac hesitated in the courtyard. He looked at the announcements and proclamations and warnings and at the posters to stir souls and at posters of excommunication and at the memorial stones, and read the names of the donors who donated money for the building, or to restore the house. Some of those tablets he had re-painted. And so he ambled from one wall to another and from one door to another, with neither wish nor will. At last, he went into a study house as they were reciting the afternoon prayer. Bent before the Ark an old man was intoning the prayer, You are One and Your Name is One. The sun was declining and the study house was filled with darkness. The congregation finished the afternoon prayer and sat down and sang, O Lord my strength, until it was time for the evening prayer. After the prayer, Isaac left the study house and went wherever it was he went, and as he went he came to the valley of Beit Israel west of the Hungarian quarter.

4 |

The sky above is bereft of light and the earth below is so quiet that Isaac heard the sound of his own footsteps swallowed up in the si-lence and falling of the rocks. From the distant houses steeped in gloom sparks of light are twinkling. They have already celebrated the end of the Sabbath with wine, and the women are lighting fires to heat water. Isaac looked toward the lighted windows, but in his heart he contemplated things that have nothing to do with those houses or those windows, about his trip to Jaffa and about Sonya, who he had to finish his affairs with, and about his father, who chastised him that the time had come to take a wife, and about Yudele, who wants to ascend to the Land of Israel, and about thoughts that come to you on their own.

And so Isaac walks around in a gloomy land under a sky bereft of light. And between heaven and earth, moving like living clouds, is a herd of goats that came to the Jews' neighborhoods to be milked. The goats follow the goatherd and watch for the women who will come and relieve them of their milk. The goatherd kneels and milks into the women's jars and the fragrance of warm milk wafts among the rocks like the fragrance of field and village.

A girl came holding a jar. Isaac called in a whisper, Shifra. Shifra raised her head and was amazed. Who said, Shifra, and who called her by name on this night when you can't see your comrade in front of you. Her ears must have deceived her, even though she clearly heard someone calling her. Isaac called again, Shifra. Shifra lifted her eyes and looked in front of her.

Said Isaac, A good week, Shifra. Shifra replied in a whisper, A good and blessed week. And out of the sleepy darkness Shifra's sweet essence sparkled. Never had she been so close to his heart and never did his heart hum like that. His body trembled and he almost fell down. He held out his hand and said, From heaven were you summoned here. Shifra raised her eyes upward. The sky was black and coils of gloom rolled from the firmament to the earth, and not a trace of anything was heard there. Her soul grew frightened and her spirit was faint. She lowered her eyes to the jar in her hand and said, I came out to buy an ounce of milk for Father, and she lifted the jar to Isaac and said, I'm in a hurry to bring the milk to Father. Isaac put his hand on his heart and said, If only I could talk with you. Shifra stood in amazement, Here he is talking with me and finally he says, If only I could talk with you. Amazed as she was, she wanted to hear more.

His strength gave out and his heart struggled to come out. He feared that if he were silent, Shifra would go away and leave him. He pulled himself together and said, Is that the only reason you're in a hurry? Shifra had already forgotten what she had said at first and waited for him to say something to her, maybe his words would relieve her a bit. Said Isaac, I know what's in your heart, Shifra. His words frightened her, for she saw that Isaac knew the secret she hid even from herself. She lowered her head and dropped her eyes and her ears flamed as if they were on fire, and they heard not a trace of a word. She wanted to comprehend but didn't.

Isaac stood still and was sorry, for all the days he hadn't seen Shifra he had talked with her in his heart, and now that she appeared before him he was silent. Such a moment of opportunity won't fall into his hands again. If Isaac stands still and is silent, she'll go away and she won't come back, and he's got a lot of things to tell her. And if not now — when?

The Holy-One-Blessed-Be-He took pity on Isaac and did not send Shifra away from him. But if the Holy-One-Blessed-Be-He took

pity on Isaac, He did not take pity on Shifra. He took away the strength
of her legs and slackened her arms so that even the little ounce of
milk she bought for her sick father started quaking and pouring out
of the jar. Shifra lifted her eyes and looked grudgingly at Isaac who
was blocking her way like that darkness that closed in on her.

The Lord saw her troubled soul and put words in Isaac's
mouth. He talked about anything and everything. Things he didn't
want to say and things he did want to say. He told about his father
and his mother, about his brothers and his sisters. Then he started
telling about himself, about the days he had spent in his hometown
and the days in the Land of Israel.

Shifra was agitated. Even if Isaac had talked with her about
things in general, she would have been agitated, but how much more
agitated she was that he told her such personal things. As if everything she knew up to that time was nothing compared to those things
she heard from Isaac. Isaac suddenly groaned and said, Tomorrow I'll
go to Jaffa.

Shifra heard and was amazed. Why did he have to go to Jaffa,
and if he did go — so what? Shifra hesitated and didn't find any reply.
Shifra asked Isaac, Is it hard for you to leave Jerusalem? As soon as
she asked, she regretted, lest he think she was sorry he was going. Between him and her, he took the jar from her hand and took her hand
in his. Shifra pulled her hand out in panic, for never in her life had
she given her hand to a boy, and she took the jar and went on her
way. Isaac watched her as she went down to the valley and climbed
up on the rocks and disappeared in the dell and appeared on the hill
and once again disappeared until she disappeared and he didn't see
her again.

Isaac was sorry she had gone before he could tell her all that
was in his heart. And even though he had spoken a lot with her, the
most important things he hadn't said. Isaac stood like a person who
has entered a dark house and wants to light a candle but his matches
have fallen out of his hand. He started groping forward, once he
veered to the right and once to the left. And even though it was dark,
he saw her, as if she were walking in front of him and he were still
holding her hand, and all the things she said stirred his heart seven-

fold than when she talked with him. And even though she went on her way and was far from him, he knew she was close to him. He picked up his feet and took two or three steps. It seemed to him that she hadn't gone so far and he started running after her. And he didn't know that she had already gone far away, and that creature he saw walking wasn't a human being, but a stray dog. Isaac didn't see that it was a dog, but the dog saw Isaac. And when he saw him he barked at him. And when he barked at him, his mind became confused and his thoughts flew away.

5 |

At that time, Shifra went home. She recalled what she had done and was shocked. She looked all around. Not because she was afraid her neighbors had seen her talking with a man, but because her whole world had changed. She stood still and lifted up her eyes to ask mercy for herself and forgiveness for that transgression and she wanted to swear that she wouldn't repeat her acts. And she saw that the firmament was silent, and calm was spread over the earth. Calm came into her heart and she knew they weren't angry with her. But she still wasn't reconciled with herself, for he had talked to her and she had answered him. She resolved to ignore this thing and uproot it from her heart and not to run into him ever again. And she immediately began running with all her might lest he come back. And even though she knew that if he talked she wouldn't listen to him, even so she was scared lest a few of his words would reach her ears, for even now that he was far away from her, his words pounded in her ears. She felt her ears, which were blazing like embers, and said, Thus far and no farther. And if he comes to our house, I'll go out of the house and leave him. Let him talk with Mother, let him take care of Father, let him do what he wants, with me he won't talk.

As she said that, another thought came into her heart that was better than the first. I won't leave the house, but on the contrary, I'll sit down and do my work as if he weren't there. And if he says something to me, I'll answer him, but from my answer he will learn that he isn't important to me. Meanwhile I'll take my revenge on him for that shame he has caused me. And in her mind's eye, she already saw him coming in and saying Good evening. When she seemed to hear his voice, her heart was stunned in her and she knew she wasn't strong enough to resist him, for even now when she didn't see him face to face, her decisions were canceled and everything she had decided to do she didn't do, she didn't leave the house and she didn't say things that would show him he wasn't wanted. But praise be the name of the Lord that all the ways of the hated one were only in a vision. And praise be the name of the Lord that she had already reached her house and didn't have to be afraid, for her mother defended her.

6 |

When Rebecca saw her daughter, she was shocked. She called out in panic, What's wrong with you, my daughter? My daughter, what's wrong with you? Did something happen to you? Shifra shouted, I don't know what you want from me. As she said that, she laid her head on her mother's breast, looked into her eyes, and thought, Does Mother know what happened to me? Rebecca stroked her cheeks and her hands, and didn't know what else to do. And she didn't stop gazing at her beauty, the beauty that planted jealousy in the hearts of her neighbors and made them slander her and say that that painter had set his sights on her. Rebecca said to herself, God Forbid there is sin in her because she is beautiful and gracious. And don't we pray every morning, Grant us grace and kindness in Your eyes and in the eyes of all who see us. She recalled the tale of one Tanna who had a very handsome daughter, he saw that people were looking at her and stumbling into thoughts of sin, he asked for mercy on her to make her ugly and she was made ugly. Rebecca raised her eyes to heaven and said, Lord God, merciful and gracious, have mercy on us. Shifra lifted her eyes to her mother and asked, Mother, did you say something? Said Rebecca, what shall I say, may it be His will that He who sees the offense of the offended see our offense and save us. The voice of a dog was suddenly heard. Rebecca grasped her daughter's hand in a panic. Said Shifra, If a dog is barking outside, should you be afraid? But she was scared, too.

Shifra went to bed and pondered, What was I scared of, I don't have anything to do with him. He behaved with me as they behave with a girl. All her anger for Isaac departed, and a heavy sadness clasped her heart. And she already saw herself far away and distant from all those things that are even slightly pleasant. Lord God, merciful and gracious, whispered Shifra, help me and save me. It is already past midnight but I am still not asleep. Such a thing didn't happen to her, except on nights of Selikhot. What shall I do, what shall I do, shouted Shifra from her heart, and repeated the Shema a few times until she sank into sleep.

CHAPTER TWENTY-THREE

Why Isaac Stayed in Jerusalem and Did Not Go to Jaffa

1 |

When he wanted to go down to Jaffa, it was the anniversary of his mother's death. He postponed his trip and went to say Kaddish. He came to the synagogue during the day to get to know the congregation, and he stood in a corner and recited the Kaddish in a whisper. A Cantor went to the Ark and prayed the afternoon prayer. Isaac glanced at him and reviled himself, That man recites the whole prayer by heart and my heart is too reticent to say Kaddish in public. How did I get to this point? Because I stayed away from synagogues. He who withdraws from the public eventually dreads the public. What would Mother say about that? But Mother is lying in the grave and it's not clear if she knows or if she doesn't.

The study house smelled of books and holy objects, the smell that evokes in a man's heart the days when he would pray early and late. And when he recalled those days, he began looking in the depths of his heart, Why isn't he satisfied with himself? Said Isaac to himself, Even if you are busy during the day, you are free for prayer in the evening and the morning. Happy is he who knows how to begin in the morning and how to end at night. Shifra doesn't imagine that I eat without prayer.

But he, being full of compassion, forgave their iniquity and destroyed them not, a sad and pious voice was heard, like people who know their instincts and try to please their Creator. Isaac dismissed all his thoughts and began to pray. At first in a whisper, then aloud, like a person who was flung into a distant place and his heart hesitates to speak, for he doesn't know their tongue, as he began speaking he found that his tongue is their tongue. And when he came to the Shema, he covered his eyes and drew out the "One" until he and the whole world disappeared before the Unique One of the World Who fills all of existence. And when he came to the prayer that begins, You shall love your God with all your heart, he opened his eyes. He saw himself standing in a study house, for today was the anniversary of his mother's death. And when he recalled his mother, he recalled those days when he was a child and his mother would stand at his bed and make him recite the Shema. And two loves, the love of God and the love of his mother, stirred his heart.

After reciting the Kaddish, he studied a chapter of Mishnah. After he concluded his chapter, he saw that there were ten men there. He said to them, By your grace, I want to recite the Kaddish of learned men. He straightened his legs and bent his head and recited the Rabbi's Kaddish in fear and trembling.

Meanwhile, the candlelight waned. He turned and went to the Ark and read by the light of the candle he lit for his mother's soul. The wick floated on the oil and its sweet light illuminated. Five hundred miles away, his mother's body is lying in the ground, and five hundred years from the ground to the firmament, where her soul is hovering, and between heaven and earth stands the son and studies for the repose of her soul. Nine hundred and seventy-four generations before the world was created the Torah existed, and it will exist until the end of all generations. When a man studies Torah, all the generations before him and all those that will come after him press together and come join him.

As Isaac stood and studied, an old man came to him and greeted him and asked him, Who are you and what is your trade? Free or married? From the old man's questions, his trade was clear. Isaac pondered, It is a disgrace to choose to make a match through a matchmaker. But he felt that if a person came to intervene for him, he would be happy. Isaac looked at the old man's strange hat and at his red eyes with the flesh around the lashes already devoured, and his white hair that had turned blue in a few places. How come he doesn't take snuff? An old man who doesn't take snuff is stubborn, and I won't get rid of him in a hurry. Isaac asked the old man, How are you? Said the old man, Me you're asking? Not good, my friend, not good. Asked Isaac, What does that mean, not good? Said the old man, Simple as can be, not good. Said Isaac, But the first days were good? Said the old man in amazement, Good? Can it be good if you grumble and complain? Isaac pondered to himself, An old man whose fear is spread on his face, he might grumble. That old man said to him, There is no difference between the first days and the last days except in the past I complained that the Holy-One-Blessed-Be-He, the Almighty, wasn't watching over me, and now I complain that I am not watching over Him, the Almighty. But that's not the major grief. In the past when I had my full strength, I would also complain with all my strength, and sometimes He would answer me and do good for me, not as I wanted but as He wanted, at any rate, He would answer me. And now, my friend, now when I complain, I complain without strength. And as a result, my friend. . . I see that I am keeping you from the Torah, I'll go away. Said Isaac, Never mind, never mind. Said the old man, What are you saying, never mind. If I were you, I would pick up the stick and hit that foolish old man who clings to you and keeps you from studying. I'll go away, my friend, and you go back to studying.

In the morning, he was lazy to get up and assumed he was late for prayer. The church bells began pealing. His rest was over and he jumped out of bed. Said Isaac, If Jacob doesn't awaken by himself, Esau comes and gets him up.

2 |

The anniversary of the day his father and his mother died is a day of moral stock-taking. If the son hasn't attained their age, he worries that he won't get there. And if he has more years than they had, he fears that he was given more years only to test him more. Therefore, people used to fast on that day, to be stirred to repentance and to rummage around in deeds and to regret them, and thereby the son gives the right to his father and mother to rise to Paradise. When the Hasids multiplied and dispensed with superfluous fasts, for fasting saps a person's strength and increases sadness, and after all it is a Commandment to serve the Lord with joy, as it is written, Serve the Lord with gladness, then they annulled the fast on the death of father and mother, and made a memorial to the deceased by drinking a toast and saying a blessing on the ascent of the soul, for the drink is fit for a blessing and the blessing is fit for the living and for the dead. Most people followed this example and people do not fast on the anniversary of a death. Isaac didn't fast either. But he prayed and said Kaddish and studied some chapters of the Mishnah that begin with the letters of his mother's name and with the letters of Soul.

After he finished studying, Isaac longed to do something else for his mother. He considered going to the elders of his hometown who sit inside the Old City walls, for he had longed all the time to see them and was ashamed to go there because his sidelocks were shorn and his beard was shaved. Today when he prayed in public and hadn't removed his beard from the day before the Sabbath, he wasn't afraid to appear before them.

He went down to Jaffa Gate and entered the Old City inside the walls. He went around a few houses and courtyards and came to a dirty, narrow alley, the dirtiest of all, and entered an alley that was even dirtier. He had often been here before to visit Reb Alter the ritual slaughterer, and would turn back for the same reason, that he was ashamed to appear clean-shaven.

Reb Alter the ritual slaughterer had been one of the big landowners in his hometown and was a professional circumciser and Isaac loved him, both because he was nice to him and because he had brought him into the Covenant. Reb Alter had often stroked his cheeks and told him, Be a Jew and don't be a Goy. Reb Alter's apartment in Jerusalem was not like his apartment in his hometown, for in his hometown he had lived in a handsome house with four rooms, and in Jerusalem he lived in one room in a dreary house, the remains of one of those houses the Ishmaelites burned down in time of plague or pestilence so the disease wouldn't spread to the rest of the houses, and ever since they returned to live in it, they hadn't repaired it.

That day was laundry day in Reb Alter's courtyard and all the schoolchildren in the courtyard gathered together there, barefoot and dressed in rags. Some of them washed their face in the water of the puddles between the cobblestones, and some of them cooled their face in the laundry on the line, and some of them licked the water from it. When they saw a stranger coming into the courtyard they gathered around him and asked him, Who do you want? And each one pushed the other and was eager to lead the guest.

3 |

On a rickety bed of worn-out and tattered pillows and covers sat Reb Alter leaning over a three-legged table and reading a book. On the table stood a crushed and sooty kettle and a thick glass with bread soaking in it. Poverty chirped from the whole house, like the house itself which was mean and poor. That house was no different from most of the houses inside the Old City wall, but Isaac, whose work brought him to the houses of the well-to-do, had never in his life seen such a house and such poverty. Isaac moaned, Reb Alter, don't you know me? Reb Alter raised his eyes and squinted, his lips shook and he said, Isaac? And he went on, Aren't you the son of Simon? Wait a little and I'll get up and greet you. Reb Alter straightened up a bit and took his hand and said, Itzikl, I didn't recognize you. My sight is afflicted. But praise the Living God I can recognize a voice. Sit down, my son, sit down. So you're in Jerusalem and not in the agricultural settlements. Sit down first and then we'll talk. He sat him at his right and started talking.

After Reb Alter succeeded in sending his sons out into the world, he saw that his time had come to return his body to his mother's bosom. He divided his fortune, two thirds he gave to his sons and a third he took for himself. Moreover, the new ritual slaughterer paid him to take over his position. He took his money and set out, alert, happy and goodhearted, without grief or pain, he and his modest wife, Mrs. Hinda Puah. Happy that he would eat on his own, and goodhearted that he wouldn't need anyone. But living in the Land of Israel is a Commandment and not a pleasure. When they sniffed money on him, the inspectors of the Torat Haim Yeshiva came and persuaded him to put his money in their shares. He was persuaded by them and was happy, for he would aid those who study Torah and his money would bring him profit, for shares are wont to bring profit to their owners. But divine justice hovers over Jerusalem. It wasn't long before he lost his money and had nothing left but the shirt on his back. As he spoke, Reb Alter put on his clothing and covered his knees, which were seen in the torn trousers. He sensed that Isaac was looking at him. He raised both hands and clapped them together, and said, One way or another, at any rate, we are in Jerusalem.

At that moment, Reb Alter's wife was not at home. Isaac was afraid to ask about her, lest she had passed away. Said Reb Alter, You don't ask about the old lady. She'll be so sorry she didn't see you. An hour ago, she went to blind Haim Rafael. In our hometown he knew all paths of the city like ten clever men, here he hasn't yet learned the roads. Once a week, Hinda Puah goes to his house to launder his shirt. A person who ascends to the Land of Israel receives an extra reward, for he sees the holy places and rejoices at the sight of them, but the ascent of that blind man is all for its own sake, for he cannot see and cannot rejoice at the sight.

In his hometown, Reb Alter entertained guests and guests were always found in his house, and he himself would serve them. Now that a guest from his hometown had dropped in him, he put on the kettle and put water in it to heat. The kettle was cracked and the kerosene stove didn't work properly and the wicks didn't catch fire, and when they did, the water dripped and extinguished the fire. He lit the wicks again and poured water out of the kettle so water remained up to the place where it was cracked. And he began talking with Isaac about matters of their hometown. Said Reb Alter, I did a great repair before I went. A copper ewer I made, with six handles, and every Levite holds one handle and pours water on the hands of Cohens, and the Levites praised me for that. And said Reb Alter, There may be rich men but they didn't do it, or those who follow the Commandments and yet they didn't do it, but they left the Commandment to me to distinguish myself by virtue of the Land of Israel. And I have already seen a reward of the Commandment in this world, for I stood on the last holiday before I ascended, six Levites wrapped in prayer shawls each one holding one handle of the ewer, except for bachelors and children, and they didn't jostle one another.

Isaac sat with his head down and his eyelashes trembled. Reb Alter's words conjured up the prayer house in his hometown, all the people dressed in holiday clothes and the Cantor standing before the Ark and praying a holiday prayer with a holiday melody and the Priests running to climb onto the platform and bless the people and everyone bowing their head to receive the blessings from the Priests. Reb Alter looked straight ahead into the space of his dreary room and his lips trembled between his beard and his moustache. Well, said Reb Alter, the water is boiling, let's pour us a cup of tea right away and drink. He stood up and extinguished the wicks and picked up a cup to pour tea for him. He saw that he didn't have any tea essence or any tea leaves. He sighed and said, If there's no tea here, there is sugar here. Blessed is He and blessed is His Name. He took a lump of sugar and put it in Isaac's hand and said, A person should rejoice in what he has. Isn't that so, Itzikl? Bless, my son, bless the blessing of Everything, for Him through Whose word everything came to be.

Isaac sliced himself a small piece of sugar and said, Reb Alter isn't drinking? Reb Alter smiled and said, I'm drinking, I'm drinking. We've got, thank God, a cistern full of water, something not many people can say. Here in Jerusalem, I have learned to know that everything the Holy-One-Blessed-Be-He gives is a precious gift from His hand. Outside the Land, where everything is in abundance, many times a person despises His gifts, especially water, but here we praise the Holy-One-Blessed-Be-He for every single drop that He brings down on us from heaven, as it is written, drinketh water of the rain of heaven. And on that, Isaac, I've got a tremendous argument, and I'll explain it to you with a parable. Once there was a king who had many sons. They went off into the world to conquer many lands. The king gave them abundant supplies for the journey, as is the wont of a king who has a lot. And the king had a youngest son of his old age whom he kept at home because he loved him the most and he gave him what he needed every day. As we found with Our Father Jacob, may he rest in peace, who didn't want to send his son Benjamin away because he loved him the most. Perhaps the son should envy his other brothers for the king gave them a lot all at once, and this one he gave only what he needed every day? Drink, my son, drink another glass. You don't want to?

Isaac wiped his mouth and stood up to go. Said Reb Alter, You're in a hurry? Said Isaac, Today is the anniversary of my mother's death and I am going to afternoon prayers at the Western Wall. Reb Alter was ashamed that the whole time he had talked about himself and didn't ask Isaac about his affairs. He immediately began to laud Isaac's mother and said, A great merit she earned that her son says Kaddish in Jerusalem. In truth, wherever people say Kaddish His Name Blessed-Be-He is sanctified in His worlds and He sanctifies His people Israel. But it befits the king that they play at the entrance of his palace, for the king dwells in his house and doesn't have to leave.

Said Isaac, Perhaps Reb Alter will go with me? Reb Alter stretched out a leg and Isaac saw it was swathed and bound in cotton and rags. He asked, What's that? Said Reb Alter, This is how that came about: When I was blessed to stand on the Holy Ground, I slipped and broke my leg. That old man was wandering around in the upper worlds and didn't pay attention to the few inches in front of him and slipped and fell. The punishment came from heaven, my son, for I was wandering around above my own stature, and a person in the Land of Israel has to know what is in front of him, for this ground is holy. And even though I live right near the Western Wall, I have not been blessed to pray there. Isaac groaned over that old man, how many efforts he made, how many troubles he had taken until he got to Jerusalem, and when he got to Jerusalem, he wasn't blessed to pray even once at the Western Wall. Said Reb Alter, Am I more distinguished than all other Children of Israel? It's enough for a person to dwell in Jerusalem. Now, my son, go and pray for the soul of your mother, may she rest in peace, and may she intercede for you. When Isaac left, Reb Alter called him back and said, Come and I'll show you something amazing. Reb Alter took out a little notebook where he had written all the names of the boys he had brought into the Covenant of Our Father Abraham and he showed him Isaac's name among them.

CHAPTER TWENTY-FOUR

Broken Vessels

1 |

On every single one of the stone steps on the way to the Western Wall
are flocks of paupers, cripples, and blind men, some have no arms,
some have lame legs, some have swollen necks, and some are swollen
with hunger and some are shriveled with despair, and there are other
invalids and diseased people, fragments of people whose Creator left
them in the middle of His work and didn't finish their creation, and
when He left them, He left His hand on them and increased their
torments. Or their Creator did finish them and strict justice struck
them. And every step down had a sorrow greater than the last one.
When you have descended all those stairs, you see a bundle of rags.
You think they're rags, but they are a woman and her daughter, and
it's not clear if the daughter is younger than her mother, but it is clear
that they have the same calamity of hunger. Their eyes look straight
ahead, but it's not the eyes that seem to be looking, but the pus in the
eyes. Those remnants of bodies lie before our precious Temple that
was destroyed, a place where the Holy-One-Blessed-Be-He heard
every prayer and every supplication of any child of Israel and filled
his request, and now that it is destroyed, they pray and supplicate and
request and the prayer isn't heard. And if it is heard, it achieves only
half, a person's soul is saved but his body isn't.

Old men and women come and go, and as they walk, they
bend over at every single stair and give their brothers and sisters a fig
or a date or a piece of sugar or a penny. It's forbidden to find fault
with the principles of the Holy One, that He gives this one a lot and
that one He doesn't give anything. Here it must be said that He did
not give the former much more than the latter. But some have con-

trol over their limbs and take from their own mouths and give to others. Isaac bent over every single pauper and gave him something. And as he gave them, he soothed them with his eyes, as if to say, Don't grumble at me that I am not sitting with you and don't suffer as you do. As long as there was a penny in his hand, he gave. When his pennies ran out and the paupers didn't, he spread out his hands and showed that they were empty. They started pulling him by his clothes and accompanying him with wailing until he fled and pressed into the crowded square of the Western Wall. And here other paupers joined him, who were worse off than the first ones.

2 |

The square is full of men and women, old men and old women. Some sit on benches and stools with books in their hands, others stand and recite Psalms, some in a thin murmur, others with shouts and weeping. Old men stand on this side and embrace the stones of the Western Wall, and old women stand on that side and cover the stones with tears. Between the stones grasses grow along with the letters of names and requests written there by those who are weary with grief and in need of salvation. And the strip of the firmament stands in its purity, like an eye from above watching from the abode of His holiness from heaven over Israel and over the Land He gave us. Our brothers, the sons of Ishmael our uncle, who seized the houses next to the Western Wall, come and go, this one with a dung basin on his head and a loaf of bread on it, and that one riding on a donkey carrying manure, and as they walk they press the worshippers so their prayers won't rise and bring redemption. And men and women tourists, descendants of Jacob's brother, stand and point their sticks at the stones of the Destruction and at the Jews weeping over their own destruction. When Isaac came, the Sephardi usher grabbed him and called out *Feter, tsindn a likhtl*, that is, Uncle, light a candle, and into his hand he thrust an oil wick for him to light and to give him a penny. Isaac had often been to the Western Wall before, but had never gotten close to it because of his humility. Now that he said Kaddish, he approached the holy stones as if by himself. His heart started pounding and his legs tottered. And along with the tottering of his legs and the pounding of his heart, his voice went with the voice of all those standing at the Western Wall who answered after him, Amen, May His great Name be blessed forever and ever.

Darkness fell. But daylight still gleamed between the stones of the Western Wall. The men and women tourists went off and the Arab neighbors of the Western Wall gathered in their houses, and a silence of mercy settled over the holy stones and over the square of the Western Wall. The worshippers tightened their belts and stood up to recite the evening prayer. Between the stones of the Western Wall, a sad voice was heard, Behold, bless ye the Lord, all ye servants of the Lord, which by night stand in the house of the Lord. The stones were swallowed up in the gloom, and all the worshippers became one mass before the Lord. Suddenly the moon came out to light the earth. The worshippers finished their prayer and returned to their homes, this one assisting that one and that one assisting this one to climb the stairs.

Good and sweet are the nights of Jerusalem. As if the Almighty is sorry at night for the evil He did to the city in the day. A wind blows and dust doesn't fly. The moon dispatches her light, and a fine fragrance rises from among the grasses of the rocks. Everyone who can study sits in his house or in the study house and studies, and those who can't study recite Psalms. You study a page of Talmud and you become their partner, you read the Book of Psalms and the Holy-One-Blessed-Be-He adds your tears to their tears. Everything that was far away from you is close to your heart now, even our God in Heaven is close.

B OK THREE *From One Issue to Another*

CHAPTER ONE

Isaac Is About to Go to Jaffa

1 |

Isaac found a tenant for his room, who paid him back a bit of what he had paid the landlord, and the landlord gave in to entreaties and agreed to rent it on those conditions he set for every other tenant, that he wouldn't do any work in his room that profanes the Sabbath publicly, not cook on a Primus stove on the Sabbath because it makes noise, and not stand at the window with a cigarette in his mouth on the Sabbath. If his lease was up and the landlord needed his room, he would leave and not make any claims on it. And if he brought a second tenant into the room, the same conditions applied to him, and one-third would be added to the rent. That is, if he brought one, but if he brought two or three, he would add as they agreed. And they would launder shirts and drink from the cistern like the rest of the residents of the house. And if water was scarce, they would launder their clothes somewhere else. All those conditions were written down, not because the landlord is a hard man or because clarity is good for everyone, so as not to raise any complaints about him, but because he is fond of the Holy Tongue. To show you that he mastered all its rules. When the tenant agreed and rented the room, Isaac had no more excuse to postpone his trip.

He went to Mahane Yehuda to hire a wagon to go to Jaffa tomorrow. Even though the train is more comfortable and takes less time and costs a quarter less than a Maguida, just like hiring a wagon for the trip. When the train saw that wagon owners were competing with it, it added a third car for simple people who don't want luxuries, but the train goes by day and wagons go by night, and thus is available all day long.

2 |

After he arranged the trip, he returned to his room and examined his things so as not to leave behind in Jerusalem what he needed in Jaffa, and not to take with him to Jaffa what he wanted to leave behind in Jerusalem. He examined every place he put food and ate his fill and went to bed to restore his strength for the trip.

His thoughts came and drove out his sleep. He thought about Shifra, whom he was leaving because of Sonya, and about Sonya, who had left him. And even though she had left him, he felt he had to talk with her, for as long as their relationship wasn't resolved, he couldn't regard himself as a free man. When he had eagerly pursued Sonya, he didn't ask if he was a free man, but when he moved away from her, he regarded himself as bound.

An hour passed and sleep still didn't come. He started saying soft words to himself to make himself rest, At any rate, I must not complain. All the days I have been in the Land of Israel, I have been healthy and haven't spent even one day in the hospital, unlike most of my comrades who suffer from illnesses, and all of them are sick with malaria or other diseases found in the Land, since not everybody eats regularly and they don't live like human beings and they sap their strength in assemblies and meetings and debates. And when diseases strike a person they don't leave him alone. And I make a living and my clothes are not ragged. I don't go to bed without my supper and I get up early and have something to eat, either vegetables or an egg, either a cup of tea or cocoa. Isaac dismissed his thoughts and closed his eyes to sleep. His events came into his mind. First came the small events that come before every trip, then came the other events. First came the last events, then came the first events. First they all came together, then each detail appeared individually. Suddenly he found himself with his brother Yudel in the same bed. This one pulls the blanket this way and that one pulls the blanket that way. Yudel was filled with anger and threw the pillow under their heads and Isaac fell into the sea. He picked up a hoe to hoe and the sea was filled with myriads of colors. Victor's mare saw and started cheering. Embroidered dogs dropped out of her mouth with Hirsh Wolf Atamanot written on them.

Isaac woke with a start and started thinking about his trip again. He stretched his hands up and said, You O God, help me. What do You care if my affairs end well. And in the middle of his prayer, he stopped until God would weigh his actions. He turned over and started calculating how much money he had and how many days he could be idle. His brother Yudele comes and his face is gloomy and his right sleeve is threadbare, like scribes who wear out their sleeve as they write, and he started complaining about his sisters who don't leave him even a tiny place to sit and copy his poems. Isaac was filled with pity for his brother and thought to himself, If I didn't have to go to Jaffa, I would buy him a silver pen made at Bezalel. And Isaac already saw the silver pen in the hands of his younger brother, as he sits and writes rhymes about the legend of Reb Yudel Hasid, their ancestor. Isaac wept tears of joy. But, said Isaac, how will I spend ten Francs on a pen when I have to go to Jaffa? How simple it would be if not for that action. But acting comes before thinking, and after an action is done thinking comes and says, How simple it would be if it weren't done. Where were you before we got into a bad deal?

Hope, that is wont to show a smiling face, didn't turn its face away from Isaac. It began to amuse him and show him what would be when all his business in Jaffa was finished and he returned to Jerusalem. Isaac let the power of imagination imagine what it imagined. And to add reinforcements, he evoked Shifra's grandfather and Shifra's grandmother as they welcomed him. Moreover, all the time we were on the sea, they showed me an angry face and in Jerusalem they smiled at me. And it would have been right if they had kept me at a distance, for an iron wall separates the old from the young here, and they have nothing in common, and old people who have left the vain pleasures of this world to be buried in the Land of Israel, for them our settlement in the Land is difficult to accept, for our whole settlement in the Land is earthly. Yet they were affectionate to me and were close to me as if I were their relative. They didn't foresee it, but their luck did. And even if that old man became close to me only to fill the Commandment, thou shalt in any wise rebuke thy neighbor, and not suffer sin upon him, he nevertheless blessed me that I would find my mate.

The Master of Dreams wasn't watching over the wagon Isaac hired or over the bed he lay on or the good thoughts that made his sleep pleasant. And when he dozed off, he came and took him to the railroad station, with all his belongings, even those he had left behind in Jerusalem, and he made him run from car to car. Isaac held onto his belongings and was crowded into a crowded car. Shifra came and took his hands. He threw away his belongings and took her hands. And she interlaced her fingers in his and started weeping. So he began to soothe her and stroke her head, as everyone looked at them and whispered about them. They stood and rode until they came to wherever it was they came to.

3 |

And some of what had been shown him in the dream, he saw when he was awake. There was a pharmacist in Meah Shearim and Isaac painted a sign for him. He went to collect his fee and he had it in hand. At that moment, Shifra came to get medicine for her father and that medicine wasn't in the pharmacy. The pharmacist went to bring it from somewhere else, as pharmacists are wont to take from one another and repay one another. Isaac was left alone with Shifra in the pharmacy. Isaac saw that no person was listening to them. So he said to Shifra, I'm going to Jaffa. He saw that she was sad. He said to himself, I'll count to sixty and if nobody enters in the meantime, it's a sign that her spirit is sad because I'm going. He counted to sixty and again to sixty, and no one came. He took her hand in his and said, I'll write to you. Shifra was shocked and said, May he not write me. He asked, Why? She whispered, So the neighbors won't be able to slander us. Said Isaac, If so, what shall we do? She looked at him as if asking for advice. Isaac drew up his courage and squeezed her hand and didn't let go of it until the pharmacist's footsteps were heard.

CHAPTER TWO

Tribulations of Travel

1 |

Close to sundown, the full wagon left, harnessed to three horses, loaded with nine people. The carter sat on his box and brandished the whip. The horses picked up their feet and started trotting easily and not fast. Easily, to make it easy for their owner to show the passengers they can rely on his horses, and not fast, for the road was long and the wagon was heavy.

The wagon left the city, leaving behind Jerusalem and its neighborhoods. The wheels rolled and they came to the Valley of Niftoah. And from the valley on the right, Kfar Lifta appeared, surrounded by trees and gardens. From there, the wagon rolled on and came to Motza. The horses stood still by themselves, for it is a simple custom that when they get to Motza, the horses stand still to rest a bit before they climb up the mountain. The passengers who weren't yet weary from the trip and were neither hungry nor thirsty, complained about the carter, who stopped his horses. But the carter looked benevolently at his horses who know the time for every purpose.

After they rested a bit, the carter signaled to them that the time had come for them to go. They bent their knees and bowed their heads and started going. The roads are winding, twisting and rising, they spin the cart and circle around themselves. And suddenly they seemed to descend into themselves and swallow themselves up. The cart rises up, and seems barely suspended and moving on thin air. The horses clop their feet on stones and knots and dirt, and dirt and knots and stones spray from under their feet, and they are suspended on thin air. The passengers began to fear they would fall and their bones would be strewn around. One remembered his wife and his little sons, and another remembered things he hadn't thought about all his life and now, in time of danger, he remembered them. And they asked for mercy for themselves not to leave the world until they repaired in spirit what they had broken.

The moon came out and illuminated the land. Vineyards were seen on the right and from the mountaintops, a kind of village was seen, Kiryat Yearim that is in Judea. Here the sons of Dan halted when they went to capture Laish, and here God's Ark of the Covenant dwelt for twenty years until David took it up to Jerusalem, and because of our many sins, Kiryat Yearim was destroyed and its name was changed to Abu Gosh after the deceitful highwayman who robbed all those who went up to Jerusalem. And a Christian church sits on its mound, confident and secure.

The roads were noisy. Caravans of camels loaded with merchandise file past, and the camel drivers sweeten their way with song, and the camels' bells respond to their song. The carter also started singing. The cartwheels roll with the sound of the camels' feet, who are walking as if on carpets. The moon floats between the mountains, and between the flanks of the mountains the big sea appeared along with part of the coastal plain. The carter stopped and looked at his horses and at the road they were traveling.

One of the passengers said to the carter, Perhaps, Reb Zundl, you can sing something by Bezalel Hazan, like, Then all shall come to serve You. The carter laughed and said, I knew you would call me Zundl, but Zundl isn't my name, my name is Avreml. The man said to him, Didn't I hear them calling you Zundl? Said he, They call me Zundl because my younger brother was named Abraham after me. Said the other, How can you call two brothers by one name when both of them are alive? Said he, When my brother was born, they thought I was dead, and my mother, may she rest in peace, who couldn't find consolation for me wanted them to call her newborn son after the son she thought was dead. And so they called my brother Abraham, with the nickname Avreml, as they called me. And when I returned here and my name was taken by my brother, they asked Rabbi Dovidl Biderman. Said Rabbi Dovidl, Call him Zundl. And so they call me Zundl.

One man responded, What do you mean, they thought you were dead? Said the carter, Everything you want to know. If I tell you everything on this trip, what will be left for you to hear on the way back to Jerusalem? Aren't you going back to Jerusalem with me? Said the man, I swear to you that I am going back to Jerusalem with you, and now tell me Reb Zundl, what was the story? Said the carter, When my brother isn't with us, you can call me Avreml. I like the name they gave me the day I entered the Covenant and I like when people call me Avreml. The man said to him, And that story, what is it? Said the carter, There wasn't any story, just simply, when I was a boy I ran away Outside the Land. I wandered around the world a little until the war came between the English and the Boers. I went and hired myself to the English army. After the war was over, I had enough of the world and I came back to Jerusalem. All those years when I was outside the Land, I didn't write anything to Father, because they didn't teach me how to write, even though I've got a good brain, and I still remember the sermon I delivered the day I was Bar Mitzvah. When a few years passed and they didn't hear a thing from me, they despaired of me and thought I had already passed away. Meanwhile, Mother gave birth to a little brother and bequeathed him my name. And now you want me to sing you Bezalel Hazan's Then all shall come to serve You. That, my friend, is impossible, for once I was traveling on the road and I started singing Then all shall come to serve You, and the horses started quaking and shaking and jumping and leaping until their yoke came undone to serve the Holy One Himself. You think I'm telling you made-up things. The God's honest truth I'm telling you, just as my name is Avreml and not Zundl.

Another man answered, Then sing us whatever tune you want. Said Avreml, Wait until I want to. Said that man, Don't you want to? Said he, How do I know if I want to or not? If I sing I know that I want to, if I don't sing I know that I don't want to. That man sighed and said, If I had a fine voice like yours, I wouldn't stop singing all day and all night. As he was sorry he didn't have a fine voice like Avreml's, Avreml started singing the Kedushah, A crown will they give You. Said that man, Such a Crown I never heard in my life.

Avreml straightened his neck and said, You think I heard such a Crown? I never heard it either until now. Said that man, Did you compose it? Said he, By itself it was composed. Another man responded, How good you are, Reb Avreml. Said Avreml, Why will I be bad when I can be good? But in truth, I'm not good. But you're a good man, and therefore you think that I'm a good man. Whoa. Where are you going, you bastards? Once again the horses turned off the road. You want to go straight and your animal doesn't let you. And can a person be good if he's mixed up with animals?

The horses went the way their master led them. Sometimes the sound of the horses' feet was heard and sometimes the sound of the cartwheels was heard. Isaac sat and listened. And the assembly of the sounds with the wind rattling among them made him sleepy. But he didn't doze off. He was amazed that he had feared the trip when there was no need to fear. He stuck his head out and looked at the roads retreating and coming toward him. A mountain chain suddenly closed on them. When he got there he found nothing but shadows. But far from them rose a real mountain. And stars quivering on it. Some of them shrouded and some of them like drops of water. And a sound like a sound of bells emerges from the mountain. What will Avreml do when he gets there, and how will he get his wagon through? When they got there, there was nothing but a flock of shadows. And an abundance of camels came and the bells around their necks emitted their sound.

Isaac sits and doesn't know if the thoughts he is thinking now had visited him before, or as they appeared to him it now seemed he had already thought them. He passed his hand over his eyes and was amazed. What is this? Before, other horses were harnessed to this same wagon. And the carter was also different, not Avreml and not Zundl, but Neta, the companion of Reb Yudel Hasid who traveled around with him to collect money for dowries. Isaac passed his hand over his eyes like a person who removes the sleep from his eyes. And he heard his heart talk to him, Since we are talking about your ancestor, let's say something about him. Your ancestor Reb Yudel was a great Hasid and never in his life did he do a thing that wasn't for the sake of Heaven. Now, let's go back to our current affairs. So, we're going to Jaffa, what will we say to Sonya when we come to her house? Whoa, where are you taking us, you bastards? You might think these words were said about the horses, but no, they were said about ourselves. You think they were said as parables. No, they were said literally.

Avreml said to Isaac, And you, young fellow, songs you don't sing, words you don't say, and so what do you do? Isaac woke with a start and asked in a panic, I? Avreml started singing, I, I was greatly afflicted: I said in my haste, All men are liars. So what do you do? Said Isaac, I don't do anything. Said Avreml, Which means you're idle. When I studied in Heder, my teacher would say, Scratch yourself, just so you don't sit idle. Another man said to his companion, What is sparkling so much, the sea? Avreml started singing, What ailed thee, O thou sea, that thou fleddest? By the time he finished, the sea disappeared and from both sides of the road, the mountains rose up straight and stopped, and the road began descending. They passed one ruin, and another ruin and they came to the coastal plain, to the Gate of the Valley, Sha'ar HaGai.

2 |

The carter stopped the horses and the horses stopped the cart. And all the carts that had left before it and after it stood still. Sha'ar HaGai was beginning to fill up with vehicles and horses and donkeys and mules. Some were going from Jerusalem to Jaffa and others were going from Jaffa to Jerusalem. Countless people came and stood among the carts. Some looked at the moon and others set their watches. Some wanted to rest from the travail of the road, and others were looking for the carters. The carters disappeared. This one found himself a corner to rest, and that one went to tend to another need. Only the horses stood like sedate creatures, who know their season and their time, and as long as their hour to go hasn't come, there is no need to quake and shake.

Time slows down and doesn't budge, boredom sets in, and boredom progresses. A person stands next to another person and knows that this isn't the one he is looking for. And a chill comes from a person's body and mates with the chill that comes from outside and gives birth to a chill of boredom. Here, in this place, stands an old house, from its navel on down it is a stable and from its navel on up it is a coffee house. A big stove is lit with big kettles on it. A few travelers go in. Some of them stretched out on the ground, and some of them are looking for a place for their bones. All the places are already taken. This one is lying next to that one, and that one has his hands on his belly. This one is curled up like a fetus in his mother's belly, and that one has his head on the belly of this one and his feet next to the nose of his companion. The servants of the house are running around holding cups and jugs of coffee, spilling half of it on those who are sleeping and pouring half of it for those who are awake, whether they want to drink or whether they don't want to drink, and in spite of themselves, they pay several times more than that little cup is worth. And they grumble at themselves for coming into this den of thieves, for they could have done like the others who stayed in their cart and don't have to pay for coffee. At that moment, the servants of the house go serve those who are sleeping in the cart, whether they want to drink or whether they don't want to drink, and in spite of themselves, they pay several times more than that little cup is worth, and they envy their companions who hurried into the house. And since they had been awakened, they got up and took out their bags and extracted all the provisions they had prepared for the trip, bread and olives and sardines and vegetables, and sat down and ate their fill.

Between one thing and another, midnight passed. The carter came back and started shouting to his companions who were scattered to all four winds and were delaying the trip. They hurried and scurried into the cart. They wrapped themselves in all kinds of clothing and all kinds of blankets, for when midnight comes, a great chill makes its way in and anyone who is not wrapped up well is liable to catch cold. Zundl looked into the cart and asked, Is everybody here? When he saw that they were all here, he picked up the reins. The horses started walking without grumbling, for they were refreshed now, and yet they didn't hurry and didn't run, so the carter wouldn't get used to that and give them less rest tomorrow.

They passed Latrun. A cool wind came and a smell like the smell of wet wheat stalks wafted over the whole road. The passengers leaned their head on their shoulders and began dozing off. Only the cart wheels were awake. From time to time Zundl waved his whip over the horses' heads, to announce that he still had his eye on them and to prove to himself that he was awake. In an hour they reached Ramle, the last stopping place for carts going to Jaffa. The passengers shook themselves awake, their limbs pressed and their tongues dry and their heads heavy and their whole body broken. Zundl agreed to stop the wagon for a little while. They went into the inn for a hot drink. The samovar was still hot, but its fire was about to go out. The innkeeper blew on the fire and brought glasses. Between one thing and another, the passengers asked him about the local people and their livelihood, for in those days about thirty Jewish families were settled in Ramle, cobblers and harness-makers and tailors who hadn't found work in Jerusalem and went to seek their fortune in Ramle, and a League For Zion in Germany aided them a bit. When the passengers had quenched their thirst with tea, they got back into the cart.

Silence reigned. The sky was full of stars and the moon moved between the stars. All those with a watch took out their watch and informed their companions of the hour. Waves of sand rose and appeared, and the sight of the city of Jaffa and its gardens sprouts up. The horses suddenly picked up their feet and started hurrying, and the passengers started preparing for the city, place of their desire.

CHAPTER THREE

At Sonya's Place

1 |

When Isaac left Jerusalem, he didn't know what he would say to Sonya. But he relied on himself to come up with something on the way. By the time he got to Motza, he had taken his mind off Sonya, and when he entered Jaffa and came to Sonya's place, he was back where he was when he left Jerusalem, and didn't know what he would say.

It was twilight. Sonya was sitting in an easy chair made of canvas, and under her head was a little pillow tied to the chair with loops. The two windows were open, and a sweet darkness from outside mated with that darkness in the room. And in the space of the room was a sweetness of dusk that's special to Jaffa at sunset. The air in the room was still and Sonya's whole being filled the room. It had been weeks and months since Sonya had left the kindergarten and tried other kinds of things, but nothing came of all the things she tried to do. So, she considered going to Paris. And she relied on Paris to find something for her to do there. And she had already pictured to herself all that was in store for her in the big city. Suddenly she heard that Yarkoni, whom she thought was in Paris, had returned to the Land of Israel, and she was waiting for him to come to her place. Now she heard the sound of his footsteps and his fingers tapping on her door, like a person who wants to surprise his comrade and comes with a whisper and doesn't know that his comrade is waiting for him. God in Heaven, how blind are the eyes of fellows who think they are surprising a girl! But if Yarkoni wants to surprise me, I'll pretend I don't know he came back and that I'm surprised. And in a simple voice, Sonya called out, Come in.

Isaac Kumer came in and stood before Sonya. Ages ago they had stopped writing to one another and she hadn't heard a thing about him. All of a sudden he comes in. Sonya got up and said hello. She lit the lamp and sat down again. She took out a comb and combed her hair and looked at Isaac as if he were a stranger. And indeed, there was something strange about Isaac. When Isaac left Jaffa, he left without a trace of a beard and now he had a sort of beard, for ever since the anniversary of his mother's death, he hadn't passed a razor over his beard. His Jerusalem clothes added to his strangeness. And so, said Sonya, so you're Isaac, and you come from Jerusalem. What's new in the world?

Isaac dropped his eyes and gazed at the chair whose paint was peeling and repeated her words, What's new? Said she, Shouldn't the guest tell first? Said Isaac, What's there to tell? You yourself wrote me, the old news became obsolete and no new news appeared. Sonya squinted her eyes and a whitish yellowish light gleamed between her lashes. She shook her head and said, You're festive, Isaac, your face is like the face of a bridegroom. Isaac's face blushed and he thought to himself, Sonya knows every issue and everything. Said Sonya, Why are you standing? Take a chair and sit down. Isaac moved a chair and sat opposite her and said, Right away I'll sit. Sonya smiled and said, You're already sitting. Yes, yes, said Isaac, I'm already sitting. Said Sonya, So, Mr. Kumer, it seems you wish to say something. Said Isaac, In fact, I did want to tell you something, but I see there's no need. Said Sonya, But what? Should we sit silently, Isaac? Silence is nice for romance. She squinted again, and once again a kind of yellowish-whitish light glowed from between her lashes. Isaac licked his lips and said, It wasn't for romance that I came, but to speak clearly.

Sonya put out her fingertip and rubbed her lip and said, Clear speaking I want to hear. Clear speaking I want to hear. Even before he finished speaking, she put her hands on her knees and laughed. Said she, Oh dear, *kh'shtarb aveket fun lakhn*, I'll die laughing. Finally she stopped laughing and said, A great thing you told me. And so, for the same price, I won't refrain from telling you something too. I wrote you that a lot of men want to marry me, but I don't remember writing you that, if I cast off the yoke of father and mother, I won't put on the yoke of a husband. And I'll also tell you, that as long as I'm young, I want to be free. But. . . And here she gazed at him. Isaac's heart weakened. Sonya went on, But you know what came into my mind, let's go and eat ice cream. She got out of her chair, wrapped herself in a light shawl, and turned down the wick of the lamp. She went out with Isaac.

2 |

The moon shone and illuminated the earth. No wind blew, but a warm fragrant damp emanated from the sea. Once again, Isaac hesitated in the sand of Jaffa, which got into his shoes and bothered him until they got to Neve Shalom, where the ground was hardened like solid earth, for it was constantly trampled by the feet of passersby.

The street is hustling and bustling. From the two hotels of Zussman and Levi Isaac to the Arab coffeehouse stretches a strip of human beings, and a smell of roasting and cooking and frying bubbles up. In the coffeehouse and on the square in front of it, where the coffeehouse owner stretched colorful sheets and hung colorful lanterns on them, sat Moslems, white-skinned ones and black-skinned ones, bearded ones and mustachioed ones, and eunuchs whose faces are wrinkled and hairless, and they ate a lot and drank a lot, for those were the days of the Fast of Ramadan and the Faithful tried to do at night what they were forbidden to do during the day. A gramophone stood and sang joyful songs. Opposite it an old parrot shrieked words from the Koran. Passersby stood and drank colorful sweet and sour cold water, while the coffeehouse owner walks around among them and sprinkles eau de cologne on them and smiles, and his two boys take the coins with their fingertips and toss them into the air and catch them in their mouth. Meanwhile, the Faithful ogle the daughters of Israel and are amazed that Allah granted His beauty to the daughters of Infidels. As Isaac and Sonya are strolling, Yarkoni came toward them. Good God Almighty, yesterday and today she had been waiting for him to come, and when she despaired of him he comes and doesn't apologize to her or anything. But Yarkoni isn't to be scolded. Yarkoni has something that silences all complaints about him. Sonya put Yarkoni on her right and put her hand on his shoulder until they came to Café Hermon. The café owner looked into Isaac's childish eyes and wanted to say, I know you, and he looked at Yarkoni, whom he also knew, but whose name he had forgotten.

The garden of the café was full of men and women teachers, clerks and activists, and ordinary people who wanted to be teachers or writers or activists. Some of them were playing chess and some were playing with balls. Some said hello to Isaac and some said hello to Yarkoni. And some greeted Sonya who was lucky enough to have two guests at the same time. Sonya peered at all the seats until she found an empty one under a palm tree near the wall and ordered four portions of ice cream, so that if someone wants a second portion he won't have to wait.

The café owner brought the ice cream and looked at Miss Zweiering's two guests whom he knew, but couldn't remember which one's name he had forgotten. When Sonya ate her portion, she said, I see an extra portion here which you two are too lazy to eat. She thrust her spoon in and ate, and as she ate she said, If I had known there was no difference between this one and the one I ate, I wouldn't have eaten it. Yarkoni, over there in France, did you eat better ice cream than this. Yarkoni shook his heavy pompadour and said, I don't remember if I ate ice cream there. Said Sonya, Then what did you do there? Said Yarkoni, What did I do? I didn't do anything. Said Sonya, Then what, they did to you? Said Yarkoni, They didn't do to me. Said Sonya, They already came and told us your whole love affair with that little milliner. So, so, said Yarkoni dismissively and knocked the ice cream spoon on the little plate like a sad refrain.

Happy was that affair at the beginning and sad at the end, like most love affairs with their aftermaths. All he had left of that tale was regret and shame. Said Sonya, What are you humming to yourself? Better tell us about Paris. As he began telling, she raised herself and adjusted her dress like someone preparing for a journey. A moment later, she said, back onto the chair and pondered to herself, And I'm buried here in the sands of Jaffa between the sea and the desert, and wherever you turn, it's either camels and creatures or writers and teachers. Yarkoni sat and told his story, and the more he told, the more he wanted to stop, and the more he wanted to stop, the more he went on telling. Sonya sat and listened with her eyes closed and her heart open. Suddenly she opened her eyes and saw Isaac. She tapped him on the shoulder and said, I would leave my paw in a black man's maw if this guy heard any of that.

In truth, Isaac hadn't heard anything, but he was thinking of his first night in Petach Tikva, when Rabinovitch took him to Yarkoni's room after Yarkoni had left the Land. Meanwhile, Rabinovitch left and Yarkoni came back, and here he is sitting between him and Sonya. Said Sonya, A man sits here and his head is somewhere else. Where are you looking, Isaac? Isaac looked at the chessplayers' table. One was sitting with his back to the table and the other one was moving the pieces as he instructed. Isaac wasn't an expert at chess, yet he watched to see who would win, the one who was playing normally or the one who was playing blindfold. Yarkoni stopped talking and said, There's Mr. Makherovitch with Makheranski, and also, if I'm not mistaken, Makherson. No. . . Yes, yes, Makherson as he lives and breathes.

Mr. Makherovitch came in wiping the sweat off the back of his neck and looking at the people, like a speaker checking out his audience and replying to greetings on all sides. Isaac lifted his eyes and looked at him, as someone who enjoys the fruit of his own toil looks at a slacker, and bowed his head to him submissively and was angry at himself for doing that out of habit.

Mr. Makherovitch came and sat down. He put his hat in front of him and asked, Well, what are we drinking, hot or cold? Accustomed to public speaking, he spoke loudly and looked at his audience. Well, so what were we talking about the Eretz-Israel office. That is what I said, David Wolfson wouldn't have installed that office and wouldn't have sent two Germans to us, except to prove that it's impossible to do anything in the Land of Israel. Yarkoni, are you here? Welcome. Where were you, in Berlin? Said Yarkoni, No, in Paris. Said Makherovitch, Indeed, you were in Paris. And how is Miss Zweiering? Hello, Miss, fine, fine. No doubt a great livelihood is in store for the Land of Israel from the castor oil plants. What are you eating there, ice cream? How is it today? What did I want to say?

Makheranski and Makherson nodded in agreement. Mr. Makherovitch added, Well, in Eyn Ganim, things aren't going right. Yes, yes, you can't say the tea is hot, said Makheranski. Said Mr. Makherson, This is my cup, but whose lemon is this. Whose lemon? It is indeed mine, said Mr. Makherovitch. A fine story, a fine story, if Gilboa were here, he would write a whole novel about that. Mr. Makherovitch wasn't fond of the writers because they turn a blind eye to the building of the Land and go on writing about the Shtetl and the Yeshiva and the study house, except for Gilboa, who only writes about the Land of Israel and its settlements.

The three activists were getting bored with themselves. Deep in his heart, each one of them still sought something to interest his comrades. By the time they mated one word with another, that desire ended and the face grew slack and a stupid sadness made their mouth droop, the sadness of people whose acts and words have neither root nor branch. Mr. Makherovitch tightened the kerchief on his neck and said, Tomorrow is a great day, tomorrow a ship comes from Odessa and it will surely bring letters from the Odessa Committee.

3 |

Sonya gestured to Isaac and said, You see that one, that's Yael Hayyot. She's clinging to Hemdat, but her eyes are on Shammai. Isaac loved Hemdat as the young men of Israel love their poets. When he heard he was here, he longed to see him. Said Sonya, Let's go to Hemdat's place. Said Yarkoni, And what will Yael say? Said Sonya, In the meantime, Yael will court you.

Hemdat rejoiced to see Yarkoni and was cordial to Isaac, as he was with everyone, for Hemdat said, If a person drops in on me it surely has to be, for if not, would Divine Providence have taken the trouble to bring us to the same place? And since I encountered him, I have to be nice to him. And so, Hemdat was cordial to Yarkoni and rejoiced to see Isaac. Two guests at the same time, one from Europe and one from Jerusalem. And since the whole world is secondary to Jerusalem, let us ask first what's new in Jerusalem? Said Sonya, You don't see? Jerusalem makes a beard grow. Hemdat looked at Isaac pleasantly and said, Whenever I shave my beard, my hands tremble as if I were wounding the image of God. Said Sonya, Then why don't you grow a beard? Said Hemdat, Why? So I won't be innocent in my own eyes and I won't be arrogant and too proud. Said Sonya, And what's the real reason? Said Hemdat, The real reason is what is already written in the book of the first Adam, that Hemdat shall not grow a beard.

At that moment, Hemdat was in a good mood. That, said Hemdat, was only because Mr. Kumer brought the Jerusalem air with him. Said Sonya, Well, since you're so fond of Jerusalem, why don't you live there? Said Hemdat, A great question you asked, Miss Zweiering, but I shall tell you, A certain Hasid wanted to ascend to the Land of Israel. He went to the Rizhin Rebbe. The Rizhin Rebbe told him, Do not ascend. When the Rizhin Rebbe saw that he was amazed, he said to him, It is said the eyes of the Lord Your God are in the Land of Israel, so why do you want to get under the wheel of the eyes of the Holy-One-Blessed-Be-He, the Almighty. And what is true for the Land of Israel, is especially so for Jerusalem. Who is this coming? Dr. Schimmelmann in person.

4 |

Doctor Schimmelmann nodded here and there and inquired about the health of all those sitting there. Ah, Miss Zweiering, said Schimmelmann, you're here, fine, fine. A new face I see here, a new immigrant. Said Yarkoni, I see that Doctor Schimmelmann doesn't recognize me. Ah, ah, ah, said Schimmelmann, Mr. Mittelman? Oh, no, I was mistaken, when did you return, Mr. Rabinovitch? Said Yarkoni, You were mistaken, Doctor. I'm not Rabinovitch. Said Schimmelmann, I thought you were Rabinovitch. Said Hemdat, What's the wonder that Doctor Schimmelmann doesn't recognize you. Every son of Israel is one letter of the Torah, and since Doctor Schimmelmann is used to confusing the Torah anyway, he confuses the people, too. Said Schimmelmann, The gentleman doesn't like Scriptural criticism? If so, what do you do with the contradictions in the Scriptures? Said Hemdat, A person has enough Scriptures that do fit. Said Schimmelmann, If so, I shall show you some Scriptures that appear to be comprehensible, but really aren't. In spite of yourself, you cannot maintain the formulation as it is and you have to correct it.

Hemdat took Schimmelmann's hands and said to him, Dear Doctor, you may have heard the name of Hirsh Mendel Pineles. All his days that sage sat diligently over the books of our first sages. Once, on the Sabbath, after the meal, he sat and read as was his wont, *The Guide to the Perplexed,* and his father-in-law sat and read a book by some preacher. Said his father-in-law, Come and see how sweet are the words of this preacher. Hirsh Mendel looked at the preacher's book and immediately removed his eyes from it. Said his father-in-law, What do you say? Said he, Today is the Sabbath and we shouldn't speak frivolous words. When the Sabbath was over, after the Havdalah blessings, his father-in-law said to him, And now, what do you reply to me? Pineles took a piece of chalk and opened that preacher's book. That Sabbath was the Sabbath of the Torah portion that begins, Then Judah came near unto him. The preachers raised a few questions about that portion. One question why is it written *came near* and not "neared," and they said in the Talmud, A teacher should always teach his pupil succinctly. Pineles wrote, "neared" on the slate. A second question, since they said that a teacher should always teach the short way, why is it written *unto him* and not 'to him.' Pineles wrote on the slate, 'to him.' Third question, since the Torah prefers the long way, why did it change here and write Judah, and not 'Judah the *lion's whelp,*' as Jacob called his son in the Torah portion that begins, And it came to pass after these things. Pineles wrote on the slate, 'Judah the lion's whelp.' Fourth question, Why is it written 'he said' and not 'he had spoken,' as we find later on in *Let thy servant, I pray thee, speak a word,* for he spoke harsh things to him. Pineles wrote on his slate, 'speak.' Fifth question, Why did Judah choose to soothe Joseph with 'Pray my lord,' for didn't we find Our Teacher Moses, who said O *my Lord, I am not eloquent,* which means that 'pray' is used by someone who is not used to speaking, and here we see that he speaks at length. And the Ramban of blessed memory was already amazed in his commentary at the length of Judah's speech. So, he should have written 'please,' which is a synonym of 'pray'; indeed, the Onkelos translation says in both cases, 'if you please.' And if you conclude that it was nice here to write 'will you please,' for they said in the Talmud *that the last expression alone is regarded*. After Pineles wrote the whole verse as the preacher explained it, he read, Neared to him Judah the lion's whelp and spoke please, etc. Said Hirsh Mendel to his father-in-law, Dear father-in-law, what's nicer, the language of Our Teacher Moses or the language of the preacher. Doctor Schimmelmann took his hand out of Hemdat's and said, I don't understand what you're talking about. Said Hemdat, Whose language does Your Honor not understand, the language of the preacher or the language of Our Teacher Moses?

Said Sonya, Will Doctor Schimmelmann have an ice cream with us? Said Doctor Schimmelmann, I really came to drink something hot, but if the lady wants, I am willing to eat ice cream. So, you're not Mr. Rabinovitch and you're not Mr. Mittelman? Then, who are you? I'm Yarkoni. Schimmelmann rubbed his hands and said, Ah, ah, ah, obviously, obviously, of course you're Yarkoni. When did you come back, Mr. Yarkoni? Said Yarkoni, I came yesterday, Doctor, and already I am sitting in your presence. Said Sonya, You taught your tongue to speak politely. Said Schimmelmann, I assume Mr. Yarkoni's words come from the heart. So, let us have some ice cream. Oh dear, these mosquitoes. If a person wants to sit quietly, a mosquito jumps on him and stings him. Said Sonya, I heard that Jacob Rachnitz found some seaweed that keeps off the mosquitoes. Said Schimmelmann, That still needs to be clarified. Here's Tamara. What happened to little Tamara that she's so sad? Where is Yael? Yael Hayyot was about to leave, when Shammai got up to accompany her.

Hemdat and Shammai went to accompany Yael and Isaac and Yarkoni accompanied Sonya. After Isaac parted from Yarkoni, he said to himself, Apparently I finished all my business with Sonya. Yet Isaac's joy was only short-lived, for if he had settled his account with Sonya, with Rabinovitch he hadn't settled. A hundred times he said to himself, Rabinovitch has already taken his mind off her, and he doesn't care about anything. But Isaac wasn't satisfied. He started trembling and he started sweating like someone in the grip of malaria. But this wasn't malaria, but the sweat of shame covered him and remorse racked his body.

Delays Isaac in Jaffa

1 |

When Isaac opened his eyes he said to himself, Well, here I am in Jaffa, in this inn where I stayed the day I ascended to the Land of Israel, though its owners have changed, and I too have changed a little, and yet here I am again in this very same inn where I stayed the day I ascended to the Land. This matter, that he had come upon the same inn and so forth, seemed to warrant examination. But since he didn't know what the matter was, he repeated the words, perhaps this way he might comprehend it.

His sleep didn't open his bones, and he still was as tired as when he lay down to sleep, for he had sat eight hours crowded in a cart and all night long he hadn't tasted sleep, and when he got to Jaffa, he had trouble finding an inn, and when he did find an inn he ran around until the day passed and went to Sonya's place and sat with her until after midnight, something he wasn't used to doing in Jerusalem, for if he went to bed late, he caught up with his sleep the next night.

He stayed in bed and started thinking about the events that had happened to him the night before. Everything went well, Isaac said aloud. But his voice wasn't nice. He stretched his hands in front of him and asked, Why did I come down to Jaffa? Isaac knew very well why he had come down to Jaffa, to get things straight with Sonya, so he would be a free man and ready for Shifra. And in that he had succeeded very easily. And even though he should have been glad that he separated from Sonya without any difficulty, his mood was spoiled, for she regarded him as so unimportant, that she separated from him without a murmur.

He lay and examined her words in detail, the ones she said last night in her room and the ones she said afterward as they walked with Yarkoni and the ones she said in the coffeehouse. Like that skein that drops out of your hands and all the threads scatter and you have to wear yourself out to get them back into a skein, so Isaac wore himself out over the words until he came back to the beginning of the matter. And none of the words soothed the offended soul. He threw the blanket off and jumped out of bed. He put on his few clothes and thrust his feet into his sandals, picked up a towel and went to the sea.

2 |

Isaac went down to Jaffa to talk with Sonya, and now that he had talked with her, he could go back to Jerusalem. But people like Isaac, if they make such a long trip from Jerusalem to Jaffa, are not wont to return immediately, and even if they intend to return immediately, they find excuses and they tarry. That year was a drought year and Jerusalem, which drinks cistern water, drinks water with measure, and needless to say, doesn't bathe very much. And now that he had come to Jaffa, he wanted to bathe in the sea.

Isaac remained at the inn. Since his relations with Sonya were over, why did he need a private room? The owner of that hotel didn't rent it as a hotel, but used it for himself and his family, and since there were extra rooms there, he rented out two or three rooms. And since he didn't get his livelihood from them, he didn't charge much for his rooms and a person like Isaac, whose funds were limited, could live there. And there was another advantage there, that the hotel owner, who hadn't come to the Land of Israel because of Zionism, saw himself as a foreigner and all the people of the Land of Israel as natives, and therefore he made a special effort for every guest. There was another advantage there, that the house was close to the sea, and if you wanted you could bathe right after getting up and eat right after bathing and sleep right after eating.

Even though Isaac was idle, he wasn't bored. If you bathe in the sea and don't need to work, your days pass and you don't feel them passing, for bathing in the sea brings fatigue, and fatigue needs rest. All the days that Isaac was in the Land of Israel, he had never seen better days than those days he spent in Jaffa. The roar of the waves of the sea sweetened his sleep at night, and during the day his limbs dozed off by themselves. When he has slept his fill and eaten his fill, he goes off to Sweet Foot. He sits with him for an hour or two, looks at what he has done and hears tales of his deeds. One story evolves into another story and the next story into another story, and every story gives birth to other stories. There are people who could live as long as Methuselah, and nothing would happen in their lives. When Sweet Foot surveys himself, his whole life is a chain of events.

Sweet Foot doesn't make up things, but his stories are chronicles of his eyes, that is, he sees and tells what he sees. Just as he tells about human beings, so he tells about his dogs. About the dog he had and about the dog he has and about the dog who wandered by between the two of them. The one he had was a gadabout. Once he went out and didn't come back. Later, he came back, wounded and bleeding. He gave him bread with milk and healed his wounds. After he recovered, he told him, A gadabout you are, go and get yourself other masters. And the one he has is a thief, but he recognizes his transgression and accepts his punishment and doesn't get angry. And the one between them, what about him? Once a man passed by, the dog recognized him as his first master, and ran after him. A few days later, the man encountered Sweet Foot, and said to him, Your dog came to me. Said Sweet Foot, If he came to you, let him stay with you. But the man said, I don't want him. Said Sweet Foot, I don't want him either. Why? Because if he left me and went to you, it means he doesn't find satisfaction in my house, and a dog who leaves his masters and goes off, you mustn't bring him back. Now that he is living with you, he misses me, afterward, when he stays with me, he'll miss you. So the man said to him, If so, who's guarding your house? Said Sweet Foot, If there's no one to call out bow-wow here, the burglars don't notice my hut and don't come to burgle.

Sweet Foot speaks Yiddish with his dogs, not Russian and not Hebrew. Not Russian so that the dog won't understand the language of the intellectual girls who sometimes take a walk by his hut. Not Hebrew because of the students of the Hebrew Gymnasium. So the dog won't get too friendly with them, for Sweet Foot is angry with the kids of the Hebrew schools, who go out with a big fuss on the fifteenth day of the month of Shevat and plant saplings and don't take care of them afterward, don't water them, and don't hoe around them and abandon them and they wither. And why isn't he angry with the teachers? The teachers are supposed to deliver speeches and speeches they do deliver.

Sweet Foot welcomed Isaac as if he had parted from him just an hour ago and didn't ask him where he had been all those days. Just as he doesn't get angry if you come to him, so he doesn't get angry if you don't come to him. As he spoke, he told that he was in Jerusalem, too, that he went to visit his father and ask him for his tools. But his father didn't give them to him so that he wouldn't do profane work with them. After Father worked in the great synagogue in Jerusalem, he has guarded his tools from all profane work. But a person doesn't live forever, and after a hundred and twenty years, they'll get his tools. But Father says, in the winter, pilgrims come from Russia and when they go to Jordan and to the Dead Sea, he'll go with them and bring his tools to the Dead Sea. Two months Sweet Foot spent in Jerusalem and there wasn't a place he hadn't been. He walked mostly in the vaulted markets among the perfume vendors and the goldsmiths, and from there he went to the Western Wall. Once he stayed there until midnight. The Bratslav Hasids came to lament the destruction. They gave him a pamphlet and told him, Here you find what you need for your soul. He put the pamphlet in his pocket. That night in his dream he saw an orchard full of fragrant trees. He wanted to enter the orchard but they didn't let him. The owner of the orchard peered at him, called him Rabbi, held out his hand to him, and brought him in. The next day, he went to the Western Wall. The Bratslav Hasids asked him, Did you look at our Rebbe's book? He told them, I didn't look at it. Said they, Why? Said he, I don't know. Said they, Your face is shining, what happened to you? He told them, Nothing happened to me. Said they, Something did. He remembered his dream and told them. Said they, Blessed are you who were granted the right to see our Rebbe in a dream. They asked him how our Rebbe was at that time. He told them. Said they, That's it, that's it.

CHAPTER FIVE

Over a Cup of Tea

1 |

One day, Isaac found Hemdat sitting at Sweet Foot's place. Hemdat doesn't have anything to do and doesn't do anything. As long as he was Outside the Land and his heart was in the Land of Israel, he composed poems; now that he lives in the Land of Israel, what shall he do? Would he compose poems about the longings he once had?

But that is not why he was idle, but because if he would write, it seemed to him that this thing he wants to write would be his final work, and he was afraid he would die. As we were scared in our childhood, when we came to the saying of the Tanna, and repent one day before you die, for we were scared that that day was our last day and we wouldn't have time to repent.

Hemdat and Isaac are the same age, and should have been conscripted into the army. They slipped away and ascended to the Land of Israel on one and the same day in two different ships. Hemdat was friendly to Isaac, even though he wasn't comfortable with the craft Isaac practiced, for there is something misleading in it, since painters are wont to embellish ugly things.

Sweet Foot doesn't talk to two people at the same time, for talking to two is like talking to many, and talking to many is like orating, and there is no lack of orators in Jaffa. And since Hemdat and Isaac are both here, Sweet Foot withdraws from them and applies himself to his work.

When they were alone, Hemdat asked Isaac, What news do you hear from there? (From there means from Galicia), and his eyes became misty like a person remembering a beloved place. Isaac wasn't able to tell him a thing. Hemdat took him and said, Let's take a walk. They walked in the sand, the sand of Jaffa that makes you stumble. Isaac, who was used to the ground of Jerusalem was amazed that he found his footing in that sand. By the time you've extracted one foot, the other foot sinks in the sand. Hemdat, who was used to Jaffa, walked on the sand as if he were walking on a carpet.

Hemdat still lived in Neve Tsedek and intended to invite Isaac to his place for a cup of coffee. Before he could invite him, they came to the inn of Jacob Malkhov. Said Hemdat to Isaac, If you want, let's go in.

Jacob Malkhov was a ChaBaD Hasid and something of a writer. A day when an article of his was published in *Havatselet* was a good day for him, for a lot of readers read his articles and he was one who contributed something to many. Because his voice was hoarse, he chose to live in Jaffa, not in Hebron and not in Jerusalem, for the sea is good for the throat. Jaffa wasn't counted as one of the holy cities and its inhabitants don't receive the Distribution. But a Jew has to support his wife and children, so he made himself an inn. Three rooms he had, a dining room and a living room and a room for himself and his family. And when there are a lot of summer guests, he spreads a mat in the courtyard and shifts his apartment there and rents out his room to the bathers from Jerusalem.

His house was fit to be an inn for the members of the Old Yishuv, but it was occupied by our comrades who ran away from the noise of the hotels of Levi Isaac and Zussman where they gather every night and hold assemblies. But it was to Malkhov's credit that he took pains with his guests and asked nothing in payment except the little bit allowed us by the Torah and he gave them healthy food, for every day is destined for salvation, and when the Holy-One-Blessed-Be-He returns the children of Israel to their home, all the children of Israel will repent, and Malkhov gives them good food so they will have strength to repent. And when Malkhov gets excited about his generation that was blessed to settle here in the Chosen Land and acts here as if it were living in the lands of the Gentiles, he sings a beautiful, sad tune, like a teacher teaching the children, and says, Come, ye children, hearken unto me: I will teach you the fear of the Lord. Sometimes he says HASHEM, and sometimes he says the Lord. And just as he gets excited about his generation, so he marvels at the patience of the Holy-One-Blessed-Be-He Who sees their deeds and is silent.

2 |

When Hemdat and Isaac came, there weren't any guests there, except for one old man whose old age wasn't obvious either from his cinnamon-colored beard or from his movements. But his good-heartedness and agility were obvious. A black felt hat was on his head and his clothes were white cloth, not short and not long, like the clothes of many simple pious people in Jaffa, who wear light white cloth clothes on hot days.

That old man was sitting there drinking tea. He drank one cup and paid and said a blessing, and asked for another cup and paid. When he stood up to leave, he saw Hemdat and asked about his well-being. Said Hemdat, In your well-being is my well-being. Said the old man, That is the finest blessing of all blessings, that a Jew makes his well-being depend on the well-being of his fellow Jew. And that Jew, who is he? Said Hemdat, It is my comrade who came to bathe in the sea. Said the old man to Isaac, You do well, my friend, the waters of the sea are healing. Are you worried about your limbs, my friend? Said Jacob Malkhov, He's worried about his loins. The old man shook his head in grief and said, May HASHEM send you full healing. Said Jacob Malkhov, A pile of Dinars he has loaded on his loins, so he's worried about his loins. Jacob Malkhov laughed and the old man laughed.

When he left, Malkhov followed him out and said to him, Reb Zerakh, I've got a great matter for you. Said Reb Zerakh, My heart is not haughty. He said to him, It is a matter of charity, and our Sages of Blessed Memory said, great is charity that lengthens the days and years of a person and prepares the person for life in the World-To-Come. Said Reb Zerakh, How much do you want? Said Malkhov, Thousands on thousands and ten thousands on ten thousands, I want, but by the time all the coins are counted, a poor person can pass away, God Forbid, and so I am satisfied for the time being with one Bishlik. Reb Zerakh took out his purse and gave him. Malkhov took the coins and wanted to put them in his pocket. Reb Zerakh said to him, Everyone who receives coins has to count them. Said Malkhov, You can count on Reb Zerakh, who knows how to count coins. Reb Zerakh said to him, Nevertheless. Malkhov counted and found a Bishlik missing a Matlik. Reb Zerakh said to him, One Matlik I deducted for the charity of Rachel Leah, my wife. Said Malkhov, And for the charity of Rachel Leah is the pauper deprived? Said Reb Zarakh, So that you won't be angry at my Rachel Leah, I'll give you the Matlik.

When Malkhov came back from Reb Zerakh, Hemdat asked him, How is that worrying about loins related to a pile of Dinars, and why did you two laugh so much? Said Malkhov, I referred to when Reb Zerakh bought this land where Neve Shalom was built, he gave the sellers a bill they call a check. They didn't want to accept it, for in those days there was no bank in Jaffa. So he went up to Valero in Jerusalem and exchanged his bill for coins. He sewed himself a long pocket and put the Dinars in his pocket and fastened it to his loins so the highway robbers wouldn't notice it. The highway robbers didn't notice it, but his loins did notice it, until he bathed in the sea and was healed.

Isaac asked Hemdat, Who is that Reb Zerakh? He said to him, He's Reb Zerakh Barnett, one of the builders of Meah Shearim, the Hundred Gates, in Jerusalem and one of the builders of Petach Tikva, the Opening of Hope, and one of the builders of Jaffa, the Belle of the Sea. When Reb Zerakh ascended to Jaffa, before he went to Petach Tikva, there weren't a Minyan of Ashenazi Jews here, and after he was forced to leave Petach Tikva, for he saw that he couldn't make a living from working the soil, he went to Jaffa and bought land and built houses and made a settlement. I'm amazed you've never heard of Reb Zerakh. Said Isaac, I heard and didn't hear.

Even though Isaac had lived a long time in Jaffa, he didn't know Reb Zerakh, for Reb Zerakh wasn't distinguished in his outward appearance from the other people of Jaffa. And even though Isaac had often worked in the Barnett houses, he hadn't asked who was this Barnett that a row of houses was named for him, just as he hadn't asked about the other houses and streets to know who they were named for. And it may be that he hadn't encountered him at all, for in those days when Isaac lived in Jaffa, Reb Zerakh was Outside the Land. When Reb Zerakh saw that his money ran out and that he couldn't make any more in Jaffa, he went back to London to his workshop. And because all his deeds were for the sake of the Land of Israel, his labor was blessed. And when his hands were filled with the grace of God, he returned to the Land of Israel and divided his money into three parts, one third to build houses, one third for Heders, and one third for himself.

Said Malkhov, Generation of ingrates, who don't know their builders. If not for Reb Zerakh and his comrades, you wouldn't even have a place to spend the night here. You know Makheranski and Makherovitch and Makherson who came to the table after it was set, and eat what others have made for them, and take a fee for eating. And here Malkhov glared at Isaac and added, *Ha-Po'el Ha-Tsa'ir* has already shown their true faces, and those things should be said. And I will add this, you criticize the Distribution and say that all Distribution is distributed to the pockets of the officers. Aside from the fact that that was exposed as a lie, those officers are raising their children for the Torah and staying in the Land of Israel, and the Land is being built. While those who get the new Distribution who take several times more — what does the Land get from them? They make congresses to travel outside the Land, and they go to theaters and circuses and enrich the Gentiles with money that Jews saved up from their own mouths, and their children they send to schools Outside the Land and they become complete Gentiles. But let us not deprive sinners of any reward. When they become Goyim, they settle in the lands of the Gentiles and don't return here and don't pollute the Land like their fathers.

Said Hemdat, I saw that Reb Zerakh drank and paid and drank and paid again. How come he doesn't pay all at once? Said Malkhov, He thinks he'll have enough with one glass, and when he isn't satisfied with it, he drinks and pays again. While the whole world pays half a Matlik, he pays a whole Matlik, to make up for those who drink and don't pay. And Reb Zerakh has a house full of delicacies, so why does he come to drink in my place, except that he has mercy on his wife not to bother her, for she is busy cooking for the Talmud scholars studying in the study house he built for them.

3 |

As they are talking, a man with a big blond beard and beautiful blue eyes comes in. His movements are casual and his clothes are tattered, and he is timid in the presence of folks. This timidity isn't because he values folks highly, but because he regards himself as humble. But beyond his timidity, you can detect his wisdom that didn't overcome his naïveté. When Malkhov saw him, he called his daughter, Yetele, Yetele, hurry and bring a cup of tea for Brenner. Malkhov doesn't usually use his daughter, but when Brenner came, he didn't want to miss a single moment with him, so he called his daughter.

Malkhov and Brenner studied Torah from the same rabbi, Rabbi Heshel the scion of Gnessin, father of the writer Uri Nissan Gnessin, and because of that, there was a kind of camaraderie between them, even though they didn't study at the same time, for Malkhov was older than Brenner. And even though Brenner studied and withdrew, that didn't change Malkhov's love for him, because of his learning and his piety which he excelled in when he was young, and because of his good nature and his generosity, and because even after he became a heretic, he didn't try to attract others to heresy.

Brenner said to Hemdat, I passed by your room last night and saw a lamp lit. He said to him, Why didn't you come in? Said he, Haven't you made your room a kind of fetish? How will I come in? Hemdat was silent and pondered, Brenner's words were right. If I hadn't made my room into a fetish, would I be sitting here? I would sit in my room with this fellow from my homeland and we would tell each other things about Galicia. Said Hemdat to Brenner, And you're content with your room? Said Brenner, I'm content. Hemdat said to him, Why, it's dark. Said Brenner, I moved the table to the window. Said Hemdat, And the noise in the street deprives you of your repose. Said he, Hemdat, Hemdat, you still think repose is something that depends on outside, repose is something inside.

That whole time, Isaac didn't take his eyes off that great writer, brother of the oppressed, whose clothing and everything else were no different from all the other simple workers. Brenner noticed him and said hello. Isaac returned his greeting and was stunned that he had said hello to Brenner and didn't notice that he was Brenner.

Happy Deeds and Sad Thoughts

1 |

At sundown, the laborers returned from their work, dirty with plaster and dust and sand. They put down their tools and went, this one to wash his face and hands and that one to rinse his throat with a glass of soda, this one rummaged in his window in case there was a letter for him there, and that one picked up *Havatselet* and started reading. One of them saw Brenner, ran up, and greeted him. Brenner held his hand and looked at him affectionately, like a person who wants to give his brother a gift and has nothing but the affection in his eyes. He whispered to him, Order yourself a cup of tea. The other replied excitedly, as if he had suddenly discovered what he had been lacking and said, Right away I'll order a cup of tea. But he didn't go order tea for himself, for it was hard for him to get away from Brenner, whom he had just met by chance.

Malkhov wrapped himself in a long heavy cloak that came down to the bottom of his legs and put a hat on his head that was designated especially for prayer and for every Commandment, and said, If we were blessed, we would pray here in public, but as we are not blessed, I leave you and run to the synagogue. Our comrades who rejoiced to see Brenner said, Pray for us too, Reb Jacob. Malkhov turned his head around and said, May this person pray for himself.

Malkhov's prayer house isn't far from his hotel, but the road is all sand and the long cloak he wears for prayer, because it is his garb of honor, weighs him down and bangs his feet, and whenever he goes to pray, all his limbs are stirred, as if he were going to do something beyond his strength.

Malkhov's wife came in and saw the fellows who had come back from work. She sighed and said, You've already come back from work, and I don't know what I'll give you. I cooked a little bit of groats in gravy, I cooked a little bit of eggplant, I fried bread in the skillet, God knows if that's enough for a meal. Said little Yankele, I give up my portion. Said Malkhov's wife, All the time you give up, and you of all people mustn't give it up, look at your face, Yankele, skin and bones. Said big Yankele, Don't worry about him, Mrs. Malkhov, it's a good deal he's making, he gives up in this world for the World-to-Come. Do you have malaria again, Yanekele? Said Yankele, No, but. . . But what? But today is the anniversary of your father's death and you make it a fast day. If you don't eat, you'll die, just like your father. You should have gone with Malkhov to the study house and have a little drink there with the Hasids.

Malkhov's wife spread her hands in front of her, hunched her shoulders, and asked anxiously, So, what shall we do? Said Podolsky, Don't worry too much, Mrs. Malkhov, but do what all the other innkeepers do, add a jar of water to the soup, and if that isn't enough, add two jars. Said Malkhov's wife, The kids stand all day in the sun and the dust, and when they come to eat they don't find anything. And whose fault is that, my Jacob, Long-May-He-Live, who runs after Commandments all day long, and this Commandment that lies in his own house, he neglects. Now he went off to the study house, and from the study house he'll run to the blind seer, and from the blind seer he'll run to get supporters for the old people's home in Jerusalem, and you are hungry and thirsty. And wouldn't it be better if he took care of the business of his own inn? I guarantee you he won't come back so fast. And there's nothing I can do. Nothing. After all, I only have two hands. Two frail hands, a pity to move them. Oh dear God, You tell me, is it worth it to live in Your world? And this one sits in his study house and doesn't think of coming back. And why should he come back, it's good over there. There's a kerosene lamp de luxe there and the Torah and Hasidism, and here there's a pair of weak hands and nothing. And my feet, oh, Master of the Universe, may all the enemies of Zion have such feet. And the whole body, it's not a body, a heap of the plagues of Egypt. And this Jacob, Long-May-He-Live, wraps himself in his cloak his father made for him on his wedding day and runs off to the study house like a groom to his wedding and doesn't think about coming back. I'm telling you, he won't come back soon. Here, he's coming.

2 |

Malkhov rushed in and called out joyously, Good evening, fellows, good evening, fellows. He took off his heavy cloak and hung it on a peg in the wall, and he took off his hat and stroked it affectionately. He saw his wife standing in the room, scolded her, She stands and preaches sermons like a preacher, go back to your cooking, woman, and don't stick your nose into things that are none of your business. Joseph Haim, will you eat here? I won't eat, answered Brenner. Said Malkhov, Did the woman frighten you, that there's nothing here to eat? Delicacies her father and mother fed her are in her mind's eye, and she thinks all Children of Israel are obliged to eat delicacies. Sit down, my brother, and eat. And you Hemdat, a piece of fish is waiting for you, may you see the reflection of his tail in the World-to-Come. Mapku, you're one of the family, go to Azulai and bring me forty or fifty eggs. (Mapku is Gorishkin, whom Malkhov named after Abraham Mapu, because he wrote stories.)

Said little Yankele, Reb Jacob, I'll go. Said Malkhov, Sit down, you're a Cohen, and I don't use Cohanim. You didn't come to the prayer house and you didn't say Kaddish. Your father isn't worth bothering about? One Kaddish I stole from the mourners. Tomorrow, come and say Kaddish yourself. And here Malkhov turned to Brenner and said, I knew his father, may he rest in peace. He was a worker, he worked for the Lord and worked his own land. A strip of ground he had in Hadera and he died on it from yellow fever. When he got sick and they wanted to take him someplace else, he refused. He said, It isn't the Land that kills and it isn't malaria that kills, but forsaking the Land kills. As he passed away, he pointed to part of his land and said, How we are spoiled! *We are greatly confounded because we have forsaken the land.* And you Polishkin, put down

Havatselet. If you want to laugh, read Ben-Yehuda's newspapers, or maybe you're scared of the scorn of idolators. Joseph Haim, you're a new person in the Land and you don't know the wisdom of its sages. So I shall tell you a little bit. Brenner didn't like to hear about Ben-Yehuda, neither praise nor blame, but because of his respect for the landlord, and so he wouldn't look fed up with his talk, he didn't stop his ears, but shut his eyes, like sensitive people who express their sensitivity with their body.

Said Malkhov, When Professor Boris Schatz made his Bezalel, Hanukkah came upon him, that holy holiday they started calling the holiday of the Maccabees. They went and made him a joyous party. They put up a statue of the High Priest Mattithiah, holding a sword in his hand to pierce the tyrant who was sacrificing a pig on the altar they had made in honor of Antiochus the Wicked. They spent all night in riot and gluttony. The next day, Ben-Yehuda wrote affectionately about the party in his newspaper, just that he wasn't comfortable with that statue they had put up in the hall, for this Mattithiah was a zealot for his religion, for his religion and not for his land, for as long as the Greeks were spreading over our land and robbing and oppressing and murdering and killing and destroying cities and villages, Mattithiah and his sons sat in Modiyin, their city, and didn't lift a finger, but when the Greeks started offending the religion, as the prayer says, to force Thy people Israel to forget Thy Torah and transgress the commands of Thy will, he leaped like a lion, he and his sons the heroes, and so on and so forth, and they decided to honor the event with an eight-day holiday. And now, says Ben-Yehuda in his article, and now I wonder, when they gathered last night to honor him, if they had breathed life into the statue, or if he himself were alive, if he wouldn't have stabbed every single one of us with the sword in his hand, and sacrificed all of us on the altar.

The whole time, Brenner sat with his eyes shut, as if that was how he saw what Malkhov told. After Malkhov concluded, Brenner's eyes opened and his lips burst and he started rocking with laughter. Gorishkin shouted, Lies, Malkhov, lies. Malkhov grabbed his beard and said, Mapku, shut up. Just because you're used to profanity, you even profane the words of Ben-Yehuda. Brenner grabbed the table to keep from collapsing with laughter. When he rested a bit from laughing, he laughed again and said, A vulgar man am I. Forgive me, comrades, for that wild laughter.

Malkhov's wife called from the kitchen, Jacob, Jacob, the soup's getting cold. Malkhov ran to the kitchen along with his son Zalman Leyb. They brought a bowl of soup to this one and a plate of vegetables to that one, a piece of roasted fish to this one, and radish chopped with eggs and onions to that one. Finally, from the box under the window, Malkhov took eight or nine loaves of bread and put them on the table. Our comrades sliced the loaves, some with their fingers and some with a knife. Malkhov looked at them with kindly eyes and said, Before apostasy enters your ears, food and drink will enter your bellies. Who didn't get his share? You all did. Well then, eat, children, eat. Hemdat, how's that fish? An incarnation of a monthly synagogue officer or of a Rabbi from Poland? What's that, Yosef Haim, you're idle. Somebody make yourself thin and squeeze in between your comrades. Fellows, make room for this guy from Jerusalem. Said Brenner to Malkhov, You're a clown, Reb Jacob. Said Malkhov to Brenner, Yosef Haim, my brother, you laugh and I cry. They take a delightsome and good land and make it into a desert. No Torah and no Commandments and no respect. There are children here in their Gymnasium who don't know the first chapter of Psalms. A generation will rise here whose whole wisdom will be knowing how to say How are you, Madame.

When they had eaten and drunk, some of them went to bed, and some of them took books out of their packs and sat down to read. Some of them strolled around the room, and some of them went to accompany Brenner. Malkhov looked at them and started reciting, Come, ye children, hearken unto me: I will teach you the fear of the Lord. Brenner turned around and said to him in a gentle voice, Goodnight, Malkhov. Malkhov replied in a hoarse voice, Goodbye and blessings, Joseph Haim, and he walked three paces behind him to accompany him.

3 |

The night was beautiful, like most nights in Jaffa when there is no hot wind. And the sea, the sea that guards us against the aridity of the desert, smelled of saturated damp, the sandy soil was trodden flat and shone from inside. It didn't bother the people strolling, on the contrary it was mild, as it is mild at night. And as the ground was mild, so the mood of our comrades is mild. Everyone ate his fill and knew he had the wherewithal in hand to pay for his dinner. The bad days were past when we stayed at home because we didn't have the strength to move around, because we were hungry, because we didn't find any way to make money, because they gave our work to Arabs, and didn't let us earn enough even for dry bread. At long last, the activists of Jaffa had to turn over the task of building the school to our comrades, and all those who said we couldn't compete with Gentile craftsmen admitted that our work was perfect. Stephan saw and admitted it was fine. Urban saw and admitted it was fine. Now Ahuzat Bayit, the Home Estate Company, is about to build its houses, and it too will give the construction work to Jewish laborers. And Akiva Weiss, the founder of the society, has already published an announcement in *The Young Laborer*, that contractors are invited to propose their terms to the building committee. Who would have imagined that disputes and conflicts would have led to action? People who fled to the Land of Israel because of oppression and persecution and kept their bags packed like emigrants and made the prices rise, and they watched ships leaving the Land and wondered when would they leave with them, now those same people gathered their strength and their courage and worked with the builders of our land, and you couldn't tell who came to be built and who came to build. Even the LeKaKh Company (the initials of Lomir Klappn Khissinen, that is: Let's Beat Up Khissin, Dr. Khissin, the representative of the Lovers of Zion who wouldn't give them unemployment wages), even they recognized that there is no place for grumbling, but there is a place for work. All the activists of the Yishuv got involved in the building work for Ahuzat Bayit, led by Dizengoff, who deals with every issue and every matter seriously and calmly. For the time being, they're building sixty houses. Sixty houses aren't sixty cities, but we who do not aim too high, even smallness is great for us.

4 |

Brenner doesn't share the rejoicing. What do you want with joy here? And if they build sixty houses, have they caught even the tail of the Messiah's donkey? Jews are wont to build houses. One mortgage lender in Lodz has more houses than all the Ahuzat Bayit Company will build, and they don't hold him up as a model for the salvation of Israel. But he builds Outside the Land and they build in Palestine. Jerusalem is also building houses and neighborhoods, and what will all their houses and their neighborhoods add, aside from a multitude of unemployed idlers, flatterers and hypocrites, quarrel mongers, those who eat the bread of Distribution and expect all their days the charity of their brothers, the donors of the nation, the God of Abraham, the remnants of Israel sitting by the fleshpots and making *gesheftn,* who will throw them bones to gnaw on with their rotten teeth, and for that, they will pray for them at the Western Wall and at all the other holy places for the Holy-One-Blessed-Be-He to send blessing and success to all the works of their hands and for them to see reward in this world and the World-to-Come. One thing we have to do, to work the land and to bring bread out of the earth. But plowing doesn't make a fuss, and so few demand it. And so they make a new Exile here, the Exile of Ishmael, and they see themselves as the emissaries of the nation, saviors of Israel. But the nation doesn't recognize them, and doesn't want to know them. Only a very small handful of people who are poor in deed and lazy in thought follow them like cattle in a valley, for they are not yet freed from the spell of the splendid past and expect a good future when their work will be done by Arabs, and they will sit in their houses and drink Wissotsky tea. Except for the members of Bilu, my brothers and friends, aside from the members of Bilu, everything here is humbug, humbug, humbug. Yankele, what did your father say when he passed away, *How we are spoiled! We are greatly confounded because we have for-*

saken the land, because we have forsaken the land, that's the greatest confounding of all, and about that, the lamenter is lamenting. Tell us a little of your father's deeds, Yankele.

Yankele blushed and was silent. Brenner put his hand on his shoulder and looked at him with great affection. Yankele's heart was filled and he said, I didn't know Father. When the yellow fever began bringing people down, they took us out of Hadera and brought us to Zikhron Ya'akov. But one thing I did hear. Once they asked my father, Are you satisfied, Reb Israel, with living in the Land of Israel? Father answered, I could be satisfied, but one thing I lack. Outside the Land, when I went to pray, I would encounter city policemen and other wicked Goyim, this one slapped my face and that one spat on my beard and another one looked at me with loathing, and I knew that we were in Exile, and when I prayed, I prayed with a broken heart. And here, Jews are sitting on their own land, no policeman and no Exile, and my mind gets proud and I am ashamed for my Creator to stand before him with an arrogant heart. Brenner fell on Yankele's neck and began reciting, *Come, ye children, hearken unto me: I will teach you the fear of the Lord.*

And when our comrade Yankele mentioned the village where he was born, he started telling how much territory was in Hadera. A space of thirty thousand Dunams it was, and of them, three thousand five hundred Dunams are swamps full of mold, that brought plague and pestilence, yet the people of Hadera didn't leave their place, but said, We came to establish a settlement, and as long as there is breath in our bodies, we won't budge. The Baron took pity on them and sent to drain the swamps. They took the women and children out of the settlement, only the men remained to gather their harvest. They brought three hundred Egyptians who were used to the work of draining and were accustomed to malaria. There were nine of the members of the settlement who wanted to show that a Jew isn't afraid of any danger and they urged the supervisor to let them stay in the settlement. The supervisor agreed and let them. They stomped around up to their knees in mire eight hours every day for nine months. A miracle from heaven that not one of them got sick. They drained the swamps and planted twenty-five thousand eucalyptus trees, and planted another twenty-four thousand eucalyptus trees, until they surrounded all of Hadera with a wall of trees, so the plague wouldn't reach the houses of their settlement. And needless to say, all the saplings they planted — Jews planted with their own hands. And when the trees grew, they went on planting, until Hadera became a flourishing settlement unlike any other in the whole Land. And when little Yankele told that tale, he also told other things. Some bitter as wormwood and some sweeter than honey.

The night was fine and the sea was fine and Brenner's conversation was fine. The things Brenner said most of our comrades had thought about in days gone by, days when they didn't give us work and we were idle and didn't see a piece of bread. Now that there is work and a person works and makes money, our comrades were like the one who regretted that his heart wasn't broken. And yet every single one thought of his own affairs, this one about making new clothes and that one about bringing his girlfriend to the Land of Israel, this one about saving for travel expenses and going Outside the Land to study at a university. And our comrade Isaac, what was he thinking about? Our comrade Isaac was thinking about Shifra.

CHAPTER SEVEN

Night Thoughts

1 |

The second watch of the night passed. The voice of the sea changed and its waves donned foam. A chill wind began blowing and furrows began bursting and raising water. Brenner looked at the sea, striving to grasp some of the splendor of its force. He dropped his hands and grasped Hemdat's hand, as he grasped his pen when he strove to conjure up an idea that wasn't completely clear to him, and said, The time has come to sleep. Said Podolsky, Ye, *m' darf geyn aheym* (yes, we better go home), and emphasized the word *heym* and laughed, for there is no man here who has his own *heym*. Brenner responded with a melody and said, *Kinderlakh, m'darf geyn aheym*. When Brenner withdrew from the group along with Hemdat, everyone felt weary. They parted from one another and went their way, this one to his room, and that one to the corner of his bed in the cheap hotels in Neve Shalom.

2 |

A small lamp stood at the bed of one of the guests of the hotel who was sleeping with his face covered with a sheet of *Ha-Or*. Isaac picked up the lamp and took a copy of Lunz's almanac he had found in the hotel. He put the lamp near his bed and put the almanac on his pillow to read before he went to sleep. When he lay down he forgot the almanac and put out the light.

Isaac lay on his bed and thought about everything that came into his mind, about Sweet Foot and about that day when the artisans in Jaffa made a banquet and made him drink a lot of wine and Isaac brought him to his room and lay him on his bed and they had become friends. They never mentioned that deed, but their friendship didn't cease. From Sweet Foot, Isaac came to Jacob Malkhov, and from Jacob Malkhov to Reb Zerakh Barnett. Brenner disparages those houses and the neighborhoods they're building in the Land of Israel because he's a pessimist.

With no connection, his mind came to Arzef. A lot of stuffed skins Isaac had seen at Arzef's, but the stuffed skin of a dog he hadn't seen. It's a bad quality in dogs that they bark and stop and bark again. If they barked incessantly, we would get used to their barking. Since they bark and stop and bark again, they confound the heart.

Blurry thoughts that came in a jumble confounded his soul. He fluttered his eyelids hoping to evoke the figure of Shifra. But Sonya came and then Reb Fayesh, lying in bed and both eyes crusted over like turgid ice peeping at him, at Isaac, and the bed was covered with a blanket on which the figure of a dog was embroidered with a stick in its mouth. Isaac was stunned, if Reb Fayesh slept in a bed, how was the bed covered. Isaac fluttered his eyelids. The stick in the dog's mouth fluttered and he barked, Bow-wow.

Am I sleeping? Isaac asked himself in his sleep. Am I dreaming? Isaac asked himself in a dream. For that dog is on Sonya's blanket, so how did he wind up at Shifra's father's house? Shifra came, beautiful and handsome, and different from Shifra. And her hair wasn't gold, but black. And it was flat on her head and smooth, as if an iron were passed over her hair, and her cheeks were reddish, and a dark glow gleamed on them. Such beauty isn't found in every girl. But her tongue was thick and filled her whole mouth, and her nose bent down toward her upper lip. She asked him, Do you love me? He wanted to take her in his arms, but his hands were slack because he was hugging Sonya.

A dream or not a dream? Isaac asked himself in his dream. This couldn't be a dream, for I hear my roommate sneezing. Who's here? A statue of the High Priest Mattithiah. But you don't look like Mattithiah. And if you look like anybody, pal, you look like, for instance, Professor Schatz. But Professor Schatz dressed in a Bedouin cloak, but the sword in your hand is stabbing.

Isaac woke with a start from a mosquito sting. He rubbed his cheeks and thought about his dream. A bad dream or a good dream? In any case, I did well to come to Jaffa. Here is society, here is life. It would be nice if I knew how Shifra was. In fact, I should write to her, but what will I do since I promised her I wouldn't write? And even if I do write to her, how will the letter reach her? For I don't know her last name. Yankele, why don't you say Kaddish? Bloykof hired a man to say Kaddish, and you are cruel to your father and don't say Kaddish for him. Who is this who appeared to me? Isn't that Lydia, secretary of the director of the seminary? The director of the seminary doesn't behave nicely. A Hebrew seminary he made in Jerusalem, so they had to increase Hebrew studies there, and in the end, they cram the students with German literature and its history, and rumor has it that Reb Yehiel Mikhl Pines teaches Talmud in Yiddish, but when guests come, he teaches in Hebrew. How come I haven't seen Orgelbrand? Mapku, tomorrow, we'll go to Orgelbrand. But before we go, we'll shut our eyes and doze off.

How did I climb up these steep steps? Lo, they're from the Hungarian houses, their Talmud Torah. One hundred twenty students sit there, crowded and packed together and the teacher sings to them, I have loved you, saith the Lord. Yet ye say, Wherein hast thou loved us? Was not Esau Jacob's brother? saith the Lord: yet I loved Jacob. What can my sisters do here? Would I let my sisters be like those seamstresses and milliners who live in the convert's house. I see that the cisterns lack water, if so, where will we drink? The well of Job is emptied and the waters of Shiloh, says Lunz in his almanac, are not good for drinking, and aren't brought to the city, and even in a drought year, the waters of the Shiloh are used only for cooking and other household needs, and my neighbor pours a full jar of water on his head. Good morning, said his neighbor to Isaac. Good morning, Isaac answered his neighbor and turned over onto his other side.

CHAPTER EIGHT

Between Jaffa and Jerusalem

1 |

Isaac got out of bed. He washed his face and hands, but he didn't go to the sea, for it was already noontime, and in those days, we didn't go walking at the sea in the afternoon on hot days, except for Doctor Rekhnitz, who used to hunt for seaweed, and now that he has left for America, you don't see a person at the sea in the afternoon.

After he put on his clothes, he ordered himself a cup of tea, even though it was already time for lunch. Isaac thought, like all our other comrades, that drinking something hot after sleep was obligatory. They brought him a cup of tea and sugar and a round cake, one of those cakes of dough and cinnamon that are found in Jaffa in every hotel and every restaurant and every teahouse, and we thought at the time they were good, for we had already forgotten the taste of the cakes we ate in our father's house. He drank and sliced himself a slice and thought about all kinds of people he had come across yesterday. And once again he said to himself, I did well to come to Jaffa, now let's check how much money I have left and how long I can stay here. He took out his pocketbook and started counting his coins, like Simon his father. But while Simon his father counts over an empty heart and sighs, Isaac counted his coins over cake and a cup of sweet tea, for sugar is cheap here, and you can put as much as you want into a cup, but nature gave a limit to sweetness so that a person won't eat too much of it.

After he drank and ate his cake, he asked himself, And now what shall we do? Now we'll eat lunch and we'll lie down in bed and we'll read the almanac of the Land of Israel. Afterward, we'll go perhaps to Hemdat. And even though he wrote on his door, "I'm not in," so that guests won't interrupt him, he welcomes a guest and makes him coffee. And if we don't find Hemdat, we'll go to Orgelbrand. A sad man, Orgelbrand, but the sadness in him isn't depressing. How beautiful were the walks we took in Sarona and the Saturday evenings we spent in Petach Tikva. I really should put on my work clothes and look for work, for if I stay here, I need money. Our best critics are used to seeing Brenner as a pessimist, for they judge from his books and they don't know his laughter. A letter from Father has certainly come and is lying around in Jerusalem. There certainly isn't anything new in it, and if there is something new in it, it's only added to the old troubles. And Shifra doesn't write anything and I don't know anything about her. Isaac recalled days when he would come to her house and bring food with him, and the two things, that is what she lacked and what he lacked combined into one sad thing. Isaac regretted he had agreed with Shifra not to write to her, and that he didn't ask her to write to him. Avreml, the carter, didn't write to his father because he didn't know how to write, perhaps Shifra doesn't know how to write either. In school, she didn't learn, and her father certainly wouldn't hire teachers for her. Once Wilhelm Gross reproached one of the dignitaries of Jerusalem for not teaching his daughters to write. That Rabbi told him, Why should they learn to write? He told him, When they are betrothed, they will want to write a letter to the bridegroom. Said he, I'll get them bridegrooms from Jerusalem and they don't have to write letters. That Rabbi got bridegrooms for his daughters from Jerusalem, which isn't true of Shifra, whose bridegroom is in Jaffa. And will that upholsterer, that Hungarian who is a neighbor of Shifra's, tell her he saw me? He doesn't know that she knows me. I hope he didn't know, because if he did know, he would tease her. What did I hear about him? They say he is going to divorce his wife because he set his sights on Sweet Foot's ex-wife. Now it's time for lunch. I'll eat first and then I'll consider my return to Jerusalem.

2 |

When he had eaten and drunk, he stretched out on his bed and went back to ruminating at the point where he was interrupted. But the brain which is wont to be tired after the midday meal, when the shutters are drawn and the heat is pressed in the room, the brain is too lazy to think thoughts. On the other hand, the eyes which are wont to be shut at that hour, were filled with valor and began wandering from Jaffa to Jerusalem. He saw what a person sees on sunny days in Jerusalem. A flaming dust covers the eye of the city, its walls and its houses and its inhabitants. Even a bird in the sky, even a dog in the street are covered with dust. You may have heard that the people of Jerusalem wear clothes of various hues, but their color cannot be seen because of the dust on them. And if that is true of normal years, how much truer of a drought year. From Jaffa Gate to Mahane Yehuda a pillar of dust ascends to the heart of the sky and covers the eyes of Jerusalem. And every house is like a box of dust. People walk around wrapped up, wiping their bleary eyes and groaning parched groans, like that parched earth of Jerusalem. A person takes one step and sinks into potholes and ditches of dust, he lifts his eyes up, a dusty sun dries the mucous in his eyes. The roads are full of pits and pocks, cracks and grooves, dirt and stones, and desolate lawns extend here and there. If not for carcasses of cats and dogs and reptiles and insects, Jerusalem would be like a desert and a bad smell bubbles up from the carcasses and all kinds of flies and mosquitoes swarm among the carcasses and they are wrapped in dust so you won't recognize them, so they come upon you suddenly and sting you. And the walls of the houses turn dark with excoriations, a boycott on secular schools and a boycott on libraries, a boycott on this one who excommunicated that one, and a boycott on that one who excommunicated this one. A person brings plasterers and plasters the walls of his house, and as soon as he pays for their work, all the walls are once again covered with excoriations. We thought that most of the excoriations were those of Reb Fayesh, and when Reb Fayesh got sick and his hands don't obey him, we know that his students have gone beyond him.

3 |

And here the sea of Jaffa cheers the heart and the green citrus groves gladden the eyes and the red pomegranate trees are suffused with a

loveliness of beauty like a sweet promise. Date palms sway in the
wind and ancient sycamores spread their shoots and give you shade.
And white houses basking in sun sit within the citrus groves, and
vineyards spread out into the distance, and every day they bring wet
grapes from the settlements, and every grape is like a glass of good
wine, and the grapes here are cheap. If you want, you get yourself
half a Rotel of grapes, and you sit yourself down in the shade of a tree
in the Baron's garden, and you pick a grape and eat it, pick a grape
and eat it. If you want, you climb a high hill and look down on Jaffa
the Belle of the Seas.

And Jaffa also has this advantage over Jerusalem, that everywhere you go there, you find comrades. You go into a café and you
find the activists of the Yishuv and you hear how the deeds of the
Land are done. Sometimes Mordechai Ben-Hillel Ha-Cohen comes
in. Mordechai Ben-Hillel isn't one of those who sits in a café, but between one assembly and another, he comes in and sits at the head
and tells what he said to Deputy Minister So-and-So in Petersburg,
and what the Russian Consul in Jerusalem said to him, on the day
he came to him adorned with all the medals he had received from
the government, and it seems to you that the world is revolving right
in front of your eyes. You go into a restaurant and no one turns up
his nose because you're a painter, for here a craft honors those who
practice it. Sons of good families who practice a craft beautify the
craft. While in Jerusalem, the educated people preach in praise of
crafts and welcome the labor leaders, but a simple laborer doesn't see
a welcome. Great is a craft so long as you don't smell the smell of its
sweat. And it is no wonder, a city that heard that a vocational school
is banned and excommunicated, how will it honor a craft. Therefore,
all artisans in Jerusalem are lowly in the eyes of the folks, and lowly
in their own eyes, and they don't see an hour of satisfaction and not
a voice is heard singing at their work. And the students of Bezalel,
who should have brought Isaac close to them, stay far away from him,
so that painter will not be counted as one of them. Isaac still remembers that artist he met in Jerusalem when Isaac asked him about
his fellow artisans, the housepainters, and he looked at him as some
triviality that doesn't deserve to be looked at.

CHAPTER NINE

Happy People

1 |

On the eve of the Sabbath, before dark, Isaac went down to the sea, as the people of Jaffa are wont to do, to bathe in honor of the Sabbath. He found a few of his comrades. Some stood naked and warmed themselves in the sun, and some split the blue waves, this one lay supine and that one lay on his side, this one suddenly disappeared into the mighty waters and floated up again to the surface of the water, and that one grabbed his comrade by the heel as if he wanted to drown him, but his comrade overcame him and rode on his shoulders, and the two of them rose up like a two-headed creature. Meanwhile, a third jumped onto their backs, raising both hands up, as if he were holding up the sun so it wouldn't fall into the sea. Thus they played like Gymnasium students who don't have the yoke of a livelihood on them, for from Friday afternoon until Sunday morning, they were free from work.

Said one to his comrade, It's good that there's the Sabbath in the world, isn't it. Said his comrade, If the Sabbath day is good I don't know, but the eve of the Sabbath is certainly good. Said he, If there were no Sabbath, there would be no Sabbath eve, would there. Said he, Aren't you from the Lida Yeshiva, where they teach Talmud through logic. Said he, And you who didn't learn Talmud, there isn't a trace of logic in your skull, is there.

Between this and that, the sun sank and fell into the sea. The gate of the west turned red and the waves of the sea grew bigger. The sea uttered a sound, and within the sound was silence. The sea brought up foam and the foam covered the tops of the waves, which changed their hues like that world between heaven and earth and between sea and firmament. And the heaven and the earth also changed their nature, and hidden yearnings began permeating the space of the world, yearnings that aren't grasped by any of the five senses, but the heart grasps them because it is part of those yearnings. Everyone who was in the water separated from the waves and came up, dried himself off and got dressed, every single one with his beard shaved and his moustache trimmed, for before they went to the sea, they went to the barber.

They put on clean Sabbath clothes, cloth trousers with a white or gray or blue shirt. They belted their shirt, this one with a woven belt and that one with a leather belt. They put shoes on their feet, not camel skin ones and not torn ones, but light shoes like the shoes worn by strollers. On their head, this one put a straw hat and that one a cap. At that time, in the heavens above, the Sabbath candles were lit and their light was seen from the sea. Some members of the group recalled their mother's candles and some their father's table. Rhymes of Sabbath songs emanated from their heart and yearnings of yearnings surrounded the melody and became another melody, like those waves of the sea, which are the same as they were at first, but are heavier and bolder and gloomier than they were at first.

One laughed and said, You guys haven't eaten yet and you're already singing songs. Hey gang, let's go eat. Another one heard it and said, If you're hungry, go eat. And the first one answered, And you, you're not hungry? Said he, Whether I'm hungry or not, I'm willing to eat any time and any hour. This one got up and went to Levi Isaac and that one to Sussman, this one to Malkhov and that one to another restaurant, for our comrades were already used to celebrating their Sabbath in a restaurant, and even those who dined in their rooms every night, on the Sabbath they dined in the restaurant, for the restaurants in Jaffa are jolly on Sabbath nights. Don't look in the bowl to see if there is meat and fish in it or if there isn't meat and fish in it, but look at the joy between one bowl and the next. Everyone who can sing sings and all the rest assist him and bang a spoon or a fork like singers and musicians, until they get up from the table and move the chairs aside and dance, and continue into the street of the city. Other comrades of ours come from other restaurants and accompany them, dancing. Isaac who ordered his meal in his hotel which our comrades don't frequent, was sorry to sit alone, as on Sabbath nights in Jerusalem.

2 |

Behold, that hotel, of all places, was joyous. That night was the birthday of the owner's only daughter, who was born on the ship on the way to the Land of Israel and some of the passengers of that ship came to wish her happy birthday, and with them came the two ex-wives of Vittorio Lordswill. The owner brought out muscat wine and his wife brought fruit and sweets. They ate and they drank and they ate. And Masha Yesinovsky Lordswill, whom Lordswill the wonderful musician had courted for her fine voice, raised her voice and sang some splendid songs. And the princess Mira Ramishvili Lordswill, her friend, who had left her husband Prince Ramishvili for Vittorio Lordswill, got up and danced, and as she danced, she took her friend Masha and danced before her the dance of a bridegroom trying to please his bride, until sparks of fire sprayed from their eyes and from our eyes too. And Masha Yesinovsky Lordswill put her handsome head on the heart of Mira the princess, like a girl who puts her head on the heart of her lover. The sea roared and a wind came from the sea. The wind put out the candles and a sweet gloom swathed the space of the house.

Afterward, we went out to the balcony and from the balcony to the courtyard and from the courtyard to the street, and from the street we went into Levi Isaac's house, for there was great joy in Levi Isaac's hotel, where Michael Heilperin made himself a new suit of Lebanese silk, with a light blue belt around his waist and an immense straw hat on his head, and he danced in a circle they formed, and he held a dagger in his hand, the dagger he grabbed from the hand of an Arab who was about to kill him with it. His golden curls that had turned gray in a few spots were waving in the wind, and two blue fringes hung down from his hat below his neck, and his blond beard was neatly trimmed and came down to his long neck, and his blue eyes sprayed sparks of molten steel. Six kinds of dances he danced that night, until Mira came and put her big hand on his shoulder and danced with him the dance of the seven bayonets. And you, Hemdat, used to say that dancing was given only to the Hasids. But that moment, you shook your head and said, Great, great. A happy group we were in those days in Jaffa, the Belle of the Seas.

Hemdat shook his head and said, Great, great. Little by little, his eyes cooled down, like someone who sees a person approaching, and thinks it's his comrade, but when he gets to him he sees it isn't his comrade. Brenner sat with Aharon David Gordon, who came from Eyn Ganim on the Sabbath eve. Levy Isaac ran to and fro. And as he ran, he dropped a word here and a word there and his bald head gleamed, as if he were Heilperin and Mira and Brenner and Gordon all at the same time. Right away, said Levi Isaac to someone who didn't ask him for anything. Zhelde Zhlate, he called to his wife, Zhelde Zhlate, a cup of tea for comrade Brenner. Won't you spend the night here, comrade Gordon. Falk Shpaltleder explained the essence of dancing to Pnina. You see, Pnina, this thing, namely the dancing, in fact it's nothing but a result of the legs, but it raises the body to the level of the soul. A man walking aimlessly doesn't make an impression on us, he is one of thousands, tens of thousands, millions of people, for it is the nature of man to walk, just as on the other hand, man is wont to stand or sit or lie, for all those functions are in the nature of man. And yet let a man lift his feet and launch into a dance, then his spirit is exalted, and his soul soars so high that we say that all his limbs, all his body are transformed into soul, for thus the body was elated and his whole body became all soul.

Pnina wasn't listening. Her small eyes narrowed and her lashes meshed together, like a person making a bundle and tying up everything in it. Heilperin's golden curls and Mira's dark eyes suddenly merged into one face, and the sound of their feet answered, That's how we are, one face are we. Pnina opened her eyes wide and as she went on looking, she saw that it was true, Michael and Mira were one person. And they, that is he, his curls caress her cheeks and his eyes look at her with love. If not for Yael Hayyot's laughter, she could have stood like that to the end of her days. Pnina shut her small eyes so that vision wouldn't be swallowed up in that sight. And yet, from Yael's full lips rolled a jolly laugh. Shortly before that, Shammai whispered something to her, and now that she fathomed his meaning, she started laughing, and the whole delightful existence Pnina saw went off.

Gorishkin, our comrade in distress, sat and pondered, This Heilperin ascended to the Land when he was rich and, with his own money, he built a big flour mill in Nes Tsiona and taught his workers how to strike, the first strike in the Land of Israel. Heilperin lost his money and became a guard in the Herziliya Gymnasium. Events are in abundance here and there's no author to put them into writing. Brenner writes about the miserable and the bereaved, and all the other authors write as they are wont about beggars and Yeshiva students. In that generation, not all readers were happy with their stories, some complained about the authors, Why doesn't this author write like that author, and others complained, Why doesn't that author write like this author? But Gorishkin wasn't happy, because the authors leave the Land of our Resurrection and do dwell on the small towns of Diaspora.

In honor of Gordon, some began singing a song Gordon had composed against the zealots in Petach Tikva and against Yehoshua Shtemper, the leader of the zealots, who loathed the young workers who didn't follow the Torah. That Shtemper who had risked ascending on foot to the Land of Israel, and was blessed to be one of the first three founders who established the first settlement in the Land of Israel and defended it with his life against the Bedouins, and finally when they were about to establish a settlement of young workers next to Petach Tikva, he said it was better that German Gentiles settled near us rather than heretics. Gordon gathered his beard in his hands, as he was wont to do when his soul was upset, and said to Brenner, I hear, I hear. Said Brenner, An Englishman walks around in the streets of Jerusalem and addresses me in English, and it doesn't occur to that gentleman that these aren't English people here, and no one here understands English. Fortunately for him, I lived in London and I understand a little English and I answered him, even though it vexed me a bit, for am I obligated to understand his tongue. So is that nation, wherever they go, they imagine they're at home, for all the lands of the globe are theirs, only theirs.

Heilperin danced a new dance like a fellow who speeds up in the lightness of his movement, and when he came to Mira, she turned her face away from him and glanced behind her shoulder with a fondness for seduction, like a bride who urges her fiancé to follow her. And when he approached her and enjoyed seeing her, she slipped off and slid away, making her arm a kind of a bow and peeping at him from there. He jumped up and slipped his head through the bow of her arm and thus he danced.

Gordon stroked his beard and asked Hemdat, my prince, what do you say about that? Hemdat shook his head and said, Great, great. But his cold eyes revealed what was on his mind. Gordon gathered his beard in his hand and said, Never will I understand the heart of our youth. It's almost six years since I've been here in the Land of Israel, and at every time and every hour and everywhere I set foot, I see our fellows sad as mourners. Is it because of the short perspective visible to us from our work in the Land that you are sad, or is the suffering of your heart so much more important to you than our work in the Land of our Resurrection that you don't find a bit of solace for your souls in forgetting your personal troubles.

CHAPTER TEN

Continuation

1 |

Sonya came with Yarkoni. Isaac stood up from the bench and gave her his seat. Between Isaac and Sonya there was neither love nor hate, neither envy nor rancor. All the time they had been friendly with one another, they were close to one another, when they grew apart, they behaved like all the other couples who separated, that is, like people who have nothing to do with one another and have nothing for one another. Man has free will, if he wants to, he gets close, if he wants to, he goes away, and if they go away, that's not a tragedy, and if they chance to meet among folks, they don't make a comedy of running away from one another. Sonya had already stopped thinking of Isaac, and Isaac had stopped thinking of Sonya, and since he met Shifra, he no longer tried to get close to Sonya. Sonya didn't want to know Isaac's business, and Isaac, who was afraid at first that he would have to reveal it to her, wasn't afraid anymore, for Sonya was concerned with the whole world, but not with Isaac.

When she sat down, she raised her eyes and looked at him, as if she suddenly noticed him and said, You're still here? Isaac didn't know what to answer, whether to apologize to her for not having yet returned to Jerusalem or whether to agree with her that he was still here. He nodded at her and was silent. Sonya laughed and said, If I see you, it's clear that you're still here. As she talked with Isaac, she looked at Yarkoni.

Yarkoni was sad and was depressed. His heart was obviously remorseful and bitter. And just a little while ago, he was happy. Sonya sat and thought about several men she knew, the Russian journalist and Grisha, Rabinovitch and Isaac. Aside from Grisha that pest who was wont to be raging, no one had treated her like Yarkoni. She pouted and wanted to scold him. She recalled that moment when his hands were laid on her head and her head was laid on his heart and it seemed to her that in all the years that she had lived, there had never been a greater moment than that. The golden freckles on her cheeks began hopping and the thoughts of her heart began smiling, as if Yarkoni was still standing and stroking her hair. Not like one who wants to cool off, and not like one who strokes any girl who happens to be in front of him, but like a person whose deeds come from his affection. That time she humbled herself because of that marvelous existence, for she thought it would never stop. Suddenly it did stop and everything changed and by the time they left her room, she sensed that change. What caused that change? And how come he is so sad? He should have been happy. Once again she looked at him and once again she wanted to say something, not as she wanted to say at first, but just something that neither adds nor detracts. When she saw his face, she remained silent.

She turned her face from him and shut her eyes. His sad face vanished and that jolly youth was revealed to her, his delicate fingers trembling on her hair and his eyes smiling into her eyes, and she also smiled a secret smile. The golden freckles on her cheeks trembled and a hot veil was drawn over her cheeks. Why aren't you happy like me? Sonya wanted to ask and held her hand out to him to take his hand and put it on her heart. Look, she wanted to tell him, look at my heart trembling. She opened her eyes wide and was amazed that everything here was like all other nights. And nevertheless, there is a change here. Not because Michael Heilperin and Mira Ramishvili were dancing together, and not because Gordon and Brenner had happened by here, but because Yarkoni is here. In the distance, Hemdat appeared. Hemdat isn't happy either. Surely not because Shammai is playing with Yael, but because. . . Before she found a reason for it, she went back to thinking about Yarkoni. Like sad roses your lips will flower, no poet wrote that, but that was what she said about Yarkoni, and the golden freckles in her cheeks turned red as flame. And those lips, those sad roses, a short while ago, they had kissed her jolly lips.

Sonya stood up and waved her hands. It was the kind of wave her poor uncle made when he dined at her father's house and Father would pass him some treat so he would eat more. What is the meaning of that wave? Doesn't it mean, What will I do tomorrow when I don't have such a good treat? She sat down again. When she sat down her dreaming soul dozed off as if nothing had happened. What does that old man with the gray beret want, Sonya asked herself and looked at Gordon, and why is he stroking his beard, and what do all those fellows surrounding him see in him? She started worrying that Yarkoni would go to Gordon or to Brenner and leave her alone, she said to herself, I have to say something to keep him. She turned to Isaac and said, Did you thank Yarkoni yet? Yarkoni woke with a start and looked at her. Said Sonya, Yarkoni, the first night Kumer slept in Petach Tikva, he slept in your room, in your bed. Yarkoni shrugged, but looked amiably at Isaac, like a man saying, I didn't shrug at you. And once again his face became sad.

2 |

Seventeen years old was Yarkoni the first time he ascended to the Land and three years he spent in the Land and was one of the carefree fellows who had nothing whatever to do with the ideas our comrades are devoted to. If he found work, he worked. If he didn't, he wasn't sorry, for he got what he needed from his father and didn't need employers. When the days of his youth ripened and he began thinking about his future, he observed that it was impossible for him to cast his burden on his father all his life. Nor could he return to his hometown and go into business with his father, for if he had planned to be a merchant, he wouldn't have ascended to the Land of Israel. Nor did he want to go to Switzerland and enter a university. And even if he did, he wasn't prepared for that. There was nothing for him to do but be a laborer, but he had already experienced that and had seen that a Jewish laborer couldn't hope to make a living, for the employers prefer an Arab laborer to a Jewish laborer, for the Arab laborer is obedient, is used to work, and is cheap, while the Jewish laborer isn't experienced, doesn't accept authority, and doesn't give up his opinions. An example of that is Petach Tikva. About three thousand laborers work in Petach Tikva, two thousand eight hundred of them are Arabs, and two hundred are Jews. After our comrade Yarkoni examined everything that was before him, he decided to leave the Land and study agriculture.

At that period, Ruppin was already guiding the settlement effort in the Land. When Ruppin came the first time as a tourist, he saw that the land was weary and that the Jewish farmers of Judea, Samaria, and the upper Galilee grew old before their time. Those settlements were a score of years old and their founders had founded them in their youth, and because of hard work, old age had come upon them and they became negligent. And the sons who weren't imbued with the excitement or hope of their fathers, forsook the settlements and went to seek their fortune somewhere else. Some of them went to the city and some of them went Outside the Land. There are settlements that look like old age homes. To complain about the sons is impossible, for reality slapped their fathers in the face. They saw no reward for their toil and their hope was thwarted too. When they ascended from the Diaspora, they thought their will would stand them in good stead and they would cover the whole Land with villages and would make all the children of Israel ascend to the Land of Israel. And in the end, after twenty-five years of efforts, not one new settlement was added, and even what they succeeded in doing grew weak and came undone.

Said Ruppin, I don't see any cure for the Land unless we restore to the settlements the strength of their youth. And if we are poor in money, we are rich in people. Bring young people and train them in the farms we are making for them. When they get as much training as they need, they'll go to work in settlements and will form cooperative unions, every union of members who think alike, and they will vouch for one another. When each one sees himself as responsible for his comrades, a sense of responsibility with grow strong in him and he will devote himself to his work, and in the end, expert laborers will come out of them. Those experts examine every technical innovation and examine which ways of working are desirable for the settlement of the Land of Israel and the special qualities of the Jew. And since the laborers are young and they ascended to the Land on their own and of their own free will, the Land will become a source of blessing and a center of pure national life, and these laborers will serve as a model for others.

For that purpose, we need Jewish agronomists, who, along with their preparation and expertise, admit the existence of our nation and want the settlement of our Land, and know the soul of our fellows, and don't tend to prefer the Arab laborer to them because he is obedient or cheap. And what Ruppin demanded he carried out. He founded Kinneret and Degania. And some of our comrades began finding succor and work there. Some went to work immediately and some wanted first to study agriculture to prepare themselves for working the Land. Eliezer Yarkoni, who came from a well-off family and whose father supplied him with money to attend school, left for France to study there. When he completed his studies and thought about returning to the Land, he went to his hometown to see how his father and mother were. He found Raya, his cousin, a beautiful and charming maiden who still loved him from their youth. His heart was drawn to her and he gave her his pledge. He returned to the Land and waited for the day he would get a position and would bring his fiancée. He was appointed to a position. He went and telegraphed his intended to come. Sonya met him. Yarkoni, who was happy about the position and about his intended who was to come, smiled at Sonya, and Sonya, who was glad she found Yarkoni, smiled at him and invited him to her room. And since he was happy, he stroked her head and kissed her. When he realized what he had done, he was sad.

Sonya looked at him obliquely. She patted her hair and straightened the folds of her dress, as average people are wont to do if their soul is disheveled, they exchange their need for things that are secondary to the body. She took out a comb and a mirror and combed her hair. Yarkoni's reflection was seen peeping out of the mirror. She pursed her lips and looked at him interrogating and observing. She waved her hand in front of her face, as if she wanted to shift an expression of anger, and said, Dammit, we thought he threw himself in the sea, and it turns out he's walking around in Jerusalem dressed like a monk. That is simply ridiculous. Grisha a monk, Grisha a monk. A monk.

By now, everyone knew that story. For Silman had already come from Jerusalem and said that he had seen Grisha in the Russian Compound dressed as a monk. As Silman told Sonya, so he told others. Some of them were glad to get rid of that parasite who took his food from others and showed them his rage. And some of them were worried that if the Russians came to know him, they would reproach the Children of Israel for the deeds of that convert. Said Podolsky, Once upon a time, in our city, a reckless character changed his religion, the Jews were sad and the Gentiles were glad. There was one clever Gentile there. He told the Jews, You expelled filth and we took in filth.

Falk Shpaltleder came, stroking his beard, and asked, What are Jews talking about? Pnina, tell them what I told you. What? asked Gorishkin, straightened his shirt, pulled the tips of his moustache with the tips of his fingers, and looked at Pnina.

Zhelde Zhlate, Zhelde Zhlate, called Levi Isaac. Zhelde Zhlate shouted, What do you want from me, what do you want from me, you saw that character, all night long he shouts Zhelde Zhlate, Zhelde Zhlate, like he's scared I'll forget my name. Zhelde Zhlate, Zhelde Zhlate — again he shrieks. What do you want from me? Can I cut myself into a few pieces and throw them wherever you want? Zhelde Zhlate here, Zhelde Zhlate there. Zhelde Zhlate, shouted Shammai in Levi Isaac's voice. Zhelde Zhlate jumped up and came to Levi Isaac and shouted, What do you want, Levi Isaac? Levi Isaac replied, I don't want anything from you. Zhelde Zhlate said, He bleats like a beheaded heifer and in the end he says I don't want anything from you. Said Levi Isaac, By your life, Zhelde Zhlate, I didn't shout. Yael Hayyot laughed and hugged Shammai. Levi Isaac understood who had shouted here. He patted his bald head and laughed and said to Shammai, Young devil, what do you want from my Zhelde Zhlate? Shammai replied, I want your Zhelde Zhlate to be your shpouse and to sherve you.

Well, are you tired? Shpaltleder asked Heilperin. Heilperin opened his blue eyes and looked at him contemptuously. At last he replied with malicious placidity, Did I hear your lecture, that I should be tired? Said Shpaltleder, If you had heard it, you would have enjoyed it. Heilperin shrugged his shoulders and turned and went on his way, not because Shpaltleder was a pest, but because he had already stopped thinking of him. Who is that old man? asked someone, pointing to Gordon. There are no old men here, said Heilperin, we're all young. Levi Isaac, give us something and we'll drink a toast to all the young people here.

3 |

The house was filled to the rafters. Not everyone who came ate at Levi Isaac's table, and not everyone who ate at his table was a regular customer. But everyone who came in regarded himself as a member of the family, for Levi Isaac's hotel was open to every single person, whether he ate or whether he didn't. If a person wants to eat and there's nothing ready, he doesn't leave hungry, for with every customer, Levi Isaac adds water to the soup, not that he wants to get rich, but so as not to refuse someone who wants to eat. That night, people came from Petach Tikva and from Eyn Ganim and from Rehovoth and from Nes Tsiona, and from Be'er Yakov, along with the Jaffaites who are used to coming here when they see a lot of people. A big group gathered, for everyone who saw a large gathering saw a need to join them. And even though there were a lot of them, every one was known by name or nickname, like Father of Hair for his long hair and Father of Shirts because he took pride in his shirts at a time when nobody was fussy about clothing. And some called themselves by the name of the settlement where they found work. And just as the men were called by name or nickname, so were the girls. This one was called Bint Alla, that is Daughter of God, because of her beauty. And that one was called Ladybug, for once she found a flea and never in her life had she seen a flea, and she thought it was a ladybug, and they started calling her Ladybug.

Levi Isaac walked from one to the other, asked this one: Did you eat, did you drink, and before he could answer, Levi Isaac shouted out, Zhelde Zhlate, Zhelde Zhlate, give Father of Hair something to eat, Zhelde Zhlate, did Ladybug drink milk? Father of Shirts, did you take your medicine? Be'er Yakovite, have you made peace with the Georgians? And as for those he didn't find anything to say to, he just looked at them, as if to say, Even though I'm busy, I haven't forgotten you. Comrade Gordon, comrade Gordon, where is Gordon? Gordon went to Aronovitch. That day, Aronovitch received a package of books from Outside the Land, including books of Bible criticism, and Gordon was eager to see them, and so he went off quietly, so they wouldn't keep him.

Brenner stood up and said, *Kinderlakh, m'darf geyn aheym,* children, we've got to go home. Where is Hemdat? Hemdat had already left an hour earlier. Said Shammai, Gang, let's go to Hemdat's, I promise you we'll find a drop of wine at his place. Said Sonya, I heard that full bottles of wine are standing in his room in rows all along the wall. Isaac, isn't Hemdat from your hometown? Said Isaac, I met him here through you. Said Sonya, You see, Isaac, all good things come from me.

Sonya and Yarkoni and Yael Hayyot and Shammai and Isaac, too, slipped out of the hotel and were about to go. Pnina came and joined them and Gorishkin dragged along behind her. When they came to the Hill of Love, they parted from the group and stayed there.

CHAPTER ELEVEN

In Hemdat's Garret

1 |

Hemdat lived in his garret at the edge of Neve Tsedek at the edge of Jaffa. You go there from Neve Shalom through the houses of Zerakh Barnett until you get to the old school for girls. When you get there, you see some houses burgeoning out of the sand, including the ChaBaD study house on the right and the house of Rabbi Kook on the left. You walk between heaps of sand until you come to the new school for girls. When you get there, you see a row of small houses of the Akhva quarter. You turn right and you turn left. There you see a small house with a kind of garret on top, half of it floats on the house and half seems to flutter in the air. You enter the courtyard and go up to the garret, that's Hemdat's garret.

Our comrades in the Land of Israel call every roofed space a room. If its walls aren't split, they call it a fine room. But Hemdat's room is a room and in fact it is fine. He lives there all by himself, and it has five windows. In one window you see the big sea that has no end, and in another window you see the green citrus groves that have no measure, and in another window you see the valley where the train passes, and in another window you see the desert where Tel Aviv was built later on, and one window faces Neve Tsedek. And just as the room is fine outside, so it is fine inside. Its ceiling is made of boards, and its walls are painted green, and green curtains hang on the windows, and when a wind blows, the curtains wave like a fan. Real furnishings are there, a table and a chair and a sofa and a lamp and a kerosene stove, and a kettle and cups. A curtain is stretched over a corner of the room, and Hemdat's clothes are hanging behind the curtain. And there is no dust there. And that is no exaggeration, but the honest truth. And so Hemdat is fond of his room. He is especially fond of that small balcony in front of the room, which overlooks the valley where the train passes. The train meanders in the valley and the steam of the locomotive rises. And beneath the balcony a little garden is planted and a lemon tree grows there and a well is there. And the whole yard is surrounded by a wall, and in the daytime the sun dwells on it and at night there are shadows. And it is quiet there in the garden and in the yard. The landlady does her cooking, and her daughters sew dresses for themselves, and the landlord chants a Turkish melody from the songs of Reb Israel Nageara. There was another family there, an old man and his wife and their daughter, Germans from the remnants of the Templars. The old man was retired now and sits idly and writes letters to his relatives who have already died. And the daughter is preparing to go to her relatives in Germany, where a bridegroom is waiting for her, for the German fellows from Sarona and Wilhelmina and Jerusalem and Jaffa have deviated from the true path, and some of them go dancing with virgins, and so her parents are sending her to their homeland where there are still fellows who aren't flawed. And since the room and the balcony and the yard and the neighbors are nice and quiet, Hemdat doesn't make much noise either, and doesn't bring guests into his home. But if a guest comes to him, he puts on the kettle and makes coffee for him, or drinks a glass of wine with him, for wine and coffee are always found in Hemdat's house, for wine maketh glad the heart and coffee stirs one for work. And even though he doesn't do any work, the coffee doesn't move from his house, for if he gets work, he wouldn't have to go looking for coffee.

And so, our comrades went off to Hemdat. And Sonya hurried them on and told them not to dawdle, for she was yearning to see Hemdat's room, for she had heard a lot about it and hadn't yet seen it. They plodded along in the sand from the knolls to the valley and from the valley to the knolls. And since the road was hard, Yael linked her arm in Shammai's. And what Yael did with Shammai, Sonya wanted to do with Yarkoni. But not all minds are the same. Sonya wanted to link her arm with Yarkoni's arm, and Yarkoni wanted to walk alone. And so he took a few steps forward, pulling off a few hairs on his right arm, and didn't notice Sonya, or he did notice and pretended he didn't. Sonya bit her lip and stretched her empty hand toward Hemdat's garret and said, Dark, no light there. Yael pressed Shammai's arm and said, He's already sleeping.

Hush, children, hush, said Shammai. It's too bad he lives alone. If he didn't, we would have done to him what we did to Miltzman, who lived in Litvinovski's house. One night the whole Litvinovski family went to a concert and left Miltzman alone, for he had an attack of headache or liver or spleen or kidneys. We went to his house and found him sleeping. We tied him to the bed and took him with his bed to Mr. and Mrs. Litvinovski's bedroom. And when they came back from the concert and found him... Here Shammai started laughing and repeated, And found him... And again he started laughing until he and Yael were rolling in the sand. Said Sonya, Hold your tongue, man, you're waking up Hemdat. Shammai repeated, And found him... And laughed again. Yael put her hand on his mouth to cover the laughter. His lips tickled her hand and she started laughing too.

2 |

At that moment, Hemdat was sitting on the balcony in front of his room and looking into the gloom, where all kinds of shadows strolled among the trees in the garden. The shadows suddenly vanished and the figure of an old man rose up from the gloom. His face was long and his beard was big, made of one reddish-brown bloc, with a sable fedora on his head, one hand was on his heart, and a luster of modesty and humility emanated from him. One day before Passover a few years earlier, Hemdat dropped in on his old aunt Rebecca and found her waving a picture to shake off the dust. Hemdat looked and was amazed, for never in his life had he looked at a portrait of a man with such clear awareness. His aunt noticed that and said to him, This is a picture of Rabbi Nahman Krokhmal who made a book. And Hemdat didn't yet know that people made books, for he thought you take books from the case as you take flowers from the garden and wine from the cellar. When he grew up, that book fell into his hands, *The Guide to the Perplexed of our Time*. He read a few things in it that perplexed him. His spirit was struck and his questing soul awoke, and the gleam of the icon of Rabbi Nahman Krokhmal, who made that book, lighted his way. He ascended to the Land of Israel and didn't meet anyone who could discuss Rabbi Nahman Krokhmal or Rabbi Nahman Krokhmal's book. He forgot about the book and its author. Last night he went to Brenner's. He found him sitting sadly in front of his house. Brenner said to him, I recalled a summer I spent in Zolkov, and I recalled its friendly Jews who were a bit childish and a bit lyrical and festive, who attract the heart like a legend with their fantastic simplicity, and among them, one stands out, Rabbi Nahman Krokhmal, a giant of a man. Indeed I long to write a few chapters on that giant. Not a big tome filled with troubles on the anomaly in our lives, but to unfurl a bit the scroll of a human life who was endowed with the spirit for profound investigation of the spirit of the nation, and who could truthfully observe its qualities. If I had a style befitting that, I would approach the task. Now that Hemdat sat alone, he recalled Rabbi Nahman Krokhmal, for all our literature that came after him is like an evening prayer after Neila, the closing prayer of Yom Kippur. Hemdat's soul was filled with sublime longings, like the soul of a son of Israel when he recalls the great men of Israel.

Hemdat woke with a start at the young people's shouts of joy. Where am I, Hemdat whispered to himself, as if he were afraid he would wake himself up. He wrinkled his brow and looked straight ahead. His hometown Shibush appeared to him with the old study house and the waters of the Stripa flowing slowly between two forests. And once again he skipped from that Jaffa and that neighborhood he lived in, and Rabbi Jacob Goldman comes and calls to him, and they stroll together, as he used to walk with the elders of his hometown. Rabbi Jacob Goldman doesn't talk about research or about Hasidism, for never in his life did he even look at the original *Guide to the Perplexed,* and in his eyes the Hasidim are among those who make the ideal real, for they set their sights on the mediating deeds. But he offers him an interpretation of the Mishnah and clarifies his doubt about whether Jaffa is sanctified with the sanctity of the Land. And even though his doubt deprives Jaffa of sanctity, he is fond of his words, for Hemdat regretted not feeling in Jaffa what a son of Israel should find in living in the Land of Israel, and he used to place the onus on himself. When he heard the doubt of Rabbi Jacob Goldman, he was relieved, for if he dwelt in city in the Land of Israel, he would feel the holiness of the Land. And once again he was transported to his comrades who mock him for making up a Land of Israel that doesn't exist in reality. He put his head in his hands to hide his face from his comrades. Shammai and Yael and Sonya and Yarkoni came, along with Isaac Kumer, Hemdat's compatriot.

3 |

Said Yael, You're sitting in the dark. What shall I reply to her, thought Hemdat, and didn't reply at all. Said Shammai, Where's your lamp? Said Hemdat, It went up in flame. Said he, Then, light a candle. Said Hemdat, If a candle, we have to search for candles, and candles I don't have. Said Shammai, Gang, I tell you, this person is awed by the Sabbath. Said Yarkoni, Hemdat, we heard you've got wine in your house. Give us a drop and we'll drink. Hemdat went into his room and brought out wine.

Yarkoni made peace with his soul. After all, Raya didn't see me kiss Sonya, and I'm not obligated to tell her. I take on my work and I'll bring Raya, and everything between me and Sonya will be forgotten, just like the affairs I had in Paris were forgotten. A person has to forget what should be forgotten, otherwise it's impossible to exist. As he pondered to himself, he looked at Isaac. Could it be true, what I heard, that there was something between Sonya and Kumer? But Yarkoni isn't one of those who lets his bad mood dominate him for long. He got rid of his jealousy and started thinking about the position he was appointed to and about Raya his intended who was to come to him. He was content and was sorry he had grieved Sonya. When he looked at her, he saw her eyes gazing at Hemdat. What do I care if her eyes gaze at Hemdat? Yarkoni asked himself and poured himself a glass and drank it at one gulp, bending his head back and supporting it with his left hand, and called out, L'haim to Hemdat, To your health. After he emptied his glass, he turned toward Sonya and said, If I had another glass I would drink a toast to you. Sonya offered him her glass. He took the glass, raised it toward Isaac, and said,

L'haim Mr. Kumer, here's to Mr. Kumer. Isaac clutched his glass in a panic, touched it to the edge of his lips and answered, L'haim to you. Yarkoni looked around and asked, To whom shall we drink a third glass? Said Sonya, Enough, Yarkoni, you've had enough. Said Yarkoni, I wish it would be as you say, Sonya. What did you tell me, Sonitshka, who spent the night in my room? Ah, Mr. Kumer. Isaac was confused and stammered, This is how it was, that day when I came to Petach Tikva, Yedidya Rabinovitch took me to your room and I slept for less than half a night. Yarkoni picked up a bottle of wine and said, To Rabinovitch, to Rabinovitch, L'haim. L'haim, answered Isaac, and hunched his shoulders as if he suddenly felt a shudder.

They sat and drank one glass and two glasses and three glasses, and Hemdat sat and told stories about the first sages of Galicia. Hemdat was from a small town once full of Torah and wisdom, and even though it is emptied now of its learning, vestiges of aspirations still permeated it and the old men of the generation who still knew the first sages loved to tell about them, and Hemdat would sit and listen and put one tale together with another, and when he encountered people who wanted to hear, he would sit and tell them.

From the first sages, Hemdat came to the sages who came after them, who were lesser than them, but were greater than those who came after them. From them Hemdat came to Velvl Zbarazher, and to Reuben Asher Broydes, and the other writers and poets. From Velvl Zbarazher and Broydes, he came to Eleazar Rokakh. For when Eleazar Rokakh wandered Outside the Land to win souls for the settlement of the Land of Israel, he dropped in on Hemdat's hometown and Hemdat heard a lot of things from him about the people of Jerusalem and the people of Safed, who look like imaginary creatures today, for the generations have changed and everything that was simple and usual and common in generations past looks exaggerated and outlandish to us. From days gone by, Hemdat came to the Land of Israel in this time and told some adventures that had befallen him. When did these adventures befall me? he asked himself. And as he went on telling, it was clear to him that all those adventures did indeed befall him, but he didn't know when. But the mystery of the date wasn't a reason to deny them. This is what befell me, this is what befell me, Hemdat said to himself, as if to remove the doubt from his heart, and went on telling tales of things he had seen in a dream, as if they were real events. Yael was irritated, You never told me those things. I'm probably not important or worthwhile in your eyes. And to show him that he wasn't important in her eyes either, she turned her face away from him and took Shammai's head in her arms.

4 |

The moon still stood in the firmament. But the footsteps were already heard of people rising early for prayer and going to the study house. Said Shammai, We should envy them, now that we've emptied all the wine, the Sabbath blessing of the wine is in store for them. Said Sonya, Did you hear, Yael, he lies in your arms and envies others. Yael glared at her. Sonya thought to herself, Too bad Hemdat doesn't see those eyes that make her face ugly. Yarkoni looked at Sonya and grimaced. Isaac thought to himself, Now when I'm having a good time, Shifra is sitting alone and forlorn. He resolved to return to Jerusalem right after the Sabbath. But not every trip we plan on the Sabbath comes to pass. Thus this trip. He thought of going right after the Sabbath and the Sabbath went out and he didn't go.

CHAPTER TWELVE

In the House of Reb Fayesh

1 |

In the house of Reb Fayesh there is quiet and silence. In the house, there is no one but Reb Fayesh and Reb Fayesh's wife and Reb Fayesh's daughter. Gone were the days when the Guardians of the Walls would gather in Reb Fayesh's home and Reb Fayesh would sit at the head with his head leaning on his left arm and his eyes sleeping and seeing everything in the heart of every single one of them, and when he opened his mouth everyone shrank without a word in awe and trembling and sweat, and the house of Reb Fayesh was so full they would sit on Reb Fayesh's bed. Now Reb Fayesh himself lies on that bed and everyone stays away from the house of Reb Fayesh, for Reb Fayesh has already abandoned the world and the world has abandoned Reb Fayesh.

Rebecca sits at the window and knits a white Kippa, which she meant at first to make for her father, for all he has are black velvet Kippas and he looks strange in them, for everyone here wears white Kippas. But before she could finish her work, her father had gone to Safed, and Reb Fayesh got sick and all his Kippas have become tattered from lying down in them. She went back to knitting the Kippa for her husband. Rebecca sits with her work. Sometimes she wipes her eyes and sometimes she wipes her eyelids. Across from her sits Shifra, and polishes the Etrog box, which is about to be pawned, for ever since the day Reb Fayesh got sick, a curse fell on income, and expenses increased, and Isaac, who used to ease their needs, had gone to Jaffa and didn't come back.

There they sit, the mother and the daughter, one busy at her work and her grief and the other busy at her work and her grief. And even though they should have gotten used to their grief because it is old, they can't resign themselves to getting used to it. They both turn their head to the sick man and their eyes encounter one another. A groan rises from their heart and they sigh and complain, this one sighs and complains about that one and that one sighs and complains about this one, that the time has come to get used to troubles, so why does she rouse the heart with her moans.

Reb Fayesh lies on his bed and doesn't notice. His ascetic face had grown fat and his eyes were sunk in their orbits, and two lines of encrusted fat were hanging under his eyes. The wrath of his eyes had vanished, and a kind of mute panic lay on his face, and his whole being was like a dumb, mindless creature. Rebecca raises her eyes and looks at the husband of her youth. How did he change so much, and how did he come to that? Rebecca represses the moan in her heart, so as not to stir her daughter's anger, and she doesn't know that a moan already rose from her heart. She complains about Shifra as if she started moaning first. If I moan, she moans, and if I don't moan she moans. In either case, alas. At that moment, Shifra is pondering and saying to herself, If I moan she moans, and if I don't moan she moans. This one raises her head to the sick man, and that one raises her head to the sick man, a moan blurts out of the heart of this one and a moan from the heart of that one. The women look reproachfully at one another, Once again you moaned, once again you moaned, the time has come to get accustomed and not to stir the heart every once in a while. As they looked at one another, Shifra stood up and went to her mother and put her head on her heart and said, Good mother, good mother, let me weep with you, and they weep on one another, as this one wipes the tears of that one, and that one wipes the tears of this one, until their tears dry up and they have no more strength to weep. This one returns to her work to make a Kippa for her husband, for all his Kippas have become tattered from lying down, and that one returns to polishing the Etrog box, which is about to be pawned. Rebecca thinks to herself, A person gets older every day and every day a person comes closer to his end. Not as he was yesterday is he today, and not as he is today will he be tomorrow. Yesterday he was like a wet garden and today even the stick he leans on is dry in his hand. Yesterday they rocked him in a cradle, and today he goes to get himself a grave. Today he walks around on his feet, and tomorrow he will be carried on their shoulders. She looks at her husband and is shocked at her thoughts.

2 |

Shifra sees all that grief and doesn't complain about her mother anymore, but she does complain about Isaac, for until Isaac came, they lived serenely, and she behaved like all other modest daughters of Israel, but when Isaac came, her mind was distracted. If she wants to turn her mind to her mother or her father or her Father in Heaven, this one comes and reduces that love, which exalted and elevated her. Why did he come, Shifra complains and grumbles, why did he come, Shifra growls in her heart. And since she knows that he did well to come, she complains and protests, If he did come, why did he go? And if he went, why doesn't he come back? She removed her anger from him and then went back to being angry at him, for he was the cause of all those effects. She was appeased about him a little, and she complained about herself, for she caused that herself, and in the end she places all that blame on him. For if she hadn't paid attention to him, he wouldn't have had a pretext to approach her. And when she realized that, she grumbled about him again, for just because she paid attention to him, just for that it was his fault.

The cares of her soul paralyzed her hands. Now all the household affairs are cast onto her mother. She turns Father over and washes him, she makes the fire and cooks and runs to the market to get a tiny bit of meat from the butcher, and if she happens to buy a chicken, she runs by herself to the ritual slaughterer to slaughter the chicken. Aside from those jobs, she roasts coffee for her neighbors for a small profit. If Shifra has any free time to do something, she does what isn't necessary or what isn't necessary at the time. And even those things, she abandons before they are done. As Shifra treated housework, so she treated her body in dressing and feeding it. She didn't comb her hair and she didn't change her dress and she didn't eat at mealtimes, and when she noticed that, she changed one dress for another and then another, and she combed her hair several times a day, and she ate more than usual. If she noticed that she would glare straight ahead, as if to show the one who stands over her, to tell him, See what I have come to because of you. And when she saw that he wasn't here, she would look into the void and wipe her eyes, like someone wiping his eyes to prepare them to see, but she saw nothing except her fingers wet with tears. Once she thought she saw him in a crowd of people. She wanted to turn her face away from him. But what was he doing, wherever she turned he was standing and chuckling, like that crowd whose faces look like one another and he looks like them too.

Shifra got up from her chair and sneaked out so he wouldn't hear and wouldn't follow her. She came and sat at the cistern. She lowered her head and put her hands on the mouth of the cistern. A tepid wetness rose from the water and a kind of dizziness took hold of her. She was startled and shouted in a hoarse voice, He's bathing in the sea, and she shut her eyes so as not to look at him. She saw a reflection of a man and heard the sound of footsteps. That reflection donned flesh and took on a voice and said, Did you hear, Mendel Tokay, the upholsterer, is divorcing his wife. Why? Because he found another one more beautiful than she. He went to Jaffa to get seaweed and there he saw a woman and is getting rid of his wife to marry her. You're shaking, Shifra, you have a cold. Go inside and don't sit on the cistern.

Shifra returned home and sat perplexed. In her limbs, she noticed neither cold nor heat, but her heart oppressed and weighed on her like a kind of harsh dream that weighs and presses. She woke with a start and saw that there was nothing here but a dream. She regretted that there was nothing here but a dream. She raised her hands and looked at her fingers as if Isaac's hands still held them. She shrieked from her heart, Why don't you come? Says her heart inside her, He's in Jaffa now, among Zionists who have forgotten God, and surely he has also forgotten me. Father in Heaven, how is it possible to forget You? She sat down and wept for him and for herself and for the whole world who have forgotten God. Shifra said to herself, I won't forget my God, who in His mercy for me gave me a mind to return as long as I have not sunk into the abyss of sin. I shall repent,

I shall repent, and when Yom Kippur comes, I won't move from the synagogue and I shall pray all the prayers in the prayer book, those I usually pray and those every Saint and Hasid prays, and if it is Your will, Master of the Universe, and You send me my mate, I shall fast on my wedding day, and You in Your great mercy, do not remember the thoughts I thought ever since the day I met the fellow and do act as if I hadn't thought any thoughts. As she talks to her Father in Heaven, she gets up and goes to her father. She caresses his brow and wipes his mouth, Reb Fayesh moves his lips. Said Shifra, Father, did you say something to me? Her father looks at her with frozen eyes. She is shocked and shouts, Woe is me, Father, that this befell you for my sins.

She began to make an accounting of the days. When did she meet Isaac, before or after her father got sick? And it turned out that Isaac already came and went in their house before her father got sick. Shifra raised her hands and said, My God, my God, do good to me, and don't bring down this man for all the evil he has brought on us. The Lord did good to her and spoke with her from her heart and said to her, Don't be a fool, Shifra, all that is done is done from My mind and My will, and you mustn't complain either about yourself or about Isaac. Shifra replied, If only it were so. She went back to her work as she was taught and took up the yoke of the house and didn't let her mother do anything. Her mother noticed that and the eyes of her mercy accompanied her movements and she prayed for her. God heard her prayer and gave her her heart's desire. Whether for good or for bad will be clarified in the following chapters.

CHAPTER THIRTEEN

On the Sabbath Day

1 |

Isaac returned to his hotel. That air prevailed in the house that prevails in new hotels on the Sabbath morning. The hotel owners hadn't yet gotten out of bed because the guests get up late, and the guests get up late because today is the Sabbath and they don't have anything to do. But it isn't like that in other inns, where everyone gets up early on the Sabbath, Hasidim to immerse at dawn and Mitnagdim for prayer, and average people sit over a cup of hot tea and read Scripture, twice in the original and once in the Aramaic Targum.

On the table in the corridor stood a sooty lamp with overturned glasses and empty bottles and almond shells and date pits left over from the little girl's birthday party, and buttons that dropped off and flowers that withered were scattered on the floor and a smell of dampness came from the sea and a smell of burned kerosene bubbled up from the kitchen. The hotel owners didn't abstain from lighting the samovar on the Sabbath, but they also put a kettle on the stove from the Sabbath eve, either for a guest who was used to Sabbath tea or because everybody does that. At that moment, Isaac longed for two things, for a cup of tea and for a bed. Since they hadn't yet set the table, he went into his room and stretched out on his bed.

He found someone lying in his bed. Isaac took pity and didn't make him get up and was afraid to take another bed lest the owner of that bed would come and make him get out of it. The sleeping man woke with a start and looked around in alarm like a baby. Isaac, too, was scared that he had woken a sleeping man out of his sleep. That man said to Isaac, Is this your bed? My horse took sick and I went to get doctors and I was tired and lay down. Isaac recognized him as fat Victor, whom he had seen in the market of Petach Tikva when he went with his comrade Rabinovitch to look for work. Said Isaac, Lie down, sir, lie down. Victor turned his face to the wall and started snoring, his hands clenched like a sleeping baby, the smell of the stable and the smell of soap emanating from him. Tears came to Isaac's eyes and he thought in his heart, Everyone needs pity, and a person needs to pity his fellow man. Too bad a person doesn't see his fellow man at a time when he needs pity. That day when I went out with Rabinovitch to look for work, Victor didn't notice us because he didn't look at us. If he had looked at us, he would have hired us, and I would have stood on the ground, and Rabinovitch wouldn't have left the Land and would have married Sonya, and I would have looked at the world with proper eyes. He left the room and went back to the dining hall. They are still sleeping, whispered Isaac, and went into the kitchen to pour himself tea. He saw that the water had evaporated. So, he went out. And so, mumbled Isaac, today is Lydia's birthday, and she was born on the ship to the Land of Israel, and some of the passengers of that ship came to congratulate her parents, and Lordswill's two ex-wives danced in her honor, and afterward we went to Levi Isaac's and we found Michael Heilperin dancing because he had made himself new clothes. Afterward we drank wine at Hemdat's, and the wine needs to be blended, and they haven't yet lit the samovar. He left and went on his way.

The sun wasn't yet at its height and a quiet light illuminated the firmament. And within the silence, the voice of the sea was heard, and a kind of blue reflection fluttered in the air. No one was outside. Those who got up in the morning were sitting in the prayer house, and those who hadn't yet gotten up were lying in their bed. What Bible chapter are they reading today? Here is an Arab coffeehouse. Those Arabs know how to make coffee, I'll go in and drink a cup of coffee. As he is about to go in, he considers and goes to Sweet Foot.

2 |

The door of the hut was open, and Sweet Foot was lying on his bunk, wearing his clothes and holding an American journal. Who's here? he asked and scowled at the visitor. Said Isaac, I don't mean to disturb you. So, said Sweet Foot, as a person saying, So, why did you come? Sweet Foot's dog jumped on him and started barking at him. Sweet Foot got out of bed and said to the dog, *Gey in dayn ru areyn* (Go rest). The dog shrank off to his bed under the bench. Sweet Foot smiled and said, Such a clever dog, understands every word and is obedient. If only human beings would understand and obey like he does. That Rabbi's wife, you tell her one thing and she understands the opposite. Last night she came back. To consult about match-making she came. Some Hungarian is clinging to her and wants to marry her. I told her, Well that's good. Said she, Why do I need him? I told her, If you don't want him, don't marry him. Said she, My love, let's go to Cairo and have a good time. I told her, I don't want to go to Cairo or to have a good time. She said to me, Well then, what do you want? I told her, What I want I know. She said to me, Tell me what it is. I told her, At any rate, it isn't what you want. Said she, Why don't you want what I want? I didn't answer her at all. She wept all night and kept the dog from sleeping, so he's irritated. But maybe you haven't eaten today? Sit down and eat. I read a great story in this jour-nal. A Duke went to war. A sword hit his nose and cut it off. The duke remained without a nose. He said to his doctor, Take as much gold as you want from my treasury and make me a nose. The doctor went out and found a pauper. He told him, Give me your nose for the duke and I'll give you so-many gold Dinars. The pauper thought it over, here he was, a pauper without even a grain of snuff, and here the duke was giving him a lot of money for his nose. He consented and agreed to give him his nose. The doctor took out his scalpel and cut off the nose and stuck it on the duke's face. And because the poor man loved the duke, the nose stuck to him and they became one flesh. Eventu-ally, the pauper died. That nose started rotting and dropped off. Why? Because the pauper's love for the duke ceased with the pauper's death. As long as he was alive and his sympathy for the duke was alive, the nose was also alive, when he died the sympathy ceased and the nose dropped off. Look how the dog is upset. He wants to come out but doesn't dare. Sweetiepie, if you have to come out, come out.

Sweet Foot said to Isaac, There is a lot of food here that the Rabbi's wife brought, sit down and eat. What do you think about the

Hungarians, Isaac? I don't know many of them, aside from that upholsterer who is wooing the Rabbi's wife. That man comes to me and
tells me, That woman, I want to marry her. I told him, If so, that's
good. He said to me, What's good here, she doesn't want to. I told
him, If so, that's no good. He said to me, If she gave in to my pleas
that would be good. I told him, If so, that's good. He said to me, How
can you say that's good, after all, I've got a wife. I said to him, If so,
that's no good. Said he, I could get rid of her with a divorce. I said to
him, If so, that's good. He said to me, Her marriage terms cost a lot.
I said to him, If so, that's no good. He said to me, If I marry the Rabbi's
wife, she can pay my wife for her marriage terms. I said to him, If so,
that's good. He said to me, What's good here, the Rabbi's wife won't
listen to me. I said to him, If so, that's no good. He said to me, If you
plead with her, she'll listen to you. I said to him, Why should I plead
with her? Said he, To do a favor for a Jew. I said to him, If she's good
for you, I don't know, but it's clear as day that that woman you're divorcing will get a good deal. He said to me, How come my wife is
closer to you than I am? I said to him, Because she's your wife. Said
he, If I'm so important to you, plead with the Rabbi's wife for me. I
said to him, She doesn't listen to me. He said to me, You're telling
me, all this time she doesn't stop praising you. I said to him, Many
times I told her, Sister, don't bother coming to my house, and she
doesn't listen and she comes. His face turned yellow and he started
shouting, That's strictly forbidden, she's your ex-wife and you're forbidden to be alone with her. I said to him, Don't get mad, Reb
Mendel, anger is idolatry. He said to me, Boor, you're teaching me,
I was one of the outstanding Yeshiva students. I said to him, Too bad
for that man who didn't remain a Yeshiva student. He said to me,
What's too bad here? I said to him, If you had remained a Yeshiva
student, your wife wouldn't have had to take care of husbands. He
said to me, Husbands you say, why? She has only one husband. I said
to him, And even he is too much. He said to me, How do you dare
tell me to my face I'm too much. I said to him, Why, if you want to
get rid of her, it means that you see yourself as superfluous for her.
He said to me, And you, why did you divorce the Rabbi's wife? I told
him, Better she's freed by a divorce and not by the death of the hus-

band, for if it's by the death of the husband, she's called a fatal female, and it is dangerous to marry a fatal female. As we talk, the Rabbi's wife comes. The Hungarian said to her, What are you doing here? Said she, And you, Mister Mendel, what are you doing here? Said he, To consult about us I came. She said to him, I too came only for that. Said he, And what does he say about that? Said she, Here he is right in front of you, ask him. He said to me, So? I said to him, I don't think that whole matter is nice. Why? You've got a wife, why do you need another one? Said he, What does it mean, why do I need another one? I'm divorcing the first one, aren't I? I said to him, And she agrees? Said he, Whether she agrees or not. Never in my life have I paid any attention to what women want. The Rabbi's wife shook a finger at him and said, Watch out, mister.

3 |

Isaac had a headache and wanted to go back to his hotel and close his weary eyes. But he didn't have the strength to go. He wrinkled his brow and put his hand over his eyes, thinking, What am I doing here and why didn't I go back to Jerusalem?

Jerusalem shrank to the size of a human eyeball and looked to him as it looks on the Sabbath morning. All the neighborhoods in Jerusalem go to the Western Wall. Some come from the southwest, and some come from the west of the city, some come from the north, and some come from the east, and some climb up to the top of the city from the south. All are wrapped in prayer shawls and dressed in Sabbath clothing. When they get to the Western Wall, they find several Minyans. One Minyan is reciting the morning prayers and one Minyan is reciting the Musaf prayers, one Minyan is reading the Torah and one Minyan is reading the excerpts from the Prophets, and the Priests are blessing the people in the morning prayer and the Musaf prayers. Some with the Volyn chants and some with the Lithuanian chants, some with ChaBaD chants and some with Karlin chants, some with Sadigura chants and others with all kinds of prayer chants, and between them all, some old men and young men who have already prayed are sitting on the benches and reciting Psalms.

Isaac has now forgotten that he is standing in Sweet Foot's hut in the sand of Jaffa, and it seems to him that he too is in Jerusalem. He gets up and goes to Nablus Gate, and from there, outside the Old City wall, and from there to the Hungarian Houses. And on his way he sees Shifra standing in the window, wearing her Sabbath dress. Isaac asks in a whisper, Shifra, why are you so sad? Shifra replies, You ask me, ask yourself. And even though she is sad, her voice is sweet. Isaac wants to stand still and listen. Suddenly the dog jumped on him and stopped him. Sweet Foot growled at him, Go rest, Sweetiepie. The dog didn't obey him and jumped up and went outside. Sweet Foot laughed and said, The world has stopped obeying me.

Said Sweet Foot, Abu Hassan sent for me. He wants to paint his house. But I can't go to him, for I already promised Shakhnai the surveyor to help him survey the roads to Gaza. But I can't go with him, because I already promised Goldman to go with him to Nablus, for the Pasha has appointed him engineer of all Nablus. But I don't want to go with him, because I don't like the Arabs who are idle as women and give their work to you like women, and after you do their job, they think they've done you a favor. Skin yourself alive, my love, and make me a nice fur. And since you flayed the skin off your flesh, the woman has turned her eyes to somebody else's skin. And so, that Effendi sent for me. If you want, go to him, but not today, for he hates a Jew who violates the Sabbath. What portion of the Bible are they reading today? You don't know either. It seems to me that we are at the chapter that starts, And Balak the son of Zippor saw all that Israel had done to the Amorites. Sweetiepie, what do you want? Isn't this our friend Isaac? Once, on the seventh day of Passover, in the morning, I was sitting on the ledge in front of the government office in Segera. I heard strange sounds like voices of Russians. How can there be Russians here? I pricked up my ears and I heard *Bokh ata elogey Abragam elogey Isaak and elogey Yakov*. I went in and saw a congregation of Russkies wrapped in prayer shawls and I knew they were converts. Some of them came to Saul Cohen, that ardent Zionist Saul Cohen, who later went to Australia, and asked him to go up to the stage to read the Torah. He shrugged his shoulders and didn't want to go up. He said, Am I religious that I should go up to the stage.

Hemdat was there. He grabbed Saul Cohen and didn't let go of him until he went up to the stage and blessed them with the Priests' Blessing and the Russkies answered Amen at the top of their voices. If they hadn't been converts, I would have been scared they would make a pogrom there. The Holy-One-Blessed-Be-He watches over His world. If Jews don't want to pray he puts a spirit in Russkies and they convert and they form a Minyan and they pray and they force a heretic to go up to the stage. What was I talking about? That Arab. If we don't distinguish between Sabbath and weekday, the Gentile says, To me, you are contemptible. You see, Isaac, when I was in Jerusalem, I didn't profane the Sabbath. And when I saw a man committing a transgression in Jerusalem, I was amazed, can a person commit a transgression in Jerusalem. In truth, I don't know what a transgression is. But when I want to do something and my heart tells me don't do that, I know there is a transgression here. I ask myself, if this is a transgression, why do I desire to do it? Since I ponder, I don't do it, and since I don't do it, my heart is at peace, as if I did something good. And I still don't know what is good here, but I do know that peace of heart is a good thing. And so I refrain from everything that looks to me like a transgression. And if so, the Commandments may be the same, for a Commandment is doing, and doing drives out peace. If I have a chance to do a Commandment, and I do it, nevertheless peace doesn't leave me, on the contrary it increases, not the peace of Sit still and don't do anything, but peace that stirs the soul. And here is the amazing thing, if it's peace, it's not stirring, and if it's stirring it's not peace. And even though there is something and its opposite here, I reach a state of equanimity. If so, why don't we do Commandments and why do we transgress? This is a question and I don't know how to answer it. And I'm sure, I shall leave the world full of transgressions. You see, Isaac, when a man is dead, his nose, worth all the gold in the duke's coffers, will rot and drop off. And here, Sweet Foot grabbed his nose and started laughing, Ha ha ha. And he immediately changed his voice and said sadly, What good is sympathy if the strength of will is dead?

The hut began to heat up and the junk in the hut glowed and a hum of boredom hummed in the hut. The food in the hut smelled and a coarse fly came to the hut and pestered Isaac. Isaac hit his own face and his nose. Sweet Foot looked and said, He heard a rumor and came. For Mr. Kumer doesn't love the prince and isn't ready to give him his nose. And you, Isaac, you want to return to Jerusalem. Sweetiepie, a fly is pestering Isaac and you're silent? The dog heard and jumped on Isaac. Sweet Foot shook his finger at him and said, You, dog's brain, I tell him, Hit the fly who's hitting Isaac, and he hits Isaac who was hit by the fly.

CHAPTER FOURTEEN

Miracles

1 |

Ever since the day Isaac went down to Jaffa, Shifra hadn't heard a thing from him. Shifra could have known everything about him, but she had already forbade him to write her because of slander. But the slander didn't stop anyway. When folks get their teeth into a Jewish girl, they don't let go of her.

Mystifying and mysterious are the ways of the neighbor women. Some turn angry faces to her, and some twist their faces at her, and some pretend to be friendly and tell her stories to make her tell them stories. Oh, God, what is there to tell here? Once upon a time, a fellow sailed in the same ship with her grandfather to the Land of Israel. Later he came to visit him. Her grandmother welcomed him warmly. The fellow started coming and going as a member of the family. Once on a dark night she met him outside and he took her hand in his and told her things, and whenever she thinks about them, she feels good, but she is sad. And that's impossible to fit together, if she feels good why is she sad, and if she is sad, why does she feel good?

2 |

Rebecca recognized that something had happened here. Sometimes Shifra is sad and sometimes she is hasty. Rebecca knows it is all because of that painter, for ever since the day he started coming and going in her house, Shifra's nature changed. But now that he went away, why should she be sad? Perhaps she did set her sights on that fellow as the neighbor women say? In truth, he is a decent fellow and a lot of favors he did for them, and if not for him whom the Holy-

One-Blessed-Be-He sent, they would have perished. At any rate, things are hard to fit together. And if Fayesh is sick, is the whole world lawless? If he were healthy, he would tear out her hair and yank her out of that fellow's hands. When Rebecca recalls everything Fayesh was liable to do to her daughter she was filled with pity for her.

A neighbor woman says to Rebecca, That Russian is a heretic. Says Rebecca, I won't be in his hell. Says the neighbor woman, He has set his sights on your daughter. Says Rebecca, Oh, God, aren't there Russian girls, that he has to woo Shifra? Says the neighbor woman, I ask the same thing, at any rate, you have to do something. Says Rebecca, What shall I do? Fayesh is sick and I am only a woman. Says the neighbor woman, If you're a woman, you're a mother, too, and if you want your daughter's good, you have to do something. Says Rebecca, What shall I do? Says the neighbor woman, There's a lot to do, and I am saying only a little. There's a herb in Jerusalem, if you put it in a glass of tea, you can cancel love. Once upon a time, there was a man from Istanbul whose daughter was offered a match, a fellow from Bukhara. Once the fellow came to his aunt and said to her, This girl, who is she? She told him, She's the daughter of Hakham Nissim. He told her, I like her. The aunt came to Hakham Nissim's house. He said to her, Sit down, and she sat. Many things she told. Afterward, she said, I got a fellow at my house and he wants your daughter. And he's a good match. Said Hakham Nissim, If it came from the Lord, it will be good; but we have to ask the girl. Hakham Nissim asked the girl, Such-and-such a fellow, you want him? She said yes. The aunt and uncle came and fixed the time to set the conditions. And they prepared a few things for five Bishliks. When the matter became known, the neighbors became jealous. There was one Mugrahban woman there. She had a relative she wanted to marry to that fellow. On the morning of the betrothal, she invited the fellow to her house and gave him a glass of tea. He drank it, returned home and said, I don't want Hakham Nissim's girl. The uncle was sorry because he had invited a few people and because of the shame of the girl. There was another neighbor there, a good woman. She asked the bridegroom, Where were you today? He told her, I was at So-and-So's. She understood that that woman had practiced sorcery on him. She invited him to her house and made him come in and fixed tea for him and gave it to him to drink. And she knew what to put in the tea. When he drank it he wanted to vomit. He excused himself and went out and vomited a lot. The sorcery departed. When he returned home, he washed his face and said to his uncle, Where is Hakham Nissim's girl, why doesn't she come? And he didn't remember anything. A messenger went to Hakham Nissim's and told him. Said the daughter, Now that he wants me, I don't want him. They explained the whole matter to her and she agreed to take him.

Rebecca asked Shifra, What's wrong with you, Shifra? When she asked she was scared that Shifra would answer her and reveal to her what was in her heart. Suddenly, a voice was heard, and she thought it was Fayesh's voice. Rebbeca jumped up and spread out her hands and made them a kind of barrier between him and Shifra.

3 |

Rebecca said to her daughter, Shifra, tell me, is there anything I can do? Shifra laid her head on her mother's heart and wept. Rebecca stroked her cheeks and didn't know what else to do. She looked into her beautiful and sad face, that gloomy beauty that caused the trouble that that fellow set his sights on her. Rebecca hadn't been blessed with such beauty, nevertheless Fayesh had married her. It's doubtful if he even looked at her, either before they were married or after they were married. And if she hadn't known that all her husband's deeds were for the sake of Heaven, she would have said that that was why he never showed her any sign of affection.

Shifra's head lies on her mother's heart. Rebecca strokes her daughter's cheeks and thinks, How many years did she live with Fayesh until they were blessed with that daughter. Reb Fayesh was a ritual slaughterer Outside the Land and he always had a dispute with butchers, for they said he unjustly disqualified their livestock. And the dispute destroyed his strength. Finally he put away his knife and they ascended to the Land of Israel to get away from the sinners and to be blessed with sons. Sons he wasn't blessed with, but only this one daughter. And when she was born, Rebecca was afraid Fayesh would be angry at her for giving birth to a daughter and not to a son, but Fayesh wasn't angry, but on the contrary, he blessed her with great joy. Now this daughter is grieving and there's no way her mother can save her.

CHAPTER FIFTEEN

Peace

1 |

Isaac didn't go to Abu Hassan because he was eager to return to Jerusalem, and he didn't return to Jerusalem because he found an apartment for free here, for Sweet Foot was going with Shakhnai the surveyor or with Goldman the engineer or with neither one nor the other, but was fleeing from his ex-wife and from the upholsterer who was wooing her to marry her. He gave Isaac his hut to live in. Isaac was glad to stay in Jaffa, for living there is pleasurable, and he was glad he had chanced to get an apartment for free.

Deserts of sand stretch from the hut to the great sea, and a broad sky is stretched over them and over the hut, and a sprout blossoms from the sand, and sometimes a bird comes down from the sky and settles on the blossom. That bird isn't one of those birds that Isaac saw on the ship on the sea. But the same wonderment he felt for the birds he saw on the ship on the sea, he felt for that bird.

Isaac stands in the doorway of his hut and compares his voice to the voice of the bird. But the bird doesn't pay any heed to him, for he isn't directing his song at a creature like him, but at the mate he desires. At that moment, another bird comes flying in, and now they spread their wings and fly among the blue waves between the sky and the land, sometimes with one another and sometimes against one another, and they come back to where they started. And it is a great joy in the world that two creatures who longed for one another mated in one place and you stand there and are glad, too. Peace and tranquility all around him and peace in his heart.

And since there is peace and tranquility here and there isn't a person here, sometimes a person comes here to be alone with himself. Once Arzef from Jerusalem passed by here. Not looking for a phoenix did Arzef come to the deserts of sand, but a pair of stuffed skins Arzef sent Outside the Land and was bothered by the customs officials, who had trouble assessing how much customs duties to impose on them, either the rate for live animals but they weren't alive, or the rate for inanimate objects but they did have skin and they did have bones. Arzef debated with them until his soul grew weary and he went to divert himself on the seashore. Isaac saw him and came out to greet him. Arzef didn't recognize Isaac, but Isaac recognized Arzef, for once on the Sabbath, he had gone to him in Eyn Rogel with his comrades. Isaac brought him to his hut and put the kettle on and made him tea. And as is the way of our comrades, for whom every issue and matter is close to their hearts, he talked about the fowls of the heaven and the beast of the earth. And Arzef nodded at every single thing and stroked him with his eyes, as he was wont to do with man and beast and stuffed animal skin.

2

Everyone who goes to live in a dwelling that has no neighbors seems to be relieved of all his constraints. Like most sons of the poor whom the Lord placed in a crowded world, from the moment he was born, Isaac found himself closed in on all sides, for he was given only a narrow place for his body. When he ascended to the Land of Israel and rented a private room for himself, his domain didn't expand, for his room was shrunk among a lot of rooms among a lot of neighbors. But from the day he went to live in Sweet Foot's hut, that stood alone in the deserts of sand, Isaac's boundaries burst open and his domain expanded, for wherever he turned, he saw himself alone. When he returned home at night, he doesn't have to watch his steps because of the neighbors, when he gets out of bed in the morning, he can raise his voice in song, for there is no one here but the tranquil wind moving among the sands and the roar of the waves of the sea.

Isaac removed his mind from the world and lived on what he found in the hut, rusks and smoked meat and canned fish and various jams and tinned milk and coffee and tea and cocoa and chocolate and sugar and wine and cognac and liquor and fruit juices, which Sweet Foot's ex-wife brought Sweet Foot. The dead husband of that Rabbi's wife left her money, along with what she inherited from her father, and she was bored and didn't know what to do. She went round to the shops and got whatever she laid eyes on, and hired herself a carriage and came to Sweet Foot, for she was afraid he would starve to death, for he was busy with various inventions and didn't look for paid work. But Sweet Foot doesn't like delicacies because delicacies lead to laziness, and when he gave his hut to Isaac, he did it on condition that he eat everything and not leave anything for the mice.

3 |

Isaac feels good and doesn't do anything. You don't know how much man is prone to be idle. The moralists think that man's purpose in the world is to do good deeds, and those with a purpose think that man's purpose is to reach a purpose. If we look at Isaac, we see that if he has a bed and a table, he has his purpose. If a thought comes to him to return to Jerusalem, another thought comes that, as long as he can sit here, there's no point moving. And if his heart was drawn to Shifra, his thoughts brought him closer to her than he could be in reality. Thoughts have no limits, wherever the heart wishes, they enter. And if you say, what will we eat after Sweet Foot comes back and Isaac has to clear out of his place, there is enough in his purse to support himself for a month or two. And in the winter, what will he do, when the painters are idle because the paint doesn't dry fast, and there are landlords who keep a lid on their fees, wait for winter and live on their debts. Even the winter itself that reduces his income brings him profit. How? For when the great rains fell and got into their churches and blurred the paints, the priests called him to re-paint in honor of the pilgrims who come from Outside the Land for Christmas. And sign-painting also brings him a penny or two.

4 |

In those days when Isaac lived in the hut, he relived his first days, except that in the past he was idle because he didn't have anything to do, and now he is idle because he doesn't have to do anything. And

Isaac has now forgotten the days of hunger, the days of despair, the days when he didn't see a cent and didn't see how he would earn any money for tomorrow. A bit of good makes us forget a lot of bad. And since he is steeped in goodness, his mind is fine and his heart expands. And he sees the Land from another perspective. Not like Brenner, who says a moneylender in Poland owns more houses than Ahuzat Bayit will build, and not like those who sneer at everything that is done in the Land of Israel, but like those who say houses Outside the Land of Israel are houses, but the houses in the Land of Israel build the Land, and all those deeds they sneer at today may one day be the foundation of our life in the Land.

In Jaffa, Isaac found some of his first comrades with whom he humbled himself looking for work from the farmers and with whom he beat his feet on the doorsills of the activists. Like all our comrades, they too came to build and to be rebuilt. Years went by and they weren't rebuilt, not them and not the Land. Their eyes grew dim and their backs grew bent. Now they are erect as cypresses and their eyes are smiling. They were joined by new people who ascended from the Diaspora, and they have the enthusiasm of the first ones but they don't have the doubts of the first ones. They do whatever work comes along and they don't split hairs about what should be done and what shouldn't be done. Some of them went out to the new settlements founded by Ruppin, and some find their livelihood in the city, building houses. The people of Jaffa abhorred the Arab houses whose filth was great and whose air was heavy. There are houses whose cesspools are close to the water cisterns and their waters blend and bring all kinds of diseases, and there are houses where there is no cesspool and they pour their waste in front of the house and raise mosquitoes and gnats and flies that bring malaria. And the Arabs raise the rent from one year to the next, for every ship brings new immigrants and all the houses in Jaffa cannot absorb all those who come. So the people of Jaffa formed an association to build themselves decent houses in a separate neighborhood, that's the neighborhood of Tel Aviv, which became a major city in Israel.

CHAPTER SIXTEEN

Beginning of Tel Aviv

1 |

At first, they planned to build summer houses where a person could find rest after the toil of the day, and his wife and sons and daughters could sit in fresh air and not fear trachoma and all the other diseases of the Land, for the Land made its inhabitants sick ever since the first day we were exiled from our Land, with diseases the children catch from their Arab neighbors. Money to buy land and build houses they didn't have. After all, they didn't bring money from Outside the Land, and what a person earns here isn't enough for anything but a modest livelihood. But their heart's desire and their will grew strong. And since they got the idea in their heads, they didn't let go of it. And furthermore, they decided to build themselves a regular neighborhood for all seasons, summer and winter.

About sixty people gathered together and formed a company and called that company Ahuzat Bayit, because every one of them wanted to make himself a house in the Land of our possession. Some wanted to build their neighborhood within the city of Jaffa for their livelihood was in the city and if their houses were far away from the city, they would be weary from the sun in summer and from the rain in winter and far away from social life, for all social life was in the city. Furthermore, a settlement outside the city is far from the foreign consuls and there is danger in that. And some said, No, on the contrary, we'll build ourselves a special quarter outside the city, and we'll build ourselves fine houses, and in front of every house we'll plant ourselves a little garden and we'll make ourselves straight, broad streets, and we'll make our spirit, the pure spirit of Israel, prevail in that place. And when we achieve that, we'll make ourselves a kind of autonomy. For it's impossible to do that unless we're far away from the city. The latter defeated the former and they agreed to make the neighborhood outside the city. Everyone gave twenty Francs for the first expenses and they started looking for land. They found land in the wasteland of the city, but they couldn't pay the price of the land. They made an effort to get a loan. They appealed here and there and didn't get an answer. At last, the Jewish National Fund did respond and lent them three hundred thousand Francs.

They got themselves land, part sand dunes and part ravines and valleys. They hired themselves workers to prepare the land and ready it for building houses. Our comrades move mountains and pour the sand into the valleys and bring stones from the sea and set them in the sand and fill in ditches. And camels and mules carry sand and wheelbarrows run, and hammers strike, and a stone crusher crushes the stones, and our comrades scatter gravel among the stones and make the valleys and hills into a plain. Our comrades stand sunk in sand, and a forest of wide hats waves in the air, and a supervisor wearing high boots up over his knees runs from place to place, and looks here a little and there a little, and has a word with this one and half a word with that one. And the workers run, not like the Arabs who have to be prodded. And our comrades don't stop except to drink water and wipe their sweat, and sometimes, near dark, a person asks his comrade what time it is. And a sound of blasting comes from the quarry where they bring building stones and a smell of burned dust bubbles up. Not the sound of war and not the smell of war, but the sound of building and the smell of settlement. And a sort of road now sprouts from the sands and it lets a person's feet stand firm. And men and women and children come from Jaffa and try out their feet on the road. Behold that wonder, the road doesn't sink and the foot doesn't drown in the sand.

There are those who slander the Jewish National Fund for lending money to the members of Ahuzat Bayit, for they include merchants and shopowners and some of them are moneylenders, who are saving their own money that brings them high interest, and are asking for public money at low interest. And there are those who mock the members of Ahuzat Bayit, who want to build on the sand,

and whose end is inherent from the start, like the well-known proverb about those who build on sand. Furthermore, expenses will be added on top of expenses, for their livelihood is in the city and they will have to hire a wagon, and needless to say the children need a school.

2 |

Not all opinions are the same. Some mock and some rejoice, some grumble and slander and some build and respond, This place that was desolate and without a settlement will be full of big and fine houses and beautiful trees, and right in the center of the neighborhood, we'll plant a big garden, and around the garden we'll build a synagogue and a library and a town hall and schools, and all the streets will be filled with boys and girls. The Herziliya Gymnasium already started building its school in our neighborhood and everyone who wants to give his sons and daughters a Hebrew schooling along with a general education will send his sons and daughters to us, and will send their mother along with them, and then he himself will come.

The sun flames and blazes and the sand bubbles. From morning till night, our comrades stand up to their navels in sand and move mountains and fill valleys and pave streets and smooth roads. Mountains and hills are moved and valleys and dales are filled. The lizards and snakes flee, and ravens and the offspring of ravens spread their wings and fly away. Small carts race, and our comrades accompany them with song. They wring the sweat out of their clothes and dry them in the sun. Scores of our comrades who were wrapped in tatters and were yellow with malaria, stand half naked and rejoice at their work and are happy at their building.

Sometimes a cool wind passes by and a smell of sycamore refreshes the heart with its sweetness. Young men who had already despaired of the Land ask themselves what was wrong with us. Gorishkin pulls his wagon and drives it. His face is tanned and his eyes are red. By day he transports sand and at night he writes memoirs. Like the number of wagons he transports by day is the number of pages he writes at night. Today his memoirs aren't important, but in the future, when houses stand and people are dwelling in them, they'll open the book of his memoirs and read how their houses were built and who built them. Mendele and Bialik write about beggars and Yeshiva students, while he writes about the Land and the builders of the Land. The world takes off one shape and puts on another, anyone who will want to know how the Land was built will pick up Gorishkin's book and read it.

Tourists who came later on to tour the Land and saw that fine new neighborhood of sixty small houses called Tel Aviv, and every house is surrounded by a small garden and all the streets are clean, and boys and girls play in the streets, and old people sit leaning on their canes and warm themselves in the sun — those tourists couldn't have imagined that that place was desolate without a settlement and that there were a lot of quarrels among the builders. It doesn't occur to a man who sees a perfect, beautiful girl that that girl wasn't so beautiful and perfect at the beginning of her creation, but her parents put a lot of toil into her, and often would quarrel about her. When the daughter grew up and stands at the height of her charm and grace, her father and mother quarrel about her and each one claims that it was only because of him that she had come to be what she was. The same with Tel Aviv. The tourists think Tel Aviv was like that from the beginning and each one of her forefathers, the builders of Tel Aviv, attributes the splendor of Tel Aviv to himself. But we who know God the Eternal, the Creator and Shaper and the Almighty, and by His will He gives life and grace and favor, we laugh heartily at all those who, in their innocence, err in thinking that they made Tel Aviv by their own power and by the strength of their hand. Tel Aviv became Tel Aviv by the life force of the Living God, the complete opposite of what the founders of Tel Aviv wanted to make of Tel Aviv, for if they really thought of making Tel Aviv as it is now, why did they make narrow streets that aren't fit for a city?

CHAPTER SEVENTEEN

Isaac Wants to Return to Jerusalem and Cannot

1 |

In those days, Rabinovitch returned from Outside the Land. At first, we didn't recognize him because his hair had turned white and because he was dressed like a tourist, until he tapped us on the shoulder and then we recognized him. Everyone who returns to the Land of Israel even dressed in foreign garb, when his foot touches its soil, he is no longer estranged from it.

Isaac heard that Rabinovitch had returned and longed to see him but was afraid of him. Even though his affairs with Sonya were over, his affairs with himself weren't over. And if Rabinovitch had never been out of his mind's eye for a day, those days he grew severalfold. And as he grew so did that sin grow and none of his justifications justified his deeds. And if he put Shifra before his mind's eye to prove that he has nothing with Sonya, He Who reproaches him evokes Sonya in his mind's eye. Isaac's love for Shifra made him forget Sonya's good qualities and he was amazed at himself and asked, What did I see in her to trail along after her? And He Who reproaches him says to him, That's the same question I ask. Isaac's peace was gone and he found no satisfaction staying in that Jaffa he had been so fond of just a short time ago. When he wanted to return to Jerusalem, his hut held him. That hut which had made him stay in Jaffa longer than he had planned at first didn't let him go, for he had to deliver the key and he didn't know who to deliver it to.

Sweet Foot went and no one knows where he went. Two or three times, the Rabbi's Wife came to ask about him and Isaac replied that he doesn't know. An hour or two after the Rabbi's Wife left, Mendel the upholsterer came to spy on her. Since he didn't find her, he got angry. Finally he asked Isaac, Where is Leichtfuss? Isaac told him, I don't know. Said Mendel, If so, who does know? Said Isaac, You know? Mendel mocked him and said, You think I don't have anything else to do besides this? Said Isaac, I see that you have something else to do here. Mendel raised his face to him and scowled at him and said, So, this matter, in your opinion, what is it, for example? Said Isaac, In my opinion, I set before my mind that it is clear enough to you. Mendel stroked his beard and replied calmly, You want to know what I set before my mind. A Jew who follows the ways of the Lord always sets before him what he is commanded to do in paragraph one of the Shulkhan Arukh, I have set the Lord always before me.

Isaac wanders outside from the hut and from outside to the hut. Aside from Hemdat, there isn't anyone here to whom he can deliver the key, and Hemdat can suddenly get up and go his way for several days and when Sweet Foot comes back, he'll find his hut locked and no key. Isaac decided to consult with Mr. Orgelbrand, maybe he would find some advice. Meanwhile, wherever Isaac goes, the image of Rabinovitch goes before him. If he sits in his hut, it seems to him that Rabinovitch came. If he closed the door, he went to see if he had come. If he heard footsteps, he feared it was Rabinovitch. If he didn't hear anything, he feared he was walking stealthily and would come upon him suddenly. Because Isaac was afraid of meeting Rabinovitch, he was eager to return to Jerusalem. He hurried to Mr. Orgelbrand to consult with him about delivering the key.

2 |

Orgelbrand still lives in the German quarter in Rabinovitch's attic. Orgelbrand is satisfied with his apartment and is satisfied with the landlady and is satisfied with the neighborhood. When he comes home from his work, he sits down at the window with his little pipe in his mouth and looks at the trees, and at night he puts on his beret and goes for a stroll with his walking stick. What does a bachelor need? A bed and a table. And here's a bed and a table. And if you want peace, is there more peace than here. Here there are no assemblies and no meetings, no debates and no quarrels, but every person sits within his own home and enjoys whatever can be enjoyed.

Since the day Isaac last saw Orgelbrand, his hair had turned a bit silver and his eyes had become more sorrowful. Nothing new had occurred to him, but something new was approaching, for the director of the Anglo-Palestine Company was planning to make him director of a branch. Orgelbrand was still evading it, but he would be forced to accept the position because it's impossible to refuse, and because his stepmother's husband needed money for doctors. Orgelbrand has another need for money, for when he was a lad, his father's hand weighed heavy on him, he escaped to the town of Baruch Zweiering, his relative, Zweiering greeted him warmly and supported him. Now that Zweiering has become poor, it is only proper that he help him in his hour of need, but he doesn't know how. Perhaps he should return to him his expenses, but he doesn't know how much he spent on him, and perhaps he should estimate, but Orgelbrand doesn't like estimates. And sending him a gift of money involves some shame. After Orgelbrand examined all the ways, he wanted to make a conspiracy with Sonya to give her what she needs to live on, and let her write her father that she found a job and doesn't need his money. Thus Barukh Zweiering would be freed from Sonya's expenses. And if she wants to go to Berlin to study, Orgelbrand is willing to pay her expenses. When he observed the matter more closely, he began to worry that if she went, she would distance herself from him. It occurred to him that, ever since the day he went to work in the bank, he hadn't missed a single day and hadn't taken any vacation. Now he would take a vacation and go with Sonya, to assist her on her trip and to help her settle in Berlin. And on the days when the school is closed, he would take her to the museum and the theaters. And when they are in Berlin, where she doesn't know anyone except him, she'll see all the favors he is doing for her and will see that she has no one better in the world than him. She turns her mind away from all the other fellows in the world and goes with him to the Rabbiner to marry them. The Rabbiner wears rabbinical garb and marries them, while the big organ in the temple plays and the temple is lighted with many candles, and heavy, expensive carpets are rolled outside from the temple, and all the Zionist dignitaries in Berlin come and join their celebration. Finally he takes Sonya on a honeymoon, etc.

3 |

Isaac enters the group of citrus groves which extends to the German quarter, where Mr. Orgelbrand lives. In these houses, amid gardens and orchards, our comrade Isaac had found his livelihood at a time when he despaired of everything, and here he strolled with Sonya at the time when he thought he had everything. And even if he had taken his mind off of her, the roads still exist. And nearby is the Hebrew Gymnasium. Once, in those days when he was despondent, he went to visit one of his friends who was a secretary at the Gymnasium. He found him sitting with the teachers and drinking tea. He sensed that Isaac hadn't eaten a thing that day, and brought him tea and cake. Where is the one who helped him in his hour of hunger? His wife couldn't stand the afflictions of the Land and he returned with her Outside the Land. If he hadn't found a job here, he wouldn't have had money for the travel expenses and would have stayed in the Land. Now that he lived Outside the Land, his sons are growing up without Torah and he mourns for them and for himself. Years later perhaps he will return to the Land and won't find any work to do, for his job had already been given to someone else and new jobs you don't find every day. What does Rabinovitch want to do in the Land? Oh, God, Isaac shouted in his heart, will I never be free of my thoughts of Rabinovitch?

Rabinovitch

1 |

A gentleman encountered him and said, If my eyes don't deceive me, you are Mr. Kumer. Said Isaac, And what is your name, sir? Said that gentleman, The name of your "sir" you should know by yourself. Said Isaac, Your voice I do recognize, but your face I don't. Rabinovitch? Said Rabinovitch, Have I changed so much that it's hard to recognize me? Isaac looked at him and said, In fact, you haven't changed, but it seems to me you didn't use to smoke. Rabinovitch stretched and said, I didn't smoke? Said Isaac, At any rate, not black cigars. Said Rabinovitch, You are right about that, my friend. Isaac pondered, He says, You are right about that, which means I wasn't right about something else. At any rate, from his face it doesn't look like he has any grudge against me. On the contrary, he greeted me nicely and even gave me a friendly kiss.

Rabinovitch asked Isaac, Where are you going? He told him. Rabinovitch said to him, If I'm not mistaken, Lorentz's coffeehouse is near here, let's go in and have something cold to drink. Confound it, such a fat lizard I've never seen before, how nimble she is, hopping like a devil and hiding behind the shutter. And she doesn't know that when they open the shutter, she'll be crushed. Lorentz has enlarged his coffeehouse. Do you come here often? Said Isaac, Me? Said Rabinovitch, Who am I talking to? Not you? Said Isaac, I don't live in Jaffa. Said Rabinovitch, Where do you live? Said Isaac, In Jerusalem. Said Rabinovitch, Then you're a visitor here? What do you do there in Jerusalem? You paint to cover up? Will you smoke a cigar? Said Isaac, I don't smoke. Said Rabinovitch, Why not? Said Isaac, Because I don't get any pleasure from smoking. Said Rabinovitch, A person has to educate himself for pleasures.

2

Isaac saw that Rabinovitch didn't have anything at all against him in his heart. On the contrary, he treated him affectionately, maybe even more than before. If we weren't apprehensive about making comparisons, we would compare him to a big brother who left his father's house in time of trouble and when he returned, he is grateful to his little brother for staying and protecting the house.

As they sat in the coffeehouse, Isaac asked his comrade, Why didn't you write to us at all? Rabinovitch smiled and said, Us, you say, that is, you and Sonya. What will you drink, maybe a cold beer? I'll tell you the truth, as long as I was deep in troubles, I didn't want to write. And when I came out of the troubles, I was busy earning a living. And do you think it's easy, my dear, to support a wife? Women Outside the Land aren't satisfied with bread and tomatoes. Waiter, two bottles of beer and some rolls. Isaac, take the beer and drink. What are you contemplating?

Isaac sat and contemplated. Now that Rabinovitch was married, he wouldn't mention the offense of Sonya to him. Nevertheless, if he asked him, what would he tell him? Said Rabinovitch, If it's my marriage, I'll tell you some other time. I plan to settle down here and we'll find time to talk. Isaac asked Rabinovitch, What do you say about Jaffa? It's grown, hasn't it? Did you see Sonya? Rabinovitch picked up his hat and waved it like a fan, and said, I saw her, I saw her. A supple girl. So supple she slips through your fingers. Waiter, another bottle. Where did the corkscrew disappear? Here. Thank you. Now, my dear boy, let's drop the subject of Madame Zweiering. At any rate, we mustn't be ungrateful. Here's to life, Isaac, here's to life.

Isaac put his mouth on his glass and cooled his lips. He says we mustn't be ungrateful, which means he knows there was something between me and Sonya. Isaac tightened his fingers around his glass and pondered to himself, Not good, not good that I didn't return to Jerusalem and I met Rabinovitch. He put his glass down and said, I've got a lot of things to ask you and I don't know what to ask first. Said Rabinovitch, There's plenty of time for that. In fact, I don't know why I came back to the Land of Israel, if not to fulfill what they say, that a covenant was made with the Land of Israel that everyone who leaves her ends up coming back. Said Isaac, Which means you came to settle down. Said Rabinovitch, What else, you think I came as a tourist. For the time being, I don't know what I'll do, I've got one offer to buy a citrus grove near Jaffa, and I have another offer for almond groves in Hadera, and I have another offer to go into partnership with a carpenter who wants to expand his workshop. In short, a lot of deals are waiting for me here, and it doesn't occur to anybody that this Rabinovitch, an expert in the clothing business, should perhaps open a clothing store. But it's not a man's training that counts, but money. And Makherovitch, as usual, stands me in front of a map of the Land of Israel and offers me lands in the east and in the west, in all four corners of the Land, on the palm of his hand and on the smooth place of his bald head. Even though on the other hand, he says I should set up a new printing house here. And Makheranski concurs in that advice. Makheranski says that there is only one printing house in Jaffa, and in a place where there is one there is a place for two. If one Jew eats bread why not have another one join his repast. And Makherson agrees with him, for the writers of Jaffa are about to publish a daily newspaper and need a big printing house. And Mordechai Ben-Hillel has already composed a prospectus to send to the Odessa Committee, and Doctor Luria is willing to sign the prospectus, and needless to say, Ludvipol, who is willing to edit the newspaper, but they've got to beware of S. Ben-Zion in case Ussishkin asks him, for S. Ben-Zion claims there are no writers here, that those who regard themselves as writers aren't writers. On the other hand, Dizengoff is an optimist. Says Dizengoff, There are writers or there aren't writers, I'll send you a barrel of ink and you write as much as you want. Meanwhile, Sheinkin comes to me with shares in the Gymnasium and Mrs. Buchmil with shares of Shiloh. A handsome woman is Mrs. Buchmil. Isn't she? Waiter. Check. You see, Isaac, a lot of livelihoods are in store for me in the Land of Israel, but I don't like any of those deals. So what shall I do? When the time comes, I'll tell you.

3 |

Ahuzat Bayit began building its houses. One day, Ruben lays a foundation for his house and one day Simon lays a foundation for his
house. They come from Neve Tsedek and from Neve Shalom and
from the street along the sea and from Hobard Street and from the
Ajami quarter and from gloomy alleys with no light and no air and
they bring wafers from Albert and wine and seltzer. They drink and
they dance and they sing, offer the sacrifices of righteousness and put
your trust in the Lord. There be many that say, Who will shew us any
good? And the workers burgeon forth from piles of sand and partici-
pate in the rejoicing of the homeowners and no one knows who is
happier, the one who owns the house or the ones who are building
the house. Some weep out of joy and some weep for joy. They went
through a lot before they could start building Tel Aviv. The Anglo-
Palestine Company embittered their lives and middlemen changed
the conditions of the sale seven times a day and Turkish government
officials invented complications every day, and every day benefactors
appeared who had to be appeased with a tribute so they wouldn't go
and harm them. Now they are standing on that ground and building
houses for themselves with the hope and expectation that they will
be blessed to dwell in them in peace and righteousness and that they
will be blessed to see the building of the whole Land.

Some owners are occupied themselves with the building,
and some are occupied with their occupations and entrust the building of their houses to contractors, and the contractors make partner-
ships with financiers. Rabinovitch, who brought money with him,
agreed to become a partner of contractors. When our comrade Rabinovitch ascended to the Land of Israel, it was to work the Land that
he ascended, it didn't respond to him, and he engaged in trade.
When he saw that trade needed innovation but his bosses didn't want
to change their ways, he left the Land and became an expert in his
profession, and married a rich woman, and returned to the Land to
derive profit from his learning for his own benefit and for the benefit of the Land. Before he got started, he got into that business of
contracting. When our comrade Rabinovitch left the Land, he left
poor, when he came back he came back rich, and as a rich man he

doesn't have to go looking for a livelihood, for the livelihood comes looking for him.

Rabinovitch forgot Sonya. Rabinovitch had managed to learn that man wasn't created to spend his days and his years with girls who don't know what they want or what they're looking for. Rabinovitch forgot Sonya, but Isaac he didn't forget. And even though many people want to be close to him, he turns to Isaac. And that is amazing, for Isaac doesn't have a name or anything at all. Moreover, something they do share, that is, the matter of Sonya, they don't even hint at. But they talk about all other matters. And Isaac had already told Yedidya a few of his adventures, even his events with Shifra, to whom his heart was drawn, and he is waiting for the compassion of the Lord.

For years, Rabinovitch hadn't heard the Lord's Name, and today he hears the Name of the Holy-One-Blessed-Be-He every single time he talks with Isaac. Those Galicians, they like all men, but when they want something, they immediately put their trust in the Holy-One-Blessed-Be-He and aren't ashamed to mention Him. Rabinovitch has nothing to do with his Creator and nothing against his Creator. Ever since the day Rabinovitch left his hometown, it's doubtful that he remembered Him. Many are the issues concerning a person and he hasn't got time to remember everything. But Rabinovitch should be remembered for he remembers his comrade. Out of his affection for Isaac, he decided to bring him into his business, and give him the job of painting as a contractor or otherwise, whatever Isaac liked. And Isaac had already agreed to work with him, as a contractor or otherwise, whatever Rabinovitch liked.

4 |

Isaac remained in Jaffa another day and another day, on account of business and everything relating to it. And Rabinovitch was a busy man and delayed Isaac another day and another day. Isaac frequented Rabinovitch's house and supped at his table, for our comrade Rabinovitch was a generous soul and loved guests. In the past, when Rabinovitch was a poor worker and lived in a rundown hut, he entertained his guests with coarse bread and tea, and now that he is a rich man, he entertained them with fine bread and wine and various foods. And his wife is happy with the guests, for what is left for a woman in the Eastern lands aside from the kitchen and entertaining guests? In truth, there are activist women and women lobbyists and women orators here. Hilda Rabinovitch isn't one of them and doesn't want to be like them. Women are of many minds, and her mind was given to herself and her house.

Among Rabinovitch's guests, you also find Mr. Orgelbrand. Mr. Orgelbrand does not visit any house in Jaffa, but Rabinovitch made him come to his home, and sometimes even to sup at his table. And as he dines, Rabinovitch laughs at Mr. Orgelbrand and his boss, the director of the Anglo-Palestine Company. Says Rabinovitch, Why doesn't our friend Orgelbrand get married? Because if he does get married and have a son, he will have to honor his boss as the godfather, and therefore he foregoes marriage. And may he not remain a bachelor all his life.

Sonya Zweiering also frequents Rabinovitch's house, for there is love and affection between her and Hilda Rabinovitch, for once they met each other and Mrs. Rabinovitch saw Miss Zweiering's shoes which were beautiful and asked her who made her shoes here, and Sonya Zweiering took her to a small cobbler from Homel, who makes nicer shoes than all the cobblers in Jaffa, even nicer than the Greek cobblers, whose shoes were all the rage among most of the ladies of Jaffa and the nearby settlements. From then on, a great friendship developed between Mrs. Rabinovitch and Miss Zweiering and Mrs. Rabinovitch invited her to her home. And Rabinovitch honored his wife's guests, just as she honored his guests, even Isaac Kumer, although she wonders what Rabinovitch found in him to be so close to him. And Sonya agrees with her that that Jerusalemite is a boring person. In fact, every person here is a fund of boredom. And if somebody tells you, Hemdat isn't boring, you tell him, But that maiden he chose, that Yael Hayyot, is boredom times two. Does Hilda Rabinovitch know what went on between her husband and Sonya? Even if she did know, she wouldn't care. Hilda Rabinovitch isn't provincial and doesn't bother about the sort of frivolous things you see as serious.

Isaac sits at the home of his comrade Rabinovitch among special people and among frivolous people, and Rabinovitch sits at the head of the table and his words fill the house, about everything there is in the Land of Israel and about everything there isn't in the Land of Israel, about public activists the public doesn't need and about Turkey and its leaders and about the situation of the Jews in Turkish law, about industry and manufacturing and about the craft of laying floor tiles, which didn't exist among Jews a few years before, aside from one Mughraban who carved tombstones, who hired Gentile workers but not Jews. From the industry we have and the industry we don't yet have, Rabinovitch returned to the issues of our national institutions, and from them to our leading institution, the Anglo-Palestine Company in Jaffa, and from the Anglo-Palestine Company to the head of the Anglo-Palestine Company, who is a cautious man and protects the national treasure, but so much caution makes him most punctilious with the customers and he doesn't give credit to those who need credit, like a certain Jewish factoryowner, while the German bank did give him credit. But that credit of the German bank is limited, and he has to go looking for moneylenders who are usurers and charge him eighteen percent and that is why he can't start up his business.

From issues of credit and banks and industry, Rabinovitch turns to the issues of our comrades who were afflicted with malaria and torments and spent their days in debates, or sat in couples on the beach and sang Take me in under your wing and Be a mother to me and a sister. Rabinovitch calls out, Confound it, you found yourself a mate, why are you prattling on about a mother and a sister? Worse than them were the people of Jerusalem, they don't sit on the beach and they don't sing songs about mother and sister, but they run from grave to grave, and from prayer to prayer. If they won't go to hell for their idleness, they will be sent back to this world to be workers and artisans so that, in the next incarnation, they can repair what they have damaged in this one. And when Rabinovitch mentions Jerusalem, he praises Isaac and praises his modest girlfriend from Jerusalem, who never raised her eyes to another man, for no joy is greater than a man's joy at a woman like that. At that moment, Ra-

binovitch is thinking of his own wife, who was married to somebody
else before. At that moment, he feels a lack, but he judges himself
fairly, for he didn't enter the marriage clean of all impurity either,
and if he makes a fair accounting, the Holy-One-Blessed-Be-He
might have some change coming. How did Rabinovitch get to that
woman? A little dog she had and Rabinovitch gave it chocolate and
sugar. Rabinovitch became fond of the dog and of the dog's mistress,
she left her husband and went with Rabinovitch. And behold, what
happened to Rabinovitch, something like that happened to Isaac.
Once Isaac was working in one of the neighborhoods of Jerusalem,
and a dog came and lay down in front of him. Isaac didn't pet the dog
and didn't give him sugar and chocolate, but on the contrary, he
kicked him and wrote slandering words on his skin. But if he hadn't
kicked him, the dog wouldn't have been driven away to the place of
Reb Fayesh and wouldn't have barked at him, and Reb Fayesh
wouldn't have been shocked and wouldn't have gotten sick and Isaac
wouldn't have frequented his house and wouldn't have become close
to Shifra. In everything, the Holy-One-Blessed-Be-He carries out His
mission, sometimes in the open and sometimes in secret. What is
done in the open, we see, what is done in secret, we don't see.

Our comrade Isaac sits at Rabinovitch's house at a fine table,
where several kinds of good foods are served. Such food Isaac had
never seen, neither in his father's house nor in the inns of the Land
of Israel, where most of the innkeepers he frequented had never seen
an inn in their lives, and don't know what is proper for a guest and
what isn't, they provide whatever they provide, just so they receive
payment, and most of the guests are poor and don't go looking for
what befits them, just so they fill their bellies and won't be hungry.
Several people sit at Rabinovitch's table and eat for their enjoyment
and spice the table with fine conversation. Some of those sitting
there had stood with them to hire themselves out as laborers, and
some of them had refused to hire our comrades. When God makes
things better for folks, folks too are nice to one another.

And behold, once Victor came to Rabinovitch's house.
How? That summer Victor went to Karlsbad to repair his body and
reduce his fat. There in Karlsbad, he met a maiden. She heard he

was from Palestine. She told him, I have a sister in Jaffa, and that sister was Hilda Rabinovitch. Victor agreed to deliver her regards. And so Victor came to Rabinovitch.

Victor knows how to behave with people. As long as Rabinovitch was barefoot and looking for work, he treated him the way you treat the barefoot; now that he is rich, he treats him as you treat the rich. And our comrade Rabinovitch, you know him. Rabinovitch is a practical man and doesn't waste his time in accounts of revenge and grudges. And when Victor came to him he greeted him warmly and sat him down among our comrades. But some of our comrades like arguments at every hour and in every place and with every person. One of our comrades says to Victor, By what right do you farmers feel superior to us workers. Didn't we all come here empty-handed, didn't we. But you got land given to you by the Baron, by IKA, by the Lovers of Zion, didn't you. And you became farmers, didn't you. And we who weren't given an estate in the Land, we became workers, didn't we. So, all of us live because of the Lovers of Zion, don't we. So how are we worse than you? Aren't we. While the latter asks and the former has no answer, the host pours a glass of beer for the former and a glass of beer for the latter, Mrs. Hilda takes the latter's hand and puts the former's hand in it and says, I'm not moving away from you until you drink to each other. They raise their glasses and drink and toast each other, and everyone drinks with them. The joy of peace they make in Rabinovitch's house, as if nothing was wrong between workers and farmers. Of such things our comrade Naftali Zamir would sing, on a glass of liquor and wine. Brothers in mind, of one descent. Can't tell farmer from worker, or a hundred from a cent.

Isaac is satisfied and isn't satisfied. Before Rabinovitch went Outside the Land, there wasn't a place and time that Isaac didn't seek him out, when he came back to the Land, sometimes he seemed to be a stranger to him. Isaac avoided visiting his friend. Rabinovitch found him and brought him back. On the way, Rabinovitch got flowers for his wife. Isaac looked at him and wondered why he wasted his money on luxuries like flowers, Rabinovitch lit himself a thick cigar and said, A person has to get accustomed to luxuries. If he hasn't got a great desire for luxuries, he must desire them, for if you have great desires, you desire to fill them, and when you do you increase your strength of will, you don't sit idle, for lusts require money, and money requires activity. You get rid of laziness and bring yourself to activity and thus you are building yourself, and the Land will be built along with you. The Land of Israel is not given to those who eat manna. I'm not a great scholar, but I do know that when the children of Israel entered the Land of Israel, the manna stopped.

Isaac inhales the smell of the flowers blended with the smell of the black cigar and doesn't know what to answer his comrade. Rabinovitch's opinions have changed, but his heart is as fine as it was. Our two comrades, Isaac Kumer and Yedidya Rabinovitch, walk along. Sometimes Isaac walks beside his comrade and sometimes he keeps his distance from him, keeps his distance and is drawn to him, until they reach the house. When they come, Hilda takes the flowers and smells them and says, Thank you very much, Rabinovitch, and she puts them in special vases, and enjoys how they look and how they smell. Perhaps our apartments in Jaffa aren't handsome, and perhaps the other things in the Land don't match our style, but the flowers in the Land are beautiful and worth giving up some of our necessities for them. Says Rabinovitch to his wife, Wait five or six months and we'll move into a new dwelling which isn't inferior, even to those in Europe. And to Isaac he says, You too will move out of your apartment and live here with your wife. Mrs. Rabinovitch suddenly turns her beautiful eyes on Isaac and sings in the tongue of the German poet, which we translate simply, There is room even in a small hut for a pair of lovers. Isaac blushed. Even though all his thoughts were on Shifra, he hadn't yet imagined where he would live with her. Isaac ponders to himself, I'll move out of my apartment and I'll live with Shifra in Jaffa. I'll take her out of the nest of gossips and bring her to friendly people and I'll make us a house and I'll buy us furniture and I'll expand her mind with everything the Lord puts in my hands.

5 |

Our comrade Rabinovitch didn't exaggerate and didn't overstate. When you go out to that desert that Ahuzat Bayit bought, you see some sort of buildings glittering from the sands. Not yet real houses there, but there will be houses. And there are already people in Jaffa who call that place by the new name of Tel Aviv. And so that Jewish quarter they call Tel Aviv is being built, and every day new workers come, tamp down the sand and make houses. And that place which was desolate and without inhabitants is humming like a settled land.

There are some Children of Israel who prophesy that those houses built by the hands of Jewish workers won't possibly stand, just as a farmer can't possibly exist with Jewish workers. And sometimes, chance supports them, a wall fell or a beam collapsed. And behold this miracle, from the place of the defeat comes relief and salvation, for every wall that fell and every beam that collapsed teaches the workers what to do and what not to do, and they become expert in their work to their own enjoyment and to the enjoyment of their boss. And now our comrades in Jaffa have bread to eat and money to pay rent, to relax their bones and draw strength for their work, until folks are amazed and say, How they have changed. And as folks are amazed, so is Heaven amazed. And when the sun blazes in the firmament and the whole world is seething, it comes there to cool itself a bit among the wood scaffolding. And at night, couples come there and stroll among the new buildings, for all the places on the beach are taken by the new immigrants who are coming with every ship. Waves and ripples rise from the sea and hug one another, and the moon now floats on the sea and now goes to see the new houses rising from the sands, like a strong city in a dry land.

Many times Isaac saw Sonya, sometimes at Rabinovitch's and sometimes on the beach or among the houses of Ahuzat Bayit which is called Tel Aviv. Sometimes he found her strolling with Yarkoni and sometimes with somebody else, for Yarkoni was busy at work arranging his affairs and wasn't available to Sonya all the time. Once Isaac found Sonya strolling with a tall, skinny fellow, with an artist's beret on his head and a roll of canvas in his arm. If we're not mistaken, this is the one who scolded Isaac when Isaac asked him about his fellow painters. A lot of pictures he "picted" in Jerusalem, and now Jaffa is ripe for him to "pict" pictures of it. Isaac doesn't hold a grudge against him and isn't jealous to see him with Sonya, and doesn't care to know what they are talking about, whether it's Apollo or Venus or Beatrice, or other creatures who are already dead.

In fact, they aren't talking about anything, but are walking along with one another, and each one is thinking his own thoughts in his heart and doesn't raise his thoughts to his lips. Sonya is thinking about Yael Hayyot who is two-faced, her face is the face of the Madonna, but her heart is full of deceit. She walks around with Shammai but doesn't let go of Hemdat. From Yael Hayyot, Sonya's mind wanders to Tamara Levi. That little girl who still has ink on her fingers from school is already preparing to go to university Outside the Land. From Tamara Levi, Sonya returned to thinking about Yarkoni, he doesn't seem to have anyone in the world but her, yet she and the whole world seem superfluous to him.

While Sonya was thinking about the whole world, that artist was walking next to her and thinking to himself, You are walking around with a girl and nothing happens. Good God Almighty, how can you paint pictures if you have never in your life seen the bare calf of a woman's leg. Paint whatever you may paint, the blind and the lame, the sidelocks of the Yemenites and the beggars scrabbling in the dung, but not a living soul whose smell you inhale. This land is a strange land, a land without women. The Arab women are veiled, and as for the girls of the Old Yishuv, Heaven separates you from them. What do you have left outside of those old virgins whose purses are full of quinine pills and a thermometer and bicarbonate of soda. And if you went down to Jaffa and are strolling with this erect girl, you have to fulfill your affection, in thought only. That man takes on the manner of an artist, stretches out his arm to the sea, and says, How beautiful is that sea. Sonya nods in agreement, and her head nods at Isaac Kumer who passed by and asked how she was. Isaac often encountered her. Sometimes he spoke with her and sometimes he got off with a simple hello, like people who know one another but aren't close to one another.

One day, Isaac went into his hut. He found the owner of the hut sleeping on his bed. How did he get in if Isaac has the key? He waited for him one hour, two hours, but he didn't wake up. Sweet

Foot returned from wherever he returned from, where he made a pulley for a room that stands on top of a room, and if the Turkish officials come to spy on the place, you turn a kind of spring and that lower room rises so they don't notice anything. Sweet Foot noticed Isaac but didn't want to engage him, because he was tired and wanted to sleep. Isaac got up and went to a hotel. He said, Tonight I shall sleep in a hotel and tomorrow I shall return to Jerusalem.

All the rooms of the hotel were taken, for this was the season for bathing and some came from Jerusalem and some from the settlements to bathe in the sea. The landlady of the hotel set up a bed for him in a small room where Teplitsky the overseer lived, who supervised the estate of his uncle Spokoyny. Amazing, said Isaac to himself. When I left here I found Victor, and when I came back here I found Teplitsky. As if all those who wouldn't let me work the Land are passing before me. Teplitsky didn't recognize Isaac, for never in his life did Teplitsky raise his eyes to a person. But he was glad to see him, for if he has a roommate, they lower the rent.

That day, a great calamity befell Teplitsky. An orphan girl had grown up in the house of his uncle Spokoyny, who had been appointed her guardian by the girl's father. Teplitsky set his sights on her to marry her because he knew that that citrus grove he supervised belonged not to his uncle, but to that orphan girl, and he was already secretly congratulating himself, for if he married her, the citrus grove would fall into his hands. What did his uncle do? He went and married her off to an idler, a medical student in Beirut who agreed to marry her as she was, without a dowry.

Isaac lay on his bed and recited the Bedtime Shema as he sometimes did. Drowsiness fell on his eyelids, and he wasn't frightened by bad dreams, or by dreams that seem good but aren't. But close to morning, he heard the sound of studying the Talmud. And since that Teplitsky who shared his room was not a scholar, Isaac understood that it was Reb Yudel his ancestor who was studying. And since his ancestor was no longer in this world, he imagined that this was no one but himself. A matchmaker entered and proposed a match to him. He put his handkerchief on the Talmud to hear what the matchmaker said. The entire room was filled with men wearing prayer shawls and wrapped in Tefillin, and the Tefillin of some touch the Tefillin of others.

After Isaac ate breakfast, he went to the hut, packed his things, and went out to find a porter to take them to the railroad station. The porters saw him and started wrangling with each other to serve him. Isaac saw one man standing alone with his hands folded behind his back, he called him. That porter was a porter of the Burial Society whose work was to serve the dead, but since he had called him, he didn't refuse the profit that fell into his hands. He untied his ropes and followed Isaac.

BOOK FOUR *Epilogue*

CHAPTER ONE

Leaves Isaac and Returns to Balak

1 |

Whenever Balak appeared in the neighborhoods of the Jews, they hurled stones at him, when he moved away from them, they cast false charges at him. There was not one mouth that did not throw mud at him and not one newspaper that did not blacken his name. The newspapers were filled with nothing but the misfortunes of Balak. *Havatselet* called him a heathen and heretic, who behaves insolently and goes bareheaded with the letters of the Holy Tongue on his skin. And *Ha-Or*, which was lavish in his praise at first for the same reason, because he went bareheaded, changed its opinion about him for the worse, and suspected him of a touch of hypocrisy, because he moved away from the neighborhoods of the Jews for he feared *Havatselet*. Harsher than both of them was *Ha-Herut*, which reprinted the words of both *Havatselet* and *Ha-Or*, but added, Why do *Havatselet* and *Ha-Or* turn their eyes away from that event? Because they get hush-money.

When the Jerusalem newspapers reached Jaffa, Jaffa thought that dog was a parable, like Mendele's horse and other stories of livestock and animals and birds which a person reads for pleasure, and if he's intelligent, he applies his intelligence to the moral. The people of Jaffa, who are all intelligent, applied their intelligence to that, but they didn't know who they were against. This one says, There's something to this; and that one says, We have to derive the implicit from the explicit. But what is explicit here no one explained. Meanwhile, opinions were divided, and there were as many opinions as there were inhabitants of the city.

Suddenly a rumor spread in the city that the whole episode of Balak referred to the administrators of education in Jerusalem. One person told his comrade and that comrade told his comrade, Why should we rack our brains and express another opinion every time, obviously this concerns so-and-so and so-and-so, who run like dogs after their masters the ministers of the nations and the foreign consuls, some because they are servile and others to win a medal, and impose all kinds of foreign tongues in the Land. But the newspapers of Jerusalem, who are afraid of them because they depend on them for money, talk in allusions.

By the end of the day, Jaffa had left its business and come to a protest meeting. The courtyard of the Gates of Zion Library was filled with a big crowd, and all the slopes leading to it were crowded with people. Some above others and others even higher, and everyone who preceded his comrade felt as if he had achieved a temporary success. And still they came. The leaders of the meeting saw that there was no room for all the people who were coming and they declared that the meeting would be outside in the open. All the people who had crowded in started going out. The ones on top suddenly found themselves on the bottom and the ones on the bottom who stood below were on top, for the temporary successes turned away from their possessors. They brought a bench and somebody climbed up on it and delivered a speech. And he was followed by his comrade, who was followed by his comrade. Thirty-six speeches were delivered that night and every speaker said something new. (A phenomenon that may not have happened since the day Jaffa became a metropolis for speakers.) Since the principals of the schools of Jerusalem were administrators of education, every single person had a different opinion, and just as his opinion was different so his language was different. The Alliance Israelite spoke French. The Gehilfsverein spoke German. At Evelyn Rothschild's they spoke English. And thus they impose all kinds of languages on their students and bring a turmoil upon the Land. And if they don't have the Children of Israel as teachers, they hire Gentile teachers and even complete anti-Semites, famous Jew-haters whose hatred bubbles up like venom. And any student who doesn't want to hear slander about the Jews is disgraced. And there was the tale of one student who left the classroom of a wicked teacher and went out to answer the call of nature, and the principal followed him and locked him in the outhouse and took away the key.

What the activists of Jaffa did orally, the workers of the Land of Israel did in writing. They wrote stinging articles in *The Young Laborer* against the Alliance Israélite Universelle and against Miss Landau and against the Gehilfsverein and against the other schools, because every one of them confounds another language, until the Land of Israel is confounded in seventy languages like the Tower of Babel. And when they attacked those schools for adapting the tongues of the Gentiles to Jewish mouths, they didn't refrain from assaulting the Yeshivas and the Heders that forbid their students to speak Hebrew and cut our tongue from our mouth.

The enlightened of Jerusalem were teachers in those schools themselves, or their sons or their sons-in-law were, and they could not make open war against their breadgivers, but they couldn't remain silent either; they assaulted the missionary schools that hunted the schoolchildren of Israel deceitfully and introduced into their hearts hatred of their own nation and converted them to their own faith and forced them to deny the holiness of the nation until they departed from the community of Israel. The missionaries took vengeance on them and raised the price of the Bible severalfold. The teachers lost heart and withdrew from the quarrel. Things settled down and the world went back to business as usual.

2 |

Since the war for Hebrew was aroused again, the Rabbis of Jerusalem started a war for Torah, until all the walls were filled with excommunications against atheists who breached the fence that was fenced and bounded by our ancestors who were like angels, those aged Rabbis and ancient geniuses, the mighty ones of the Land of Israel, to impose a strict and total ban on all schools in all the cities of the Holy Land that adopted as the essence of their religion the Hebrew language and the Holy Tongue and they profane everything holy. Because of that quarrel, Jerusalem took its mind off Balak. And Balak thought the world had returned to a good state.

When the newspapers of Jerusalem arrived outside the Land, the Jews of Diaspora understood that they said dog only as a euphemism. The newspapers which are wont to criticize the Distribution of Charity and its managers, made the tale of the dog the prime feature of their editorials about the distribution of charity and its corruption. The newspapers that have no interest in the Distribution of Charity, but are interested in political issues found that everything in the Jerusalem newspapers hinted at the Turks. They immediately launched a war against Turkey and its tactics. And they wrote again and again that anyone who thought Asiatic brutality had passed out of the world should read the Jerusalem newspapers and see how far it goes. When practical people saw all their newspapers writing, they gathered together and sent letters to their emperors and their kings to order their plenipotentiaries and consuls to keep an eye on the deeds of the Sultan to remind him that this world hasn't gone to the dogs.

When the newspapers of Diaspora arrived in the Land of Israel, the Land of Israel understood that the kingdom of Turkey had imposed a harsh persecution on the Children of Israel, but that the leaders of the Children of Israel in all lands stood in the breach and abolished it. The whole Land of Israel gathered together and lauded the Children of Israel in Diaspora, whose eyes were wide open every day upon those who dwell before the Lord on the holy mountain in Jerusalem. And all poets wrote poems made cleverly in the shape of our destroyed Temple and in gold letters, curled and curlicued, to honor our champions, the defenders of the Land, the leaders of the Children of Israel who stand in the breach, who hold king and nobles in their hand, and their eyes and their heart are on the precious sons of Zion to urge them to put off every persecution without delay from the nation of the Lord that dwells in Jerusalem.

And Jerusalem went back to its disputes and its rivalries and to the Big Quarrel, for all the national groups were divided about the episode of Balak. The Ashkenazi Geniuses and Rabbis said he was the reincarnation of that heretic who denied the entire Torah and accepted the Holy Tongue. The Sephardi Sages and Rabbis said he was the well-known fox who emerged from the Holy of Holies, but the sages of the congregations were divided about the profound issue. Some said he came for good, and some said that wasn't the case, but that harsh persecutions that were about to come down — may they strike the foes of Israel and not Israel. Babylonians say don't rejoice, Aleppans say rejoice. Iraqis say don't rejoice, Yemenites say rejoice. Moroccans say don't rejoice, Georgians say rejoice. Bukharans and Persians didn't stand apart. The Persians separated from the Bukharans, Persians say don't rejoice, Bukharans say rejoice. But they all agreed that penance had to be done.

3 |

The tale of the dog was not confined solely to the borders of the Land of Israel, but began influencing science and life and art both within the Land and Outside the Land. And even Hasidism was enriched by its rejection of Balak. We shall not exaggerate if we say that the story of Balak was more significant than most deeds of a lot of people.

How did it influence science? Aside from those who reside here permanently, there are Gentile sages who come to the Holy Land now and then to study its climate, its flora, or the manners of livestock, animals, and birds there, or the inhabitants of the Land and their customs, or other kinds of research whose name hasn't yet been researched by research. They sit in a hotel and record in their notebooks what they hear from the innkeepers and the carters and the guides, and when they return to their own country, they write books and pamphlets. One sage came by here. He saw the dog and his skin. He sat down and wrote, It is a simple custom in Jerusalem, and no doubt throughout Palestine that the Jews write on the skin of dogs in the Hebrew language and in block letters: Crazy Dog. This seems to be done as a form of a "placatory act," that is, someone who has a crazy person in his house goes and catches a white dog and writes on his skin, as those Jews do on the eve of their Day of Atonement with chickens, which they twirl over their head and say, This is my atonement this is my exchange. And it is still open to investigation why they chose a dog of all animals, and not a cow or some other animal. Further study is required to elucidate if this is because in Islamic countries the dog is abandoned, or because of some other reason. At any rate, the Jews of Palestine are to be condemned, for after they do that, they throw big stones at the dog and chase him furiously. This, however, is not within the realm of science, and it is not the task of the genuine scholar whose sights are set solely on science, to be concerned with mores. But this should be called to the attention of the Humane Society, if there is such a society in the Oriental lands, so that they may pay heed to this brutal custom which brings more brutality in its wake. And if they can, they should stop the Jews from doing whatever their heart desires.

How did it influence life? When the scholar's words were published, another scholar came along and added, From his words we learned that the Jews hate animals, and when they see a cow or an animal or a bird that isn't fit to eat, they kill them with stones. And when he condemned the Children of Israel, he fabricated slanders that caused us many troubles, Heaven Forfend.

If we were amiss in one place, we benefited in another place. How? There was a group of artists in Jerusalem and that group came up with an idea to paint the dog everybody was talking about. They were afraid to use a real dog as a model, so they went on to paint a likeness of a likeness of him. And if I didn't fear a trace of apostasy, I would say that the deeds of artists are greater than the deeds of our God, for the Creator May-He-Be-Blessed sometimes produces repulsive and ugly and defective creatures, while the artist makes everything beautiful. And we can say without fear or doubt that if not for Balak, we would lack several things in art. Moreover, a few years later, a few streets in Tel Aviv were added because of him. For when the artists became famous, a few streets were named after them. Moreover, we gained other streets which were named after writers who wrote books about the painters.

4

Even Hasidism was enriched by the adventures of Balak. How? There was an old Hasid in Jerusalem who was an expert in tales of old deeds and used to tell tales of the Saints. That Hasid regretted that everyone was talking about a dog, as if they were talking about dukes and counts, and they neglected his stories for that unclean animal. Once he went to the butcher to get meat for the Sabbath. At night, he saw in a dream a lamb with a Shtrayml on its head, and carved on it were the words, O my dove, that art in the clefts of the rock, and next to it stood a butcher his arms as strong as Pharaoh in the time of Moses. But he wasn't Pharaoh, he was Bismarck. And he wasn't Bismarck but the Military Commander of the King of Poland. He interpreted his dream. The lamb refers to the Children of Israel who live amongst the Gentiles like this lamb among seventy wolves, and they sacrifice themselves for the Torah like lambs on the altar. And the Shtrayml is the Saint of the Generation who defends the Children of Israel who stretch their neck like an innocent dove to the slaughter, and Bismarck is just a Gentile. But he was still puzzled, for first he looked like Pharaoh with strong arms and afterward like the Military Commander of the King of Poland. At night they read him a verse, Now shalt thou see what I will do to Pharaoh: for with a strong hand shall he let them go, and with a strong hand shall he drive them out of his land. And he interpreted it as the Gentiles driving Israel out of the Land. But he was still puzzled about why the Military Commander of the King of Poland appeared. He recalled a Mishnah, And one sticks in even a pole, even a reed into dripping water which one made into flowing water, and he knew that this referred to the dark cisterns, for if a Jew owed them money, the Polish nobles would throw him into a dark cistern until he settled his debt.

Came the anniversary of the death of a certain Saint. A group of his Hasids entered the prayer house named after him and feasted and fêted. They sat and drank toasts and blessed one another with the wish that the merit of that Saint would defend them, and between one glass and another they told awesome and miraculous stories of that Saint and of the other Saints of the world. Some of them you may have heard, and some you probably haven't heard. What you heard you heard, and what you haven't heard you must hear, especially since it's about a dog.

Once upon a time, a man claimed to be a Saint. He attracted a big group of Hasids to him. But he wasn't a Saint at all, but a complete villain, who presented himself as a Saint, with that Satanic force, Heaven Forfend, for in every generation where a genuine Saint comes into the world, Satan puts an evil man against him and makes him a Saint in the eyes of the folks so they will be led astray by him and won't follow the Saint of the generation. And he is aided by heaven, for even honest Hasids are led astray by him. Why? Because the first generations were full of genuine Saints and the people didn't believe in them, and the Holy-One-Blessed-Be-He said, I gave you great Saints and you didn't heed them, so I put false Saints to rule you and you will follow them.

There was one of the genuine Saints who wasn't famous at all and who behaved like all the other simple Hasids, traveled to all the Saints and humbled himself before every single one of them. He heard that a great Saint was revealed and he went to him, to spend a Sabbath in his presence. And that famous man was of high stature for Satan endowed him with high qualities. He sensed that this was a simple Saint, and greeted him with great honor. The Saint sniffed a trace of a bad smell in him. Nevertheless, he bowed down to him, for in his modesty and simplicity, he thought he was not worthy to follow that Saint, and that Heaven had led him astray in the contro-versial issue of whether smell is a substantial thing or not. He waited for the entrance of the Sabbath, for by virtue of the Sabbath, when the holy Children of Israel purify themselves, he would be blessed to inhale some of the holiness of the Saint, for a Saint is considered as if he were the Sabbath, and that smell won't come to lead him astray. Comes the Sabbath. Comes that famous man to the study house with joy and dancing and prays at the top of his lungs until the walls are shaken by his prayer. Both when he greets you and when he recites the Kiddush. Said that Saint to himself, Thank God I didn't take pains for nothing, for the more we get into the Sabbath, the more ex-alted we are and rise from one degree to another. And he didn't sense a trace of a bad smell. And it is only right that he didn't smell it, for that faker immersed himself before the Sabbath, and a ritual bath pu-rifies. He waited until the Sabbath meal, where a good drink brings hearts together.

And that Saint was wont to starve himself in honor of the Sabbath so that he would come to the Sabbath meal with a hearty appetite, and he would eat only a pittance on the eve of the Sabbath so that he wouldn't enter the Sabbath in torments. When they sat at the meal, that famous man took his full share and gave him the remainder. The leftovers dropped from his hand and fell under the table. He bent down to pick them up. He hit them with his shoe and they were rejected. And no one noticed it, for their eyes were directed at their Saint. And their Saint didn't notice it either because all hands were stretched to him to ask for leftovers. That Saint sat with a heavy heart and a hungry stomach and thought to himself, It's a Commandment to celebrate the Sabbath with food and drink, but except for a slice of bread of the blessing, I haven't tasted a thing. And if I ask for something to eat, my voice won't be heard over the singing of the Sabbath songs. The next day, the false Saint again gave him the first portion. He took it with great haste. Before the leftovers reached his mouth someone jumped up and snatched them out of his hand. He had no mouth to speak, because of weakness, because he was hungry, because he hadn't eaten on the Sabbath night or the Sabbath eve. And even if he had said something, his voice wouldn't have been heard over the voice of the Torah of the fake Saint. That Saint regretted his fast and consoled himself that at the third meal he would repair the misdeed. Came the time for the third meal, the false one sat the Saint at his right hand and gave him the first portion. He took his full portion and recited the blessing. Suddenly a black dog, menacing and horrible, jumped up and snatched the leftovers from his hand. And that Saint knew what he knew and recognized what he recognized. And may we too know and distinguish between true Saints and false Saints, for by our many transgressions the false Saints have multiplied many times more than the true Saints.

All the while, that old man was sitting and pondering his dream, and he didn't know if he was dreaming a dream or pondering a dream he had already dreamed. The dream began evolving from issue to issue, from lamb to lamb, and from a Shtrayml to a Saint and from one Goy to another Goy. With the tips of his eyes, he looked at those around the table and said, Be quiet and I shall tell you something you've never heard in your life. But if you think you'll hear tales about dogs, you're simply wrong. Blessed be the Lord Who didn't make me a duke and I have nothing to do with abominable animals. He passed his glass from here to here and from there to there and filled his nose with snuff and started talking. And that tale has already been published in the books of the Hasids, but because of its length and its double language, no one could grasp it. And we present it in short, so that our book will not lack anything.

Once upon a time, there was a Hasid who owed money to a nobleman and couldn't pay. The nobleman ordered the Hasid's wife and daughters thrown into the cistern until he settled his debt. He went to his Rebbe and wept before him. Said his Rebbe, Go to the market and buy every object they offer you — buy and don't notice what it is or whether it is worth the price or not. He went to the market. Elijah the Prophet of blessed memory came to him in the form of a Christian peasant and offered him a lambskin. The Hasid asked him, How much will you sell it for? He replied, One gold coin. He put his hand in his pocket and took out a gold coin. He gave him the gold coin and took the skin. He went back to his Rebbe. Said his Rebbe, Tomorrow is the nobleman's birthday, go and bring him the lambskin. He went to the nobleman and brought him the skin. The nobleman was angry that he brought him such a simple birthday gift that would shame him before the noblemen and women who came to honor him. He took the skin and hit the Hasid with it. When he struck him, the skin spread out and it was made of letters upon letters, and the nobleman's name was written there. The nobleman saw that and was amazed, for even if he assembled all the artisans in the world, they couldn't have made anything so marvelous. But surely it came from Heaven. The nobleman immediately forgave the Jew all his debts and ordered him to take his wife and daughters out of the cistern and he appeased him with a great deal of money, and all the noblemen and noblewomen who were there gave him gifts of silver and gold. Finally, the nobleman made himself a lambskin hat and he wore that hat every single year on his birthday.

CHAPTER TWO

Balak's Nature and Pedigree

1 |

We don't know if Balak knew what the newspapers wrote about him and what people said about him. And if he did know — if he paid any heed to them. And if he did pay heed to them — if he was offended. And if he was offended — how much he was offended. As long as they offended him with words and didn't hit his body, he feared neither the newspaper articles nor the scholarly studies nor was he sorry about the woes of the Children of Israel who are slandered by wicked Gentiles, whose studies bring one calamity after another. And if this assumption is true, we may add to it an important rule, that Balak was bereft of any critical spirit, for if he was critical, he would have attributed everything that happened to him to ancient dialogues based completely on false superstitions, stemming from the imagination, and have nothing to do with reality. And you can't bring a counter argument from what was written on his skin, Crazy Dog, for precisely here it is easy to prove that there is nothing here, for according to the rules of the language, it should have said Mad Dog. And since it says Crazy Dog — it is a distortion, and if it is a distortion, the whole issue is a distortion, and is as if it were zero. And even his name itself belies it, as one diligent critic proved that the Jews are not wont to call animals by name, while he was called Balak. Hence, it is clear that this does not allude to an event that occurred, but there is a hint here that has not yet been understood by scholars and it warrants study. And if you say, He sticks out his tongue and barks, it may be countered that all other dogs bark too, as witnessed by books on the history of animals, that every dog is wont to stick out his tongue and bark. And while those described in the books of the history of an-

| 495

imals have not even one letter on their skin, even more so must we say that the writing on his skin does not exist.

2 |

Since we know that Balak was bereft of a critical spirit and didn't deny his own reality, there is room for a hypothesis, which we see as a complete certainty that Balak was a simple dog and wasn't concerned with what was beyond his understanding. Therefore, it is easy for us to grasp his nature, both physically and spiritually, for from the beginning of his creation, he was created like all other creatures who have nothing in the world except to protect their survival and to take care of getting their food. If they threw him a bone, he would lick and bark, sometimes out of pleasure and sometimes to ask for more, like any creature; if it gets enough of what it lacks, it enjoys; if it gets less it asks for more. And we shall not be mistaken if we say that he imagined that if he took pains to acquire his sustenance and supported his body, he was fulfilling the Commandments of his Creator Who created him to eat and to bark. The soul of a boor was incarnated in Balak, and a boor has nothing in his world aside from boorish matters. Not in vain are boors compared to dogs in the Zohar book, The Faithful Shepherd. All of Balak's behavior was taught by the precept of dogs. In the second watch of the night, he would shout, and if the Angel of Death came to the city, Balak would weep; and if the Prophet Elijah came to the city, Balak would smile. And when he finished fulfilling what he was commanded, he would go back to his corporeal affairs. In general, Balak was not exalted above all his brother dogs. And if he did have a few bits of knowledge — the hairs of his tail were more numerous than such bits.

Those bits of knowledge that Balak boasted of were mostly fragmentary, and even those concerning him and his pedigree did not reach an historic scope, or needless to say, a general scope. Balak knew that he had a father and that his name was such-and-such, and that his father also had a father and his name was thus-and-so. But what they changed in the world and what they added to the world, Balak didn't know. Like most Yeshiva boys in our time who occupy all their days studying Kabalah and know how many angels there are in the firmament and what their names are, but not one of them knows a thing about their rôle or what purpose they serve.

Here one of Balak's forefather dogs deserves mention. This was Tuval, the dog who was the leader of a pack of dogs in Jerusalem and ruled by force from Jaffa Gate to the street of the greengrocers at the edge of the upper market next to the street of the Anglican Church. That Tuval had a flat head and lopped-off ears and his hair was hard and so sparse that many people mistook him for a hyena. He was also concerned with public needs and cleaned the streets of Jerusalem from their filth and watched over the city's inhabitants at night, and if he heard any moving around he would raise his voice and shout until the ears of the thieves were deafened and they ran away. Because of that, most of the shopowners were fond of him and welcomed him and treated him with all kinds of food. And even the Ishmaelites would pet him (through a garment) and flatter him. They were especially fond of Tuval on the day he went up to the top of the tower of the Russian Church and struck the big bell the Russians had brought for themselves from Moscow and there was great laughter in Jerusalem. But if you asked Balak, When did this Tuval live whom you boast of so much, in the time of the war of Plevne or in the time of the great debate of the Herdskovici court — I doubt if he would know. As we said, even his historical information was defective and didn't go beyond knowing names and a few events, and even those events, if they weren't mentioned in the Almanac of the Land of Israel, it's doubtful if Balak would know anything about them.

Aside from that ancestor, Balak had other relatives who were also famous for their exploits, like those who aided the Sages and Rabbis of the Ashkenazim in their war against the secular schools. And when Ludwig August Frankel ascended to the Land to establish schools in Jerusalem, some of them volunteered their tails and the Sages and Rabbis tied notes to them saying, I am Ludwig Frankel excommunicated and ostracized; and moreover, the dogs behaved more heroically than the humans, for when Frankel complained to the consuls, most of the disputants withdrew and said they had had no part in that, while Balak's relatives didn't withdraw, and moreover they carried their tails with pride, and when the humans wanted to take the notes off them, they barked. As a result of that, in the days when the wife of the Rabbi of Brisk, may she rest in peace, ruled, some of Balak's relatives helped her in her war against the enlightened. The historian will have to conduct an exhaustive study to determine where the adventures of human beings end and the adventures of dogs begin.

Study of Impurity

1 |

But from the day Balak was exiled from Meah Shearim and bereft of his livelihood and wandered from place to place and from neighborhood to neighborhood and from quarter to quarter and from nation to nation and from sect to sect, an intelligent mind entered into him and he started thinking thoughts, like tourists and travelers. But tourists and travelers see every part of the world as different from every other part and creatures in the world as different from one another, while Balak saw the world as one whole. The earth is the same everywhere, said Balak, and there is no distinction between the people of this place and the people of that place. And if there is a difference, it is an external difference, for the end of every creation is flesh and bone, that is sustenance, whether they say a blessing over slaughter like the Jews, and say Who hath sanctified us with his commandments and commanded us to slaughter, or say a blessing like the Karaites, who say, Who allowed us to slaughter, or say a blessing like the Ishmaelites, who bless in the name of the merciful and compassionate Allah, or they slit the neck like all other nations, they all intend the same thing, sustenance.

Ever since the day Balak came to that worthless knowledge, he didn't regard the rich more than the poor or the boors more than the sages. Things came to such a pass that he didn't make any distinction between those clothed in rabbinical garb and those in dung and straw. Said Balak, Both the former and the latter intend the same thing and both the former and the latter shout give, give, alf alf, but the latter take their food with the toil of their arms and with the labor of their hands, and the former by grace of their long garments and their fedoras. But he was very clever and concealed his thoughts in his heart so that he wouldn't end up like those dogs whose mouths are muzzled. And when he restrained his wisdom, his head became like a beehive, until it was amazing how this simple creature could exist. To his thoughts he added his dreams. We already said that Balak was wont to dream a lot of dreams and to forget them immediately, but sometimes he remembered them. And when he remembered he would think they were actual events that had happened. But dreams sometimes have a bit of truth, whereas most studies of them are nonsense. And it wasn't enough that Balak held onto his nonsense, but he attached hypotheses to them and hypotheses to hypotheses and worked out systems and reinforced them with systems weaker than they were.

There is a view among dogs that they too were once human creatures, but because they revolted against their master, he turned them into dogs. Some of them repented and were restored to their original form, and some of them maintained their rebellion and remained dogs. Needless to say, this view has no scientific support. And scholars now agree that the dog came from the fox or from the wolf or from the hyena or from some primeval dog who is extinct now. It seems that the dogs heard the rumor about Nebuchadnezzar, who was turned into a bear and repented and went back to being a man. The dogs latched onto that tale and translated it for themselves. We don't know if it was out of extreme naïveté that Balak held that view or out of conviction, for he saw many human creatures who had a canine temperament.

2 |

From that view, he came to a worse view about the story of creation. And why do we mention it if it is incorrect? If another sage comes and says, I know that from tradition, we will tell him, It was the words of Balak the dog you heard.

In the beginning was the camel. Once he ate a field of prickly pears, and another field and another field. His belly exploded and he died. All the livestock, animals, birds, insects, and reptiles gathered in his belly. Vegetarians lived on the vegetables that re-

mained in his belly, carnivores lived on his meat. And since they
didn't spare him and ate his flesh, they became cruel. At last, nothing was left but the bowels of the camel. Came the pig and ate the
bowels. At last nothing was left of the camel but his skin. Came the
mice to nibble on his skin. The dog and the vulture stood to guard it
from the mice, the dog down below and the vulture up above. They
stood one day and two days and three days, until seven days. They
grew impatient and became bored. They started playing with the
skin. This one pulled it this way and that one pulled it that way. The
skin stretched and became the firmament. It rose up and stretched
over the earth, for the firmament is wont to be up above. The dog
saw and was amazed. He said to the vulture, What is that? Said the
vulture, I'll go and see. He spread his wings and began flapping them.
That created a wind that stirred up the whole world. The dog shuddered and pounded the ground with his tail. The whole land became
mountains and valleys and dales and rifts. The dog shouted from the
earth and the vulture shrieked in the air. The firmament grew frightened and wept. From its tears, the whole land was filled with water.
Came livestock and animals and birds to drink until they drank up
all the water and there was no more water left except the water in the
seas and the streams and the rivers and the springs. As they drank they
kicked their feet. The earth was plowed and brought up grass and
trees. And the firmament went on weeping. With his wings, the vulture dried the eyes of the firmament and wiped away its tears. The
firmament dried up and the world was about to be destroyed. They
came to the dog. The dog sent to the vulture. The vulture wrapped
himself in his wings and wasn't responding. Once again he wrapped
himself and wasn't responding. He said to the dog, If my prayer
doesn't work, perhaps your teeth will. Come and I'll ride you on my
wings and you'll rise with me to the firmament and bite it the same
way you bit that Arab merchant. Once an Arab merchant brought a
waterskin to Jerusalem. You bit the skin and the skin brought down
tears. The dog rode on the back of the vulture up to the firmament,
the dog bit the firmament and the firmament began weeping. The
whole land was soaked with its tears and filled with water. From those
bites, the firmament was cracked and the moon and the stars

emerged. That's why when the moon comes out, all the dogs bark, for the dogs remember all the efforts of their forefather, the Great Dog, and they shout.

At first, when Balak dwelt among the Jews and adhered to the ideas of his forefathers, he believed like all Jerusalem that the rains come only when the Shofar is blown, and when the rains stop, they take up the Shofar and blow, and the whole firmament starts trembling and bringing down rain. Some of it the land drinks and brings out bread for human beings, some of it livestock and animals and birds drink so their flesh will be sweet to human beings. Ever since the day Balak was exiled from his place and the faith of his forefathers shattered in him, he denied the power of human creatures and took issue with those who say that everything created in the world is created only for human beings. Said Balak, It's enough for man that he is like a dog and like all other creatures. And what led Balak to that conclusion? They said, Once seventy died in Jerusalem from dog bites. Said Balak, Where is the strength of man and where is the power of his awe? And there are those who say, He saw people behaving like animals. So, he went and sinned.

3 |

When does Balak deny the valor of human beings? When no person is before him. When Balak sees a person before him holding a stick in his hand, his mind immediately becomes meek and his spirit is humiliated and he subjugates himself before him and flatters him. How awed is Balak of man? There was a convert in Balak's neighborhood, the convert saw Balak and his writing, he went and denounced him to the Gentiles and they wanted to kill him. That convert is a worthless person, they don't even believe his faith, but they accepted his testimony and were prepared to kill a creature on his say-so.

Balak shouts in torment, Oh, why am I hounded out of the whole world, everyone who sees me wants to kill me. Did I ever do anybody any harm, did I ever bite any one of them. So why do they hound me and not leave my bones alone. Balak complains to Heaven and shouts, Arf arf, give me a place to rest, give me righteousness and justice. And when Balak's shout is heard, they assault him with stones and sticks. Balak bites the stones and the dirt and screams. The stones and dirt say, Why are you shouting at us? Do we have a choice? Evil humans hurl us and do with us whatever their hearts desire. If it's revenge you want, go and bite them. Says Balak to the dirt and stones, Do you think I'm a mad dog to go and bite humans? The dirt and stones say to Balak, Then, go and complain to them. Says Balak, Do they want to hear complaints, you didn't hear them saying whichever is stronger can take possession. The dirt and stones say, In that case, show them your strength. Says Balak to himself, Maybe they're right and I can rely only on my own strength. Great is the strength, for just bringing it out imposes fear. And what is the strength of a dog? To bark. A dog has to bark even if no one is attacking him. It's a shame for a dog to shout just when humans come upon him, as if barking depends on humans, but rather you should shout whenever you want to. Just as man is scared of the strength, so he is scared of the voice. Moreover, superior is the voice that frightens even from a distance.

Balak began shouting. Sometimes he shouted sporadically and sometimes he shouted incessantly. If he stopped, he stood amazed, imagining that his voice had got rusty. Said Balak to himself, Why did my voice get rusty? Because I don't use it enough, so I shall shout again until it gets strong again. He barked and shouted and whined day and night, whether there was a man or whether there wasn't. He who didn't hear Balak's groans, may he not hear them. Even dogs were shocked by his voice. And once upon a time, Balak was wooing a bitch. When he jumped at her, she leaped onto the top of the rock and fell down and died.

Balak wanted to shut his mouth and subdue his groaning, but habit does a lot. At first, it was he who ruled his voice, now his voice ruled him. He shouted and his tail was between his legs and he walked on the side for fear of the Angel of Death, for Balak was afraid they would poison him like a pig that strayed among the Ishmaelites. From now on, he kept away from all food and drink lest they had put a drug of death in it. Of all deaths, the one Balak feared most was death by poison, for if he was healthy in his body and healthy in his limbs, suddenly the Angel of Death would come from his guts as if he himself had lodged him there.

Said Balak to himself, Woe unto me from the Jews and woe unto me from the Gentiles. If I dwell among the Gentiles, Gentiles will poison me, and if I dwell among the Jews, Jews will split my skull. Between the former and the latter, woe unto me. Even Heaven fought with him, for the radiance of the late summer sun seemed to him like ropes used to bind mad dogs.

Out of extreme caution, Balak's ears pricked up, and every ripple and trace of a ripple would wander into his ears and hum like a military drum and stir his soul and he would bob up and down like a Cantor's Adam's apple. But Balak didn't produce melodies, for he already knew that the world doesn't need singing. His stormy soul was filled and a shout was wrenched out of his throat, and he added to it a dry wail to make the shout forgotten, and lay back prostrate on his belly and was silent again. As if he hadn't barked. All those days when he was away from home, he followed the maxim: A dog away from home doesn't bark for seven years.

Along with the sense of hearing, the sense of smell was so well developed in him that he would smell the trace of the trace of a smell. The sense of hearing Balak ruled by himself, the sense of smell ruled him. If he was following a smell, before he got there, another smell came to him, and when that smell came to him, another smell came and grabbed him by his nose and led him away. If he ran with it here, another smell came from there, and before he arrived, another smell ran to meet him. The garbage of Jerusalem could deprive anyone with a nose of his sense of smell, but not Balak, every single heap of garbage reveals its smells to him.

Impossible to dwell in many places at the same time and impossible to stay in one place when all kinds of voices are bustling in the soul, and so Balak ran around from place to place, and listened and smelled and smelled and listened. And what sounds didn't do to him, smells did; and what smells didn't do to him, sounds did. Balak reverted to shouting and he smelled and poked his nose into garbage, so they wouldn't think it was he who was shouting, but that garbage.

4 |

This abundance bestowed upon him made him sad. All those senses couldn't have been given in vain. There must be a great design to it, but why were they given and what is the design? As the abundance increased, his understanding diminished.

Balak straightened up from the garbage and went somewhere else, like someone walking in the middle of the night and gloom, and a candle is placed at his feet, and he moves away from where he is standing so the candle will illuminate him. He went up to the cliff and opened his eyes and shook his ears, and tried to grasp something of that design with his eyes or his ears, for like most primitive creatures, Balak didn't distinguish between his mental images, his internal organs and external organs. And so he stood, and all the things in front of him were deafening and didn't tell him anything. He stretched out his legs and started scratching on the ground until he dug a hole in it, either to force it to open its mouth or to make it a new mouth. Came a dust storm and darkened his eyes, and after the dust, from the earth appeared the head of a brush that had been discarded by some painter. Balak sniffed this handful of hairs. His skin shuddered as on the day he spent in the neighborhood of the Bukharans, the day when the man with the wet instrument plastered his moisture on him. But that throb wasn't a throb of pleasure, but a throb of fear. His eyes were filled with blood and a voice was torn out of his mouth. Not the voice of wailing and not the voice of whining and not the voice of groaning, but a new voice, a voice of revenge.

And when Balak heard his voice, an arrogant power overpowered his heart and a tough rind enveloped his body like armor. He turned his head to his tail which rose erect as an arrow. Balak was filled with valor and gnashed his teeth on top of one another, and sank his mouth in the space of the world, to bite the whole world. And yet his spirit weakened at once and the skin of his face began changing, changing, and his heart didn't let him rest. Balak swayed and knelt, sometimes on his hind legs and sometimes on his forelegs and his heart fluttered and pounded vigorously inside him. And he too dreaded and feared, and his teeth, which just recently were gnashing in valor, were chattering against one another, like those cowards that Homer, the master of the Gentile poets, condemned in his poems. On top of that, his tail became flaccid, and every single hair sat in its spring as if the spring dried up and the hair dried up. On top of that, the fear. Not that fear that Homer praises in his heroes, which accompanies them wherever they go, and it terrifies even brave men until they flee from it, but that fear that imposes dread on itself. Sometimes his eyes were enveloped in awful sadness, sometimes his eyes became empty, sometimes his heart was crushed, sometimes his heart was mashed, as if someone had brought a wooden or stone pestle there and crushed and mashed and mashed and crushed.

Balak stood dejected, his tail drooping, until he stole down from the cliff. He lay down wherever he lay down and closed his eyes to sleep. But his eyes jolted open by themselves. His sleep was jolted and fled. And when sleep returned to him, it didn't bring him rest, but on the contrary, brought weariness on top of weariness with it. And when he shook himself awake, he found himself much more fatigued than he was at first. Because of the bad dreams and because of the bad thoughts that had mated with him in his sleep. He waved his leg to shoo them away, like flies you shoo away but they weren't to be shooed. He opened his mouth to swallow them. But his tongue dropped and was about to fall out of his mouth. Now, even if a person threw him some bread, he didn't have the strength to shut his mouth.

In those days, his nose began to dry up like a shard, and some harsh and turbid warmth emanated from his muzzle and returned there. And his nails shuddered from his blunted paws, as if his whole being was gathered in them. But his mouth was weak and his tongue was hanging down. If he wanted to put his tongue back into his mouth, he confused it with his tail and put his tail between his legs. He turned his head around and searched for his tail and didn't find it, because it was lying between his legs. And since the body is composed of a head and a tail, it's easy to understand Balak's grief when he turned his head around to his tail and didn't find it.

CHAPTER FOUR

Leaves the Dog and Returns to Isaac

1 |

Whole in body and whole in spirit, Isaac returned to the Holy City. His soul, heavy when he left, was light when he returned. Sonya didn't complain about him and Rabinovitch didn't mention his transgression. On the contrary, he made him a partner in work and livelihood. Now all he had to do was go to Shifra's mother and ask her for her daughter's hand. The days Isaac had spent in Jaffa had expanded him, and he didn't see that he was an artisan and she was the daughter of important people, that he was from Galicia and she was from Hungary. Reb Fayesh's illness and the assistance Isaac had provided for Shifra and Rebecca also helped bring down the barriers. Even in the bad days, Isaac didn't despair, and now that his mood was good and his heart was open, there was even less reason.

The bare mountains roll and run with the train and sublime clouds are attached to them. And olive-green cliffs and rocks are suspended between the mountains and tend to fall but don't. And wild goats leap from cliff to cliff and from rock to rock, some raise their horns and look amazed, and with others, bunches of dirt roll away beneath their hooves and they don't make a sound. And a breeze goes among the mountains and refreshes a person's bones. Just this morning, deserts of sand were stumbling at your feet and the sea was roaring in front of you as far as the eye could see, and now solid mountains of the earth are on your right, and on your left a strip of blue is stretched above the mountains and a still small voice rises, and the mountains develop in silence, rise and fall, fall and rise, and the wheels of the train rattle below, and a big bird soars above and disappears in the blue of the sky or in the smoke rising from the train.

And the train winds and goes from valley to dale and from dale to mountain on the way to Jerusalem. Before the day is over, he will arrive in Jerusalem and will go to Shifra. If she has prepared her mother's heart, fine, and if not, he has his own mouth.

2 |

Isaac's train was full of Jerusalemites who went down to Jaffa to bathe in the sea. The change of place and bathing in the sea gave them tanned faces, refreshed spirits, and control over their limbs. They sat comfortably, this one on a pillow and that one on a quilt, with a basket of food at the feet of every single one, and this one looked at his expanding belly and that one at his neighbor's full face. They felt good and started joking about that custom of changing air and bathing in the sea, which is simply a stupid custom the doctors introduced, for after the doctors try all remedies and don't find a cure, they send the patients to Jaffa and order them to do this and that, so that afterward they will have an excuse to say, You certainly didn't follow our orders, and they start tormenting them with medications all over again. For if it's air, Jerusalem is the holiest of all places, and it stands to reason that her air is better than the air of Jaffa. And if it's the sea, if we were worthy, the sea of Solomon would exist, and when they mentioned the sea, they started explicating the sea that Solomon made and the seven seas that surround the Land of Israel, and why are the waters of the sea better for the body? Because the planets have no control over the sea, only the Holy-One-Blessed-Be-He does Himself, and it is His wont, as it were, to be good to His creatures, especially the Children of Israel. There is a special closeness between the sea and the Children of Israel, for the sea gives salt which they take for sacrifices, and He remembers the Children of Israel for the sacrifices they sacrificed on the altar. And when they praised the sea, they mentioned creatures in the sea that aren't defiled, for the First Adam didn't give them names. Hence we don't find names of fish anywhere in the Torah. And when they mentioned fish, they praised them, for even if they have no personal providence and have no astrological sign as man does, they fulfill their obligation to fate and the obligation to providence through man, for sometimes fish is prepared for him in honor of the Sabbath, in accordance with the person's astrological sign and personal providence, for the Sabbath is the mating season of the scholars and Leviathan is in charge of the lust for copulation, as Rashi explains in his commentary on Job, who are ready to raise up their mourning. And that is the reason why the Holy-One-Blessed-Be-He castrated the male and killed the female preserving it in salt for the righteous in the world to come. And when they mentioned Leviathan, they mentioned his power and his valor, when he is thirsty he makes numerous furrows in the sea. The deep does not return to its strength until seventy years, and nevertheless it was created only for man, as the MaHaRSHA wrote in the Tractate Babba Batra. That goodness in the World-to-Come did not make them forget the goodness of Jaffa, where living is fine and food is plentiful. And when they remembered Jaffa, they sighed, for living in Jaffa makes a person take care of the body, as if it were the essence of man and man is nothing but body. In fact a person does need a body to maintain the soul, but what is the value of the body and how much do we have to take care of it. It's enough for the body that it exists for the soul, yet in the end it takes everything at first and enjoys first. Indeed, its hand and its head are the first for the Commandment of Tefillin. And for the Commandment of the Sukkah, who enters it first if not the body. And it is first for all Commandments, not to mention eating on the Sabbath and the Commandment to perform a Commandment.

3 |

Another group that isn't so learned in the Torah tell about this Jaffa, for their forefathers told them that when they came to the Land of Israel, there was nothing in Jaffa but a mere Minyan, and even a few years afterward, when people from Jerusalem came down and established a settlement there, they wanted to make a Talmud society, but there wasn't a complete Talmud in the whole city, just one tractate here and another tractate there. Now Jaffa is full of synagogues and study houses, and you don't have one single study house that doesn't have several Talmuds and several Minyans. And Jaffa now regards it-self as one of the cities of the Land of Israel and wants a portion of the Distribution. And two preachers are already fighting and deliv-ering slanderous sermons against one another. And even about the Rabbi there's a Quarrel, for some tend to follow the son of the de-ceased Rabbi and help him assume authority. And when they came to the Rabbi of Jaffa, they praised him, for aside from his great ex-pertise in overt and mysterious knowledge, he truly sacrifices himself for every single son of Israel.

Someone groaned, What difference does it make to us if he's a genius and a saint, if shops are open there on the Sabbath and he sees and keeps silent. Someone else groaned, On the contrary, he does well not to do anything, for if you act, you ruin things. Last year, the Rabbi wanted to expel one of the whorehouse owners from Jaffa. Not only did he not succeed in expelling him, but that filth joined other sinners like him and they brought a trouble-maker and made him Rabbi, and the breach grew wider and wider, and the city was torn into several sections and every section expanded.

4

As some tell of Jaffa and its quarrels, others began lauding Jerusalem and Rabbi Samuel, who knows how to lead his community wisely, and knows what is in the heart of every single person in Jerusalem. How far? Once upon a time, they came and told Rabbi Samuel that they saw a Jew lying dead on the road to Jericho and already rotting and worms were swarming over his body. Rabbi Samuel ordered them to hurry and bring him to the city to be buried in a Jewish grave, so that the issue wouldn't be known to the government, for that year there was a fear of plague. That day was the Sabbath eve and by the time they brought him, the sun had gone down and they buried him in the dark. At night, Rabbi Samuel called Rabbi Haim and told him the whole deed. Rabbi Samuel asked Rabbi Haim, What should I have done? Said Rabbi Haim, You taught well, Rabbi Samuel. In the morning, all the Hungarians made a turmoil and shouted, as if Rabbi Samuel had ordered to profane the Sabbath, for they could have bribed the government officials with Bakshish. What did the Hungarians care if Jerusalem spent five hundred Napoleons? At that moment, Rabbi Haim wasn't in the study house. When he came they told him the issue. Said Rabbi Haim, Rabbi Samuel did well. The Quarrel subsided immediately. For Rabbi Samuel is a wise man, who knew that the Hungarians would disagree with him, but they wouldn't disagree with their own Rabbi, and he anticipated them and called Rabbi Haim.

On the train was one man who, with his father and his father's father, as well as his son and his son's son had known Rabbi Samuel. He waved his hand dismissively and said, I'll tell you all something and you'll understand how far Rabbi Samuel's wisdom reached. Someone else interrupted him and said, We know what you want to tell. But I'll tell you something you never heard in your life. Before he could tell, someone else interrupted. Before he could tell, someone else interrupted and told.

Every day before the afternoon prayer, Rabbi Samuel would go out to stroll in the courtyard of the Hurbah Synagogue. In those days, the hospice was still there, and the whole courtyard was full of male and female beggars of Jerusalem and other places. Some were cooking and frying and some were laundering their garments. Some were chatting and some were bickering. Once a question about a wife deserted Outside the Land came before Rabbi Samuel, he found the issue very difficult and didn't find any grounds for leniency. Before the afternoon prayer, he went to stroll in the courtyard, pondering the question of the deserted wife, and his eyes weren't yet afflicted. Among the beggars, he saw a man. He recognized in him all the identifying marks of the deserted wife's husband. He asked him, What's your name? But the man didn't tell him. He said to him, Aren't you so-and-so, son of so-and-so, from the city of such-and-such, who deserted your wife? If you don't confess the truth, I shall call a policeman and have you locked up, for I have authority from the government. The pauper was about to run away. They caught him and brought him to court and Rabbi Samuel forced him to give his wife a divorce.

The first one who wanted to tell said, I used to visit Rabbi Samuel frequently and I can testify that whoever Rabbi Samuel talked to, he knew immediately what was in his heart. All Rabbi Samuel had to do was glance at you and immediately all your secrets were revealed to him. And even after he lost the light of his eyes, Heaven Forfend, he recognized every person by his voice. And if a child passed and said, Sabbath greetings, Rabbi, Rabbi Samuel would say to him, Aren't you the son of the daughter of so-and-so who lives in such-and-such a courtyard, and never did Rabbi Samuel make a mistake.

As some tell of the wisdom of Rabbi Samuel, others told of the genius of the Rabbi of Brisk of blessed memory, who could innovate everything every author had innovated in his writings. Once upon a time, the Rabbi of Brisk found a student poring over a book. He said to him, What's that in your hand? He said to him, A new book full of marvelous innovations. He said to him, Tell me one thing from the book. He told him. He said, If so, I'll tell you what that author innovated in this passage of the Talmud and in that problem. And his words conformed to the words of the author.

Someone else started talking, And I'll tell you something you never heard in your life. Someone else interrupted him and said, And I'll tell something even you haven't heard. Another one interrupted him and said, You want to tell him a tale you heard from me. Well, gentlemen, this was the story. Before he got started, someone else jumped into his words and said, I'll tell you something that will make you sorry you have only two ears. Since everyone knew that if he opened his mouth there was something to hear, everyone pricked up his ears. He started telling, What made the Rabbi of Brisk marry Sonya? This is how it was. After Sonya was divorced from her first husband, all the great men of the state sent to marry her, but she rejected them all. At that time, the Rabbi of Brisk was widowed. One matchmaker, two matchmakers, three matchmakers she sent to him and they couldn't do anything. She went to him in Brisk. That Rabbi didn't let her in. She said to his close friends, Go and tell your Rabbi that I have one thing to say to him, and when he hears that thing, he will change his mind immediately. The Rabbi recognized that this wasn't just idle talk and ordered them to bring her in. She told him, When I was a little child, my grandfather, Rabbi Joseph

Yampola, son-in-law of Yehuda Landau, the author of *The Famous of Yehuda*, was fond of me. Once he sat me on his lap, put both his hands on my head and blessed me that I would marry the genius of the generation. And since the Rabbi of Brisk is the genius of the generation, it is fitting that he should marry me to fulfill the blessing of that Rebbe. The Rabbi of Brisk said to her, I have heard of you that you don't bear sons. Said she, That doesn't depend on me. Within a few days, he married her. And when they mentioned the wife of the Rabbi of Brisk, they started telling of her greatness, that in her time, no one raised his head, and even Rabbis and Geniuses were scared of her, not to mention the Rabbi of Brisk, who himself followed the biblical injunction, in all that Sarah hath said unto thee, hearken unto her voice.

As some praise the Rabbi of Brisk, others tell of the greatness of the Rabbi of Lublin, a holy man of God whose face was like an angel of the Lord of Hosts, and he didn't forget a single thing he learned. And when they would ask him something about the Rabbinic Law, he would open a Talmud and immediately show the answer. And never in his life did he have to turn over the page, for he would point to the place and even to the line with his finger. And not only that, but things that other men would struggle over for an hour or two, he would grasp in a wink, quite unnaturally. And once upon a time, people came from Hebron with a question written on several sheets. He looked at it and made some answer. They told him, Our Rabbi hasn't yet read the whole question and is already answering it. He said to them, So, listen and I'll tell you everything that is written here, and his words were correct word for word. A small fraction of his genius is seen in his book *Torat Hesed* which he didn't publish to boast of his learning, but when he saw that his strength was waning and it was hard for him to teach students, he wrote his book, to take the place of studying with students. All his life, he didn't waste a minute, and at the end of his days, he would recite Mishnahs by heart, for as that Saint said, every Jew should know the Six Orders of Mishnah by heart, for if he dies on the Sabbath and is laid out until the close of the Sabbath when he is buried, what will he do to keep from wasting his time. And clearly the words were meant for himself, for he saw with the holy spirit that he would depart on the Sabbath. That Sabbath when the Rabbi of Lublin passed away was the time of the Greeting of the Sabbath, and all Jerusalem was standing in the synagogues and study houses to greet the Sabbath. Suddenly a roar was heard, as if heaven and earth were stunned. And everyone knew that the Rabbi of Lublin had departed. After the prayer they went to his house but they no longer found him alive.

As some praise the great scholars of the Torah, others sat and told tales of miraculous people of Jerusalem, who weren't experts in Torah, but who were great Saints, like Reb Noah Hayatt, who was tall and skinny and behaved like a complete ignoramus, and when Rabbi Samuel had difficulties about releasing a deserted wife, he would call him to tell him where the deserter was, and he was always right. Once Rabbi Samuel started teaching him the Torah. Reb Noah pretended he didn't know what he was talking about. Rabbi Samuel said to him, I know that you know. Said he, I don't know, I don't know. Just one thing I do know, I know how to find men who deserted their wives, so as to release the daughters of Israel from the bonds of desertion. Rabbi Samuel said to him, I order you to reveal yourself to me. He said to him, Shut up or I shall order you to do whatever I want. Rabbi Samuel was frightened and fell silent.

5 |

As the Poles and the Lithuanians praised the geniuses of Poland and Lithuania, the Hungarians praised the great men of Hungary. In that train was a stooped, suffering man, who didn't travel to heal the body, but went to the Rabbi of Jaffa for he needed his judgment because his wife went mad right after the wedding night and the Rabbis of Jerusalem won't let him divorce her, even though they write a divorce decree for everyone who can pay for the scribe. That man looked with disfavor at those carefree people, everyone sitting on his pillow and his quilt, dressed in fine clothes, his bed made and his table set, while he lives with a madwoman in a humble house with no bed and no table. He clicked his tongue contemptuously at them and their stories. One young Yeshiva student scolded him, Why are you squeaking at us like a mouse? That man drew himself up to face him and said, If it's stories you want I'll tell you stories that will curdle the milk in your bellies. And you can tell your father who will excommunicate me as he excommunicated Rabbi Akiva Yosef the author of A *Hebrew Heart*, who had a real Hebrew heart. And when he mentioned Rabbi Akiva Yosef, he started telling how many troubles befell that Saint who wanted to undo the ban of Rabbi Gershom against taking two wives, and when he wanted to make other great repairs, the officers rose up against him and outlawed him. His father-in-law, Rabbi Hillel of Kolomea, heard and wrote to him, When the holy ARI, Isaac Luria of blessed memory, was in Jerusalem, he saw Satan standing with one foot on the holy place and his other foot standing on his house, and the holy ARI Luria was forced to run away from Jerusalem. You run away too. Replied Rabbi Akiva Yosef, I won't run away. And he still lives in Jerusalem and Satan dances in the city to keep the Children of Israel away from good fortune.

And when they mentioned the officers, they mentioned Reb Naftali Haim, who knew the root of the soul of every single officer and the secret of his metamorphosis. When Reb Naftali Haim walked around the marketplace and saw watercarriers bringing waterskins on their donkeys, and poking the donkeys with a spiked stick until they bled, he called every donkey by the name of one of the famous officers who had already departed this world and had been metamorphosed into donkeys, and the donkeys looked pleadingly and imploringly at that Saint. Sometimes he would say to a donkey, So-and-So, son of So-and-So, you already have repair, and the donkey would shake his head at him in thanks and go on his way; and sometimes he would say to a donkey, Many torments are still demanded of you and many woes are in store for you in this world until you find your repair, and the donkey would drop his head and not budge, not even if they poked him, even if he bled.

Once a man came to Reb Naftali Haim to request an amulet for his son who had gone mad, Heaven Forfend. Reb Naftali Haim told him, I don't write amulets. But I do bless you that your son may recover, and my blessing is enough for you. That man didn't budge from him until he was forced to write him an amulet. The man hung it on his son's neck and the boy's mind was restored. His neighbors asked to see what names could drive out madness and they opened the amulet. They found written Nissim Bek and Eleazar Shapiro, two officers of Jerusalem. They went to Reb Naftali Haim and told him, What is this? He told them, Even the demons are scared of those people.

Reb Naftali Haim lived on Hebron Street in a small room, and not everyone could come to him, and those who were allowed in his house saw great wonders. In his room were two beds, his and his wife's, and two small tables, his and his wife's. On his table not a fly was seen, and his wife's table was full of flies. Once, one of the people close to him came to his house. He told him, Sit down. He wanted to sit on the bed of the Rabbi's wife. He told him, Sit on my bed. Not that I am strict about sitting on her bed, but her bed is full of fleas and my bed is clean. And in fact that was so. And no wonder, for everyone who doesn't flee from his deeds, the fleas have no power over him.

Reb Naftali Haim's landlord was a wicked Arab, and every day he would aggravate his Jewish tenants. Once, he troubled Reb Naftali Haim very much. Reb Naftali Haim told him, Please go. The Arab got angry and said to him, You tell me to go, I'll throw you right out of the apartment. And that wicked man didn't calm down until he locked the cistern to Reb Naftali Haim. Said Rabbi Naftali Haim, I don't want to fight with you, the water and the cistern will fight with you. The next day, they found the Arab lying dead in the cistern in his courtyard. The entire city was amazed, for the stone opening of the cistern was narrow and that Arab was fat and fleshy.

6 |

When they mentioned water and a cistern, everyone mentioned his own cistern, whose water was low that year, and if the rains didn't come on time, there wouldn't be water to drink, for the reservoirs were already starting to raise the price of their water, as the Arab watercarriers, when they see that Jerusalem is thirsty for water, raise their price. Everyone became sad. Said one of them, Gentlemen, sufficient unto the hour is the trouble thereof, it will be better to speak of happy things. They went back to talking about Jaffa, where they drink well water and don't need to bring their water for money. And in addition, they have a sea there, and if you bathe in it, it's like bathing in the ritual bath, which removes the pollution on your body. And the sea has a great advantage over the ritual bath, for when a man comes out of the ritual bath he is sick from the smell, while the sea smells good. And those who aren't strong enough to go down to the sea take sand baths. How? You dig yourself a kind of grave and you sit up to your navel in the sand and you are healed, for a man is created from four elements, fire, wind, water, and earth, and the sand of the sea includes four elements, fire wind water and earth. Fire is the sun that inflames the sand. Wind is what blows the sand apart. Water, for the sand comes from the sea. Earth, for the sand is also a kind of earth. Those four elements come and bring healing to man who was created of four elements.

But a person has to be careful not to go far away from the settlement so that the grave he digs for his cure does not become an eternal grave, God Forbid, as happened once upon a time to one old man from Jerusalem who went into the sand up to his neck, and three young Ishmaelites passed by him with donkeys loaded with dung. They dumped the dung on him and buried him alive. Jews came and saw what they did to that old man. They chased the vandals and caught one of the three donkeys and cracked open the heap and pulled out the old man and put him on the donkey naked as he was and took him to his Consul and told him the whole tale. The Consul got angry that the Ishmaelites had humiliated his subject. He sent his deputy to the Saraya, the police chief. Police came immediately and arrested the donkey. The leaders of the city agreed to pay the donkey's board until his trial came up, and they took the old man to the hospital and wrote to Jerusalem that his society would pay for medical expenses and lodging. Meanwhile, all the Fellahin of the village of Yazoor assembled and attacked Mikveh Israel with rifles and bows and spears to avenge the donkey. The officials of Mikveh Israel ran away along with the teachers and the students. One jumped out of the window and broke his leg, and was put in the hospital. He lay in one bed and that old man in another bed, and all Jaffa discussed which came first, the trial of that old man or the trial of Mikveh Israel, for it was impossible to win both trials at the same time, for the community isn't capable of bribing all the judges. Before some finished boasting of the greatness of the sons of Israel and others finished moaning over the troubles of the sons of Israel, the train approached Jerusalem.

He Goes to Shifra

1 |

Even before Isaac reached Jerusalem, Jaffa was uprooted from his heart, and all the things he had seen there vanished as if they had never been real. And when he reached Jerusalem, his soul woke up and his heart began to beat. In this city, every hour has something of the life of the World-to-Come. He wiped the dust of Jerusalem out of his eyes and the Holy City was revealed to him as it is revealed to those who love it. He recalled something the painter Bloykof had said to him, Come, let us embrace one another that we are graced to dwell in Jerusalem, and Isaac wiped a tear from his eyes and rented a seat in a wagon. He went to the inn of Shoel Hirshl, as he had done the first time he had ascended, but now he went on his own. Every inn is good and bad. The inn of Shoel Hirshl has a special advantage, that it embraces its guests.

There were no guests in the inn. Not even Shoel Hirshl or his sons and daughters were there. The sons and daughters weren't there because they had bickered and left, and Shoel Hirshl wasn't there because he had gone across the Jordan. Shoel Hirshl loved business and couldn't sit idle. Now that the inn was empty, he had joined the Lulav merchants and went with them across the Jordan to bring Lulavs.

What were those Lulavs? Across the Jordan, along the Dead Sea, on the way to Kir-Moab, between the mountains and in the mountains, you find little groves of palms. The palms grow by themselves and the Bedouins don't tend them, since they don't bear fruit. Once a Jew from Jerusalem went to Kir-Moab to get wheat. He cut some palm branches and brought them to Jerusalem. The people of

Jerusalem saw the Lulavs and found them fit and fine and beautiful and good for waving. And another advantage of those Lulavs is that, since they grow without water, they are hard and can last a long time, and are suitable for export Outside the Land. One of the distinguished families of Jerusalem got permission from the Wali in Damascus to cut Lulavs there. Every year, they cross the Jordan and bring Lulavs. The people of Jerusalem rejoice at the Lulavs that come from across the Jordan, which the Lord prepared for them to perform the Commandment in utmost beauty and perfection, and even the poorest of the poor stints on necessities to buy himself a Lulav from across the Jordan. On the other hand, there were a group of people in Jerusalem who washed their hands of them, for the Torah says *the branches of palm trees,* and those Lulavs are palm-branches that don't bear fruit. But it didn't get as far as a Quarrel. And they already exported more than fifty thousand Lulavs Outside the Land and they wrote from abroad, Send us more like those.

2 |

Since the inn had no guests and all the rooms were empty, the landlady opened a nice room for Isaac, and asked money only for the bed. And as she made up his bed, she told him her troubles. Strife befell the house between her daughters and her daughters-in-law. Everyone moved out. And when did they leave? When the inn was empty. Why? To make Shoel Hirshl angry. They know he can't sit alone and they left him at the moment of isolation. Shoel Hirshl is good-natured and loves folks, but what pleasure does a person get if he's good and the world's bad. Such a Sabbath as that Sabbath when the house emptied out—the day of mourning for the Destruction of the Temple, Tisha b'Av, is nicer than that. The table is set, the candles are lit, Shoel Hirshl comes back from the synagogue and says Shabbat Shalom and may you have a peaceful, blessed Sabbath, and I return his greeting. Said Shoel Hirshl, Tsippa Riva, I tell you Shabbat Shalom and you don't reply. Said I, You accuse me falsely, Shoel Hirshl. I did reply to you, but you are used to many people answering you, and now when there is nobody but me here, you didn't even notice my blessing. He started to say Peace Unto You. But suddenly he turned his head around and asked, Where are they? I thought he was asking about the children. But he was only asking about the Ministering Angels. After he recited the Kiddush, he waited as he did every Sabbath until our sons and sons-in-law recited the Kiddush, but every one of them was making his own Sabbath. He groaned and washed his hands and broke off the bread and started chanting Sabbath songs. He chanted and stopped, chanted and stopped, like a Cantor who stops for his choir. And here there is no choir and no one to assist. He said to me, Bring the soup. I brought the soup. He took one sip and put down the spoon. I said to him, Shoel Hirshl, why aren't you eating? He said to me, Who cooked the soup? I told him, The one who cooks every Sabbath cooked this Sabbath. He said to me, And who cooks every Sabbath? I told him, I am the one who cooks every Sabbath, and I am the one who cooked this Sabbath. He said to me, Why doesn't the soup have the flavor of the Sabbath? That's what he said about every single dish. When the Sabbath was over, I went to the children and shouted, Murderers, you are, there is no God in your heart. And what did they answer me? Oy, Isaac, the days of the Messiah have come. A daughter riseth up against her mother, the daughter-in-law against her mother-in-law; a man's enemies are the men of his own house. So Shoel Hirshl went out across the Jordan to amuse himself a bit, for from all his trouble, he won't earn a red cent, for that whole trade in Transjordanian Lulavs is in the hands of others, and it was only for the sake of friendship that they took him along on the trip. And I sit here forlorn, and in the whole inn, there isn't anyone except one single guest in mourning, Heaven Forfend, and sits Shiva.

Isaac asked the owner, And where is that little girl who helped you in the inn? Said Tsippa Riva, That little girl is lying in the mission hospital, and may she recover. And if she does recover, may she keep her Judaism. There in the hospital, they tell her, if not for us, that is them, may-their-name-be-wiped-out, who took pity on her and took care of her, she would be dead by now. Oy, Master of the Universe, Jews come to Jerusalem, Your city, to serve You in truth and You send them troubles and suffering and diseases and converts and inciters who seduce them to idolatry. I ponder to myself, all the

Children of Israel are responsible for one another and if, God forbid, one is alienated from us, what shall we reply to God on High. And Noah, you remember him? Noah scratched himself with his tarboosh and went on his way. Why? I also ask why. All the days he would roar, I'm worried about you, Reb Shoel Hirshl, that you'll go to hell because you enslave me. Shoel Hirshl got fed up with the thing and expelled him with a reprimand. And that fool doesn't know that all the work Shoel Hirshl threw at him he threw at him only because he can't bear to see a person walking around idle. Go teach others wisdom if your own sons and your own daughters don't want to learn. Right away I'll bring you a cup of tea. After he drank, he put on his good clothes, wiped his shoes with a dustrag, and went to Shifra's house.

3 |

The sun was about to set. The carters were bringing their horses to their stables and the shopkeepers were locking their shops. The streets grew wide and the earth grew still. Nothing was heard but the sound of a blind man's cane or the sound of an old woman's footsteps as she tottered from one holy place to another to bring a candle to the Ark. In the houses, candles hadn't yet been lit, but the light of the synagogues fell on them, and every window gleamed like stained glass. In the doorways of their houses, girls stood and looked at Isaac walking calmly, as if he had already finished all his prayers. Isaac stroked his beard and entered the Hungarian Houses.

The doorways stood open, and from every threshold whispered an earthenware stove with a pot or a kettle on it, and in the prayer houses, the sound of prayer was heard. Leaning on their canes, old women stood outside to hear the Kedushah, the sanctification, and the Barkhu, the blessing. Near them, schoolchildren played hide-and-seek. One old woman lifted her head to Isaac and said, Run, my son, run, you may still find a Minyan. Suddenly the whole courtyard fell silent for the silent prayer.

Shifra stood at a washtub of water and laundered her father's small prayer shawl. She rolled down her sleeves and raised up her eyes. Those were not eyes called dreamy eyes or eyes of gold. And if they were dreamy, they were like a dream that wasn't interpreted, and if gold — like tarnished gold, as if that wasn't the Shifra he had always known. But she was more handsome than ever. Rebecca was sitting in a corner and knitting. When she saw Isaac, she looked at him in amazement. Said Isaac, I come from Jaffa, and he looked at Shifra. Rebecca shook her head and said, I heard you went to Jaffa. Said Isaac, I just now returned from there and here I am. How is Reb Fayesh? Rebecca tilted the lamp toward her husband and groaned.

Reb Fayesh lay on his bed. His eyes were sunk, and under his eyes were bags of flesh that moved by themselves. Rebecca looked at her husband and said, May the health of all the foes of Zion be as the health of Fayesh. Said Isaac, Which means that nothing has changed. Said Rebecca, Praise God nothing has changed. For if there was a change, it wouldn't be for the good. Reb Fayesh stirred and peeped at Isaac. Rebecca tilted the lamp to the other side and said, Why don't you sit down? Sit, Isaac, sit. So, you've come back to Jerusalem. Right away I'll bring you something hot to drink. Said Isaac, Thank you. Jaffa is getting bigger. They're building a new neighborhood there. Sixty houses all at once. All hands are busy building. I found work there, too. Said Rebecca, You plan to return to Jaffa? Said Isaac, If you ladies agree, I'll return. Shifra blushed and lowered her eyes. Isaac gazed into her eyes, asking and pleading. And he blushed, too.

A dog's shout was heard outside. Rebecca said to Shifra, Go to father. And she said to Isaac, When Fayesh hears the sound of a dog, he right away gets scared. Shifra went to her father and stood and stroked his brow. Reb Fayesh closed his eyes and his chin quivered. Rebecca adjusted the kerchief on her head and wiped her eyes. Shifra returned from her father, took the prayer shawl out of the washtub and hung it on the chair, and went and poured a cup of tea for Isaac. Drink, Isaac, said Rebecca, my father, Long-May-He-Live, says, tea is above any drink, and you should know that outside the Land, he wasn't used to tea. Said Isaac, How is Reb Moyshe Amram? Said Rebecca, God be praised. Just today a letter came from Safed Both he, God be praised, and mother, God be praised, are healthy.

But they are weak. Drink, Isaac, drink. What were we talking about, Jaffa. Who's at the door?

The door opened and a neighbor woman came in. When she saw Isaac, she wanted to leave. Isaac held the cube of sugar in his hand and said, Auntie, you don't have to run away from me. He took the last sip and put down the sugar, he stroked his beard and said, The time has come for me to go. He stood up from his chair, nodded to Rebecca, and said, Goodnight. And he went to Shifra and took her hand and said goodbye. Rebecca looked and was amazed. Said the neighbor woman, That's the fellow? Isaac smiled at her and said, That's him, that's him, and clasped Shifra's hand. Shifra slipped her hand out of his and said, Goodnight. Isaac stroked his beard and left. Rebecca picked up the lamp and stood in the doorway to light his way out. And Shifra stood still and absorbed the sound of his steps. When he disappeared from sight, Rebecca came back and hung the lamp on the peg in the wall.

Said the neighbor woman, He still walks around and scares folks. Who? Rebecca called out furiously. Said that woman, My ex-husband got sick. They say it's a fever of panic. The dog barked at him. Yesterday he went out as usual to collect the torn books the heretics, May-Their-Names-Be-Wiped-Out, throw away. He saw Hebrew letters lying in the dung. And he didn't know that those were the letters of the famous dog who has Crazy Dog written on his skin. When he touched the letters, the dog woke with a start and barked at him. He fainted dead away and got sick. Why are you trembling, Shifra? Atchoo! I have waited for thy salvation, O Lord.

4 |

When Isaac returned to his room, he lit the lamp and took off his hat, he examined his bed, and started pacing back and forth, and as he walked he dipped his fingers in water and moistened his temples, he poured himself a glass of water, put on his hat, and recited a blessing. All the beds in the room, except for his bed, were made up. Clearly there were no guests here aside from him. That would have been good if he had wanted to sleep, but was not good since he was wide awake. He opened his bag and put it on his lap, took out a nightshirt and once again rummaged around in the bag. He came upon a garment with ritual fringes. He put down the bag and examined the fringes. The garment was whole, the moths hadn't gotten to it. Unlike the other garments he had brought from his father's home, which were mostly ruined by now. At that moment, an image of Father came into his mind's eye, sitting and tying the fringes in the garment, counting the threads and holding one thread in his mouth. At that moment, Isaac understood why Father took special pains over that small prayer shawl, while he let his sons tie the other prayer shawls, but Father surely wanted that garment his son wore on his heart in the Land of Israel to be made by his own hands, and perhaps Father prayed a special prayer for him. Tears flowed from Isaac's eyes. He brought the fringes over his eyes and kissed them. He hung his prayer shawl on the chair and went into the dining room.

He heard the voice of a man reciting the blessing after his meal, sitting on a stool, with a chair in front of him. The landlady came in and waited until he concluded the blessing on the food, and said, The bed is made up, and she took the dishes off the chair. That man stood up from the stool and went out, dragging his slippers on his feet. The landlady watched him and said to Isaac, That man is a guest who was hit by mourning for his father, and now he sits Shiva, God have mercy.

Isaac remained in the dining room and was sad, like a man whose business has made him stay in a hotel at night and he doesn't know what to do. He saw pen and ink lying on the windowsill. He said to himself, I'll sit down and write a letter to Father. He picked up paper and turned up the wick of the lamp and started writing. When the pen was in his hand, he looked behind him. When he saw that no one was there, he went back to writing. I shall not hide from my father, Long-May-He-Live, something that will rejoice a father's heart, even though for the time being, the matter is still emerging. But, Is any thing too hard for the Lord? For I have been silent for a long time and haven't informed my father so far. But how will I tell it. And Isaac thrust the pen in the ink again and went on in plain language a bit about his affairs with Shifra. And once again, he thrust the pen in the ink and went on in florid language, May it please heaven that I shall herald the end from the beginning, to give joy to the heart of my father, and may my father will not withhold good from me and will impart a blessing on me, for this time my father will be content with me, as the desire of his loving son Isaac.

After he signed his name on the letter, he put commas and periods in it, changed a few letters, some "y's" for "i's" and some "j's" for "g's," and other letters that sounded the same, as he imagined they were spelled at that moment. And he was amazed at the rhetorical flourishes he had written, for Isaac, like most of our comrades in the Land of Israel, who speak Hebrew as a living language, wasn't used to rhetoric. But as he wrote he saw his father showing the letter to the educated men of his city and he wove some rhetoric into it.

For the Time Being

1 |

In the morning, Isaac had a slight headache because at night his sleep was troubled by a dog barking at his window. He got up and went into the dining room to eat breakfast. He found the room full of worshippers and that guest who was in mourning was standing before the Ark. Isaac returned to his room until the worshippers finished their prayer and thought about all he had to do. He started arranging his things. He picked up his valise and rummaged around in his belongings, he picked up an item and put it down, picked up an item and put it down, like things he had no desire for.

Once again, the sound of mourning reached him, the sound of a subdued melody. What am I looking for, what am I looking for, Isaac asked himself. It's my Tefillin I'm looking for, my Tefillin I'm looking for, and I don't have them, I don't have them, because before I went to Jaffa I left them with the belongings I don't need. And with every single biblical verse heard from the house of mourning, it seemed to Isaac that something was taking place there. He left his belongings and went back to the dining room, where the mourner was forming a Minyan. Isaac stood among the worshippers and scowled, ready to defend himself against anyone who challenged him. No one did challenge him, but on the contrary, they offered him Tefillin. He took them grudgingly and put them on, and once again he scowled at them to see if they were watching him. But he soon shifted his eyes from the others and started praying.

After all the worshippers left, the landlady came and brought Isaac breakfast. After he ate and drank, he recited the blessing after food with a tune like Reb Fayesh, whom he had heard reciting the

blessing on the day he went to visit Reb Moyshe Amram, and in that
tune was blended his own tune from the days when he was observant.

2 |

The mourner entered and sat on the stool, the landlady came and
brought him his meal. He saw Isaac and said to him, It seems to me
that I saw you at prayers. Aren't you from Galicia? From what town?
Isaac told him the name of his town, and said, How does the gentleman know I'm from Galicia? He said to him, We sons of the Land of
Israel are perceptive. Said Isaac, Then the gentleman is a native of
the Land of Israel. The man said to him, I am a native of the Land
of Israel. But woe is me, that my deeds have turned bad and I am
forced to live Outside the Land. By the by, he started telling a bit
about his affairs. If we add one thing to another, this is the story.

That man was the son of a farmer of Mahanayim, that village of Mahanayim that was established by people from Galicia, and
before they saw it exist on its own, it was destroyed, and it still stands
ruined and desolate. Forty thousand Francs Galicia had invested in
that settlement, a lot of money for the Jews of Galicia, most of whom
are extremely poor, and even those who are well-off barely get along.
A few families gathered together who had a bit of money, close to five
hundred Gulden per family, and ascended to settle in the Land. But
to maintain a family on the ground requires eight or nine thousand
Gulden.

They came to the Land and settled in Mahanayim. They
made tents for themselves of reed mats and went out to plow and sow,
out of poverty and out of all the other sorrows and suffering that befall every new person in the Land, but they accepted the sorrows well
and waited for salvation. Until the last cent they brought with them
from Outside the Land was gone, they led a difficult existence, and
when the last cent was gone, they had nothing to exist on. But they
still didn't despair and hoped for the best. And if a traveler came and
proved to them that they were committing suicide, they would silence him. And if the newspapers told things about them as they
were, they would deny them and write, On the contrary, thus and
so is what the Land does and thus and so is the goodness in store

for those who work it. Some of them did that because they were ashamed of their poverty, and some did that because of honor for the Land of Israel. And the officers of Mahanayim in Galicia reinforced their words and exaggerated them perhaps too much, so their foes wouldn't say they uprooted naïve Jews from their home and sent them to the deserts of the Land of Israel to starve to death.

And so, as long as they had a cent in their hand, they held out. When their last cent was gone, the colonization official began borrowing money from moneylenders in Safed on pledges and charity that would come from Outside the Land, and every family was given forty Francs a month to keep them from starving to death. And they found some help from the Gehilfsverein in Berlin, and other Lovers of Zion societies promised them their help, too. But the charity came little by little and the interest kept growing bigger and bigger, and the farmers were mostly forty-year-olds and their strength was sapped by the climate and hunger and they weren't fit for work.

If not for a new calamity that came, we might have been able to hold out on the land. But you cannot derive If from If Not. And indeed a new blow came, the locust, which covered the eye of the Land and devoured every tree and every blade of grass. We stood there, young and old, sons and daughters, day and night, and we banged all kinds of pots and pans, to make a noise to frighten the locust. After the locust devoured every blade of grass in the Land and every fruit of the trees, and didn't leave even the straw in bed, he went on his way.

All the time we were busy with the locust, we forgot all the other calamities, but when we got rid of that blow, all the other calamities returned and made us remember them. Harder than anything else is the sorrow of subsistence, that's the greatest sorrow, for it brings hunger. And all those who were eager to lend us money at first, have closed their hand to us, and clenched an evil fist. And so the creditors demand and the usurers deduct their deductions and the interest multiplies and there's no way to pay up, and hunger increases and there's nowhere to borrow. And the mats they made into tents, some were eaten by the locust and some fell apart all by themselves. We dwelt in the field with no shade and no food. The colonization official got impatient and ran away. And the farmers also left their tents that were torn and their fields that weren't sown, and they ran away. One went here and one went there and Father went to Safed. There he lived in penury and poverty. In the end, he buried his wife, in the end, he buried his sons, in the end, all that was left of our whole household was him and me, who by the mercy of God had escaped death.

And in those days as in these times, Safed is idle. There is neither trade nor handicrafts there. But it does have the graves of the Tanna'im and the Amora'im and the graves of other Saints, and it does have study houses and prayer houses, and there isn't a single Saint Outside the Land who doesn't have a prayer house in Safed. The Hasids sit in the study houses and in the prayer houses and every day they have themselves a banquet and a celebration in honor of their Saint or in honor of his father or in honor of his grandfather or they go to the graves. And on their way there and on their way back they have a little drink to strengthen their heart.

Banquets and festivities and celebrations need wine. Every householder makes himself a little wine, not to mention the big pub owners whose whole business is wine. Once I went to Eyn Zeytim and an Arab came to me and said, Take some of my grapes. I said, I'm willing to take, but if I don't give you money, you won't give me grapes. He said, Take, and when you have money, you'll pay me. I looked at his grapes and I saw that they were fine and beautiful and superior to all grapes. It occurred to me to take some of them and make a little wine for Father, for Father's soul was bitter, and he didn't leave his house, but sat and hurled abuse at everyone, even the Saints. He would say, Wouldn't it be better to strengthen those who work the holy soil with the same money they use to fill the throats of those idlers. And so I took some of the grapes and I selected them very very carefully and I made me a little wine. But why should I praise it? Its quality made itself known. To make a long story short, I made myself a little bit of wine. And when you do something in Safed, word spreads. So with that wine. Once the Zunz Hasids sat at a banquet they made to celebrate their Saint, may-his-virtue-protect-us-and-all-Israel. They sat all night and drank and ate and drank until they didn't leave a drop of wine in the glass to recite the blessing over the meal. They sent to the pub keepers and didn't find any, or they found a kind of drink that isn't worthy of a blessing. Some say that the hand of the Sadigura Hasids was in it, because of the Quarrel between Zunz and Sadigura Hasids which hadn't yet subsided, and the Sadigura Hasids made trouble to upset the Zunz Hasids who were celebrating their Saint.

There was one old man there from the remnants of the elders of the Hasids who had been graced by the Rebbe of Zunz who had put his Tefillin on him the day of his Bar Mitzvah, and that man guarded his Tefillin and didn't let anyone touch them. That old man said to me, I heard you make wine. If you bring me a glass for the blessing, I'll let you put on my Tefillin tomorrow. When I heard that, I jumped up and brought a pitcher of wine. The old man recited the blessing, For You are good and do good, and drank and said, This is worthy of the blessing. And he liked it so much he called it a wine that resurrects the dead, for every single drop of it is like dew of resurrection. And the other Hasids also lavished praise on my wine. And I didn't lose either materially or spiritually. Spiritually, for the old man let me put on his Tefillin. And when I stood and put on his Tefillin, I saw that he was dozing, for he was very old and was tired from the wine. I picked up the Tefillin and put them on, Tefillin the Zunzer Rebbe had held. So far, that's spiritually.

And materially, how? From that night on, my wines became famous and a lot of people started coming to get wine from me. And here I did what Baron Rothschild once did. How? When the Baron Rothschild got involved in improving the Land of Israel, they told him there are so-and-so many Jews in the world and so-and-so many Sabbaths and holidays in the year, and there isn't a single Jew who doesn't bless with wine and doesn't distinguish between Sabbath and weekday with wine, let alone the four glasses on Passover. The Baron planted vineyards and excavated two big wine-cellars, one in Rishon Le-Tsion and one in Zikhron Ya'akov, and made wine. So did I. So and so many relatives I have, etc. And praise the Lord, I did a good business in wines, maybe better than Rothschild, for Rothschild spent and didn't earn, and every one of my relatives lent me a hand.

I amassed some money and started thinking about myself. Why should I live in Safed? I had a relative in Galicia, a wine merchant. I went to him. My relative didn't rejoice overmuch to see me, but he did give me room and board. I stayed with my relative and observed his business. My relative saw that this man from Safed was no idler and was even expert in wines. He took me into his business and consulted me. In the end, he didn't do anything I didn't agree to. In the end, he gave me his daughter for a wife. In the end, he made me a partner in his business. And neither of us regretted it. The merit of the Land of Israel also stood me in good stead, for many of the Rabbis started buying wine from him. And they, Long-May-They-Live, when it comes to wine, they know what they're talking about. They say that every Jew understands wine, for the two drinks every son of Israel drinks, one at the time of his circumcision and one at his wedding, he isn't likely to forget. But the Rebbes really are experts in wine. If you want, you can interpret it mysteriously, as they said in the Zohar, Because of wine there is joy of the Torah, according to the biblical verse, also they saw God, and did eat and drink. And if you want a straightforward interpretation, since every single Hasid puts on his Rebbe's table a bottle of wine, the Rebbes attain perfection in wine.

And so, I lived Outside the Land and I did good business. Meanwhile, my father-in-law passed away and I took over his business. I made some innovations and I introduced some regulations. And once every three years, I would go up to the Land of Israel to maintain the Commandment to honor my father, and I would stay in the Land a few months, and make wine from the grapes of our brothers the farmers in the settlements. And for the Belzer Rebbe, Long-May-He-Live, I would make wine from the Arab grapes, because he was afraid of profaning the sabbatical year. I also imported fruit from the Land of Israel. Once I brought a gift of fruit to a Rebbe on Arbor Day, the fifteenth day of the month of Shevat, the Rebbe kissed every single piece of fruit, and gave me endless honor in honor of the Land of Israel.

Later on, I began to slack off in my business. There are many reasons for that. And the reason of all reasons was that I longed to settle down in the Land of Israel, for every time I was in the Land of Israel, it was hard for me to leave. And when I left, I wanted to go right back. But what would a person do in the Land of Israel when he has to make a living. And here that trade in wine is weak. It has no market either in the Land or Outside the Land. There are ports Outside the Land where you find barrels of wine from the Land of Israel standing for years and no one wants to buy them. And once in Trieste I got two hundred barrels of one hundred twenty liters and of one hundred seventy liters at twenty Hellers a liter, for the wine had stood there for two years and didn't even bring in enough to pay customs duties. And even in the cities of the Austrian state, no one pays attention to it. Once I went to Krakow, and there I saw barrels lying around in the customs house, some of them empty and some of them broken and some with wine pouring out, that's how much they despised the wine of the Land of Israel.

To make a long story short, I slacked off in wine because I wanted to go back to the Land of Israel. And my business, my friend, was a big business. I had one cellar of six hundred square meters, that is, more than half a Dunam. And I had one cellar in the customs house, Transit Lager, so as not to pay customs duties twice. But for the Land of Israel, I left my wines and started looking for a business where I could make a living in the Land of Israel. I saw that in the Land of Israel, beer is expensive. A three-quarter-liter bottle costs from ten to fifteen Grush, and even a simple beer costs six Grush, because there is no beer factory here. I said to myself, I'll make myself a beer factory in the Land of Israel. Well, there are no hops here, so I can import them from abroad and even grow them here. The Land of Israel is destined to grow all kinds of plants that exist in the world.

I left my business and I went to Okocin to learn how to make beer, for Okocin is the place for beer. And three kinds of beer they make there, simple, medium, and superior. That superior beer is called Bock, for Bock means billy-goat, because they make it close to their new year, a time when the billy-goats mate. And it lives up to its name, for it gives potency to those who drink it, like a billy-goat who is extraordinarily potent. And two hundred thousand liters they make there every year. Along with malt and concentrates of malt and various kinds of sweets.

And cars go into the cellar and come out of the cellar. And they have special factories for barrels and bottles. I spent two years there and went to Pilsen. There I spent three months and went to Prague. There I spent four weeks and went to Nancy. To make a long story short, I didn't miss a place where they make good beer. And in every single place they treated me nicely, for the Gentiles are fond of the Land of Israel. In addition, the nobles I had sold wine to recommended me as an honest man, and even the big merchants among my coreligionists were nice to me. I endeared myself to factory owners and they showed me things they show only to their sons. They knew I didn't intend to compete with them, but that I wanted to make a little beer in Palestine, and what did they care if I made good beer. I became an expert in that craft and returned to the Land of Israel. When I returned I saw that nothing could be done here. In fact, it was obvious to me before I left that the Land was desolate and there was little activity here, but out of my desire, I said, perhaps and maybe. I tried what I tried and didn't succeed in anything. I was compelled to go back Outside the Land. I went up to Jerusalem to pray at the Western Wall. Came the news that my father, may I be an expiation for his rest, departed from this life, and here I am sitting Shiva.

Isaac looked at him and thought to himself, While I was eager to ascend to the Land of Israel, this one was eager to descend Outside the Land. That man looked at Isaac and thought to himself, I who am a native of the Land of Israel, and my father and my mother and my brothers and my sisters died in the Land of Israel, I have to wander Outside the Land, and this one who was born Outside the Land and his father lives Outside the Land, he dwells in the Land of Israel.

3 |

After he withdrew from the mourner, Isaac went out to rent himself a room. But first he wanted to see how his tools were. And since his tools were with the landlord where he lived before his trip to Jaffa, he went there. When he came close to the house, he changed his mind. Once, twice, three times, he had already resolved to move out and was afraid the room was free and he would be tempted to return there. When did he resolve to move? From the moment he returned to Jerusalem, or from the moment he was at Shifra's? At any rate, he didn't get up his will power and didn't reach a definite decision until that moment when he went to look for a room. And not only did he want to change his place, but all his ways, too. He looked at himself to see if there was already a change in him, and was amazed that no change was obvious in him. But he soon took his mind off himself and looked straight ahead like a man who returned from a trip and wanted to see what had been done in his city.

The sun was blazing as usual, but some change was evident in the city, where the month of Av had already begun and the nine days had arrived and double sadness rested on the houses and the courtyards and the alleys, for the two Destructions of the Temple. Isaac suddenly felt that solid earth of Jerusalem, where your feet don't get lost as in the sands of Jaffa. He looked here a bit and there a bit, as if he doubted that he really was in Jerusalem. And once again, the city appeared before him. The houses and the courtyards stood in their place, and human beings were occupied as usual, but a kind of gloom lay on their faces. The butchers and all the barber shops were closed and from the synagogues and study houses rose the voice of the mourners of Zion, sitting on the ground and praying the Midnight Vigil, for from the seventeenth of Tamuz to the eve of the ninth of Av, they gather in the synagogues and in the study houses and lament over Jerusalem. And even though it wasn't yet midday, the eager ones were anticipating the hour.

Isaac walks in the streets of Jerusalem and glances here and there. Here a man is carrying an Etrog, to send it to his relative Outside the Land; and there a Yemenite is running with a watermelon in his arms. Here a dog is walking behind a butcher, and is evidently amazed that the man doesn't emanate an odor as on all other days; and there a broad she-ass walks along bent under a load of calendars for next year; and here a lame stammerer grabs the hem of your garment and hops in front of you and stammers, B-b-b-buy y-y-your-r-rs-s-s-elf a l-l-l-lam-m-m-ment-t-t-tat-t-t-ion for the n-n-ninth of A-A-Av.

And meanwhile, Doctor Mazia is going to a patient, riding on a donkey. The donkey runs where he is asked. Mazia steers him

to the other side, since he saw Lunz walking with a tourist and pointing with his stick to everything a Jerusalemite should show, for
Lunz is an expert in the paths of Jerusalem, more than any other
Jerusalemite, even though he is blind in both eyes. Mazia bows to
Lunz and starts splitting hairs over an interpretation of a word they
have been wrestling with for a few nights in the meetings of the Language Committee. A rich Bukharan came and invited Mazia to a ran-
som celebration for the first born of an ass. Mazia steers his donkey.
Two blind broomsellers come. And toward them comes a mule
loaded with writings, and two clerks are walking behind it to bring
them to the post offices to send them to our brothers in Diaspora.
The mule saw the brooms and was startled and threw the load off his
back. A few people gathered and picked up some of the letters and
read the names of the institution on them. They started laughing that
never in their lives had they heard of such an institution in Jerusalem, and in the end it sends the mule loaded with pleading letters.

And Isaac has already stopped thinking about a room because of the things he heard in the morning at the inn from that Safed
man, a native of Mahanayim. Isaac moves to another place and to
other times, when he sat in his father's house and read good tidings
from Mahanayim in old newspapers. Suddenly the printed letters
flew off the pages and became a thick swarm of locusts. And even the
pages changed their shape and turned into mats and charred fields.
Isaac wanders in the field with no shade and no roof overhead, and
the sun beats down on his head and thirst parches his throat. For half
a Matlik, Isaac could get himself a cold drink, for at that moment, a
carob water vendor passed by, banging his instruments and announcing his wares. But you, Isaac, saw him as if he were one of the
people of Mahanayim, standing and banging their pots and pans to
scare off the locusts. And when Isaac recognized that he was a drink
vendor, he said to himself, Wouldn't it be better to support workers
of the holy soil for that money than to fill the gullets of idlers. And
when he realized who said those words, he recalled everything that
native of Mahanayim had told him, about the administrator who borrowed money from usurers, and about Father, whose soul was bitter.
And I, said Isaac to himself, I walk around as if nothing happened.

Isaac's eyes filled with tears, and all the troubles that had come upon him since the day he ascended to the Land came and stood before him. He wasn't sad, but on the contrary, it seemed as if he had already come out of the valleys of troubles, and days of blessing were making their way toward him. Why? Because in his heart of hearts, he expected to take Shifra as his wife.

And when he recalled that, all the words of the letter he had written to his father the night before reappeared. I shall not conceal from my father, Long-May-He-Live, etc., even though it is still in the process of emerging, etc. Therefore, may it please Heaven that I may be able to send tidings of a happy ending, etc. Father picks up the letter and reads it, and shows it to Mr. Atamanut. Mr. Atamanut reads it and praises the language. Isaac is glad he inserted a few rhetorical flourishes in the letter, something he hadn't done before, for he usually wrote in a plain language. Mr. Atamanut returns the letter to Father, and says, Well, Reb Simon, we should congratulate you. Father bows to him and replies modestly, Now that Mr. Atamanut has congratulated me, I know that Isaac really is a bridegroom. And Isaac's heart is filled with love and affection for Shifra for the Lord brought happiness to his father through her.

4 |

He encountered a maiden. If we're not mistaken, it was the maiden he had met at Bloykof's. She gazed at him and said, I almost passed by and didn't recognize you. If I knew that you would get my meaning, I would say that you've got something, Mr. Kumer, that's hard to grasp. Your face is fenced off as if you put up a fence between yourself and the world. How come we haven't seen you? Come pay me a visit, Mr. Kumer. When he left her, he encountered the man whose house he had lived in before his trip to Jaffa. He greeted him and talked at length with him. And as they talked, the landlord hinted to him that the tenant who was living in his room was not to his liking, and that he would like to get rid of him. And when Isaac left the landlord, he encountered that teacher who lived in his neighborhood. The teacher talked with him and told him that his house was open to people like him, and if he needed a room, he had a fine room to

rent, the same room his sister-in-law had lived in. And when he mentioned his sister-in-law, he praised her. When Isaac left him he ran
into Mendel the Tokay. That Mendel who was litigating with his wife
about divorcing her, because he set his sights on the American
Rabbi's wife who was Sweet Foot's ex-wife. Before they took three or
four steps, Mendel raised his voice and shouted, What do you say
about that numbskull, that Leichtfuss who calls himself Sweet Foot.
That boor that wanton that ignoramus that criminal that heretic, who
isn't even worth my chitchat, sticks his nose between me and her to
keep her from marrying me. Me, a pious man and a scholar and of
distinguished character and distantly related to two famous Rabbis.
But why should I talk to you, you're just like him, for if you weren't
like him at all, would you have been close to him. And Rabbi Haim,
Rabbi Haim, Let the high praises of God be in their mouth, and a
two-edged sword in their hand. And because he is incorruptible,
something you can't say about all the other Rabbis, he is entitled to
scold me, for a woman who is tempted by evil people not to accept
a divorce decree from me. If she doesn't want a divorce decree, the
divorce decree will fly into her hands. Thank God, Jerusalem is full
of Rabbis and scribes we don't lack, and messengers to send a divorce
decree we won't lack. I don't envy you, Gitteshi, I don't envy you.
Not even a red cent will I give you. Now, in a peaceful way, I'm willing to give you, later on — not a thing. You know the Rabbi's wife.
You say yourself, Am I doing something wrong that I want to marry
her? And you too must intercede for me with Leichtfuss to keep him
from doing me any harm. No good will come to him out of that. If
I'm not important in his eyes, I am important in the eyes of the Consul. And don't say that Leichtfuss is a Russian, and what can the Austro-Hungarian Consul do to a Russian. If a Consul wants to, he can.
And you, don't think I walked with you to accompany you, but only
after you stuck to me did I walk with you so as not to shame you.

Isaac saw that all his turns were in vain. Here he comes on a
man who wants to drive him out of his mind and there he is simply
pestered by a hard man. And he didn't know that all the delays were
for his own good. How? Near the railroad station stands a big brewery of Richard Wagner. A few days earlier, Richard Wagner had hired

a painter to paint his furniture. The painter got drunk and left his work in the middle. Richard Wagner went out to hire a Jewish worker who won't get drunk. He saw Isaac and called to him. Isaac went to the landlord where he had left his tools and took his belongings and sent them with a porter to the inn and he picked up his tools and went to Richard Wagner's.

Richard Wagner is a short man and the hair on his head is full and black and his belly rises toward his chin, and his face is bluish and his moustache stands erect at both ends close to his eyes, and his eyes are like the eyes of Egyptian dancing girls who wink here and there and their face doesn't move, and his voice seems to emanate from his navel and sounds like a kind of scolding. Different from him is his wife, who is tall and thin and her hair is sparse and her face is blazing like a baker's oven and a kind of singsong accompanies her speech, like a woman who was suddenly jolted with fear and is calming down. The two of them were born in the Land to German fathers who ascended to the Holy Land to live a holy life on the holy soil. As long as the old folks were alive, she made railway cars and wagons with her father, and Richard made wine for the priests with his father. When the old folks died, she left her craft and he left his craft and they made themselves a brewery which gives an easy and satisfying livelihood.

5 |

Isaac did his work in the courtyard under the olive tree. From time to time, Wagner and his wife would come to look and would say to one another, That Jew is a diligent worker. When dinnertime had passed and he hadn't sat down to eat, they brought him bread and cheese and beer. Since they didn't take money from him, and because he didn't want something for nothing, he repaired the brewery sign whose colors had become blurred, and he touched up the wings of the angel on the sign and added waves of foam rising from the beer in the jug in the angel's hands.

After he repaired the sign, he went back to his main work. Meanwhile, the day declined. The brush grew thick in the hand of the painter and all the furniture he painted raised a dark moisture. The day was over, said Isaac, and a kind of sadness began entwining around him. He raised his head and looked into the twilight, thinking to himself, Now they're forming a Minyan at the inn, now they're reciting the prayer, It is You, our God, before whom our forefathers burned the incense, now the mourner is repeating the Eighteen Blessings, now he's saying, Forgive us, our Father, for we have erred. Believers feel good when they're praying. But for a man like me, what good is prayer? At any rate, if I were at the inn, I would have joined the Minyan. He raised his head again and looked at the firmament. The edges of the west were turning red and the sun rolled like a ball of fire in a flame of fire, in hosts of flame, in a pool of blood, in arrows of gold, thrown into gray clouds, into pink mists, into torches of splendor, to the purple mountains, to the dark earth. And a kind of dull bleating rises from the earth and a trace of an action is heard from the mountains. Sometimes the mountains trample the firmament and sometmes the earth walks on the slopes of the mountains, and of all the things that just filled the firmament nothing is seen anymore. And between the firmament turning silver and the earth growing dark, a pillar of gloom rises and spreads. Isaac put down his brush and picked up the jar and washed his hands and closed his eyes and started to recite the prayer, Praiseworthy are those who dwell in Your house. As he prays he asks himself, Did I want to pray? The verses came one after another until he forgot what he wanted and what he didn't want. He stood heartbroken and downcast and prayed the afternoon prayer. And when he finished the afternoon prayer, he started praying the evening prayer.

After he finished his prayers, he left his tools with his boss and went to the city. Little stars like the eye of gold, like the eye of silver, like blue fire, like red fire sparkled from the black blue of the firmament. And a sweet fragrant chill rose from the earth. And a sound like the sound of a rug being rolled up was heard from the sound of camels' feet. Sometimes the whining of jackals was heard and sometimes the sound of the wind was heard like the sound of mighty water. Isaac made his way to the city, but his heart wandered in other places. In Rabinovitch's hut, in Sonya's room, in Mahanayim, and in the house of the mourner. Thus did Isaac ponder and walk until he came to the house of Reb Fayesh.

6 |

A small lamp was hanging on the wall and the smell of coffee pervaded the house. Rebecca wasn't at home. Ever since her share of the Distribution had been taken away, she had gone peddling coffee to her neighbors. The smell of the coffee and the light of the lamp made the house seem tranquil. In addition, there were the white linens on Reb Fayesh's bed. But the tranquility was only make-believe. God in Heaven, do You know what happened here? Isaac asked in his heart as he glanced and looked at Shifra. And she glanced at him too through her tears, and all her beauty disappeared because of her grief.

What happened? On that day, Shifra's mother went to get her share of the Distribution and heard harsh words from the officer because of her daughter and that fellow she had taken up with. Rebecca heard her disgrace and didn't reply, for she herself had given a pretext to folks, for she had greeted Isaac warmly. But it wasn't she who had brought Isaac into her house, it was her father who had brought him in and brought him close, but her father had spent most of his years Outside the Land and was used to all kinds of people, while Jerusalemites are withdrawn from the world, and not every person is proper in their eyes. What bad things did they find in Isaac? Master of the Universe, to whom will she tell her troubles and to whom will she open her heart? Fayesh lies like a dead man, and she is worse than a widow, for a widow's husband is dead and she's alive, while her husband isn't alive, and she isn't dead. And her father and mother are farther than a few days away and by the time a letter arrives from them, the eyes are extinguished but the tears aren't. Rebecca wrings her hands and says, Tell me, good people, what shall I do? Her neighbors tell Rebecca, You're asking us, ask your daughter. Rebecca shouts in torment, Oh God, what do they want from my daughter? A neighbor woman replies, Her good and your good I want, as long as the fellow is in her hands, marry them off properly. Rebecca recoils and then follows her neighbor again, for it has never occurred to Rebecca that Isaac is a mate for Shifra, and that woman comes along and says marry them off properly.

CHAPTER SEVEN

A Welcome

1 |

Her neighbor's words impressed her. This wasn't the only time the neighbors had said those words, for every single day they had spread slander and advice, but she hadn't noticed them until now. And when she did notice, she resolved to keep Isaac away from her house. In her heart, Rebecca would discuss with Isaac, What did my daughter do to you and what do you want from her? And is that the reward for my father, who let you into his house, that you bring shame on his granddaughter? You think that if there are only women here, you can do whatever your heart desires. Don't worry, Fayesh, your daughter is my daughter, and I won't give her to just any man. How many times a day did Rebecca look at her daughter and say to herself, If you won't make it hard for me, I promise you that no evil shall befall you.

Rebecca returned from the market and found the house dark. She put down her things and asked in a whisper, Are you sleeping, Shifra? Shifra answered, I'm not sleeping. Said Rebecca, Then, let's light the lamp. She checked to see if there was kerosene in the lamp. She lit it and hung it on the hook in the wall and glanced with sad eyes at her husband's bed. Reb Fayesh noticed her and looked at her. She took a cloth and spread it on his heart and brought him dinner. Then she took her prayer book and recited the evening prayer. After the prayer, she returned to her husband, arranged his bed, whispered Goodnight, and looked at him to see if he had heard her blessing, and if he understood her words. And you, Mother, said Shifra, you haven't tasted a thing today. Said Rebecca, I'm eating. She took a scrap of bread with a drop of oil. After she ate and recited the blessing on bread, she turned up the wick of the lamp and brought a basket of stockings, and sat down to do her work.

She sat and did her work, raised her head and said, A letter didn't come from grandfather. No, answered Shifra. Said Rebecca, Could you imagine that he hasn't written to us? Said Shifra, Of course he's written, but the letter hasn't reached us. Said Rebecca, What does that mean, it hasn't reached us? If he wrote to us, the letter should have reached us. Said Shifra, In Safed, the only post office is the Turkish one, and everybody knows that sending a letter in the Turkish post office is like not sending it. Said Rebecca, There are people here who get letters from Safed. And we also got letters from Safed. Said Shifra, That was a miracle. Said Rebecca, Perhaps our letter didn't reach Grandfather? Said Shifra, Why do you say that? Said Rebecca, It seems to me that people are coming. Shifra blushed and fell silent. A short time passed and no one came. Rebecca looked at the door and said, I don't know what's got into me. All day long, it has seemed to me that someone's coming and going. But someone really is coming. Who's coming?

2 |

Isaac knocked on the door and came in. Rebecca raised her head in terror. What she had feared during the day came upon her at night. Rebecca thought to herself, I should say something to him. She forgot that she had resolved to keep Isaac away, and she said, Sit down, Isaac, sit down. What's new in the world? I see that you're coming from work. Have you eaten supper? And when she heard that he had worked all day for a Gentile, she said, Then you didn't eat any cooked food. She went to the stove to make him something and tried to make him a good dish that he would eat and enjoy.

Shifra heard and was amazed. Why did Mother want to bring Isaac so close? Shifra saw herself forgotten and abandoned. Father is sick and her grandparents live in Safed. All she has left was Mother. Now Mother is currying favor with Isaac. Her soul was gloomy as if she were left alone in the world.

Rebecca spread a cloth on the table and urged Isaac to eat. Isaac dipped his hands and ate heartily. For two days now he hadn't

eaten any cooked food, and here is a warm meal and a warm welcome. Eat, Isaac, eat, said Rebecca softly, and urged him to eat and
drink. When he had eaten and drunk, he recited the blessing. And
even though everyone is wont to recite the blessing after his food, Rebecca was amazed. Rebecca thought that every Zionist was a heretic,
and here she sees him recite a blessing.

On the table was an Etrog case, which Rebecca took out
every day to pawn it, and every day she forgets to take it to the pawn-
shop. Isaac looked at the box and praised its beauty. Said Rebecca to
Shifra, This case was given by my father to your father on our wedding day. Shifra looked in amazement, as if it was strange that her father and her mother got married. Rebecca groaned, How close I
came to pawning that case. And if I had pawned it, I don't think I
could ever have redeemed it. How many adventures we've been
through since the day Father gave that case to Fayesh. But even
among the troubles, there were good days.

The lamp is lit on the wall and a colorful cloth is spread on
the end of the table. The silver case absorbs the lamplight and the
flowers embroidered on the cloth and shines them on Isaac and on
Rebecca and on Shifra. Reb Fayesh is dozing and Rebecca is sitting
and talking. For many years Rebecca had been silent, now her words
flow from her mouth and with them all the times of her life rise up
before her. And it seems that even the years of troubles weren't bereft
of good. Shifra lifts her eyes. An event occurred in the house, and she
doesn't know what it was.

Rebecca said to Isaac, Isaac, you never told us where you
came from, what city you're from, if you have a father and mother, a
brother and sister. And as she spoke, she was amazed at herself that it
hadn't occurred to her to ask until now. Isaac answered, My mother,
may she rest in peace, died a year and a half before I ascended to the
Land of Israel and my father was left a widower, even though before
she died, she ordered him to get married, for the orphans were little
and needed taking care of. But Father didn't get married. Father said,
How can I bring a strange woman into the house? Said Rebecca, So
you lost your mother. And she groaned over him as if he were orphaned only now. Shifra lifted her eyes and looked at Isaac, like a baby

lying tranquilly who hears that one of its relatives is in mourning. She observed Isaac and was amazed that he didn't look as if he were in mourning, and she looked at her mother and rejoiced that she was alive. And again Shifra felt that there was something in the house that hadn't been here before. As she was serene, her mother was serene. From the day her husband took sick, Rebecca had never imagined she could take her mind off his illness. Rebecca recalled everything she had been through since the day Reb Fayesh got sick and she recalled days when her husband was healthy, and days when she was a girl. She was amazed at herself that in a short time she recalled a lot of things. If she wanted to tell them, she wouldn't have had enough time. And as if to test whether those things could be told, she started telling. If we put one item together with another, this is the gist of her story.

3 |

Reb Moyshe Amram, Rebecca's father, was a wine merchant, and everybody was fond of his wines. Lords and ladies and — quite the contrary — Rebbes and Hasids quenched their thirst with them. And he earned in one year more than he ate in three years. And she, Rebecca, was the daughter of their supplications, for she came into the world because of the prayer they had prayed for her to come into the world, and she was the daughter of a soul, for they gave up a soul for her. For when her mother was about to give birth to her, it took her thirty-three hours to be born, and all those hours, her mother's father didn't budge from Mother's bed. He didn't eat and he didn't drink and he didn't take off his clothes and he didn't lie down to sleep. In the outer room stood the elders of the city and in the inner rooms sat all the teachers in the city with their pupils and recited Psalms, while the mothers of the children stood in the cemetery, the House of Life, and measured graves. But He, May-He-Be-Blessed, demanded more. And when her mother's father saw that, he went to the synagogue and opened the Ark of the Covenant and said, My soul for hers. His words were accepted and his sacrifice was agreeable. He passed out of this world and Rebecca came into it

   Good were the days of Rebecca's childhood. Everything she asked for was given her. But she didn't ask for anything. What will a girl ask for who doesn't imagine what she doesn't see with her own eyes? Once, her father brought a fellow who was outstanding in Torah and summoned all the dignitaries of the city. Her mother brought many bowls of rose jam and put a bowl in front of every single one of them. The fellow stood up and preached a tremendous sermon. When he concluded his sermon, he picked up his bowl and ate, when the bowl was empty, he picked up his neighbors' bowls and didn't leave a single bowl that he didn't empty. What did Rebecca do? She placed the entire platter in front of him. What did he do? He picked up the platter and ate everything on it. Rebecca's mother asked Rebecca, What do you think of that fellow? Said Rebecca, I don't want him. Said her mother, I didn't think you should want him either. Father appeased him with many words and gifts and sent him off. Later on, when Rebecca ascended to the Land of Israel with her husband, they went to him to be blessed with his blessings, for in the meantime he had become famous as a holy man of God. He didn't recognize Rebecca, but Rebecca recognized him.

A few days after that event, Father brought Fayesh. A thin fellow he was, just like Shifra, and his eyes filled his whole face, and a light came from them that kindled and burned. He didn't raise his eyes to Rebecca, but Rebecca didn't take her eyes off of him. His two sidelocks lay on his cheeks like two kosher butcher knives, and his movements were swift as a butterfly. He preached no sermon, raised no hair-splitting issues, but when he opened his mouth, everyone bent their ears to hear.

Rebecca's mother asked Rebecca, You want him? Said Rebecca, Do they ask girls who they want and who they don't want? Said her mother, Father and I want to marry you off to him. Said Rebecca, If so, do you want me to disagree with Father and Mother? Her mother laughed and Rebecca laughed too.

After her wedding, the laughter stopped, for she was forced to leave her father and mother. And why was she forced to leave them? Because of Fayesh, who couldn't bear the Polaks and the Galicians who came to get wine from her father, whose voices were strange and whose movements were strange and whose pronunciation was strange. Nor did he like Father's house, because there was too much wealth there, because they ate fat meat and drank old wine and slept on soft beds and wore nice clothes, because Fayesh said that all those delicacies hinder a person from serving the Lord and from studying Torah in piety. He began to stay away from the table and fasted on Monday and Thursday and slept on a hard bed, and he didn't calm down until he resolved to leave Father's house and go to the first place he came to. He came to a small village that was looking for a kosher slaughterer. He took Rebecca and went there with her.

For Father and Mother, the separation from their only daughter was hard, and it was harder for their only daughter to separate from Father and Mother and to leave a house full of love and affection and go to a place where no one knew her and where she knew no one. When they came there, a new trouble came. Fayesh refused to slaughter fattened geese, which the Rabbis of every state allow, and the people of the village didn't want to give up fattened geese, and so a Quarrel erupted between them and Fayesh. And when it started, it didn't stop. And if he declared an animal unkosher, they shouted that he was jealous of them because they would eat meat. Fayesh got angry at them and shouted, Wicked people, you want me to allow you animals that are carcasses or aren't kosher, if it's meat of carcasses you want, a lot of carcasses are thrown in the garbage, go and eat. They got mad at him and said that all his disqualified meat was nothing but revenge. Fayesh got mad at them for suspecting him of making the Torah a matter of revenge. They got mad at him for it wasn't bad enough that he gave them grief with his kosher, but he also called them wicked. The ground couldn't bear him. He resolved to go somewhere else.

He began examining various places, and didn't find a decent place. One village he found defective because they sent their sons to school; and another village he found defective because the girls wore red shoes like the Gentile girls. Finally, he came upon a kosher place, where the whole community was famous for its piety. It wasn't long before he came upon a wedding. He saw that the bride lit candles he tore her wedding and blessed the candles by HASHEM who has commanded us to kindle the light of Yom Kippur, for it was an old custom in that community that brides bless before their wedding with the blessing of the Yom Kippur candles, because they compared the wedding day to Yom Kippur, and everyone answered Amen. Fayesh scolded them, shouting, That's a vain blessing, and he almost upset the whole wedding. To make a long story short, wherever he turned, he found a defect. When you want to, you find flaws. Said Fayesh, Why should I end my days in Exile, I better immigrate to the Land of Israel, for the eyes of the Lord thy God are always upon it, and surely no wicked person can exist there, and I don't need to ruin my life among the wicked. Great joy entered his heart. And because of his joy, he stroked his wife's hand, something he wasn't in the habit of doing, and said to Rebecca, This year, God willing, we shall ascend to the Land of Israel. Rebecca heard and was scared. How would she leave her homeland and go to a faraway place overseas and never see her father and her mother. She wailed and wept, and he rejoiced that the Lord had given him the idea of ascending to the Land of Israel to serve the Creator Blessed-Be-He in His own home. And he was a stubborn man, if something came up into his heart, he didn't let go of it.

It's hard for a woman whose husband is a stubborn man, and yet there is a bit of good in his stubbornness. There are men who want something today, and when their wife starts getting used to it, they set their sights on something else, and when their wife starts getting used to that, they have already set their sights on something else again. But that's not so when her husband is resolute, for a woman doesn't have to change her deeds all the time. Father and Mother heard that Fayesh wanted to ascend to the Land of Israel and reluctantly they answered Amen. They knew Fayesh and knew he wouldn't change his mind, whether they agreed or whether they didn't. And they consoled themselves that the Land of Israel is propitious for children. And indeed it was. Within one year, Shifra was born. Now this same Reb Fayesh, who feared no one in the world, lay on his sickbed because he was frightened by a dog, and our comrade Isaac who couldn't set foot in Reb Fayesh's house, frequented Reb Fayesh's house because he wrote silly words on the dog's skin. And neither

Isaac nor Reb Fayesh knows that it was that dog and those words that caused whatever they caused.

4 |

Rebecca asked Isaac, And don't you miss your father? Said Isaac, At first I missed my father and my brothers and my sisters, even my hometown. Now I don't know if I miss them. Shifra lowered her eyes and blushed. Said Rebecca, What has changed now from before? Isaac blushed. He took his handkerchief out of his pocket and wiped his forehead and said, It's hot here. Said Shifra, Not like in Jaffa at any rate. Said Isaac, But in Jaffa, a sea wind blows. Said Rebecca, But the sun of Jaffa is twice as strong as in Jerusalem and the sand is searing. When I went to greet Father and Mother on the ship, I thought I was condemned to be boiled, all day long I wiped the sweat off my face and the sweat kept coming back. Said Isaac, That day was hot. Said Rebecca, Blessed is He Who reminds us of what is forgotten. Didn't you travel with Father and Mother in the same ship?

Isaac recalled that moment when his ship reached the port and Rebecca came to greet her father and mother and he was jealous of them because as soon as they entered the Land they found a home and family. All his experiences began unfurling before him, everything that had happened to him from that moment until now, and he wondered. Wouldn't it have been better if he had gone from the ship with Rebecca and hadn't hesitated so much.

Said Rebecca, Now you're sitting here and Father and Mother are in Safed. How many years did I pray that I would be blessed to see them. God heard my prayer and they came. And in the end they went to Safed. Will I ever be blessed to see them? Said Shifra, Why not? Said Rebecca, Father is sick and Mother isn't healthy. Master of the Universe, take pity on us. Said Shifra, Go to them. Rebecca glanced at her husband's bed and said, What are you talking about, daughter, he's sick, and I should go?

Isaac pondered, If I . . . Then she . . . That is, if I marry Shifra, she, that is, my mother-in-law, can travel to her parents. Said Rebecca, Just imagine, my father and mother are in the Land of Israel and I can't see them. Go, they tell me. It's fine for the two of you to say go. Why are you laughing, Shifra? Said Shifra, I'm the only one who said it, and you say the two of you. Rebecca recalled everything she had determined about Isaac, and was furious that everything she had done was the complete opposite of everything she had wanted to do. Shifra looked at her mother and was amazed.

5 |

The day after that and the one after that, Isaac worked for Richard Wagner. When Wagner hired Isaac for one day he hired him to finish the painting job the others had left. When he saw that Isaac did fine work, he brought him his other items. And so did his wife. Whenever she came to see, she brought him things to paint. Isaac spent two days, three days, four days. He painted the benches and the chairs and the tables in the garden and the garden shed and the boards of the screen and the posts the screen was stretched over to keep out the sun. When Wagner's wife saw the garden and its things, she said, The Jew will spend another day with us and will repaint the furniture in the house. When Wagner saw that the furniture in the house that Isaac did was more handsome than it had been, he said, Let him spend another two days and repaint the whole house. Isaac spent another day and another day, and didn't have any free time to look for a room, so he lived in the inn.

Shoel Hirshl returned from the trip across the Jordan. Business he didn't do. But he didn't regret the trip. For years he had been stuck in the city without air to breath and had just four cubits to walk from the inn to the study house and from the study house to the inn; and all of a sudden he has a chance to walk around in the Land and to see the Jordan and the Dead Sea and the land of Moab and the other places mentioned in the Torah. The Holy-One-Blessed-Be-He smiled upon the Children of Israel and gave us a delightsome, good, and spacious land, and for our great transgressions it was taken from us. But in His anger, He recalled His mercy, and gave us good Commandments. A son of Israel can go out and wander around in the Land to get wheat for Matzo and Lulavs for the holiday, and see some of the goodness we have had. Shoel Hirshl walks around in his inn like the First Adam after he was expelled from the Garden of Eden and all kinds of sights he saw on his trip are romping before his eyes. Now he sees himself rising among the palm trees and now he sees himself cruising in a ship on the Dead Sea. And the heavy water is greenish-blue with the reflection of the green palm trees, with a greenish glow of silk hovering over them, evokes yearnings in his heart that he had never known before. He walks around and hums a sad tune, Who remembered us in our low estate: for his mercy endureth forever, and he tells everything he saw on the Jordan and on the Dead Sea and everywhere he went, and groans and says, And for our great transgressions, everything was taken out of our hands. And you, Isaac Effendi, said Shoel Hirshl to Isaac, you were in Jaffa. What's new in Jaffa? I heard they're building a city. Sixty houses all at once. You advise me to learn to be a scribe. I can earn more from Mezuzas than what I earned from Lulavs. Or maybe we'll cross the Jordan and make ourselves a butter factory. They sell a Rotel of lambs' milk there for two Matliks, and there are two fingers of fat on it, and in the morning it's frozen and you have to cut it with a knife.

After he finished his work at Wagner's, Isaac went to Ephraim the plasterer. Isaac said to Ephraim, You're involved with folks, maybe you know of a room for me? Ephraim took him to a woodcarver who was hard up for money and had to sublet a room.

CHAPTER EIGHT

A *Chapter unto Itself*

1 |

That woodcarver was one of the remnants of artisans in Jerusalem, whose forefathers got fed up with the bread of idleness and learned to enjoy the labor of their hands. The people of Jerusalem saw their poverty and destitution, living in cramped and dreary apartments, and wearing tatters, and their children's only food was one dried fig in the morning and a slice of bread and oil fried with onion in the evening, and all day long they sit in Heder or in Yeshiva without food, while from all corners of the Diaspora crowds and crowds come because of the Distribution, and even at the beginning, the Distribution wasn't enough to provide one fourth of a person's needs. Discerning people started asking, How are the Children of Israel different from the Gentiles that live in the Land? For this Land wasn't given to their forefathers, and now they live in the Land as we do, and yet they make a living from the produce of the Land, while we are meager with poverty and shriveled with suffering. Is it not because of our sins that we eat the bread of sorrows, and no one raises a finger to improve his deeds? Some of them considered commerce and some considered working the land or finding a trade. But wherever a person turned, success turned away from him, for Jerusalem is solitary and forsaken and her events are meager and penurious. And these things are known, so there is no need to detail them.

Some philanthropists of the nation of the God of Abraham, led by the dignitary Reb Moses Montefiore, of blessed memory, saw the trouble of their brothers, and wanted to save them. They negotiated with the Sages and Rabbis of Jerusalem. There was a lot of advice and little action. A lot of money Montefiore invested in

Jerusalem and a lot of money he scattered was lavished on the destitute. But giving money is an ephemeral salvation, money goes and
trouble remains. For two things Montefiore won merit and brought
merit to the community, for raising the prestige of Israel with the
Gentiles and for building houses and neighborhoods in Jerusalem.

The name of Reb Moses Montefiore began ringing like a
golden bell, and his good deeds won great fame throughout the Diaspora. And many who yearned to ascend to Jerusalem relied on the
generosity of that dignitary and came.

Poverty from all over the whole world descended on Jerusalem and gave birth to a lot of troubles there. Some accepted their
sufferings with love, and rejoiced their heart with Torah and prayer;
and poverty drove some of them out of their mind and away from
their Creator and they did all kinds of contemptible things, for resentment of the Lord of Hosts, for resentment of themselves, for
money, for honor, for futile hatred, for belligerence. And sometimes
they brought the Consuls into their quarrels, and gave Jerusalem a
bad name among the Gentiles. Those who degenerated, degenerated, those who weren't yet degenerate shrieked, O Heaven, where
am I and what will happen to my sons? Will we ever get out of this
abject poverty? Some considered returning Outside the Land or
sending their children away, but they said, Was all the trouble our
forefathers took to ascend to the Land of Israel only so their sons
would return Outside the Land? They started reflecting that pun-
ishments came only because of idlers, for idleness leads to boredom,
and boredom leads to bad deeds, and as long as they sit idle, there is
no solution. They tried to repair what had been broken by generations before them. They were unable to save themselves, for many
obstacles were placed in the Holy City, and everyone who tried to
act had a lot of idlers against him.

There were in Jerusalem some artisans, who engraved tombstones and carved seals. They knew how to draw and mold ceramics
and make handsome objects. Some made holy instruments and ritual articles. Some knew how to write the whole Bible story of Human
on a grain of wheat, and some drew pictures for the Christians of
Bethlehem to engrave on their chalices of black stone. And when

Jerusalem had to send a gift to the Kaiser, the heads of the Societies asked them to make splendid figures of silver and gold, wood and stone. And never did they receive pay, but did as the Torah teachers and prayer leaders in Jerusalem, who serve the community not for reward. Individuals began coming to them to study.

They heard about that in the Diaspora and were filled with joy that Jerusalem, which had been idle, had turned to work. They started reinforcing their spirit and promising them good things and established committees and associations to support the craftsmen in Jerusalem, and wrote articles about them. The sound of words was heard but no action was seen. But those who had tasted the taste of work didn't let go of it. Before long, handsome and well-made figures came from their hands. But they found no profit from the products of their hands, for because of the poverty in Jerusalem, no one could buy himself an art object. And not only did they not see a blessing from their toil, but they became an example for the lazy, who said, You see them? They work like slaves and are starving like dogs.

2 |

One craft that some Children of Israel practiced in Jerusalem was carving olive wood figures, bought as souvenirs by all the travelers who come to the Holy Land. This craft was mostly in the hands of the Children of Israel, and a German Christian buys from them and sells in the Land and Outside the Land. That Christian attained wealth and honor, but those who do the work are poor and wretched. They work like slaves and their master eats their wealth.

They practiced their craft in grief and suffering, in poverty and humiliation, lacking food, and they bowed their head under every single trouble, until their boss intended to lower their salary by a third. Then, some of them banded together and said, How long will we wear ourselves out for others while we barely make a living. Let's make our own shop and sell our wares ourselves and share the profit. They wrote to some philanthropists of Israel to lend them money. The long expectation disappointed the artisans. The Holy-One-Blessed-Be-He advised them to help themselves. They borrowed money at interest and made themselves a workshop. Within three or four years they paid the debt, principal and interest, and still had seven hundred Pounds Sterling in hand.

Some of the Christian artisans saw it and were jealous of them. One night, they sneaked into the workshop. They took all the portable tools and what wasn't portable they burned down. The artisans were left with no tools and without anything. One Austrian Deputy Consul in Jerusalem took pity on them. He went to his fellow consuls in Jerusalem and collected about twenty Pounds Sterling. The dignitaries of the House of Rothschild also sent a contribution of two hundred Francs. And the artisans went back to their work. One day, they recognized their tools in the hands of the thieves. They brought them to trial in the municipal court. The proceedings lasted about three months. The thieves, who came from distinguished families, were supported by their relatives and they intervened to pervert justice. But the leader of the artisans, Reb Haim Jacob, didn't rest until he had brought them to trial before great dignitaries who came from Damascus. What did the thieves do? Not only had they damaged the property, but they also wanted to hurt the people. In those days, an Ishmaelite baby was lost. Witnesses came and testified that that Jew Jacob stole the baby and slaughtered him and brought his blood to the Rabbis for Passover. The royal guards came and beat Reb Haim and wounded him and dragged him off to prison. The leaders of the community gathered and went to the Pasha. The Pasha sent to search for the baby and they found him alive in the home of one of his relatives outside the city. They let Reb Haim Jacob out of prison, but he didn't recover from the blows. Fear of the foes descended on him and he dropped his lawsuit, lest they slander him again and bring evil upon him. He became weak and the business declined because money had to be borrowed at eighteen percent interest, and the mortgaged merchandise was in the home of the lender. If a tourist came to buy an item and he didn't have it — he went to the home of the lender. The lender didn't want to give it to him unless he gave him money. The workshop was shut down and the artisans dispersed.

Sometime later, they made themselves a new company. They found agents in the Diaspora who bought from them on credit.

Some paid them back a little and some didn't. They wrote to them. They replied from Diaspora, We didn't succeed in selling the merchandise, send shipping charges and we'll return it to you. They had no money to send. The merchandise sank in the hands of the agents and the artisans had neither merchandise nor money. They despaired of companies and agents and every one of them went back to acting on his own and sold to Christian shopowners, and the Christian shopowners sold them as items made in Bethlehem and Nazareth. Once that engraver where Isaac rented a room saw that they carved a cross on his figures and he didn't want to sell his figures to the shopowners. He was hard pressed for money and needed to rent his workroom. Isaac saw the room and found it nice, and he saw the people of the house and found them decent. He paid them rent and went to live there.

3 |

Isaac was mistaken neither about the room nor about the people of the house. The room was small but looked handsome, and the people of the house were good people, their spirit was humble, and their soul was meek and they looked kindly on all people, as is the wont of artisans of Jerusalem who enjoy what comes from the work of their hands and don't ask for anything except bread to eat and raiment to put on and good teachers for their sons and suitable sons-in-law for their daughters.

Isaac lived in the woodcarver's house like an artisan among his comrades. The landlord does his work inside and Isaac works outside. And since Isaac didn't need his room during the day, the landlord got to work in it as he was accustomed. The landlord worked in the tenant's room and was amazed that he took rent. Great are the works of HASHEM, from the place where He narrows, from there He expands. And His mercy is not yet done, Blessed-Be-He. When Isaac saw how the people of the house were crowded, he took a child into his room and made a bed for him on two chairs as he had learned in his father's house at the time when his mother was alive. The child lorded it over his brothers for they slept on the ground and he lay on a bed, the child hugs Isaac and whispers in his ear, Isaac, I love you.

Isaac kisses his forehead and says, Good good, the main thing is for you to sleep well. Says the child to Isaac, I'm already sleeping, and he peeps between his eyelashes to see if Isaac sees that he isn't sleeping. Meanwhile, sleep descends upon him and he dozes off, and when he wakes up in the morning he looks and wonders where Isaac is. Why, just a little while ago, he was hugging his neck.

Ever since the day Isaac first dwelt in the Land of Israel, he had never lived with others, aside from the first days when he wandered among his comrades' places and afterward at the inn in Jaffa. All of a sudden he found himself living like a member of the family with members of the family. And more than that. Ever since the day he first dwelt in the Land of Israel, he had never played with a child, for most of our comrades in the Land were either single or didn't have children. And now that he has come upon that child, the child endeared himself to Isaac and Isaac endeared himself to the child. Isaac amused himself with the boy and sat him on his lap as Yudele did with Vove, and recited a rhyme to him, *Av* is a father, *le'troakh* is to bother, *kedar* is a Tartar, *kadosh* is a martyr, and so on. The child sits and is amazed at the rhymes rolling out of Isaac's mouth, and Isaac is amazed at the child, at how great is the wisdom of the little one, he grasps many words at once. Says Isaac to himself, If my brother Yudele was here, he would tell him more rhymes. Yudele is a poet and makes rhymes. But Isaac has another advantage that Yudele doesn't have, for Isaac can draw, and he draws funny shapes for the child, like a dog holding a stick in his mouth, and all kinds of other amusing pictures.

Isaac sits in Jerusalem and one of the children of Jerusalem is entertained on his lap. As if he were his own brother. Isaac ponders to himself, My father and my brothers and my sisters live in Diaspora and I dwell in Jerusalem. Isaac looks all around, Am I really in Jerusalem? And in his mind's eye emerges a host of early visions he had envisioned when he was in Diaspora. And two loves, the love of Jerusalem in the vision and the love of Jerusalem in reality, come and mate and give birth to a new love, which has some of the former and some of the latter.

Next to him sits the landlord and carves his figures and engraves images of Jerusalem on them and inscribes on them the name

Jerusalem, and fills the letters with all kinds of ink. The figures are exported Outside the Land and are sold all over the Diaspora, and the holy Children of Israel who are fond of the Land of Israel come and buy them. This one buys himself a box for the Etrog and that one buys a spice box, this one buys a pair of Sabbath candlesticks, and that one buys a spoon or a fork. The woodcarver recalls that everyone who buys his figures lives in Diaspora and has nothing of the Land of Israel except that little olive wood figure, while he sits in the holy city with his wife and his sons and his daughters. How will he thank the One on High and how will he appease his God? If by reciting Psalms, there is not a single one of the Psalms they haven't recited thousands on thousands of times, but he has one craft and he tries to do it well so that those who buy his figures will find satisfaction from them. On one figure he draws the place of the Temple, and on another figure he engraves the Western Wall, on one figure he makes an image of the tomb of Our Mother Rachel, and on another figure the Cave of Makhpelah, and on one figure he carves the Tower of David. Our brothers in Diaspora, if you are not blessed to see the holy places, look at their images. And sometimes the artisan draws the image of the synagogue of the Hurbah, with its study rooms and high Yeshivas. Ever since the day the Temple was destroyed, the Holy-One-Blessed-Be-He has nothing but the four cubits of the Law, and it's enough for the slave to be like his Master and to rejoice that in our destruction we have been blessed with houses of study.

As Isaac treated them so they treated him. He gave his room to the landlord — and the landlady cleaned his room. He put the child to sleep in his room, the landlady made his bed. Within two or three days Isaac became a member of the family. When he became a member of the family, he started behaving like the people of the house, he went to bed early and got up early. And in the morning, he would pray in public. When the Sabbath eve came, Isaac asked the landlady if she could make him a Sabbath dish. Said she, Why not? The fire that cooks her dishes will also cook his dish.

On Sabbath eve at sundown, Isaac went with the landlord to pray. That prayer house belonged to the Mitnagdim. No one there wore Shtraymls and no one wore robes, but everyone wore clean clothes and a special Sabbath hat. Those simple clothes didn't change those who wore them, as the clothes of the Hasids do, but accorded them a shining countenance. Every single one stood in his place, like a person who knows before Whom he stands. And when he prays, he makes his prayer a request and a plea. Someone who is accustomed to the Hasids may say that their prayer is more beautiful than the prayer of the Mitnagdim, for the Hasids pray with sounds of joy and excitement, and the Mitnagdim pray quietly. But someone who has the excitement of the Hasids gets excited with them, and someone who doesn't have it to that extent stands like a mourner among the merrymakers, but that's not so here where the prayer is open to every soul.

On his return from the prayer house, Isaac found the house lighted and the table set and the landlady in her Sabbath clothes. The ten candles lit in a glass bowl filled with olive oil created a serene calm over the house. Between one dish and another, they sang songs, and between one song and another, the father examined his sons on the Torah portion of the week. After the meal, Isaac borrowed a Humash and read the whole portion. Ever since the day he had left his father's house, Isaac had not been blessed with a Sabbath night like that one. And perhaps even in his father's house he had not seen such a fine Sabbath night as that, for the shining countenance of the Sabbath Outside the Land is not like the shining countenance of the Sabbath in the Land of Israel.

With His Townsfolk

1 |

After the midday meal, Isaac went to his fellow townsman, Reb Alter Shub the ritual slaughterer. Reb Alter saw him and didn't recognize him, not as on the first visit when he recognized him as soon as he entered. Hinda Puah, Reb Alter's wife, saw him and cried out, Isn't this the son of Judith. Reb Alter asked Isaac, How come you haven't come all this time. When he started telling that he had been in Jaffa and had found himself a good livelihood there, he stopped him and said in a singsong, Desires you may not entertain, Consider your accounts as paid, Thoughts allowed and not in vain, Making matches with a maid. As it says in Psalms 128:2, For thou shalt eat the labour of thine hands: happy shalt thou be, and it shall be well with thee. Go to the next verse. What is written there, Thy wife shall be as a fruitful vine by the sides of thine house. Isaac smiled and said, That's just what Reb Moyshe Amram told me. Said Reb Alter, Moyshe spoke well. Who is that Reb Moyshe Amram? Isaac told him. Said Reb Alter, According to my accounting, Itzikl, you're approaching twenty-five. Tell me, my son, isn't there among your Zionists here a person who has a decent daughter? Are all of them bachelors like you? Isaac sighed and was silent. Reb Alter looked at him and said, Heaviness in the heart of man maketh it stoop. Do you know how they interpreted that verse in the Talmud? One interpretation is that he will tell it to others. Reb Alter saw that Isaac wanted to weep. He scolded him and put a soft hand on his shoulder affectionately and said, Today is the Sabbath, to rest from any regrets. What is it, Itzikl, that troubles you and oppresses you. Said Isaac, Nothing, Reb Alter. Said Reb Alter, Don't be a fool, Itzikl, heaviness in the heart of a man maketh him talk. Said Hinda Puah, Itzikl, your eyes are more reliable than your mouth. If your mouth is silent, your eyes are speaking. Said Isaac, What shall I tell? Said Reb Alter, Open up, my son, open up, and the Lord will help you to speak words of truth, by virtue of our holy Sabbath that protects us. Isaac started telling.

2 |

After he finished, said Reb Alter, We can discuss things with them. Isaac looked at Reb Alter's foot wrapped in cotton dressings and dropped his hands in despair. Said Reb Alter, You see, my son, how good it is for a man who has himself a wife? What I can't do, she can do. Said Hinda Puah, Where do those Hungarians live? Isn't the neighborhood of the Hungarian Society also in Jerusalem? And if it's outside the Old City walls, Jews also live there and they'll show me. And I rely on His grace May-He-Be-Blessed to put words in my mouth by virtue of your mother may-she-rest-in-peace, who will be our advocate in Heaven. Did you see Haim Rafael? Go to him, Itzikl. It's a good deed to cheer a blind man. And when you come to him, don't talk Lithuanian, but talk Jewish with him. Isaac called out in amazement, Do I speak Lithuanian? Said Hinda Puah, You mix in words which we used to laugh at in our hometown. So, the Hungarian Houses are near Meah Shearim, so I know where they are. And if I don't find them, the Holy-One-Blessed-Be-He gave me a mouth to ask a person. And you, Itzikl, are dwelling in Jerusalem and painting furniture and making signs. Who would have pictured Jerusalem as a city like other cities, with houses and shops. I remember how Jerusalem was pictured in my eyes, and I'm ashamed of my stupidity. Can a person exist without an apartment and without a shop the way I pictured Jerusalem to myself. In spite of yourself you need a house to live in and a shop to get your food. And I thought people fed on Torah and prayer here. For even when the children of Israel were living in the desert and had Moyshe and Aharon and Miriam and Sarah the daughter of Asher and all the other saints, they couldn't get along without food, until the Holy-One-Blessed-Be-He brought down manna and quails from the sky for them, and so in the World-to-Come, the Holy-One-Blessed-Be-He will feed Leviathan and

Wild Bull to all who are worthy. And now that I know it's impossible to exist without an apartment and without food, once again I'm amazed that they call this ruin we live in an apartment and the food we eat here food. But praise God, on the Sabbath we don't lack anything. Isn't that so, Alter? Wait, Itzikl, right away we'll drink a glass of tea.

3 |

After Isaac left Reb Alter and his wife he went to Reb Haim Rafael. Reb Haim Rafael was blind and had never seen light in his life, and all his days he sat in the dust of the study house, and was expert in the Five Books of the Torah and in the Six Orders of the Mishnah, for ever since the day he knew his own mind, he yearned for the words of Torah, and for him the Lord summoned good people who read to him and taught him and explained to him, and he would re-peat his learning until the words were incised on his mouth.

Reb Haim Rafael lived in a dark room without windows, on the bottom floor in the courtyard of the deserted wife. Since he was blind in both eyes and didn't need light, he made do with an abode that didn't have any windows, and since he didn't find champions to champion his cause with the officers, he made do with a cramped room. But he was grieved by the bad smell in the courtyard, and was amazed at his neighbors, for was it possible that holy Jews who were blessed to dwell in the Holy City that is sanctified with an abundance of sanctity, could they be so contemptuous of its purity? Not that Reb Haim Rafael had been pampered in his youth, but he did yearn for fresh air. Little by little, he grew accustomed to the smell of the court-yard, and when he grew accustomed he found something good in the courtyard, for in the upper story in the courtyard, the Bratslavers had set up their prayer house, and sometimes when they needed a tenth man for the Minyan, they called him, and their prayer was a delight to the soul. And after the prayer, when they danced, they took him among them. And even though he didn't know the basics of dancing, he did know that it was nice for his feet to fling them about. Another advantage there is that they sit day and night and study together and he lends an ear and hears. And on the Sabbath morning, after the prayer, when the head of the group reads the stories of Rebbe Nakhman of Bratslav, there's no greater pleasure than that. In the prayer house of the Bratslaver Hasids, Reb Haim Rafael made himself a friend, a simple man who patched shoes in Jaffa, who left his work and his house and ascended to Jerusalem to serve the Lord humbly. He brought Reb Haim Rafael water from the cistern and filtered it and removed the worms from the vegetables, and led him to market to get his food.

Isaac found Reb Haim Rafael sitting and reading by heart the Torah portion of the week, and since he knew him by his voice, he said to him, From heaven you were sent to me. I'm having trouble with one place in Rashi's commentary. Do me a favor and read it to me. But first I'll open the door and bring in a little light for you. Isaac sat down and read to him until it was time for the afternoon prayer. From now on, every Sabbath, Isaac went to Reb Haim Rafael and read Rashi to him. And if he had enough time, he read to him from *Or Ha-Haim*. If Isaac made a mistake in reading, Reb Haim Rafael would correct him, for Isaac had learned little and had forgotten a lot.

CHAPTER TEN

Isaac Is About to Marry Shifra

1 |

Hinda Puah's visit made an impression. Even though Rebecca welcomed Isaac, she was ashamed to give her daughter to a fellow whose family they didn't know. Now that decent people had come and testified that he was from a respectable family, her heart was relieved and she could hold her head up in public.

What was left out by Hinda Puah was filled up by Reb Haim Rafael who accompanied her. She praised Isaac's forefathers back to Reb Yudel Hasid of blessed memory, and he praised Isaac who studied together with him every single Sabbath. The opinion of that blind man who knew the Six Orders of the Mishnah by heart eased folks' minds about Isaac for they had thought he was just some Zionist, like most of the Polaks and Lithuanians who come to the Land of Israel to anger the Creator in His own home.

After Isaac paid his landlady for his Sabbath expenses, he asked her if he could eat in her house on weekdays too. She told him, The stove that cooks for the whole house will also cook for him, but not every day does she cook. Sometimes she warms up what is left over from the Sabbath, and sometimes they make a meal of bread and oil and onion. But if he wants cooked food, she's willing to cook for him, and meanwhile the children will also benefit. And when the landlady laundered the linens, she also took his linens to launder. Isaac was freed from the bother of food and all the trouble. From the bother of food since he didn't have to go to restaurants. From all the trouble since he didn't know the language of the Russian laundresses.

Ever since the day he came to live in the woodcarver's house, most of his time was his to do with as he wanted, like praying in public or studying a book. And if he wants to study a book, he doesn't have to go to the People's Center, and doesn't have to wait until the person in charge of the books answers him. The study houses of Jerusalem are full of books, and anyone who wants to study takes a book from the shelf and studies, and nobody asks his name or his father's name and his profession and his place of residence, and they don't write down what he read, and they don't ask for library fees. And as for newspapers, good news they don't announce, and bad news flies by itself. And if we are blessed to live until salvation comes, the Shofar of the Messiah will inform us. Little by little, Isaac ceased to frequent most of the places he had frequented and he moved away from most of his original comrades and he became like one of the Jerusalem people. If Isaac's cradle had stood in Hungary, Rebecca's neighbors would have regarded him as one of their own. But since he was a Pole, not all minds were easy about him. In the future, when the Holy-One-Blessed-Be-He returns to reign over Jerusalem, all the Children of Israel will be as important as princes. But now that Jerusalem is in the hands of the Societies and the officers, every Society regards itself as pedigreed and all other Societies as stepsons of the Lord.

Isaac wrote to his father in great detail what he had already indicated and hinted, that he was about to take a wife, a beautiful and pious bride, the daughter of a famous man known for his proclamations even outside the Land.

But he didn't mention that the match was not made with the consent of the father of the bride, who was paralyzed and couldn't tell his right hand from his left, and if he had been healthy, he wouldn't have given Isaac leave to set foot in his house, not to mention to marry his daughter. After all the grief, Father would see that Isaac's ascent to the Land was from Heaven, for it is the way of a man to go to his mate. And who is Isaac's mate? The daughter of one of the great men of Jerusalem. Another letter Isaac wrote to Shifra's grandfather in Safed and he wove into it a few biblical verses, like, The thing proceedeth from the Lord, for she is from the Lord, and, A prudent wife is from the Lord. And he added a few words about cause and effect, that he didn't just happen to be with Shifra's grandfather on the same ship, but that the One Who causes all causes in His Sublime Wisdom brought them together for the main cause, and so on.

On his way to the mailbox, a dog barked at him. Isaac stretched out his foot and kicked him. The dog rolled around and fell. The dog's heart was bitter and the thoughts of his heart were evil. The dog lay as long as he lay. What he did to Isaac he forgot, what Isaac did to him he remembered. We don't want to poke our nose into a quarrel, but this was the way things were. A man walks along innocently, following his train of thought, and suddenly a dog jumps on him and startles him. If he hadn't barked at him, Isaac wouldn't have kicked him. Finally, the dog stands up on his legs and shakes the dust off himself. Finally, he shakes his two ears and opens his mouth and sticks out his tongue. Isaac's footsteps are silent now, but Balak's voice is still resounding, not the weak voice of pain, but a voice like the voice of a war monger. Two or three times he stopped, pricked up his ears and restrained his teeth, sniffed the air and went back to barking.

2 |

Satisfied with his affairs, Isaac went to bed. And no wonder he was satisfied. His livelihood was at hand, his shirt was clean and his stockings were mended, his food was prepared for him every day among humble and modest people who were happy with their lot and rejoiced at his good fortune. The fathers who put their trust in the Lord, the mothers who manage their house loyally, the sons who go to Heder, and the daughters who take care of their little sisters, became as close to him as the members of his own family. The silence of the street and the bustle of the courtyards, the turmoil of the market and the sound of the Yeshivas, and everything in the houses and the courtyards and the market and the study houses was close to his heart, like his whole new being. And when he went out to work in the morning and saw the old men and women walking with their stick and running to prayer and the women going to the market, he bowed his head and blessed them and they blessed him. And at night when he came back from work and a kind of sweet blue illuminated him from the firmament and a tranquility settled over everything, he blessed his Lord who gave him the wisdom to settle here in this place. But when he recalled the contract he had made with Rabinovitch, his soul grew sad, for he would have to leave his place and return to Jaffa.

Isaac lay on his bed and thought about things that occupied his heart. He asked himself, Why have I merited all this good fortune? And since he didn't find in himself any merit, he attributed it to the mercy of the Holy-One-Blessed-Be-He Who is good to His creatures and sometimes overlooks their transgressions. And since Isaac didn't want to think about things that reminded him of his early deeds, he started thinking about the affairs of others, people he wasn't concerned with, but who were close to him here, like Zundl the carter who had inherited the courtyard of his brother Avreml who died without sons, and who became Isaac's neighbor. And since the courtyard was called Avreml's courtyard, and Zundl came to live there instead of Avreml who died, they started calling Zundl by Avreml's name, and the name returned to its rightful owner. And when Isaac came to Avreml, he recalled that trip he made to Jaffa for the sake of Sonya, and recalled that contract he had made with Rabinovitch. Isaac was amazed, at the moment he made a partnership with Rabinovitch he was happy, but he should have been sad for he would have to leave Jerusalem and return to Jaffa. But he was sure he'd find an excuse to get out of the deal. He turned his face to the wall and closed his eyes.

When he closed his eyes, all those roads he had traveled came and he suddenly found himself in Jaffa. He knocks himself out, going from hotel to hotel and hides from Rabinovitch. Sonya laughs at him. He went to Sweet Foot. A dog barked at him. Said Sweet Foot, Sweetiepie, if you don't shut up, I'll take you to Arzef. Zundl patted the dog with his feet and told him, Don't be scared, never did Arzef make a stuffed skin of a dog. And you, Isaac, where do you want to go? Isaac got into the car and went, and wrote to Rabinovitch from the road, I've got to cancel the contract for cause and effect. And what Isaac wrote on the road he wrote afterward at home, for he resolved not to budge from Jerusalem and not to return to Jaffa.

Isaac wrote Rabinovitch that he wouldn't return to Jaffa and wouldn't budge from Jerusalem. And Isaac wrote that with full consciousness. Little by little, Isaac stripped off his old shape and began to look like his neighbors, and he took his mind off many of the things that had preoccupied him at first, until he had removed them from his heart, as if he had never had anything to do with them. Once he got some work for Mr. Posek who was fixing up a new house for himself after his marriage to Lydia, and Mr. Posek said to him, It seems to me that I know you. Said Isaac, You are mistaken, sir. Said Posek, Didn't I see you in the People's Center? He said to him, I was never there. Mr. Posek looked at him and said, Then, where did I see you? He said to him, I don't know. Lydia came and said, I am glad, Mr. Kumer, that I found you and can ask your forgiveness. I know that I didn't behave properly. Will you forgive me. Mr. Posek was amazed. Said Lydia to her husband, I'm ashamed, my love, to tell you. I've changed so much because of you. Things I did and didn't know they weren't nice, I see them now as revolting and repulsive. Don't look at me so much. I'm telling you. Mr. Kumer was a boarder where I was a boarder and I was furious at the landlord for boarding a laborer at my table. Won't you forgive me, Mr. Kumer. Mr. Posek said to Isaac, How come you're hiding? Did you rob a church? And if you did rob a church, God certainly wasn't there anyway.

3 |

Isaac left Posek, saying to himself, Thank God I got away from that old man safely. And that Lydia who apologized to me. Forgive me, she said. I know I didn't behave well, she said. I've changed so much, she said. Not nice! And I denied ever having been in the People's Center. In other words, I lied.

Isaac recalled those days when he dined at the same table as Lydia and those nights when he sat in the People's Center. He passed his hand over his eyes and got rid of them. When he got rid of them, there came those days when he knocked himself out going around in Jaffa, and all the evils that hapened to him there stood before him. Impossible that he didn't have good times in Jaffa, but all that was good at first didn't seem good to him now. And once again he passed his hand over his eyes, as if it were possible to cancel the past with a wave of his hand. At any rate, all those things went away, and fine and

good things came in their place. Ever since we trudged along looking for work, the Land had changed its deeds. Workers' farms and
workers' settlements were made in the Land, and the soil that was
worked there belonged to the whole nation, and anyone who became
a partner in the work devotes himself to the work of the nation. They
don't talk of expropriation anymore. Words that inspired terror in the
farmers are forgotten. And even the farmers want to consign their earlier deeds to oblivion. We won't exaggerate if we say that a new period was making its way in, and the joy of its creativity was evident in
everything. And Isaac at that moment was like that Isaac we saw outside the Land, but outside the Land his fantasies were fantasies, and
now they are reality. On the face of it, it seems problematic, but since
he was ardently devoted to the soil, why didn't he do as our comrades
in Kinneret and in Merhavia and in Eyn Ganim and in Ben Shemen? Was he afraid Shifra would hold him back? But the years Isaac
had spent in the city had tied his hands.

Isaac asked himself, How would I be now if I had stood the
test and didn't run away to the city? He started enumerating the feats
of those who stood on the soil, and for what merits did they stand on
the soil. And he was amazed at himself, why was he thinking about
things he had already removed from his heart? He started striding
until he neared his room. He saw Menahem. That same Menahem
he had dined with in Petach Tikva. But since he didn't see him, but
only his back, he wasn't sure it was Menahem. Meanwhile, the man
disappeared. When he disappeared, Isaac no longer had any doubt
that he had seen Menahem.

Isaac brought his tools to his room and washed his face and
hands and changed his clothes and thought of going to Shifra, even
though the time wasn't right, for Shifra was busy preparing her
trousseau. But precisely because it wasn't right for him to go to her,
his heart was drawn to see her. Shifra was handsome every day, especially when she was busy with her wedding clothes. Her eyes of
gold rested on those fabrics, and her fingers moved nimbly. And you
sit and see that those fabrics lying across her lap are becoming a dress.
But sometimes Shifra had to measure her dress, and a girl is not wont
to measure her dress while a stranger is in the house, and as long as

they haven't stood beneath the wedding canopy, he was a stranger. So Isaac gave up and didn't go to Shifra's house, but he did go to pray, for it was already time for the afternoon prayer.

4 |

Isaac came to the study house and there he found Menahem standing in front of the bookcase consulting a book. He greeted him and asked him, What is Reb Menahem doing here? Menahem smiled and replied, When a Jew dwells in Jerusalem you don't ask him what he's doing here, for the very existence of the Children of Israel in Jerusalem is a deed in itself. But I came here only on business. Isaac glanced at him in amazement. Said Menahem, One of the householders of my city died and left young heirs and bequeathed them an estate in Motza and the religious court in my hometown appointed me guardian of the property of the orphans and I went to see the property. But I don't know if I'm entitled to accept the guardianship, for according to the law, the guardian has to be a person with abilities in the business of this world so he can protect the property and make a profit on it, and I know that I have no abilities in the business of this world. So I'm investigating the law. Perhaps I should accept the property as a tenant and divide the profit with the orphans.

Isaac went on to another issue and asked him if he was still living in Petach Tikva and if he had a livelihood. Said Menahem, My home is still in Petach Tikva, which was my first lodging in the Land of Israel. And as for a livelihood, what a person needs is a matter of determination, for a person determines how much he needs for his livelihood, and since my need is according to what I earn, it follows that I can say I have a livelihood. And you, my dear, how do you support yourself? Said Isaac, Bless God. Said Menahem, When a man says Bless God, I don't know if that's good or bad, for a person has to bless the bad just as he blesses the good. Said Isaac, I haven't yet gotten to that state. At any rate, I can't complain. Please, Reb Menahem, come dine with me. Menahem's face turned pale and he fell silent. Isaac said to him, I remember, Reb Menahem, that day when I dined at your table, and I ask you to dine with me as I dined with you. Menahem was careful not to eat a piece of bread that wasn't his own, and was careful not to disappoint anyone. To reject Isaac's offer was hard for him and to dine with him was hard for him, so he replied to Isaac, It may be that you might live in an inn and I'm not used to eating in inns. Said Isaac, I live with decent people and the landlady makes my meals. Said Menahem, And should we bother a woman? Said Isaac, I won't leave you until you dine with me.

Isaac brought him to his room. They sat and ate and drank. During the meal, Isaac said to Menahem, Do you remember, Reb Menahem, when I was at your house and we spoke about work? Said Menahem, I remember. Said Isaac, I'm amazed at you, Reb Menahem, that you remember. Said Menahem, Why shouldn't I remember? Are the words of a man husks that are thrown out of his mouth? Said Isaac, When I think about it, I must say that those who exalt work to a religion are precisely the ones who stood on the soil. Said Menahem, He who won won, but not because of his words.

Said Isaac, When I look at myself, I'm sorry I didn't stand the test and didn't become a farmer. Said Menahem, No matter what, you would be sorry. Said Isaac, What reason do you have to say that? Said Menahem, Everyone who is sorry about the thing he didn't do will be sorry about every single thing. Isaac asked Menahem, And what could a person do not to be sorry? Said Menahem, You're asking me? I don't know what sorrow is. Said Isaac, That is, you are happy with your lot? Said Menahem, I don't know what happiness is. Said Isaac, That is, you have reached a state of equanimity? Said Menahem, That state I haven't reached, but if a day passes and I'm not ashamed of it, I'm satisfied. Said Isaac, That you already told me when I was at your house in Petach Tikva. Said Menahem, In Petach Tikva, I told you I wish we didn't have to be ashamed of the Land, and now I told you if a day passes and I'm not ashamed of it, I'm satisfied. Said Isaac, What's the difference? Said Menahem, I wish there were no difference, but sometimes a man is fed up with living in the Land, therefore a person has to remember, at any rate, every day that passes. As Menahem talked, the voice of Avreml the carter was heard singing. Menahem stood and closed his eyes, as if sleep had descended on him. Said Isaac, Once I traveled in his cart, and the passengers asked him to sing *Then all shall come to serve You* and he didn't want to. Why? said Menahem, I am amazed that the soul of that man doesn't evaporate in singing.

After Avreml stopped, Menahem said to Isaac, I'll sit and say a blessing and I'll go on my way. Said Isaac, Where do you want to go, Reb Menahem? Said Menahem, I'll go to some study house. And where will you sleep, said Isaac. Said Menahem, Wherever I chance to come, I will put my head down and sleep. Said Isaac, Spend the night with me. Menahem looked at the room and said, If you make me a bed on the floor, I'll lie down. Said Isaac, No, I'll give you my bed. Said Menahem, What I don't do for others I don't want others to do for me. Said Isaac, And if I entreat you? Said Menahem, I won't be moved by entreaties. Said Isaac, Why? Menahem smiled and said, I see that you regard me as an all-round sage who can reply to all the conundrums in the world. Said Isaac, What study house do you want to go to? He said, To a study house that has books and a lamp. As they entered the study house, Isaac said to Menahem, I would like to see you tomorrow. Said Menahem, Aren't you a day laborer? Said he, I'm my own boss and I can postpone my work for a day. Said Menahem, And you won't be ashamed of the day you waste in idleness? Said Isaac, Reb Menahem is worth wasting a day for. Said Menahem, And all that for the sake of words? In any case, I'm not free, I want to go to Motza. Said Isaac, I'll go with you. Said Menahem, I'm used to going alone, for if I go alone, I'm free to look. Said Isaac, When you went to Jerusalem, you didn't go alone. Or did you ascend on foot? Menahem nodded his head. Said Isaac, For the honor of the city did you walk on foot? Said Menahem, No, but because I don't want horses pulling me. He said to him, Then, you could ride the train? Said Menahem, Can it be that I should ride the train that deprives the poor carters of a livelihood? Isaac asked Menahem, And wasn't the road hard for you? Said Menahem, The road wasn't hard, but I did have another difficulty. They said a person walks from Jaffa to Jerusalem in twelve hours, and I walked in eleven hours. He said to him, You certainly replied to the conundrum. Menahem smiled and said, They meant an average man, and I'm below average.

Menahem picked up a book and stood and read until the sun flashed and they recited the morning prayers, and Isaac returned to his room. The child was lying on his bed and his face was smiling with a good dream he was shown in his sleep. Isaac's paints and the engraver's woods exhaled an odor. Isaac took off his clothes and got into his bed. He recited the Bedtime Shema and extinguished the lamp. For a little while, a mosquito buzzed. Little by little the voice of the mosquito fell silent and a silent darkness covered the room.

5

In those days when Isaac lived in an enviable good fortune, he got up early for prayer and so forth and observed his Judaism as a Jew, in those days a bitter drop fell into the goblet of his happiness. It seemd that evil angels who received their vitality from his early transgressions envied him and wanted to annoy him. And since they had no control during the day, for in the day a person governs his mind, they came to him at night. For at night a person's mind is not in his own hands. And since they could not approach him, for their force was sapped by his good deeds, they sent the Lord of Dreams as an agent, for he is halfway between good and bad. The Lord of Dreams came to Isaac and pulled him to the sea. There he forgot his shoes. He went back to his shoes and the wind flew his hat off. A man encountered him and said to him, Come and I'll show you where your hat is. When he went with him, the man disappeared. Isaac stood in the street barefoot without shoes, his head bare. He heard the sound of prayer and followed the sound. He came to a two-story house, the bottom story in ruins and you climbed a ladder to the top story where they were praying. And the ladder stood straight. He leaned the ladder and ascended. When he put his head in, the door closed on him from inside and his body was outside. That's how it was one night and two nights and three nights. And he thought he would never get rid of his bad dream. Finally, the dream went and didn't come back. His soul came back to him and he forgot the dream, as he had forgotten many things he saw while awake, like Jaffa and all its pleasures. And the good people who had been good to him, and the bad people who had been bad to him, he removed them all from his heart, Not out of ingratitude for the good ones and not because of pardon and forgiveness for the bad ones, but because that soul that wanted rest wanted to forget the whole chapter of the past.

6 |

Isaac began frequenting the elders of his hometown who were in Jerusalem and when he conversed with them in that tongue he was used to in his hometown, that whole world seemed to rise up before him, and he would think to himself, If HASHEM grants me, I'll invite them to my wedding. And he was amazed at himself, I who am not learned in the Torah or in wisdom am sitting with the pious. He recalled his comrades in the fields and cities, recalled them only in pity, like one who is sorry about his dear ones who haven't been blessed with what he has.

When we look at all the events of the past, we are simply amazed. We saw Isaac in Jaffa and didn't find him different from our other comrades, aside from the handful of hairs in his beard. And even in that he wasn't any different from some of our comrades who leave themselves a beard. And if we examine his early deeds, we are even more amazed. Perhaps Jerusalem caused that, but there are several fellows in Jerusalem and we didn't find any who did what Isaac did. But Isaac was a simple fellow who didn't engage in profound inquiry. And like the simple Children of Israel, who, if they sometimes stray from the path, in the end they return.

On the face of it, Isaac looked like a tree with few roots, and every wind that comes along uproots it and overturns it. But if we observe his deeds very closely, we shall see that that's not how it is. As long as Isaac observed the Commandments as a learned habit, the Commandments weren't important in his eyes, therefore wherever he went he behaved like the people of the place. But when his rational soul awoke in him, he changed his opinions and along with them his deeds.

Not in one day and not in one month and not in one year did he change his opinions and his deeds, but little by little, he changed his opinions. And not because of the pious did he change them, but even back when he was living among his comrades in Jaffa and in the settlements, he saw that the soul was searching for something that was withheld from her. In those days, he didn't yet know what the soul was seeking. And when did he discover it? Here too we have to say, not all at once did he discover it, but little by little. In the end, he became a tree with many roots, and even if all the winds in the world came upon it, they couldn't move it from its place.

In those days, when he saw himself as if he had reached the desired purpose, he would recall some of the events that had occurred to him ever since the day he entered the Land. Things he didn't consider worthy, he dismissed; things that were worthy he lingered over. And the same with humans. Anyone he considered worthy he dwelled on, anyone he didn't consider worthy he removed from his heart. But it was precisely those he found nice who were dissatisfied with him, and sometimes it seemed to Isaac that someone was complaining about him. Isaac replied, Many ascended to the Land of Israel to work the soil, and when they didn't succeed they turned to whatever they turned to, everyone according to his merit. But this is true, if I had stood the test and hadn't run away immediately, I would now own an estate in Eyn Ganim or in the Galilee, and Shifra and I would have worked the soil, and maybe I would have brought my brothers and my sisters and my father. But when Isaac observed his chain of events, he said, Blessed art Thou for what is done.

Once in his dream, Isaac found himself standing in a hot place without any shade. His thirst assailed him and he was afraid he was swooning. He saw a channel of water flowing by but he couldn't get to it, worse than the thirst is the fact that he doesn't know the place and doesn't know how or why he wound up here, and why his shoulders are heavy. He saw Pnina standing and plowing, Isaac asked Pnina, Where are we? Pnina replied, Don't you see that we're in Um G'uni? And now he wasn't amazed that he was here, but he was amazed that the voice was Shifra's voice. He took the hoe off his shoulder and started hoeing. Makherovitch came with a photographer, while he was among those who were plowing. Isaac woke up with a start from the sound of a dog barking in front of the window Isaac groaned and said, When I get out of bed in the morning, my head will be heavy as on the day I met that man from Safed, the native of Mahanayim. Meanwhile, he was sitting in his father's house reading wonderful things about the farmers of Mahanayim in an old issue of *Ha-Magid*. Isaac scolded himself for wasting his days in Diaspora when the Land of Israel was so beautiful. Said Shifra, Don't get upset, Isaac. If you were living in Mahanayim, you wouldn't have met me. Isaac replied, You are right, Shifra, if I had settled in Mahanayim, I wouldn't have met you. And now I shall tell you something logical, you, Shifra, wouldn't have met me either. Who's shouting here? How many times have I shooed him away and he doesn't move.

7 |

The summer passed but Reb Fayesh's illness didn't. The lines on his face grew fatter and his eyes seemed to congeal. Sometimes his lips stirred. Speech they did not attain. His neighbors had already stopped asking about him, and even his friends and students didn't come to visit him, for they were already used to the fact that he was incurably ill. If one of them recalled that one should visit the sick, he didn't go visit him because he didn't want to sit with women. If Isaac didn't come and go, there wouldn't have been a sign of life in the house. Rebecca and Shifra understood one another by a hint, and even their winks were only about the sick man, whether he ate, whether he drank, whether his clothes were clean.

Rebecca didn't complain or protest. Whatever folks did, she regarded as something obvious. And Sonitskhe, the wife of the Rabbi of Brisk, who was dreaded by all Jerusalem and all the geniuses and Rebbes of the city were terrified of her, when her husband, the Rabbi of Brisk, passed away, no one paid any attention to her. So much more was it true of Rebecca, a simple and humble woman, and even when her husband was healthy, she didn't raise her voice, and now that her husband lay like a dead man, why should she complain and why should she protest? It's a miracle from Heaven that they still exist. How? In the days when Isaac was in Jaffa, they were hardpressed, and Rebecca went to the tomb of Simon the Saint to ask for herself. There she found women crushing glass shards and pottery shards and selling them to builders to put in the cement they used for roofs and cisterns. She sat down to work with them, but she wasn't strong enough, for she was a delicate woman and her hands weren't used to rough jobs. After an hour or two her hands swelled up and her fingers started bleeding. A woman said to her, Go back home and take a reed, a tube of coffee beans, and roast some coffee and grind it and sell it to your neighbors. That is what she did. She roasted coffee and ground it and went round to her neighbors and made a little money for herself and her daughter.

Joy mixed with grief came in the letter of Reb Moyshe Amram. Joy that he blessed them for the match and grief that neither he nor Disha could come to the wedding. And this is what he wrote in his letter from Safed: We would be so very happy to see with our own eyes the wedding of our blessed granddaughter Long-May-She-Live, the only daughter of our only daughter, with the fellow Mr. Isaac Long-May-He-Live, whom we saw on the sea and met in Jerusalem the Holy City, for he is a paragon of virtue. But because of the hand that was dispatched against us, we cannot ascend to Zion, for our legs have become heavy with old age and our strength has departed. But the Lord will give good fortune and will send you the holy blessing that the match will succeed and we shall be blessed to see a generation of upright people from them walking on the paths of God. And you, Isaac, now you are like a son to us, and like a father who will love his son so will we love you, and with our love, we beseech you to walk in the paths of God, for all who walk in His paths will never be ashamed. And now, I send you ten Reinish to buy yourself a prayer shawl and a Torah and prayer books, and I give ten Reinish as a blessing for your intended, my granddaughter Shifra, Long-May-She-Live, and may she have them to buy bridal embellishments, for the jewels her grandmother, Long-May-She-Live, brought with her from outside the Land, which we were supposed to bequeath to our granddaugher, Long-May-She-Live, are no longer in our possession, for the illness has eaten the fruit of our toil and with the rest we bought a plot of ground for ourselves for the End of Days. For that we are sick at heart and our eyes are dim, for we are unable to send a Napoleon or even half to you, Rebecca our daughter, Long-May-You-Live, for the wedding expenses to make a fitting and proper feast and party for all who come to rejoice with you on the day of the celebration of the nuptials of Shifra, Long-May-She-Live. But after my return I was consoled for I heard that all the great founders of the Yishuv, May-God-Protect-and-Preserve-Them, agreed to forbid the bridegroom to invite more than ten men aside from friends and family to the celebration, so as not to increase expenses, for that we shall rejoice seven times over with great joy, when Our God will bestow on us the joy of Zion and Jerusalem by gathering her sons there in joy, soon in our own time, amen.

When Rebecca read her father's letter, she took heart and started preparing for her daughter's marriage. She fixed the time of the wedding and set aside a place for the couple to live with her in her house because Shifra couldn't live anywhere else for Fayesh needed a lot of care and he couldn't be left only to Rebecca, who had to go to the market and return with the coffee she roasted for her neighbors.

Isaac Invites His Guests

1 |

Three days before his wedding, Isaac went to Reb Alter to invite
Hinda Puah to his wedding. That day, Reb Alter was sick in bed.
Since he wasn't used to lying idle, and since he couldn't study a book
because of his illness, he lay and read in his notebook the names of
the children he had circumcised. Quite often he wanted to know
how many there were, but refrained from counting them. Finally he
put his hands on his notebook and whispered, Master of all the Uni-
verses, Creator of all Souls, You know the number of them all, may
it be Your will that by virtue of the seed of Abraham Your beloved,
that I brought into Your Covenant, You will bring me safely out of
my bed and give me strength to serve You in truth. Finally, he put his
notebook down at the head of his bed and started evoking the children he had brought into the Covenant, and was glad that all of them
were God-fearing, and even Isaac the son of Simon, who was ru-
mored to have strayed from the path, even he changed his mind and
returned to Him.

Isaac entered. Reb Alter raised his head and said, Welcome,
Itzikl, a guest who comes in time. I was just thinking about you and
here you come. You see, Itzikl, there is power in the thought of a Jew,
that it draws to us those who are dear to our heart, like a magnet drawing iron to it. And if we purified our thoughts we would do wonders.
And on that, Itzikl, I have a tremendous argument, as the Bible says,
I thought on my ways and turned my feet unto thy testimonies, that
is, if a person thinks cunningly on his ways, in the end he returns his
feet to Torah. This is why Torah is called the art of the Tabernacle
and its vessels cunning work. For by the power of the good thoughts

they were blessed to make the Tabernacle and its vessels. And that is the secret of what is written, For them that feared the Lord, and that thought upon his name, for since they thought upon His Name, they became God-fearing. In other words, because they feared the Lord all their thought was blessed anyway. For when a son of Israel is blessed to forge his thought in the service of the Lord, and thinks on all his ways, he returns his feet to the service of Him, the Blessed One. And there is no need to go on talking about it for anyone who observes the world a little bit sees that this is the absolute truth. And you, Itzikl, you came just as I was thinking good things about you. In general, a person should think good things about his fellow man, for a good thought raises the sparks captive in the dark. And even a man in the depths of the Underworld, God Forbid, when good things are mentioned about him, that mention gleams for him in the dark. And even he, that is, the one who thinks a good thought about his fellow man, benefits in his light from the force of his good thought, as the Bible says, the Lord lighteneth both their eyes. Now let's leave the arguments aside and hear something from your mouth. Why don't you sit down. Take a chair and sit down.

2 |

Isaac took a chair and sat down and looked sorrowfully at Reb Alter. Said Reb Alter, You look to me like a man who is grieving. Said Isaac, I see that Reb Alter is lying in bed. God Forbid that he might be sick. Reb Alter smiled and said, Sick I definitely am not. If I were in my hometown I would be sick. How? Hinda Puah, Long-May-She-Live, would call the doctor. The doctor would come and write me a prescription for medicine, and would warn the people in my house to take very good care of me. My sons and daughters and sons-in-law and daughters-in-law would immediately gather together and surround my bed with gloomy faces. This one asks, Father, is the pain lighter? And that one asks, Father, is your illness heavier? And every single one of them indulges me in his own way. Meanwhile, respectable householders come visit me in my illness, and groan about that exquisite one who is wasted in bed, and I groan with them, so they'll see that they didn't bother in vain. In the end, I really would be sick. Now that, Praise God, I dwell in Jerusalem and we don't have extra money to waste on doctors and medicines, and human beings aren't scared for me, aside from my spouse, Long-May-She-Live, I am sure that by tomorrow, God willing, I'll get up healthy. Isn't that so, Hinda Puah? Said Hinda Puah, If you lived in our hometown, you would live like a human being and eat like a human being and cover yourself like a human being and you wouldn't drink the bad water and you wouldn't get sick. Said Reb Alter, Is it nice to talk like that? By virtue of saintly women was the Nation of Israel redeemed from Egypt, and this woman is blessed to dwell in the Land of Israel, in Jerusalem the Holy City, and she says things the mind cannot endure. Said Hinda Puah, Is it forbidden to speak the truth? Said Reb Alter, The remnant of the Children of Israel may make a sacrifice and may not talk falsehoods, but the essence of truth is truth from beginning to end, that is, when you truly believe that everything is by His Will, Blessed-Be-He. And for that one needs a good mind, as we find in Daniel, a man greatly loved who prayed, to understand Thy truth. And thus said King David, May he rest in peace, God shall send forth his mercy and his truth. And when we attain the truth that is mercy, that is when we reach the truth of truth, we rejoice at every single thing that comes upon us, especially here in the Land of Israel, the source of the truth, as the Bible says, truth shall spring out of the earth, for the truth shall spring out of the earth of the Land of Israel. And the Scripture concludes, and righteousness shall look down from heaven, for all the observation of the Blessed One is righteousness. And so, Itzikl, you came at a good time, and there are certainly good tidings on your tongue. Let us hear and rejoice.

3 |

Said Isaac, I know that Reb Alter's legs are sick and he cannot come to my wedding, but perhaps Hinda Puah may honor me and come. Said Hinda Puah, A great request you asked. Did you think I wouldn't come. Even if you don't invite me, wouldn't I come. A child solitary as a stone in the field and I would refrain from dancing at his wedding. Itzikl, where is your mind? Weren't I and your mother, May-we-be-set-apart-for-a-long-and-good-life, close neighbors, and you say

perhaps Hinda Puah may honor me and come. It's befitting for a polite person to speak polite words, but for a thing like this, Itzikl, all
words are simply superfluous. Now allow me to bring a few refresh-
ments and we'll congratulate you.

Hinda Puah took out a slice of cake and went to her neighbor to borrow something to drink. Reb Alter put his hand on Isaac's
hands and said to him, You've brought me back to life, Itzikl, with
good tidings, but I'm sorry I can't come to your wedding. You know
that sometimes I like to talk in rhymes, and if I were at your wedding
the Holy-One-Blessed-Be-He would put fine rhymes in my mouth to
rejoice the bride and groom. And as for the rhymes the wedding
jesters say to the people at the wedding celebration, I've got a tremendous argument. On the face of it, that matter, that is, rhymes, comes
from the power of the wedding jester, who trains his tongue to speak
in rhymes, but that really isn't so, but all the jester's power comes
from the power of the mating, for rhymes are a kind of mating, for
when a word mates with her fellow word, and when the mating succeeds, the rhymes also succeed, and sometimes even ordinary people who aren't wedding jesters succeed in entertaining at a wedding
celebration with fine rhymes that emerge from the power of mating,
which derives from the secret of the divine mating. Therefore, those
books of rhetoric made by the transgressors are not nice, since they
come from another power of mating, that is from the power of the
mating of the Other Side, Heaven Forfend, and there's no point
going on with that, so as not to give them power, God Forbid, from
the power of our words, for the essence of all powers comes from the
power of the words that a son of Israel brings out of his mouth. So,
let's go back to the essence of the matter. So, Itzikl, you're getting
married at a good and successful time. Hinda Puah already brought
a drop to drink. Let's drink a toast and bless you with a glass, may the
mating succeed.

4 |

And when Reb Alter had a drop to drink he took Isaac's hand and
blessed him. And when he completed all the blessings in his mouth,
he looked here and there and was searching for some gift to give Isaac

for his wedding day. When he didn't find anything, he said to Isaac, A custom among the Jews is a law that you give a gift to the groom on his wedding day, and so I have to give you a gift. But I am in your debt, for I should have given you a gift on the day I circumcised you, for we found in Our Father Abraham, May he rest in peace, that the Holy-One-Blessed-Be-He gave him the Land of Israel on the day he circumcised himself. Silver and gold and rubies I don't have, but I shall tell you a word of wisdom, and the price of wisdom is above rubies. And King Solomon, May he rest in peace, also said, For wisdom is better than rubies and all the things that may be desired are not to be compared to it.

It is written in the Torah, And Adam knew Eve his wife, hence the sages of research specified that when Adam took a wife he came to total knowledge. Sixty-two times we found the word knowledge in the Torah. Sixty-two corresponds to the numerical value of the letters of TURN. Turn, my beloved, and be thou like a roe, turns on the man who takes a wife, may he run like a roe to do the will of his Father in Heaven. And it is also written, Know therefore this day, that is, the Torah hints to us that this day, that is, the day you came to knowing, know and consider it in thine heart that the Lord is God.

Our sages of blessed memory said in the Talmud that a bridegroom on his wedding day is forgiven all his sins, and on Yom Kippur it is said, For on that day shall the priest make an atonement for you, to cleanse you, that ye may be clean from all your sins. Hence the wedding day is like Yom Kippur, and so on their wedding day, bridegrooms fast and say the confession of Yom Kippur. And it is a great mercy from the Creator May-He-Be-Blessed that He gave the Children of Israel great and festive days like those to forgive them for all our transgressions. And remember and don't forget, Yom Kippur we have every single year, but not this day. May it be His Will, Itzikl, that He will fulfill in you the Scripture, O, satisfy us early with thy mercy that we may rejoice and be glad all our days. Dawn is called the time of the wedding, when a man's light begins to shine. If a man does good with his Maker and satisfies his dawn with purification, he is blessed with rejoicing and gladness all his days.

And that I gave you a word from the Torah, Itzikl, I'll give you a blessing. When the Holy-One-Blessed-Be-He gave the Torah, our betrothed, to the Children of Israel, He gave us forty years of nourishment. May it be His Will that you are blessed with a good livelihood. And don't worry about the future, for between one day and the next, the Messiah of our righteousness will come and we will be worthy of it, we shall sit with our crowns on our heads and enjoy the splendor of the *Shekhina*.

5 |

When Isaac departed from Reb Alter and Reb Alter's wife, he went to Reb Haim Rafael. He found him sitting on the edge of his bed, shaking his head back and forth. Reb Haim Rafael said to him, I'm sitting and contemplating, here I am in Jerusalem and I don't see a thing, and I may, God Forbid, doubt whether I am in Jerusalem, for a man has nothing but what his eyes see, and I'm blind in my two eyes, may you not have them. It's true that the holiness of Jerusalem is so great a person can feel it. But who does that apply to? To a person with elevated thoughts. But I, all my strength is in the sense of touch, who am I to say I am blessed to feel the holiness. It's enough for that blind man that he gropes along the walls and doesn't stumble, feels his way with his stick and doesn't fall. For I could, God Forbid, despair that after all the troubles and roaming around on land and sea, I have here nothing but the walls I grope and the stick I walk with. But behold, how great are the words of the Sages who said, The air of the Land of Israel makes you wise. Perhaps you ask, what wisdom is here, for even what I came for I didn't get, for I ascended to Jerusalem to bury my body in her dirt, and this earth hasn't yet absorbed me. But the air of the Land of Israel really does make you wise, and even I have become wise here, from the force of the Land of Israel whose air makes you wise, for the Lord has enlightened the eyes of my understanding and wisdom has come to my heart. That is, that the earth hasn't absorbed me, even though all my ascendance is to bury myself in her dirt, is a mercy from the Creator May-He-Be-Blessed, for as long as I'm alive I can snatch Commandments and even do Good Deeds, which wouldn't be the case if I were dead, for when a man dies he is exempt from all the Commandments in the Torah. And when I sit all by myself and ponder that I dwell in Jerusalem, the Holy City, and I am not blessed to see it, I am still allowed to pray in it and to eat my bread and to say a blessing before and after. The great mercy is from the One Who sees and is not seen, Who gave me days of grace, I who am seen and don't see. What do you want to say, Isaac? I feel that you want to tell me something. Said Isaac, I came to ask you, Reb Haim Rafael, to come to the day of my celebration. In three days, God willing, I shall get married. Said Reb Haim Rafael, Give me your hand and I shall bless you. Isaac held our his hand and placed it in the hand of the blind Reb Haim Rafael. Reb Haim Rafael shook his head back and forth and blessed him. And when he completed all his blessings, he smiled and said, You know, Isaac, I was at the wedding of your grandfather, may he rest in peace. And even though fifty-seven years have passed, I remember it as if it happened today. Sit down and I'll tell you.

Here is how it happened. One night, I woke up and was amazed that the whole house was silent and I didn't hear any movement, not from Father's bed and not from Mother's bed. That was amazing, why is the whole house silent? I was scared and I shouted, Mother, Mother. After a while, when I didn't get an answer, I was terrified, for a mouse could come out of its hole and gnaw my face or a wild animal could come suddenly and tear me to pieces, for I'm blind and I can't resist a mouse or wild animals, and here I am left alone, and if I shout nobody will hear and come to save me. I took pity on myself and I wept, How can they leave a blind child alone? And when I stopped crying for a little while my heart was filled with anger and rage for my father and mother, who left me and went off. I went back to crying. And when I felt that nobody heard my voice, I decided to take revenge on my father and mother, who had left me alone. I got out of my bed and put on ritual fringes and pants and went outside, and I didn't know where I wanted to go, but I did know that I wanted to take revenge on father and mother, so that when they came back home they wouldn't find me. When I was outside, I heard musical instruments. I followed the sound until I came to a house and I heard dancing and music. I started crying again because the music was so pleasant. I took pity on myself for there were such nice melodies and I was angry at father and mother for not taking me to hear the wonderful melodies. A woman came and said to me, Child, why are you standing with your eyes closed? I didn't tell her that I was blind, but I told her, Because I want to. That woman said, Open your eyes, child, and don't be stubborn. I took pity on myself that I was blind and couldn't open my eyes, and my heart was filled with anger at that woman who didn't know I was blind. I answered, To spite you, I won't open my eyes. And as I spoke I burst into such weeping that my voice was heard from one end of the house to the other. Mother heard and rushed over, for she and my father were among the guests. Mother took me in her arms and hugged me and shouted and cried, My chick, oy what got into us? And when she came to, she reproached me for disgracing her and Father and coming barefoot to the wedding. I took pity on myself, it wasn't bad enough that she left me alone, but she also accused me. And as I took pity on myself, I was angry at her and at my father and at the whole world, that had no pity in their heart for a defective little child. And when I started crying again I didn't stop. Nothing helped, not my father's scolding nor my mother's pleas, nor the cakes they gave me. Finally an old woman came and took me and lay me down on a bed and I fell silent, because I didn't have any more strength to cry. All that I remember as if it were today, even though fifty-seven years have passed. Now that you came to invite me to your wedding, I am really restored. Sometimes a person asks himself why he is alive in the world, and doesn't know if they do him a favor to make his days long so that he can repair his deeds. And I hope I may repair at your wedding what I ruined at your grandfather's wedding.

6 |

At the same time that Isaac was inviting his guests, Rebecca was going round to her neighbors to invite them to the wedding. Some of them promised her they would come and they didn't, and some of them said plainly, We won't come. Rebecca didn't give up her daughter's celebration and got challahs and wine and sardines, as well as sweets and nuts and brandy so the guests would dip their hands and recite the Seven Blessings. She also invited a pair of drummers and a flutist to rejoice the bride and groom at their wedding. And before the wedding she dressed her husband in Sabbath clothes, a Caftan and a Shtrayml, and she washed his beard, and took him outside in his bed so he could see the wedding of his only daughter.

Reb Fayesh lay on his bed. Two fat, blue bags hung under his eyes and his congealed eyes saw and didn't know what they saw. Opposite him stood Reb Haim Rafael, the blind man, peeping with his blind eyes, with a kind of smile bound in them. He was not yet used to the Jerusalemites and groped with his hands and shook his head and smiled his blind smile that scared folks.

Not many guests came to celebrate the happiness of the bride and groom. Hinda Puah didn't come because of Reb Alter's illness. The engraver and his wife didn't come because they went to Giv'at Shaul for the Pidyon Ha-Ben, the Redemption of their daughter's firstborn son, which took place that day. Efraim the plasterer didn't come because he was ill, for the night before, when he went to wake the sleepers to serve the Creator, he found the Mughrabi guard removing a shop door to steal the merchandise, the guard jumped on him and dropped him in one of the pits. Unlike the guests who didn't come, young men and women came to see Reb Fayesh's daughter marrying a Polak. Whenever a neighbor would appear, Rebecca would hold both her hands to them and say, Come, come, good people, come to the wedding of my only daughter. Before she could pull them in, they dropped off and went on their way. Anyone who saw Rebecca's grief that day will not see the face of hell.

Isaac and Shifra didn't notice either those who came to their wedding or those who came to look at them, for Isaac's mind clung to Shifra and Shifra's mind clung to Isaac, and there wasn't any room left in their heart for others. And when they brought him a telegram of congratulations on his marriage from his comrade Rabinovitch, he stuffed it in his pocket and didn't finish reading it. Things had reached such a pass that he forgot Sonya's last name. And, before the wedding, when he went to cut his hair and had to wait a little, and the barber gave him a copy of *The Young Laborer*, and he saw there the story of Hemdat and Yael, that Hemdat was attracted to Yael

Hayyot and Yael Hayyot was attracted to other fellows, Isaac put down the paper and didn't notice Hemdat's grief, like a bridegroom who puts down the grief of the whole world because of his joy.

Shifra and Isaac didn't notice those who came to their wedding or those who came to look and sneer. Nor did they even notice the grief of that wretched Rebecca, who was sorry that her daughter's wedding was without joy and without honor, and she said to herself, What is this and why did God do this to me. But in the end, the Lord took pity on her and gave her joy and honor before all her neighbors.

How? In those days, a great Rabbi ascended to Jerusalem from the land of Hungary, a holy man of God, a genius and a Saint, and great as his genius was the goodness of his heart and his righteousness. That tale reached his ears, and he recalled that once, in his youth, he had come to the house of Reb Moyshe Amram, who proposed a match for him with his daughter, and he recalled all the honor Reb Moyshe Amram had paid him. And like all the Saints and Hasids who are honest in their heart, who remember the good and don't remember the bad, that Saint remembered the goodness of Reb Moyshe Amram. He told his attendant, I shall go and repay a kindness with the daughter of one who was good to me. He dressed in his Sabbath clothes and went to Reb Fayesh. And anyone who saw that Saint walking went with him. Soon he was accompanied by scholars and practical people and they brought bread and wine and meat and fish and other delicacies. They made a big feast and the Rabbi recited the Seven Blessings. The whole house was filled with joy and rejoicing and all the neighbors came, men and women and children, to rejoice in the celebration of the bride and groom, until the house couldn't hold all those who came.

CHAPTER TWELVE

About Diseases

1 |

The festivities passed and all the joy turned to gloom. Malaria which is wont to strike most days of the year went on striking. There wasn't a house where someone wasn't sick. Add to that an epidemic of influenza. And to those two evil diseases Jerusalem is used to, add meningitis, called stiff neck. Sick paupers, especially among the Ashkenazim, decayed in their diseases.

There are some doctors who say disease comes from the bad water, for at that time, the water in the cisterns ran out and only foul water remained. And there are other doctors who say that the dung and the filth in the city bring the disease. And there are some doctors who say that the prayer shawl and the Shtrayml bring the disease with them. In the home of the sick person, they are placed on the sickbed, and on the Sabbath a person goes to the synagogue, and spreads the evil germs from the private sphere to the public sphere. In addition, there is the ritual bath. There are ritual baths filled with turgid water changed only once in two moths, and the water in the women's ritual bath that must be filled with rainwater is changed only three times a year. In addition to all these reasons is the poverty, for they live in crowded apartments and they eat tuna that is one or two years old, and they drink the bad water, and latrines overflow and stink up the air.

Fear increases. One doctor says the situation is dangerous. And his colleague adds, It is dreadful. And things are terrifying even to the healthy. And everyone who can is ready to take his family and get out of the city, but there's no place to flee, for bad rumors come from other places, until they see all kinds of hallucinations. The doctors run from patient to patient, write prescriptions and take fees, and if they are sent for at night, the fee is double and quadruple.

The officials and leaders of the city do all they can, they discuss renting a house for the sick, and they call on people to fast every Monday and Thursday, pray and prostrate themselves on the graves and to examine their sins. Every day, announcements are posted by the Rabbis and the rabbinical court, Nation of the Lord be of good courage, Daughter of my people, do not be silent, sons of Israel, do not rest. And new pamphlets with old bans on secular schools are printed, and individuals stick amulets and remedies on their doors, and they've already held a wedding for two orphans on the Mount of Olives to stop the plague.

Shepherds of the holy flock follow their custom and those with a license to sell lamb follow their custom. Announcements are posted in the streets, Have mercy on your sucklings and children, don't eat beef and don't drink cow's milk, for all diseases come from them. And everyone who is used to beef and cow's milk eats mutton and drinks sheep's milk, and the price of mutton and sheep's milk go up from one day to the next. Prices rise. The lack of income combined with helplessness make folks despondent. And yet the sun is at its zenith and toys with the world on earth.

The Young Laborer, which doesn't refrain from criticizing any event in the Yishuv, wrote about that matter. There are brazen people in Jerusalem who say that there is no epidemic here at all, but merely that the diseases of the Land usually come every year and kill a few souls, and thus last year, two hundred people got sick and thirty of them died, but a few Rabbis and officials made all that noise to evoke pity in the heart of the Jewish philanthropists Outside the Land so they would send them money. But that is not the truth, for even the schools of the freethinkers were closed. But when we challenge the words of *The Young Laborer*, the paper presents evidence that not all the schools were closed, it was just that the principals of the schools are wont to go Outside the Land every year, and some were delayed and didn't leave and they want to leave now — their doctors ordered them to send the students home for fear of disease, while the principals who came back from Outside the Land and who don't intend to leave again this year — their doctors allowed them to study in their schools.

2 |

The month of Kislev is over and the rain hadn't fallen. The downpour doesn't come and the Land is parched. Landlords plaster their roofs and once again they crack. Sometimes clouds appear in the morning and look like they are loaded with rain, but in fact there isn't any moisture in them at all. As they come so they vanish. And once again the skies are pure and the sun stands in its glory and every bush and every tree are like corpses. The same is true for all two-legged creatures, and the same is true for all four-legged creatures. The empty cisterns have no water, but they do have maggots and earthworms and snails, all of them twisted, greenish, reddish, terrifying. Every drop of water costs a Matlik and every goatskin of water the Arabs brought from Eyn Rogel is fought over by ten women. Every day a black chicken appears and shrieks in a voice dry as a shard. At the sound of that voice, the lambs shudder and hide their heads in their wool. At the sight of them folks prophesy that a hard year will come may it be on the enemies of the Jews and not on the Jews. One way or another, prices go through the roof, merchandise becomes expensive, and storekeepers conceal foodstuffs to sell them for more money later.

Some individuals begin fasting and doing acts of charity, and preachers and reproachers pop up to stir the people to repentance. Jerusalem stands like an uninhabited wasteland, and the sun kindles the dust and the filth in its streets like fire. But the synagogues and study houses are full. Every day they recite Slikhot and the Thirteen Rules for expounding the Law, Our Father Our King, and Save Us, and they blow the Shofar, and the Cantor intones the prayer for rain, and after the prayer they recite Psalms, and after the afternoon prayers the preacher stands up and moralizes to stir the heart. And he counts and enumerates the transgressions of the Children of Israel that block up the skies and won't let the rain come down. Every day Rabbi Grunam May-Salvation-Arise comes to Meah Shearim and preaches, sometimes in the courtyard of the Yeshuot Jacob Synagogue and sometimes on the stairs of the tabernacle of the Yeshiva. And when he comes, most of the people follow him, for he can preach and he can stir the heart and humble the soul, for he was an expert in the transgressions of the generation as were the destructive angels, and all the transgressions and sins and crimes they committed and sinned and transgressed he knows by heart, as if Satan had deposited his notebook with him.

Right from the start, Isaac's heart was drawn to the preachers, because he loved to hear the words of the Torah or a fine parable. Unlike most of our comrades who go to hear for some other reason. A generation that emptied itself of the deeds of their fathers and was not blessed with deeds of their own seeks a smell of those deeds, even if their smell is dissipated. Some are eager for stories of Hasids, for a melody of the Days of Awe, for preachers' sermons. That generation, which has not created a new life and has gone away from the old, when they see themselves naked, they pick up a garment left over from their fathers and cover themselves with it. And they don't know that all the time the garment was in the hands of their fathers, their fathers preserved it from moths and from dust and every day it was like new and would provide warmth from the cold and shade from the heat. But the sons didn't preserve it from the moths and didn't shake the dust out of it. Not only doesn't it warm, but it also raises dust. In fact, Rabbi Grunam was also dressed in tatters, but you can't see the tatters because of the dust.

That day was the last day of the seven days of wedding feast. Isaac came out of his father-in-law's house dressed in his wedding clothes and his heart rejoiced and he came and stood before Rabbi Grunam. At that moment, Rabbi Grunam was standing on the steps of the tabernacle of the Yeshiva and his voice was bursting. But let us leave Rabbi Grunam in his crowd and Isaac in his wedding clothes, and let us return to Balak.

CHAPTER THIRTEEN

Returns to Balak

1 |

How Balak's soul longed for a place of rest, but wherever he went, his luck went with him. Here they showed him the stick, and here they threw stones at him, and here they showered contempt on him, that would shame even a pig. Three or four times, he came across that painter and Balak expected him to say why they hounded him so much. But before he heard from him, the painter kicked him and chased him away, because Balak came to him at the top of his voice, because his heart urged him in grief. When Balak saw that, he said, I'll go to him calmly, then I'll grab him by his trousers, then I'll grab him by his flesh, and then he'll tell me why they hound me. When Balak came to this resolution, he went back to running after the painter. Either the footsteps of the painter were revealed to him in one place, or in another place, or sometimes the whole Land smelled of him. When he followed the smell, the smell ran and rolled before him like the shadow of a creature running. Balak saw that the Land was laughing at him, and that there was no hope or expectation of reaching what his soul desired and coveted and sought and he returned to his main issue, that is, subsistence, which is the main issue of every single creature.

In those days, Balak found himself a place of rest in Richard Wagner's brewery at the railroad station. There he found his food, and perhaps more than in other places, for aside from bones he also found real meat. How? Because sometimes a Jew came to dine there, not only on the nine days, and suddenly another Jew appeared and he was ashamed to be eating unkosher food in front of him, so he would throw the meat under the table and Balak would come and snatch the food.

Balak did not find satisfaction from his food. We may assume that he abhorred forbidden food and longed for kosher meat. Even though the Torah allowed him to eat animals that were not ritually slaughtered and non-kosher meat, he wanted to sanctify himself with what is allowed him. It is with reluctance that we come to this assumption, for if not, why did Balak need to leave his place, where he lacked for nothing. Not because his mind was not rational, for everything Isaac wrote on his skin he wrote only as a joke. Hence, it was with clear awareness and a lucid mind that he got disgusted with the inn and was fed up with Germans, because he desired to eat kosher food. This desire made him want to return to the neighborhoods of the Children of Israel so much that he forgot all the insults he had experienced, and didn't sense the insults in store for him there. And if his heart told him, Be careful and don't go, he barked at it and replied, I'll go, I'll go, because I want to go. On the face of it, a primitive answer did Balak reply, but in fact you find a philosophical reasoning here, that is, that the will is an autonomous force and cannot be denied with reasons of causality.

To make a long story short, Balak prepared to go to Meah Shearim, for he was already disgusted with Richard Wagner and the other Germans, and all the other places were disgusted with Balak. And if his heart told him, Don't go to Meah Shearim, so that you won't die, he answered, No matter what, my death is in store for me, better I die in the place where I was born and not in some makeshift hole. And when he reached this state, new life started flowing in him. He saw himself already as if he were in Meah Shearim, and his neighbors put out good food for him, whose like you don't find even in the *Yoreh De'ah*. And after he filled his belly with food and drink, he got up and went off to hear a sermon by Rabbi Grunam May-Salvation-Arise. And Balak's share of that was nicer than the other listeners, for all the other listeners were pressed and pressing, while Balak wasn't pressed and wasn't pressing, but was lying between the feet of Rabbi Grunam, if he wanted to he wallowed in Rabbi Grunam's cloak, which dragged down below his feet, if he wanted to he slept, and Rabbi Grunam's cloak served as his blanket.

Balak knew that he had to come to Meah Shearim by stealth, for if they saw him, they wouldn't leave a bone on his flesh. In Balak's place, you would have tied an amulet of invisibility around you. Balak was skeptical of amulets just as he was skeptical of other charms and remedies, for he had already learned from experience that they don't help. Balak relied on himself. How? Said Balak, here I come clandestinely. First I don't show anything but my tail, then I show my body, then I show my head. If they don't pester me, it's good; and if not, I'll show them my teeth.

2 |

Balak left Richard Wagner and the brewery, urinated, and looked at all four corners of the sky for which way he would choose. Finally, he stuck his legs to his body and started running until he came to the neighborhood of Abu Tor, the Father of the Bull. He sniffed a little here and a little there and took himself to the neighborhood of Beit Yosef, the smallest neighborhood in Jerusalem, where in those days it was settled by Jews, with fourteen houses and a synagogue. And for our great transgressions, they sold them to foreigners. And since he intended to go to Meah Shearim, why didn't he go to Meah Shearim? Yet he wanted to hear the opinion of folks about whether there was going to be war or peace.

And so Balak entered the neighborhood of Beit Yosef. Rest and peace were spread on the neighborhood and its houses. And next to every house stood a barrel full of dried figs or a heap of straw. And poultry roamed around them. And next to them, a blind donkey, who had been working in the oil press, walked in circles as if he were still turning a wheel in the oil press. Next to him, tied to a cliff stood an old horse. Next to him played five or six dogs. One of them noticed Balak and withdrew from the group. His comrade noticed that and went off. Then all of them noticed him and took off. Finally, of all the dogs, the only one left was Balak. Balak was wroth that the dogs were disgusted with him. He swallowed his anger and pretended to be dumb, like those of whom the Bible says, They are all dumb dogs, they cannot bark. And he did well to be silent, for if he had opened his mouth, all the dogs would have barked at him and the people of the place would have heard and been horrified. For he didn't come to scare the Children of Israel, but to get accustomed to them.

At that moment, there was not a man, woman, or child of the Children of Israel there. Those whose work was in the city were in the city and those whose work was in the villages walked through the villages. And the women, where were they? The girls went to launder their clothes in the waters of the Shiloh, and their little sisters accompanied them to splash their feet in the water. And the married woman, the ones whose time had come to give birth were giving birth, and those whose time had not yet come to give birth went to the Western Wall or to the Tomb of Our Mother Rachel or to the Mount of Olives, or to the grave of Simon the Saint to pray that their sisters would have an easy birth of sons for the Lord. And the sons, where were they? Some of them were sitting in the Talmud Torah in the city and reciting psalms, and some of them went to the Cave of Kalba Savoua, the Cave of the Sated Dog, to pray for rain, and some of them were sitting in the Alliance Israelite school studying art, and some of them I don't know where they were at that moment. There was no one there but Gentiles, who don't know the shape of a Hebrew letter.

When Balak saw himself in tranquility and safety, he lifted his tail and started strolling around, sniffing in every courtyard and rummaging through all dungheaps. Finally, he went down to the nearby gardens beneath the neighborhood which continued on into the valley and wound around each other, one above another and one below another, full of trees and bushes, whose shadow rises and falls, one shadow on top of another, as if every tree and every bush is the reflection of the other, and the other is also a reflection of the first. And above the bushes flew a big bee and it cast a shadow too. Balak asked himself, If this buzzer stings me, what shall I do? He opened his mouth and jumped at the bee's shadow to swallow it alive, according to the law, Kill him first who rises to kill you. The bee noticed that. It laughed and said, Dust in your mouth, mad dog, I won't sting you and my shadow won't give you honey. Balak heard it and was ashamed and went off.

He came to a big cave in the rock of the mountain, the burial place of their pilgrims. From there they brought shiploads full of dirt to Italy in Rome to sanctify their graveyards. This is the place the Christians call Aceldama, and it is a cave in the rock of the mountain the Christians call the Mount of Evil Counsel, for there, they say, was the summer house of the High Priest Caiaphas.

The sun declined and the lower parts of the firmament turned gold with seven kinds of gold, and a flock of clouds red as alabaster floated and surrounded the sun, and opposite, the Mountains of Moab turned gray and turned blue and turned gray. Monks came from doing their good works in the city and entered their prayer house. Opposite them stood the Muezzin and called the faithful to prayer, and opposite him the bells of their churches tolled, and opposite them the Muezzin raised his voice. At last all the voices fell silent and a small still voice of prayers and weeping rose from the city. This is the voice of the Children of Israel imprisoned among the Gentiles and all the Gentiles want to silence them, but the Holy-One-Blessed-Be-He picks up their voice and raises it to the firmament and conceals it in the Trumpet of the Messiah, and when the Trumpet of the Messiah, May it Come Soon in Our Days, is full with the voice of the Children of Israel, the Prophet Elijah May-He-Be-Remembered-For-Good will come and stand on the top of the Mount of Olives and will blow the Trumpet.

A shepherd wrapped in a coarse brown woolen blanket came from the mountains leading goats without number, all of them black and the same height, and in his arms, a day-old kid. The householders came out and brought their goats into the folds, and a smell of fragrant woods drying and a smell of new milk and a smell of dry droppings bubbled up from every house and from every courtyard and a small fire started flickering and glowing from the doorways of the houses, where they were cooking the evening meal in clay ovens. The moon rose and looked like a scythe, and as it came out it disappeared among the clouds and then came out again. Dogs started shouting. Balak opened his mouth and wanted to add his voice to theirs. He recalled something and fulfilled by himself the saying, A dog away from home doesn't bark for seven years.

God arranged the stars in the firmament and they all sat each and every one in his own place calmly and quietly, silently and comfortably, and illuminated the earth and those who dwell on it with great affection, and every single star landed in the place the Lord fixed for it as He determined, Blessed-Be-He, for the stars have no will or purpose of their own, aside from doing His commands, Blessed-Be-He. And if you ever saw a star jumping out of its place and getting out of line, know that it is His will, Blessed-Be-He, for even things that look out of line are lined up. And all the sages of truth have already applied their proof to it, there is no need to go on.

CHAPTER FOURTEEN

Balak Gets Out of Line

1 |

A smell of meat fried in oil and onions started bubbling up. All the air was saturated and smelled good. Such a fine smell as that Balak hadn't sniffed in many a day, for in Richard Wagner's brewery they fried meat in butter as the Germans do. Balak raised his nose and the smell began to attract him. He subordinated himself to his nose and plodded along behind it, until he came to the priests' house where the smell was coming from. He looked at the entrance and saw that the gate was closed. He groaned and said, They're already sitting down to dinner, for when the priests come in to eat, they lock the gate. Balak stood at the locked door and that smell bubbled up much stronger. Balak pictured to himself all that they were eating and drinking. He longed to join the meal. He postponed his return to Meah Shearim, like fickle people, who, when a pleasurable thing comes their way, they immediately postpone their repentance.

He licked the gate as if it were meat. There was a little wicket there that wasn't locked. The wicket gave way and opened a bit. Balak stuck his head inside and his whole body was drawn after it. He leaped into the courtyard, and from the courtyard to the vestibule, and from the vestibule to the great hall, where the priests were having their meal. He saw one fat, fleshy bishop, his belly broad and rising to his double chin. Said Balak to himself, Everybody like that is dear to me, for if he is fat and has a round belly, his portion is double, and even a light creature lying underneath will draw comfort from a full stomach. Balak went up to him and got into the hem of his cloak, as he did during the sermons of Rabbi Grunam May-Salvation-Arise, quite to the contrary.

2 |

The monks sat at the table made in the form of a horse-shoe. That old bishop who had come to tour the monastery sat in the middle, and at his right was the head of the monastery, and behind him the principal of the seminary, and behind him the keeper of the holy bones, and behind him the keeper of the keys. All of them were important and dignified priests. And behind them the brothers, the keeper of the holy vessels and the keeper of the icons and the keeper of the candles. And to the left of the bishop sat the students of the seminary. One student arose and read a chapter of Holy Scripture. That day it was a chapter from I Samuel telling that the priests' custom with the people was, that, when any man offered sacrifice, the priest's servant came, while the flesh was in seething with a fleshhook of three teeth in his hand so he could take a lot with it, and he struck it into the pan, or kettle, or cauldron, or pot; all that the fleshhook brought up the priest took for himself. After the student concluded his chapter, the other seminary students stood up and brought all kinds of dishes to the table. Some were made according to the local custom, and some were made according to the customs of other lands to honor every single land, and some were made according to the custom of the monastery and some were made according to the custom of the early monks, because you don't throw out the old for the new, if you can maintain both of them. And old Father Zenon, in charge of the tables, takes the portions from the hands of the young men and puts them before the bishop and the dignitaries of the monastery. And the man in charge of the wine stands and pours.

After they ate and drank and said grace, the old men gathered in the prior's room. They were brought narghilas and cigars and cigarettes and fruit and various sweets. They smoked and drank and ate, and ate and drank and smoked, and refreshed themselves with stories of their saints and with the tale of the Father of the Bull for whom the neighborhood is named and with other amusing stories. From those stories they came to stories of ordinary men, and from them to the daughters of man, whose heart God sealed and you can't know their mystery. They told this, that, and the other thing. One thing we shall tell.

A rich peasant's wife died. He made her a big funeral and married another woman. Soon after, she died too. He made her a big funeral and married another woman. She died too. He made her a big funeral and married another woman. Soon after, she died too. He made her a big funeral and married another woman. She died too. He made her a big funeral and wanted to marry a virgin. He came upon a maiden who agreed to marry him. Her girlfriends came to her and said, That assassin you want to marry, won't he bury you as he buried the first six or seven? She said to them, Instead of looking at their deaths, look at the nice funeral he made for them.

Let's go back to Balak. So Balak lay in the monks' house at the feet of the bishop and ate what the bishop ate and drank what the bishop drank (aside from the alcoholic beverages a dog isn't easy with), and didn't turn away his ears even from the spiritual things, especially from the story of that maiden, who didn't look at her death but at the fine funeral her husband would make for her, for in most cases, what is desired vanquishes good sense and impels actions. Similarly, said Balak, I know that if I go to Meah Shearim I'll end up killed, but even so I will go, for all my being is there already, and if my tail wanders here, the core of my vitality is there. And I don't need to seek an intelligent reason, for the will is reason enough for everything.

CHAPTER FIFTEEN

About the Spirits

1 |

Balak left the priests' house and set off for Meah Shearim. He saw that his body was heavy and his belly dragged him to the ground, and he was also tired from so much eating and drinking. He did what he did and postponed his walk to the next day, and sought a place to put himself until he digested the food in his guts. And why didn't he go back to the priests' house? Because of the tolling of the bells. In the past, when Ishmael was assertive, no bell struck in Jerusalem, and the Christians got around their obligation with a mortar, now that the Christians are powerful, they ring the bells in their churches and disturb sleep. And so Balak sought a place for his bones. He knew he couldn't sleep outside, in case a Jew saw him. And he didn't have the strength to dig himself a hole. He gazed up and saw that he was standing near Djurat El-Anab in the Valley of the Spirits below Yemin Moshe near the Abu Tor neighborhood. But he didn't go there for the same reason, in case a Jew saw him, for that poor neighborhood is populated by Jews, and in every single one of the forty-seven houses in the neighborhood, there are two score Jews. Some of them are porters, some of them are cobblers, some of them are shoemakers, some of them are peddlers, and if they saw him they would do to him what they do to Negroes. Once upon a time, some Negroes came to Djurat El-Anab to steal, the porters overpowered them and bound their hands and feet, and the peddlers came and beat them with their measuring rod, and the cobblers cobbled them with their awls. Balak looked at the four corners of the sky, where is a place for his bones. And wherever Balak turned his eyes, it locked itself before him. Here the sky lowered its head to the ground and here the hills rose up to the firmament, and he wasn't an expert in the laws of the sky and didn't understand the way of the horizon, and thought the world was closed down on him. He took himself south of Jaffa Gate and hid there among the big houses standing on a landfill of dung that was taken out of the city and poured into the valley and those houses were built on it. A wind came and turned the windmills. A menacing sound was heard like the sound of the windmills at night when the winds gather to grind the black flour. Another menace mated with that menace, that they would sequester and harness him as one of the businessmen of Jerusalem did who leased a windmill, but didn't have the money to rent the mules to turn the millwheel, so he went and brought a pack of dogs and tied them up to grind his flour. And since Balak didn't have the strength to run away, he stood still and lamented for himself, as if he were already chained and as if he were already forced to work and would never have salvation. Balak groaned from his heart and thought, What has happened to me and what will become of me? Is it possible for a weak creature like me to endure such hard work? Won't I die, and I will surely die and there's no doubt I will die, and if I don't die from that work, I will die from boredom. How do you take a free dog and make him a slave forever to walk around here and there like a mule of a mill until he dies, and when he dies you throw him into the dungheap just like that.

But Balak's luck at that moment was extraordinary. And when he imagined that he was already chained, he looked out of the corner of his eye to see what they were doing to him. He saw that he was standing in a safe neighborhood, in Yemin Moshe near Montefiore's windmill. And when Balak saw himself at Montifiore's windmill he was no longer scared, for the windmill was idle and they weren't working in it, and even if it wasn't idle, there was no danger because it was worked by wind power and not by animal power, for that dignitary Reb Moses Montefiore was a great saint and all his works were designed to make things easy for folks and not to bother them, and he built that windmill only for the good of folks. How? When he saw that the poverty was immense, and everything he wanted to do for the good of Jerusalem, the sages and Rabbis of Jerusalem came and prevented him, for they were afraid of everything new that could lead to heresy, he built a windmill to make it a little easier for the poor, who wouldn't have to take the grain to the city to the windmills of the Arabs, who took a lot of money and produced a little flour. He built a fine windmill of square-cut stones, fifty feet high, and sent machinery and tools and an English artisan who was expert in that work. The pieces came to Jaffa and were taken up to Jerusalem, every single part separately, and four or five porters loaded them because they were so heavy, and four months they were busy bringing them up. The windmill was built and the wind revolved four pairs of big stones. They ground and made flour. The Arabs saw and were jealous. They hired an old man to curse the windmill. He turned his eyes to the windmill and said, I guarantee you that when the rains come and the winds come, they will make it into an everlasting ruin. The winds came and the rains came and didn't do anything to it. The old man saw it and said, This is the Devil's work here and no mortal can uproot it. And even the great Dervishes agreed with him. Within a few years, two or three of the pieces were broken and there wasn't anyone in Jerusalem who could repair them. They wrote to Montefiore but he didn't respond, for steam mills were already built in Jerusalem that didn't depend on the winds. That windmill remained idle and ground the wind. Said Balak, I shall lie here until tomorrow and shall rest a bit from my toil.

2 |

Balak went inside and lay down to sleep. He lay down wherever he lay as the wind roamed around and called, Do Vilna, Do Vilna, as the wind is wont to do while roaming in a windmill and it seemed to be calling Vilna Vilna. Said Balak, Why are you rattling To Vilna To Vilna, when I'm from the Hungarian Society? And he immediately considered himself very important as if he were receiving Hungarian Distribution.

There was an old night owl there, Lilith, who knew the world and knew everything that was done in every house, under every roof. She flapped her black wings and told him, Aren't you Balak that the whole world envies because you are feeding at the table of that Prussian? And even though Richard Wagner who owns the brewery is from Würtemberg, they called him a Prussian, like the Arabs of Jerusalem who call every German Gentile a Prussian. Said he, I am he. She said to him, Does your table lack something that you came here? Balak groaned and told her, My table lacks nothing, but I lack a lot. She said to him, There isn't a creature in the world who doesn't lack, like the proverb they tell in Jerusalem, one person lacks an eighth thread in his ritual fringes and another one lacks the heart for a ritual garment. And you, my friend, what do you lack? Balak looked all around to see if anyone was listening. He whispered, Meah Shearim I lack. And he was immediately filled with valor and added, Tomorrow I am going there. The night owl looked at him out of the corner of her eye and said, Meah Shearim you lack? And I thought that Meah Shearim doesn't lack creatures like you. But let me hear why you want to go to Meah Shearim of all places. Said Balak, Why? Because I want a meaningful life. Said the night owl, And so it is signed, sealed, and delivered in your mind to go there. Said Balak, Signed and sealed. Said the night owl, I'll tell you something, think about it on the way and you won't get bored. Said Balak, If the story isn't long, I'm willing to listen. Said the night owl, The story isn't long, but your mind is short. Said Balak, May your house be destroyed, you clump of feathers, behold the wisdom she took to herself. He swallowed the curse in his mouth so as not to increase his foes, for he was dejected and he feared every creature. He stretched his legs to show her that he was eager to go, but was willing to do her the satisfaction of listening. The night owl smiled and said, Put down your feet and load your ears, as Ben Sira said, There is no cure for the proud man's malady since an evil growth has taken root in him, and Solomon said, The ear of the wise seeketh knowledge. And may I not be one of those who holds the ear of a passing dog. Balak barked, Arf arf. Said the night owl, Throw away your arf arf, Balak, you won't get any meat with that. Said Balak, Didn't you want to tell me something? Said the night owl, Be patient, Balak, lest you perish before you hear. Balak softened his tail and put his head between his legs. The night owl flapped her wings and said, Are you sleeping, Balak? Perhaps we should ask the Lord of Dreams to come and show you a good dream? Said Balak, I'm not sleeping. Said the night owl, Then listen.

Once upon a time, there was a hyena who passed by the door of Arzef's house in Eyn Rogel and found him busy stuffing a fox. The hyena asked Arzef, What's that? Said he, A fox. Said the hyena, And his bones and his flesh, where are they? He told him he threw them away and took straw and stubble instead. Asked the hyena, Why? He told him, As long as your flesh exists you're considered dead, for everyone wants to eat your flesh and break your bones, and if you are saved from the foes and you die in the hands of Heaven, your end is dust and vermin and worms, which is not the case if you threw away your flesh and tossed off your bones and put straw instead of flesh and bones, for then you live forever and exist for eternity, and moreover, they put you in a museum and everyone desires and yearns to see you.

Said the hyena to Arzef, Mr. Arzef, I know there is no flaw uglier than envy, as we learned, envy and lust and honor take the person out of the world, and so King Solomon, may-he-rest-in-peace, said, Envy the rottenness of the bones, and the Talmud said, He who has envy in his heart, his bones rot away. And every person has to remove envy from his heart and to make do with what he has and rejoice at the good fortune of his fellow man, for He is the Rock, his work is perfect, and whatever the Merciful One does is good. But there is envy that is good, that is the envy to do good, and all who would lengthen his days and his years will have time to do commandments and good deeds. And so may it be your will Mr. Arzef that you do with me as you did with that fox. And I swear to you by my teeth that I will not rob you of your fee and I will bring you meat for the Sabbath.

Arzef glanced at him and saw that he was a great lad and his skin was bristly and fine. He told him, By your virtue and by virtue of your good deeds and by the charity of your honest and innocent forefathers I am willing to be gracious unto you and bring you to life in the World-to-Come. Arzef went and brought an Egyptian rope and tied the hyena's legs and picked up a knife and slaughtered him, as he had done with the fox. He took out his flesh and threw it wherever he threw it and filled his skin with straw and stubble and set big glass eyes in his face.

A few days went by and the hyena didn't return. His brothers saw that their father was worried. They said to him, Father, don't worry, don't you know that your son has become the leader of a gang of searchers of sin, and he is surely busy with the evil instincts of others. The hyena's father was happy for his son who became the leader of a gang of searchers of sin, but his heart feared for his son lest the transgressors overcome him and harm him. His sons told him, Father, do not fear the transgressors, even though they are many they cannot do anything to him, for transgressions sap the strength of those who practice them and even a small fly can overcome them, but tonight is the time for the Sanctification of the New Moon, tonight we shall go out and greet him.

When they went out, they smelled meat. They followed the smell until they came to Eyn Rogel. At that moment, the moon shone and the eyes of the stuffed animal were gleaming brightly. His brothers stood still in amazement and said to him, Our brother, son of our mother, son of our father, please tell us where did you get that light and what was your merit that your eyes come to be so gleaming? Arzef heard their voice. He made his voice sound like the voice of the hyena and said to them, Who are you, mortals, race of wretched hyenas, today you are here and tomorrow dust and vermin and worms, who are you that you assembled to annoy me. Don't you see that I live and exist forever and ever? And moreover, I expect to be put in a museum and all the painters of Jerusalem will come and make a picture of me, and moreover, they'll publish my picture in textbooks, and everyone who wants to study will come and look at me. They said to him, Our brother, what things are you saying and what tales are you telling? Please explain your words, for our soul is dying for them and we long to hear. Behind the back of the hyena, Arzef replied to them as he had replied to their brother.

When they heard his words, they began whispering among themselves, Woe unto us from our brother who will live forever, for he inherits our legacy. Envy entered their heart and they discussed what they would do. They flattered the stuffed animal and said Aren't we your brothers, are you not of our flesh and bone, why are you estranged from us, why don't you give us the secret that has made you become what you have become? Behind the back of the stuffed animal, Arzef answered them, Tell the artist who made me live forever, perhaps he will do to you as he did to me. Arzef came and stood before them. They greeted him and prostrated themselves before him and said, You are Arzef who dwells in peace with all creatures, by your life, we will not budge from here until you make peace between us and our brother. But as long as we expect to die and our brother lives forever, there is no peace at all. So we ask you, do with us as you did to our brother so we will be equal in this world and in the next. And if our brother swore to bring you meat on the Sabbath and holidays, we also swear to bring you meat for the nine days every day you finish a tractate of the Talmud. Arzef agreed and granted their request.

After the night owl finished her tale, she went on, Rise up, Balak, and hear; hearken unto me thou son of barking. It wasn't a parable I told you and it wasn't made up words I made up. But I shall ask you, Tell me, instead of flesh what will you wish and instead of skin what will you desire? Either stones of the streets or a furious rod. And now shut your eyes, Balak, maybe you'll rest. And I am going to my place and I shall not see your misfortune. The night owl flew off and left Balak.

3 |

Balak folded his paws and shut his eyes and lay and thought of the same thing all the scholars of all generations are toiling to discover, What are we and what is our life, and are all the sufferings and pains and insults and grief that come to us worthwhile for the sake of a little bit of ephemeral pleasure. Especially me, since I don't have even a bit of pleasure, but I do have many pains, and on top of every pain comes an even harder pain. Black bile overcame him and he wanted to die. But death is wont to come when you don't want it and not to come when you do want it. With so many thoughts, Balak's brain grew weak and his mind was about to go mad. Nevertheless, Balak did not tend to the opinion of the philosophers who say that madness comes from black bile and not from demons, but he did admit their error, that the cause is black bile, and the black bile itself comes from the demons who inject their venom and give rise to black bile. There is no doubt that that black bile that clasped him like scabies and bubbled up all over his body came from them, from the demons in the windmill, for as is well known, nothing in the world can endure emptiness, and since the windmill is empty of humans, demons came to take up residence in it. And he didn't know that in the sign of the month of Heshvan black bile dominates. Balak began to be frightened and wanted to run away.

When he was about to run away, his legs became heavy. Even the spleen that attracts the waste of the black bile ejected by the liver, to purify the blood, also stopped acting right. Black bile overcame him and all kinds of evil thoughts were born in him, until he was filled with them and couldn't lift himself up, not to mention to run away. Even though dogs are creatures who walk on their toes, and walkers on toes are light and nimble, and easily raise their legs off the ground, not like those creatures who walk on soles of their feet, like the bear and the human, who roll the soles of their feet from the heel to the toes.

Balak saw that he was doomed to stay here. He pretended to join the three philosophers who deny the reality of demons, as if he didn't know that the Ishmaelites and the Greeks and — quite the contrary — the Children of Israel had all agreed on their complete reality. And even though he saw them with his senses, he denied their reality here, because they were composed of air and fire, and here there was complete darkness, while if there were a demon here, his fire would be seen, and since his fire isn't seen, that we must conclude there is no demon here. And when he denied their reality here, he also completely denied their reality altogether, for as is known, demons are invisible, and if they are seen they aren't demons.

Suddenly a noise was heard and the sound of words. His bones were shaken by a tremor and he was scared and shocked and stunned. The fear that paralyzes the body and makes it heavy as lead, suddenly behaved differently and made Balak as light as a feather. He took off and fled for his life. And he flattered himself that his wisdom stood him in good stead to run away before the demons could harm him. And when he retreated from his error and admitted that there were demons, he began envying them for the length of their days, for from the day the world was created until now, only three kings had ruled them, Asmodeus and Hind and Bil'ad, and Bil'ad who is still alive. But here Balak saw something and was wrong. That sound wasn't of demons but of a man, for there are human beings who want to study secular wisdom, but they are afraid to study in public because of the zealots, so they go to hidden places to study in secret. Now too, there was no demon here but one of Isaac's comrades, who came every night to the empty windmill to study foreign tongues.

Balak fled outside and raised his tail in freedom, as if no dread or fear were facing him. And in fact, he had no need to fear, for even if a son of Israel had passed by him, he wouldn't have seen him, for the Land was black and darkness and gloominess was over it. He opened his eyes wide and looked once here and once there. The darkness suddenly burst open and lanterns began running urgently and hastily like meteors, running and appearing as if they were falling down to earth. Balak who was neither an astronomer nor an astrologer, but who was expert in matters of Jerusalem understood immediately that they were carrying a corpse to be buried, and those were the lanterns of the Burial Society. He wanted to pay his last respects to the corpse and accompany him to his resting place. But to save his life, he pulled in his paws and didn't go to the funeral, for if they had seen him they would have made him into a corpse too.

Balak stood at a distance and pondered what a living being ponders when a dead person passes by him. This dead person was alive two or three hours before, and perhaps he didn't know he was going to die, and in the end his soul departed and he died. For ever since the day Adam was condemned to die, there isn't a creature who doesn't die, for there is no way to get out of dying, and everyone passes away and dies and everyone is given into the hands of the Angel of Death by the will of the Creator Blessed-Be-He, for by His will He gives life and by His will He takes it. And just as that dead person died, so Balak will die and that painter will die, too. And perhaps he already died, and the one they were taking to be buried was the painter. And since the painter died, Balak will never know the reason for the contempt and persecution and hatred, for the dead man has already taken his secret with him to the grave. Balak became melancholy, like someone who has suffered an irreparable loss, for if the painter died, all Balak's hope for knowledge is lost forever. And once again, Balak saw the greatness of Man, for everything is in the hands of Man, and as long as man lives you have hope, when he dies your hope is lost. And even death itself comes from Man, for if Adam, that is, Man, hadn't eaten from the tree of knowledge, death wouldn't have come into the world. Meanwhile, everything is destined to die, both man and dog.

Darkness covered the land and everything on it is gloomy. But when Balak raised his head up, he saw that the world wasn't as dark as it looked from below. The planet of Jupiter shone and Procyon and Sirius, two knightly dogs in the firmament, hastened to Jupiter. Balak lifted his eyes to the sky and asked the stars and the planets, If I and man are equal in death, why does he exalt himself over me and why is he eager for my death? What does he care if I exist, do I eat his world, do I hurt what is his? If the end of both of us is to die, let him wait for me until my years are out and I shall die by the hand of Heaven and let him not sin with my blood.

Jupiter is called Justice, since he governs justice and law, and the eye of his justice illuminated the whole world. But everyone who observed him carefully saw that his eye was damp. That he looked over the earth and saw that there was no just judge and no one was judged by law, and so a tear flowed from his eye and the gleam of his justice shed a tear. Balak despaired of the planet of Jupiter and put his trust in Procyon and Sirius. At that moment, the two knightly dogs in the firmament were preoccupied with their desire to don light, to appear beautiful before the stars of Virgo, the Virgin, and Balak knew that when the stars are conjoined, one who asks them something is answered immediately, therefore he put his faith in them.

Suddenly a star fell from the sky. Balak was startled and all his bones began trembling. He called with all his might, Not me and not my family, until the Angel of Death comes and say your star fell and your constellation died. At last, he dropped his head and took his mind off the stars on high for we don't get anything from them, for they frighten us and don't do us any good.

A north wind blew and midnight came. The Children of Israel awoke, as they awake for a midnight vigil to mourn the Destruction of the Temple. The trees heard and rustled and quivered. Few and meager are the trees of Jerusalem and their force isn't visible during the day because of the dust that covers them. But when midnight comes and the Children of Israel lament the Destruction of the Temple, they remember the ancient days, when the city stood in her glory and the Children of Israel dwelt in tranquility and all the mountains were crowned with olive trees and all kinds of beautiful trees, and all kinds of songbirds nested in them and sang songs to the Lord, the kind of song they heard from the Levites in the Temple, immediately all those trees remaining from the Destruction rustle and quiver and moan, and their voice is heard from one end of Jerusalem to the other.

CHAPTER SIXTEEN

Hell Opens Beneath Him

1 |

That moan filled Balak with pity for the Children of Israel and he wanted to remove his anger from them. But his anger was greater than he was, because of the troubles that had come upon him. His guts started rumbling and his pity turned back on himself. His eyes rolled up, as if to say, Did you see my suffering?

A few of the stars began to decline, and the other stars followed and declined, except for the morning star that ruled at that moment and shone and twinkled. Little by little, the firmament emptied out and a kind of dark whiteness or whitish darkness rose from the earth. And from the mountains beyond the Jordan a kind of light flickered, like the flicker of sunlight, for the sun had already begun digging herself a place in the firmament, but her effulgence hadn't yet risen.

Balak saw that the sun was about to come out, and when the sun comes out, human beings are wont to get out of their bed, and when they get out of their bed, they are wont to go outside, and when they go outside, they will see him, and when they see him, woe unto him. He looked here and there for a place to hide from them. He saw a dungheap and crept into it. And we will cover it up and will not reveal the location of that heap where he hid.

Balak lay down wherever he lay down. Sleep descended upon him and he dozed off. But he didn't admit that he had dozed off, as suffering people are wont to do, for since they don't enjoy sleep, it seems to them that they haven't been sleeping at all. And how do we know he dozed off? If he hadn't dozed off, would he have dreamed? He dreamed of this, that, and the other thing. Four dreams

Balak dreamed during that sleep. Three dreams he forgot and one he remembered. And this was that dream: Balak was strolling in Meah Shearim and two wild animals came toward him, a jackal and a fox, one from Lifta and the other from Eyn Kerem. And the head of the jackal is erect like the head of the legendary bird Bar Yokhani, and spectacles of flesh cover his eyes from below halfway up, and the spectacles gleam like a peacock's tail. Smaller than the jackal is the fox, and he had no spectacles of flesh, but his eyes are big and bulging, and they look purple and black like the turban of Hakham Bashi. And the mouths of the animals, oh, their mouths, herald evil. They walked and walked until they came to that neighborhood called Abu Tor, Father of the Bull. At that time, turkeys were strutting around the street of the neighborhood. Balak recognized from the mouths of the animals that they wanted to devour the turkeys. He wanted to warn the neighborhood. But his throat was parched and he couldn't shout. The animals came to the fowls. The fowls raised their necks and lifted up their heads, until their heads came up to the heads of the animals. The animals stood still and didn't do a thing to the fowls.

2 |

When he awoke, he didn't linger long, but set off for the place where all his thoughts were, to Meah Shearim. He turned southeast and descended to the Valley of Hinnom, to get used to human creatures. When an hour had passed and they didn't say a thing to him, he raised his eyes a bit and started looking here and there. He saw this, that, and the other thing. Aside from carcasses of dogs and carcasses of cats and carcasses of mice and cadavers of reptiles and maggots and bones and other kinds of garbage, it's doubtful if he saw anything.

Balak slipped from dungheap to dungheap and sank until nothing was seen of him but his tail. Like a mouse swallowed by a cat and his tail is hanging outside. Said Balak, I won't budge from here until the dung covers me and I am released from all trouble. But suffering was still in store for him. A blind man who had lost his cane chanced by there. The blind man was groping with his hand for what he had lost. He came upon Balak's tail. The blind man grabbed the tail and pulled it. Balak was pulled after his tail and came out of the garbage. When he came out he ran away. The blind man spread out his hands and was stunned at the cane that fled from his hand. Balak turned his head around and looked behind him to see if they weren't pursuing him. All his bones were scared and his whole body trembled.

We have no specific information about what terrified Balak. Whether it was because he was about to lose his tail or because he feared for his whole body. Since the place he had happened upon was the Valley of Hinnom, where sons and daughters were put through fire as a sacrifice to Moloch, Balak feared he would be sacrificed. And he already saw Moloch, as if his hands were reaching out to receive him, and the priests were banging drums to Moloch and bellowing and telling him, May you enjoy it and may you find pleasure in it. And he didn't know that they sacrificed human beings and not dogs, and he didn't know that that pagan ritual was no longer practiced.

Balak ran away and fled for his life. He urinated and started running to the left of his tail, that is toward Yemin Moshe, and didn't enter Yemin Moshe but threaded between one rock and another and between one valley and another below Yemin Moshe, until he came to Jaffa Road. At that moment, the whole street was empty of the Children of Israel, not a peddler nor a dweller, not a buyer nor a seller, no stringer of beads, no dealer in seeds, no pastry chef who bakes, no customer to eat his cakes, neither a castigator nor a prestidigitator, no charity collector, no lottery winners, no slanderers or other sinners, no one preaching, none beseeching, no emissaries and no missionaries. No Ashkenazim and no Afghanistanis and no Babylonians and no Bukharim and no Georgians and no Dagestanis and no Caucasians and no Aleppans and no Sephardim and no Persians and no Crimeans and no Yemenites. Not to mention those who didn't amount to a national community, like Urmeans and Urpalis and Iranians and Arbals and Assyrians and Garmoklites and Damascans and Zukuuans and Mochodans and Suidicilans and Adenites and Kurds and Arameans. To make a long story short, not a single one of the Children of Israel was to be seen in the street, for everyone with ears went to hear the word of the preachers. There were only Ishmaelites and Edomites there, sitting on a stool or sitting on a chair, some smoking a narghila and on the qui vive, some thinking about Adam, and some about Eve, some playing darts and some playing dice, all of them wearing striped clothes that are nice, with chains in their hands counting the beads, and listening with one ear to tales of great deeds, waving their hand to shoo the flies away, who pester human beings all the livelong day. If you shoo them away from here they come there, if you shoo them away from there they come here. The flies ask, Since we don't come to you secretly like lice, that's what you do to us? If you don't like us dwelling with you on your forehead, we'll dwell on the bridge of your nose. And if you don't like us dwelling on the bridge of your nose, we'll dwell in your eyes. All Gentiles pick up a swatter to expel them. The flies immediately take wing and fly into their mouth. Meanwhile, they don't see Balak. And if they had seen him, they wouldn't have done anything to him. For *Havatselet* and *Ha-Or* and *Ha-Herut* they don't read, and their newspapers hadn't yet printed things from our newspapers.

3 |

The sun was at its zenith and neither weariness nor fatigue was to be seen in it. On the contrary, it was clearly coming up and overcoming. Opposite it stood the ground scraped and arid. And between Heaven and earth the air was blazing and ablaze, covered with a garb of dust, and when it shook its garment, the eyes of human creatures were blocked and so were the eyes of Balak. Balak stuck out his dry tongue and shouted Arf arf arf, bring us a downpour, bring us a drop of water, I am going mad from thirst. He bared his teeth and looked at the firmament. Presumably he recalled the deed of his forefather, the Great Dog who, during a drought, poked a hole in the firmament and brought down rain.

The firmament stood as was its wont in those days, white hot with the blue steel of the blacksmith's shop and laughed at Balak. Balak put his tail between his legs and drooled and thought to himself, Maybe those who blow the Shofar are right, that the sounds coming from the Shofar burst all four firmaments and they are shocked and bring down rain. But there are seven firmaments, so why does he say four firmaments? Because, like all the other beasts and animals, Balak could only count up to four. Less than them, are birds who count to two. Less then them are those racehorses who have eight legs, four to run on and four to rest on, who don't count at all, for they are busy with weariness and rest, and haven't got enough time to consider intellectual matters. And when Balak recalled those who blow the Shofar, he recalled Meah Shearim. And when he recalled Meah Shearim, he picked up his feet and ran there.

It's not known what route he ran, whether the route of Hotel Kamenetz, where the old post office was, and from there to Musrara Street; or whether he went through Jaffa Road and jumped up to the street of the Diskin Orphanage. Or perhaps he didn't take the former route or the latter route, but opened himself another route. But presumably he walked on the sides of the roads and barked, and his voice wasn't heard. And it seems that our assumption was close to the truth, for if he had walked in the middle and his voice had been heard, they would have seen him and stopped him, for all those places are inhabited, Thank God, by our brothers the sons of Israel, and they are wont to read the newspapers, either secretly or openly, and if they had seen him, he wouldn't have reached Meah Shearim alive.

CHAPTER SEVENTEEN

Balak Reaches His Place

1 |

Balak enters Meah Shearim walking on the sides of the roads and his mouth gapes open and his saliva drools and his ears droop and his tail is between his legs and his eyes are bloodshot and he barks and his voice isn't heard. He stood still and cleansed his body of the forbidden food in it. He folded two of his legs beneath him and sat on them in the style of an Ishmaelite and put out his tongue and breathed like a blacksmith's bellows and looked all around and didn't see a living soul, for Meah Shearim was gathered inside to hear Rabbi Grunam May-Salvation-Arise. When Balak saw that he was alone, he prostrated himself in prayer and asked mercy for himself that his tongue wouldn't stumble and his voice would please human beings.

At that moment, Rabbi Grunam was standing on the stairs of the tabernacle of the Yeshiva and a few score people surrounded him on all sides, aside from women who stood in the doorways of the shops and were eager to hear. And his words flew like arrows and his face burned like a torch and his voice went from one end of Meah Shearim to the other, and whenever a sigh or a groan or a whine or a wail came out of his mouth, it also came from the hearts of his listeners, and he tossed his body back and forth and shut his eyes and opened them and tossed out his hands and brought them back and beat his heart. We shall copy a bit of his sermon here, and everyone who can cry will sigh and cry.

Our holy sages, of blessed memory, said in the Talmud Tractate Ta'anit, Rain is withheld only when the enemies of Israel have merited destruction. Gentlemen, what is the meaning here of *the enemies of Israel?* For we know that the world stands only for the sake of the Children of Israel, especially the rains that were promised to the Children of Israel that they would come down for their sake. And that is known by all the nations, as we find in the book A *Bundle of Myrrh* on the Torah portion that begins, If ye walk in my statutes, on the verse then I will give you rain in due season, and he didn't say the rains, to indicate that the rains are ours. And that was the glory of our might when the nations accepted us, because we could bring water in due season.

And here I shall tell you an original reading. When I went to repair Eruvs, I went into the home of one of the notables of Jerusalem to drink some water. That week was the Torah portion that begins with the verse "If ye walk in my statutes and keep my commandments and do them," and I explained to him that I had found new meaning in the two reproofs in the Bible, that is the reproof in Leviticus 26 and the reproof in Deuteronomy 26, in the Torah portion that begins with the verse "And it shall be when thou art come in unto the land which the Lord thy God giveth thee for an inheritance, and possessest it, and dwellest therein," for on the face of it, it is a difficulty that reproofs of the Holy-One-Blessed-Be-He are less than the reproofs of our Teacher Moses. Is the Lord's hand waxed short? Finally, to conclude with a happy ending, I told him the words of A *Bundle of Myrrh* about rains. The dignitary took out one of his books and showed me that in the time of the exile from Germany, the Jews were received in Poland with great honor and the king stipulated a condition with them that they would beseech HASHEM to bring down the rain in due season, for the king knew that that was the power of the Children of Israel to bring down the rains with their prayers. And it is still a custom among the uncircumcised in those places, to sow their fields at the time of Shmini Atseret, when the Children of Israel recite the prayer for rain. Hence, gentlemen, the conundrum still stands, if the enemies of Israel have merited destruction, why should the Children of Israel be sorry for them? Don't we have enough troubles and all the harsh decrees and all the destructions, Heaven Forfend, that the Gentiles bring down on us, that we should also be sorry when the rain is withhold? For they we have fields that need a downpour, or do we have gardens and orchards, isn't our whole need for rain just to fulfill a Commandment to immerse our hands, etcetera, and so on? For it was proper for the Holy-One-Blessed-Be-He that He should see to our needs so that we can keep His Commandments, and He will bring down rain for us. But in the end He includes us with the Goyim, quite to the contrary, whose whole need is simply material. But in another place, the Sages of blessed memory say, What trouble do the Gentiles and the Children of Israel share? The trouble of the withholding of rain. That was in the days of the Temple when the Children of Israel were living on their own land and needed rains to make their fields produce to bring sheaves and the two breads and to give contributions and tithes and to pour water on the altar. But now, gentlemen, now alas that we have lost everything, how much does a Jew need as a Jew, especially in this time, alas, in these hard times, when through our many transgressions the words of Lamentations, We have drunken our water for money, have been realized in us.

But, gentlemen, what the Talmud means by the *enemies of Israel* is the Children of Israel themselves because, for the honor of the Children of Israel, our Holy Sages spoke in euphemisms, as we know, and so there are a lot of passages like that in the Talmud. And so, gentlemen, we have an enormous conundrum. Can it be that the Sages of the Talmud, who are all holy and pure, can it be that in their generation there were people who merited destruction that they said in the Talmud that the heavens withhold rain because they merited destruction? And should that generation not have learned a bit from the virtues of our holy sages and performed Commandments and good deeds and not merit destruction?

Another, greater conundrum we must pose, Can it be that the great Sages, the Sages of the Talmud, who taught all the generations Torah that protects us in all seasons and in all times, can it be that they didn't teach their own generation Torah and didn't defend them so that they wouldn't merit destruction?

But, gentlemen, those two conundrums are solved with one answer, that everything according to the generation, and according to their measure of greatness and holiness. And always those the Talmud called the enemies of Israel were enemies according to their generation, for they lived in a holy generation and didn't learn from their deeds and didn't become holy and pure too, and hence the Talmud accused them and called them enemies of Israel, for they had teachers and they didn't learn, but if they lived in our generation they were considered Saints, as they say, If you want to find a Saint go and search for him among the wicked of the past generations. Oh, gentlemen! How great is our descent for our many transgressions that the wicked of the past generations who merited destruction were considered complete Saints in our generation. Gentlemen, I am not so old, and yet I can tell you what I saw with my own eyes in Jerusalem our Holy City. I remember that there were people here who went from dawn to dusk to the synagogues and to the study houses and prayed and studied and did great works of charity and yet they were slandered because that generation was such a righteous generation that human beings like them were considered heretics and atheists. And now, gentlemen, what shall we say and what shall we claim, for we see the face of the generation as the face of a dog. And not just an ordinary dog, but a mad dog, and they are even worse than a mad dog, for they think that they are great sages, logical philosophers, and want to spread their net over all the Children of Israel, especially over the children who haven't sinned, and make secular schools for them to divert them from their religion, Heaven Forfend. While the mad dog, gentlemen, is better than them, for he declares that he is mad, as we found in that dog that tormented Jerusalem who had Crazy Dog written on his skin to warn folks to stay away from him. This is what I say, the face of the generation is like the face of a dog. And not just an ordinary dog, but a crazy dog.

2 |

As Rabbi Grunam stood and preached, his face suddenly turned pale, and even his beard seemed to turn pale. He opened his mouth in panic and wanted to shout. His jaw contorted and he lost the power of speech. And both his eyes bulged like two bullets coming out of a rifle toward the crowd. He glared at all the people. All the people thought Reb Grunam had become so excited from the transgression of the generation and they became excited too. Anyone who could groaned, anyone who couldn't rolled his eyes upward. And they didn't yet know that that proverb, the face of the generation is the face of a dog, had donned skin and bones and put on flesh.

Reb Grunam shut his eyes and started striking the air and shouting, The crazy dog, the crazy dog. His eyes recovered their force and opened by themselves, and stood like two bulging boils, and looked in panic at the dog. And Reb Grunam still wasn't sure if the dog was a dog or a phantom. The dog raised himself and showed him his skin, as if he were saying, If you're not sure, Rabbi Grunam, read what is written here. Reb Grunam put his hands on his eyes and shouted in a loud shout, The crazy dog, the crazy dog.

Everybody thought he was shouting that to shock the heart, as he was accustomed to do in his sermons, when he took a word and repeated it at the top of his voice. They waited until his shout would die out and he would come back to the subject. He took his hands off his eyes to see if the dog was standing there. The dog saw that Reb Grunam's eyes were full of panic and fear and dread. The dog was frightened and shocked and shouted, Arf Arf, and Reb Grunam shouted at him, and the shout of the former blended with the shout of the latter, and the shout burst out until the crowd recognized that the dog was standing among them.

Panic descended on the crowd, a panic as never before and never after. They clung to one another and stood nailed to the spot, and hid their head one on the breast of the other and one on the back of the other, until they took off and started running. They ran here, there, and everywhere. From the place where they had come they returned. And when they returned, they were pressed and they pressed, pushed and were pushed, until they all stood as one and didn't move again, but only their eyes still ran back and forth, with a panic of dread hacking from them. Suddenly that dread in their eyes congealed, and their eyes didn't move either. Balak was scared and stunned. So much that he forgot to bark.

When Balak saw that they didn't do anything to him, he was amazed. Can it be that this big crowd is scared of me? How many feet are here, how many sticks are here, if they lifted their feet to me and kicked me or if they raised their sticks to me to hit me, I would run away. And since they didn't lift their feet to him and didn't raise their stick to him, his opinion was reinforced that everyone was scared of him. He raised his head and stretched his tail and looked with arrogant eyes. Finally he raised his voice. When the voice of Balak was heard, all the feet were shocked and all the sticks were dropped and everyone took off and started running away. Balak became haughty and said, If their feet are strong, I am stronger, and if their sticks are strong, my voice brings them all down.

He became proud and started bragging, like the scholars who brag about their research, for since they are so proud of it, they don't accept anything literally, unless they heap piles of vain research on it, and in the end they think the world behaves according to their research. His put his tail down wherever he put it down, as thinkers deep in thought put their hand on their forehead. And thus he stood and questioned, Where do the sticks get their power to hit if not from the dog who attracts the stick to him. The proof of this is that, as long as the stick doesn't see the dog it doesn't hit him. And not only the stick, but also human feet, as long as they don't see the face of a dog they pass by or creep by. If so, why should I be scared? And if the stick is strong, my voice makes it droop, and if the human feet are strong, my teeth terrify them. And when Balak came to that conclusion, he didn't bury his voice in his mouth. Strange was Balak's voice at that moment. Even fetuses in their mothers' wombs were shocked.

3 |

At that moment, Isaac stood and didn't see anything, for his soul clung to his wife like a bridegroom in the wedding week. His thoughts wandered off to Sonya and Rabinovitch and he was amazed, like someone who recalled things that he was afraid of, and in the end he sees he doesn't have to be afraid. Isaac was suddenly jostled aside and jostled aside again, and didn't know why he was jostled or why they were jostling him. Someone grabbed him, shouting in his face, The dog, the dog. And still shouting, he let go of Isaac and ran away. Others did the same thing. Isaac, who was used to dogs, wondered, Why is everybody scaring him with a dog?

Isaac was dragged here and pushed there. Somebody came to him and shrieked at him, Don't you see what's written on the dog? Isaac saw the dog and didn't worry about what they said. They thought Isaac was mad, and a mad person doesn't notice anything. They yanked him away and shouted, Don't you see the crazy dog. Isaac looked at him in amazement, and finally replied calmly, Who says he's crazy? Said they, Isn't that what's written explicitly? Said Isaac, And if it is written, so what? Are we obligated to believe everything that's written? But I'll tell you, I myself wrote on his skin, and I know that he's a healthy dog, for if he were mad, would I have bothered with him at all.

Some of them believed Isaac and some of them didn't believe him. Those who did believe him calmed down, like someone who gets a spark in his beard and in the end it's nothing but an ember that dies out at night. But they stood amazed and wondered, What does it mean that he himself wrote on the dog's skin, and if he did write, why did he write?

On reflection, we can only wonder. When Isaac saw all that panic, why didn't he panic, and furthermore, why did he announce that he himself had done that deed? But when he saw that everybody was scared of the dog, he revealed the matter only so they wouldn't be scared, for Isaac our comrade was honest and decent and didn't cover up his deeds, even if they redounded to his disgrace, especially in a matter concerning the general good.

A spirit of peace and consolation descended. And even those who weren't sure if it was Isaac who had written on the dog's skin, even they lost some of their fear and weren't so scared. And the curious approached Isaac and peeped at him and studied him, and some of them clicked their tongue, Good work, good work. They asked Isaac, What made you write that? Said Isaac, Once upon a time, I had to paint a marble tablet. A dog came and pestered me. I pushed him with the brush in my hand and he didn't budge. One, twice, three times. I dipped my brush and wrote on the dog's skin D O G, that is dog. When I saw that he wasn't satisfied with that, I added C R A Z Y, that is crazy.

If Isaac had stayed in Jerusalem all summer and heard all the troubles the dog had caused, he would have lowered his face to the ground. But he had gone to Sonya in Jaffa and stayed there as long as he stayed there and didn't hear anything about the dog, and after he had done that deed, he hadn't thought about the dog or what he had written on his skin.

When the fear of the dog was removed and the whole people were relieved of their grief, they lifted their eyes and looked at Isaac. Some looked at him with eyes of grief and some looked at him with anger. The plasterer Efraim came to him and said, Isaac, how could you, Isaac, what did you do? Isaac dropped his eyes and said, If I had known, I wouldn't have done it. And thus Isaac stood, full of shame and disgrace, grief and torments, like a person who has sinned and is waiting for his sentence.

And now there wasn't a person who feared the dog. And since the fear of the dog was removed, they wondered how they could have feared him. They became arrogant and started making fun of timid people, who if they see a dog, they run away. And even the cowards donned boldness and cast all the blame on the newspapers, which made them afraid of a dog. Those newspapers have nothing to write, so they write whatever it is they write. Yesterday they scared us with dogs and tomorrow they'll scare us with flies.

And thus there wasn't a person who was afraid of the dog, not to mention Isaac, who had done the deed and forgotten it as soon as he did it. But the dog didn't forget Isaac, for Balak recognized that all the tribulations that had come to him had come from the man with the brush. Balak ran after the man with the brush. Whenever he encountered him he barked at him, and if he didn't encounter him, the man's image went before him and he barked. Everyone who heard his voice or saw his shadow was afraid. When they heard that story, their fear of the dog was removed. Lo and behold, as long as Balak was sane, they were afraid of him as of a mad dog, when Balak began to doubt if he was sane, no one was afraid of him.

CHAPTER EIGHTEEN

Evil Encounter

1 |

As soon as Balak entered Meah Shearim, he sniffed the smell of the painter. And even though Isaac's form had changed, as a bridegroom in the week of his wedding, and even though his clothes were different, Balak noticed him and wanted to go to him. That panic came and he delayed. When all the voices died down, he remembered him. Balak's heart began trembling and both his eyes got bloodshot. His leg tottered and his ears shook and his mouth was filled with foam. He looked at Isaac malevolently and asked himself, Why doesn't he run away from me, the way everybody else does? Am I so contemptible in his eyes that he despises my power? His heart was filled with wrath. He looked at him again. He saw his face was serene without a trace of fear. It occurred to Balak that the lack of fear was the consequence of the truth, that is, because that human creature knows the truth, therefore he isn't afraid.

Once again a desire for truth stirred in Balak's heart. And when the desire for truth stirred in him, his heart started pounding. What can we tell and why should we go on? Because of Balak's yearnings for the truth, his heart pounded like a pestle in a mortar. And in his innocence, he imagined he would grasp the truth, and wondered, Now I should rejoice but in the end, I don't. His insides shriveled and his kidneys grew cold and he couldn't bear the coldness of his spleen. Black bile overcame him and he saw himself leaving the world and not grasping the truth. Oh, how many weeks and how many months had he been pursuing the truth, and when he is about to grasp it, they are about to remove him from the world.

Balak picked up his weary eyes and looked at the feet of the man with the brush. He saw that the feet were standing in their place. Balak groaned from his heart and thought, He who knows the truth isn't scared of anything in the world, but the truth is heavy and those who bear it are few. I shall bend my shoulders and I shall bear the truth with them. At that moment, Isaac was filled with shame and disgrace and grief and torments, like a person who has erred and is waiting to receive his punishment. When Isaac noticed the dog, he tapped him with his fingers and said to him, Did you hear what they say about you, crazy dog they call you. Needless to say, Isaac didn't mean to provoke the dog, but because he was ashamed to talk with a human, he talked with Balak. But Balak was of another mind. He raised his head in panic and looked at Isaac, the wrinkle in Balak's eyes grew dark and the white disappeared from them. His mouth was filled with foam and his teeth began rattling. And he was rattling too. He wanted to leap on Isaac. In the end, he turned his face away from him and buried his mouth in the ground.

All the events that had occurred to him ever since the day the painter had encountered him in the neighborhood of the Bukharim revolved in his mind's eye. How many troubles and how many torments and how many insults and how many injuries had come upon him since that day and how many were in store for him in the future. Why and what for? The smell of the painter rose before him and his heart screamed inside him, Here he is standing right close by, ask him. His spirit drooped much lower than it was, for he knew that if he asked the man wouldn't answer him. Once again he put his mouth down into the ground so his instinct wouldn't make him raise his voice, for if he raised his voice, the painter would kick him, and he didn't have the strength to accept new torments. But the desire for truth overcame his fear. He shook his ears, like someone who shakes off a malevolent whisper and he lay on his guts to consider his affairs. Said Balak, What shall I do? If I ask him, he won't answer me. And if I raise my voice, he'll kick me. His mouth began shuddering and his teeth began chattering. He shook his ears here and there, not as he had shaken them at first the way you shake a flea off your clothes, but like someone who nods his ears in agreement.

Said Balak, I won't approach him calmly and I won't raise my voice, but I'll bite him and the truth will leak out of his body. And Balak already saw the truth leaking from the blood of the painter like the bountiful rains, as when the Great Dog bit the firmament. But he immediately lowered his eyes from Isaac, and took his mind off him. He banged his head on the ground, and all those visions that he saw at first grew blurry. He was at a loss and he forgot everything he wanted to do. He lowered his tail between his legs, as if that was all that was left for him. At last, he lowered his muzzle down over his mouth in total sadness like someone who realizes that all his acts have come to naught. If he could fall asleep at will, he would have laid down and lulled all his apprehensions.

His sleep didn't come. Either because of the black bile that attacked him or because of the smell of the painter that swirled in his nose. Whatever it was, his guts began grinding inside him like the grinding stones of a windmill, and even his spleen caused him grief and torments. He wanted to put his tail on them, like a bandage you put on a sore. But his tail didn't budge from between his legs. Your guts dwell inside you and they do whatever they want, and you stand there and can't do a thing to them. He raised his head and looked a bit here and a bit there, as if he were searching for somewhere to bury his wrath. He saw the man with the brush standing. The wrinkle in Balak's eyes turned dark again and his teeth rattled. He began to fear he would bite himself and blood would come out of him as on the day the painter kicked him in the mouth. His lips started foaming and his tongue started bubbling up bitter foam, as if his gall had dissolved and flooded his mouth. He raised himself up and looked straight ahead in panic. He saw Isaac standing and it seemed to him that he was smiling. Balak shook his head and thought, What does he have to smile about, and who is he smiling at, at such a wretched and despised and persecuted and downtrodden creature that even the dogs of the Goyim stay away from me. He lowered his eyes from him and got up to go.

But his bones were weak and his thighs were exhausted and his legs stumbled and his paws were dull and his soul was heavy, and he didn't have strength to move his body and go. He turned here and there, searching for a place to disappear. He started scrabbling in the ground to dig himself a hole and bury himself like a fieldmouse in the earth. His legs slid and he fell on his belly. He raised his eyes to see if the man with the brush saw him and if he was smiling at him. When he looked at him again, he didn't take his eyes off him.

2 |

Isaac was about to return home to his wife, whom he yearned for like a bridegroom after his wedding. At that moment, Shifra was sitting all by herself and was amazed, for from the wedding ceremony until now, she hadn't stopped thinking about Isaac. Shifra raised her eyes to see if anyone noticed that. Her eyes encountered the mirror on the wall and was surprised. Aside from the kerchief on her head, no change was apparent in her. Yet she thought she had become a new creature. She straightened the kerchief and shifted her eyes away from the mirror, but she looked between the mirror and the wall, where her wedding contract was placed. She recalled the moment when she had stood with Isaac under the wedding canopy and thought she would never have a greater moment than the moment of her wedding, and now she sees that every moment is great. She went to the stove and checked the food her mother was preparing for the day's meal and was stunned that the food had already cooked and Isaac hadn't yet come. She turned to the window and her fingers began trembling, like a young wife who wants to beckon to her husband to hurry home. And you, Isaac, you stood in the street and talked nonsense about a dog on whose skin you wrote things you shouldn't have written. But it must be said that even when Isaac stood in the street, he didn't take his mind off Shifra. And Isaac already saw himself returning to Shifra and she greeting him in joy and embarrassment, like a woman who rejoices to see her husband and is embarrassed about her joy. And he was also joyous and embarrassed, joyous about his wife and embarrassed at his early deeds. In the end, he picked up his feet to go home to his wife. And when he took two or three steps, he forgot all his early deeds, not to mention the dog.

Balak shook his head, thinking to himself, He goes on his way, and I — I stay here despised and downtrodden and forsaken. He stuck out his tongue until it was about to drop out. He tried to put it back in its place, but couldn't. A sweet bubble began bubbling between his teeth. All his heartaches were drowned and a kind of longing gushed in him like a spring, up to his teeth. His teeth stood erect and his whole body was taut. Before Isaac could start walking, the dog leaped on him and sank his teeth in him and bit him. And when he bit him, the dog picked up his feet and ran off.

Those standing near Isaac screamed and ran away, and those who heard their scream leaped up and came to him. They looked at him in panic and asked him, How did that happen? Isaac tried to tell but his throat was dry and he fell silent. He put his hand on the place where the dog had bitten him. Fire came from the bite and entered into his fingers, and fire came out of his fingers and entered into his wound. He took a few steps. At last, he returned to where he had been standing at first. Someone pointed to someplace and asked Isaac, Here he bit you? Isaac gazed and replied in a whisper, Here. And a kind of smile spread over his lips, like a sick man who has a hard time talking and soothes you with his eyes. Somebody said, If so, there's no danger here, for the venom of a mad dog is in his saliva, and since he bit you through your clothes, his saliva didn't reach your flesh. Isaac shook his head at him and rubbed his wound, and the fire of his wound and the fire of his fingers held onto one another and both burned together, for after the dog bit him, he sank his teeth once again in his fingers. Someone else added, And even in the opinion of those who say that a worm lies in the tongue of a mad dog and that's what is dangerous, even so there's no need to worry, for the clothing stopped the worm and it didn't injure the flesh. Now we'll take you home and you'll rest from the scene. While some accompanied Isaac, others spread out over the whole city to search for the dog, to kill him and feed his liver to the bitten man. They searched for him, but they didn't find him.

The dog ran away wherever he ran and was lying in the dust of his hole and peeping out, looking straight ahead as if he were wondering why the truth he had sought all the days still eluded him. And after he dug himself a hole in the flesh of the painter and dripped the truth from it, the truth should have filled all his being, but in the end there is no truth and no nothing. And he is still as at the beginning, as if he hadn't done a thing. Could it be that all his trouble was for nothing? Balak became sad and angry. But his teeth that had tasted human flesh began longing and wanting more. Those teeth that Balak had made into emissaries made themselves into tools for their own pleasure. Meanwhile, Balak called out about himself, He ate a human. And even though he had tasted only enough human flesh to wet his mouth, he began to boast as if he had filled his belly with it. And once again he was amazed, for man is made of special material, yet in the end, his flesh is no different from most animals. Now let's go back to Isaac.

They brought Isaac to his house and lay him on his bed. The specialist heard and came. He made Isaac a compress of salted olive oil and pressed his wound and squeezed the blood and slaughtered a pigeon on it and placed the pigeon on the wound. Another compress he made him of pigeon droppings mixed with mustard and nuts and yeast and salt and honey and onions. And as he left, he looked benevolently at Isaac, as a specialist who did what had to be done and knows that from now on there's no need to worry.

3 |

All night long, Isaac strove to remember the name of a man he and his comrades had gone to visit in Eyn Rogel. That man's dwelling, and the mat he lay on and the books he read, as well as all kinds of stuffed animals he saw there stood all that while before Isaac's eyes, and even the voices of his comrades calling him by name did Isaac hear, but the name he couldn't remember. At last, when Isaac did succeed in remembering Arzef's name, he found him standing in Sweet Foot's hut, stroking Sweetiepie's teeth and calling him as a female, Come, girlie, come, and Sweetiepie enjoys and is pampered by him like a female. At last Sweetiepie leaps up and runs to the old Baron who held a pot of paints in his hand. Sweetiepie grabbed the pot in his teeth and ran away with it. Once again, Isaac saw Arzef, lying on his mat and reading *The Fables of Foxes*. And the book was strange for it wasn't made of letters but of voices. Even stranger was that all those voices were composed of two syllables. Isaac looked at the book to see what those syllables were and saw that his own hand strolls over to the book and writes Arf arf. And even stranger was that he stood apart from the owner of the writing hand, and even though there was no doubt that both of them, that is he and the one with the writing hand, were one, nevertheless the former stood apart from the latter. All those things Isaac saw clearly, but it seemed to be a dream. And he wondered why he thought it was a dream for everything was clear and explicit.

That's how I'll know it isn't a dream, said Isaac in his dream. Before he could explain to himself how he knew that, the black man guarding the German colony stopped him. Isaac squeezed through a closed gate and entered the quarter and went to Rabinovitch. Rabinovitch said to him, Aren't you amazed? Said Isaac, In truth, I am amazed. Said Rabinovitch, But you don't know why you're amazed. You're amazed that you found me dressed like a woman. Isaac nodded and said, It seems I should be stunned at that. Said Rabinovitch, Then know, it's not I who is dressed like that, but a peacock. And if you don't believe me, here's his voice. Said Isaac, How can I tell, for I've never seen a live peacock in my life. Said Rabinovitch, A little brother you have and he learns the alphabet, take his ABCs and read E and O, and you've got the voice of a peacock. Said Isaac, I can do that. Said Rabinovitch, You see, my friend, we can do anything, and everything a person wants to do he does. And you in your naïveté thought the peacock speaks Russian or Hungarian. Tell me, Isaac, isn't that what you were thinking? Vove came with the engraver's child and they surrounded Isaac, dancing and singing, *kedar* is a Tartar, *kadosh* is a martyr. Hilda Rabinovitch made herself into a kind of ball and said, Hush, children, hush. Isaac glanced at her and saw that her shoes were Sonya's shoes, and were made of gold colored leather, or maybe from an orange rind. And since shoes aren't usually made of orange rinds, Isaac understood that he himself had painted the shoes with his paints, but he didn't remember when he had painted them. He was sorry that his power of memory had weakened when he was about to get married, and worried that he would forget when his wedding day was. He woke up in pain and his dream stopped.

4 |

When he woke up because of the pain, Isaac didn't know what limb he was worried about. But he immediately felt as if his throat were wounded with searing slivers of glass. And when he stretched out his hand and stroked his neck, the pain stuck to his fingers. He tossed and turned from side to side. Then his bedclothes began stabbing him like thorns. He stretched out his hand to clear the thorns away and his fingers pounced as if a thorn had struck them. He squinted his eyes and rubbed his body, and wherever he touched, the pain sprouted from there. Harder than that was another pain he couldn't locate. Meanwhile, the walls of the house were filled with shadows, and from the shadows loomed a strange shape and started pursuing him. No good, no good, whispered Isaac, trying to lie comfortably, not to wake up Shifra. But he was amazed at Shifra that she was sleeping and didn't notice his torments. Good mother, good mother, Isaac called in his heart and looked at the shadows on the walls growing thicker. One shape stood out from the shadows and started sticking its tongue out at him. Isaac pulled the blanket up and covered his head. The pain he had felt at first in his throat stopped, but a malevolent pain capered in all his other limbs.

Won't I sleep at all tonight? grumbled Isaac. But he didn't close his eyes because he wanted to see the shadows on the wall who were running urgently and panicky, and because he wanted to see if that shape was still sticking its tongue out at him. Finally his eyes closed, and when his eyes closed and he began to doze off, he was suddenly jolted awake by the voice of the one whose name he couldn't remember, calling: Come here, girlie, come.

5 |

All that time, Shifra was asleep. But she found no rest in sleep, because a cold wind blew on her head. Until her wedding night, her head was covered with soft, warm hair that came down below her waist, and when she lay in her bed at night, it was as if she lay on a soft couch of gold filaments And now that they had shaved her head and taken away her hair, her bed pressed her and she found no rest. In her sleep, Shifra said, I'll get up and cover my head. She got out of bed and went to the mirror to wrap a kerchief around her head. From the mirror, the figure of a girl looked out at her. She wanted to ask the girl, What do you want here? But she was frightened to ask lest the girl answer things that shouldn't be heard. Meanwhile, the new Rabbi who had ascended from Hungary came and sat at the head of the table and read the Seven Blessings. All those present nodded and sang, *in the cities of Judah and in the streets of Jerusalem, the voice of joy and gladness will be heard, the voice of the bridegroom and the voice of the bride.* But their voices were only the voice of Efraim the plasterer, who walks around at night and calls people to serve the Creator, and the voice is threatening and awesome, as if he were warning the sleeping people of great trouble about to appear. Shifra raised her eyes to look at her husband's bed to see if he had heard and was warned. Her eyes closed in a heavy sleep.

CHAPTER NINETEEN

End of the Tale

1 |

Before three weeks had passed, Isaac began feeling pain in his body in all the places where the dog had bitten him. His wounds began to swell up and turn red, and finally they opened by themselves and a stinking pus began bubbling out of them. His spirit turned bad, and he was so angry and afraid as if someone were pursuing him, that he grew restive and wanted to die. In those days, his swallowing apparatus contorted and his breathing apparatus shriveled and so did the muscles of his body and the muscles of his legs. He wanted to eat or drink and couldn't, as the membrane shriveled in his mouth. And now Isaac was no longer thinking of his wife or anything else in the world. But he complained about the chill in his body and about his breathing which was heavy and about his heart that oppressed him and about the pain in his guts. His pulse became irregular. Sometimes it was weak and sometimes it was erratic. Because of bad thoughts and bad dreams, his sleep was scrambled. All those days, he sweated and sweated some more, and thirst seared his throat. If he saw water or something liquid or heard the sound of water, he quivered and contorted, and even a candle and a mirror caused him torments, perhaps because the candle and the mirror resemble water. Finally, his voice grew hoarse and his saliva began dripping, and when he tried to swallow it, he couldn't. His face flushed and the pupils of his eyes became fixed. Finally, his contortions stopped and he seemed to be all right again and they could feed him. But because he was so weak, he couldn't eat. His melancholy and his depression kept increasing. Sometimes Reb Fayesh looked at him from his pillows and blankets, and he seemed to know why that man was living in his house, and his colorless eyes turned dark with anger because everyone was busy with Isaac. And with special anger at Shifra. And Shifra who was always calm and quiet and never in her life had she made a useless gesture, and when her hand had moved, it had seemed to Isaac that something in the world had changed, now she was busy with him necessarily and unnecessarily, and he didn't notice her. And once emotional serenity had beamed from her golden eyes, as if a gold radiance emanated from them, now panic was looming up from them.

2 |

Shifra and Rebecca took care of Isaac but didn't neglect Reb Fayesh. In those days, Reb Fayesh seemed to have taken a slight turn for the better, and was already raising his head on his pillow and blurting out half words. Whenever Rebecca or Shifra heard Reb Fayesh's voice, they would hurry to him. When they came to him, he fell silent. No doubt Reb Fayesh was trying to recover his tongue, but he didn't mean for them to understand what he said. Whatever it was, they took great pains with him, in case they would hear a word from his mouth. They ran from Reb Fayesh to Isaac, and from Isaac to Reb Fayesh, until their strength gave out and they couldn't stand up. And if not for Gitteshi, the wife of Mendel the upholsterer, who helped them, they wouldn't have held out. That wretched woman was fearful that her husband's emissaries would suddenly come to her house and serve her a writ of divorce, and from early morning to late at night she was in Reb Fayesh's home, so that if the fiends came with the writ of divorce, Rebecca and Shifra would see them and warn her. And so she came every day and helped Rebecca and Shifra as much as she could. Help in trouble they found in Efraim the plasterer, for when he finished going around at night to wake the sleeping people to serve the Creator, he came and helped the sick.

Once Menahem happened to come to Jerusalem. For the sake of two things had Menahem come up from Motza to Jerusalem, to buy himself a new pitchfork and to exchange one tractate of the Talmud for another, for the tractate he had brought with him from his hometown he already knew by heart, and the pitchfork he had brought with him from Petach Tikva was broken. And his success in those two matters exceeded his expectations. The pitchfork could be mended and he didn't have to spend his money on a new one, and since that was the case, he could get himself a new tractate and keep the old one as well. As he walked in the marketplace and looked into the Talmud, he came upon the woodcarver who told him all that had happened to Isaac. Menahem went to visit the sick man. As he stood at his bed, he took out the new Talmud to look at it. When he looked at the Talmud he didn't budge from it. Rebecca and Shifra who were weary lay down to rest from their toil and Menahem's voice sweetened their sleep as in the days when Reb Fayesh was healthy and the world was in its proper order.

Once Hinda Puah came. She didn't know what had happened to Isaac, but one night Isaac's mother Judith came to her in a dream and her face was dark and her winding sheet was torn and she said to her, Perhaps you have heard what my Itzikl is doing? My heart tells me that wrath has been poured out on him. Hinda Puah got up in the morning and told her dream to her Alter, and she thought her Alter would laugh at her and her dreams. Her Alter said to her, There is something to it. I looked in my notebook and I saw that the letters of Isaac's name were blurred. And so, she left her house and her Alter and dashed over to see why Itzikl's mother shocked her at night. When she came to the houses of the Hungarians, she heard what had happened. She grew faint and thought she was dying. But she took herself in hand and came.

Hinda Puah saw Isaac. She repressed the tears in her eyes and scolded him, *Feh, feh, Itzikl, vos makhtsi dikh narish. Iz epes a koved far dayn mame aleya hasholem az ihr libe kind lebn zol zikh azoy oyffihrn.* That is, Itzikl, why are you playing the fool? Is it an honor for your mother, may she rest in peace, that her beloved son should behave like that? Isaac looked at her with saliva dripping and he tried to gulp it and couldn't. Hinda Puah took her apron and wiped her eyes. Rebecca took her in her arms and said to her, Tell me, good woman, why did he do that to my daughter? Said Hinda Puah to Rebecca, Who do you mean? Said Rebecca, Who do I mean? I mean the Holy-One-Blessed-Be-He. Said Hinda Puah, Why did He do that to our Itzikl? Said Rebecca, A baby who never in her life ever even harmed a fly, oh what has befallen her?

Efraim the plasterer heard the women's conversation. He shook his head from side to side and said, Instead of asking why the Holy-One-Blessed-Be-He did that to Isaac and Shifra, ask what are we and what are our merits, that The Blessed One gives us mercy to make us a living. The Holy-One-Blessed-Be-He knows what He's doing, and everything He does He does according to the law, and it's not for us to ponder His judgment. And if we do ponder, what do we gain, this is stupidity and nothing. Reb Fayesh is certainly a proper person. And now I'll ask you, Rebecca, why did that befall him? Let me see, can you answer my question. Oh, good women, there is one answer to all the questions in the world, that's an answer coming from our bad deeds. And now I'll ask you, is there in the world a city that is holier and dearer and nicer than Jerusalem, and why have so many troubles come upon it? And it's not bad enough that all those troubles often come upon it, but we don't even have water to drink. Or I'll ask you, is there in the world a nation finer than the Children of Israel, and yet we are stricken and afflicted. And if a person tells me all kinds of reasons, will that get you anything? Said Hinda Puah, At any rate, it's a hard question. Don't we know that the mercy of the Holy-One-Blessed-Be-He is great, so why doesn't He have mercy on us? Efraim shook his head from side to side and said, King David already screamed, Why standest thou afar off, O Lord? Why hidest thou thyself in times of trouble? And what did the Holy-One-Blessed-Be-He reply to David? He said to him, I am the one whose glory fills the world, before the Lord there is neither near nor far, but times of trouble cause a man to think that The Blessed One is far away from him.

Thus they wrestled with the issue that everyone who has ever come into the world has wrestled with from the day the world was created until now. And to every single question that Rebecca or Hinda Puah asked, Efraim answered them from the Psalms, and stressed the verse to them with a fine melody, and they repeated their questions. They didn't find an answer to their questions and Efraim didn't see that there was a question after his answers. At last, Efraim hunched his shoulders and said in a pleasant voice in a melody of Psalms, My soul cleaveth unto the dust: quicken thou me according to thy word.

Efraim wasn't content only with words, but went with a group of ten men to the Wailing Wall, and didn't budge from there until they had completed the entire Book of Psalms. And when they came to the chapter Deliver my soul from the sword; my darling from the power of the dog, he wrote Isaac's name and his mother's name on a slip of paper and put the slip of paper between the stones of the Wailing Wall. And since the breath of children who haven't sinned is very important to the Lord, he gathered a few children from the streets and recited Psalms with them. And when he came to the verse Deliver my soul, etc., my darling from the power of the dog, he repeated the verse two hundred and eight times as the numerical value of Isaac's name. But none of those things helped, for the decree was already sealed.

And now, good friends, as we observe the adventures of Isaac, we are shaken and stunned. This Isaac who is no worse than any other person, why is he punished so harshly? Is it because he teased a dog? He meant it only as a joke. Moreover, the end of Isaac Kumer is not inherent in his beginning. By his nature and his aptitudes, Isaac should have stood on the soil and seen life on the earth and brought his father and his brothers and sisters up to the Land of Israel. Those miserable people who hadn't seen a good moment in their lives, how devoted they were to the Land. Isaac's sisters would have found their mates here and Yudele would have plowed his land and composed pleasant lyrics for her. And Reb Simon Kumer, the father of our comrade Isaac, who was still hounded by usurers, would have seen the happiness of his sons and daughters and would have been happy. And you, Rock of Our Salvation great in counsel and mighty in work, from the mouths of those who thirst for Your Salvation You would have heard Your praise all the days. It's easy for those who don't bother with too much thinking, either because of too much innocence or because of too much wisdom but a person who is not very innocent and not very wise, what will he answer and what will he say?

3 |

And now the neighbors were talking about Isaac and saying that Reb Fayesh's son-in-law's mind is not sane. And imaginative people imagined they saw him crawling on all fours and shouting like a dog and running after every person to bite him. Fear fell on folks and they complained about the officers of the society for letting a dangerous person walk around in public. The officers of the society heard those words and sent a doctor to him. The doctor saw Isaac and said, We have to take him to Egypt to the Pasteur Institute. Meanwhile, the bitten man has to be bound with ropes and put in a separate room behind a locked door.

They bound Isaac with ropes and put him in a room by himself and locked the door behind him and closed the shutters, and they brought him water and food. Because he was so weak, he didn't eat and didn't drink. Isaac sat alone in the dark room and lamented from the Book of Lamentations, She weepeth sore in the night and her tears were on her cheeks. And everyone who heard his voice wept for him and for his wife. Sometimes, his mind would come back and he would warn his attendants to be careful that he didn't bite them, and sometimes he tried to sleep. But sleep didn't come. And sometimes he looked with vacant eyes and didn't want anything.

The dog's venom penetrated all of Isaac's limbs. His face turned dark, his eyes glazed over like glass, his tongue swelled up like a shriveled date. A harsh thirst choked and strangled him. If he took some water to drink, he imagined a delegation of small dogs was dancing in the water. (And people said that he too started barking like a dog.) In the end, the muscles of his body and the muscles of his face became paralyzed. Finally, his pained soul passed away and he returned his spirit to the God of spirits for whom there is no joke and no frivolity.

The dog disappeared, but his bites indicated that he was alive. Since he had tasted the taste of human flesh, he went on biting. Many were injured by him and many mentioned him with horror. Until the troubles of the great war came and that trouble was forgotten.

4 |

On the day that Isaac was buried, the sky was covered with clouds. The sun was overcast and a wind came and with it came lightning flashes and thunderbolts. The firmament was shaken with the rumble of their might and began to bring down rare, warm drops. The next day, the clouds scattered and the sun shone, and we knew that all our expectations were in vain. And even the winds we imagined would refresh us didn't bring any gain, as they were hot and piercing as leeches.

But at night the winds cooled and the world began to cool off. And the next day the sun was dull and pressed and squeezed between the clouds. Before it finished its course, it was pushed out of the firmament. That sun, that devouring fire, that had blazed with its strong heat and burned all the grass of the field and parched the trees and dried up the springs of water — darkening clouds pushed her out until there wasn't a corner in the firmament that it wasn't pushed out of. And when we lifted our eyes to the sky to see if the clouds weren't lying, abundant rain began coming down. Only yesterday we had stood in prayer and pleading and we increased the number of Slikhot and we blew Shofars and we recited Hosanna, and today we read aloud the Praising, thanking and singing.

When the rains began coming down they didn't stop coming down by day or by night. The water flowed from above and from below, on the roofs of our houses and underneath our houses, it swept away furnishings and brought down houses. But the cisterns were filled with water. And now we have water to drink and even to cook our food and to bake our bread and to dip our hands. For six or seven days the rains came down, and when they stopped they started coming down again. Finally, the rains stopped and the clouds dispersed and the sun shone. And when we came outside we saw that the earth was smiling with its plants and its flowers. And from one end of the Land to the other came shepherds and their flocks, and from the soaked earth rose the voice of the sheep, and they were answered by the birds of the sking. And a great rejoicing was in the world. Such rejoicing had never been seen. All the villages in Judea and the Galilee, in the plain and in the mountains produced crops and the whole Land was like a Garden of the Lord. And every bush and every blade of grass emitted a good smell, and needless to say, so did the oranges. Like a blessed dwelling was the whole Land and its inhabitants were blessed by the Lord. And you our brothers, the elite of our salvation in Kinneret and Merhavia, in Eyn Ganim and in Um Juni, which is now Degania, you went out to your work in the fields and the gardens, the work our comrade Isaac wasn't blessed with. Our comrade Isaac wasn't blessed to stand on the ground and plow and sow, but like his ancestor Reb Yudel Hasid and like some other Saints and Hasids, he was blessed to be given an estate of a grave in the holy earth. May all mourners mourn for that tortured man who died in a sorry affair. And we shall tell the deeds of our brothers and sisters, the children of the living God, the nation of the Lord, who work the earth of Israel for a monument and fame and glory.

Completed are the deeds of Isaac
The deeds of our other comrades
The men and the women
Will come in the book A *Parcel of Land*

Abu Tor ("Father of the Bull") Arab section of Jerusalem outside the walls, near the Bethlehem Road, established in the 1870s.

Adjami Quarter Quarter in Jaffa.

Ahad Ha-Am ("One of the People") Asher Hirsh Ginsberg (1856–1927) Hebrew essayist and philosopher, theoretician of the revival of Zion as the "Spiritual Center" against Herzl's political Zionism.

Ahuzat Bayit ("Home Estate") A committee in Jaffa that founded a settlement by that name north of Jaffa, subsequently considered the inception of the first Hebrew city, Tel Aviv.

Aliyah (literally: Ascent) Zionist immigration to the Land of Israel. Each wave of Aliyah is known by its number, indicating the period and countries of origin. The First Aliyah, 1882–1904, was initiated by BILU and the Lovers of Zion in Odessa, even before Theodor Herzl's political Zionist organization was established. Its members, independent farmers, created the first modern settlements in Palestine, supported by Baron Edmond de Rothschild and the Jewish Colonization Association. The Second Aliyah, 1904–1914, was dominated by young idealists coming from the Russian pogroms and revolution. It was carried by a Zionist Socialist ideology, fighting for "Jewish labor" and creating the first Hebrew-speaking collectives of workers. At the same time, the urban Jewish population in Jaffa grew and the first Hebrew city was established in 1909.

Alliance Israélite Universelle First modern international Jewish organization, founded in 1860, centered in Paris. Starting in the 1890s, the Alliance focussed its efforts on creating an international network of French-language schools, including Palestine.

Anglo-Palestine Company (APC, pronounced "APAK") Later renamed Anglo-Palestine Bank. In 1951, renamed Bank Leumi le-Israel, the National Bank of Israel.

Antebi Albert Abraham Antebi (1869–1918), leader of the Jewish community in Eretz Israel, born in Damascus, knew Turkish, and had good relations with the Turkish authorities. Was the representative of the Alliance Israelite Universelle and ICA (Jewish Colonization Association) in the Land of Israel.

Antipatris Ancient Palestinian city in the valley of Kfar Saba, built by Herod.

Aramaic Targum The Aramaic translation of the Bible, printed on the margins of the Torah text.

Ark The receptacle in the synagogue in which the Torah scrolls are kept.

Aronovitch, Joseph (1877–1937) Hebrew writer and Palestinian labor leader, first editor of the influential journal of the Labor Movement, Ha-Po'el Ha-Tsa'ir.

Asch, Scholem (1880–1957) Yiddish novelist and playwright.

Ashkenazi European Jews as opposed to

Sephardi (Spanish) Jews; the name derives from "Ashkenaz," Germany.

Av   Fifth month in the Jewish year, usually July-August.

Ba'al Ha-Ness, Rabbi Meir   The tomb of
Rabbi Meir the Miracle Worker is near
Tiberias; from the eighteenth century
on, a Ba'al Ness alms box was found in
almost every Jewish home. It was customary to contribute money or candles
as protection against ailments and
dangers.

Baksheesh   Turkish for bribe.

Bar Yokhani   Or Ziz, a big legendary
bird like the phoenix, mentioned in
the Talmud: "once an egg of a Bar
Yokhani fell and drowned sixty cities,
and broke three hundred cypresses."

Barnett, Zerakh (1843–1935)   Pioneer of
settlement in modern Eretz-Israel and
one of the founders of Petach Tikva.

Basel, Congress   The founding Congress of the World Zionist Organization
in 1897, in Basel, Switzerland.

Be'er Tuviya   A *moshav* (labor coopera-
tive) in the southern coastal plain of
Israel, founded in 1887 by Jews from
Bessarabia, with the help of Baron
Edmond de Rothschild.

Be'er Yakov   Town in the coastal plain
of Israel, founded in 1907 by a group of
56 Jews from Russia.

Belzer Rebbe   Hasidic Rebbe, heir of
a dynasty founded in the Galician
city of Belz by Shalom Rokeah (1779–
1855).

Ben Shemen   Youth village and *moshav*
(labor cooperative) in central Israel.
Land bought here in 1904 by the
Anglo-Palestine Bank was transferred to
the Jewish National Fund in 1907, and
became one of its first holdings in the
country.

Ben Sirah   Simeon ben Jesus, also
called Ecclesiasticus, Hebrew aphorist,
sage, and scribe of the second century
BCE whose wisdom literature was included in the Apocrypha.

Ben Zion, S. (Simhah Alter Gutmann;

1870–1932)   Hebrew and Yiddish author, came to Palestine in 1905.

Ben-Yehuda, Eliezer (1858–1922)   Hebrew writer and lexicographer, generally considered the father of modern,
spoken Hebrew. Immigrated to Palestine in 1881.

Bezalel   Academy of Arts and Design in
Jerusalem, founded in 1906 by Profes-
sor Boris Schatz, court sculptor to King
Ferdinand of Bulgaria.

Bialik, Hayyim Nahman (1873–1934)
Considered the greatest Hebrew poet
of the period of the Hebrew Renaissance, essayist, storywriter, translator,
and editor, who exercised a profound
influence on modern Hebrew culture.

BILU[im]   Hebrew initials of "House of
Jacob, come ye and let us go" (Isaiah
2:5). An organized group of young Russian Jews who emigrated to Palestine in
1881 and launched the First *Aliyah*.

Bishlik   Turkish coin.

Black Hundreds   The secret fighting
squads of the anti-Semitic Union of the
Russian People, largely responsible for
the pogroms of 1905.

Braslav Hasids   Followers of Nahman of
Braslav (1772–1811), one of the great spiritual leaders of Hasidism. His followers
are called the "Dead Hasids" because it
is the only Hasidic sect that has had no
successor to the dead leader.

Brenner, Yosef Hayyim (1881–1921)   Hebrew writer, leading spiritual figure of
the Second *Aliyah*, murdered during
an Arab riot in Jaffa.

Brith   Ceremony of circumcision of
Jewish boys on the eighth day after
their birth.

Brod   In Polish, Brody; a central city in
eastern Galicia, in the Austro-Hungarian Empire, on the Russian border, famous for its enlightenment figures.

Broydes, Reuben Asher, or Braudes
(1851–1902)   Hebrew novelist and enlightenment figure, born in Vilna.

Buchmil, Joshua Heshel (1869–1938)
Zionist leader.

Bukharan Houses in Jerusalem   Housing project of Jews from Bukhara in Central Asia.

Burial Society   Khevre Kadisha, the official society observing Orthodox Jewish burial rituals.

Carmel Wine   Wine produced in the Rothschild wine cellars in the settlement of Rishon Le-Tsion ("The First in Zion"). Drinking Carmel Wine was considered a patriotic deed in the Diaspora.

ChaBaD Society   The society of the Lubavitcher Hasidim.

Chamberlain, Houston Stuart (1855–1927)   An enthusiastic Germanophile and theoretician of anti-Semitism.

Cholent   A stew traditionally prepared on Friday and placed in the oven before the Sabbath to keep hot without having to light a fire on the Sabbath.

Commandment (of Commission and of Omission)   Mitsvah, or ordinance. There are 613 such Mitsvot in the Torah.

Damascus Gate (Sha'ar Shekhem)   One of the gates of the Old City of Jerusalem.

Days of Awe   The days between Rosh Hashanah and Yom Kippur.

Degania   A kibbutz on the Jordan-Yarmuk Plain south of Lake Kinneret, founded in 1909.

Diskin Orphanage   An orphanage in Jerusalem, established in 1880 by Moses Diskin (1817–1898) to "save" children from another orphanage where foreign languages were taught.

Distribution   *Halukah*, charity fees distributed among poor Jewish settlers in Jerusalem by the community organization of their country of origin.

Dizengoff, Meir (1861–1937)   A founder and first mayor of Tel Aviv.

Dr. tor Thon, Ozias (Yehoshua) Thon (1870–1936)   Rabbi and early Zionist, Polish-Jewish leader, born in Lemberg. Assisted Dr. Herzl in preparing the first Zionist Congress in 1897.

Effendi   "Landowner" in Arabic; here used ironically to refer to Jewish landowners as "bourgeois."

Eruv   A thread around a city neighborhood that symbolically makes it one courtyard, in which things may be carried even on the Sabbath.

Esrog (Ethrog)   Rare citrus fruit, among the Four Species used on Sukkoth.

Etz Hayim Yeshiva ("Tree of Life")   The central Ashkenazi Yeshiva in Jerusalem, founded in the mid-nineteenth century by Shmuel Salant.

Exile   *Galuth*, Ashkenazi: *Goles*, the condition of Jews in Diaspora being expelled from the Land of Israel.

Eyn Ganim   A *moshav* (labor cooperative) of Hebrew laborers founded in 1907.

Eyn Zeytim   An Arabic village in the Galilee with four Jewish households

Fables of Foxes   *Mishley Shualim*, a collection of fables by Berekhiah Ha-Nakdan who lived in Normandy in the twelfth-thirteenth century, mostly adapted from the fables of Marie de France. (English translation by Moses Hadas, *Fables of a Jewish Aesop*).

Faithful Shepherd   A part of the Zohar dealing with the justification of commandments.

Frankl, Ludwig August   Ritter von Frankl-Hochwart (1810–1894), Austrian poet, secretary of the Vienna Jewish Community and founder of the Laemel School in Jerusalem.

Gate of Flowers   A gate in the Old City walls.

Gate of Mercy   A gate in the Old City walls.

Gate of Tribes   A gate in the Old City walls.

Gates of Zion Library ("Sha'arey Tsion")   Hebrew public library in Jaffa.

Gershom   Elder son of Moses and Zipporah (Exodus 2:22; 26:24).

Gilboa   Mountain range branching off to the northeast from the Samarian Hills, above the Jezreel Valley.

Gnessin, Uri Nissan (1881–1913) Hebrew fiction writer introduced a proto-
stream-of-consciousness prose into
Hebrew literature.

Golden Book (of the Jewish National
Fund) In which major contributions
were recorded.

Gordon, Aharon David (1856–1922) Hebrew writer and revered spiritual leader
of the Zionist Labor movement in
Palestine, who emphasized self-
realization through settlement on
the land and the "religion of
labor."

Gordon, Judah Leib (1831–1892) Major
Hebrew poet of the Haskalah.

Gross, Wilhelm Delegate to the first
Zionist Congress in Basel in 1897.

Guardians of the Walls Strict adherents
of the Orthodox tradition.

Guide to the Perplexed The classical
book in religious philosophy by Moses
Maimonides (1135–1204).

HaCohen, Adam, Abraham Dov Leben-
sohn (1794–1878) Major Hebrew
poet of the Vilna Haskalah.

Ha-Cohen, Mordechai Ben-Hillel (1856–
1936) Hebrew writer and Zionist,
settled in Palestine in 1907.

Hadera Settlement in central Israel,
founded in 1890 by members of
Hovevey Tsion from Vilna, Kovno, and
Riga.

Haftorah Hebrew: *Haftarah*, passage
from the Prophets read in the synagogue after the weekly Torah portion.

Ha-Herut daily newspaper, edited by
Ben-Yehuda, published in 1908.

Hakham Bashi the title of the chief
rabbi in the Ottoman Empire, composed of the Hebrew word for "sage"
and the Turkish word for "chief."

Ha-Magid the first Hebrew newspaper,
began publication in 1856 in Lyck in
Eastern Prussia, and ended in 1903 in
Berlin.

Ha-Mitspe Hebrew weekly newspaper,
published in Krakow, 1904–1921.

Hamsin (Arabic, Hebrew: *sharav*) A
hot, dry desert wind that creates a
dusty, intense heatwave.

Hanukkah Dreidl A kind of spinning
top used in a children's game on
Hanukkah.

Ha-Or Ben-Yehuda's Hebrew daily,
published in Jerusalem, 1910–1915.

Ha-Po'el Ha-Tsa'ir ("The Young Worker")
The non-Marxist Socialist Zionist
party in Ottoman Palestine, as well
as the name of the most influential
Labor Zionist and literary weekly
journal of the Second *Aliyah*, 1907–
1970.

HASHEM The Name, referring to the
ineffable Name of the Lord.

HaShiloah Central Hebrew literary and
cultural journal, founded by Ahad Ha-
Am, in Russia in 1896.

Hasid Follower of one of the dynasties
of Hasidism, an emotional, even ecsta-
tic form of Jewish worship.

Hatam Sofer Moses Sofer (1762–1839),
leader of Orthodox Jewry and Rabbi of
Pressburg (Bratislava), where he
founded his famous Orthodox Yeshiva
engaged in the struggle against the Re-
form movement.

Ha-Tsvi Ben-Yehuda's Hebrew newspaper, founded as a weekly in Jerusalem
in 1884, and published as a daily after
1908; later renamed *Ha-Or*.

Havatselet Hebrew newspaper first published in Jerusalem in 1863–1864, and
resumed publication in 1870 and continued until the outbreak of World War
I. The paper was the organ of the Hasidim, who were the minority in the
Ashkenazi community in Jerusalem,
and eventually became a loyal sup-
porter of the Distribution.

Heder Jewish religious primary school.

Helperin, Michael (1860–1919) Socialist Zionist in Russia, settled in Rishon
Le-Tsion in 1886.

Herzeliya Gymnasium The first Hebrew high school, founded in Jaffa in
1906, moved to Tel Aviv in 1909.

Herzl, Theodor (1860–1904) Ideologue

of political Zionism and founder of the World Zionist Organization.

Hilfsverein, Relief Organization of German Jewry (Hebrew: *Ezra*) Founded in 1901 to improve the social and political conditions of Eastern European and Oriental Jews; established German-speaking schools for Jews in Palestine.

Holy ARI, "the Sacred Lion" Initials of Isaac Ben Solomon Luria (1534–1572), the founder of the Lurianic Kabalah in Safed, Galilee, under Ottoman rule.

Horodna Houses (or Grodno) A town in Jewish Lithuania.

Hoshana Raba A name for the seventh and last day of the Sukkoth festival.

Humash The Pentateuch, the Five Books of Moses.

Hungarian Houses Housing for Hungarian Jews in Jerusalem.

Hurbah (literally: ruin) The name given to the synagogue of Rabbi Yehuda Hasid in the Old City of Jerusalem, which fell into ruin in the early nineteenth century, when Jews from Eastern Europe were forbidden to settle in Jerusalem.

ICA Jewish Colonization Association, founded by Baron Maurice de Hirsch in 1891, philanthropic association to assist Jews around the world and foster agricultural settlements. From 1896, provided active support to settlements in Palestine.

Issar (Judah ben Nehemiah of Brisk; d. 1876) Lithuanian rabbi who immigrated to the Land of Israel at the end of his life, and died there.

Jaffa Gate One of the main entrances to the Old City of Jerusalem.

Jewish National Fund Founded in December 1901 at the Fifth Zionist Congress in Basel, with the goal of redeeming land for Jewish development in Eretz Israel.

Kabbalah The traditional term for the esoteric teachings of Jewish mysticism.

Kaddish The memorial prayer for the dead.

Kalba Savoua Ben Kalba Savoua, a wealthy man in Jerusalem in the first century CE, who provided food for the inhabitants during the Roman siege.

Kapores *Kapparot*, the sacrifice of a fowl on Yom Kippur to atone for human sins.

Karaites A Jewish fundamentalist sect that emerged at the beginning of the eighth century and rejected the talmudic-rabbinic tradition.

Karlin Study House Of the Hasidic sect of the followers of the Rebbe of Karlin in Lithuania.

Kaymakam Turkish governor of a city or region.

Kedusha The third blessing of the Amidah, recited by pious Jews every morning.

Kfar Lifta Arab village on the western outskirts of Jerusalem.

Kfar Saba Town in central Israel, in the southern Sharon, settled in 1896.

Kiddush Prayer recited over a cup of wine in the home or synagogue to consecrate the Sabbath or festival.

Kinneret Agricultural settlement at the Sea of Galilee, founded in 1909.

Kippa (yarmulke) Skullcap always worn by pious Jewish men.

Kiryat Yearim City of the Hivites, part of the Gibeonite confederation (see Joshua 9:17).

Kishinev (Pogrom) Kishinev is the capital of Moldavia, known in the Jewish world for a major pogrom that took place there in 1903.

Kislev Jewish month, corresponding to November-December.

Kook (Abraham Isaac; 1865–1935) Rabbinical authority and thinker, first Ashkenazi Chief Rabbi of modern Israel.

Krochmal, Nahman (1785–1840) Philosopher, historian, one of the founders of the "Science of Judaism," and a leader of the Haskalah movement in Eastern Europe.

Kugel   Noodle pudding.

Lag b'Omer   The thirty-third day of the counting of the *Omer,* the period between Passover and Shavuot.

Land of Israel (Eretz-Israel)   A reference to the land of Israel before modern statehood.

Landau, Ezekiel ben Judah (1713–1793)   Halakhic authority known by the name of his book, *The Famous of Yehuda (nodah bi-yehuda).*

Language Committee   Committee to promote the Hebrew language, first founded by Eliezer ben Yehuda in Jerusalem in the 1880s. Now: the Academy of the Hebrew Language.

Latrun   Crossroads in the southern Ayalon Valley in Israel, where the Judean Hills and the coastal plain intersect.

Lemberg   Lvov, the capital of eastern Galicia.

Lida Yeshiva   Lithuanian Yeshiva in Palestine that originated in the city of Lida.

Lovers of Zion (Hovevey Tsion)   Followers of the Hibbat Tsion movement founded in the early 1880s, a generation before Herzl's political Zionism.

Ludvipol, Abraham (1865–1921)   Hebrew journalist, settled in Palestine in 1907.

Lunz, Abraham Moses (1854–1918)   Immigrated to Jerusalem in 1869. Author, publisher, and enlightenment figure who published his famous *Yearbook for the Diffusion of an Accurate Knowledge of Ancient and Modern Palestine.* Between 1895 and 1915, he published annual literary almanacs, called *Luakh Eretz Israel* ("Calendar of the Land of Israel").

Mahanayim   A settlement founded by Orthodox Jews from Galicia in 1898, was soon abandoned, and attempts to revive it failed until a kibbutz was established there in 1933.

MaHaRSHA   Rabbi Shmuel Eidels, famous seventeenth-century Talmudist.

Makhpelah   The burial cave in Hebron bought by the Patriarch Abraham from Ephron the Hittite (Genesis 23).

Mamila   Street in Jerusalem.

Mapu, Abraham (1808–1867)   Born in Kovno, Lithuania, famous for his novel *Ahavat Tsion* ("The Love of Zion"), published in Vilna in 1853.

Masie, Aaron Meir (1858–1930)   Physician specializing in ophthalmology. Settled in Rishon Le-Tsion in 1888, and then in Jerusalem in 1900. Author of a comprehensive dictionary of Hebrew terms for medicine and natural sciences.

Maskil   Adherent of the Haskalah, the Hebrew enlightenment, generally applied to persons who acquired a secular education and culture.

Matzo   Unleavened bread, eaten during the week of Passover.

May-Salvation-Arise   An Aramaic prayer, read every Sabbath after the Torah reading. It includes a blessing for the Rabbis and their pupils and a blessing for the whole congregation.

Meah Shearim   Neighborhood of ultra-Orthodox Jews in Jerusalem.

Melaveh Malkah   The festive meal to accompany the Queen Sabbath on her departure at the end of the Sabbath.

Mendele Mokher Sfarim (Seforim; literally: "The Bookseller")   Pseudonym of Shalom Yakov Abramovitch 1835–1917), nicknamed the Grandfather of Yiddish literature; founder of modern Yiddish and Hebrew prose and the "synthetic style" of Hebrew, including words from all historical layers of the language.

Meron   Town in the Galilee near Safed, site of the tomb of Simeon bar Yokhay, where thousands of pilgrims assemble on Lag b'Omer.

Midnight Vigil   Reading of Psalms and lamentations on the Destruction of the Temple, which Hasidim wake up at midnight to recite.

Mikveh Israel   Jewish agricultural school east of Jaffa, established in 1870, by the Alliance Universelle Israélite.

Minyan   A group of ten adult men required for Jewish public prayer.

Mishkenot Sha'ananim ("Dwellings of the Peaceful")   First neighborhood outside the Old City walls in Jerusalem, established and built by Moses Montefiore in 1858.

Mishnah   Collection of oral laws compiled by Rabbi Yehudah ha-Nasi in the second century, which forms the basis of the Talmud.

Montefiore, Moses (1784–1885)   Grew up in England and was involved in the rebuilding of Palestine.

Motza   Jewish settlement west of Jerusalem.

Mount of Olives Cemetery   Ancient Jewish cemetery outside the Old City of Jerusalem.

Mughrabi   A Jew from North Africa.

Musar Movement   Movement for the education of the individual toward strict, ethical religious behavior. Arose in the mid-nineteenth century among the Mitnagdim in Lithuania.

Najara, Israel (1555?–1625?)   Hebrew poet in Ottoman Empire, lived in Damascus and Safed.

Narghila   A Middle Eastern tobacco pipe whose smoke is filtered through water.

Ne'ila   The closing prayer of Yom Kippur.

Nes Tsiona   A Zionist settlement near Rehovoth.

Neve Tsedek   Neighborhood between Jaffa and Tel Aviv.

Nissan   The first month of the ancient Hebrew calendar or the seventh month in the accepted current calendar, roughly in April.

Odessa Committee (short for: Society for the Support of Jewish Farmers and Artisans in Syria and Palestine)   Legal framework of Hovevey Tsion ("The Lovers of Zion"), founded in Odessa in 1890.

Old City   The area of Jerusalem within the seventeenth-century walls, comprising Christian, Moslem, Armenian, and Jewish quarters.

Oliphant, Laurence (1829–1888)   English writer, traveler, and Christian mystic, who supported the return of the Jews to the Land of Israel.

Oppenheimer, Franz (1864–1943)   German sociologist and economist, initiated the cooperative agricultural settlements in the Land of Israel.

Our Bard   The Hebrew national poet, Bialik (allusion to the poem "To the Bird").

Our Father Our King   Avinu Malkenu, prayer.

Outside the Land   Diaspora, according to the binary opposition: the Land of Israel / Outside the Land.

Ovadia of Bartanura (Bertinoro; popularly called Bartinura)   Italian Rabbi of the fifteenth and sixteenth centuries, canonical commentator of the Mishnah.

Peretz, Isaac Leyb (1852–1915)   Classical Yiddish fiction writer.

Petach Tikva   Literally: Opening of Hope. The first new agricultural settlement near Tel Aviv, founded by observant Jews from Jerusalem in 1878. In 1883, BILU immigrants renewed the settlement.

PICA   Palestine Jewish Colonization Association (1924–1957), established by Baron Edmond de Rothschild for the development of Jewish settlements in Palestine. Agnon mistakenly refers to ICA by its later name.

Pidyon Ha-Ben   Redemption of the firstborn son (see Numbers 18:16–17).

Pineles, Hirsh Mendel (1806–1870)   Galician scholar and writer, lived in Brody.

Plevne   City in northern Bulgaria; site of battles between the Russian and Turkish armies in 1877.

Poaley Tsion   The Marxist Labor Zionist party, originated in the 1890s in Russia and established as World Union of Poaley Tsion in 1907. Mainspring of the Israeli Labor Movement.

Prayer shawl (Tallis)   Worn by Jewish men during prayers.

Przemysl   City and fortress in Galicia.

Purim Rattle   A noisemaker used to drown out the name of the wicked Haman, during the reading of the Book of Esther at Purim.

Rabbi Benjamin, pseudonym of Yehoshua Radler-Feldmann (1880–1957)   Hebrew journalist born in Galicia. Arrived in Palestine in 1907, worked as a laborer and became secretary of Herzeliya Gymnasium in Tel Aviv. One of the few Galician writers in the Second *Aliyah*.

Rabbi Meirle of Peremyshlyany (1780–1850)   Grandson of Rabbi Meir of Peremyshlyany, known as "the First" or "the Great," founder of a Hassidic dynasty. One of the most outstanding personalities among the Hasidic rebbes of Galicia.

Rabinovitch, Alexander Ziskind (known by his acronym, AZAR, 1854–1945)   Hebrew writer, settled in Palestine in 1906.

RaMA (Rabbi Moses Isserlish, 1525–1572)   Polish rabbi, one of the great Halakhic authorities.

Ramle   Arab city on the road from Jaffa to Jerusalem.

Rashi (Rabbi Shlomo Yitzhaki, 1040–1105)   Born in Troyes, France; major author of the canonical commentary of the Bible and the Talmud.

Reb Yudel Hasid   Hero of Agnon's novel, *The Bridal Canopy.*

Rebbe   Dynastic leader of a Hasidic sect.

Rehovoth   Settlement in the coastal plain near Jaffa, founded in 1890 by First *Aliyah* immigrants.

Religion of Work   A cornerstone of A. D. Gordon's labor ideology.

Rishon Le-Tsion   "The First in Zion," a settlement twelve kilometers from Jaffa. Founded in 1882.

Rivlin, Yoshi   Yosef Yitzhak (1837–1896), born in Jerusalem, initiated the building of the first Jewish quarters outside the Old City walls, such as Nahalat Shiv'a and Meah Shearim.

Rizhin Rebbe (Israel Ruzhin, 1797–1850)   Founder of the Ruzhin or Rizhin dynasty.

Rokakh, Eleazar (1854–1914)   Born in Jerusalem, lived in Safed. From 1880 he lived in Romania and Galicia, where he encouraged Jews to settle in Eretz-Israel.

Rosh Hashanah   The Jewish New Year in the autumn.

Rothschild, Baron Edmond James de Rothschild (1845–1934)   Patron of Jewish settlement in the Land of Israel.

Ruppin, Arthur (1876–1943)   Economist, sociologist, and "father of the Zionist settlement" in the Land of Israel.

Sabbath boundary   See *Eruv.*

Sabbath Goy   A non-Jew hired to perform necessary chores forbidden to Jews on the Sabbath.

Sabbath Keepers   A Russian Christian fundamentalist sect (called Subotniks) that observed the Sabbath on Saturday instead of Sunday; many of them immigrated to the Holy Land, settled in the Galilee and eventually merged with the Jews.

Sadigura Hasids   A Hasidic dynasty.

Sarona (Sharona)   German colony in what is now central Tel Aviv.

Schatz, Boris   Professor Boris Schatz; see Bezalel.

Selikhot   Lamentations.

Sephardi   Descendant of former Spanish Jews.

Seven Blessings   Traditional formula of blessings recited in the wedding ceremony.

Sha'ar HaGai (Gate of the Valley)   The exit from the Judean mountains, on the road from Jerusalem to the coastal plain.

Sha'arey Zion Library   See Gates of Zion Library.

Shavuoth   Holiday, seven weeks after the end of Passover.

Sheid, Elijah (or Elie Scheid, 1841–1922) Wrote historical studies of Alsatian Jewry, was appointed by Baron Edmond de Rothschild as inspector of the Baron's settlements in the Land of Israel, 1883–1899.

Sheinkin, Menahem (1871–1924) Zionist leader in Russia and Palestine.

Shekel The membership contribution of the Zionist organization.

Shekhina The Divine Spirit in Jewish mysticism.

Shema Jewish credo ("Hear, O Israel, the Lord our God, the Lord is One").

Shiv'a The Jewish week of mourning following a funeral.

Shofar Ram's horn, trumpet.

Sholem Aleichem (literally: How-Do-You-Do; pseudonym of Shalom Rabinovitch, 1859–1916) Major Yiddish classical writer.

Shtemper, Yehoshua (or Stampfer, 1852–1908) Religious Jew from Jerusalem, cofounder of the first Jewish agricultural settlement in Petach Tikva.

Shtrayml The festive fur hat worn by Orthodox Jewish men.

Shulhan Arukh Code of Jewish laws written by Joseph Caro (1488–1575).

Silman, Kaddish Yehuda Leyb (1880–1937) Hebrew teacher, writer, and satirist. Immigrated to Palestine in 1907.

Sukkah Booth erected for the Feast of Tabernacles where, for seven days, religious Jews dwell, or at least eat.

Sukkoth Feast of Tabernacles, in the autumn.

Tamuz The fourth month of the Jewish calendar.

Tefillin Phylacteries, cube-shaped cases containing Torah texts worn by worshippers.

The Young Laborer See *Ha-Po'el Ha-Tsa'ir.*

Thirty-Six Just Men According to legend, the world exists on the basis of thirty-six just men, hidden among humanity.

Trietsch, Davis (1870–1935) Attended the First Zionist Congress in 1897, but opposed Herzl's political Zionism and insisted on immediate practical settlement in Palestine and its vicinity. In 1905, he opened an Information Office for Immigration in Jaffa.

Tsena Ve-Rena The women's Bible in Yiddish.

Ussishkin, Abraham Menahem Mendel (1863–1941) Member of Hovevey Tsion in Odessa and President of the Jewish National Fund.

Valero Sephardi family in Jerusalem. Jacob Valero (d. 1880) founded the first modern bank in Jerusalem in 1848; his son Haim Aaron (1845–1923) was director of the bank after 1875.

Warburg, Otto (1859–1938) Botanist and the third president of the World Zionist Organization.

Wessely, Naftali Herz (in Hebrew: Vayzeli, 1725–1805) Hebrew epic poet in Germany, one of the founders of the Haskalah.

Western Wall Hebrew: Kotel. A retaining wall at the foot of the Temple Mount; the last remnant of the Second Temple and the holiest site in Judaism.

Windischgrätz, Alfred Fürst zu (1787–1862) Austrian field marshall, suppressed the Hungarian revolt of 1848.

Wolffson, David (1856–1914) Second president of the World Zionist Organization.

Yad Avshalom Gravestone and monument to Avshalom, at the foot of the Mount of Olives.

Yehuda the Hasid (Segal ha-Levi; 1660?–1700) Active in the Shabbatean movement in Poland, arrived in Jerusalem in 1700 and died a few days later. His group was the first organized Ashkenazi immigration to Eretz-Israel. One hundred fifty years later, the main synagogue of the Ashkenazi community in the old city of Jerusalem was founded in his name.

Yemin Moshe The first Jewish settle

ment outside the walls of the Old City of Jerusalem; named for the British Jewish philanthropist Moses Montefiore.

Yeshiva   An Orthodox Jewish higher school.

Yishuv   Settlement in the Land of Israel. The *Old Yishuv* was the ultra-Orthodox presence of elderly people in the Holy Land; the *New Yishuv* was the Zionist settlement in the Land of Israel since the late 1870s.

Yortseit   Anniversary of a death.

Yosiphon   Or Josippon; historical narrative in Hebrew, describing the Second Temple Period, written in southern Italy in the tenth century.

Zanz Hasids   Or Nowy Sacz. A Hasidic dynasty was founded there by Haim Halberstam (1793–1876).

Zbarazher, Velvl (pseudonym of Ehrenkranz, Binyamin Ze'ev, 1819–1883)   Popular Yiddish and Hebrew poet and songwriter in eastern Galicia.

Zikhron Ya'akov   Settlement founded in 1882 by Jews from Romania.

Zohar   Book of Jewish mysticism presumed to have been written in the thirteenth century by Rabbi Moshe de Leon.